Great Horror STORIES

101 CHILLING TALES

Great Horror STORIES

◆

COMPILED BY STEFAN DZIEMIANOWICZ

FALL RIVER PRESS

New York

FALL RIVER PRESS

New York

An Imprint of Sterling Publishing Co., Inc.
1166 Avenue of the Americas
New York, NY 10036

ISBN 978-1-4351-6441-3

Manufactured in the United States of America

2 4 6 8 10 9 7 5 3

www.sterlingpublishing.com

Contents

64000

0

0

0

0

0

0

0

0

0

0

0

0

0

0

0

0

0

0

0

0

0

0

0

0

0

0

0

0

0

0

0

0

0

0

0

0

0

Introduction

In his posthumously published essay "The Poetic Principle," Edgar Allan Poe had this to say about poetry:

> I need scarcely observe that a poem deserves its title only inasmuch as it excites, by elevating the soul. The value of the poem is in the ratio of this elevating excitement. But all excitements are, through a psychal necessity, transient. That degree of excitement which would entitle a poem to be so called at all, cannot be sustained throughout a composition of any great length. After the lapse of half an hour, at the very utmost, it flags—fails—a revulsion ensues—and then the poem is, in effect, and in fact, no longer such.

The unity of effect that Poe mandated for good poetry has often been applied to the tale of horror. Certainly there are many novel-length works of horror fiction—horror as a branch of popular fiction was launched with the gothic novel, and one has only to think of Bram Stoker's classic *Dracula* and the contemporary work of Stephen King to recognize that there are distinguished works of horror in long form. For much of the nineteenth and early twentieth century, however, horror was a story type whose reputation rested predominantly on its shorter works. It's not hard to understand why: traditionally, the tale of horror begins on ordinary footing and then builds relentlessly to a crescendo of its terrifying narrative elements. Anything that would impede its pacing or protract the amount of time needed to read it to its conclusion would make for a lesser story.

The 101 stories collected in this volume were chosen to showcase the achievements that are possible in the short tale of horror. Each runs no more than a few thousand words in length and requires little more than a few minutes to read. Although their origins span a wide swath of the globe from North and South America to England and the European continent, they cover considerably more ground in terms of their imaginative reach. Here you have tales of horror's iconic monsters: the vampire, the werewolf, the mummy, the witch, the ghoul, and the ghost. Here, as well, are horrors not so easily classified: the malevolent thoughts that drive the narrator of Fitz-James

O'Brien's "A Terrible Night" to his tragic actions, the mirage that only one person in a group of people can see in Robert S. Hichens's "The Figure in the Mirage," the fatal miasma that pervades Ralph Adams Cram's "The Dead Valley," and the mania verging on madness that motivates the point-of-view character in John Metcalfe's "The Tunnel." There are horrors here to suit every taste: physical horrors of the gruesomest sort in Ambrose Bierce's "A Tough Tussle" and Bram Stoker's "The Squaw," and supernatural horrors that defy human reasoning (although not logical explanation) in Lewis Spence's "The Archer in the Arras" and J. Sheridan Le Fanu's "The Fortunes of Sir Robert Ardagh." There are even horrors that fall somewhere between these two extremes in William Hope Hodgson's "A Tropical Horror," H. G. Wells's "The Strange Orchid," and Clive Pemberton's "The Spider," whose monsters originate in the natural world. There are psychological horrors in the inescapable precognitive vision of William Fryer Harvey's "August Heat" and the overwhelming sense of guilt that burdens the protagonist of Nathaniel Hawthorne's "The Hollow of the Three Hills," and horrors of human depravity characteristic of the *conte cruel* in Villiers de l'Isle Adam's "The Torture by Hope," Maurice Level's "The Kennel," and W. C. Morrow's "His Unconquerable Enemy." And what are we to make of the nightmare world revealed at the end of H. P. Lovecraft's "The Music of Erich Zann" other than horror of a cosmic scope that mocks the narrow parameters of our perceived reality.

Returning to the words of Edgar Allan Poe quoted at the beginning of this introduction, all of the tales collected in this volume succeed by their brevity in achieving the "excitement" requisite for effective art. But they differ from Poe's poetic ideal in one crucial regard: there is nothing transient about the emotional responses they provoke. The horrors to be encountered in *Great Horror Stories* make an impact that readers will feel long after the book is closed.

—Stefan Dziemianowicz
New York, 2016

Amina

Edward Lucas White

Waldo, brought face to face with the actuality of the unbelievable—as he himself would have worded it—was completely dazed. In silence he suffered the consul to lead him from the tepid gloom of the interior, through the ruinous doorway, out into the hot, stunning brilliance of the desert landscape. Hassan followed, with never a look behind him. Without any word he had taken Waldo's gun from his nerveless hand and carried it, with his own and the consul's.

The consul strode across the gravelly sand, some fifty paces from the southwest corner of the tomb, to a bit of not wholly ruined wall from which there was a clear view of the doorway side of the tomb and of the side with the larger crevice.

"Hassan," he commanded, "watch here."

Hassan said something in Persian.

"How many cubs were there?" the consul asked Waldo.

Waldo stared mute.

"How many young ones did you see?" the consul asked again.

"Twenty or more," Waldo made answer.

"That's impossible," snapped the consul.

"There seemed to be sixteen or eighteen," Waldo reasserted. Hassan smiled and grunted. The consul took from him two guns, handed Waldo his, and they walked around the tomb to a point about equally distant from the opposite corner. There was another bit of ruin, and in front of it, on the side toward the tomb, was a block of stone mostly in the shadow of the wall.

"Convenient," said the consul. "Sit on that stone and lean against the wall; make yourself comfortable. You are a bit shaken, but you will be all right in a moment. You should have something to eat, but we have nothing. Anyhow, take a good swallow of this."

He stood by him as Waldo gasped over the raw brandy.

"Hassan will bring you his water bottle before he goes," the consul went on; "drink plenty, for you must stay here for some time. And now, pay attention to me. We must extirpate these vermin. The male, I judge, is absent. If he had been anywhere about, you would not now be alive. The young cannot be as many as you say, but, I take it, we have to deal with ten, a full litter. We must smoke them out. Hassan will go back to camp after fuel and the guard. Meanwhile, you and I must see that none escape."

He took Waldo's gun, opened the breech, shut it, examined the magazine and handed it back to him.

"Now watch me closely," he said. He paced off, looking to his left past the tomb. Presently he stopped and gathered several stones together.

"You see these?" he called.

Waldo shouted an affirmation.

The consul came back, passed on in the same line, looking to his right past the tomb, and presently, at a similar distance, put up another tiny cairn, shouted again and was again answered. Again he returned.

"Now you are sure you cannot mistake those two marks I have made?"

"Very sure indeed," said Waldo.

"It is important," warned the consul. "I am going back to where I left Hassan, to watch there while he is gone. You will watch here. You may pace as often as you like to either of those stone heaps. From either you can see me on my beat. Do not diverge from the line from one to the other. For as soon as Hassan is out of sight I shall shoot any moving thing I see nearer. Sit here till you see me set up similar limits for my sentry-go on the farther side, then shoot any moving thing not on my line of patrol. Keep a lookout all around you. There is one chance in a million that the male might return in daylight—mostly they are nocturnal, but this lair is evidently exceptional. Keep a bright lookout.

"And now listen to me. You must not feel any foolish sentimentalism about any fancied resemblance of these vermin to human beings. Shoot, and shoot to kill. Not only is it our duty, in general, to abolish them, but it will be very dangerous for us if we do not. There is little or no solidarity in Mohammedan communities, but on the comparatively few points upon which public opinion exists it acts with amazing promptitude and vigor. One matter as to which there is no disagreement is that it is incumbent upon every man to assist in eradicating these creatures. The good old Biblical custom of stoning to death is the mode of lynching indigenous hereabouts. These modern Asiatics are quite capable of applying it to any one believed derelict against any of these inimical monsters. If we let one escape and the rumor of it gets about, we may precipitate an outburst of racial prejudice difficult to cope with. Shoot, I say, without hesitation or mercy."

"I understand," said Waldo.

"I don't care whether you understand or not," said the consul. "I want you to act. Shoot if needful, and shoot straight." And he tramped off.

Hassan presently appeared, and Waldo drank from his water bottle as nearly all of its contents as Hassan would permit. After his departure Waldo's first alertness soon gave place to mere endurance of the monotony of watching and the intensity of the heat. His discomfort became suffering, and what with the fury of the dry glare, the pangs of thirst and his bewilderment of mind, Waldo was moving in a waking dream by the time Hassan returned with two donkeys and a mule laden with brushwood. Behind the beasts straggled the guard.

Waldo's trance became a nightmare when the smoke took effect and the battle began. He was, however, not only not required to join in the killing, but was enjoined to keep back. He did keep very much in the background, seeing only so much of the slaughter as his curiosity would not let him refrain from viewing. Yet he felt all a murderer as he gazed at the ten small carcasses laid out arow, and the memory of his vigil and its end, indeed of the whole day, though it was the day of his most marvelous adventure, remains to him as the broken recollections of a phantasmagoria.

On the morning of his memorable peril Waldo had waked early. The experiences of his sea-voyage, the sights at Gibraltar, at Port Said, in the canal, at Suez, at Aden, at Muscat, and at Basrah had formed an altogether inadequate transition from the decorous regularity of house and school-life in New England to the breathless wonder of the desert immensities.

Everything seemed unreal, and yet the reality of its strangeness so besieged him that he could not feel at home in it, he could not sleep heavily in a tent. After composing himself to sleep, he lay long conscious and awakened early, as on this morning, just at the beginning of the false-dawn.

The consul was fast asleep, snoring loudly. Waldo dressed quietly and went out; mechanically, without any purpose or forethought, taking his gun. Outside he found Hassan, seated, his gun across his knees, his head sunk forward, as fast asleep as the consul. Ali and Ibrahim had left the camp the day before for supplies. Waldo was the only waking creature about; for the guards, camped some little distance off, were but logs about the ashes of their fire.

When he had begun camp life he had expected to find the consul, that combination of sportsman, explorer and archaeologist, a particularly easygoing guardian. He had looked forward to absolutely untrammeled liberty in the spacious expanse of the limitless wastes. The reality he had found exactly the reverse of his preconceptions. The consul's first injunction was:

"Never let yourself get out of sight of me or of Hassan unless he or I send you off with Ali or Ibrahim. Let nothing tempt you to roam about alone. Even a ramble is dangerous. You might lose sight of the camp before you knew it."

At first Waldo acquiesced, later he protested. "I have a good pocket compass. I know how to use it. I never lost my way in the Maine woods."

"No Kourds in the Maine woods," said the consul.

Yet before long Waldo noticed that the few Kourds they encountered seemed simple-hearted, peaceful folk. No semblance of danger or even of adventure had appeared. Their armed guard of a dozen greasy tatterdemalions had passed their time in uneasy loafing.

Likewise Waldo noticed that the consul seemed indifferent to the ruins they passed by or encamped among, that his feeling for sites and topography was cooler than luke-warm, that he showed no ardor in the pursuit of the scanty and uninteresting game. He had picked up enough of several dialects to hear repeated conversations about "them." "Have you heard of any about here?" "Has one been killed?" "Any traces of them in this district?" And such queries he could make out in the various talks with the natives they met; as to what "they" were he received no enlightenment.

Then he had questioned Hassan as to why he was so restricted in his movements. Hassan spoke some English and regaled him with tales of Afrits, ghouls, specters and other uncanny legendary presences; of the jinn of the waste, appearing in human shape, talking all languages, ever on the alert to ensnare infidels; of the woman whose feet turned the wrong way at the ankles, luring the unwary to a pool and there drowning her victims; of the malignant ghosts of dead brigands, more terrible than their living fellows; of the spirit in the shape of a wild ass, or of a gazelle, enticing its pursuers to the brink of a precipice and itself seeming to run ahead upon an expanse of sand, a mere mirage, dissolving as the victim passed the brink and fell to death; of the sprite in the semblance of a hare feigning a limp, or of a ground-bird feigning a broken wing, draw-ing its pursuer after it till he met death in an unseen pit or well-shaft.

Ali and Ibrahim spoke no English. As far as Waldo could understand their long harangues, they told similar stories or hinted at dangers equally vague and imaginary. These childish bogy-tales merely whetted Waldo's craving for independence.

Now, as he sat on a rock, longing to enjoy the perfect sky, the clear, early air, the wide, lonely landscape, along with the sense of having it to himself, it seemed to him that the consul was merely innately cautious, over-cautious. There was no danger. He would have a fine, leisurely stroll, kill something perhaps, and certainly be back in camp before the sun grew hot. He stood up.

Some hours later he was seated on a fallen coping-stone in the shadow of a ruined tomb. All the country they had been traversing is full of tombs and remains of tombs, prehistoric, Bactrian, old Persian, Parthian, Sassanian, or Mohammedan, scattered everywhere in groups or solitary. Vanished utterly are the faintest traces of the cities, towns, and villages, ephemeral houses or temporary huts, in which had lived the count-less generations of mourners who had reared these tombs.

The tombs, built more durably than mere dwellings of the living, remained. Complete or ruinous, or reduced to mere fragments, they were everywhere. In that district they were all of one type. Each was domed and below was square, its one door facing eastward and opening into a larger empty room, behind which were the mortuary chambers.

In the shadow of such a tomb Waldo sat. He had shot nothing, had lost his way, had no idea of the direction of the camp, was tired, warm and thirsty. He had forgotten his water bottle.

He swept his gaze over the vast, desolate prospect, the unvaried turquoise of the sky arched above the rolling desert. Far reddish hills along the skyline hooped in the less distant brown hillocks which, without diversifying it, hummocked the yellow landscape. Sand and rocks with a lean, starved bush or two made up the nearer view, broken here and there by dazzling white or streaked, grayish, crumbling ruins. The sun had not been long above the horizon, yet the whole surface of the desert was quivering with heat.

As Waldo sat viewing the outlook a woman came round the corner tomb. All the village women Waldo had seen had worn yashmaks or some other form of face-covering or veil. This woman was bareheaded and unveiled. She wore some sort of yellowish-brown garment which enveloped her from neck to ankles, showing no waist line. Her feet, in defiance of the blistering sands, were bare.

At sight of Waldo she stopped and stared at him as he at her. He remarked the un-European posture of her feet, not at all turned out, but with the inner lines parallel. She wore no anklets, he observed, no bracelets, no necklace or earrings. Her bare arms he thought the most muscular he had ever seen on a human being. Her nails were pointed and long, both on her hands and her feet. Her hair was black, short and tousled, yet she did not look wild or uncomely. Her eyes smiled and her lips had the effect of smiling, though they did not part ever so little, not showing at all the teeth behind them.

"What a pity," said Waldo aloud, "that she does not speak English."

"I do speak English," said the woman, and Waldo noticed that as she spoke, her lips did not perceptibly open. "What does the gentleman want?"

"You speak English!" Waldo exclaimed, jumping to his feet. "What luck! Where did you learn it?"

"At the mission school," she replied, an amused smile playing about the corners of her rather wide, unopening mouth. "What can be done for you?" She spoke with scarcely any foreign accent, but very slowly and with a sort of growl running along from syllable to syllable.

"I am thirsty," said Waldo, "and I have lost my way."

"Is the gentleman living in a brown tent, shaped like half a melon?" she inquired, the queer, rumbling note drawling from one word to the next, her lips barely separated.

"Yes, that is our camp," said Waldo.

"I could guide the gentleman that way," she droned; "but it is far, and there is no water on that side."

"I want water first," said Waldo, "or milk."

"If you mean cow's milk, we have none. But we have goat's milk. There is to drink where I dwell," she said, sing-songing the words. "It is not far. It is the other way."

"Show me," said he.

She began to walk, Waldo, his gun under his arm, beside her. She trod noiselessly and fast. Waldo could scarcely keep up with her. As they walked he often fell behind and noted how her swathing garments clung to a lithe, shapely back, neat waist and firm hips. Each time he hurried and caught up with her, he scanned her with intermittent glances, puzzled that her waist, so well-marked at the spine, showed no particular definition in front; that the outline of her from neck to knees, perfectly shapeless under her wrappings, was without any waist-line or suggestion of firmness or undulation. Likewise he remarked the amused flicker in her eyes and the compressed line of her red, her too red, lips.

"How long were you at the mission school?" he inquired.

"Four years," she replied.

"Are you a Christian?" he asked.

"The Free-folk do not submit to baptism," she stated simply, but with rather more of the droning growl between her words.

He felt a queer shiver as he watched the scarcely moved lips through which the syllables edged their way.

"But you are not veiled," he could not resist saying.

"The Free-folk," she rejoined, "are never veiled."

"Then you are not a Mohammedan?" he ventured.

"The Free-folk are not Moslems."

"Who are the Free-folk?" he blurted out incautiously.

She shot one baleful glance at him. Waldo remembered that he had to do with an Asiatic. He recalled the three permitted questions.

"What is your name?" he inquired.

"Amina," she told him.

"That is a name from the 'Arabian Nights,'" he hazarded.

"From the foolish tales of the believers," she sneered. "The Free-folk know nothing of such follies." The unvarying shutness of her speaking lips, the drawly burr between the syllables, struck him all the more as her lips curled but did not open.

"You utter your words in a strange way," he said.

"Your language is not mine," she replied.

"How is it that you learned my language at the mission school and are not a Christian?"

"They teach all at the mission school," she said, "and the maidens of the Free-folk are like the other maidens they teach, though the Free-folk when grown are not as town-dwellers are. Therefore they taught me as any townbred girl, not knowing me for what I am."

"They taught you well," he commented.

"I have the gift of tongues," she uttered enigmatically, with an odd note of triumph burring the words through her unmoving lips.

Waldo felt a horrid shudder all over him, not only at her uncanny words, but also from mere faintness.

"Is it far to your home?" he breathed.

"It is there," she said, pointing to the doorway of a large tomb just before them.

The wholly open arch admitted them into a fairly spacious interior, cool with the abiding temperature of thick masonry. There was no rubbish on the floor. Waldo, relieved to escape the blistering glare outside, seated himself on a block of stone midway between the door and the inner partition-wall, resting his gun-butt on the floor. For the moment he was blinded by the change from the insistent brilliance of the desert morning to the blurred gray light of the interior.

When his sight cleared he looked about and remarked, opposite the door, the ragged hole which laid open the desecrated mausoleum. As his eyes grew accustomed to the dimness he was so startled that he stood up. It seemed to him that from its four corners the room swarmed with naked children. To his inexperienced conjecture they seemed about two years old, but they moved with the assurance of boys of eight or ten.

"Whose are these children?" he exclaimed.

"Mine," she said.

"All yours?" he protested.

"All mine," she replied, a curious suppressed boisterousness in her demeanor.

"But there are twenty of them," he cried.

"You count badly in the dark," she told him. "There are fewer."

"There certainly are a dozen," he maintained, spinning round as they danced and scampered about.

"The Free-people have large families," she said.

"But they are all of one age," Waldo exclaimed, his tongue dry against the roof of his mouth.

She laughed, an unpleasant, mocking laugh, clapping her hands. She was between him and the doorway, and as most of the light came from it he could not see her lips.

"Is not that like a man! No woman would have made that mistake."

Waldo was confuted and sat down again. The children circulated around him, chattering, laughing, giggling, snickering, making noises indicative of glee.

"Please get me something cool to drink," said Waldo, and his tongue was not only dry but big in his mouth.

"We shall have to drink shortly," she said, "but it will be warm."

Waldo began to feel uneasy. The children pranced around him, jabbering strange, guttural noises, licking their lips, pointing at him, their eyes fixed on him, with now and then a glance at their mother.

"Where is the water?"

The woman stood silent, her arms hanging at her sides, and it seemed to Waldo she was shorter than she had been.

"Where is the water?" he repeated.

"Patience, patience," she growled, and came a step nearer to him.

The sunlight struck upon her back and made a sort of halo about her hips. She seemed still shorter than before. There was a something furtive in her bearing, and the little ones sniggered evilly.

At that instant two rifle shots rang out almost as one. The woman fell face downward on the floor. The babies shrieked in a shrill chorus. Then she leapt up from all fours with an explosive suddenness, staggered in a hurled, lurching rush toward the hole in the wall, and, with a frightful yell, threw up her arms and whirled backward to the ground, doubled and contorted like a dying fish, stiffened, shuddered and was still. Waldo, his horrified eyes fixed on her face, even in his amazement noted that her lips did not open.

The children, squealing faint cries of dismay, scrambled through the hole in the inner wall, vanishing into the inky void beyond. The last had hardly gone when the consul appeared in the doorway, his smoking gun in his hand.

"Not a second too soon, my boy," he ejaculated. "She was just going to spring."

He cocked his gun and prodded the body with the muzzle.

"Good and dead," he commented. "What luck! Generally it takes three or four bullets to finish one. I've known one with two bullets through her lungs to kill a man."

"Did you murder this woman?" Waldo demanded fiercely.

"Murder?" the consul snorted. "Murder! Look at that."

He knelt down and pulled open the full, close lips, disclosing not human teeth, but small incisors, cusped grinders, wide-spaced, and long, keen, overlapping canines, like those of a greyhound: a fierce, deadly, carnivorous dentition, menacing and combative.

Waldo felt a qualm, yet the face and form still swayed his horrified sympathy for their humanness.

"Do you shoot women because they have long teeth?" Waldo insisted, revolted at the horrid death he had watched.

"You are hard to convince," said the consul sternly. "Do you call that a woman?"

He stripped the clothing from the carcass.

Waldo sickened all over. What he saw was not the front of a woman, but the body of a female animal, old and flaccid—mother of a pack.

"What kind of a creature is it?" he asked faintly.

"A Ghoul, my boy," the consul answered solemnly, almost in a whisper.

"I thought they did not exist," Waldo babbled. "I thought they were mythical; I thought there were none."

"I can very well believe that there are none in Rhode Island," the consul said gravely. "This is in Persia, and Persia is in Asia."

AND THERE'S YOUR PROOF

DOUGLAS NEWTON

"I DON'T TALK MERELY FOR EFFECT EVEN TO A 'FAN' AUDIENCE, AS YOU CALL IT," Cumber said, in that fat and final way of his. "I meant exactly what I said. I have worked out an absolutely undetectable way of murdering a man."

Cumber was throwing his weight about as usual. He had, not for the first time, got on to the front pages of the papers with this absurd lecture of his, and he was not the man to miss any opportunity of a personal boost.

His big, luxurious lounge-study was emphatically and pointedly littered with all that day's news-sheets, scare headlines upward, so that everywhere their eyes turned his guests saw:

CELEBRATED AUTHOR INVENTS FOOL-PROOF MURDER

Boyington, thin, acrid, brilliant, soured by lack of public recognition, and his nerves jangled by Cumber's display, muttered:

"Oh, we've all invented that fool-proof crime at one time or other—for purposes of fiction."

"This is different. This is IT! It'd be deadly in fact as well as fiction," Cumber said, filling their glasses with a gesture that said: "You needn't stint yourselves. I, at least, can afford it."

Thoms, the he-man novelist, who veiled an utter lack of scruple behind a façade of breezy bigness, laughed:

"I noted you were precious careful not to hint at even a detail of your process in your lecture, old boy."

"Daren't. I may be only a 'shocker' writer, but I have a sense of responsibility," Cumber said. His self-sufficient solemnity made them all squirm: it was as if he'd said that being unsuccessful writers made them all crooks. Particularly Thoms looked ugly, but then it was said that Cumber had nosed out of one of Thoms' dirty pieces of work and held the power of criminal proceedings over his "friend."

Edwin Mitchel, the *Daily Front*'s crime expert, who was not above hinting in private that Cumber's colossal popularity owed not a little to a sly ability for milking the brains of one Edwin Mitchel, sneered:

"Of course, that sort of guff goes down with your West End mob, Cumber, old chap; but we know there's 'no sich thing' as the unsolvable crime. You'll back me there, won't you, Inspector?"

Inspector Ropes, C.I.D., large, hard, grim, weighed that. He would rather side with Mitchel than with Cumber. Like most men, he detested the "Best Seller." The man not only used his popularity and wealth to curry favour with the authorities and so make himself a nuisance at the Yard; but Cumber had a nasty habit of employing actual facts he had picked up from the police, and for that reason was an education to crooks, and, in Ropes' opinion, a public danger.

"I think it's harder for a killer to get away with it than it ever has been," he answered slowly. "We've got so much science on our side nowadays. Of course, it's true we can't always get convicting evidence against our man, but we generally know him—"

"That's what I meant," Mitchel put in. "And if you know your murderer, then his crime is hardly fool-proof."

"I was thinking of that, too," Cumber said pompously. "By a detection-proof murder, I mean one that leaves not a shade of trace. I dwelt expressly on that point in my lecture."

He pulled Mitchel's own paper towards him, and read in a here's-where-you-get-off voice:

> "This murder I have invented is absolutely clue-proof in every sense.
> No police detective, or even the fabled Sherlock Holmes could trace it.
> Doctors and Home Office experts would be utterly baffled. Neither acci-
> dent, nor chance, nor that well-known slip which all criminals are said
> to make, nor, indeed, even bad luck would give the crime away. I know
> what I am saying, for I am an expert in these things. I assure you as a
> matter of definite fact that this murder I have worked out simply could not
> be discovered. It is the one perfect crime in history."

"And I think you were an utter fool to say such a thing in public," came a voice from the corner, where Pennyfold sat in his shabby and aloof dignity.

"I'm of that opinion, too," said Tilbury, Cumber's nearest rival in thriller pro-duction. "To say a thing like that to a mixed crowd, knowing that the press must broadcast it—"

"Oh, no risk, I assure you," Cumber smirked. "I'm seeing to that."

"The great plan remains hidden in the vast brain?" Thoms jeered.

"Oh, no, that's not my method," Cumber said, seizing the occasion to show lesser minds how genius worked. "You know it's a matter of conscience with me that I must be exact in everything. I get the thing down on paper, study all the authorities, then I subject it to tests from every angle, so to speak, before I allow it to pass me."

"So it's on paper now," Boyington said sharply.

"Certainly. The whole murder is down in black and white, worked out in scrupulous detail. But, naturally, it's filed out of harm's way."

He crossed the big lounge to a bookcase filling one wall. He touched some spring. A whole bay of the shelves, books and all, swung outward. Behind was a smart, bright, and very large safe. It was characteristic of the man that he should indulge in tricks like this. He turned now to catch their appreciation of his dramatic quality.

"It's in here, and it will take a pretty good crook to get it out," he boasted. "This safe is one of the latest models, and practically burglar-proof. Naturally, I'm not the sort to be fobbed off with the second best."

"There isn't a best," Tilbury put in. "The safe hasn't been made that a good 'peterman' can't 'bust.' I know that. I've been pretty thoroughly into the subject."

"I agree," Mitchel said. "Lammel, the bank breaker showed me, just before he went up for his last stretch, how any safe could be mastered, no matter what make."

"I've heard that sort of story before," Cumber jeered.

"It's more than a story. The expert criminal studies each new model as it is issued— often, through secret information, before it is issued," Pennyfold put in unexpectedly. "I happen to know that. My father was head mechanic to a firm of strong-room manufacturers. I myself was apprenticed to the calling before I deserted it for the less stable industry of literature."

They were all rather impressed. Pennyfold was the sort of mind one had to respect—that is, all did except Cumber, who never had ears for any voice but his own.

"It'd certainly have been to the benefit of others if you hadn't changed your trade," he said, with the spitefulness of the contradicted. And as Pennyfold winced, and his stern old eyes blazed, the others recalled that Cumber had lent the old man a great deal of money. But Cumber went on contemptuously:

"As I say, I've heard that sort of talk before, but I'm afraid my mind isn't satisfied by such simplicity. The facts are against it. Safes are made and bought to keep criminals at bay, and the fact that nine-tenths of the safes in the world still keep their valuables intact rather shatters your romantic ideas."

"All the same," Boyington said. "I think your plan for the foolproof murder would be better burnt. If it is as perfect as you say, it's existence is a public danger."

"Definitely," Mitchel put in. "Who knows what blackguard hasn't already seen in it his great chance of killing someone he hates?"

"Oh, I'm not worrying," Cumber said as he swung the bookcase back into place. "I may bum it later, but just now—well, you know how difficult it is for an artist to destroy a perfect bit of work."

Inspector Ropes thought him a complacent and dangerous fool. He knew crime too well to feel quite safe. He knew that scores of vile minds might be mulling over Cumber's 'revelation' even now. How many men and women who had nurtured the thought of murder for hate, greed, revenge, and a dozen other motives, must have been stirred by the news that the thing could be done in perfect security, merely through possessing the papers that this fool kept in his flat.

"It's like having a cylinder of poison gas in your house," the inspector said. "It's best destroyed, Mr. Cumber."

"It's too precious," smirked the novelist. "The mere possession of it gives me a glamour with *my* public. Let's change the subject to poker— But I'll ring you up, Ropes, if one of your pet burglars should get away with it— You'll find the cards and chips in that drawer, Mitchel—"

There was a curious constraint about the party, and Inspector Ropes, when he left later, felt a sense of anxiety. He considered that pressure really ought to be brought to bear on Cumber to destroy the paper.

He meant to talk to the Chief Constable about it, but was busy for the next two days on a receiving case. It was at one o'clock the next night that Cumber rang him out of sleep to say that his burglarproof safe had been "busted" and that the "formula for the perfect murder," as he called it, had been stolen.

"Sometime this evening," the novelist shouted over the wire. "I've only just got back from Lady Stripe's ball, and I'll swear the safe was intact when I came home to dress at seven— Are you awake, Ropes? Did you hear? I'm telling you the papers for the fool-proof murder have gone."

"What do you want me to do?" Ropes said sulkily. "I'm in bed, and—"

"But don't you grasp it?" Cumber yelped. "The danger of it *to me!*"

Ropes was taken aback by the real panic in the novelist's voice, if not so much by the "me." Cumber would, naturally, think of himself first, though who'd want to kill a fool like him. . . .

But Cumber was wailing:

"But, don't you see, I told the thing to all you chaps—and you—they all hate me. Boyington's never forgiven me for killing the sales of his last 'masterpiece' by my lecture on 'Backboneless Fiction.' Thoms—I know things about Thoms that could put him in jail, and he knows I know. Mitchel's always had his knife into me because I've beaten him at his own game; yes, and because he owes me money. Same thing about Pennyfold. He owes me thousands, and knows I could blot him out by bankruptcy if I liked. Tilbury—he thinks I'm the cueman who stands between him and a 'best seller' status. He's been longing to remove me by fair means or foul for years. . . . They all hate me because I'm such a success where they aren't, because they all owe me money. . . . They pretend to be friends, but I know—"

"You're talking nonsense," Ropes began.

"I'm not," Cumber almost screamed. "I know it was one of them— Of course I know. How? Because it isn't only the details of the fool-proof murder that have been stolen, all their IOUs, too, have gone— Yes, the IOUs of all four, and some more besides; that can only be a preliminary to murder—"

"Keep your head, man," Ropes snapped. "Even if you're not talking rubbish, you're not dead yet. We'll take good care—"

"You can't," Cumber screeched. "Not if the murderer has the papers. He can kill me at once without trace. I'm in desperate— O-oh!—"

Cumber's voice ended on a wild scream. There was a crashing in Ropes' ear as the telephone fell.

He hurled into his clothes, dashed by taxi to Cumber's place. He found the flat empty, and Cumber dead on the floor.

There was nobody there. No sign of violence anywhere.

"Most baffling case this," said the Divisional Inspector as he handed in his post-mortem report. "Not a trace of how the man died, nor even an hint as to its cause. I hope you've had better luck, Ropes."

"I've had none at all," the Inspector said. "There's not even the ghost of a clue. . . . And from the look of it, there never will be."

The Divisional Surgeon stared at him queerly, wondering why he laughed.

The Archer in the Arras

Lewis Spence

Lord D'Aintry peered through the night at the overturned car.

"The chap who ended a road suddenly like this in the midst of a deserted heath," said he, "deserves a niche in the Pantheon—and I hope he has it. Idiots are born—not made."

I rubbed my haunch and groaned.

"It's hopeless," continued D'Aintry, as he gloomed at the long outline of the racer at which we had toiled for over an hour. "In short, as a colonial friend of mine used to say, 'It's a blue duck.' Come on, Steuart, let's see what the locality can do for us. Isn't that a light over yonder among the trees? It looks cosy—like supper, eh?"

"I suppose it is," I moaned, "but I have seen so many stars recently that I'm incapable of saying whether it's astronomical or gastronomical. Oh Lord, here it comes!"

"It" was the rain. It fairly slashed. It might have been South African hail, so keen was the edge of it. Pulling up our coat-collars we ran, or rather limped, in the direction of the light, which was no very great distance away. As we passed through the belt of poplars which screened it from the road a great building loomed into sight, such a château as only Touraine and the fifteenth century could have produced. Its turrets and tourelles soared sheer and ghostly in a bewildering array above a solid yet fantastic façade, and the whole rose out of a broad moat which reflected the thin, watery moonlight in luminous patches.

As we saw whither we were bound we halted. At least I did, for I was no Lord D'Aintry, Earl of Chalbury to be, but merely that exalted stripling's travelling tutor, and so unaccustomed to look for lodgings for the night in fifteenth-century French châteaux.

"What's up?" snapped his lordship, as I stopped. "Won't this do?"

"Oh, it'll *do* all right, but—"

"But what, eh?" asked the boy testily. "You're an awful fidget, Steuart; never contented. It's just *got* to do, I tell you."

"As you like," I murmured humbly, for I had long ago given up the attempt to influence the youngster in any way. If you happen to know anything of the D'Aintrys you'll know why. "Let's hope they'll have us," I added, as we crossed the moat by a stone bridge and entered an imposing courtyard.

"Oh, I always carry cards," said D'Aintry sufficiently; "besides they're probably Americans. The whole front's dark, although it's only ten o'clock. The light's showing in that postern window. Where's the bell—ah!" and he tugged it resoundingly.

After some delay the door was opened about three inches, and a feminine voice, nasal and precise, inquired our business. D'Aintry took upon himself the task of explanation, but the lady behind the door did not seem at all convinced. The family were in Paris, she said, and she was alone in the house with the exception of two servant maids. Yes, she was the housekeeper. She was sorry for Messieurs, and the car would of course vouch for their respectability, but—

The doubtings were accentuated by the gradual closing of the door, and I was preparing for a ten-mile tramp through the rain, when the shutting process was suddenly arrested, a hand stole out, to a sound of tinkling sovereigns, and the door swung open. We were shown into a cosy little room, evidently the housekeeper's snuggery. The great living-rooms of the chateau were all closed, a circumstance we in no wise lamented as the room in which we were was warm and comfortable after the chill, rainy night, and French salons are usually more elegant than cheerful.

At first we were more inquisitive concerning our supper than our surroundings, but when the edge of appetite had been blunted, by ragoût, cream-cheese and excellent Bordeaux, curiosity returned, and I asked the old woman who was waiting upon us the name of the place we had so unceremoniously stormed. She looked very much astonished, laughed, and mentioned a name equally well known with Blois and Chambord as a show-place. As she uttered it, Denzil D'Aintry laid down his knife and fork with a clatter and stared at her open-mouthed. A moment later the housekeeper left the room to get us coffee, and he turned sharply to me and said in a strange voice, almost a whisper: "A D'Aintry in Brécourt! Isn't it odd? Surely we've done enough damage here without my butting in, eh? But I see you don't remember."

I shook my head. D'Aintry made a grimace of annoyance.

"You're as bad as the housekeeper," I said; "she expected us to know the name of her château, you expect me to know all about your family affairs."

D'Aintry groaned aloud. "The dear, good bourgeois!" he cried, more in sorrow than anger, "and he calls the annals of a house as important in the history of England as the Percys or the Cecils 'family affairs'! Well, I'm not such a conceited ass as to think that *everyone* knows our history," he continued, looking at me a little superciliously; "but, rotting apart, I'm sorry I came here, Steuart; it's like adding insult to injury."

"Was it as bad as that?" I asked; then, as he nodded affirmatively: "Please tell me about it."

"Well, Lynton, the chap who wrote our family history, you know, says that after the battle of Verneuil in 1426, by which the Duke of Bedford roped in all the country north of the Loire for England, my ancestor Denzil, first Earl of Chalbury, took prisoner the Sieur Alain de Brécourt, lord of this very château, and held him to ransom. He must have been hot stuff even for those times, for when the poor Frenchman couldn't or wouldn't pay up he heaped indignities upon him, and, suspecting him of concealing hidden treasure, tortured him so unmercifully that the unfortunate beggar died."

"The age was not a tender one, nor were men lavish of the humanities," I murmured, in polite excuse of the first Earl of Chalbury.

"Yes, but that's not the worst of it," continued D'Aintry, as if determined to atone in some measure for the villainies of his forbear. "The day after the Sieur de Brécourt died, his widow, unaware of his death, set out for the English camp with his ransom, which she had succeeded in raising by the greatest possible sacrifices. Even a devil would have sent her home safe and sound. But Denzil D'Aintry, my beautiful namesake, had her waylaid as she returned sorrowing to Brécourt, robbed her of the ransom, and ill-used her so shamefully that the poor girl went clean crazy. At all events, tradition says that she afterwards became a sorceress and that her château was abhorred by the people for miles around as a place of evil name because of sights and sounds that happened there. Her one grand aim and object in life became the extermination of the House of Chalbury. Disguised as a page she succeeded in killing the Earl who had so grievously wronged her. His brother and eldest son fell victims to the daggers of assassins instigated by her, and had she lived long enough I have no doubt that she would have succeeded in wiping out the entire family, such is the hate that can spring in the heart of a brave woman from a great wrong. It isn't a nice story to have behind you, is it?"

"Probably all of us have sprung from people whose deeds were no whiter than those of Earl Denzil," I said soothingly, for I saw that the boy was upset. "Come, I see you're tired. Shall we ask about sleeping arrangements?"

As the housekeeper returned I executed a tactful yawn. Denzil took up the cue and gaped monstrously. Catching at the hint the old dame asked if Messieurs would care to be shown their room, and when we gratefully assured her that that was the goal of our desire she took up a candle and beckoned to us to follow her.

"The gentlemen are too tired to be particular," she said smilingly, "but this, the oldest portion of the château, is usually occupied by the upper servants, and, as Messieurs are aware, all the best apartments are dismantled, so I must perforce put them in the steward's room. The gentlemen will see my difficulty and excuse me, I am sure."

"Don't mention it, Madame," said D'Aintry through a gigantic yawn; "anywhere out of the rain. . . ."

We followed in her wake down what seemed an interminable stone corridor.

"This is all of the fifteenth century," she said impressively, with an explanatory wave of her hand towards the grained roof. "But you are tired and I will not fatigue you with its history, which is sombre and gloomy—ah, so sad, so very sad."

"For heaven's sake don't tell her," whispered D'Aintry. "It might mean facing the rain again."

We mounted a much-worn spiral staircase, leading to a circular chamber, evidently part of one of the flying turrets which were so prominent a feature of the château from the outside. The great, gaunt room was lit by a single candle and occasional flashes from a newly lit fire which hummed and crackled in the huge, draughty fireplace. The housekeeper, giving a last glance around the room to assure herself that we had all we wanted, left us with a courteous "good-night." Fagged as we were, there was something so fantastic and striking about our sleeping-place that, instead of throwing off our clothes and jumping into the four-poster opposite the fireplace, we set about examining it by the light of the candles the housekeeper had left us. Its solidity was eloquent of its antiquity. The huge, canopied bed, raised on a dais, occupied most of the space; there was a wonderful sixteenth-century settle in a corner, and such stonework as peeped from beneath the tapestry was sumptuously chiselled. But the arras which concealed most of it was more remarkable than anything else in the apartment. As D'Aintry raised the candle into the reaches of gloom above us we drew breath sharply and stared at one another. Never had I seen such marvellous hangings. Not only were the designs with which they were covered harmonious and elegant in colour and grouping, but their wonderful state of preservation was most remarkable. As I looked at them more attentively I started, for, beginning next the door and continued around the circular wall of the chamber, I became aware first by a strange intuition, then by actual examination, that *they illustrated the tale of medieval barbarism which D'Aintry had just related to me!* The first group represented the battle of Verneuil, the central figures evidently being intended for the Sieur de Brécourt and the Earl of Chalbury. The French knight, surrounded by men-at-arms, one of whom bore the Chalbury banner, was seen in the act of handing his sword to his captor, whose visor was closed. In the second group was depicted the torture of the Sieur de Brécourt. Stretched on a rack, his tightly compressed lips revealed the degree of torment he suffered. Over him stood Denzil, Earl of Chalbury, a sinister figure, with knitted brows and mouth twisted in a savage sneer. The death of the hapless Sieur de Brécourt was next pathetically portrayed. Then followed the waylaying of his lady, and this—a striking and arresting panel—concluded the series.

I turned to Denzil D'Aintry. He was staring at the tapestry before him as if under a spell. Had the incidents which it portrayed been enacted in stern reality before him he could not have shown greater astonishment.

"Steuart," he whispered hoarsely, "you know what they mean. I'm not a superstitious ass, but, by Jove, it's uncanny. And just look at this figure over the mantel. You'd think it was painted instead of woven."

I looked up and beheld a wondrous work indeed. It represented a man in a hunting-dress of the fifteenth century, a furred jerkin, belted at the waist, feathered cap of maintenance, and short boots of deerskin. The figure was of life-size and stood full face to us, and I at once recognized it as the same as that which represented the Sieur de Brécourt in the other tableaux. The face was that of a man of perhaps thirty-five, stern, resolved, and military in aspect. The figure held in its left hand a bow at full stretch with an arrow notched to the string, as if ready for discharge. If the other pieces were spirited and lifelike the reality and vividness of this were positively startling in the similitude of the flesh tints, the vivacity of the expression, and the natural pose which distinguished it.

"Gad, there's writing beneath!" cried D'Aintry excitedly. "It's old French, I think. Can you make it out, Steuart?"

An acquaintance with medieval scripts enabled me to negotiate the crabbed, woven figures, and I read as follows, translating as I did so: "This tapestry, the labour of love and grief, was woven in memory of the murdered Alain, Sieur de Brécourt, by his heartbroken spouse Elise, and finished in the year 1433." Then followed cabalistic figures such as I had seen in the magical grimoires of the late Middle Ages.

I looked again at D'Aintry. His face was white and strained, and his hand shook as he held the candle above his head.

"Come," I said, "this room is enough to give anyone a fit of the blues. Let's ask the housekeeper to give us another."

"No, no, Steuart," said the lad decidedly, as if ashamed of the weakness he had displayed. "Let's dowse the glim and hop into bed. We can have a good look at all this to-morrow morning." And throwing off our clothes we blew out the candies and dived into the depths of the great four-poster.

I leapt up in bed, a strange light before my eyes. Rubbing them, and looking about me, I saw that it proceeded from the neighborhood of the tapestry above the mantel, which was now dim illumined by a thin, watery gleam, uncertain and phosphorescent, which seemed to concentrate itself upon the figure of the man with the bow. The light, whatever it was, had also aroused D'Aintry, for he sat up in bed and, seizing me convulsively by the wrist, pointed in what seemed an ecstasy of terror at the figure above us.

"Good heavens, Steuart, what's that?" he cried.

As I gazed I became transfixed with horror, for the face that stared down upon us with eyes full of dire and malignant hatred no longer wore the immobility of a figured thing, but was instinct with expression and movement, and informed with the hues of life. Fascinated, I watched for a few brief seconds the workings of that furious and hate-inspired countenance as with anguished eyes and distorted lips it glared upon us from above as if in a frenzy of loathing. D'Aintry's nails ate into my flesh, and his voice rose to a shriek as he cried:

"Good God! Steuart, it's moving; see, it's—"

As he spoke came a humming sound as of a loosened bowstring, followed by a shriek of mortal agony and a horrid sob. Instantly all was dark—a darkness that brought with it an agonizing silence. Leaping from the bed I stumbled madly towards the table on which we had left our candles, and struck a light.

"D'Aintry," I cried thickly, "it's all right now, old fellow, it's gone . . . gone." But the sound of my own voice terrified me, and I went over to the bed, candle in hand, full of a hideous fear and with averted eyes. With a mighty effort I looked at that which was heaped upon the tangled sheets.

For there with terrible dead eyes, which yet glared with a horror unspeakable, lay Denzil, Lord D'Aintry—a great cloth-yard shaft in his heart!

At the Article of Death

John Buchan

"Nullum
Sacra caput Proserpina fugit."

A NOISELESS EVENING FELL CHILL AND DANK ON THE MOORLANDS. THE DREICHIL was mist to the very rim of its precipitous face, and the long, dun sides of the Little Muneraw faded into grey vapour. Underfoot were plashy moss and dripping heather, and all the air was choked with autumnal heaviness. The herd of the Lanely Bield stumbled wearily homeward in this, the late afternoon, with the roof-tree of his cottage to guide him over the waste.

For weeks, months, he had been ill, fighting the battle of a lonely sickness. Two years agone his wife had died, and as there had been no child, he was left to fend for himself. He had no need for any woman, he declared, for his wants were few and his means of the scantiest, so he had cooked his own meals and done his own household work since the day he had stood by the grave in the Gledsmuir kirkyard. And for a little he did well; and then, inch by inch, trouble crept upon him. He would come home late in the winter nights, soaked to the skin, and sit in the peat-reek till his clothes dried on his body. The countless little ways in which a woman's hand makes a place healthy and habitable were unknown to him, and soon he began to pay the price of his folly. For he was not a strong man, though a careless onlooker might have guessed the opposite from his mighty frame. His folk had all been short-lived, and already his was the age of his father at his death. Such a fact might have warned him to circumspection; but he took little heed till that night in the March before, when, coming up the Little Muneraw and breathing hard, a chill wind on the summit cut him to the bone. He rose the next morn, shaking like a leaf, and then for weeks he lay ill in bed, while a younger shepherd from the next sheep-farm did his work on the hill. In the early summer he rose a broken man, without strength or nerve, and always oppressed with an ominous sinking in the chest; but he toiled through his duties, and told no man his sorrow. The summer was parchingly hot, and the hillsides grew brown and dry as ashes. Often as he laboured up the interminable ridges, he found himself sickening at heart with a poignant regret. These were the places where once he had strode so freely with the crisp air cool on his forehead. Now he had no eye for the pastoral loveliness, no ear for the witch-song of the desert. When he reached a summit, it was only to fall panting, and when he came home at nightfall he sank wearily on a seat.

And so through the lingering summer the year waned to an autumn of storm. Now his malady seemed nearing its end. He had seen no man's face for a week, for long miles of moor severed him from a homestead. He could scarce struggle from his bed by mid-day, and his daily round of the hill was gone through with tottering feet. The time would soon come for drawing the ewes and driving them to the Gledsmuir market. If he could but hold on till the word came, he might yet have speech of a fellow man and bequeath his duties to another. But if he died first, the charge would wander uncared for, while he himself would lie in that lonely cot till such time as the lowland farmer sent the messenger. With anxious care he tended his flickering spark of life—he had long ceased to hope—and with something like heroism looked blankly towards his end.

But on this afternoon all things had changed. At the edge of the water-meadow he had found blood dripping from his lips, and half-swooned under an agonising pain at his heart. With burning eyes he turned his face to home, and fought his way inch by inch through the desert. He counted the steps crazily, and with pitiful sobs looked upon mist and moorland. A faint bleat of a sheep came to his ear; he heard it clearly, and the hearing wrung his soul. Not for him any more the hills of sheep and a shepherd's free and wholesome life. He was creeping, stricken, to his homestead to die, like a wounded fox crawling to its earth. And the loneliness of it all, the pity, choked him more than the fell grip of his sickness.

Inside the house a great banked fire of peats was smouldering. Unwashed dishes stood on the table, and the bed in the corner was unmade, for such things were of little moment in the extremity of his days. As he dragged his leaden foot over the threshold, the autumn dusk thickened through the white fog, and shadows awaited him, lurking in every corner. He dropped carelessly on the bed's edge, and lay back in deadly weakness. No sound broke the stillness, for the clock had long ago stopped for lack of winding. Only the shaggy collie which had lain down by the fire looked to the bed and whined mournfully.

In a little he raised his eyes and saw that the place was filled with darkness, save where the red eye of the fire glowed hot and silent. His strength was too far gone to light the lamp, but he could make a crackling fire. Some power other than himself made him heap bog-sticks on the peat and poke it feebly, for he shuddered at the ominous long shades which peopled floor and ceiling. If he had but a leaping blaze he might yet die in a less gross mockery of comfort.

Long he lay in the firelight, sunk in the lethargy of illimitable feebleness. Then the strong spirit of the man began to flicker within him and rise to sight ere it sank in death.

He had always been a godly liver, one who had no youth of folly to look back upon, but a well-spent life of toil lit by the lamp of a half-understood devotion. He it was who at his wife's death-bed had administered words of comfort and hope; and had passed all his days with the thought of his own end fixed like a bull's eye in the target of his meditations. In his lonely hill-watches, in the weariful lambing days, and on droving journeys to faraway towns, he had whiled the hours with self-communing, and self-examination, by the help of a rigid Word. Nay, there had been far more than the mere punctilios of obedience to the letter; there had been the living fire of love, the heroical altitude of self-denial, to be the halo of his solitary life. And now God had sent him the last fiery trial, and he was left alone to put off the garments of mortality.

He dragged himself to a cupboard where all the appurtenances of the religious life lay to his hands. There were Spurgeon's sermons in torn covers, and a dozen musty "Christian Treasuries." Some antiquated theology, which he had got from his father, lay lowest, and on the top was the gaudy Bible, which he had once received from a grateful Sabbath class while he yet sojourned in the lowlands. It was lined and re-lined, and there he had often found consolation. Now in the last faltering of mind he had braced himself to the thought that he must die as became his possession, with the Word of God in his hand, and his thoughts fixed on that better country, which is an heavenly.

The thin leaves mocked his hands, and he could not turn to any well-remembered text. In vain he struggled to reach the gospels; the obstinate leaves blew back ever to a dismal psalm or a prophet's lamentation. A word caught his eye and he read vaguely: "The Shepherds slumber, O King, . . . the people is scattered upon the mountains . . . and no man gathereth them . . . there is no healing of the hurt, for the wound is grievous." Something in the poignant sorrow of the phrase caught his attention for one second, and then he was back in a fantasy of pain and impotence. He could not fix his mind, and even as he strove he remembered the warning he had so often given to others against death-bed repentance. Then, he had often said, a man has no time to make his peace with his Maker, when he is wrestling with death. Now the adage came back to him; and gleams of comfort shot for one moment through his soul. He at any rate had long since chosen for God, and the good Lord would see and pity His servant's weakness.

A sheep bleated near the window, and then another. The flocks were huddling down, and wind and wet must be coming. Then a long dreary wind sighed round the dwelling, and at the same moment a bright tongue of flame shot up from the fire, and queer crooked shadows flickered over the ceiling. The sight caught his eyes, and he shuddered in nameless terror. He had never been a coward, but like all religious folk he had imagination and emotion. Now his fancy was perturbed, and he shrank from these uncanny shapes. In the failure of all else he had fallen to the repetition of bare phrases, telling of the fragrance and glory of the city of God. "River of the water of Life," he said to himself, . . . "the glory and honour of the nations . . . and the street of the city was pure gold . . . and the saved shall walk in the light of it . . . and God shall wipe away all tears from their eyes."

Again a sound without, the cry of sheep and the sough of a lone wind. He was sinking fast, but the noise gave him a spasm of strength. The dog rose and sniffed uneasily at the door, a trickle of rain dripped from the roofing, and all the while the silent heart of the fire glowed and hissed at his side. It seemed an uncanny thing that now in the moment of his anguish the sheep should bleat as they had done in the old strong days of herding.

Again the sound, and again the morris-dance of shadows among the rafters. The thing was too much for his failing mind. Some words of hope—"streams in the desert, and"—died on his lips, and he crawled from the bed to a cupboard. He had not tasted strong drink for a score of years, for to the true saint in the uplands abstinence is a primary virtue; but he kept brandy in the house for illness or wintry weather. Now it would give him strength, and it was no sin to cherish the spark of life.

He found the spirits and gulped down a mouthful—one, two, till the little flask was drained, and the raw fluid spilled over beard and coat. In his days of health it would have made him drunk, but now all the fibres of his being were relaxed, and it merely stung him to a fantasmal vigour. More, it maddened his brain, already tottering under the assaults of death. Before he had thought feebly and greyly, now his mind surged in an ecstasy.

The pain that lay heavy on his chest, that clutched his throat, that tugged at his heart, was as fierce as ever, but for one short second the utter weariness of spirit was gone. The old fair words of Scripture came back to him, and he murmured promises and hopes till his strength failed him for all but thought, and with closed eyes he fell back to dream.

But only for one moment; the next he was staring blankly in a mysterious terror. Again the voices of the wind, again the shapes on floor and wall and the relentless eye of the fire. He was too helpless to move and too crazy to pray; he could only lie and stare, numb with expectancy. The liquor seemed to have driven all memory from him, and left him with a child's heritage of dreams and stories.

Crazily he pattered to himself a child's charm against evil fairies, which the little folk of the moors still speak at their play,—

"Wearie, Ovie, gang awa',
Dinna show your face at a',

Ower the muir and down the burn,
Wearie, Ovie, ne'er return."

The black crook of the chimney was the object of his spells, for the kindly ingle was no less than a malignant twisted devil, with an awful red eye glowering through smoke.

His breath was winnowing through his worn chest like an autumn blast in bare rafters. The horror of the black night without, all filled with the wail of sheep, and the deeper fear of the red light within, stirred his brain, not with the far-reaching fanciful terror of men, but with the crude homely fright of a little child. He would have sought, had his strength suffered him, to cower one moment in the light as a refuge from the other, and the next to hide in darkest corner to shun the maddening glow. And with it all he was acutely conscious of the last pangs of mortality. He felt the grating of cheek-bones on skin, and the sighing, which did duty for breath, rocked him with agony.

Then a great shadow rose out of the gloom and stood shaggy in the firelight. The man's mind was tottering, and once more he was back at his Scripture memories and vague repetitions. Aforetime his fancy had toyed with green fields, now it held to the darker places. "It was the day when Evil Merodach was the king in Babylon," came the quaint recollection, and some lingering ray of thought made him link the odd name with the amorphous presence before him. The thing moved and came nearer, touched him, and brooded by his side. He made to shriek, but no sound came, only a dry rasp in the throat and a convulsive twitch of the limbs.

For a second he lay in the agony of a terror worse than the extremes of death. It was only his dog, returned from his watch by the door, and seeking his master. He, poor beast, knew of some sorrow vaguely and afar, and nuzzled into his side with dumb affection.

Then from the chaos of faculties a shred of will survived. For an instant his brain cleared, for to most there comes a lull at the very article of death. He saw the bare moorland room, he felt the dissolution of his members, the palpable ebb of life. His religion had been swept from him like a rotten garment. His mind was vacant of memories, for all were driven forth by purging terror. Only some relic of manliness, the heritage of cleanly and honest days, was with him to the uttermost. With blank thoughts, without hope or vision, with naught save an aimless resolution and a causeless bravery, he passed into the short anguish which is death.

AUGUST HEAT

WILLIAM FRYER HARVEY

Penistone Road, Clapham,
20th August, 190-.

I HAVE HAD WHAT I BELIEVE TO BE THE MOST REMARKABLE DAY IN MY LIFE, AND while the events are still fresh in my mind, I wish to put them down on paper as clearly as possible.

Let me say at the outset that my name is James Clarence Withencroft.

I am forty years old, in perfect health, never having known a day's illness.

By profession I am an artist, not a very successful one, but I earn enough money by my black-and-white work to satisfy my necessary wants.

My only near relative, a sister, died five years ago, so that I am independent.

I breakfasted this morning at nine, and after glancing through the morning paper I lighted my pipe and proceeded to let my mind wander in the hope that I might chance upon some subject for my pencil.

The room, though door and windows were open, was oppressively hot, and I had just made up my mind that the coolest and most comfortable place in the neighbour-hood would be the deep end of the public swimming-bath, when the idea came.

I began to draw. So intent was I on my work that I left my lunch untouched, only stopping work when the clock of St. Jude's struck four.

The final result, for a hurried sketch, was, I felt sure, the best thing I had done.

It showed a criminal in the dock immediately after the judge had pronounced sen-tence. The man was fat—enormously fat. The flesh hung in rolls about his chin; it creased his huge, stumpy neck. He was clean-shaven (perhaps I should say a few days before he must have been clean shaven) and almost bald. He stood in the dock, his short, clumsy fingers clasping the rail, looking straight in front of him. The feeling that his expression conveyed was not so much one of horror as of utter, absolute collapse.

There seemed nothing in the man strong enough to sustain that mountain of flesh.

I rolled up the sketch, and without quite knowing why, placed it in my pocket. Then with the rare sense of happiness which the knowledge of a good thing well done gives, I left the house.

I believe that I set out with the idea of calling upon Trenton, for I remember walk-ing along Lytton Street and turning to the right along Gilchrist Road at the bottom of the hill where the men were at work on the new tram lines.

From there onwards I have only the vaguest recollection of where I went. The one thing of which I was fully conscious was the awful heat, that came up from the dusty asphalt pavement as an almost palpable wave. I longed for the thunder promised by the great banks of copper-coloured cloud that hung low over the western sky.

I must have walked five or six miles, when a small boy roused me from my reverie by asking the time.

It was twenty minutes to seven.

When he left me I began to take stock of my bearings. I found myself standing before a gate that led into a yard bordered by a strip of thirsty earth, where there were flowers, purple stock and scarlet geranium. Above the entrance was a board with the inscription:

CHS. ATKINSON. MONUMENTAL MASON.

WORKER IN ENGLISH AND ITALIAN MARBLES.

From the yard itself came a cheery whistle, the noise of hammer blows, and the cold sound of steel meeting stone.

A sudden impulse made me enter.

A man was sitting with his back towards me, busy at work on a slab of curiously veined marble. He turned round as he heard my steps and I stopped short.

It was the man I had been drawing, whose portrait lay in my pocket.

He sat there, huge and elephantine, the sweat pouring from his scalp, which he wiped with a red silk handkerchief. But though the face was the same, the expression was absolutely different.

He greeted me smiling, as if we were old friends, and shook my hand.

I apologized for my intrusion.

"Everything is hot and glary outside," I said. "This seems an oasis in the wilderness."

"I don't know about the oasis," he replied, "but it certainly is hot, as hot as hell. Take a seat, sir!"

He pointed to the end of the gravestone on which he was at work, and I sat down.

"That's a beautiful piece of stone you've got hold of," I said.

He shook his head. "In a way it is," he answered; "the surface here is as fine as anything you could wish, but there's a big flaw at the back, though I don't expect you'd ever notice it. I could never make really a good job of a bit of marble like that. It would be all right in a summer like this; it wouldn't mind the blasted heat. But wait till the winter comes. There's nothing quite like frost to find out the weak points in stone."

"Then what's it for?" I asked.

The man burst out laughing.

"You'd hardly believe me if I was to tell you it's for an exhibition, but it's the truth. Artists have exhibitions: so do grocers and butchers; we have them too. All the latest little things in headstones, you know."

He went on to talk of marbles, which sort best withstood wind and rain, and which were easiest to work; then of his garden and a new sort of carnation he had bought. At the end of every other minute he would drop his tools, wipe his shining head, and curse the heat.

I said little, for I felt uneasy. There was something unnatural, uncanny, in meeting this man.

I tried at first to persuade myself that I had seen him before, that his face, unknown to me, had found a place in some out-of-the-way corner of my memory, but I knew that I was practising little more than a plausible piece of self-deception.

Mr. Atkinson finished his work, spat on the ground, and got up with a sigh of relief.

"There! what do you think of that?" he said, with an air of evident pride.

The inscription which I read for the first time was this:

SACRED TO THE MEMORY

OF

JAMES CLARENCE WITHENCROFT.

BORN JAN. 18TH, 1860.

HE PASSED AWAY VERY SUDDENLY

ON AUGUST 20TH, 190—

"*IN THE MIDST OF LIFE WE ARE IN DEATH*"

For some time I sat in silence. Then a cold shudder ran down my spine. I asked him where he had seen the name.

"Oh, I didn't see it anywhere," replied Mr. Atkinson. "I wanted some name, and I put down the first that came into my head. Why do you want to know?"

"It's a strange coincidence, but it happens to be mine."

He gave a long, low whistle.

"And the dates?"

"I can only answer for one of them, and that's correct."

"It's a rum go!" he said.

But he knew less than I did. I told him of my morning's work. I took the sketch from my pocket and showed it to him. As he looked, the expression of his face altered until it became more and more like that of the man I had drawn.

"And it was only the day before yesterday," he said, "that I told Maria there were no such things as ghosts!"

Neither of us had seen a ghost, but I knew what he meant.

"You probably heard my name," I said.

"And you must have seen me somewhere and have forgotten it! Were you at Clacton-on-Sea last July?"

I had never been to Clacton in my life. We were silent for some time. We were both looking at the same thing, the two dates on the gravestone, and one was right.

"Come inside and have some supper," said Mr. Atkinson.

His wife is a cheerful little woman, with the flaky red cheeks of the country-bred. Her husband introduced me as a friend of his who was an artist. The result was unfortunate, for after the sardines and watercress had been removed, she brought put a Doré Bible, and I had to sit and express my admiration for nearly half an hour.

I went outside, and found Atkinson sitting on the gravestone smoking.

We resumed the conversation at the point we had left off.

"You must excuse my asking," I said, "but do you know of anything you've done for which you could be put on trial?"

He shook his head.

"I'm not a bankrupt, the business is prosperous enough. Three years ago I gave turkeys to some of the guardians at Christmas, but that's all I can think of. And they were small ones, too," he added as an afterthought.

He got up, fetched a can from the porch, and began to water the flowers. "Twice a day regular in the hot weather," he said, "and then the heat sometimes gets the better of the delicate ones. And ferns, good Lord! they could never stand it. Where do you live?"

I told him my address. It would take an hour's quick walk to get back home.

"It's like this," he said. "We'll look at the matter straight. If you go back home to-night, you take your chance of accidents. A cart may run over you, and there's always banana skins and orange peel, to say nothing of falling ladders."

He spoke of the improbable with an intense seriousness that would have been laughable six hours before. But I did not laugh.

"The best thing we can do," he continued, "is for you to stay here till twelve o'clock. We'll go upstairs and smoke; it may be cooler inside."

To my surprise I agreed.

We are sitting now in a long, low room beneath the eaves. Atkinson has sent his wife to bed. He himself is busy sharpening some tools at a little oilstone, smoking one of my cigars the while.

The air seems charged with thunder. I am writing this at a shaky table before the open window. The leg is cracked, and Atkinson, who seems a handy man with his tools, is going to mend it as soon as he has finished putting an edge on his chisel.

It is after eleven now. I shall be gone in less than an hour.

But the heat is stifling.

It is enough to send a man mad.

THE AVENGING PHONOGRAPH

E. R. PUNSHON

THIS VERDICT OF "SUICIDE DURING TEMPORARY INSANITY" THE MAYOR HAD SO confidently anticipated, that he experienced no particular sensation of relief when he heard the foreman of the jury actually pronounce the words that assured his safety. It simply seemed to him that no other result had been possible. Every single detail of the crime he had arranged with the utmost care, and with that admirable mixture of prudence, forethought, and determination which had raised him from a barefooted boy selling newspapers in the street to be Mayor of the town and one of its most prominent business men. No one knew of the connection between him and the dead man; even if any chance suspicion of foul play did arise he was the last man on whom that suspicion would fall, and his heart swelled within him with the consciousness of his absolute and perfect safety. He looked round the court now with that decorous expression of subdued melancholy the tragic death of a fellow-citizen required, and he conceived a scorn for these smug, smiling folk whose selfcomplacence he could so shatter by a word.

"If I were just to jump on a chair and say 'This man was murdered, and I did it,' he thought to himself, "how they would all stare and shudder."

A grim smile touched his firm-set lips, and he was so confident in his own strength that he even played a little with the idea, picturing the horror and consternation of the crowd, before he set the thought aside.

The court was clearing now, and he went out with the others, who respectfully made way for His Worship. The chemist, whose place of business was next to his own, came and walked by his side, and they chatted in subdued tones about this unfortunate business which had so disturbed the even tenor of the little town's placid life.

"Frankly," said the Mayor, "while I do not blame the jury, I consider their verdict more merciful than just."

The chemist agreed. It seemed he cherished a certain resentment against the dead man. He spoke of him rather hardly, and the Mayor pleaded mildly for a more charitable judgment.

"After all, he is dead," he said, "and death covers everything."

"Yes, but the way he took to die—the way of it," insisted the chemist. "Such things may be common enough in great cities, but here one feels it as a blot upon us all—a stain upon the fair fame of the town," he said, waving a lean hand in the air.

"It is certainly most regrettable," said the Mayor; "but still, no one knows what troubles he may have had."

But the chemist would not be placated. He hinted that he wished the jury had brought in a verdict of "Felo-de-se."

"Self-murder is self-murder," he declared, sawing up and down with his lean right hand, "and there can be no excuse for it."

"Still," the mayor urged with a secret smile, "it is possible we do not know the whole truth about the affair."

"We know quite enough," said the chemist, with severity. "Besides," he added, thoughtfully, "he owed me nine and sevenpence, which I suppose now I shall never get."

The Mayor agreed that the recovery of this debt was doubtful, and as the chemist turned to enter his shop he glanced after him with amused scorn.

"By Jove," he said to himself lightly, "I have half a mind to tell him, just to see him shiver. The chattering fool, how he would gasp if he knew!"

It amused him greatly to think of the look that would spread over the chemist's lean and hollow countenance if he knew the truth, and he allowed his mind to play with this fancy for some minutes.

He went up to his office and answered two or three business letters, but he felt he had earned a holiday, and he returned home early. After dinner, which he ate with a keen appetite, he sat down with a good cigar and a glass of weak whisky and water, and in his mind he went over the whole affair again. In the evidence given before the coroner there had been various mistakes and small discrepancies, all of which he had noticed with keen interest.

For example, the smart detective fellow had put the time of death at half-past seven, while in reality it had been two hours later. The mistake had pleased the Mayor immensely, as showing how even the police could blunder. Why, what chance had they of finding out the truth when they began by making such a mistake as that?

Then again, the doctor had sworn that death must have been instantaneous, while the Mayor knew very well that the dying man had retained his consciousness for some minutes. He had lain and looked up at his slayer, and in his fast glazing eyes had been a stare of wild amazement, not reproach, not accusation, not anger or threat, only absolute astonishment. Even his victim in the very moment of death, reflected the Mayor, had not been able to realise his guilt, and this thought pleased him so much that he burst into a harsh laugh.

His wife, mild and frightened, sat opposite to him, engaged as usual with her knitting, and the unexpected sound so startled her that she actually spoke without being spoken to.

"This suicide," she said, "is very terrible, is it not?"

"A stain upon the fair fame of the town," he answered, mocking the babbling chemist. He always permitted himself more licence when alone with his wife than at any other time, for he knew the awe in which she held him, and his imitation of the chemist's tone was palpable. "Self-murder is a dreadful crime," he said.

"Dreadful," she agreed. She dropped a stitch in her knitting and paused to pick it up. "Dreadful," she sighed again, "and I suppose the dear Rector will not permit him to be buried in the churchyard," and her amiable and vacant countenance took on an expression of the deepest horror.

"I expect not," said the Mayor, and for the first time a real desire seized him to tell his secret. For there was a latent cruelty in his nature that now was wakening to stronger life, and he perceived quite plainly how if he told her she would gasp and shrink before the dreadful knowledge, and stare and mutter and presently die, crushed beneath its awful weight. But he set aside the thought, for to speak would be to imperil his own safety.

He sat in silence, sipping his whisky, and his thoughts were pleasant. What if there was one lay dead, branded with the name of suicide? Self-preservation was the first law of nature, and he had merely removed a man whose existence threatened his own. Even if there were a God—a point on which the Mayor entertained the gravest doubts— surely He must see quite clearly that even by the silly standard of the world the Mayor was certainly no worse than anyone else, and probably a great deal better than most.

He finished his whisky, yawned, and observed that it was bedtime. Really, the day had been more trying than he had quite realised, and he felt tired. As he undressed he pushed the window open and leaned out, enjoying the fragrant sweetness of the night air. He was not used to notice such things, but tonight he did. It all seemed wonderfully quiet and still, this little town that slumbered there so peacefully in the kindly darkness, and then it came into his mind how he could shatter all this peace and serenity by just opening his lips and shouting a certain thing aloud. How they would all stir and buzz, like an overturned hive of bees. A policeman passing by paused to throw the light of his lantern over the house, and the Mayor called down to him.

"A nice evening, Tompkins," he said; "anything stirring?"

"Yes, Your Worship, a lovely night," answered the man. "No, Your Worship, nothing stirring."

"Good night, Tompkins," said the Mayor.

"Good night, Your Worship," replied the man.

He went stolidly on his way, and the Mayor listened to his heavy and slow steps dying away in the distance. It amused him to reflect how different the man's demeanour would have been if he had only known. But he did not know, and he never would, and there lay the joke; and the Mayor was so confident in his own strength that again he was able to play with the idea of dropping into the police-station and telling them all about it, till he fell into a gentle and quiet slumber from which he woke next morning happy and refreshed.

He felt in extra good spirits, and when he got to his office he found intelligence waiting him of the unexpectedly successful completion of some business that would mean a really large sum of money in his pocket.

"If this had only come a week ago," he reflected, "perhaps he might be alive today. But, after all, it's as well as it is, for I remember," thought the Mayor, "that he always annoyed me."

Later he went to a meeting of the council and listened to an interminable discussion on the "Late sad event which has so disturbed our town and cast so dark a stain upon its fair fame." This phrase was the chemist's contribution to the lengthy argument about the most fitting successor to the office the dead man had held. Some wanted the office that had been so disgraced abolished altogether. The Mayor listened to it very patiently, amusing himself by picturing the different expressions that would come on each man's face if he were to rise and say:

"But all your talk is founded on the belief that this man committed suicide, whereas, in truth, I killed him."

But this time, bored by the long discussion, he played with the thought so long that suddenly he was aware of a quick fear lest it should change from an amusement to a necessity. He sat upright and called the councillor just then speaking to order with some asperity, and then he became angry that such an absurd idea should have had power to chill him with so deadly a fear.

After the meeting was over he walked away with the Rector, of whom he inquired whether there was not some ancient tale of a king who could not keep a secret, and so told it to the reeds on the river bank?

The Rector said there was, and told him the story, adding that a secret, when of a guilty nature, was a great burden.

"There are many I've kept," observed the Mayor, with a sudden tightening of his grim lips, as he thought of this last one he was keeping so well, and of how pale and terrified the Rector would look if he told it him.

But the story of this old burdened king, who, in his anxiety for relief from the intolerable burden of his silence, spoke at last to the treacherous reeds, though it aroused his liveliest contempt, yet somehow never left his mind. He found himself thinking of it intently one day as he stared into the window of the local bicycle maker, who also dealt in phonographs.

"One of these would have suited the old boy better than his reeds," he reflected as he went away, and that afternoon he left business early and went for a long solitary walk on the downs above the town.

A poignant desire controlled his feet, and though he said to himself that he would not and that he must not, presently he found himself in a position from which he could look down upon the actual scene of the grim tragedy of a few days before. There was the hedge behind which he had crept, there the ditch in which he had crouched, and there was the little gully down into which the dying man had fallen after receiving the fatal blow.

"I killed him," said the Mayor aloud, and he looked around him and then half in fear up at the broad blue sky above.

But the sky remained untroubled and the earth unheeding. The sun still shone, all nature still laughed with the joy of early summer, from a distance a rabbit watched him cautiously, and near by a bird perched on a bush and sang its loudest.

"I killed him," he said again; "but, Lord, where's the satisfaction of saying so where no one can hear or make any reply?"

Suddenly he perceived that his forehead was damp, and he knew that this was because what he had feared had come to pass—that what had been an idle fancy indulged in for amusement had now taken on an aspect of necessity.

"But I'll not speak," he said, "I'll keep silence."

He struck his hand upon his lips as though he held them treacherous and would chastise them, and walked straight back to the town, keeping his teeth tightly clenched all the way. Opposite the bicycle maker's he paused again and then went in to inquire about getting a new machine. From bicycles he went on to talk of phonographs, and presently inquired about their cost. It seemed he had some idea of using one in business to dictate his letters into, and he wished to know if that could be done. The bicycle maker assured him that it could, and showed him how, but the Mayor seemed captious and hard to please. Indeed, had not the bicycle maker been an adroit and persistent salesman the Mayor would probably have gone away without making any decision, and, as it was, all he would consent to was that one should be sent up to his house for him to try.

"It was only a passing fancy; I expect it would be more trouble than it would be worth," he said, and the next day he received with an angry growl the information that the phonograph he had ordered was in his study.

But, after a time, he went and sat in the study, looking oddly at the machine standing on the table. For long he sat there, staring down the brass mouth of the recorder. It had been sent up all ready, so that he knew all he had to do was to speak into the trumpet and his words would be engraved on the wax, ready to be reproduced and spoken back to him at his will. Presently he got up and locked the door and window and drew the blind as though he were preparing for an afternoon snooze. Then he went back and, picking up the poker, looked sideways at the machine as though he were about to break it into little pieces, and yet were afraid it might understand his purpose and defend itself in some way at once unexpected and terrible. The thought all the time was hot in his mind that if he once told this thing his secret and let it tell it back to him, then once he had heard another voice pronouncing those dread words of guilt and horror, he would no longer have any desire to speak them aloud in the ear of the world in the way that had first amused him and then obsessed him.

Suddenly he dropped the poker and began to talk eagerly, swiftly, very softly, and as he thus whispered to the machine, with its gulping trumpet ear, a deep peace grew within him, and a sense of certain, sweet security.

"That's done," he said exultingly, as he jumped up the moment he had finished and rushed to the window.

Throwing it open, he leaned out to draw in deep breaths of the fresh, open air, and only now, by the intensity of his relief, did he understand how great had been the strain upon him. He remained there for a little, full of his new sense of perfect security. He enjoyed this sensation of relief and the freshness of the air so much that he decided to stroll round the garden before returning to hear the machine talk and then destroying it for ever, and with it the nightmare of oppression and desire that had lain so heavily on him these last few days.

He left his study and went into the drawing-room, where his wife was knitting.

"Emily," he said, knowing that to her his word was absolute law, "I have left that phonograph on the study table. See that no one goes near it."

"Very well, dear," she answered meekly, and he was well assured of her obedience. "Are you going to keep it?" she asked.

"No," he answered violently, "they are silly things—stupid, troublesome, idiotic." He abused it angrily for a moment or two, deriving a certain pleasure from speaking scornfully of this machine that had witnessed his weakness. "No," he concluded, "I certainly shall not keep it."

"I'm very glad," said his wife, "I never liked the things. I can't think it right some-how for a voice to be speaking where no one is. Of course I know it's very clever, but I can't think it right for all that."

"Well, mind you see no one touches it," said the Mayor. He did not usually give rea-sons for what he told her to do, but now he added: "It is out of order apparently, for it won't work properly, and I don't want them to be able to say anyone else meddled with it."

"Very well," answered his wife, obediently, "I will see it is not touched."

He heard the renewed click of her knitting needles as he went out, and he was certain that she would never dream of disobeying him.

He walked for a few minutes in the garden, feeling an odd pleasure in knowing that his secret was safe in a little wooden box with a sort of trumpet on its top, that stood upon his study table. It was good to know the secret was there, and no longer on his mind, and good, too, to know that in a moment he would return and destroy the box and it together for evermore. But when he went back to the study the table was bare, and he looked at it for a long time before he went into the drawing-room and, standing softly by the door, asked in a low tone where the phonograph was.

"Oh, the man came for it from the shop, dear," his wife answered, as still her knitting needles clicked placidly on. "I told him you said it was out of order, so he took it away. He said he could soon put it to rights, and he wanted to know if he might bring another one instead."

The Mayor did not answer, but he came nearer to her, going cautiously, holding by the wall, and she watched him as the deer watches the crouching tiger, for it was in his mind that he would kill her, and somehow she understood that quite distinctly. Neither of them spoke as he drew unsteadily nearer, and then she leaped up and fled, with her ball of wool bounding grotesquely behind her. She fled, only knowing that she was very greatly afraid, but he made no attempt to follow her. She never stayed till she reached her mother's house, where she spent the night, but in the morning she came back, arriving just as some men brought in the unpleasantly wet body of the Mayor that they had just taken from the river, from the pool a little below the old mill.

"For my part," said the bicycle maker later that day, "I am certain he was not right in his mind, for yesterday night he sent me back a phonograph he said was out of order, and when I came to look at it I found it had never been started. Now," said the bicycle maker indignantly, "can a man be in his right senses when he talks into a machine without setting it going and then says it is out of order because it makes no record?"

"For my part," returned the chemist, "I regard it as a stain upon the fair fame of the town. I wonder who the council will appoint mayor."

Personally he considered he had the best right to the position, but the bicycle maker expressed no opinion on the subject. For his part, he thought the builder round the corner, his brother-in-law, ought to be offered the post.

As for the late Mayor's wife, she put up a specially fine monument to his memory, bearing the text: "He giveth his beloved sleep." Later on she married the chemist.

THE BAROMETER

VIOLET HUNT

THERE EXISTED A FEW YEARS AGO, IN THE YORKSHIRE WOLDS, A STATE OF AFFAIRS in which the barometer was more consulted than the Bible, and the only barometer in the district hung in the hall of the Vicarage and belonged to the parson, who scanned it daily and out of its abstruse lettering gave no hope to his pining household. The relentless needle stood ever at "set fair," and the terrible drought, which had already lasted for six whole weeks, continued. The dreary sheet of sky overhead stretched in its pitiless blueness over the baked brown earth that lay beneath, parched and cracked and yawning for rain. In between the rift set apart for their habitation, walked sad human beings, sighing and complaining, full of vague physical uneasiness and sense of stress of longing.

The Church and Vicarage of Barmoor, and the few cottages to which it ministered, made the only break in the wilderness of moorland that stretched away for miles to Pickering on the one side and Danby Moor on the other. Three trees grew near the Vicarage: the boughs of one hung over the roof of the lean-to, and made a land-mark over the moor. In the early spring they had been fine bunches of verdure. Now their tattered and disconsolate foliage hung motionless, shrinking day by day into the brown semblance of what were once green leaves. A little beck ran at the bottom of the parson's garden, but it was now all but dry. Everything was dried and wasted, except the heather which sprouted and thickened and browned under the desolating shine of the pitiless sun, while the air above it quivered with refraction.

"The air is dancing!" cried the parson's boys, lying in the thick tufts and looking towards the low ridges that bounded their moor to the north. Later on it grew so hot that the very sun was veiled in mist, and the air did not dance any more, but stood still with weariness, so the children said, again. A lighted candle, held in the kitchen garden, flared straight up, like a pillar.

The children tried it—they tried everything—everything permissible under the strict system of Vicarage discipline—to amuse themselves, in these days, when their elders were too tired and cross to undertake to keep them happy. They wandered about together, their arms heavily linked round each other's shoulders, dragging their feet along the cinder paths in an irritating unison. They stood now, in their baggy little home-made clothes, on the path that led down the kitchen garden, bordered with feeble flowers. It was only bordered; the middle patch of ground was, perforce, devoted to useful vegetable cultivation. The living of Barmoor was not a rich living, and the Rev. Matthew Cooper, its incumbent, stood very low in position, birth, and education.

His gardener, who was also the sexton, was digging the potatoes for early dinner. He grunted while he dug, and his back was turned to the children, who watched, with a kind of fascination born of ennui, the turn of the fork and the roll of the loose mould, and the horny hand that came down every now and then and gathered up the harvest of his toil and flung it into a basket. Saunders was careless, and let several potatoes roll back into the furrow, out of the eight or so that each turn of the fork should yield.

"Oh, Saunders, look, ye've missed one!" piped the youngest child.

"Happen I have, Master John," replied the old man. "It's ower hot to be fashed!" The child sighed.

"Won't it really rain soon, Saunders dear?" he asked wearily. He had heard so much lately of this wonderful rain that was to heal all ills and make the world a pleasant place again. Child-like, he had forgotten what rain was like, and how he hated it, since it kept him indoors, and spoiled his play.

"Happen it may, happen it mayn't!" muttered the old servant sulkily. With a sudden access of spite, he added, "Didn't the master pray for it i' church last Sunda'? But some folks has no influence with the Almighty. A'm sayin' that the Lord ought to do it for His ain sake—the bonny garden's fair perished for the want of a little kindly moisture."

"I think it will rain soon!" said the youngest child again gravely. In his blue eyes was something of the rapt look of a visionary.

"Well, it doesna' look much like it," grumbled the old fellow, pointing up with his fork to the sky that hung above, a wall of greyness, and coming very close to earth, somehow. "What for suld it rain, think'st tha'?"

"Because it must in the end," replied the child sturdily. "It wants to rain so badly. It is like me, when I want to cry and can't. Oh, Saunders, there's another potato you've left. What a lot you miss!"

"Gan awa'! Gan awa'," said Saunders impatiently, "and let me get done. Gan awa' an tew Hannah!" replied the old man. He shook his pitchfork at them with playful savagery, and they turned away.

"Listen, Willie," said the child called John, confidentially taking his brother's arm, and leading him towards the kitchen, a low, one-storied outhouse attached to the house, overshadowed by the biggest of the elm trees. "Listen, Willie; I think the sky is like a great wall, very thick, and yet very brittle. There's all sorts of queer things going on the other side of it, that we can't see."

"Tell us," said the elder boy, dimly interested.

"There's great bulls roaring, and sparks flying like in Hobbie Noble's forge, and a noise—such a noise! If there comes a hole in the wall; we shall see it." His eyes dilated; he squeezed his less poetical minded brother's hand.

"Hout!" said the listener, "I don't care for that story much. Let us go in, and bide with Hannah a bit."

The Vicarage rooms were damp and insufficiently lighted, but the Vicarage kitchen was bright and pleasant. Hannah's lime and marl floor was freshly washed, her copper vessels as bright as the mirror in Mrs. Cooper's best bedroom; but in spite of all these signs of previous activity the girl herself was sitting in a limp and weary attitude, her knees apart, and a great bowl of peas between them, which she was "podding" for dinner. Her eyes were heavy; her big lump of flaxen hair hung on one side of her head; her clumsy red hands moved among the pods lazily and inattentively. "Deary me—a deary me!" she murmured to herself at short intervals.

"Now, bairns!" She roused herself as the two slunk in. "I've not time for none of you. Gan awa' and play, there's good childer!"

"Don't be cross, Hannah!" said the eldest timidly. "We've only comed in for a sup of milk."

"The milk is all gone sour," she replied shortly. "Ye mun just content yersel's wi' a drink of water from the pump. Now be off with you!"

She gave the thin, inoffensive house-cat a hoist with her foot, and settled down to her peas again.

The pump in the garden had gone dry long since and Hannah knew it. The water they used in the household—that all the village used—came from one place, the well at the bottom of the village, which had luckily continued its functions in spite of the drought.

The children, as Hannah knew well enough, did not really want anything to drink, they wanted nothing but the antidote of human conversation to the restlessness and uneasiness that they shared with Hannah and Saunders, and what their father was apt to call "the lower animals." The house-dog was as restless as they, and would neither play with them nor stay quiet in his kennel. The hens fluttered brusquely in the hen-house, and the feverish rushing of wings that went on there made it an unpleasant abiding-place for the children. They sometimes amused themselves by going in to hunt for eggs, but they left them alone to-day, and wandered on to the open study window, where the Reverend Matthew Cooper, in hot, black clothes, was working at his sermon for next Sunday, putting his hand up to his head every now and again.

The two little boys were always somewhat in awe of their stern father, and all they dared do now was to stand and watch him, until the intermittent scraping of their feet on the walk in front of the window roused him from his meditations. He looked up; his brow was pained.

"Well, my laddies, what do you want?" He spoke kindly enough, but his voice dragged with fatigue and oppression.

"Father," asked the eldest child, "Father, tell us; why don't they send rain when you pray for it?"

"You had better go and ask your mother," said the Vicar, with the sort of grim humour in which he usually dealt. He was by nature a hard, cold, God-fearing, pains-taking, undeveloped man, conscious of having a wife who managed him. "What about your lessons? Willie, I gave you a chapter to write out. Go and do some work if you can't play."

"But we've got a headache, Father."

"So have I—splitting. Run away now, and let me go on with my sermon. I haven't even chosen my text yet. . . . '*Who doeth great things and unsearchable. . . . Behold, He withholdeth the waters and they dry up. . . . He bindeth the waters in His thick clouds, and the cloud is not rent under them. . . . He destroyeth the perfect and the wicked. . . . If the scourge slay suddenly, He will laugh at the trial of the innocent!*'"

The children left him, in desperation, and, going down to the bottom of the garden, took off their socks and sat with their feet in the diminished brook. The dog would not come with them, but snapped and growled at John when he tried to make overtures to it. Hannah, who came to look for them to fetch them to early dinner, could not find them, though they were only under the shade of the big rowan-bush near the brook-head. But she did not trouble herself to look very far, she herself could not have told you what ailed her. "I cannot find them, mistress," she said to their mother sitting, carving-knife in one hand and fork in the other, before the family joint, which Hannah had set before her, previous to going in search of the truants.

"Oh, very well! if they don't choose to come in to their meals!"

Mrs. Cooper helped her husband to a plateful, and sent it in to him to his study, which he had intimated he was too busy to leave. She ate a small portion herself—not much—it was too hot to be hungry. She was a hard woman, and the absence of her two little sons did not affect her appetite in the least.

The kind-hearted maid gave them what she called "a bite and a sup" later on, when they came and put their apprehensive heads round the door cheek. She did not scold them. The youngest boy looked very pale and white, and avoided her eyes.

"Poor bairn!" she said, "he wants setting up with the sea air."

The two children lay down after they had eaten, and slept on a heap of sacking, very clean and dry, near the woodstack. Their little bedroom was over the kitchen, and easy of access, but very dreary in the daytime because of the huge tree that overshadowed it. Hannah did not think of sending them up there, but flung a sack over their bare legs as they lay, and did not disturb them.

As the afternoon wore on to evening the hush became oppressive. Not a breath, not a sound of birds twittering, of fowls fluttering. Only the far-away moo of a discontented cow in an outhouse somewhere in the hills sounded like a faint trumpet call, and emphasized the stillness. The sky seemed nearer than ever now, and oppressively near, and all-encompassing.

As Hannah crossed the yard, just before supper, to throw a pail of scrapings into the pig-trough, she heard a noise. It was not Hodgson's cow. . . . It might have been the grinding of one of Miller Farsyde's flour wagons on the quartz that sprinkled the road up there beyond the brow—half-a-mile away. She did not know what it was—a very faint rumble. She thought no more of it, but as she crossed the courtyard on her way back something dropped on to the back of her hand which she could have sworn was a rain-drop. . . . !

The thought passed. Her country mind again was a blank. She gave the boys a shake as she passed in. "Come now, wake up! 'Tis supper time!"

The youngest boy stirred and frowned.

"Is it come?" he said—"the hole in the wall?"

"Whatten hole? Whatten wall? Whatten rubbish is the child talking about?" she said carelessly, brushing the loose straws off his jacket with strong sideway pats, and leading him in to the dining-room where supper was spread. Willie, the elder and more prosaic of the two, manifested some interest in the items of the meal. It was beans and bacon and porridge, too solid fare for such a day as this had been. The Vicar had finished his sermon, and was sitting in his place, as pale as his white tie, but otherwise placable enough. The eldest child went round to his own high chair in silence, but the youngest crossed the room to his mother's side and pulled her by the sleeve.

"What ails ye, laddie? " she asked not unkindly.

"Will you give me a kiss, Mammy?" he asked shamefacedly and in a low voice, lest his brother should hear, and taunt him for being a "mammy pet."

"What nonsense!" Mrs. Cooper said, with all the helpless shyness of a hard woman. She stooped down and kissed her little appealing son, nevertheless. "Now, sit down, and eat your supper quietly. Well, Mr. Cooper, how have ye got on with your sermon?"

"Badly!" replied her husband. "I seem to have such a weight on my brain—an oppression! It is quite dreadful. It is so bad, it really can't last—something must happen. Eat your supper, John, and don't stare."

For the youngest child's eyes were constantly fixed on his father, and little questions seemed to be trembling on his lips. He said nothing until supper was over,
when he begged his mother to read to them, in which request he was seconded by
his elder brother.

She got the big family Bible and reverently flirted the pages. . . .

"Read about the Israelites and the Plagues of Egypt," suggested Willie.

"Very well," the mother said equably. Her day's work was done, she had time now,
and was willing to please the children in their own way.

"'*And Moses Stretched forth his rod towards the heaven, and the Lord sent thunder
and hail—*'"

"I wish He would," murmured the Vicar.

"'*And the fire ran along the ground, and the Lord rained hail upon the land
of Egypt. . . .*'"

She was going on in her monotonous, uneducated voice, when the youngest child
suddenly screamed and hid his face in the cushions of the sofa.

"Whisht, whisht!" she called out, by way of soothing him. "Why, you silly body,
haven't ye heard it all before?"

The child continued to sob.

His face remained hidden. Sternly his parent ignored his hysterical outburst.

"How old were the children of Israel?" asked Willie, by way of distracting the
attention of his elders from this bad conduct on his brother's part, which would assuredly end in both being sent off to bed. Crying was never allowed. "Were they as old as
me, or only as old as John?"

Mrs. Cooper now gave her mind to the destruction of this erroneous impression
under which her children had been labouring, and when it was done she raised her
voice, and called "Hannah!" to the maid, who was to be heard moving heavily
about in the passage.

John raised his tear-stained face from the sofa, a wild terror in his eyes. Willie clasped
his hands together, and together they pleaded with an unaccountable vehemence. . . .

"Oh, no, no, Mother; please, Mother—we don't want to go to bed. We can't! We
can't!" both wailed.

"And what for no?" asked the mother, raising her strongly marked black eyebrows.
"Why not to bed, tonight, same as other nights?"

"Because—because—oh, Mother! because we want another story. We want
Abram and Isaac," pleaded William. It was only an excuse, and the mother knew it.

"One story is quite enough for one evening," she answered severely; "and John did
not behave particularly well over that; I won't hear any fond nonsense. Now you just

trot along both of you! You are both as cross and sleepy as you can be. Bed's the safest place for you!"

Her rough soothing was of no value. The children's faces, as Hannah came in, were blanched with terror. John ran up to the kindly servant-maid, and hid his face in the folds of her linsey gown.

"I want to speak to you," he sobbed.

"Noo, what then, ma honey?" said Hannah good-humouredly, stooping, till her smooth head touched his touzled one. "Well!"—as she raised her head—"did ye ever hear the like? What sets ye asking that? Mistress, he wants to know if they mayn't creep in aside of father and mother to-night?"

"Please let us, Mother," they murmured, almost inaudibly.

"I never heard anything so fond!" exclaimed Mrs. Cooper, laughing grimly. "Be off with ye both quietly, now, and let me hear no more nonsense."

"We did once, Mother!"

"Once! Yes! when they were mending the roof of your bedroom; but the roof's safe and sound over your heads now, at any rate. Why," she laughed, "why, when I give ye a nice big bed to yourselves, should I go and cram my own and the master's with two tiresome children, to kick me black and blue before morning? What are ye afeared of, I say?"

But they would own to nothing, and averted their eyes. A little underswell of sobbing, whimpering breaths testified to their distress.

"What's come to the bairns, I wonder?" She was puzzled, through her thick mental hide of unsympathy. "They're as fractious! It's this unked weather sets us all out of our wits."

"It *must* break," said her husband, "there's no sense in it. We may have rain to-morrow. I forgot to look at the glass as I passed in to-night. There may be a change soon, nay, there must be. . . . Come here, children, and say your prayers, and let's have no more crying."

They all at once realized the hopelessness of it all, and came meekly to his knee, Hannah folded her hands and looked on approvingly at the two flaxen heads, as in their innocent, pretty, piping voices they begged blessings on their hardened elders, and murmured deep contrition for the sins they had not yet committed. They wound up as usual with the prayer—

"'*Lighten our darkness, we beseech Thee, O Lord, and by Thy great mercy defend us from all perils and dangers of this night; for the love of Thine only Son, our Saviour Jesus Christ. Amen.*'"

Sadly they rose and kissed their parents, who had so carelessly crossed them in their strong instinctive desire, and murmured inaudible good-nights. Then Hannah, taking a little submissive hand of each, led them out of the room.

They went past the weather-glass in the hall, whose strongly marked signs and signals of change they were too young, and Hannah too ignorant, to understand, and walked round by half roofless passages to the kitchen. Then Hannah, laughingly propelling "mischief in front of her," inducted them up the shaky wooden staircase that led into the large room where they always slept, brooded over by the enormous overarching elm-tree. Its branches tapped the little skylight pane when it was windy, but now they hung still like a drooping banner in a calm.

"I do believe it's that ugly, girt tree they're feared of!" Hannah thought to herself.

During the passage towards their sleeping place they said nothing, but the fingers of the younger child closed and unclosed round the maid's stout thumb, and the touch struck her as very cold.

"I'd let you both creep in aside o' me," she said, "only I'm that fleyed o' the mistress! She'd find us out, as sure as my name is Hannah Cawthorne."

She set down the candle on the chest in the long, low, empty loft-room. The chest and the bed were almost the only articles of furniture in it. The wooden rafters that supported the roof made fanciful bars and arches over the white dimity quilt. The bed was large, clean and comfortless.

When the two children had undressed and lain down, Hannah Cawthorne, of a gloomy North Country turn of mind that ran continually on omens and predestinations, could not help thinking how like two corpses laid out they looked, lying so straight, their little bodies outlined under the quilt, their eyes wide open and staring at the roof. It made her uncomfortable.

"There's nought to be afeared on," she thought, trying to bring comfort to herself merely, for the children were still, submissive and past all repining now. "It's as safe as a church, but all the same. . . . Now shut your eyes," she said aloud, "there's good lads, and say 'Gentle Jesus' till ye feel the sleep coming on ye. Oh, ye'll sleep fine, trust me. Shall I leave ye the light?"

This was a wild stretch of authority. She might have lost her place over it. She was relieved when they shook their heads and declined it.

"See here," she went on, producing an apple from her pocket. "See here, ye can munch this atween ye."

She laid it down on the coverlet, but no little hand came forth to take it.

"Poor bairns, they're sad-like. . . . Eh, she's a hard woman, is the mistress! If they were mine, shouldn't I like them to nestle in aside o' me! This room is fair lonesome. Naebody could hear them if they were to skrike out. . . ."

"What are ye looking at, my honey?" she asked John curiously, for the child's eyes remained obstinately fixed on the roof, as if he saw something there.

"He's looking at the hole in the wall," volunteered the eldest boy at last. "He's shiverin'." "Hap him up in your arms, ma bonny bairn, that'll soon warm him. . . . Now I must be going, lads. . . Good-night to ye both. . . ."

Hesitating, reluctant, she took up her candle and made a start for the door.

"I don't half like leaving them," she murmured, as she stole out casting a last look at the two children, lying clasped, according to her recommendation, in each other's arms. Their faces were hidden in each other's necks, their sad apprehensive eyes were closed, obediently summoning sleep.

Gently snecking the door, she blundered down the rickety staircase, and made her way back into the other, safer part of the house. Ignorant, she passed by the mysterious oracle hanging in the hall, unable to read or understand the plain meaning which its hands now bore.

"Eh, but she's a right hard woman, is the mistress, and master follows her in all things. *He'd* have let the poor childer come in aside him, when they begged and prayed fit to turn a heart of stone. . . ."

She did not toss on her hard pallet, but lay stupefied in the heavy slumber that was the meed of her arduous existence. Upstairs, in the best bedroom, the Reverend Matthew Cooper slept off his headache. His wife did not drowse, but lay by her husband's side, straight and still as she had laid down, congratulating herself on the great healing storm that was even now breaking over the Vicarage, gloating over its promise of recomfiture and peace. . . . It thundered and lightened for two hours.

When morning dawned the great drought was over, and the air was refreshed.

Hannah, the maid, rose and went about her duties with a light heart, and presently, having started the kitchen fire, called the parson and his wife to resume theirs.

When it was time, she pulled her dirty kitchen apron aside, put the kettle where it could not for the moment boil over, and went to call the parson's children.

She went up the crooked stair and opened the door gently, "not to waken them sudden." The first thing she saw, before she screamed, was the wide, jagged hole on the rafters above the bed where they still lay in each other's arms. The lightning that, guided by the tree which hung over the roof, had passed through to the innocent children and dealt them their unearned and undeserved death, had not divided them. They were quiet and unchanged in appearance except for some little blue marks like shot in the forehead of the one and the breast of the other.

THE BLOOD DRIPS

J. E. MUDDOCK

FOR A LONG TIME—FOR YEARS, IN FACT—AT SHORT INTERVALS, THE FOLLOWING advertisement appeared in most, if not all, the London papers, and many of the provincial ones:

> To let, on long lease at low rental, or Freehold to be sold cheap, a magnificent Family Residence, complete with every convenience, suitable for a large family. The house stands in its own grounds, comprising nearly three and a half acres, part of which is natural wood, while the remainder is laid out as flower and kitchen gardens. There is stabling for four or five horses, with commodious carriage house, harness room, hay and corn lofts, and spacious apartments for coachmen, grooms, &c. The property, which is only twenty-five miles from London, enjoys an unequalled situation both as regards salubrity and views. The country is open all round, with extensive woods in the neighbourhood. The climate is bracing; gravel soil lying on chalk, an adequate supply of water, and drainage perfect. Apply in the first instance to Smeaton, Weardale & Smeaton, Estate and House Agents, Valuers and Auctioneers, &c, 105 New Bond Street, London, W.

On the first blush this advertisement was very attractive, and its *bonâ fides* was beyond question, seeing that such a well-known and old-established firm as Smeaton, Weardale & Smeaton was responsible for it. But a second reading would naturally have caused any thinking person to ask himself why, if this property was all that was represented, it should be offered at a very low rental, or cheaply if bought.

Now, it was very certain that there was something wrong, otherwise "a magnificent family residence," and "three and a half acres of ground" need not wait long for a customer. But, as already stated, this advertisement continued to appear at short intervals for years, so that those who were familiar with it knew quite well that out of the hundreds of thousands of people who must have read it, no one had yet been induced to invest. Now, what was the object in continuing the advertisement, upon which a large sum of money must have been spent, if a customer was not forthcoming? The only answer to this was that the owner or owners of the property hoped that by continuing it long enough, the advertisement would at last attract the right person, and in the end this hope was realised.

One morning—an August morning it was, brilliant with sunlight, when even grimy London looked bright and cheerful—a gentleman entered the office of Smeaton, Weardale & Smeaton. There was something about him that suggested long residence abroad—his dress and appearance generally. He wore a soft grey felt hat, a large, flowing necktie, and loose collar, and a grey check suit of clothes, which, though faultless as to their cut, had never been made in England, or, at any rate, not in London. For your London tailor has a style which, to the practised eye, is unmistakable. The gentleman was evidently an invalid or a convalescent. He was thin, languid, and delicate looking. There were dark rims under his eyes, and, though his face was tanned with sun, it was greyish in its hue, and suggestive of an undermined constitution.

Smeaton, Weardale & Smeaton's offices were extensive, and luxuriously fitted, as became a first-class firm of estate agents in so fashionable a neighbourhood as New Bond Street. The gentleman was received by a page-boy, and shown into a waiting-room, which was furnished with velvet lounges and chairs, and plentifully supplied with newspapers.

"I wish to see one of the principals," said the gentleman, handing the page-boy his card, on which was engraved:

Walter Reginald Minton, M.E.,
British Columbia.

The boy bowed, took the card, and retired. In a few minutes an obsequious clerk entered, and with many bows requested Mr. Walter Reginald Minton to "kindly step this way, sir."

Mr. Minton followed the clerk, who showed him into a large, handsomely-furnished room, the walls of which were covered with photographs of houses of all kinds and coloured plans of estates. At a massive mahogany desk sat a well-preserved gentleman long past the prime of life, but with silver hair, a bright, keen eye, and a rubicund face that suggested a fondness for good living and old crusted port.

"Do I address Mr. Smeaton?" asked the stranger.

"Yes, sir. I am the head of the firm. Pray, take a chair," and Mr. Smeaton put his white, fat hands together with professional dignity, and waited for his visitor to state his business.

"I've noticed an advertisement in the *Times*," began Mr. Minton, taking from his pocket-book a half sheet of notepaper, on which the advertisement alluded to had been neatly gummed. "It has reference to the sale of a family residence, and I should like to have some further particulars about it."

Mr. Smeaton's eyes brightened up with joyful expectancy, as, glancing at the sheet of note-paper, he recognised the advertisement which had become fossilised, so to speak, in the London dailies.

"Oh, yes," he answered pleasantly, and with a most becoming smile. "The advertisement accurately describes the property."

"Where is it situated?"

"About six miles from —— Station on the South-Eastern line—an hour's run from London."

"There will be no difficulty in my seeing it?"

"Oh, none whatever."

"I may mention that I am a mining engineer, and have been for many years in British Columbia. But having made a moderate fortune, and being in very bad health, I am anxious to settle down in my native country."

"Ah, just so," remarked Mr. Smeaton blandly, and stroking his smoothly-shaven chin. "Are you a family man, Mr. Minton, may I ask?"

"Yes, I have a wife and one daughter, twenty years of age."

Mr. Smeaton's countenance seemed to fall just ever so little, as he replied:

"Umph! I am afraid then if your family is so small you may find the house larger than you require."

"Oh, no," answered Minton quickly, and Mr. Smeaton's countenance recovered again; "we like a large house, for we keep a good deal of company."

"Then I don't think you can do better than purchase Dumthorpe Hall," said Mr. Smeaton, with a gracious smile.

"Is that the name of the place?"

"Yes. Of course, if you become the owner you will be at liberty to adopt any other name you like. Now, I suggest, before entering into any further particulars, that we go down and see the property; you couldn't have a better day. The country will be charming under this brilliant sun. If you will allow me I shall have much pleasure in accompanying you."

"That will suit me admirably. I am staying at the Tavistock Hotel; we can call there in a cab, and pick up my wife and daughter."

Mr. Smeaton struck his bell, and the page-boy appeared with such alacrity that one might have thought that the bell set some spring in motion which shot the boy into the room.

"Peter, look up the next train for ——

"Yes, sir." Two minutes later the boy came back. "There is a train at 12:50, sir."

"Good!" Mr. Smeaton looked at his massive gold watch, although a handsome clock stood on the mantelpiece, the force of habit, no doubt: "We have an hour and a half—ample time; and as I have a little business to do, perhaps you will permit me to meet you at the station?"

"Oh, certainly."

A few minutes later Mr. Minton was on his way to his hotel; and, punctual to the time, he and his wife, a charming but delicate and nervous-looking lady, and his daughter, a no less charming girl, were at the station, where Mr. Smeaton had already arrived and procured first-class tickets.

On alighting at ———, after an hour's run through a pleasant country, a brougham and pair of horses, which Mr. Smeaton had ordered by telegraph from the landlord of the hotel near the station, were waiting, and the party at once drove to Dumthorpe Hall, a distance of over six miles from the station.

"I should mention," remarked Mr. Smeaton, just before reaching the place, "that the property has, unfortunately been allowed to fall into a somewhat dilapidated condition, for the owner, who is in India, has sadly neglected it. However, that will be duly taken into consideration in fixing the purchase money."

As regards the situation, the advertisement had scarcely done it justice. The country, diversified with wood, hill and dale, was charming, and looked at its very best on this brilliant summer's day. The entrance to the grounds of Dumthorpe Hall was through a gateway, the gates being wrought-iron, and of a handsome design, but now rusty, and out of the perpendicular, owing to the sinking of the foundations of one of the pillars on which they were hung. Some difficulty, therefore, was experienced in getting in. There was a small lodge at the entrance, but it was overrun with ragged creepers, and the windows were covered with the accumulated dirt of years.

As the visitors stood for a few moments looking about them, after the difficulty of opening the gate had been overcome, Miss Minton suddenly uttered a startled cry, and clung in alarm to her father's arm.

"What is it, what is it, my dear?" he asked quickly. "Oh, look there!" she exclaimed, pointing with her parasol to the ground a few feet away; and he did look and beheld an adder leisurely moving across the pathway. Mr. Smeaton saw it too, and, springing forward, he struck the reptile with his stick, killing it at once, and he tossed it among the trees out of sight.

"If I were superstitious," remarked Mr. Minton, "I should take that as an evil omen."

"I am glad you are not superstitious," replied Mr. Smeaton with a laugh, "for the fact is this place has the reputation of being haunted."

He uttered this quickly—jerked it out, as it were—as though he was glad to get it off his mind, the incident of the snake having given him the opportunity of making the remark.

"Haunted!" exclaimed the two ladies in a breath, while something like a scared appearance came into their faces.

"Of course that won't affect you, ladies," said Mr. Smeaton with his bland smile. "You are above being affected by such silly nonsense, I am sure."

They walked on, the brougham followed slowly. The drive was all overgrown with moss and grass, and strewn with decaying leaves and pieces of branches of trees that had been whirled off by gales. Presently the drive took a turn, then expanded, and the house came in view. It was an old Elizabethan mansion, with pointed gables and a red-tiled roof that gave it a very quaint appearance; but it looked forlorn and mouldering to decay, even with the sun pouring down a flood of golden light upon it. Had it been seen under less favourable atmospheric conditions it would certainly have worn a repellent aspect. Ivy and honeysuckle had struggled to the very eaves, and hung in straggling and ragged festoons about the windows.

The interior of the Hall was worse than the exterior. Cobwebs hung from the ceilings in long ropes. The paper had peeled from the walls; the fire grates were red with rust; the windows obscured with dirt; the floors black, and in some places rotten; while pervading the whole house was a dank, earthy, mouldering smell, like that which comes from a newly-opened tomb.

The ladies shuddered, and were evidently repelled by the cheerlessness and gloom of the house. But Mr. Smeaton chatted pleasantly and glibly. He had a smooth tongue and great fluency, and knew how to say pretty things in dulcet tones. He was very anxious to get the property off his hands, and as Mr. Minton seemed a likely customer he was not going to let him slip if talking would secure him. The premises were thoroughly examined. They certainly were commodious and not ill-planned, but paint, paper, and whitewash everywhere wanted renewing. The same neglect characterised the grounds. They were howling wildernesses of ill weeds, and the conservatories were falling to pieces.

The ladies certainly were not impressed, although they expressed admiration for the position and view; and there could be no doubt that the situation was healthy, for it stood high; gravel and chalk were the geological features for miles round, and the air was singularly pure, while the water was liquid crystal.

"Well," said Mr. Minton, reflecting when the survey was over, "I can see certain potentialities in that place."

"Potentialities! I should think so, my dear sir," exclaimed the agent joyfully. "With the expenditure of a little money it can be made into a palace."

Without answering this remark, Mr. Minton, turning to his wife and daughter, said: "What is your opinion, darlings?"

"Well," answered his wife cautiously, "we have seen it under every possible disadvantage as far as neglect and dirt go, and I think it would want a lot of money-spending to put it in order."

"But what is the story about its being haunted?" asked the young lady, addressing Mr. Smeaton, and unable to suppress a little shudder.

Mr. Smeaton laughed loudly, almost boisterously, as he made reply:

"My—dear—young lady, such stories as these are always so ridiculous that they cannot be discussed by sensible people."

He dismissed the subject with his bland smile and a lofty wave of his white hand.

As they returned to town, Mr. Minton for the first time asked the price, and the figure named by Mr. Smeaton was so low that the other opened his eyes in astonishment.

"Is there anything the matter with the place?" Mr. Minton asked with great point.

"Nothing; I pledge you my honour," answered the agent equally emphatic, "beyond its reputation as a haunted house, but it is right to say that that reputation has kept the place untenanted for twenty years with one short break. It was let on a yearly tenancy to a family who only remained, however, six months."

"Why did they leave?" asked the two ladies in concert.

"They said that they heard noises, and that what looked like blood dripped from the ceilings."

"Oh!" exclaimed the mother and daughter with a little start, and nestling closer to each other, as if for mutual protection.

Mr. Minton smiled sceptically, and this smile did not escape the agent, who said quickly:

"I have told you frankly the cause of our not being able to let or sell the place. That is the sole reason; and it certainly does not say much for our boasted enlightenment that so splendid a property should go begging through such a senseless cause."

"You are right, you are right!" exclaimed Mr. Minton, and the other felt from this that the customer was secured.

The following day, Mr. Minton, not wholly with his wife's and daughter's approbation, instructed his lawyers to make further inquiries, and examine the title deeds. The inquiries elicited nothing beyond what the agent had stated, namely, that people said it was haunted; while, as for the title deeds, they were beyond dispute or quibble. The price asked was very low, but Mr. Minton's lawyers offered a still lower price, and, as the agents' instructions were to sell at any price rather than let the place fall into absolute ruin, the bargain was closed, and Mr. Minton became the absolute possessor of Dumthorpe Hall. He immediately set a little army of workmen to work—gardeners, painters, paperhangers, plumbers, &c., as he was anxious to move in before the winter. Very soon the place had been transformed, and the prejudice of the ladies gave way. As they saw the change they expressed themselves delighted. As soon as the workmen were out, the upholsterers entered, and as they had carte-blanche to furnish the house thoroughly and well, they had soon diffused comfort, warmth, and beauty where erstwhile all was decay and mildew.

It was the last week in October when the family moved in. The autumn tints were on the land, but beyond that there was no trace of the approaching winter. The days were still warm and bright and sunny, for it had been an exceptionally fine season. A number of servants were already installed. The greenhouses and conservatories were filled with flowers; the gardens were already bright and gay; while in the stables were horses and carriages. In fact, the place was complete with everything that could give comfort or enjoyment to the family. Mr. Minton was a liberal provider, and being wealthy—having made his pile out of mines in British Columbia—he spared no expense.

For the first few weeks all went merry as a marriage bell. The ladies expressed themselves charmed with the place. The dark days of November were drawing to a close, and the house was full of visitors, when one morning the cook approached Mrs. Minton, and said:

"Can I speak to you, mum, for a few minutes?"

"Certainly, cook. What is it?"

"Well, mum," she began sheepishly, "I've been awfully annoyed for several nights by somebody walking about over my head."

"Oh, nonsense, cook. That couldn't be. The room over you is a lumber-room, and it's just filled up with boxes."

"Yes, mum, I know that, and that's what makes the noise all the queerer. And then yesterday morning something came down from the ceiling in the kitchen like blood."

Mrs. Minton turned a little pale and shuddered, for she remembered that the agent had mentioned the story about blood dripping from the ceiling.

"What an extraordinary thing!" she said, with a forced laugh; "but the next time you are troubled with these phenomena, cook, pray come and call me."

The cook did not seem quite satisfied as she went away; and that night, about ten o'clock, she went to her mistress again with a scared white face, and said:

"It's there again, mum. Will you please to come to my room?"

Mrs. Minton went, and to her surprise she heard a steady measured tramp, tramp, tramp, overhead. She sent for her husband. He came, and he heard the same sounds. He went into the room above, but there was nothing to account for those footsteps. In fact, so full was the room of boxes, trunks, &c., that there was not a clear floor space of two yards.

Mrs. Minton did not go into the upper room. She waited for her husband coming down; and suddenly, as she was looking up towards the ceiling, something wet fell on her face. She uttered a little startled cry, and, taking out her handkerchief, wiped the wet off, and what was her astonishment to find that the handkerchief was stained with blood, or what seemed like blood. Such a shock did this cause her that she almost fainted, and when her husband returned she was pale and trembling. He expressed himself mystified, and it was evident that he was very much impressed. It was agreed that nothing should be said about this to anyone in the house, and the cook was enjoined to keep the matter secret for the present. But the following morning after breakfast the gentlemen retired to the smoking-room for a few whiffs, when a young fellow named Dobell called out as he filled his pipe:

"I say, Minton, old fellow, who is lodging over me?"

"I don't think anyone is over you. In fact I am sure there is not. Why?"

"Well, I don't know, but it seemed to me that some fellow with heavy boots did nothing but tramp about all night."

Mr. Minton started. He could not help it, and he who had indignantly disavowed any belief in the supernatural was becoming superstitious. He laughed the matter off, however, and told his friend that he must have been suffering from nightmare.

For the next two or three days nothing else occurred, or at any rate was mentioned, until Miss Minton went into her mother's room in a state of great fright, and exclaimed:

"Oh, mamma, I've had such a shock. As I was dressing something fell from the ceiling on to my face and neck, and when I wiped it off it was like blood."

Mrs. Minton grew deadly pale as she heard this, but, recovering herself quickly, she answered:

"Well, darling, I have experienced the same thing, but it is better to say nothing about it. As long as it is not more serious we must put up with it. When the guests have gone we will have the house examined. Possibly some trick is being played."

Although she thus dismissed the subject for the time being she could not get rid of the mystery so easily, and that strange drip from the ceilings was impartial, for it dripped on all alike, and in all parts of the house. Other ladies and gentlemen complained of it, and the ladies became alarmed; while a thorough investigation organised by the gentlemen was entirely barren of result. They could discover nothing, absolutely nothing, and the ceilings, which had all been newly whitened, were stainless. These people felt they were in the presence of some mystery which they could not solve. But what was it? Of course the gentlemen scoffed, and even some of the stronger-minded ladies pooh-poohed. But there were others who held their peace, and, as soon as they could courteously do so, they took their departure.

Mr. Minton was greatly concerned. If this sort of thing was to continue he would hardly get guests to stay with him, while, as for his wife and daughter, it was evident they were suffering in their nerves. Then a fresh trouble arose; some of the servants gave notice to leave, saying they were afraid to stay in such a place. The cook, who was an exceedingly good servant, and liked her place, was loath to go, but she said that she would certainly have to leave if the annoyances did not stop.

It need scarcely be said that the matter preyed upon Mr. Minton's mind. He had spent a large sum of money upon the house, and to be the victim of such an unsolvable annoyance was a great hardship.

As Christmas approached things seemed to get worse. Those drips from the ceilings were constantly falling, and the tramping, which was confined to two rooms, still went on. It became very obvious to Mr. Minton that his wife and daughter were suffering in health, though they tried not to show it, and he became greatly concerned.

A new set of guests came down for Christmas, and care was taken not to put anyone into the room below that where the tramping was heard. But people complained, nevertheless, of red moisture dripping on them from the ceilings, and nervous people became frightened. Mr. Minton was not a man to be easily subdued. As a mining engineer, he had faced dangers in all shapes and forms, and had overcome difficulties that would have daunted less determined and less strong-minded men. But now this constant interruption to his domestic comfort and peace was telling sorely upon his already shattered health. He had come here for quietude and rest, but in spite of his care and lavish expenditure it seemed as if his hopes were doomed to be blighted. As he was not quite able to divest himself of the idea that he was the victim of some stupid trickery, he, with the aid of a builder from the neighbouring town, examined the house from roof to basement, and all the time that he was pursuing his investigation that mysterious dripping of a fluid like blood continued from the ceilings, and the tramping in the lumber-room never ceased at night time. The examination, therefore, resulted in nothing, and the mystery was a mystery still.

At last, driven to desperation, Mr. Minton resolved to try another expedient. That was to clear out the lumber-room, have a bed put up there, and sleep in the room himself. This he did against the earnest, prayerful entreaties of his wife and daughter, and even of the servants. But he was resolute, saying he had never feared living man, and nothing dead could harm him.

The arrangements completed, he wished his wife and daughter a fond good-night, and when they exacted a promise from him that he would violently ring his bell if he required assistance, he laughed heartily, and retired to what had now come to be called in the house "the haunted room." His wife and daughter were restless and uneasy, but as the hours sped, and there was no sound of the bell, they dropped off to sleep.

In the morning, about nine o'clock, Mr. Minton's valet went up to the room with hot water. He knocked at the door, there was no response. He knocked again, still no answer, so he tried the handle; it yielded, and he entered. Then from his hand fell the hot-water jug he was carrying, and he staggered back with a wild cry of alarm. For lying on the bed, his limbs all contorted, the sheets twisted about his body like ropes, as if he had rolled and writhed in some torturing agony, his eyes starting from his head in horror, his mouth wide open, his hands clenched, the nails digging into the palms, was Mr. Minton, stone dead.

Medical men were hastily summoned, but their services were of no avail. They could only certify that Mr. Minton, being in very delicate health, had received a shock of some sort, which had caused death. "A shock of some sort!" That was only too painfully evident. It did not need a medical man to state that. What they could not state was how the shock had been produced.

Poor Mrs. Minton and her daughter were carried prostrated from the fatal house to a neighbour's, and they only entered it once again to take a last look at the remains of the husband and father. When he had been borne to his final resting-place, his widow instructed her lawyers to sell off all the furniture immediately. That done, the accursed house was shut up, and it remained shut for over a dozen years. No one could be found to take it; and, at last, only a few years ago, the estate was sold, the house razed to the ground, and some small villas erected on the land, and Dumthorpe Hall became only a memory.

Many people will no doubt remember what a fierce controversy raged at the time of Mr. Minton's tragic death, and how nearly every paper in the kingdom, big and little, advanced some theory to try and account for the phenomena which had alarmed servants and guests alike. Some of the papers discussed the affair banteringly, some with glib platitudes about the "pitiable superstition which still lingered in some of the remote country districts"; others, again, half seriously, and others still with appalling learnedness. Divines and laymen alike entered into the conflict of opinions, but in the end nothing was proved, nothing was solved, and the extraordinary mystery remains a mystery still.

BRICKETT BOTTOM

AMYAS NORTHCOTE

THE REVEREND ARTHUR MAYDEW WAS THE HARD-WORKING INCUMBENT OF A large parish in one of our manufacturing towns. He was also a student and a man of no strong physique, so that when an opportunity was presented to him to take an annual holiday by exchanging parsonages with an elderly clergyman, Mr. Roberts, the Squarson of the Parish of Overbury, and an acquaintance of his own, he was glad to avail himself of it.

Overbury is a small and very remote village in one of our most lovely and rural counties, and Mr. Roberts had long held the living of it.

Without further delay we can transport Mr. Maydew and his family, which consisted only of two daughters, to their temporary home. The two young ladies, Alice and Maggie, the heroines of this narrative, were at that time aged twenty-six and twenty-four years respectively. Both of them were attractive girls, fond of such society as they could find in their own parish and, the former especially, always pleased to extend the circle of their acquaintance. Although the elder in years, Alice in many ways yielded place to her sister, who was the more energetic and practical and upon whose shoulders the bulk of the family cares and responsibilities rested. Alice was inclined to be absent-minded and emotional and to devote more of her thoughts and time to speculations of an abstract nature than her sister.

Both of the girls, however, rejoiced at the prospect of a period of quiet and rest in a pleasant country neighbourhood, and both were gratified at knowing that their father would find in Mr. Roberts' library much that would entertain his mind, and in Mr. Roberts' garden an opportunity to indulge freely in his favourite game of croquet. They would have, no doubt, preferred some cheerful neighbours, but Mr. Roberts was positive in his assurances that there was no one in the neighbourhood whose acquaintance would be of interest to them.

The first few weeks of their new life passed pleasantly for the Maydew family. Mr. Maydew quickly gained renewed vigour in his quiet and congenial surroundings, and in the delightful air, while his daughters spent much of their time in long walks about the country and in exploring its beauties.

One evening late in August the two girls were returning from a long walk along one of their favourite paths, which led along the side of the Downs. On their right, as they walked, the ground fell away sharply to a narrow glen, named Brickett Bottom, about three-quarters of a mile in length, along the bottom of which ran a little-used country road leading to a farm, known as Blaise's Farm, and then onward and upward to lose itself as a sheep track on the higher Downs.

On their side of the slope some scattered trees and bushes grew, but beyond the lane and running up over the farther slope of the glen was a thick wood, which extended away to Carew Court, the seat of a neighbouring magnate, Lord Carew. On their left the open Down rose above them and beyond its crest lay Overbury.

The girls were walking hastily, as they were later than they had intended to be and were anxious to reach home. At a certain point at which they had now arrived the path forked, the right hand branch leading down into Brickett Bottom and the left hand turning up over the Down to Overbury.

Just as they were about to turn into the left hand path Alice suddenly stopped and pointing downwards exclaimed: "How very curious, Maggie! Look, there is a house down there in the Bottom, which we have, or at least I have, never noticed before, often as we have walked up the Bottom."

Maggie followed with her eyes her sister's pointing finger.

"I don't see any house," she said.

"Why, Maggie," said her sister, "can't you see it? A quaint-looking, old-fashioned red brick house, there just where the road bends to the right. It seems to be standing in a nice, well-kept garden too."

Maggie looked again, but the light was beginning to fade in the glen and she was short-sighted to boot.

"I certainly don't see anything," she said, "but then I am so blind and the light is getting bad; yes, perhaps I do see a house," she added, straining her eyes.

"Well, it is there," replied her sister, "and to-morrow we will come and explore it."

Maggie agreed readily enough, and the sisters went home, still speculating on how they had happened not to notice the house before and resolving firmly on an expedition thither the next day. However, the expedition did not come off as planned, for that evening Maggie slipped on the stairs and fell, spraining her ankle in such a fashion as to preclude walking for some time.

Notwithstanding the accident to her sister, Alice remained possessed by the idea of making further investigations into the house she had looked down upon from the hill the evening before; and the next day, having seen Maggie carefully settled for the after-noon, she started off for Brickett Bottom. She returned in triumph and much intrigued over her discoveries, which she eagerly narrated to her sister.

Yes. There was a nice, old-fashioned red brick house, not very large and set in a charming, old-world garden in the Bottom. It stood on a tongue of land jutting out from the woods, just at the point where the lane, after a fairly straight course from its junction with the main road half a mile away, turned sharply to the right in the direction of Blaise's Farm. More than that, Alice had seen the people of the house, whom she described as an old gentleman and a lady, presumably his wife. She had not clearly made out the gentleman, who was sitting in the porch, but the old lady, who had been in the garden busy with her flowers, had looked up and smiled pleasantly at her as she passed. She was sure, she said, that they were nice people and that it would be pleasant to make their acquaintance.

Maggie was not quite satisfied with Alice's story. She was of a more prudent and retiring nature than her sister; she had an uneasy feeling that, if the old couple had been desirable or attractive neighbours, Mr. Roberts would have mentioned them, and knowing Alice's nature she said what she could to discourage her vague idea of endeavouring to make acquaintance with the owners of the red brick house.

On the following morning, when Alice came to her sister's room to inquire how she did, Maggie noticed that she looked pale and rather absent-minded, and, after a few commonplace remarks had passed, she asked:

"What is the matter, Alice? You don't look yourself this morning."

Her sister gave a slightly embarrassed laugh.

"Oh, I am all right," she replied, "only I did not sleep very well. I kept on dreaming about the house. It was such an odd dream too: the house seemed to be home, and yet to be different."

"What, that house in Brickett Bottom?" said Maggie. "Why, what is the matter with you, you seem to be quite crazy about the place?"

"Well, it is curious, isn't it, Maggie, that we should have only just discovered it, and that it looks to be lived in by nice people? I wish we could get to know them."

Maggie did not care to resume the argument of the night before and the subject dropped, nor did Alice again refer to the house or its inhabitants for some little time. In fact, for some days the weather was wet and Alice was forced to abandon her walks, but when the weather once more became fine she resumed them, and Maggie suspected that Brickett Bottom formed one of her sister's favourite expeditions. Maggie became anxious over her sister, who seemed to grow daily more absent-minded and silent, but she refused to be drawn into any confidential talk, and Maggie was nonplussed.

One day, however, Alice returned from her afternoon walk in an unusually excited state of mind, of which Maggie sought an explanation. It came with a rush. Alice said that, that afternoon, as she approached the house in Brickett Bottom, the old lady, who as usual was busy in her garden, had walked down to the gate as she passed and had wished her good day.

Alice had replied and, pausing, a short conversation had followed. Alice could not remember the exact tenor of it, but, after she had paid a compliment to the old lady's flowers, the latter had rather diffidently asked her to enter the garden for a closer view. Alice had hesitated, and the old lady had said: "Don't be afraid of me, my dear, I like to see young ladies about me and my husband finds their society quite necessary to him." After a pause she went on: "Of course nobody has told you about us. My husband is Colonel Paxton, late of the Indian Army, and we have been here for many, many years. It's rather lonely, for so few people ever see us. Do come in and meet the Colonel."

"I hope you didn't go in," said Maggie rather sharply.

"Why not?" replied Alice.

"Well, I don't like Mrs. Paxton asking you in that way," answered Maggie.

"I don't see what harm there was in the invitation," said Alice. "I didn't go in because it was getting late and I was anxious to get home; but—"

"But what?" asked Maggie.

Alice shrugged her shoulders.

"Well," she said, "I have accepted Mrs. Paxton's invitation to pay her a little visit to-morrow." And she gazed defiantly at Maggie.

Maggie became distinctly uneasy on hearing of this resolution. She did not like the idea of her impulsive sister visiting people on such slight acquaintance, especially as they had never heard them mentioned before. She endeavoured by all means, short of appealing to Mr. Maydew, to dissuade her sister from going, at any rate until there had been time to make some inquiries as to the Paxtons. Alice, however, was obdurate.

What harm could happen to her? she asked. Mrs. Paxton was a charming old lady. She was going early in the afternoon for a short visit. She would be back for tea and croquet with her father and, anyway, now that Maggie was laid up, long solitary walks were unendurable and she was not going to let slip the chance of following up what promised to be a pleasant acquaintance.

Maggie could do nothing more. Her ankle was better and she was able to get down to the garden and sit in a long chair near her father, but walking was still quite out of the question, and it was with some misgiving that on the following day she watched Alice depart gaily for her visit, promising to be back by half-past four at the very latest.

The afternoon passed quietly till nearly five, when Mr. Maydew, looking up from his book, noticed Maggie's uneasy expression and asked:

"Where is Alice?"

"Out for a walk," replied Maggie; and then after a short pause she went on: "And she has also gone to pay a call on some neighbours whom she has recently discovered."

"Neighbours," ejaculated Mr. Maydew, "what neighbours? Mr. Roberts never spoke of any neighbours to me."

"Well, I don't know much about them," answered Maggie. "Only Alice and I were out walking the day of my accident and saw or at least she saw, for I am so blind I could not quite make it out, a house in Brickett Bottom. The next day she went to look at it closer, and yesterday she told me that she had made the acquaintance of the people living in it. She says that they are a retired Indian officer and his wife, a Colonel and Mrs. Paxton, and Alice describes Mrs. Paxton as a charming old lady, who pressed her to come and see them. So she has gone this afternoon, but she promised me she would be back long before this."

Mr. Maydew was silent for a moment and then said:

"I am not well pleased about this. Alice should not be so impulsive and scrape acquaintance with absolutely unknown people. Had there been nice neighbours in Brickett Bottom, I am certain Mr. Roberts would have told us."

The conversation dropped; but both father and daughter were disturbed and uneasy and, tea having been finished and the clock striking half-past five, Mr. Maydew asked Maggie:

"When did you say Alice would be back?"

"Before half-past four at the latest, father."

"Well, what can she be doing? What can have delayed her? You say you did not see the house," he went on.

"No," said Maggie, "I cannot say I did. It was getting dark and you know how short-sighted I am."

"But surely you must have seen it at some other time," said her father.

"That is the strangest part of the whole affair," answered Maggie. "We have often walked up the Bottom, but I never noticed the house, nor had Alice till that evening. I wonder," she went on after a short pause, "if it would not be well to ask Smith to harness the pony and drive over to bring her back. I am not happy about her—I am afraid—"

"Afraid of what?" said her father in the irritated voice of a man who is growing frightened. "What can have gone wrong in this quiet place? Still, I'll send Smith over for her."

So saying he rose from his chair and sought out Smith, the rather dull-witted gardener-groom attached to Mr. Roberts' service.

"Smith," he said, "I want you to harness the pony at once and go over to Colonel Paxton's in Brickett Bottom and bring Miss Maydew home."

The man stared at him.

"Go where, sir?" he said.

Mr. Maydew repeated the order and the man, still staring stupidly, answered:

"I never heard of Colonel Paxton, sir. I don't know what house you mean."

Mr. Maydew was now growing really anxious.

"Well, harness the pony at once," he said; and going back to Maggie he told her of what he called Smith's stupidity, and asked her if she felt that her ankle would be strong enough to permit her to go with him and Smith to the Bottom to point out the house.

Maggie agreed readily and in a few minutes the party started off. Brickett Bottom, although not more than three-quarters of a mile away over the Downs, was at least three miles by road; and as it was nearly six o'clock before Mr. Maydew left time Vicarage, and the pony was old and slow, it was getting late before the entrance to Brickett Bottom was reached. Turning into the lane the cart proceeded slowly up the Bottom, Mr. Maydew and Maggie looking anxiously from side to side, whilst Smith drove stolidly on looking neither to the right nor left.

"Where is the house?" said Mr. Maydew presently.

"At the bend of the road," answered Maggie, her heart sickening as she looked out through the failing light to see the trees stretching their ranks in unbroken formation along it. The cart reached the bend. "It should be here," whispered Maggie.

They pulled up. Just in front of them the road bent to the right round a tongue of land, which, unlike the rest of the right hand side of the road, was free from trees and was covered only by rough grass and stray bushes. A closer inspection disclosed evident signs of terraces having once been formed on it, but of a house there was no trace.

"Is this the place?" said Mr. Maydew in a low voice.

Maggie nodded.

"But there is no house here," said her father. "What does it all mean? Are you sure of yourself, Maggie? Where is Alice?"

Before Maggie could answer a voice was heard calling "Father! Maggie!" The sound of the voice was thin and high and, paradoxically, it sounded both very near and yet as if it came from some infinite distance. The cry was thrice repeated and then silence fell. Mr. Maydew and Maggie stared at each other.

"That was Alice's voice," said Mr. Maydew huskily, "she is near and in trouble, and is calling us. Which way did you think it came from, Smith?" he added, turning to the gardener.

"I didn't hear anybody calling," said the man.

"Nonsense!" answered Mr. Maydew.

And then he and Maggie both began to call "Alice. Alice. Where are you?" There was no reply and Mr. Maydew sprang from the cart, at the same time bidding Smith to hand the reins to Maggie and come and search for the missing girl. Smith obeyed him and both men, scrambling up the turfy bit of ground, began to search and call through the neighbouring wood. They heard and saw nothing, however, and after an agonised search Mr. Maydew ran down to the cart and begged Maggie to drive on to Blaise's Farm for help, leaving himself and Smith to continue the search. Maggie followed her father's instructions and was fortunate enough to find Mr. Rumbold, the farmer, his two sons and a couple of labourers just returning from the harvest field. She explained what had happened, and the farmer and his men promptly volunteered to form a search party, though Maggie, in spite of her anxiety, noticed a queer expression on Mr. Rumbold's face as she told him her tale.

The party, provided with lanterns, now went down the Bottom, joined Mr. Maydew and Smith and made an exhaustive but absolutely fruitless search of the woods near the bend of the road. No trace of the missing girl was to be found, and after a long and anxious time the search was abandoned, one of the young Rumbolds volunteering to ride into the nearest town and notify the police.

Maggie, though with little hope in her own heart, endeavoured to cheer her father on their homeward way with the idea that Alice might have returned to Overbury over the Downs whilst they were going by road to the Bottom, and that she had seen them and called to them in jest when they were opposite the tongue of land.

However, when they reached home there was no Alice and, though the next day the search was resumed and full inquiries were instituted by the police, all was to no purpose. No trace of Alice was ever found, the last human being that saw her having been an old woman, who had met her going down the path into the Bottom on the afternoon of her disappearance, and who described her as smiling but looking "queerlike."

This is the end of the story, but the following may throw some light upon it.

The history of Alice's mysterious disappearance became widely known through the medium of the Press and Mr. Roberts, distressed beyond measure at what had taken place, returned in all haste to Overbury to offer what comfort and help he could give to his afflicted friend and tenant. He called upon the Maydews and, having heard their tale, sat for a short time in silence. Then he said:

"Have you ever heard any local gossip concerning this Colonel and Mrs. Paxton?"

"No," replied Mr. Maydew, "I never heard their names until the day of my poor daughter's fatal visit."

"Well," said Mr. Roberts, "I will tell you all I can about them, which is not very much, I fear." He paused and then went on: "I am now nearly seventy-five years old, and for nearly seventy years no house has stood in Brickett Bottom. But when I was a child of about five there was an old-fashioned, red brick house standing in a garden at the bend of the road, such as you have described. It was owned and lived in by a retired Indian soldier and his wife, a Colonel and Mrs. Paxton. At the time I speak of, certain events having taken place at the house and the old couple having died, it was sold by their heirs to Lord Carew, who shortly after pulled it down on the ground that it interfered with his shooting. Colonel and Mrs. Paxton were well known to my father, who was the clergyman here before me, and to the neighbourhood in general. They lived quietly and were not unpopular, but the Colonel was supposed to possess a violent and vindictive temper. Their family consisted only of themselves, their daughter and a couple of servants, the Colonel's old Army servant and his Eurasian wife. Well, I cannot tell you details of what happened, I was only a child; my father never liked gossip and in later years, when he talked to me on the subject, he always avoided any appearance of exaggeration or sensationalism. However, it is known that Miss Paxton fell in love with and became engaged to a young man to whom her parents took a strong dislike. They used every possible means to break off the match, and many rumours were set on foot as to their conduct—undue influence, even cruelty were charged against them. I do not know the truth, all I can say is that Miss Paxton died and a very bitter feeling against her parents sprang up. My father, however, continued to call, but was rarely admitted. In fact, he never saw Colonel Paxton after his daughter's death and only saw Mrs. Paxton once or twice. He described her as an utterly broken woman, and was not surprised at her following her daughter to the grave in about three months' time. Colonel Paxton became, if possible, more of a recluse than ever after his wife's death and himself died not more than a month after her under circumstances which pointed to suicide. Again a crop of rumours sprang up, but there was no one in particular to take action, the doctor certified Death from Natural Causes, and Colonel Paxton, like his wife and daughter, was buried in this churchyard. The property passed to a distant relative, who came down to it for one night shortly afterwards; he never came again, having apparently conceived a violent dislike to the place, but arranged to pension off the servants and then sold the house to Lord Carew, who was glad to purchase this little island in the middle of his property. He pulled it down soon after he had bought it, and the garden was left to relapse into a wilderness."

Mr. Roberts paused.

"Those are all the facts," he added.

"But there is something more," said Maggie.

Mr. Roberts hesitated for a while.

"You have a right to know all," he said almost to himself; then louder he continued: "What I am now going to tell you is really rumour, vague and uncertain; I cannot fathom its truth or its meaning. About five years after the house had been pulled down a young maidservant at Carew Court was out walking one afternoon. She was a stranger to the village and a new-comer to the Court. On returning home to tea she told her fellow-servants that as she walked down Brickett Bottom, which place she described clearly, she passed a red brick house at the bend of the road and that a kind-faced old lady had asked her to step in for a while. She did not go in, not because she had any suspicions of there being anything uncanny, but simply because she feared to be late for tea.

"I do not think she ever visited the Bottom again and she had no other similar experience, so far as I am aware.

"Two or three years later, shortly after my father's death, a travelling tinker with his wife and daughter camped for the night at the foot of the Bottom. The girl strolled away up the glen to gather blackberries and was never seen or heard of again. She was searched for in vain—of course, one does not know the truth—and she may have run away voluntarily from her parents, although there was no known cause for her doing so.

"That," concluded Mr. Roberts, "is all I can tell you of either facts or rumours; all that I can now do is to pray for you and for her."

BROKEN GLASS

GEORGIA WOOD PANGBORN

"I CAN'T STAY BUT A MINUTE," SAID MRS. WARING, SPREADING HER LONG HANDS above the wood blaze. "I was taking my evening constitutional over the moors. Did you see the sunset? And the firelight dancing in your open windows was so dear and sweet and homy I had to come. Babies in bed?"

"Oh, yes. Such perfectly good six-o'clock babies! I can tuck them up myself and still have time to dress safe from sticky fingers. Delia is such a blessing. So big and soft and without any nerves, and really and truly fond of them. When she leaves me for a day I am perfectly wild and lost."

"What is the matter with us women," said Mrs. Waring frowningly, "that we can't take care of our own children and run our own houses, to say nothing of spinning and weaving as our grandmothers did? My grandmother was a Western pioneer and brought up six without help, and—buried three. Think of it! To *lose* a child—" A strong shudder went through her delicate body. "How can a woman live after that? We can gasp through the bearing—you and I know that—but to lose—" She covered her face with her ringed hands.

"But, my dear," said the sleek woman by the fire, "your babies are such little Samsons! That nightmare ought not to bother you now."

"No. It oughtn't. That it does so only shows the more our modern unfitness."

"I suppose our grandmothers must have been more of the Delia type."

"And yet we think the Delia type inferior. It's solid and quiet and stupid—not always honest, but it succeeds with children. You and I are reckoned among the cultured. We read—in three languages—and write magazine verse. Your nocturne is to be given in concert next week—yet I think that Delia and her type rather despise us because we are wrecks after spending an afternoon trying to keep a creeping baby from choking and bumping and burning and taking cold, or reading Peter Rabbit the fiftieth time to Miss Going-on-Three."

"The question is," said Mrs. Waring coiling bonelessly in the Morris chair, "what will our children be? You and I may be inferior, but," she caught her lower lip in her teeth, "my babies came to me after I was thirty, and I know their value, as your Delia type or your grandmother type doesn't for all her motherliness. When women are mothers in the early twenties they don't know. They can't. My music filled in those years. Filled them! It served to express the despair of a barren woman—that was all. Since they came fools have condoled with me because I have had to give up my 'career' for their sake. Career!" She threw back her head with a savage laugh, and stood up with her hands in her coat pocket. "Here," her voice growing very gentle and humorous as she took out the tatters of a little book gay with red and green, "give me some paste. I promised to mend it. She has read it to pieces at last. I thought I could rhyme about sunsets and love and death, but nobody ever loved my rhymes as she loves this. Let's write some children's verses, you and I—

'Goldilocks was naughty, she began to sulk and pout;
She threw aside her playthings—'

That's the way, you see, not—

'When from the sessions of sweet silent thought.'"

She had seated herself at the big flat-topped desk as she spoke and was deftly pasting and mending.

"I've written one; or Tommy has. We were sitting up with his first double tooth. We had taken a go-cart ride in the early moonlight and I was taking cows as an example of people who chew properly. So we got up a song—(past one o'clock it was and a dark and stormy morning)—

'The moon goes sailing through the sky
The cows are chewing—chewing—'

He liked that but when he'd had it fifty times he changed it—

'The cows go sailing through the sky
The moon is chewing—chewing—'

And it is better that way; I can recommend it as a lullaby."

"Thanks, but I've some of my own pretty nearly as good. A Norwegian maid left me a legacy—

'Go away du Fisker mand Catch a pretty fish fish—sh—sh
Bring it home to baby boy
Quicker than a wish—wish—shsh.'"

"That's not bad; I'll remember it when the moon's chewing palls. . . .

"As I was saying, you and I know the value of our children even if our type is inferior to the Delia type; and if we were bereft of our Delias and didn't have to dress for dinner and had no time to read we should show up quite as well as the Delias.

"We use the Delias for them because we want them to have everything of the best. Delias *are* best when they're little. We enter later on. We couldn't nurse our babies.

All that part of us was metamorphosed into brain—thanks to a mistaken education. Very well; we must nourish them with our brains. We can. And we go and get the best service we can, maids and nurses; we bring them home to our nests like cats bringing mice—for the babies. . . .

"But I'm afraid I've got to let Aileen go. She told Martha a story about Indians carrying off children and nearly scared the child to death. And when I went to find them yesterday afternoon over by the empty Taylor cottage, they were playing where a window had been broken and there was broken glass everywhere. It was like dancing on knives. My spine shivers with it still. And there sat Aileen—so lost in a dream that I had to put my hand on her shoulder to rouse her. 'Oh,' said she, when I showed her the glass, 'I thought it was ice!' She cried when I told her what a terribly dangerous thing she had done. Her tears come easily enough. A pretty little thing, but *so* stupid. I must do better for Martha."

"I thought," said Mrs. Blake hesitatingly, "that she didn't seem very warmly dressed the other day."

"I don't know why she shouldn't be. I gave her a very good coat. Come to think of it, she hasn't worn it. I wonder why?"

"My Delia told me she had a sister. Perhaps—"

"Sponging on her. Poor child! I like her—but, Martha dancing on broken glass. . . . There, that's done. Now, Martha can read it a hundred times more— 'Goldilocks was naughty.'

"Now I must go—and dress. Symbol of degeneracy, as women; but of all that raises us above the Delias, if we *are* above them."

The road was icy and ill kept. Some half-dozen cottages with boarded windows showed silent and black against the red band of sunset and the gray, waving line of moors. The pound of winter surf was like distant hoof-beats over the frozen land. The only cottages that were open had children in them. Air is what we give them now. Air and careful food for the rearing of the best of the next generation. And for that purpose the half-dozen cottages on that island kept their warmth and life all winter, just for the sake of properly reddening the cheeks of a dozen little children for whom city streets and parks are not supposed to furnish enough of air.

"Lovely—lovely," thought Mrs. Waring as she walked crisply toward her own fair window. "The moors and the winter storms shall make up to them for having a middle-aged mother. They shall have all the youth and vigor that I had not—that I had not."

Suddenly she faced about. It was not a footfall or a sigh or a spoken word, though it gave the impression of all three. Something behind her had betrayed its presence. . . .

No. There was nothing.

"The wind in the grass," she thought, but was not satisfied. A caretaker had been murdered on the other side of the island the winter before. Being the mother of a Martha makes one a coward. If there were no Martha one would go striding anywhere disregarding fantastic dangers, but *when* there is a Martha, who waits at home for a mother to read the story of Goldilocks one hundred times more, why, a mother must not let the least shadow of danger come near her. Because there are so many ways besides reading Goldilocks in which a mother may be useful.

Therefore she thought sharply about the dead care-taker and vowed that on her next constitutional she would carry a pistol in her pocket—for Martha's sake. The black hedges with their white spots of snow gave no sign; the road behind and in front showed empty but for the gleam of frozen puddles. The wind rattled lightly in the frozen grass. . . .

"I hope ye'll excuse me, mum—" The voice was deprecatory and, thank Heaven, a woman's; though where she had come from out of all that emptiness—

"Ah!" gasped Martha's mother.

"I didn't want to scare ye, mum."

"I can't stop," said Mrs. Waring. "If you want to talk to me come to the house. I must get home to—to—"

"Yes, mum; I know, mum, to your little girl. But I can keep pace with you, by your leave, mum, for I was wishin' to speak to you about Aileen—"

"My nurse maid?"

"The same. I was hearin' she was not givin' ye satisfaction, mum, and would like to speak a word for her—widout offence."

"I have not complained of Aileen. It is true she is sometimes thoughtless. May I ask—"

The woman's figure was so shrouded and huddled that Mrs. Waring, looking all she could, might not distinguish the features. She fancied a resemblance to Mrs. Magillicuddy who came every week to help with the washing. No doubt it was Mrs. Magillicuddy. That would account for her knowledge of Aileen.

Mrs. Waring felt a twinge of annoyance at the thought of Aileen's complaining to Mrs. Magillicuddy. She walked on rapidly, but the other kept as close as her shadow.

"You mean, I suppose, about the broken glass."

"It was very bad, mum; so bad that . . . yet there's worse than broken glass in the world. There's other things that seems no more than the glitter of harmless ice and is really daggers for your heart's blood . . . an' so I was wishin' to speak to ye a word about Aileen. As to the glass, mum, there was no real harm done, an' could ye have seen the lass cryin' her eyes out in her little room that night. . . . Not because ye'd scolded her, but because she'd been that careless. And she could not sleep the night, that tender heart, for seein' the baby welterin' in gore that never was shed at all. Och—those eyes wid tears in them! Surely, mum—surely, ye must have noticed the eyes of her when she looks up at ye wid the hope in them that maybe she has pleased ye? Remember this is her first place and that she was reared gently among the sisters, orphanage as it was, and knows as little of the world as a fine lady-girl when she comes out from *her* convent school. She is not yet used to the rough ways of servants. . . .

"But she will be soon. Ah, wirra, wirra, she will be soon. . . .

"I would like her to stay wid ye. . . . I little thought, ten years ago, that she would be eatin' the bitter bread of service, for bitter it must be, however soft the life; bitter and dangerous for a young girl that is all alone and knows nothin' at all of the world's wickedness. . . . Do ye blame her for not seein' the broken glass? Can ye not guess that the eyes of her were blind with tears for a harsh word ye had given her about mixin' up the big baby's stockings with the little ones? Do ye mind that each of your children has two dozen little rolled up balls of stockings to be looked after and that they are very near of a size—very near? My Aileen—she never had but two pairs at a time and she washes out the wan pair at night so she can change to the other. And do ye mind that hers are thin cotton—twelve cints the pair they are—and her feet are cold to break yer heart as she sits in the cold wind watchin' your little girl at play, so warm in her English woollen stockings and leggins. And have ye ever been into Aileen's room? Do ye know that the fine gilt radiator in it is never warm and that she has but one thin blanket and a comforter so ragged your dog would scorn it? And when she had a bit of a cough ye were afraid it might be consumption, ye said, and if so ye couldn't have her with the children—"

"You seem to know my house and my servants remarkably well, Mrs. Magillicuddy. I will see to Aileen's room at once. I have been very busy, but—really—"

"Ah, save yer anger, mum, for one that desarves it. He's not far away. I am not angry with you, mum, though well I might be. I know with what love ye love yer own. But the world is so large and in such need of the kind and wise that, when one is truly kind and wise like you, mum, it is accounted a sin to let your kindness and wisdom go no further than the soft small heads that are your own. . . . There are so many children without any mothers at all . . . as yours might be had I been what you feared but now. . . .

"Broken glass! Is it not worse than broken glass for a young thing like that, as white-souled as that bit of snow on the hedge—have ye ever heard the talk of house servants? And the only place she can go to get away from it when ye do not want her for your children is her own little room that is so cold.

"She does not understand as yet, the whiteness in her is so white and the servants' hall is warm and pleasant and full of the laughter that ye sometimes hear and frown about. She knows no more than you do of the black heart beneath the white coat of the rascal that is so soft stepping and pleasant and keeps your silver so clean and bright an' says 'Very good, sir,' to everything the boss says to him—"

"Impossible!"

"Does it not happen every day? Do men and women leave off bein' men and women because they do your housework for you? Hearts as well as platters can break in the kitchen, and what do ye care what goes on among the help so long as your house is clean and quiet?"

"Broken glass. . . ." Her voice rose with the rising wind, thinly. . . . "Wirra, wirra—an' a colleen as innocent of the danger of it as your baby that danced upon it unharmed—praise the saints!—unharmed. . . ."

Between anger and fright, Mrs. Waring leaned forward to pluck at the shawl which the other held about her head. At the moment a shaft of light, probably the searchlight from some vessel close inshore—or was it something else?—fell upon the woman's face. It was gone so quickly that Mrs. Waring could not afterward swear to what she had seen. No. Not Mrs. Magillicuddy's face, but similar. Lined and worn, singularly noble.

"*Who are you?*"

"Do ye ask me *that?*" said the Voice.

The flash of light having passed, it seemed so dark that now Mrs. Waring could not even distinguish the film of shadow that had showed where the woman stood.

"Do ye ask me that, mother that loves her children? What would *ye* do, then, if ye were dead, and your children's tears fell upon ye in purgatory? What would ye do if the feet of yer own colleen were standing among broken glass that is broken glass indeed?"

"Who are you?" whimpered Mrs. Waring. But the little moon had risen now and showed the moor empty except for the silent lights of the cottages where little children were.

As she stumbled at her own doorstep her butler opened the door with obsequious concern, and obvious amazement when she cried out—"Aileen—where is she?"

"In her room, I think, m'm; the children being asleep. Shall I call her, m'm?"

"*No!*"

She hurried to the attic room and knocked. The door was locked. Something stirred softly and opened. Aileen's frightened eyes sought her mistress's face. Mrs. Waring read dread of something having been stolen, of some terrible oversight in the nursery, of instant dismissal.

The girl coughed and shivered. She was wearing her coat but her little cap and apron were ready for instant duty. Mrs. Waring remembered with a shock of contrition that Martha had cried because Aileen's hands were cold as she dressed her.

"Aileen—" sobbed Mrs. Waring. . . .

"Oh, you poor *little* thing—Come down, child, where it is warm!"

THE BUSINESS OF MADAME JAHN

VINCENT O'SULLIVAN

HOW WE ALL STARED, HOW FRIGHTENED WE ALL WERE, HOW WE PASSED OPINIONS, on that morning when Gustave Herbout was found swinging by the neck from the ceiling of his bedroom! The whole Faubourg, even the ancient folk who had not felt a street under them for years, turned out and stood gaping at the house with amazement and loud conjecture. For why should Gustave Herbout, of all men, take to the rope? Only last week he had inherited all the money of his aunt, Madame Jahn, together with her house and the shop with the five assistants, and life looked fair enough for him. No; clearly it was not wise of Gustave to hang himself!

Besides, his aunt's death had happened at a time when Gustave was in sore straits for money. To be sure, he had his salary from the bank in which he worked; but what is a mere salary to one who (like Gustave) threw off the clerkly habit when working hours were over to assume the dress and lounge of the accustomed *boulevardier*: while he would relate to obsequious friends vague but satisfactory stories of a Russian Prince who was his uncle, and of an extremely rich English lady to whose death he looked forward with hope. Alas! with a clerk's salary one cannot make much of a figure in Paris. It took all of that, and more, to maintain the renown he had gained among his acquaintance of having to his own a certain little lady with yellow hair, who danced divinely. So he was forced to depend on the presents which Madame Jahn gave him from time to time; and for those presents he had to pay his aunt a most sedulous and irksome attention. At times, when he was almost sick from his craving for the *boulevard*, the *café*, the theatre, he would have to repair, as the day grew to an end, to our *Faubourg*, and the house behind the shop, where he would sit to an old-fashioned supper with his aunt, and listen with a sort of dull impatience while she asked him when he had last been at Confession, and told him long dreary stories of his dead father and mother. Punctually at nine o'clock the deaf servant, who was the only person besides Madame Jahn that lived in the house, would let in the fat old priest, who came for his game of dominoes, and betake herself to bed. Then the dominoes would begin, and with them the old man's prattle, which Gustave knew so well: about his daily work, about the uselessness of all things here on earth, and the happiness and glory of the Kingdom of Heaven; and, of course, our *boulevardier* noticed, with the usual cheap sneer of the modern, that whilst the priest talked of the Kingdom of

Heaven he yet shewed the greatest anxiety if he had symptoms of a cold, or any other petty malady. However, Gustave would sit there, with a hypocrite's grin and inwardly raging, till the clock chimed eleven. At that hour Madame Jahn would rise, and, if she was pleased with her nephew, would go over to her writing-desk and give him, with a rather pretty air of concealment from the priest, perhaps fifty or a hundred francs. Whereupon Gustave would bid her a manifestly affectionate good-night! and depart in the company of the priest. As soon as he could get rid of the priest, he would hasten to his favourite *cafés*, to discover that all the people worth seeing had long since grown tired of waiting, and had departed on their own affairs. The money, indeed, was a kind of consolation; but then there were nights when he did not get a *sou*. Ah! they amuse themselves in Paris, but not in this way—this is not amusing.

One cannot live a proper life upon a salary, and an occasional gift of fifty or a hundred francs. And it is not entertaining to tell men that your uncle, the Prince at Moscow, is in a sorry case, and even now lies a-dying, or that the rich English lady is in the grip of a vile consumption and is momently expected to succumb, if these men only shove up their shoulders, wink at one another, and continue to present their bills. Further, the little Mademoiselle, with yellow hair, had lately shown signs of a very pretty temper, because her usual flowers and *bon-bons* were not apparent. So, since things were come to this dismal pass, Gustave fell to attending the race-meetings at Chantilly. During the first week Gustave won largely, for that is sometimes the way with ignorant men: during that week, too, the little Mademoiselle was charming, for she had her *bouquets* and boxes of *bon-bons*. But the next week Gustave lost heavily, for that is also very often the way with ignorant men: and he was thrown into the blackest despair, when one night at a place where he used to sup, Mademoiselle took the arm of a great fellow, whom he much suspected to be a German, and tossed him a scornful nod as she went off.

On the evening after this happened, he was standing, between five and six o'clock, in the *Place de la Madeleine*, blowing on his fingers and trying to plan his next move, when he heard his name called by a familiar voice, and turned to face his aunt's adviser, the priest.

Ah, Gustave, my friend, I have just been to see a colleague of mine here!" cried the old man, pointing to the great church. "And are you going to your good aunt to-night?" he added, with a look at Gustave's neat dress.

Gustave was in a flame that the priest should have detected him in his gay clothes, for he always made a point of appearing at Madame Jahn's clad staidly in black; but he answered pleasantly enough:

"No, my Father, I'm afraid I can't to-night. You see I'm a little behind with my office work, and I have to stay at home and catch up."

"Well! well!" said the priest, with half a sigh, I suppose young men will always be the same. I myself can only be with her till nine o'clock to-night, because I must see a sick parishioner. But let me give you one bit of advice, my friend," he went on, taking hold of a button on Gustave's coat: "don't neglect your aunt; for, mark my words, one day everything of Madame Jahn's will be yours!" And the omnibus he was waiting for happening to swing by at that moment, he departed without another word.

Gustave strolled along the *Boulevard des Capucines* in a study. Yes; it was certain that the house, and the shop with the five assistants, would one day be his; for the priest knew all his aunt's affairs. But how soon would they be his? Madame Jahn was now hardly sixty; her mother had lived to be ninety; when she was ninety he would be ———. And meanwhile, what about the numerous bills, what (above all!) about the little lady with yellow hair? He paused and struck his heel on the pavement with such force, that two men passing nudged one another and smiled. Then he made certain purchases, and set about wasting his time till nine o'clock.

It is curious to consider, that although when he started out at nine o'clock, Gustave was perfectly clear as to what he meant to do, yet he was chiefly troubled by the fear that the priest had told his aunt about his fine clothes. But when he had passed through the deserted *Faubourg*, and had come to the house behind the shop, he found his aunt only very pleased to see him, and a little surprised. So he sat with her, and listened to her gentle, homely stories, and told lies about himself and his manner of life, till the clock struck eleven. Then he rose, and Madame Jahn rose too, and went to her writing-desk and opened a small drawer.

"You have been very kind to a lonely old woman to-night, my Gustave," said Madame Jahn, smiling.

"How sweet of you to say that, dearest aunt!" replied Gustave. He went over and passed his arm caressingly across her shoulders, and stabbed her in the heart.

For a full five minutes after the murder he stood still; as men often do in a great crisis when they know that any movement means decisive action. Then he started, laid hold of his hat, and made for the door. But there the stinging knowledge of his crime came to him for the first time; and he turned back into the room. Madame Jahn's bedroom candle was on a table: he lit it, and passed through a door which led from the house into the shop. Crouching below the counters covered with white sheets, lest a streak of light on the windows might attract the observation of some passenger, he proceeded to a side entrance to the shop, unbarred and unlocked the door, and put the key in his pocket. Then, in the same crouching way, he returned to the room, and started to ransack the small drawer. The notes he scattered about the floor; but two small bags of coin went into his coat. Then he took the candle and dropped some wax on the face and hands and dress of the corpse; he spilt wax, too, over the carpet, and then he broke the candle and ground it under his foot. He even tore with long nervous fingers at the dead woman's bodice until her breasts lay exposed; and plucked out a handful of her hair and threw it on the floor to stick to the wax. When all these things had been accomplished, he went to the house door and listened. The *Faubourg* is always very quiet about twelve o'clock, and a single footstep falls on the night with a great sound. He could not hear the least noise; so he darted out and ran lightly until he came to a turning. There he fell into a sauntering walk, lit a cigarette, and hailing a passing *fiacre*, directed the man to drive to the *Pont Saint-Michel*. At the bridge he alighted, and noting that he was not eyed, he threw the key of the shop into the river. Then assuming the swagger and assurance of a half-drunken man, he marched up the *Boulevard* and entered the *Café d'Harcourt*.

The place was filled with the usual crowd of men and women of the *Quartier Latin*. Gustave looked round, and observing a young student with a flushed face who was talking eagerly about the rights of man, he sat down by him. It was his part to act quickly: so before the student had quite finished a sentence for his ear, the murderer gave him the lie. The student, however, was not so ready for a fight as Gustave had supposed; and when he began to argue again, Gustave seized a glass full of brandy and water and threw the stuff in his face. Then indeed there was a row, till the *gendarmes* interfered, and haled Gustave to the station. At the police-station he bitterly lamented his misdeed, which he attributed to an extra glass of absinthe, and he begged the authorities to carry word of his plight to his good aunt, Madame Jahn, in our *Faubourg*. So to the house behind the shop they went, and there they found her—sitting with her breasts hanging out, her poor head clotted with blood, and a knife in her heart.

The next morning, Gustave was set free. A man and a woman, two of the five assistants in the shop, had been charged with the murder. The woman had been severely reprimanded by Madame Jahn on the day before, and the man was known to be the girl's paramour. It was the duty of the man to close at night all the entrances into the shop, save the main entrance, which was closed by Madame Jahn and her deaf servant: and the police had formed a theory (worked out with the amazing zeal and skill which cause the Paris police so often to overreach themselves!) that the man had failed to bolt one of the side doors, and had, by his subtilty, got possession of the key, whereby he and his accomplice re-entered the place about midnight. Working on this theory, the police had woven a web round the two unfortunates with threads of steel; and there was little doubt, that both of them would stretch their necks under the guillotine, with full consent of press and public. At least, this was Gustave's opinion; and Gustave's opinion now went for a great deal in the *Faubourg*. Of course there were a few who murmured, that it was a good thing poor Madame Jahn had not lived to see her nephew arrested for a drunken brawler; but with full remembrance of who owned the house and shop, we were most of us inclined to say, after the priest: That if the brave Gustave had been with his aunt, the shocking affair could never have occurred. And, indeed, what had we more inspiring than the inconsolable grief he shewed? Why! on the day of the funeral, when he heard the earth clatter down on the coffin-lid in *Père la Chaise*, he even swooned to the ground, and had to be carried out in the midst of the mourners. "Oh, yes," (quoth the gossips), "Gustave Herbout loved his aunt passing well!"

On the night after the funeral, Gustave was sitting alone before the fire in Madame Jahn's room, smoking and making his plans. He thought, that when all this wretched mock grief and pretence of decorum was over, he would again visit the *cafés* which he greatly savoured, and the little Mademoiselle with yellow hair would once more smile on him delicious smiles, with a gleaming regard. Thus he was thinking when the clock on the mantel-piece tinkled eleven; and at that moment a very singular thing happened. The door was suddenly opened: a girl came in, and walked straight over to the writing-desk, pulled out the small drawer, and then sat staring at the man by the fire. She was distinctly beautiful; although there was a certain old-fashionedness in her peculiar silken dress, and the manner of wearing her hair. Not once did it occur to Gustave, as he gazed in terror, that he was gazing on a mortal woman: the doors were too well bolted to allow any one from outside to enter, and besides, there was a strange baffling familiarity in the face and mien of the intruder. It might have been an hour as he sat there; and then, the silence becoming too horrible, by a supreme effort of his wonderful courage he rushed out of the room and up-stairs to get his hat. There in his murdered aunt's bedroom,— there, smiling at him from the wall—was a vivid presentment of the dread vision that sat below: a portrait of Madame Jahn as a girl. He fled into the street, and walked, perhaps two miles, before he thought at all. But when he did think, he found that he was drawn against his will back to the house to see if *It* was still there: just as the police here believe a murderer is drawn to the *Morgue* to view the body of his victim. Yes; the girl was there still, with her great reproachless eyes; and throughout that solemn night Gustave, haggard and mute, sat glaring at her. Towards dawn he fell into an uneasy doze; and when he awoke with a scream, he found that the girl was gone.

At noon the next day Gustave, heartened by several glasses of brandy, and cheered by the sunshine in the *Champs-Elysées*, endeavoured to make light of the affair. He would gladly have arranged not to go back to the house: but then people would talk so much, and he could not afford to lose any custom out of the shop. Moreover, the whole matter was only an hallucination—the effect of jaded nerves. He dined well, and went to see a musical comedy; and so contrived, that he did not return to the house until after two o'clock. There was someone waiting for him, sitting at the desk with the small drawer open; not the girl of last night, but a some-what older woman—and the same reproachless eyes. So great was the fascination of those eyes, that, although he left the house at once, with an iron resolution not to go back, he found himself drawn under them again, and he sat through the night as he had sat through the night before, sobbing and stupidly glaring. And all day long he crouched by the fire shuddering; and all the night till eleven o'clock; and then a figure of his aunt came to him again, but always a little older and more withered. And this went on for five days; the figure that sat with him becoming older and older as the days ran, till on the sixth night he gazed through the hours at his aunt as she was on the night he killed her. On these nights he was used sometimes to start up and make for the street, swearing never to return; but always he would be dragged back to the eyes. The policemen came to know him from these night walks, and people began to notice his bad looks: these could not spring from grief, folk said, and so they thought he was leading a wild life.

On the seventh night there was a delay of about five minutes after the clock had rung eleven, before the door opened. And then—then, merciful God! the body of a woman in grave-clothes came into the room, as if borne by unseen men, and lay in the air across the writing-desk, while the small drawer flew open of its own accord. Yes; there was the shroud of the brown scapular, the prim white cap, the hands folded on the shrunken breast. Gray from slimy horror, Gustave raised himself up, and went over to look for the eyes. When he saw them pressed down with pennies, he reeled back and vomited into the grate. And blind, and sick, and loathing, he stumbled up-stairs.

But as he passed by Madame Jahn's bedroom the corpse came out to meet him, with the eyes closed and the pennies pressing them down. Then, at last, reeking and dabbled with sweat, with his tongue lolling out, and the spittle running down his beard, Gustave breathed:——

"Are you alive?"

"No, no!" wailed the *thing*, with a burst of awful weeping; "I have been dead many days."

Carnivorine

Lucy H. Hooper

When I, Ellis Graham, being a man of middle age, means, and leisure, determined upon starting, last autumn, for Rome, with a view to studying up the localities for my projected history of the Cenci family, I never expected assuredly that a momentous and important task, regarding other people's affairs and not my own, should be imposed upon me. Yet I could not well refuse the mission. I had known the Lambert family for many years, and had always cherished a warm friendship for Mr. and Mrs. Lambert—a friendship which, after the demise of the former, I had continued to his widow. And Julius, the elder son, had been quite a favorite of mine in his boyish days, though I could not altogether sympathize with his craze for scientific pursuits, and especially for botany. It must be confessed, however, that his researches into the formation and functions of the vegetable kingdom had led to some curious discoveries. But these discoveries had only served to arouse in his mind, as he grew to manhood, a wild ambition for further successes in the same line. I never exactly comprehended what course his investigations had taken, but I knew he was deeply interested in the Darwinian theories, and had set himself, in that connection, some inscrutable problem that he was trying to make out. He lived such a secluded life, shut up with his plants and his theories, that I had wholly lost sight of him for some years, though my visits to Mrs. Lambert were still continued.

I was a good deal surprised, however, on the eve of my departure for Europe, to receive from my old friend a few hurried lines, begging that I would call to see her before I left and fixing the very next evening for my visit. I responded to the appeal, and found the usually serene and dignified lady in a state of unwonted emotion.

"I have sent for you, dear Mr. Graham," she said, "to ask if you will undertake for me a very important mission. It is hardly right, I know, for me to make such a request of you, involving, as your consent will surely do, a good deal of trouble and the loss of a considerable portion of your time. But my peace of mind is at stake, and I do not know what else to do if you are not willing to help me."

"Anything that is in my power to execute, dear Mrs. Lambert, I will gladly undertake," I answered. And, indeed, I was so much moved by her distress and by noticing the traces left upon her still fair features by wearing anxiety, that I was ready to promise anything or to undertake anything in her behalf.

"I want you to find Julius for me."

"Julius? Is he absent from home? I did not even know that he had gone away."

"Yes; he sailed for Europe three years ago. You know, his uncle left him a handsome fortune a little before that time, and he went abroad—to pursue, as he stated, his scientific experiments. I know that he believed himself to be on the verge of a great discovery; but, of what nature that discovery was, he never would reveal, even to me. As you may remember, I have never sympathized with him in his studies, so I suppose he did not consider me worthy of his confidence. Perhaps I did wrong. Maybe, if I had interested myself more in his pursuits, he would not have left me as he has done. He told me, before he went away, that his experiments must be perfected in thorough seclusion, and that he never meant to relinquish them till he had arrived at some great result. We heard from him, afterward, at Paris, and. later on, at Milan; but he has not written to his brothers or to me for months."

"Have you no idea as to his whereabouts at present?"

"I have reason to think that he has taken up his abode somewhere in the neighborhood of Rome. He was seen there, two winters ago, by Alan Spencer, the artist—who had quite a talk with him, but who could find out nothing from him respecting his residence or his pursuits."

"Did he seem well?"

"He looked tired and haggard, Mr. Spencer said, but was otherwise well. The reason for my anxiety is—is—well, I may as well confess it to you at once: I fear that there is some entanglement in the case—a passion for some woman, who may entrap Julius into matrimony."

"And have you any foundation for this dread?"

"Only this: he let fall something to Mr. Spencer about a personage called Carnivorine."

"What an extraordinary name! Did he give his friend any information concerning her?"

"No. He was singularly reticent on the subject, and seemed really distressed at having let even her name slip out unawares. He requested Mr. Spencer never to mention it; but Alan has always been on very intimate terms with Richard and Maude, and, seeing how uneasy we were at Julius's long silence, he did not hesitate, not having made any promise of secrecy, to tell us the little that he knew. So, when you reach Rome, if you will try to find our lost Julius for us, I shall be more indebted to you than I can tell you."

I promised to do my best, and Mrs. Lambert, visibly relieved, added some details about her son's banker in Rome and also respecting the few persons that he knew in that city, and who might have learned something concerning him during the last few months. Also, she gave me the name and address of the herbalist before whose door—and, indeed, issuing from it—Alan Spencer had met Julius in such an unexpected fashion.

"You will write to me as soon as you have any news," she said, wistfully, to me, at parting. "And, above all, let me know everything you can find out about Carnivorine. Do not hesitate to tell me the worst—even if Julius has married this creature with the singular name."

I must confess that, when I first arrived in Rome, so many personal interests claimed me that I did not at once begin my search for Julius Lambert, as I had intended to do. There were so many of my old friends and old haunts to revisit, and such numbers of new and interesting statues in the studios of the Roman sculptors, both native and foreign, to go to see, and my negotiations with the artists who were to execute the illustrations for my history of the Cenci family took up so much time, that the weeks insensibly slipped away before I had taken any steps in the matter. I had had the time to receive more than one letter from Mrs. Lambert on the subject before I commenced my investigations. I must acknowledge that I had come to the conclusion that the mystery, on investigation, would prove to be no mystery at all, and that Julius would be discovered in one of the minor hotels in Rome—too busy, or perhaps too much in love, to write. But, when I did finally set out in search of him, I found myself baffled at the very outset by an impenetrable wall of mystery. Nobody had seen him, and nobody knew anything about him. He had drawn all his funds from the banker's on his first arrival in the city. He had been in Rome some two years before, and had bought a collection of the curious insect-eating plants of South America from the old herbalist at whose door Alan Spencer had met him. That was all. If the earth had opened beneath his feet and had swallowed him up, he could not have vanished more utterly from human ken. I sought for him in every direction. I employed the services of a private detective. I offered a reward for any news of him. All was of no use. I succeeded in learning that he had not left Rome—and that was all I could find out.

Some months had elapsed, and I had pretty much abandoned the search in despair, when one day the fancy took me to go on a ride on horseback over the Campagna. I had long cherished the desire to explore the less frequented and scarcely known districts of that vast region, haunted by malaria and tenanted only by a few fever-stricken shepherds, that lies outside the beaten track of tourists and travelers beyond the city walls. As may be imagined, I found my excursion rather dreary. I rode on and on, passing now a flock of sheep watched over by a brigand-looking guardian and a fierce rough dog that looked ready, at a word or a sign from his master, to tear down my horse and throttle its rider, and then some huge arch of a ruined aqueduct that in the days of classic Rome had been musical with laughing water. Sometimes I came upon the shattered fragments of an abandoned hovel, or met with a herd of the gray-coated long-horned oxen of the region, beautiful placid-looking creatures, that gazed at me inquiringly out of their large soft eyes as I rode by, as though saying What is this stranger doing in this home of solitude and ruin? Still, I was interested by the very novelty of the dreary region, and I rode on and on, till the sun began to sink toward the western horizon. I have always considered myself fever-proof, but, all the same, a ride after sunset over the Campagna is not the healthiest experiment in the world, so I wheeled my horse round and started to return to the city. And, as I did so, I became aware of the existence of a house at a very short distance. I might very well have passed it without noticing it, as it was so embowered in a mass of vegetation, vines, and bushes, as well as trees, that its shape and architecture were barely discernible. As I rode nearer, I saw that it was a modern villa of imposing dimensions, which had been suffered to fall into almost total ruin. Whether the freak of a speculator or the wild idea of some Campagna proprietor had caused the erection, in this lonely unhealthy place, of a costly country residence, there was no evidence to reveal. The grounds, once spacious and well laid out, were overrun with a thick undergrowth of plants and grasses. Here and there, a statue in white marble, streaked with damp and green with mold, showed under the shadow of the trees, and one, a graceful figure of a nymph, overthrown from its pedestal, lay prostrate amongst the rank grass. The façade of the house itself was adorned with moss-grown sculptures, and one of the pillars supporting the doorway had been broken away and its place was supplied by the trunk of a cypress. One-half of the building showed deserted and ruinous with its broken windows and decaying roof. But there were traces elsewhere of human habitation. The roof of the right wing had been mended, the windows were in good condition, and a gleam of firelight from the lower rooms gave a cheery aspect to that part of the edifice. And, oddly enough, in spite of the universal decay and dilapidation, there were traces not only of comfort, but of luxury, in one portion of the premises, which I noticed as I drew near. This was a large conservatory adjoining the inhabited portion of the house. It was in perfect order. Not a pane was missing in its glazed walls, through which I could discern the red glare of the stove-fires within, as well as the dull green of the foliage of the plants.

Both I and my horse were weary, so I decided that I would halt for an hour or so at this singular habitation, and try for a feed of oats for my horse, as well as for a flask of Chianti and a crust of bread for myself. I drew rein at the dilapidated doorway, and, just as I was about to announce my presence by a resounding knock from the butt-end of my riding-whip, the door was suddenly opened and a man came hurriedly forth. He started when he saw me, and was about to retreat into the house; but, by the red light of the waning sunset, I discerned his features and recognized him instantly. It was the man I had so long sought for and in vain—it was Julius Lambert.

"Julius!" I cried, as he was about to vanish through the doorway. "Julius Lambert! Is it thus that you treat an old friend who has come so far to visit you?"

He turned back at the sound of my voice. "So it is really you, Mr. Graham," he said, hesitatingly. "How in the world did you ever find me or the Villa Anzieri? Nobody has come near it or me either, for over two years past. But come in—my man shall take charge of your horse—and you can tell me something about home matters."

I willingly relinquished the charge of my wearied steed to the black-eyed, bronze-complexioned, picturesque-looking young fellow who came in answer to his master's call, and I followed Julius into the house. I could hardly believe my senses, or that I had found my missing friend at last. It had all happened so simply and yet so strangely. Meanwhile Julius, after he had gotten over the first shock of my intrusion, seemed really glad to see me. He piled fresh wood on the fire, and gave orders that dinner should be served as soon as possible, and plied me with questions respecting his mother and his brother and sisters. As for himself, I found him looking far from well. He was never very stout, but he had grown lean and emaciated, and the yellowish pallor of his face gave evidence of the effects that the malaria of the Campagna had on his system. Dinner was served at last—a very palatable stew flavored with red peppers and tomatoes, with the accompaniment of some fine oranges and grapes by way of dessert, and a flask or two of Chianti wine and one of the delicate Civita Lavinia. Throughout the repast, I noticed with pain that Julius talked in a feverish incoherent way, pressing me to eat or to drink, and hurrying questions and remarks about home matters, half the time without waiting for an answer.

At last, pushing my plate aside, I remarked:

"Now, Julius, I have told you everything that you wished to know. It is my turn now to ask for a little information. What have you been doing all this long time in this solitude?"

He moved uneasily in his chair, and his wandering glance avoided mine.

"Nothing," he muttered—"I have done—I am doing—nothing."

"Nonsense! You cannot persuade me of the truth of that assertion, so ardent an experimentalist as you have always been, and so interested in the cause of science. Confess, now—have you not made, or are you not on the verge of perfecting, some great discovery?"

I had touched the right chord. His eyes flashed, and his whole countenance grew bright with animation.

"Yes!" he cried. "I have succeeded at last in my researches. For years I have tried to perfect a demonstration of the link between the vegetable and the animal kingdom. If you have come to scoff at my discoveries, go—go at once! Otherwise, follow me—and be prepared for full conviction as to the truth of what I have said."

He rose as he spoke, and, taking me by the hand, he led me to a door at the extremity of the large room in which we had dined. This door he unlocked with a key which he took from his pocket. Night had closed in, and he completed his preparations by lighting a great torch of pine-branches.

"Wait on the threshold, as you value your life," he said to me, impressively. Then he threw open the door.

It was the entrance to the conservatory. The first thing that struck me was a sort of faint rustling sound like that garment or a sweeping bird's-wing. Then, by the light of the torch which Julius held on high, I discerned, in the centre of the room, a vast tub filled with masses of spongy moss, from which rose a strange plant—a hideous shapeless monster: a sort of vegetable hydra—or, rather, octopus—gigantic in size and repulsive in aspect and in coloring. So immense were its proportions, that it filled by itself the whole space of the conservatory. It consisted of a central bladder-shaped trunk or core, from which sprang countless branches—or, rather, arms—thick, leafless, of a livid green, and streaked with blotches of a dull-crimson. Each arm terminated in an oval protuberance which had a resemblance to the human eye. Julius took, from a basket that stood near the door, a great slice of raw meat, and, fastening it to the end of a stick, he advanced it, taking infinite precautions to keep well out of reach within the circle of outstretched branches. Then I saw these great tentacle-like arms fold around their prey, which they transmitted to the central core; and then, closing around it, I saw it no more. It was this slow motion of the branches that had caused the rustling sound which had amazed me on my first entrance.

So repulsive was the aspect of this enormous creature, half plant and half animal, that I was glad to beat a retreat to the dining-room. Julius followed, flushed and elated at the healthful aspect of his monstrous creation.

"The plant you have just seen," he said, "is a Drosera, which, by dint of careful selection and persevering attention, I have developed into this unheard-of size. I have studied the discoveries of Warming and of Darwin concerning those strange plants, the Drosera and the Dionœa—which, though still vegetables, feed on the insects that they kill. It has been my desire for years to perfect the missing link and to develop the animal side of these curious vegetable natures. It has always been my theory that the hydra, the dragon, and other monstrous forms of animal life really did exist, and that, in the evolution of ages and by reason of geological changes on the surface of the earth, these creatures, deprived of their accustomed forms of nourishment, degenerated into trees and plants and took root in the earth. Some of them still preserve their primitive forms, as witness the dragon-tree of Java. It has been my aim and endeavor to resuscitate the animal in the plant. Chance threw in my way a Drosera of great size. I have fed it on animal food for years, and developed it into something that is not yet a dragon or a hydra, but which is surely something more than a plant. Had you ventured within reach of its branches, the grasp of a boa would not have been more swift or more deadly."

"And what further do you propose doing with your dreadful plant?"

"My aim now is to give it locomotion—to see it detach itself from the soil and go forth in search of prey."

"How can you contemplate the possibility of letting loose such a monster on the world?"

"For science, there is no such thing as a monster. Moreover, are there not crocodiles and anacondas and tigers upon earth, to say nothing of the shark and the octopus? Beside these, my creation—my Carnivorine—is a harmless creature."

I started as I heard the name. So this, then, was the object of my poor friend's affections—this ghastly shape, not yet wholly animal, yet scarcely vegetable, with the form of a plant and the appetites of a beast of prey?

Just then, Pietro, the man-servant, came in to announce that my horse was at the door. It was a beautiful moonlight night, promising a pleasant ride to the city. I took my leave of Julius, therefore, with something of the feeling of relief of a man who awakes from sleep after having been oppressed by a terrible nightmare. But I did not depart without leaving my address, and I begged Julius to let me know if his strange discovery took any new developments in the near future.

Weeks passed away, and I had nearly forgotten all about Julius and Carnivorine, when one day I received a letter from him, written in a strain of great exultation and excitement. "Come to me, dear friend," he wrote; "come at once! The hour of the perfecting of my experiment is at hand. Already, amid the masses that surround Carnivorine, I discern the stirring and striving of the roots, that are acquiring powers of independent locomotion. In a few days, the problem will be solved. I want you to be present as a witness of the phenomenon. My ambition is satisfied at last—my name shall be inscribed on the list of the great discoverers of the world of science. Come to me, and be at my side in the moment of my triumph."

It was not without difficulty that I once more made my way to the Villa Anzieri. It was late in the afternoon when I drew rein at the dilapidated doorway that I remembered so well. I knocked loudly at the door, but there was no response to my call. Looking around, I saw that the whole place wore an inexplicable air of desertion. No firelight was visible at the windows, and the red glare of the stove-fire no longer shone behind the dim panes of the hot-house. Finally, in vague alarm, finding that my shouts and knocking produced no response, I tied my horse to one of the door-posts, and, singling out a window of the large room in which we had dined on the occasion of my former visit, I swung myself up to it by the help of a thick stem of ivy, and peered into the room. The sight that I beheld within froze my soul with horror.

At the end of the room, near the entrance to the conservatory, rose the hideous form of Carnivorine, no longer planted in a tub, but supported on what seemed, to me, a pair of paddle-like feet or paws like those of some misshapen antediluvian animal. The powerful branches—or, rather, tentacles—were upraised and closely folded around some central object. And at the summit of these livid green, closely-pressed, serpent-like stems appeared a ghastly object: it was a livid human head—the head of a corpse—and the pallid features were those of Julius Lambert!

With one stroke of my arm, I burst open the casement. I sprang into the room and hastened toward the dreadful object. The long arms quivered and began to unfold themselves. But, before the creature could put itself in motion, a shot from the revolver that I always carried during my Campagna wanderings pierced its central core. The tentacles fell apart, and the hideous plant sank prone upon the ground, bearing with it, in its fall, the crushed and lifeless form of Julius Lambert. A stream of reddish sap that looked like blood flowed from the shattered stem and mingled with the branches, stained as they were with a ruddier crimson—the life-blood of my unhappy friend.

I never discovered how or when the catastrophe took place. From the condition of the body, death must have taken place at least twenty-four hours before my arrival. The servants, brought face to face with such a shocking—and, to them, inexplicable—catastrophe, had fled from the house, taking with them whatever money or valuables they could lay their hands upon. I tried to trace them out, but in vain. As to the rest, it was all mere conjecture on my part. The uptorn earth and mosses in the tub in which Carnivorine had originally found an abode seemed to prove that a sudden development of the long-sought-for powers of locomotion in the creature had unexpectedly taken place, and that Julius had been seized either in the act of inspecting its condition or at the moment of offering it food. At all events, the vegetable-animal or animal-vegetable had made a solitary trial of its newly-formed powers, and had found a solitary prey when the bullet from my pistol put an end to its existence.

Among the papers left behind by Julius was a series of memoranda respecting the experiments he had tried and the processes he had used to bring his dread creation to full perfection. These I destroyed without hesitation. It would not have been well to have suffered the race of the vegetable octopus to be extended and propagated by curious scientists in the future. Then, lest a new growth should spring from the stem or branches of the accursed tree, I hewed them to pieces with my own hand and burned the fragments to ashes. The annihilation of my friend's discovery may be a loss to science, but humanity will only have cause to rejoice in the total destruction of CARNIVORINE.

THE CASE OF LADY SANNOX

ARTHUR CONAN DOYLE

THE RELATIONS BETWEEN DOUGLAS STONE AND THE NOTORIOUS LADY SANNOX were very well known both among the fashionable circles of which she was a brilliant member, and the scientific bodies which numbered him among their most illustrious confrères. There was naturally, therefore, a very widespread interest when it was announced one morning that the lady had absolutely and for ever taken the veil, and that the world would see her no more. When, at the very tail of this rumour, there came the assurance that the celebrated operating surgeon, the man of steel nerves, had been found in the morning by his valet, seated on one side of his bed, smiling pleasantly upon the universe, with both legs jammed into one side of his breeches and his great brain about as valuable as a cap full of porridge, the matter was strong enough to give quite a little thrill of interest to folk who had never hoped that their jaded nerves were capable of such a sensation.

Douglas Stone in his prime was one of the most remarkable men in England. Indeed, he could hardly be said to have ever reached his prime, for he was but nine-and-thirty at the time of this little incident. Those who knew him best were aware that famous as he was as a surgeon, he might have succeeded with even greater rapidity in any of a dozen lines of life. He could have cut his way to fame as a soldier, struggled to it as an explorer, bullied for it in the courts, or built it out of stone and iron as an engineer. He was born to be great, for he could plan what another man dare not plan. In surgery none could follow him. His nerve, his judgment, his intuition, were things apart. Again and again his knife cut away death, but grazed the very springs of life in doing it, until his assistants were as white as the patient. His energy, his audacity, his full-blooded self-confidence—does not the memory of them still linger to the south of Marylebone Road and the north of Oxford Street?

His vices were as magnificent as his virtues, and infinitely more picturesque. Large as was his income, and it was the third largest of all professional men in London, it was far beneath the luxury of his living. Deep in his complex nature lay a rich vein of sensualism, at the sport of which he placed all the prizes of his life. The eye, the ear, the touch, the palate, all were his masters. The bouquet of old vintages, the scent of rare exotics, the curves and tints of the daintiest potteries of Europe, it was to these that the quick-running stream of gold was transformed. And then there came his sudden mad passion for Lady Sannox, when a single interview with two challenging glances and a whispered word set him ablaze. She was the loveliest woman in London and the only one to him. He was one of the handsomest men in London, but not the only one to her. She had a liking for new experiences, and was gracious to most men who wooed her. It may have been cause or it may have been effect that Lord Sannox looked fifty, though he was but six-and-thirty.

He was a quiet, silent, neutral-tinted man, this lord, with thin lips and heavy eye-lids, much given to gardening, and full of home-like habits. He had at one time been fond of acting, had even rented a theatre in London, and on its boards had first seen Miss Marion Dawson, to whom he had offered his hand, his title, and the third of a county. Since his marriage this early hobby had become distasteful to him. Even in private theatricals it was no longer possible to persuade him to exercise the talent which he had often showed that he possessed. He was happier with a spud and a water-ing can among his orchids and chrysanthemums.

It was quite an interesting problem whether he was absolutely devoid of sense, or miserably wanting in spirit. Did he know his lady's ways and condone them, or was he a mere blind, doting fool? It was a point to be discussed over the teacups in snug little drawing-rooms, or with the aid of a cigar in the bow windows of clubs. Bitter and plain were the comments among men upon his conduct. There was but one who had a good word to say for him, and he was the most silent member in the smoking-room. He had seen him break in a horse at the University, and it seemed to have left an impression upon his mind.

But when Douglas Stone became the favourite all doubts as to Lord Sannox's knowledge or ignorance were set for ever at rest. There was no subterfuge about Stone. In his high-handed, impetuous fashion, he set all caution and discretion at defi-ance. The scandal became notorious. A learned body intimated that his name had been struck from the list of its vice-presidents. Two friends implored him to consider his professional credit. He cursed them all three, and spent forty guineas on a bangle to take with him to the lady. He was at her house every evening, and she drove in his carriage in the afternoons. There was not an attempt on either side to conceal their relations; but there came at last a little incident to interrupt them.

It was a dismal winter's night, very cold and gusty, with the wind whooping in the chimneys and blustering against the window-panes. A thin spatter of rain tinkled on the glass with each fresh sough of the gale, drowning for the instant the dull gurgle and drip from the eaves. Douglas Stone had finished his dinner, and sat by his fire in the study, a glass of rich port upon the malachite table at his elbow. As he raised it to his lips, he held it up against the lamplight, and watched with the eye of a connoisseur the tiny scales of beeswing which floated in its rich ruby depths. The fire, as it spurted up, threw fitful lights upon his bold, clear-cut face, with its widely-opened grey eyes, its thick and yet firm lips, and the deep, square jaw, which had something Roman in its strength and its animalism. He smiled from time to time as he nestled back in his luxurious chair. Indeed, he had a right to feel well pleased, for, against the advice of six colleagues, he had performed an operation that day of which only two cases were on record, and the result had been brilliant beyond all expectation. No other man in London would have had the daring to plan, or the skill to execute, such a heroic measure.

But he had promised Lady Sannox to see her that evening and it was already half-past eight. His hand was outstretched to the bell to order the carriage when he heard the dull thud of the knocker. An instant later there was the shuffling of feet in the hall, and the sharp closing of a door.

"A patient to see you, sir, in the consulting room," said the butler.

"About himself?"

"No, sir; I think he wants you to go out."

"It is too late," cried Douglas Stone peevishly. "I won't go."

"This is his card, sir."

The butler presented it upon the gold salver which had been given to his master by the wife of a Prime Minister.

"'Hamil Ali, Smyrna.' Hum! The fellow is a Turk, I suppose."

"Yes, sir. He seems as if he came from abroad, sir. And he's in a terrible way."

"Tut, tut! I have an engagement. I must go somewhere else. But I'll see him. Show him in here, Pim."

A few moments later the butler swung open the door and ushered in a small and decrepit man, who walked with a bent back and with the forward push of the face and blink of the eyes which goes with extreme short sight. His face was swarthy, and his hair and beard of the deepest black. In one hand he held a turban of white muslin striped with red, in the other a small chamois leather bag.

"Good evening," said Douglas Stone, when the butler had closed the door. "You speak English, I presume?"

"Yes, sir. I am from Asia Minor, but I speak English when I speak slow."

"You wanted me to go out, I understand?"

"Yes, sir. I wanted very much that you should see my wife."

"I could come in the morning, but I have an engagement which prevents me from seeing your wife tonight."

The Turk's answer was a singular one. He pulled the string which closed the mouth of the chamois leather bag, and poured a flood of gold on to the table.

"There are one hundred pounds there," said he, "and I promise you that it will not take you an hour. I have a cab ready at the door."

Douglas Stone glanced at his watch. An hour would not make it too late to visit Lady Sannox. He had been there later. And the fee was an extraordinarily high one. He had been pressed by his creditors lately, and he could not afford to let such a chance pass. He would go.

"What is the case?" he asked.

"Oh, it is so sad a one! So sad a one! You have not, perhaps, heard of the daggers of the Almohades?"

"Never."

"Ah, they are Eastern daggers of a great age and of a singular shape, with the hilt like what you call a stirrup. I am a curiosity dealer, you understand, and that is why I have come to England from Smyrna, but next week I go back once more. Many things I brought with me, and I have a few things left, but among them, to my sorrow, is one of these daggers."

"You will remember that I have an appointment, sir," said the surgeon, with some irritation; "pray confine yourself to the necessary details."

"You will see that it is necessary. To-day my wife fell down in a faint in the room in which I keep my wares, and she cut her lower lip upon this cursed dagger of Almohades."

"I see," said Douglas Stone, rising. "And you wish me to dress the wound?"

"No, no, it is worse than that."

"What then?"

"These daggers are poisoned."

"Poisoned!"

"Yes, and there is no man, East or West, who can tell now what is the poison or what the cure. But all that is known I know, for my father was in this trade before me, and we have had much to do with these poisoned weapons."

"What are the symptoms?"

"Deep sleep, and death in thirty hours."

"And you say there is no cure. Why then should you pay me this considerable fee?"

"No drug can cure, but the knife may."

"And how?"

"The poison is slow of absorption. It remains for hours in the wound."

"Washing, then, might cleanse it?"

"No more than in a snake bite. It is too subtle and too deadly."

"Excision of the wound, then?"

"That is it. If it be on the finger, take the finger off. So said my father always. But think of where this wound is, and that it is my wife. It is dreadful!"

But familiarity with such grim matters may take the finer edge from a man's sympathy. To Douglas Stone this was already an interesting case, and he brushed aside as irrelevant the feeble objections of the husband.

"It appears to be that or nothing," said he brusquely. "It is better to lose a lip than a life."

"Ah, yes, I know that you are right. Well, well, it is kismet, and it must be faced. I have the cab, and you will come with me and do this thing."

Douglas Stone took his case of bistouries from a drawer, and placed it with a roll of bandage and a compress of lint in his pocket. He must waste no more time if he were to see Lady Sannox.

"I am ready," said he, pulling on his overcoat. "Will you take a glass of wine before you go out into this cold air?"

His visitor shrank away, with a protesting hand upraised.

"You forget that I am a Mussulman, and a true follower of the Prophet," said he. "But tell me what is the bottle of green glass which you have placed in your pocket?"

"It is chloroform."

"Ah, that also is forbidden to us. It is a spirit, and we make no use of such things."

"What! You would allow your wife to go through an operation without an anæsthetic?" "Ah! she will feel nothing, poor soul. The deep sleep has already come on, which is the first working of the poison. And then I have given her of our Smyrna opium. Come, sir, for already an hour has passed."

As they stepped out into the darkness, a sheet of rain was driven in upon their faces, and the hall lamp, which dangled from the arm of a marble Caryatid, went out with a fluff. Pim, the butler, pushed the heavy door to, straining hard with his shoulder against the wind, while the two men groped their way towards the yellow glare which showed where the cab was waiting. An instant later they were rattling upon their journey.

"Is it far?" asked Douglas Stone.

"Oh, no. We have a very little quiet place off the Euston Road."

The surgeon pressed the spring of his repeater and listened to the little tings which told him the hour. It was a quarter past nine. He calculated the distances, and the short time which it would take him to perform so trivial an operation. He ought to reach Lady Sannox by ten o'clock. Through the fogged windows he saw the blurred gas lamps dancing past, with occasionally the broader glare of a shop front. The rain was pelting and rattling upon the leathern top of the carriage, and the wheels swashed as they rolled through puddle and mud. Opposite to him the white headgear of his companion gleamed faintly through the obscurity. The surgeon felt in his pockets and arranged his needles, his ligatures and his safety-pins, that no time might be wasted when they arrived. He chafed with impatience and drummed his foot upon the floor.

But the cab slowed down at last and pulled up. In an instant Douglas Stone was out, and the Smyrna merchant's toe was at his very heel.

"You can wait," said he to the driver.

It was a mean-looking house in a narrow and sordid street. The surgeon, who knew his London well, cast a swift glance into the shadows, but there was nothing distinctive—no shop, no movement, nothing but a double line of dull, flat-faced houses, a double stretch of wet flagstones which gleamed in the lamplight, and a double rush of water in the gutters which swirled and gurgled towards the sewer gratings. The door which faced them was blotched and discoloured, and a faint light in the fan pane above, it served to show the dust and the grime which covered it. Above, in one of the bedroom windows, there was a dull yellow glimmer. The merchant knocked loudly, and, as he turned his dark face towards the light, Douglas Stone could see that it was contracted with anxiety. A bolt was drawn, and an elderly woman with a taper stood in the doorway, shielding the thin flame with her gnarled hand.

"Is all well?" gasped the merchant.

"She is as you left her, sir."

"She has not spoken?"

"No, she is in a deep sleep."

The merchant closed the door, and Douglas Stone walked down the narrow passage, glancing about him in some surprise as he did so. There was no oil-cloth, no mat, no hat-rack. Deep grey dust and heavy festoons of cobwebs met his eyes everywhere. Following the old woman up the winding stair, his firm footfall echoed harshly through the silent house. There was no carpet.

The bedroom was on the second landing. Douglas Stone followed the old nurse into it, with the merchant at his heels. Here, at least, there was furniture and to spare. The floor was littered and the corners piled with Turkish cabinets, inlaid tables, coats of chain mail, strange pipes, and grotesque weapons. A single small lamp stood upon a bracket on the wall. Douglas Stone took it down, and picking his way among the lumber, walked over to a couch in the corner, on which lay a woman dressed in the Turkish fashion, with yashmak and veil. The lower part of the face was exposed, and the surgeon saw a jagged cut which zigzagged along the border of the under lip.

"You will forgive the yashmak," said the Turk. "You know our views about women in the East."

But the surgeon was not thinking about the yashmak. This was no longer a woman to him. It was a case. He stooped and examined the wound carefully.

"There are no signs of irritation," said he. "We might delay the operation until local symptoms develop."

The husband wrung his hands in uncontrollable agitation.

"Oh! sir, sir," he cried. "Do not trifle. You do not know. It is deadly. I know, and I give you my assurance that an operation is absolutely necessary. Only the knife can save her."

"And yet I am inclined to wait," said Douglas Stone.

"That is enough," the Turk cried, angrily. "Every minute is of importance, and I cannot stand here and see my wife allowed to sink. It only remains for me to give you my thanks for having come, and to call in some other surgeon before it is too late."

Douglas Stone hesitated. To refund that hundred pounds was no pleasant matter. But of course if he left the case he must return the money. And if the Turk were right and the woman died, his position before a coroner might be an embarrassing one.

"You have had personal experience of this poison?" he asked.

"I have."

"And you assure me that an operation is needful."

"I swear it by all that I hold sacred."

"The disfigurement will be frightful."

"I can understand that the mouth will not be a pretty one to kiss."

Douglas Stone turned fiercely upon the man. The speech was a brutal one. But the Turk has his own fashion of talk and of thought, and there was no time for wrangling. Douglas Stone drew a bistoury from his case, opened it and felt the keen straight edge with his forefinger. Then he held the lamp closer to the bed. Two dark eyes were gazing up at him through the slit in the yashmak. They were all iris, and the pupil was hardly to be seen.

"You have given her a very heavy dose of opium."

"Yes, she has had a good dose."

He glanced again at the dark eyes which looked straight at his own. They were dull and lustreless, but, even as he gazed, a little shifting sparkle came into them, and the lips quivered. "She is not absolutely unconscious," said he.

"Would it not be well to use the knife while it will be painless?"

The same thought had crossed the surgeon's mind. He grasped the wounded lip with his forceps, and with two swift cuts he took out a broad V-shaped piece. The woman sprang up on the couch with a dreadful gurgling scream. Her covering was torn from her face. It was a face that he knew. In spite of that protruding upper lip and that slobber of blood, it was a face that he knew. She kept on putting her hand up to the gap and screaming. Douglas Stone sat down at the foot of the couch with his knife and his forceps. The room was whirling round, and he had felt something go like a ripping seam behind his ear. A bystander would have said that his face was the more ghastly of the two. As in a dream, or as if he had been looking at something at the play, he was conscious that the Turk's hair and beard lay upon the table, and that Lord Sannox was leaning against the wall with his hand to his side, laughing silently. The screams had died away now, and the dreadful head had dropped back again upon the pillow, but Douglas Stone still sat motionless, and Lord Sannox still chuckled quietly to himself.

"It was really very necessary for Marion, this operation," said he, "not physically, but morally, you know, morally."

Douglas Stone stooped for yards and began to play with the fringe of the coverlet. His knife tinkled down upon the ground, but he still held the forceps and something more.

"I had long intended to make a little example," said Lord Sannox, suavely. "Your note of Wednesday miscarried, and I have it here in my pocket-book. I took some pains in carrying out my idea. The wound, by the way, was from nothing more dangerous than my signet ring."

He glanced keenly at his silent companion, and cocked the small revolver which he held in his coat pocket. But Douglas Stone was still picking at the coverlet.

"You see you have kept your appointment after all," said Lord Sannox.

And at that Douglas Stone began to laugh. He laughed long and loudly. But Lord Sannox did not laugh now. Something like fear sharpened and hardened his features. He walked from the room, and he walked on tiptoe. The old woman was waiting outside.

"Attend to your mistress when she awakes," said Lord Sannox.

Then he went down to the street. The cab was at the door, and the driver raised his hand to his hat.

"John," said Lord Sannox, "you will take the doctor home first. He will want leading down-stairs, I think. Tell his butler that he has been taken ill at a case."

"Very good, sir."

"Then you can take Lady Sannox home."

"And how about yourself, sir?"

"Oh, my address for the next few months will be Hotel di Roma, Venice. Just see that the letters are sent on. And tell Stevens to exhibit all the purple chrysanthemums next Monday, and to wire me the result."

The Cigarette Case

Oliver Onions

"A cigarette, Loder?" I said, offering my case. For the moment Loder was not smoking; for long enough he had not been talking.

"Thanks," he replied, taking not only the cigarette, but the case also. The others went on talking; Loder became silent again; but I noticed that he kept my cigarette case in his hand, and looked at it from time to time with an interest that neither its design nor its costliness seemed to explain. Presently I caught his eye.

"A pretty case," he remarked, putting it down on the table. "I once had one exactly like it."

I answered that they were in every shop window.

"Oh yes," he said, putting aside any question of rarity. . . . "I lost mine."

"Oh? . . ."

He laughed. "Oh, that's all right—I got it back again—don't be afraid I'm going to claim yours. But the way I lost it—found it—the whole thing—was rather curious. I've never been able to explain it. I wonder if you could?"

I answered that I certainly couldn't till I'd heard it, whereupon Loder, taking up the silver case again and holding it in his hand as he talked, began:

"This happened in Provence, when I was about as old as Marsham there—and every bit as romantic. I was there with Carroll—you remember poor old Carroll and what a blade of a boy he was—as romantic as four Marshams rolled into one. (Excuse me, Marsham, won't you? It's a romantic tale, you see, or at least the setting is.) . . . We were in Provence, Carroll and I; twenty-four or thereabouts; romantic, as I say; and—and this happened.

"And it happened on the top of a whole lot of other things, you must understand, the things that do happen when you're twenty-four. If it hadn't been Provence, it would have been somewhere else, I suppose, nearly, if not quite as good; but this was Provence, that smells (as you might say) of twenty-four as it smells of argelasse and wild lavender and broom. . .

"We'd had the dickens of a walk of it, just with knapsacks—had started somewhere in the Ardèche and tramped south through the vines and almonds and olives—Montélimar, Orange, Avignon, and a fortnight at that blanched skeleton of a town,

Les Baux. We'd nothing to do, and had gone just where we liked, or rather just where Carroll had liked; and Carroll had had the *De Bello Gallico* in his pocket, and had had a notion, I fancy, of taking in the whole ground of the Roman conquest—I remember he lugged me off to some place or other, Pourrières I believe its name was, because— I forget how many thousands—were killed in a river-bed there, and they stove in the watercasks so that if the men wanted water they'd have to go forward and fight for it. And then we'd gone on to Arles, where Carroll had fallen in love with everything that had a bow of black velvet in her hair, and after that Tarascon, Nîmes, and so on, the usual round—I won't bother you with that. In a word, we'd had two months of it, eating almonds and apricots from the trees, watching the women at the communal washing-fountains under the dark plane-trees, singing *Magali* and the *Qué Cantes*, and Carroll yarning away all the time about Caesar and Vercingetorix and Dante, and trying to learn Provençal so that he could read the stuff in the *Journal des Félibriges* that he'd never have looked at if it had been in English. . . .

"Well, we got to Darbisson. We'd run across some young chap or other—Rangon his name was—who was a vine-planter in those parts, and Rangon had asked us to spend a couple of days with him, with him and his mother, if we happened to be in the neighbourhood. So as we might as well happen to be there as anywhere else, we sent him a postcard and went. This would be in June or early in July. All day we walked across a plain of vines, past hurdles of wattled *cannes* and great wind-screens of velvety cypresses, sixty feet high, all white with dust on the north side of 'em, for the mistral was having its three-days' revel, and it whistled and roared through the *cannes* till scores of yards of 'em at a time were bowed nearly to the earth. A roaring day it was, I remember. . . . But the wind fell a little late in the afternoon, and we were poring over what it had left of our Ordnance Survey—like fools, we'd got the unmounted paper maps instead of the linen ones—when Rangon himself found us, coming out to meet us in a very badly turned-out trap. He drove us back himself, through Darbisson, to the house, a mile and a half beyond it, where he lived with his mother.

"He spoke no English, Rangon didn't, though, of course, both French and Provençal; and as he drove us, there was Carroll, using him as a Franco-Provençal dictionary, peppering him with questions about the names of things in the patois— I beg its pardon, the language—though there's a good deal of my eye and Betty Martin about that, and I fancy this Félibrige business will be in a good many pieces when Frédéric Mistral is under that Court-of-Love pavilion arrangement he's had put up for himself in the graveyard at Maillanne. If the language has got to go, well, it's got to go, I suppose; and while I personally don't want to give it a kick, I rather sympathise with the Government. Those jaunts of a Sunday out to Les Baux, for instance, with paper lanterns and Bengal fire and a fellow spouting *O blanche Venus d'Arles*—they're well enough, and compare favourably with our Bank Holidays and Sunday League picnics, but . . . but that's nothing to do with my tale after all. . . . So he drove on, and by the time we got to Rangon's house Carroll had learned the greater part of *Magali*. . . .

"As you, no doubt, know, it's a restricted sort of life in some respects that a young *vigneron* lives in those parts, and it was as we reached the house that Rangon remembered something—or he might have been trying to tell us as we came along for all I know, and not been able to get a word in edgeways for Carroll and his Provençal. It seemed that his mother was away from home for some days—apologies of the most profound, of course; our host was the soul of courtesy, though he did try to get at us a bit later. . . . We expressed our polite regrets, naturally; but I didn't quite see at first what difference it made. I only began to see when Rangon, with more apologies, told us that we should have to go back to Darbisson for dinner. It appeared that when Madame Rangon went away for a few days she dispersed the whole of the female side of her establishment also, and she'd left her son with nobody to look after him except an old man we'd seen in the yard mending one of these double-cylindered sulphur-sprinklers they clap across the horse's back and drive between the rows of vines. . . . Rangon explained all this as we stood in the hall drinking an *apéritif*—a hall crowded with oak furniture and photographs and a cradle-like bread-crib and doors opening to right and left to the other rooms of the ground floor. He had also, it seemed, to ask us to be so infinitely obliging as to excuse him for one hour after dinner—our postcard had come unexpectedly, he said, and already he had made an appointment with his agent about the *vendange* for the coming autumn. . . . We begged him, of course, not to allow us to interfere with his business in the slightest degree. He thanked us a thousand times.

"'But though we dine in the village, we will take our own wine with us,' he said, 'a wine *surfin*—one of my wines—you shall see—'

"Then he showed us round his place—I forget how many hundreds of acres of vines, and into the great building with the presses and pumps and casks and the huge barrel they call the thunderbolt—and about seven o'clock we walked back to Darbisson to dinner, carrying our wine with us. I think the restaurant we dined in was the only one in the place, and our gaillard of a host—he was a straight-backed, well-set-up chap, with rather fine eyes—did us on the whole pretty well. His wine certainly was good stuff, and set our tongues going. . . .

"A moment ago I said a fellow like Rangon leads a restricted sort of life in those parts. I saw this more clearly as dinner went on. We dined by an open window, from which we could see the stream with the planks across it where the women washed clothes during the day and assembled in the evening for gossip. There were a dozen or so of them there as we dined, laughing and chatting in low tones—they all seemed pretty—it was quickly falling dusk—all the girls are pretty then, and are quite conscious of it—*you* know, Marsham. Behind them, at the end of the street, one of these great cypress wind-screens showed black against the sky, a ragged edge something like the line the needle draws on a rainfall chart; and you could only tell whether they were men or women under the plantains by their voices rippling and chattering and suddenly a deeper note. . . . Once I heard a muffled scuffle and a sound like a kiss. . . . It was then that Rangon's little trouble came out. . . .

"It seemed that he didn't know any girls—wasn't allowed to know any girls. The girls of the village were pretty enough, but you see how it was—he'd a position to keep up—appearances to maintain—couldn't be familiar during the year with the girls who gathered his grapes for him in the autumn. . . . And as soon as Carroll gave him a chance, *he* began to ask *us* questions, about England, English girls, the liberty they had, and so on.

"Of course, we couldn't tell him much he hadn't heard already, but that made no difference; he could stand any amount of that, our strapping young *vigneron*; and he asked us questions by the dozen, that we both tried to answer at once. And his delight and envy! . . . What! In England did the young men see the young women of their own class without restraint—the sisters of their friends *même*—*even* at the house? Was it permitted that they drank tea with them in the afternoon, or went without invitation to pass the *soirée*? . . . He had all the later Prévosts in his room, he told us (I don't doubt he had the earlier ones also); Prévost and the Disestablishment between them must be playing the mischief with the convent system of education for young girls; and our young man was—what d'you call it?—'Co-ed?'—co-educationalist—by Jove, yes! . . . He seemed to marvel that we should have left a country so blessed as England to visit his dusty, wild-lavender-smelling, girl-less Provence. . . . You don't know half your luck, Marsham. . . .

"Well, we talked after this fashion—we'd left the dining-room of the restaurant and had planted ourselves on a bench outside with Rangon between us—when Rangon suddenly looked at his watch and said it was time he was off to see this agent of his. Would we take a walk, he asked us, and meet him again there? he said. . . . But as his agent lived in the direction of his own home, we said we'd meet him at the house in an hour or so. Off he went, envying every Englishman who stepped, I don't doubt. . . . I told you how old—how young—we were. . . . Heigho! . . .

"Well, off goes Rangon, and Carroll and I got up, stretched ourselves, and took a walk. We walked a mile or so, until it began to get pretty dark, and then turned; and it was as we came into the blackness of one of these cypress hedges that the thing I'm telling you of happened. The hedge took a sharp turn at that point; as we came round the angle we saw a couple of women's figures hardly more than twenty yards ahead— don't know how they got there so suddenly, I'm sure; and that same moment I found my foot on something small and white and glimmering on the grass.

"I picked it up. It was a handkerchief—a woman's—embroidered—

"The two figures ahead of us were walking in our direction; there was every probability that the handkerchief belonged to one of them; so we stepped out. . . .

"At my 'Pardon, madame,' and lifted hat one of the figures turned her head; then, to my surprise, she spoke in English—cultivated English. I held out the handkerchief. It belonged to the elder lady of the two, the one who had spoken, a very gentle-voiced old lady, older by very many years than her companion. She took the handkerchief and thanked me. . . .

"Somebody—Sterne, isn't it?—says that Englishmen don't travel to see Englishmen. I don't know whether he'd stand to that in the case of Englishwomen; Carroll and I didn't. . . . We were walking rather slowly along, four abreast across the road; we asked permission to introduce ourselves, did so, and received some name in return which, strangely enough, I've entirely forgotten—I only remember that the ladies were aunt and niece, and lived at Darbisson. They shook their heads when I mentioned M. Rangon's name and said we were visiting him. They didn't know him. . . .

"I'd never been in Darbisson before, and I haven't been since, so I don't know the map of the village very well. But the place isn't very big, and the house at which we stopped in twenty minutes or so is probably there yet. It had a large double door—a double door in two senses, for it was a big *porte-cochère* with a smaller door inside it, and an iron grille shutting in the whole. The gentle-voiced old lady had already taken a key from her reticule and was thanking us again for the little service of the handkerchief; then, with the little gesture one makes when one has found oneself on the point of omitting a courtesy, she gave a little musical laugh.

"'But,' she said with a little movement of invitation, 'one sees so few compatriots here—if you have the time to come in and smoke a cigarette . . . also the cigarette,' she added, with another rippling laugh, 'for we have few callers, and live alone—'

"Hastily as I was about to accept, Carroll was before me, professing a nostalgia for the sound of the English tongue that made his recent protestations about Provençal a shameless hypocrisy. Persuasive young rascal, Carroll was—poor chap. . . . So the elder lady opened the grille and the wooden door beyond it, and we entered.

"By the light of the candle which the younger lady took from a bracket just within the door we saw that we were in a handsome hall or vestibule; and my wonder that Rangon had made no mention of what was apparently a considerable establishment was increased by the fact that its tenants must be known to be English and could be seen to be entirely charming. I couldn't understand it, and I'm afraid hypotheses rushed into my head that cast doubts on the Rangons—you know—whether they were all right. We knew nothing about our young planter, you see. . . .

"I looked about me. There were tubs here and there against the walls, gaily painted, with glossy-leaved aloes and palms in them—one of the aloes, I remember, was flowering; a little fountain in the middle made a tinkling noise; we put our caps on a carved and gilt console table; and before us rose a broad staircase with shallow steps of spotless stone and a beautiful wrought-iron handrail. At the top of the staircase were more palms and aloes, and double doors painted in a clear grey.

"We followed our hostesses up the staircase. I can hear yet the sharp clean click our boots made on that hard shiny stone—see the lights of the candle gleaming on the handrail. . . . The young girl—she was not much more than a girl—pushed at the doors, and we went in.

"The room we entered was all of a piece with the rest for rather old-fashioned fineness. It was large, lofty, beautifully kept. Carroll went round for Miss . . . whatever her name was . . . lighting candles in sconces; and as the flames crept up they glimmered on a beautifully polished floor, which was bare except for an Eastern rug here and there. The elder lady had sat down in a gilt chair, Louis Fourteenth I should say, with a striped rep of the colour of a petunia; and I really don't know—don't smile, Smith—what induced me to lead her to it by the finger-tips, bending over her hand for a moment as she sat down. There was an old tambour-frame behind her chair, I remember, and a vast oval mirror with clustered candle-brackets filled the greater part of the farther wall, the brightest and clearest glass I've ever seen. . . ."

He paused, looking at my cigarette case, which he had taken into his hand again. He smiled at some recollection or other, and it was a minute or so before he continued.

"I must admit that I found it a little annoying, after what we'd been talking about at dinner an hour before, that Rangon wasn't with us. I still couldn't understand how he could have neighbours so charming without knowing about them, but I didn't care to insist on this to the old lady, who for all I knew might have her own reasons for keeping to herself. And, after all, it was our place to return Rangon's hospitality in London if he ever came there, not, so to speak, on his own doorstep. . . . So presently I forgot all about Rangon, and I'm pretty sure that Carroll, who was talking to his companion of some Félibrige junketing or other and having the air of Gounod's *Mireille* hummed softly over to him, didn't waste a thought on him either. Soon Carroll—you remember what a pretty crooning, humming voice he had—soon Carroll was murmuring what they call 'seconds,' but so low that the sound hardly came across the room; and I came in with a soft bass note from time to time. No instrument, you know; just an unaccompanied murmur no louder than an Æolian harp; and it sounded infinitely sweet and plaintive and—what shall I say?—weak—attenuated—faint—'pale' you might almost say—in that formal, rather old-fashioned *salon*, with that great clear oval mirror throwing back the still flames of the candles in the sconces on the walls. Outside the wind had now fallen completely; all was very quiet; and suddenly in a voice not much louder than a sigh, Carroll's companion was singing *Oft in the Stilly Night*—you know it. . . ."

He broke off again to murmur the beginning of the air. Then, with a little laugh for which we saw no reason, he went on again:

"Well, I'm not going to try to convince you of such a special and delicate thing as the charm of that hour—it wasn't more than an hour—it would be all about an hour we stayed. Things like that just have to be said and left; you destroy them the moment you begin to insist on them; we've every one of us had experiences like that, and don't say much about them. I was as much in love with my old lady as Carroll evidently was with his young one—I can't tell you why—being in love has just to be taken for granted too, I suppose . . . Marsham understands. . . . We smoked our cigarettes, and sang again, once more filling that clear-painted, quiet apartment with a murmuring no louder than if a light breeze found that the bells of a bed of flowers were really bells and played on 'em. The old lady moved her fingers gently on the round table by the side of her chair . . . oh, infinitely pretty it was. . . . Then Carroll wandered off into the *Qué Cantes*—awfully pretty—'It is not for myself I sing, but for my friend who is near me'—and I can't tell you how like four old friends we were, those two so oddly met ladies and Carroll and myself. . . . And so to *Oft in the Stilly Night* again. . . .

"But for all the sweetness and the glamour of it, we couldn't stay on indefinitely, and I wondered what time it was, but didn't ask—anything to do with clocks and watches would have seemed a cold and mechanical sort of thing just then. . . . And when presently we both got up neither Carroll nor I asked to be allowed to call again in the morning to thank them for a charming hour. . . . And they seemed to feel the same as we did about it. There was no 'hoping that we should meet again in London'—neither an au revoir nor a good-bye—just a tacit understanding that that hour should remain isolated, accepted like a good gift without looking the gift-horse in the mouth, single, unattached to any hours before or after—I don't know whether you see what I mean. . . . Give me a match somebody. . . .

"And so we left, with no more than looks exchanged and finger-tips resting between the back of our hands and our lips for a moment. We found our way out by ourselves, down that shallow-stepped staircase with the handsome handrail, and let ourselves out of the double door and grille, closing it softly. We made for the village without speaking a word. . . . Heigho! . . ."

Loder had picked up the cigarette case again, but for all the way his eyes rested on it I doubt whether he really saw it. I'm pretty sure he didn't; I knew when he did by the glance he shot at me, as much as to say "I see you're wondering where the cigarette case comes in." . . . He resumed with another little laugh.

"Well," he continued, "we got back to Rangon's house. I really don't blame Rangon for the way he took it when we told him, you know—he thought we were pulling his leg, of course, and he wasn't having any; not he! There were no English ladies in Darbisson, he said. . . . We told him as nearly as we could just where the house was—we weren't very precise, I'm afraid, for the village had been in darkness as we had come through it, and I had to admit that the cypress hedge I tried to describe where we'd met our friends was a good deal like other cypress hedges—and, as I say, Rangon wasn't taking any. I myself was rather annoyed that he should think we were returning his hospitality by trying to get at him, and it wasn't very easy either to explain in my French and Carroll's Provençal that we were going to let the thing stand as it was and weren't going to call on our charming friends again. . . . The end of it was that Rangon just laughed and yawned. . . .

"'I knew it was good, my wine,' he said, 'but—' a shrug said the rest. 'Not so good as all that,' he meant. . . .

"Then he gave us our candles, showed us to our rooms, shook hands, and marched off to his own room and the Prévosts.

"I dreamed of my old lady half the night.

"After coffee the next morning I put my hand into my pocket for my cigarette case and didn't find it. I went through all my pockets, and then I asked Carroll if he'd got it.

"'No,' he replied. . . . 'Think you left it behind at that place last night!'

"'Yes; did you?' Rangon popped in with a twinkle.

"I went through all my pockets again. No cigarette case. . . .

"Of course, it was possible that I'd left it behind, and I was annoyed again. I didn't want to go back, you see. . . . But, on the other hand, I didn't want to lose the case—it was a present—and Rangon's smile nettled me a good deal, too. It was both a challenge to our truthfulness and a testimonial to that very good wine of his. . . .

"'Might have done,' I grunted. . . . 'Well, in that case we'll go and get it.'

"'If one tried the restaurant first—?' Rangon suggested, smiling again.

"'By all means,' said I stuffily, though I remembered having the case after we'd left the restaurant.

"We were round at the restaurant by half-past nine. The case wasn't there. I'd known jolly well beforehand it wasn't, and I saw Rangon's mouth twitching with amusement.

"'So we now seek the abode of these English ladies, *hein*?' he said.

"'Yes,' said I; and we left the restaurant and strode through the village by the way we'd taken the evening before. . . .

"That *vigneron's* smile became more and more irritating to me. . . . 'It is then the *next* village?' he said presently, as we left the last house and came out into the open plain.

"We went back. . . .

"I was irritated because we were two to one, you see, and Carroll backed me up. 'A double door, with a grille in front of it,' he repeated for the fiftieth time. . . . Rangon merely replied that it wasn't our good faith he doubted. He didn't actually use the word 'drunk.' . . .

"'*Mais tiens,*' he said suddenly, trying to conceal his mirth. '*Si c'est possible . . . si c'est possible . . .* a double door with a grille? But perhaps that I know it, the domicile of these so elusive ladies. . . . Come this way.'

"He took us back along a plantain-groved street, and suddenly turned up an alley that was little more than two gutters and a crack of sky overhead between two broken-tiled roofs. It was a dilapidated, deserted *ruelle*, and I was positively angry when Rangon pointed to a blistered old *porte-cochère* with a half-unhinged raïling in front of it.

"'Is it that, your house?' he asked.

"'No,' says I, and 'No,' says Carroll . . . and off we started again. . . .

"But another half-hour brought us back to the same place, and Carroll scratched his head.

"'Who lives there, anyway?' he said, glowering at the *porte-cochère*, chin forward, hands in pockets.

"'Nobody,' says Rangon, as much as to say 'look at it!' 'M'sieu then meditates taking it?' . . .

"Then I struck in, quite out of temper by this time.

"'How much would the rent be?' I asked, as if I really thought of taking the place just to get back at him.

"He mentioned something ridiculously small in the way of francs.

"'One might at least see the place,' says I. 'Can the key be got?'

"He bowed. The key was at the baker's, not a hundred yards away, he said. . . .

"We got the key. It was the key of the inner wooden door—that grid of rusty iron didn't need one—it came clean off its single hinge when Carroll touched it. Carroll opened, and we stood for a moment motioning to one another to step in. Then Rangon went in first, and I heard him murmur 'Pardon, Mesdames'. . . .

"Now this is the odd part. We passed into a sort of vestibule or hall, with a burst lead pipe in the middle of a dry tank in the centre of it. There was a broad staircase rising in front of us to the first floor, and double doors just seen in the half-light at the head of the stairs. Old tubs stood against the walls, but the palms and aloes in them were dead—only a cabbage-stalk or two—and the rusty hoops lay on the ground about them. One tub had come to pieces entirely and was no more than a heap of staves on a pile of spilt earth. And everywhere, everywhere was dust—the floor was an inch deep in dust and old plaster that muffled our footsteps, cobwebs hung like old dusters on the walls, a regular goblin's tatter of cobwebs draped the little bracket inside the door, and the wrought-iron of the hand-rail was closed up with webs in which not even a spider moved. The whole thing was preposterous. . . .

"'It is possible that for even a less rental—' Rangon murmured, dragging his fore-finger across the hand-rail and leaving an inch-deep furrow. . . .

"'Come upstairs,' said I suddenly. . . .

"Up we went. All was in the same state there. A clutter of stuff came down as I pushed at the double doors of the *salon*, and I had to strike a stinking French sulphur match to see into the room at all. Underfoot was like walking on thicknesses of flannel, and except where we put our feet the place was as printless as a snowfield—dust, dust, unbroken grey dust. My match burned down. . . .

"'Wait a minute—I've a *bougie*,' said Carroll, and struck the wax match. . . .

"There were the old sconces, with never a candle-end in them. There was the large oval mirror, but hardly reflecting Carroll's match for the dust on it. And the broken chairs were there, all giltless, and the rickety old round table. . . .

"But suddenly I darted forward. Something new and bright on the table twinkled with the light of Carroll's match. The match went out, and by the time Carroll had lighted another I had stopped. I wanted Rangon to see what was on the table. . . .

"'You'll see by my footprints how far from that table *I've* been,' I said. 'Will you pick it up?'

"And Rangon, stepping forward, picked up from the middle of the table—my cigarette case."

Loder had finished. Nobody spoke. For quite a minute nobody spoke, and then Loder himself broke the silence, turning to me.

"Make anything of it?" he said.

I lifted my eyebrows. "Only your *vigneron's* explanation—" I began, but stopped again, seeing that wouldn't do.

"*Any*body make anything of it?" said Loder, turning from one to another.

I gathered from Smith's face that he thought *one* thing might be made of it—namely, that Loder had invented the whole tale. But even Smith didn't speak.

"Were any English ladies ever found to have lived in the place—murdered, you know—bodies found and all that?" young Marsham asked diffidently, yearning for an obvious completeness.

"Not that we could ever learn," Loder replied. "We made inquiries too. . . . So you all give it up? Well, so do I. . . ."

And he rose. As he walked to the door, myself following him to get his hat and stick, I heard him humming softly the lines—they are from Oft in the Stilly Night—

> "I seem like one who treads alone
> Some banquet-hall deserted,
> Whose guests are fled, whose garlands dead,
> And all but he—departed!"

The Closed Window

A. C. Benson

The Tower of Nort stood in a deep angle of the downs; formerly an old road led over the hill, but it is now a green track covered with turf; the later highway choosing rather to cross a low saddle of the ridge, for the sake of the beasts of burden. The tower, originally built to guard the great road, was a plain, strong, thick-walled fortress. To the tower had been added a plain and seemly house, where the young Sir Mark de Nort lived very easily and plentifully. To the south stretched the great wood of Nort, but the Tower stood high on an elbow of the down, sheltered from the north by the great green hills. The villagers had an odd ugly name for the Tower, which they called the Tower of Fear; but the name was falling into disuse, and was only spoken, and that heedlessly, by ancient men, because Sir Mark was vexed to hear it so called. Sir Mark was not yet thirty, and had begun to say that he must marry a wife; but he seemed in no great haste to do so, and loved his easy, lonely life, with plenty of hunting and hawking on the down. With him lived his cousin and heir, Roland Ellice, a heedless good-tempered man, a few years older than Sir Mark; he had come on a visit to Sir Mark, when he first took possession of the Tower; and there had seemed no reason why he should go away; the two suited each other; Sir Mark was sparing of speech, fond of books and of rhymes. Roland was different, loving ease and wine and talk, and finding in Mark a good listener. Mark loved his cousin, and thought it praiseworthy of him to stay and help to cheer so sequestered a house, since there were few neighbours within reach.

And yet Mark was not wholly content with his easy life; there were many days when he asked himself why he should go thus quietly on, day by day, like a stalled ox; still, there appeared no reason why he should do otherwise; there were but few folk on his land, and they were content; yet he sometimes envied them their bondage and their round of daily duties. The only place where he could else have been was with the army, or even with the Court; but Sir Mark was no soldier, and even less of a courtier; he hated tedious gaiety, and it was a time of peace. So because he loved solitude and quiet he lived at home, and sometimes thought himself but half a man; yet was he happy after a sort, but for a kind of little hunger of the heart.

What gave the Tower so dark a name was the memory of old Sir James de Nort, Mark's grandfather, an evil and secret man, who had dwelt at Nort under some strange shadow; he had driven his son from his doors, and lived at the end of his life with his books and his own close thoughts, spying upon the stars and tracing strange figures in books; since his death the old room in the turret top, where he came by his end in a dreadful way, had been closed; it was entered by a turret-door, with a flight of steps from the chamber below. It had four windows, one to each of the winds; but the window which looked upon the down was fastened up, and secured with a great shutter of oak.

One day of heavy rain, Roland, being wearied of doing nothing, and vexed because Mark sat so still in a great chair, reading in a book, said to his cousin at last that he must go and visit the old room, in which he had never set foot. Mark closed his book, and smiling indulgently at Roland's restlessness, rose, stretching himself, and got the key; and together they went up the turret stairs. The key groaned loudly in the lock, and, when the door was thrown back, there appeared a high faded room, with a timbered roof, and with a close, dull smell. Round the walls were presses, with the doors fast; a large oak table, with a chair beside it, stood in the middle. The walls were otherwise bare and rough; the spiders had spun busily over the windows and in the angles. Roland was full of questions, and Mark told him all he had heard of old Sir James and his silent ways, but said that he knew nothing of the disgrace that had seemed to envelop him, or of the reasons why he had so evil a name. Roland said that he thought it a shame that so fair a room should lie so nastily, and pulled one of the casements open, when a sharp gust broke into the room, with so angry a burst of rain, that he closed it again in haste; little by little, as they talked, a shadow began to fall upon their spirits, till Roland declared that there was still a blight upon the place; and Mark told him of the death of old Sir James, who had been found after a day of silence, when he had not set foot outside his chamber, lying on the floor of the room, strangely bedabbled with wet and mud, as though he had come off a difficult journey, speechless, and with a look of anguish on his face; and that he had died soon after they had found him, muttering words that no one understood. Then the two young men drew near to the closed window; the shutters were tightly barred, and across the panels was scrawled in red, in an uncertain hand, the words CLAUDIT ET NEMO APERIT, which Mark explained was the Latin for the text, *He shutteth and none openeth*. And then Mark said that the story went that it was ill for the man that opened the window, and that shut it should remain, for him. But Roland girded at him for his want of curiosity, and had laid a hand upon the bar as though to open it, but Mark forbade him urgently. "Nay," said he, "let it remain so—we must not meddle with the will of the dead!" and as he said the word, there came so furious a gust upon the windows that it seemed as though some stormy thing would beat them open; so they left the room together, and presently descending, found the sun struggling through the rain.

But both Mark and Roland were sad and silent all that day; for though they spake not of it, there was a desire in their minds to open the closed window, and to see what would befall; in Roland's mind it was like the desire of a child to peep into what is forbidden; but in Mark's mind a sort of shame to be so bound by an old and weak tale of superstition.

Now it seemed to Mark, for many days, that the visit to the turret-room had brought a kind of shadow down between them. Roland was peevish and ill-at-ease; and ever the longing grew upon Mark, so strongly that it seemed to him that something drew him to the room, some beckoning of a hand or calling of a voice.

Now one bright and sunshiny morning it happened that Mark was left alone within the house. Roland had ridden out early, not saying where he was bound. And Mark sat, more listlessly than was his wont, and played with the ears of his great dog, that sat with his head upon his master's knee, looking at him with liquid eyes, and doubtless wondering why Mark went not abroad.

Suddenly Sir Mark's eye fell upon the key of the upper room, which lay on the window ledge where he had thrown it; and the desire to go up and pluck the heart from the little mystery came upon him with a strength that he could not resist; he rose twice and took up the key, and fingering it doubtfully, laid it down again; then suddenly he took it up, and went swiftly into the turret-stair, and up, turning, turning, till his head was dizzy with the bright peeps of the world through the loophole windows. Now all was green, where a window gave on the down; and now it was all clear air and sun, the warm breeze coming pleasantly into the cold stairway; presently Mark heard the pattering of feet on the stair below, and knew that the old hound had determined to follow him; and he waited a moment at the door, half pleased, in his strange mood, to have the company of a living thing. So when the dog was at his side, he stayed no longer, but opened the door and stepped within the room.

The room, for all its faded look, had a strange air about it, and though he could not say why, Mark felt that he was surely expected. He did not hesitate, but walked to the shutter and considered it for a moment; he heard a sound behind him. It was the old hound who sat with his head aloft, sniffing the air uneasily; Mark called him and held out his hand, but the hound would not move; he wagged his tail as though to acknowledge that he was called, and then he returned to his uneasy quest. Mark watched him for a moment, and saw that the old dog had made up his mind that all was not well in the room, for he lay down, gathering his legs under him, on the threshold, and watched his master with frightened eyes, quivering visibly. Mark, no lighter of heart, and in a kind of fearful haste, pulled the great staple off the shutter and set it on the ground, and then wrenched the shutters back; the space revealed was largely filled by old and dusty webs of spiders, which Mark lightly tore down, using the staple of the shutters to do this; it was with a strange shock of surprise that he saw that the window was dark, or nearly so; it seemed as though there were some further obstacle outside; yet Mark knew that from below the leaded panes of the window were visible. He drew back for a moment, but, unable to restrain his curiosity, wrenched the rusted casement open. But still all was dark without; and there came in a gust of icy wind from outside; it was as though something had passed him swiftly, and he heard the old hound utter a strangled howl; then turning, he saw him spring to his feet with his hair bristling and his teeth bare, and next moment the dog turned and leapt out of the room.

Mark, left alone, tried to curb a tide of horror that swept through his veins; he looked round at the room, flooded with the southerly sunlight, and then he turned again to the dark window, and putting a strong constraint upon himself, leaned out, and saw a thing which bewildered him so strangely that he thought for a moment his senses had deserted him. He looked out on a lonely dim hillside, covered with rocks and stones; the hill came up close to the window, so that he could have jumped down upon it, the wall below seeming to be built into the rocks. It was all dark and silent, like a clouded night, with a faint light coming from whence he could not see. The hill sloped away very steeply from the tower, and he seemed to see a plain beyond, where at the same time he knew that the down ought to lie. In the plain there was a light, like the firelit window of a house; a little below him some shape like a crouching man seemed to run and slip among the stones, as though suddenly surprised, and seeking to escape. Side by side with a deadly fear which began to invade his heart, came an uncontrollable desire to leap down among the rocks; and then it seemed to him that the figure below stood upright, and began to beckon him. There came over him a sense that he was in deadly peril; and, like a man on the edge of a precipice, who has just enough will left to try to escape, he drew himself by main force away from the window, closed it, put the shutters back, replaced the staple, and, his limbs all trembling, crept out of the room, feeling along the walls like a palsied man. He locked the door, and then, his terror overpowering him, he fled down the turret-stairs. Hardly thinking what he did, he came out on the court, and going to the great well that stood in the centre of the yard, he went to it and flung the key down, hearing it clink on the sides as it fell. Even then he dared not re-enter the house, but glanced up and down, gazing about him, while the cloud of fear and horror by insensible degrees dispersed, leaving him weak and melancholy.

Presently Roland returned, full of talk, but broke off to ask if Mark were ill. Mark, with a kind of surliness, an unusual mood for him, denied it somewhat sharply. Roland raised his eyebrows, and said no more, but prattled on. Presently after a silence he said to Mark, "What did you do all the morning?" and it seemed to Mark as though this were accompanied with a spying look. An unreasonable anger seized him. "What does it matter to you what I did?" he said. "May not I do what I like in my own house?"

"Doubtless," said Roland, and sate silent with uplifted brows; then he hummed a tune, and presently went out.

They sate at dinner that evening with long silences, contrary to their wont, though Mark bestirred himself to ask questions. When they were left alone, Mark stretched out his hand to Roland, saying, "Roland, forgive me! I spoke to you this morning in a way of which I am ashamed; we have lived so long together—and yet we came nearer to quarrelling to-day than we have ever done before; and it was my fault."

Roland smiled, and held Mark's hand for a moment. "Oh, I had not given it another thought," he said; "the wonder is that you can bear with an idle fellow as you do." Then they talked for awhile with the pleasant glow of friendliness that two good comrades feel when they have been reconciled. But late in the evening Roland said, "Was there any story, Mark, about your grandfather's leaving any treasure of money behind him?"

The question grated somewhat unpleasantly upon Mark's mood; but he controlled himself and said, "No, none that I know of—except that he found the estate rich and left it poor—and what he did with his revenues no one knows—you had better ask the old men of the village; they know more about the house than I do. But, Roland, forgive me once more if I say that I do not desire Sir James's name to be mentioned between us. I wish we had not entered his room; I do not know how to express it, but it seems to me as though he had sate there, waiting quietly to be summoned, and as though we had troubled him, and—as though he had joined us. I think he was an evil man, close and evil. And there hangs in my mind a verse of Scripture, where Samuel said to the witch, 'Why hast thou disquieted me to bring me up?' Oh," he went on, "I do not know why I talk wildly thus"; for he saw that Roland was looking at him with astonishment, with parted lips; "but a shadow has fallen upon me, and there seems evil abroad."

From that day forward a heaviness lay on the spirit of Mark that could not be scattered. He felt, he said to himself, as though he had meddled light-heartedly with something far deeper and more dangerous than he had supposed—like a child that has aroused some evil beast that slept. He had dark dreams too. The figure that he had seen among the rocks seemed to peep and beckon him, with a mocking smile, over perilous places, where he followed unwilling. But the heavier he grew the lighter-hearted Roland became; he seemed to walk in some bright vision of his own, intent upon a large and gracious design.

One day he came into the hall in the morning, looking so radiant that Mark asked him half enviously what he had to make him so glad. "Glad," said Roland, "oh, I know it! Merry dreams, perhaps. What do you think of a good grave fellow who beckons me on with a brisk smile, and shows me places, wonderful places, under banks and in woodland pits, where riches lie piled together? I am sure that some good fortune is preparing for me, Mark—but you shall share it." Then Mark, seeing in his words a certain likeness, with a difference, to his own dark visions, pressed his lips together and sate looking stonily before him.

At last, one still evening of spring, when the air was intolerably languid and heavy for mankind, but full of sweet promises for trees and hidden peeping things, though a lurid redness of secret thunder had lain all day among the heavy clouds in the plain, the two dined together. Mark had walked alone that day, and had lain upon the turf of the down, fighting against a weariness that seemed to be poisoning the very springs of life within him. But Roland had been brisk and alert, coming and going upon some secret and busy errand, with a fragment of a song upon his lips, like a man preparing to set off for a far country, who is glad to be gone. In the evening, after they had dined, Roland had let his fancy rove in talk. "If we were rich," he said, "how we would transform this old place!"

"It is fair enough for me," said Mark heavily; and Roland had chidden him lightly for his sombre ways, and sketched new plans of life.

Mark, wearied and yet excited, with an intolerable heaviness of spirit, went early to bed, leaving Roland in the hall. After a short and broken sleep, he awoke, and lighting a candle, read idly and gloomily to pass the heavy hours. The house seemed full of strange noises that night. Once or twice came a scraping and a faint hammering in the wall; light footsteps seemed to pass in the turret—but the tower was always full of noises, and Mark heeded them not; at last he fell asleep again, to be suddenly awakened by a strange and desolate crying, that came he knew not whence, but seemed to wail upon the air. The old dog, who slept in Mark's room, heard it too; he was sitting up in a fearful expectancy. Mark rose in haste, and taking the candle, went into the passage that led to Roland's room. It was empty, but a light burned there and showed that the room had not been slept in. Full of a horrible fear, Mark returned, and went in hot haste up the turret steps, fear and anxiety struggling together in his mind. When he reached the top, he found the little door broken forcibly open, and a light within. He cast a haggard look round the room, and then the crying came again, this time very faint and desolate.

Mark cast a shuddering glance at the window; it was wide open and showed a horrible liquid blackness; round the bar in the centre that divided the casements, there was something knotted. He hastened to the window, and saw that it was a rope, which hung heavily. Leaning out he saw that something dangled from the rope below him— and then came the crying again out of the darkness, like the crying of a lost spirit.

He could see as in a bitter dream the outline of the hateful hillside; but there seemed to his disordered fancy to be a tumult of some kind below; pale lights moved about, and he saw a group of forms which scattered like a shoal of fish when he leaned out. He knew that he was looking upon a scene that no mortal eye ought to behold, and it seemed to him at the moment as though he was staring straight into hell.

The rope went down among the rocks and disappeared; but Mark clenched it firmly and using all his strength, which was great, drew it up hand over hand; as he drew it up he secured it in loops round the great oak table; he began to be afraid that his strength would not hold out, and once when he returned to the window after securing a loop, a great hooded thing like a bird flew noiselessly at the window and beat its wings.

Presently he saw that the form which dangled on the rope was clear of the rocks below; it had come up through them, as though they were but smoke; and then his task seemed to him more sore than ever. Inch by painful inch he drew it up, working fiercely and silently; his muscles were tense, and drops stood on his brow, and the veins hammered in his ears; his breath came and went in sharp sobs. At last the form was near enough for him to seize it; he grasped it by the middle and drew Roland, for it was Roland, over the window-sill. His head dangled and drooped from side to side; his face was dark with strangled blood and his limbs hung helpless. Mark drew his knife and cut the rope that was tied under his arms; the helpless limbs sank huddling on the floor; then Mark looked up; at the window a few feet from him was a face, more horrible than he had supposed a human face, if it was human indeed, could be. It was deadly white, and hatred, baffled rage, and a sort of devilish malignity glared from the white set eyes, and the drawn mouth. There was a rush from behind him; the old hound, who had crept up unawares into the room, with a fierce outcry of rage sprang on to the window-sill; Mark heard the scraping of his claws upon the stone. Then the hound leapt through the window, and in a moment there was the sound of a heavy fall outside. At the same instant the darkness seemed to lift and draw up like a cloud; a bank of blackness rose past the window, and left the dark outline of the down, with a sky sown with tranquil stars.

The cloud of fear and horror that hung over Mark lifted too; he felt in some dim way that his adversary was vanquished; he carried Roland down the stairs and laid him on his bed; he roused the household, who looked fearfully at him, and then his own strength failed; he sank upon the floor of his room, and the dark tide of unconsciousness closed over him.

Mark's return to health was slow. One who has looked into the Unknown finds it hard to believe again in the outward shows of life. His first conscious speech was to ask for his hound; they told him that the body of the dog had been found, horribly mangled as though by the teeth of some fierce animal, at the foot of the tower. The dog was buried in the garden, with a slab above him, on which are the words:—

EUGE SERVE BONE ET FIDELIS

A silly priest once said to Mark that it was not meet to write Scripture over the grave of a beast. But Mark said warily that an inscription was for those who read it, to make them humble, and not to increase the pride of what lay below.

When Mark could leave his bed, his first care was to send for builders, and the old tower of Nort was taken down, stone by stone, to the ground, and a fair chapel built on the site; in the wall there was a secret stairway, which led from the top chamber, and came out among the elder-bushes that grew below the tower, and here was found a coffer of gold, which paid for the church; because, until it was found, it was Mark's design to leave the place desolate. Mark is wedded since, and has his children about his knee; those who come to the house see a strange and wan man, who sits at Mark's board, and whom he uses very tenderly; sometimes this man is merry, and tells a long tale of his being beckoned and led by a tall and handsome person, smiling, down a hillside to fetch gold; though he can never remember the end of the matter; but about the springtime he is silent or mutters to himself: and this is Roland; his spirit seems shut up within him in some close cell, and Mark prays for his release, but till God call him, he treats him like a dear brother, and with the reverence due to one who has looked out on the other side of Death, and who may not say what his eyes beheld.

THE COFFIN MERCHANT

RICHARD MIDDLETON

I

London on a November Sunday inspired Eustace Reynolds with a melancholy too insistent to be ignored and too causeless to be enjoyed. The grey sky overhead between the house-tops, the cold wind round every street-corner, the sad faces of the men and women on the pavements, combined to create an atmosphere of ineloquent misery. Eustace was sensitive to impressions, and in spite of a half-conscious effort to remain a dispassionate spectator of the world's melancholy, he felt the chill of the aimless day creeping over his spirit. Why was there no sun, no warmth, no laughter on the earth? What had become of all the children who keep laughter like a mask on the faces of disillusioned men? The wind blew down Southampton Street, and chilled Eustace to a shiver that passed away in a shudder of disgust at the sombre colour of life. A windy Sunday in London before the lamps are lit, tempts a man to believe in the nobility of work.

At the corner by Charing Cross Telegraph Office a man thrust a handbill under his eyes, but he shook his head impatiently. The blueness of the fingers that offered him the paper was alone sufficient to make him disinclined to remove his hands from his pockets even for an instant. But the man would not be dismissed so lightly.

"Excuse me, sir," he said, following him, "you have not looked to see what my bills are."

"Whatever they are I do not want them."

"That's where you are wrong, sir," the man said earnestly. "You will never find life interesting if you do not lie in wait for the unexpected. As a matter of fact, I believe that my bill contains exactly what you do want."

Eustace looked at the man with quick curiosity. His clothes were ragged, and the visible parts of his flesh were blue with cold, but his eyes were bright with intelligence and his speech was that of an educated man. It seemed to Eustace that he was being regarded with a keen expectancy, as though his decision on the trivial point was of real importance.

"I don't know what you are driving at," he said, "but if it will give you any pleasure I will take one of your bills; though if you argue with all your clients as you have with me, it must take you a long time to get rid of them."

"I only offer them to suitable persons," the man said, folding up one of the handbills while he spoke, "and I'm sure you will not regret taking it," and he slipped the paper into Eustace's hand and walked rapidly away.

Eustace looked after him curiously for a moment, and then opened the paper in his hand. When his eyes comprehended its significance, he gave a low whistle of astonishment. "You will soon be wanting a coffin!" it read. "At 606, Gray's Inn Road, your order will be attended to with civility and despatch. Call and see us!!"

Eustace swung round quickly to look for the man, but he was out of sight. The wind was growing colder, and the lamps were beginning to shine out in the greying streets. Eustace crumpled the paper into his overcoat pocket, and turned homewards.

"How silly!" he said to himself, in conscious amusement. The sound of his footsteps on the pavement rang like an echo to his laugh.

II

Eustace was impressionable but not temperamentally morbid, and he was troubled a little by the fact that the gruesomely bizarre handbill continued to recur to his mind. The thing was so manifestly absurd, he told himself with conviction, that it was not worth a second thought, but this did not prevent him from thinking of it again and again. What manner of undertaker could hope to obtain business by giving away foolish handbills in the street? Really, the whole thing had the air of a brainless practical joke, yet his intellectual fairness forced him to admit that as far as the man who had given him the bill was concerned, brainlessness was out of the question, and joking improbable. There had been depths in those little bright eyes which his glance had not been able to sound, and the man's manner in making him accept the handbill had given the whole transaction a kind of ludicrous significance.

"You will soon be wanting a coffin—!"

Eustace found himself turning the words over and over in his mind. If he had had any near relations he might have construed the thing as an elaborate threat, but he was practically alone in the world, and it seemed to him that he was not likely to want a coffin for any one but himself.

"Oh damn the thing!" he said impatiently, as he opened the door of his flat, "it isn't worth worrying about. I mustn't let the whim of some mad tradesman get on my nerves. I've got no one to bury, anyhow."

Nevertheless the thing lingered with him all the evening, and when his neighbour the doctor came in for a chat at ten o'clock, Eustace was glad to show him the strange handbill. The doctor, who had experienced the queer magics that are practised to this day on the West Coast of Africa, and who, therefore, had no nerves, was delighted with so striking an example of British commercial enterprise.

"Though, mind you," he added gravely, smoothing the crumpled paper on his knee, "this sort of thing might do a lot of harm if it fell into the hands of a nervous subject. I should be inclined to punch the head of the ass who perpetrated it. Have you turned that address up in the Post Office Directory?"

Eustace shook his head, and rose and fetched the fat red book which makes London an English city. Together they found the Gray's Inn Road, and ran their eyes down to No. 606.

"'Harding, G. J., Coffin Merchant and Undertaker.' Not much information there," muttered the doctor.

"Coffin merchant's a bit unusual, isn't it?" queried Eustace.

"I suppose he manufactures coffins wholesale for the trade. Still, I didn't know they called themselves that. Anyhow, it seems as though that handbill is a genuine piece of downright foolishness. The idiot ought to be stopped advertising in that way."

"I'll go and see him myself to-morrow," said Eustace bluntly.

"Well, he's given you an invitation," said the doctor, "so it's only polite of you to go. I'll drop in here in the evening to hear what he's like. I expect that you'll find him as mad as a hatter."

"Something like that," said Eustace, "or he wouldn't give handbills to people like me. I have no one to bury except myself."

"No," said the doctor in the hall, "I suppose you haven't. Don't let him measure you for a coffin, Reynolds!"

Eustace laughed.

"We never know," he said sententiously.

III

Next day was one of those gorgeous blue days of which November gives but few, and Eustace was glad to run out to Wimbledon for a game of golf, or rather for two. It was therefore dusk before he made his way to the Gray's Inn Road in search of the unexpected. His attitude towards his errand despite the doctor's laughter and the prosaic entry in the directory, was a little confused. He could not help reflecting that after all the doctor had not seen the man with the little wise eyes, nor could he forget that Mr. G. J. Harding's description of himself as a coffin merchant, to say the least of it, approached the unusual. Yet he felt that it would be intolerable to chop the whole business without finding out what it all meant. On the whole he would have preferred not to have discovered the riddle at all; but having found it, he could not rest without an answer.

No. 606, Gray's Inn Road, was not like an ordinary undertaker's shop. The window was heavily draped with black cloth, but was otherwise unadorned. There were no letters from grateful mourners, no little model coffins, no photographs of marble memorials. Even more surprising was the absence of any name over the shop-door, so that the uninformed stranger could not possibly tell what trade was carried on within, or who was responsible for the management of the business. This uncommercial modesty did not tend to remove Eustace's doubts as to the sanity of Mr. G. J. Harding; but he opened the shop-door which started a large bell swinging noisily, and stepped over the threshold. The shop was hardly more expressive inside than out. A broad counter ran across it, cutting it in two, and in the partial gloom overhead a naked gas-burner whistled a noisy song. Beyond this the shop contained no furniture whatever, and no stock-in-trade except a few planks leaning against the wall in one corner. There was a large ink-stand on the counter. Eustace waited patiently for a minute or two, and then as no one came he began stamping on the floor with his foot. This proved efficacious, for soon he heard the sound of footsteps ascending wooden stairs, the door behind the counter opened and a man came into the shop.

He was dressed quite neatly now, and his hands were no longer blue with cold, but Eustace knew at once that it was the man who had given him the handbill. Nevertheless he looked at Eustace without a sign of recognition.

"What can I do for you, sir?" he asked pleasantly.

Eustace laid the handbill down on the counter.

"I want to know about this," he said. "It strikes me as being in pretty bad taste, and if a nervous person got hold of it, it might be dangerous."

"You think so, sir? Yet our representative," he lingered affectionately on the words, "our representative told you, I believe, that the handbill was only distributed to suitable cases."

"That's where you are wrong," said Eustace, sharply, "for I have no one to bury."

"Except yourself," said the coffin merchant suavely.

Eustace looked at him keenly. "I don't see——" he began. But the coffin merchant interrupted him.

"You must know, sir," he said, "that this is no ordinary undertaker's business. We possess information that enables us to defy competition in our special class of trade."

"Information!"

"Well, if you prefer it, you may say intuitions. If our representative handed you that advertisement, it was because he knew you would need it."

"Excuse me," said Eustace, "you appear to be sane, but your words do not convey to me any reasonable significance. You gave me that foolish advertisement yourself, and now you say that you did so because you knew I would need it. I ask you why?"

The coffin merchant shrugged his shoulders. "Ours is a sentimental trade," he said, "I do not know why dead men want coffins, but they do. For my part I would wish to be cremated."

"Dead men?"

"Ah, I was coming to that. You see Mr.———?"

"Reynolds."

"Thank you, my name is Harding—G. J. Harding. You see, Mr. Reynolds, our intuitions are of a very special character, and if we say that you will need a coffin, it is—probable that you will need one."

"You mean to say that I—"

"Precisely. In twenty-four hours or less, Mr. Reynolds, you will need our services."

The revelation of the coffin merchant's insanity came to Eustace with a certain relief. For the first time in the interview he had a sense of the dark empty shop and the whistling gas-jet over his head.

"Why, it sounds like a threat, Mr. Harding!" he said gaily.

The coffin merchant looked at him oddly, and produced a printed form from his pocket. "If you would fill this up," he said.

Eustace picked it up off the counter and laughed aloud. It was an order for a hundred-guinea funeral.

"I don't know what your game is," he said, "but this has gone on long enough."

"Perhaps it has, Mr. Reynolds," said the coffin merchant, and he leant across the counter and looked Eustace straight in the face.

For a moment Eustace was amused; then he was suddenly afraid. "I think it's time I—" he began slowly, and then he was silent, his whole will intent on fighting the eyes of the coffin merchant. The song of the gas-jet waned to a point in his ears, and then rose steadily till it was like the beating of the world's heart. The eyes of the coffin merchant grew larger and larger, till they blended in one great circle of fire. Then Eustace picked a pen off the counter and filled in the form.

"Thank you very much, Mr. Reynolds," said the coffin merchant, shaking hands with him politely. "I can promise you every civility and despatch. Good-day, sir."

Outside on the pavement Eustace stood for a while trying to recall exactly what had happened. There was a slight scratch on his hand, and when he automatically touched it with his lips, it made them burn. The lit lamps in the Gray's Inn Road seemed to him a little unsteady, and the passers-by showed a disposition to blunder into him.

"Queer business," he said to himself dimly; "I'd better have a cab."

He reached home in a dream.

It was nearly ten o'clock before the doctor remembered his promise, and went upstairs to Eustace's flat. The outer door was half-open so that he thought he was expected, and he switched on the light in the little hall, and shut the door behind him with the simplicity of habit. But when he swung round from the door he gave a cry of astonishment. Eustace was lying asleep in a chair before him with his face flushed and drooping on his shoulder, and his breath hissing noisily through his parted lips. The doctor looked at him quizzically, "If I did not know you, my young friend," he remarked, "I should say that you were as drunk as a lord."

And he went up to Eustace and shook him by the shoulder; but Eustace did not wake.

"Queer!" the doctor muttered, sniffing at Eustace's lips; "he hasn't been drinking."

The Corpse Light

Dick Donovan

My name is John Patmore Lindsay. By profession I am a medical man, and a Fellow of the Royal College of Surgeons, and Member of the Royal College of Physicians, London. I am also the author of numerous medical works, the best known, perhaps, being "How to Keep in Good Health and Live Long." I was educated at one of the large public schools, and took my degree at Oxford. I have generally been regarded as "a hard-headed man," and sceptical about all phenomena that were not capable of being explained by rational and known laws. Mysticism, occultism, spiritualism, and the like only served to excite my ridicule; and I entertained anything but a flattering opinion of those people who professed belief in such things. I was pleased to think it argued a weakness of mind.

I have referred to the few foregoing facts about myself because I wish to make it clear that I do not belong to that class of nervous and excitable people who fall a prey to their own fancies; conjure up shapes and scenes out of their imaginings, and then vow and declare that they have been confronted with stern realities. What I am about to relate is so marvellous, so weird and startling, that I am fain to begin my story in a half apologetic way; and even now, as I dwell upon it all, I wonder why I of all men should have been subjected to the unnatural and unearthly influence. But so it is, and though in a sense I am only half convinced, I no longer scoff when somebody reminds me that there is more in heaven and earth than is dreamt of in our philosophy.

But to my story, and when it is told the reader can judge for himself how powerful must have been the effect of what I witnessed, when it could induce a man of my mental fibre to commit to paper so astounding a narrative as the one I now pen. It is about twenty years ago that I took up a practice in the old-fashioned and picturesque little town of Brinton-on-sea. At that time there was no railway into Brinton, the nearest station being some seven or eight miles away. The result was, the town still retained a delightful old-time air, while the people were as primitive and old-fashioned as their town. Nevertheless, Brinton was far ahead of its neighbours, and, though in a purely agricultural district, was enterprising and business-like, while its weekly Tuesday market brought an enormous influx of the population of the district for miles around, and very large sums of money changed hands. Being the chief town of the parish, and boasting of a very curious and ancient church, and a still more ancient market cross, to say nothing of several delightful old hostelries, and a small though excellent museum of local curiosities, consisting principally of Roman remains and fossils, for which the district was renowned, it attracted not only the antiquary and the gourmand, but artists, tourists, and lovers of the picturesque, as well as those in search of quietude and repose. The nearest village was High Lea, about three miles away. Between the two places was a wide sweep of magnificent rolling down, delightful at all times, but especially so in the summer. Many an ancient farmhouse was dotted about, with here and there a windmill. The down on the seaside terminated in a high headland, from which a splendid lighthouse sent forth its warning beams over the fierce North Sea. Second only in conspicuousness to this lighthouse was an old and half ruined windmill, known all over the country side as "The Haunted Mill."

When I first went to live in Brinton this mill early attracted my attention, for it was one of the most picturesque old places of its kind I had ever seen; and as I had some artistic instincts, and could sketch with, as my too flattering friends said, "no mean ability," the haunted mill appealed to me. It stood on rising ground, close to the high-road that ran between Brinton and High Lea. I gathered that there had been some dispute about the ownership, and, as is usually the case, the suckers of the harpies of the law had fastened upon it, so to speak, and drained all its vitality, away after the manner of lawyers generally. The old-fashioned, legal luminaries of the country were a slow-going set, and for over a quarter of a century that disputed claim had remained unsettled; and during that long period the old mill had been gradually falling into ruin. The foundations had from some cause sunk, throwing the main building out of the perpendicular. Part of the roof had fallen in, and the fierce gales of a quarter of a century had battered the sails pretty well to match-wood. A long flight of wooden steps led up to the principal door, but these steps had rotted away in places, and the door itself had partly fallen inwards. Needless to say, this mill had become the home of bats and owls, and, according to the yokels, of something more fearsome than either. It was a forlorn and mournful-looking place, any way, even in the full blaze of sunshine; but seen in moonlight its appearance was singularly weird, and well calculated to beget in the rustic mind a feeling of horror, and to produce a creepy and uncanny sensation in anyone susceptible to the influence of *outre* appearances. To me it did not appeal in any of these aspects. I saw in it only subject matter for an exceedingly effective picture, and yet I am bound to confess that even when transferred to board or canvas there was a certain grim suggestiveness of things uncanny, and I easily understood how the superstitious and unreasoning rustic mind was awed into a belief that this mouldering old mill was haunted by something more creepy and harrowing than bats and owls. Any way, I heard wonderful tales, at which I laughed, and when I learned that the country people generally gave the mill a wide berth at night, I blamed them for their stupidity.

But it was a fact that worthy, and in other respects intelligent, farmers and market folk coming or going between Brinton and High Lea after dark preferred the much longer and dangerous route by the sea cliffs, even in the wildest weather.

I have dwelt thus long on the "Haunted Mill" because it bulks largely in my story, as will presently be seen, and I came in time to regard it with scarcely less awe than the rustics did.

It was during the second year of my residence in Brinton that a young man named Charles Royce came home after having been absent at sea for three years. Royce's people occupied Gorse Hill Farm, about two miles to the south of Brinton. Young Charley, a fine, handsome, but rather wild youngster, had, it appears, fallen desperately in love with Hannah Trowzell, who was a domestic in the employ of the Rector of the parish. But Charley's people did not approve of his choice, and, thinking to cure him, packed him off to sea, and after an absence of three years and a month the young fellow, bronzed, hearty, more rollicking and handsome than ever, returned to his native village. I had known nothing of Charles Royce or his history up to the day of his return; but it chanced on that very day I had to pay a professional visit to the Rectory, and the Rector pressed me to lunch with him. Greatly interested in all his parishioners, and knowing something of the private history of most of the families in his district, the rev. gentleman very naturally fell to talking about young Royce, and he told me the story, adding, "Hannah is a good girl, and I think it's rather a pity Charley's people objected to his courting her. I believe she would have made him a capital wife."

"Has she given him up entirely?" I asked.

"Oh, yes, and is engaged to Silas Hartrop, whose father owns the fishing smack the *North Sea Beauty*. I've never had a very high opinion of Silas. I'm afraid he is a little too fond of skittles and beer. However, Hannah seems determined to have him in spite of anything I can say, so she must take her course. But I hope she will be able to reform him, and that the marriage will be a happy one. I really shouldn't be a bit surprised, however, if the girl took up with her old lover again, for I have reason to know she was much attached to him, and I fancy Charley, if he were so minded, could easily influence her to throw Silas overboard."

This little story of love and disappointment naturally interested me, for in a country town the affairs of one's neighbours are matter of greater moment than is the case in a big city.

So it came to pass that a few weeks after Charley's return it was pretty generally known that, even as the Rector had suggested it might be, young Royce and pretty Hannah Trowzell were spooning again, and Silas had virtually been told to go about his business. It was further known that Silas had taken his dismissal so much to heart that he had been seeking consolation in the beer-pot. Of course, folk talked a good deal, and most of them sympathised with Silas, and blamed Hannah. Very soon it began to be bruited about that Royce's people no longer opposed any objections to the wooing, and that in consequence Hannah and Charley were to become husband and wife at Christmas, that was in about seven weeks' time. A month of the time had passed, and the "askings" were up in the parish church, when one day there went forth a rumour that Charles Royce was missing. Rumour took a more definite shape a few hours later when it was positively stated that two nights previously Charles had left his father's house in high spirits and the best of health to visit Hannah, and walk with her, as she was going into the town to make some purchases. On his way he called at the *Two Waggoners*, a wayside inn, where he had a pint of beer and purchased an ounce of tobacco. From the time he left the inn, all trace of him was lost, and he was seen no more. Hannah waited his coming until long past the appointed hour, and when he failed to put in an appearance, she became angry and went off to the town by herself. Next day her anger gave place to anxiety when she learnt that he had left his home to visit her, and had not since returned; and anxiety became alarm when two and three days slipped by without bringing any tidings of the truant. On the night that he left his home, the weather was very tempestuous, and it had been wild and stormy since. It was therefore suggested that on leaving the *Two Waggoners* he might have got confused when he reached the common, which he had to cross to get to the Rectory; and as there were several pools and treacherous hollows on the common, it was thought he had come to grief, but the most diligent search failed to justify the surmise.

Such an event as this was well calculated to cause a sensation, not only in Brinton and its neighbourhood, but throughout the county. Indeed, for many days it was a common topic of conversation, and at the Brinton weekly market the farmers and the rustics dwelt upon it to the exclusion of other things; and, of course, everybody, or nearly everybody, had some wonderful theory of his or her own to account for the missing man's disappearance. One old lady, who every week for twenty years had trudged in from a village five miles off with poultry and eggs for the Brinton market, declared her belief that young Royce had been spirited away, and she recommended an appeal to a wondrous wise woman, locally known as "Cracked Moll," but whose reputation for solving mysteries and discovering lost persons and things was very great. Ultimately Royce's people did call in the services of this ancient fraud, but without any result. And despite of wide publicity and every effort on the part of the rural and county police, to say nothing of a hundred and one amateur detectives, the mystery remained unsolved. Charles Royce had apparently disappeared from off the face of the earth, leaving not a trace behind.

In the process of time the nine days' wonder gave place to something else, and excepting by those directly interested in him, Charles Royce was forgotten. Hannah took the matter very seriously to heart, and for a while lay dangerously ill. Silas Hartrop, who was much affected by his disappointment with regard to Hannah, went to the dogs, as the saying is, and drank so heavily that it ended in an attack of delirium tremens. I was called in to attend him, and had hard work to pull him through. On his recovery his father sent him to an uncle at Yarmouth, who was in the fishing trade, and soon afterwards news came that young Hartrop had been drowned at sea. He was out in the North Sea in his uncle's fishing smack, and, though nobody saw him go, it was supposed that he fell overboard in the night. This set the local tongues wagging again for a time, but even the affairs of Brinton could not stand still because the ne'er-do-weel Silas Hartrop was drowned. So sympathy was expressed with his people, and then the affair was dismissed.

About two years later I received an urgent message late one afternoon to hasten with all speed to High Lea, to attend to the Squire there, who had been taken suddenly and, as report said, seriously ill. I had had rather a heavy day of it, as there had been a good deal of sickness about for some time past, and it had taken me several hours to get through my list of patients. I had just refreshed myself with a cup of tea and was about to enjoy a cigar when the messenger came. Telling him to ride back as quickly as possible and say that I was coming, I busied myself with a few important matters which had to be attended to, as I might be absent for some hours, and then I ordered my favourite mare, Princess, to be saddled.

I set off from Brinton soon after seven. It was a November night, bitterly cold, dark as Erebus, while every now and then violent squalls swept the land from seaward. Princess knew the road well, so I gave the mare her head, and she went splendidly until we reached the ruined mill, when suddenly she wheeled round with such abruptness that, though I was a good horseman, I was nearly pitched from the saddle. At the same moment I was struck in the face by something that seemed cold and clammy. I thought at first it was a bat, but remembered that bats do not fly in November; an owl, but an owl would not have felt cold and clammy. However, I had little time for thought, as my attention had to be given to the mare. She seemed disposed to bolt, and was trembling with fear. Then, to my intense astonishment, I noticed what seemed to be a large luminous body lying on the roadway. It had the appearance of a corpse illuminated in some wonderful and mysterious manner. Had it not been for the fright of my mare I should have thought I was the victim of some optical delusion; but Princess evidently saw the weird object, and refused to pass it. So impressed was I with the idea that a real and substantial body was lying on the road, notwithstanding the strange unearthly light, that I slipped from the saddle, intending to investigate the matter, when suddenly it disappeared, and the cold and clammy something again struck me in the face.

I confess that for the first time in my life I felt a strange, nervous, unaccountable fear. I say "unaccountable," because it would have been difficult for me to have given any explanation of my fear. Why and of what was I afraid? Now, whatever the phenomenon was, there was the hard, stern fact to face that my horse had seen what I had seen, and was terrified. There was something strangely uncanny about the whole business, and when a terrific squall, bringing with it sleet and rain, came howling from the sea, it seemed to emphasise the uncanniness, and the ruined mill, looming gaunt and grim in the darkness, caused me to shake with an involuntary shudder. The next moment I was trying to laugh myself out of my nervousness. "Princess and I," I mentally argued, "have been the victims of some atmospheric delusion." That was all very well, but the something cold and clammy that struck me in the face, and which may have struck the mare in the face also, was no atmospheric delusion. With an alacrity I did not often display, I sprang into the saddle, spoke some encouraging words to the mare, for she was still trembling, and when she bounded forward, and the haunted mill was behind me, I experienced a positive sense of relief.

I found my patient at High Lea in a very bad way. He was suffering from an attack of apoplexy, and though I used all my skill on his behalf he passed away towards midnight. His wife very kindly offered me a bed for the night, but as I had important matters to attend to early in the morning I declined the hospitality, though I was thankful for a glass or two of generous port wine and some sandwiches. It was half-past twelve when I left the house on my return journey. The incident by the haunted mill had been put out of my head by the case I had been called upon to attend, but as I mounted my mare the groom, who had brought her round from the stable, said, "It be a bad night, doctor, for riding; the kind o' night when dead things come out o' their graves."

I laughed, and replied:

"Tom, lad, I am surprised to hear you talk such rubbish. I thought you had more sense than that."

"Well, I tell 'ee what, doctor; if I had to ride to Brinton to-night I'd go by the cliffs and chance being drowned, rather than pass yon old mill."

These words for the moment unnerved me, and I honestly confess that I resolved to go by the cliffs, dangerous as the road was in the dark. Nevertheless, I laughed at Tom's fears, and ridiculed him, though when I left the squire's grounds I turned the mare's head towards the cliffs. In a few minutes I was ridiculing myself.

"John Patmore Lindsay," I mentally exclaimed, "you are a fool. All your life you have been ridiculing stories of the supernatural, and now, at your time of life, are you going to allow yourself to be frightened by a bogey? Shame on you."

I bucked up, grew bold, and thereupon altered my course, and got into the high road again.

There had been a slight improvement in the weather. It had ceased to rain, but the wind had settled down into a steady gale, and screeched and screamed over the moorland with a demoniacal fury. The darkness, however, was not so intense as it was, and a star here and there was visible through the torn clouds. But it was an eerie sort of night, and I was strangely impressed with a sense of my loneliness. It was absolutely unusual for me to feel like this, and I suggested to myself that my nerves were a little unstrung by overwork and the anxiety the squire's illness had caused me. And so I rode on, bowing my head to the storm, while the mare stepped out well, and I anticipated that in little more than half an hour I should be snug in bed. As we got abreast of the haunted mill the mare once more gibbed, and all but threw me, and again I was struck in the face by the cold clammy something.

I have generally prided myself on being a bold man, but my boldness had evaporated now, and I almost think my hair rose on end as I observed that the illuminated corpse was lying in the roadway again; but now it appeared to be surrounded by a lake of blood. It was the most horrible, weird, marrow-curdling sight that ever human eyes looked upon. I tried to urge Princess forward, but she was stricken with terror, and, wheeling right round, was setting off towards High Lea again. But once more I was struck in the face by the invisible *something*, and its coldness and clamminess made me shudder, while there in front of us lay the corpse in the pool of blood. The mare reared and plunged, but I got her head round, determining to make a wild gallop for Brinton and leave the horrors of the haunted mill behind. But the corpse was again in front of us, and I shrank back almost appalled as the *something* once more touched my face.

I cannot hope to describe what my feelings were at this supreme moment. I don't believe anything human could have daunted me; but I was confronted by a supernatural mystery that not only terrified me but the mare I was riding. Whichever way I turned, that awful, ghastly object confronted me, and the blow in the face was repeated again and again.

How long I endured the unutterable horrors of the situation I really don't know. Possibly the time was measured by brief minutes. It seemed to me hours. At last my presence of mind returned. I dismounted, and reasoned with myself that, whatever the apparition was, it had some import. I soothed the mare by patting her neck and talking to her, and I determined then to try and find a solution of the mystery. But now a more wonderful thing happened. The corpse, which was still made visible by the unearthly light, rose straight up, and as it did so the blood seemed to flow away from it in great, gurgling streams, for I solemnly declare that I distinctly heard gurgling sounds. The figure glided past me, and a sense of extraordinary coldness made me shiver. Slowly and gracefully the shining corpse glided up the rotting steps of the old mill, and disappeared through the doorway. No sooner had it gone than the mill itself seemed to glow with phosphorescent light, and to become transparent, and I beheld a sight that took my breath away. I am disposed to think that for some moments my brain became so numbed that insensibility ensued, for I am conscious of a blank. When the power of thought returned, I was still holding the bridle of the mare, and she was cropping the grass at her feet. The mill loomed blackly against the night sky. It had resumed its normal appearance again. The wind shrieked about it. The ragged scud raced through the heavens, and the air was filled with the sounds of the raging wind. At first I was inclined to doubt the evidence of my own senses. I tried to reason myself into a belief that my imagination had played me a trick; but I didn't succeed, although the mystery was too profound for my fathoming. So I mounted the mare, urged her to her fastest pace, galloped into Brinton, and entered my house with a feeling of intense relief.

Thoroughly exhausted by the prolonged physical and mental strain I had endured, I speedily sank into a deep though troubled slumber as soon as I got into bed. I was unusually late in rising the next day. I found that I had no appetite for breakfast. Indeed, I felt ill and out of sorts; and, though I busied myself with my professional duties, I was haunted by the strange incidents of the preceding night. Never before in the whole course of my career had I been so impressed, so unnerved, and so dispirited. I wanted to believe that I was still as sceptical as ever, but it was no use. What I had seen might have been unearthly; but I *had seen it*, and it was no use trying to argue myself out of that fact. The result was, in the course of the afternoon I called on my old friend, Mr. Goodyear, who was chief of the county constabulary. He was a strong-minded man, and, like myself, a hardened sceptic about all things that smacked of the supernatural.

"Goodyear," I said, "I'm out of sorts, and I want you to humour a strange fancy I have. Bring one of your best men, and come with me to the haunted mill. But first let me exact from you a pledge of honour that, if our journey should result in nothing, you will keep the matter secret, as I am very sensitive to ridicule."

He looked at me in amazement, and then, as he burst into a hearty laugh, exclaimed:

"I say, my friend, you are over-working yourself. It's time you got a *locum tenens*, and took a holiday."

I told him that I agreed with him; nevertheless, I begged him to humour me, and accompany me to the mill. At last he reluctantly consented to do so, and an hour later we drove out of the town in my dog-cart. There were four of us, as I took Peter, my groom, with me. We had provided ourselves with lanterns, but Goodyear's man and Peter knew nothing of the object of our journey.

When we got abreast of the mill I drew up, and giving the reins to Peter, I alighted, and Goodyear did the same. Taking him on one side, I said, "I have had a vision, and unless I am the victim of incipient madness we shall find a dead body in the mill."

The light of the dog-cart was shining full on his face, and I saw the expression of alarm that my words brought.

"Look here, old chap," he said in a cheery, kindly way, as he put his arm through mine, "you are not going into that mill, but straight home again. Come, now, get into the cart, and don't let's have any more of this nonsense."

I felt disposed to yield to him, and had actually placed my foot on the step to mount, when I staggered back and exclaimed—

"My God! am I going mad, or is this a reality?"

Once again I had been struck in the face by the cold clammy *something*; and I saw Goodyear suddenly clap his hand to his face as he cried out—"Hullo, what the deuce is that?"

"Aha," I exclaimed exultantly, for I no longer thought my brain was giving way, "you have felt it too?"

"Well, something cold and nasty-like struck me in the face. A bat, I expect. Confound 'em."

"Bats don't fly at this time of the year," I replied.

"By Jove, no more they do."

I approached him, and said in a low tone—

"Goodyear, this is a mystery beyond our solving. I am resolved to go into that mill."

He was a brave man, though for a moment or two he hesitated; but on my insisting he consented to humour me, and so we lit the lantern, and leaving the groom in charge of the horse and trap, I, Goodyear, and his man made our way with difficulty up the rotting steps, which were slimy and sodden with wet. As we entered the mill an extraordinary scene of desolation and ruin met our gaze as we flashed the light of the lantern about. In places the floor had broken away, leaving yawning chasms of blackness. From the mouldering rafters huge festoons of cobwebs hung. The accumulated dust and dampness of years had given them the appearance of cords. And oh, how the wind moaned eerily through the rifts and crannies and broken windows! If ever there was a place on this earth where evil spirits might dwell it was surely that ghoul-haunted old mill. The startling aspect of the place impressed us all, perhaps me more than the other two. We advanced gingerly, for the floor was so rotten we were afraid it would crumble beneath our feet.

My companions were a little bewildered, I think, and were evidently at a loss to know what we had come there for. But some strange feeling impelled me to seek for something;

though if I had been asked to define that something, for the life of me I could not have done it. Forward I went, however, taking the lead, and holding the lantern above my head so that its rays might fall afar. But they revealed nothing save the rotting floor and slimy walls. A ladder led to the upper storey, and I expressed my intention of mounting it. Goodyear tried to dissuade me, but I was resolute, and led the way. The ladder was so creaky and fragile that it was not safe for more than one to be on it at a time. When I reached the second floor and drew myself up through the trap, I am absolutely certain I heard a sigh. You may say it was the wind. I swear it was not. The wind was moaning drearily enough, but the sigh was a distinctive note, and unmistakable. As I turned the lantern round so that its light might sweep every hole and corner of the place, I noticed what seemed to be a sack full of something lying in a corner. I approached and touched it with my foot, and drew back in alarm, for touch and sound told me it contained neither corn nor chaff. I waited until my companions had joined me. Then I said to Goodyear, "Unless I am mistaken there is something dreadful in that sack."

He stooped and placed his hand on the sack, and I saw him start back. In another moment he recovered himself, and whipping out his knife cut the string which fastened up the mouth of the sack, and revealed a human skull with the hair and shrivelled mummified flesh still adhering to it.

"Great heavens!" he exclaimed, "here is a human body."

We held a hurried conversation, and decided to leave the ghastly thing undisturbed until the morrow. So we scuttled down as fast as we could, and went home. I did not return to the mill again myself. My part had been played. Investigation made it absolutely certain that the mouldering remains were those of poor Charley Royce, and it was no less absolutely certain that he had been foully murdered. For not only was there a bullet-hole in the skull, and a bullet inside, but his throat had been cut. It was murder horrible and damnable. The verdict of the coroner's jury pronounced it murder, but there was no evidence to prove who had done the deed. Circumstances, however, pointed to Charley's rival, Silas Hartrop. Was it a guilty conscience that drove him to drink? And did the Furies who avenge such deeds impel him on that dark and stormy night in the North Sea to end the torture of his accursed earthly life? Who can tell? The sea holds its secrets, and not a scrap of legal evidence could be obtained. But though the law declined the responsibility of fixing the guilt of the dark deed on Silas, there was a consensus of opinion that he was the guilty party. It was a mystery, but the greatest mystery of all was that I, the sceptic, should have been selected by some supernatural power to be the instrument for bringing the foul crime to light. For myself, I attempt no explanation. I have told a true story. Let those who can explain it. I admit now that "there are more things in heaven and earth than are dreamt of in our philosophy."

The Dead Valley

Ralph Adams Cram

I have a friend, Olof Ehrensvärd, a Swede by birth, who yet, by reason of a strange and melancholy mischance of his early boyhood, has thrown his lot with that of the New World. It is a curious story of a headstrong boy and a proud and relentless family: the details do not matter here, but they are sufficient to weave a web of romance around the tall yellow-bearded man with the sad eyes and the voice that gives itself perfectly to plaintive little Swedish songs remembered out of childhood. In the winter evenings we play chess together, he and I, and after some close, fierce battle has been fought to a finish—usually with my own defeat—we fill our pipes again, and Ehrensvärd tells me stories of the far, half-remembered days in the fatherland, before he went to sea: stories that grow very strange and incredible as the night deepens and the fire falls together, but stories that, nevertheless, I fully believe.

One of them made a strong impression on me, so I set it down here, only regretting that I cannot reproduce the curiously perfect English and the delicate accent which to me increased the fascination of the tale. Yet, as best I can remember it, here it is.

"I never told you how Nils and I went over the hills to Hallsberg, and how we found the Dead Valley, did I? Well, this is the way it happened. I must have been about twelve years old, and Nils Sjöberg, whose father's estate joined ours, was a few months younger. We were inseparable just at that time, and whatever we did, we did together.

"Once a week it was market day in Engelholm, and Nils and I went always there to see the strange sights that the market gathered from all the surrounding country. One day we quite lost our hearts, for an old man from across the Elfborg had brought a little dog to sell, that seemed to us the most beautiful dog in all the world. He was a round, woolly puppy, so funny that Nils and I sat down on the ground and laughed at him, until he came and played with us in so jolly a way that we felt that there was only one really desirable thing in life, and that was the little dog of the old man from across the hills. But alas! we had not half money enough wherewith to buy him, so we were forced to beg the old man not to sell him before the next market day, promising that we would bring the money for him then. He gave us his word, and we ran home very fast and implored our mothers to give us money for the little dog.

"We got the money, but we could not wait for the next market day. Suppose the puppy should be sold! The thought frightened us so that we begged and implored that we might be allowed to go over the hills to Hallsberg where the old man lived, and get the little dog ourselves, and at last they told us we might go. By starting early in the morning we should reach Hallsberg by three o'clock, and it was arranged that we should stay there that night with Nils's aunt, and, leaving by noon the next day, be home again by sunset.

"Soon after sunrise we were on our way, after having received minute instructions as to just what we should do in all possible and impossible circumstances, and finally a repeated injunction that we should start for home at the same hour the next day, so that we might get safely back before nightfall.

"For us, it was magnificent sport, and we started off with our rifles, full of the sense of our very great importance: yet the journey was simple enough, along a good road, across the big hills we knew so well, for Nils and I had shot over half the territory this side of the dividing ridge of the Elfborg. Back of Engelholm lay a long valley, from which rose the low mountains, and we had to cross this, and then follow the road along the side of the hills for three or four miles, before a narrow path branched off to the left, leading up through the pass.

"Nothing occurred of interest on the way over, and we reached Hallsberg in due season, found to our inexpressible joy that the little dog was not sold, secured him, and so went to the house of Nils's aunt to spend the night.

"Why we did not leave early on the following day, I can't quite remember; at all events, I know we stopped at a shooting range just outside of the town, where most attractive pasteboard pigs were sliding slowly through painted foliage, serving so as beautiful marks. The result was that we did not get fairly started for home until afternoon, and as we found ourselves at last pushing up the side of the mountain with the sun dangerously near their summits, I think we were a little scared at the prospect of the examination and possible punishment that awaited us when we got home at midnight.

"Therefore we hurried as fast as possible up the mountain side, while the blue dusk closed in about us, and the light died in the purple sky. At first we had talked hilariously, and the little dog had leaped ahead of us with the utmost joy. Latterly, however, a curious oppression came on us; we did not speak or even whistle, while the dog fell behind, following us with hesitation in every muscle.

"We had passed through the foothills and the low spurs of the mountains, and were almost at the top of the main range, when life seemed to go out of everything, leaving the world dead, so suddenly silent the forest became, so stagnant the air. Instinctively we halted to listen.

"Perfect silence,—the crushing silence of deep forests at night; and more, for always, even in the most impenetrable fastnesses of the wooded mountains, is the multitudinous murmur of little lives, awakened by the darkness, exaggerated and intensified by the stillness of the air and the great dark: but here and now the silence seemed unbroken even by the turn of a leaf, the movement of a twig, the note of night bird or insect. I could hear the blood beat through my veins; and the crushing of the grass under our feet as we advanced with hesitating steps sounded like the falling of trees.

"And the air was stagnant,—dead. The atmosphere seemed to lie upon the body like the weight of sea on a diver who has ventured too far into its awful depths. What we usually call silence seems so only in relation to the din of ordinary experience. This was silence in the absolute, and it crushed the mind while it intensified the senses, bringing down the awful weight of inextinguishable fear.

"I know that Nils and I stared towards each other in abject terror, listening to our quick, heavy breathing, that sounded to our acute senses like the fitful rush of waters. And the poor little dog we were leading justified our terror. The black oppression seemed to crush him even as it did us. He lay close on the ground, moaning feebly, and dragging himself painfully and slowly closer to Nils's feet. I think this exhibition of utter animal fear was the last touch, and must inevitably have blasted our reason—mine anyway; but just then, as we stood quaking on the bounds of madness, came a sound, so awful, so ghastly, so horrible, that it seemed to rouse us from the dead spell that was on us.

"In the depth of the silence came a cry, beginning as a low, sorrowful moan, rising to a tremulous shriek, culminating in a yell that seemed to tear the night in sunder and rend the world as by a cataclysm. So fearful was it that I could not believe it had actual existence: it passed previous experience, the powers of belief, and for a moment I thought it the result of my own animal terror, an hallucination born of tottering reason.

"A glance at Nils dispelled this thought in a flash. In the pale light of the high stars he was the embodiment of all possible human fear, quaking with an ague, his jaw fallen, his tongue out, his eyes protruding like those of a hanged man. Without a word we fled, the panic of fear giving us strength, and together, the little dog caught close in Nils's arms, we sped down the side of the cursed mountains,—anywhere, goal was of no account: we had but one impulse—to get away from that place.

"So under the black trees and the far white stars that flashed through the still leaves overhead, we leaped down the mountain side, regardless of path or landmark, straight through the tangled underbrush, across mountain streams, through fens and copses, anywhere, so only that our course was downward.

"How long we ran thus, I have no idea, but by and by the forest fell behind, and we found ourselves among the foothills, and fell exhausted on the dry short grass, panting like tired dogs.

"It was lighter here in the open, and presently we looked around to see where we were, and how we were to strike out in order to find the path that would lead us home. We looked in vain for a familiar sign. Behind us rose the great wall of black forest on the flank of the mountain: before us lay the undulating mounds of low foothills, unbroken by trees or rocks, and beyond, only the fall of black sky bright with multitudinous stars that turned its velvet depth to a luminous gray.

"As I remember, we did not speak to each other once: the terror was too heavy on us for that, but by and by we rose simultaneously and started out across the hills.

"Still the same silence, the same dead, motionless air—air that was at once sultry and chilling: a heavy heat struck through with an icy chill that felt almost like the burning of frozen steel. Still carrying the helpless dog, Nils pressed on through the hills, and I followed close behind. At last, in front of us, rose a slope of moor touching the white stars. We climbed it wearily, reached the top, and found ourselves gazing down into a great, smooth valley, filled half way to the brim with—what?

"As far as the eye could see stretched a level plain of ashy white, faintly phosphorescent, a sea of velvet fog that lay like motionless water, or rather like a floor of alabaster, so dense did it appear, so seemingly capable of sustaining weight. If it were possible, I think that sea of dead white mist struck even greater terror into my soul than the heavy silence or the deadly cry—so ominous was it, so utterly unreal, so phantasmal, so impossible, as it lay there like a dead ocean under the steady stars. Yet through that mist *we must go*! there seemed no other way home, and, shattered with abject fear, mad with the one desire to get back, we started down the slope to where the sea of milky mist ceased, sharp and distinct around the stems of the rough grass.

"I put one foot into the ghostly fog. A chill as of death struck through me, stopping my heart, and I threw myself backward on the slope. At that instant came again the shriek, close, close, right in our ears, in ourselves, and far out across that damnable sea I saw the cold fog lift like a water-spout and toss itself high in writhing convolutions towards the sky. The stars began to grow dim as thick vapor swept across them, and in the growing dark I saw a great, watery moon lift itself slowly above the palpitating sea, vast and vague in the gathering mist.

"This was enough: we turned and fled along the margin of the white sea that throbbed now with fitful motion below us, rising, rising, slowly and steadily, driving us higher and higher up the side of the foothills.

"It was a race for life; that we knew. How we kept it up I cannot understand, but we did, and at last we saw the white sea fall behind us as we staggered up the end of the valley, and then down into a region that we knew, and so into the old path. The last thing

I remember was hearing a strange voice, that of Nils, but horribly changed, stammer brokenly, 'The dog is dead!' and then the whole world turned around twice, slowly and resistlessly, and consciousness went out with a crash.

"It was some three weeks later, as I remember, that I awoke in my own room, and found my mother sitting beside the bed. I could not think very well at first, but as I slowly grew strong again, vague flashes of recollection began to come to me, and little by little the whole sequence of events of that awful night in the Dead Valley came back. All that I could gain from what was told me was that three weeks before I had been found in my own bed, raging sick, and that my illness grew fast into brain fever. I tried to speak of the dread things that had happened to me, but I saw at once that no one looked on them save as the hauntings of a dying frenzy, and so I closed my mouth and kept my own counsel.

"I must see Nils, however, and so I asked for him. My mother told me that he also had been ill with a strange fever, but that he was now quite well again. Presently they brought him in, and when we were alone I began to speak to him of the night on the mountain. I shall never forget the shock that struck me down on my pillow when the boy denied everything: denied having gone with me, ever having heard the cry, having seen the valley, or feeling the deadly chill of the ghostly fog. Nothing would shake his determined ignorance, and in spite of myself I was forced to admit that his denials came from no policy of concealment, but from blank oblivion.

"My weakened brain was in a turmoil. Was it all but the floating phantasm of delirium? Or had the horror of the real thing blotted Nils's mind into blankness so far as the events of the night in the Dead Valley were concerned? The latter explanation seemed the only one, else how explain the sudden illness which in a night had struck us both down? I said nothing more, either to Nils or to my own people, but waited, with a growing determination that, once well again, I would find that valley if it really existed.

"It was some weeks before I was really well enough to go, but finally, late in September, I chose a bright, warm, still day, the last smile of the dying summer, and started early in the morning along the path that led to Hallsberg. I was sure I knew where the trail struck off to the right, down which we had come from the valley of dead water, for a great tree grew by the Hallsberg path at the point where, with a sense of salvation, we had found the home road. Presently I saw it to the right, a little distance ahead.

"I think the bright sunlight and the clear air had worked as a tonic to me, for by the time I came to the foot of the great pine, I had quite lost faith in the verity of the vision that haunted me, believing at last that it was indeed but the nightmare of madness. Nevertheless, I turned sharply to the right, at the base of the tree, into a narrow path that led through a dense thicket. As I did so I tripped over something. A swarm of flies sung into the air around me, and looking down I saw the matted fleece, with the poor little bones thrusting through, of the dog we had bought in Hallsberg.

"Then my courage went out with a puff, and I knew that it all was true, and that now I was frightened. Pride and the desire for adventure urged me on, however, and I pressed into the close thicket that barred my way. The path was hardly visible: merely the worn road of some small beasts, for, though it showed in the crisp grass, the bushes above grew thick and hardly penetrable. The land rose slowly, and rising grew clearer, until at last I came out on a great slope of hill, unbroken by trees or shrubs, very like my memory of that rise of land we had topped in order that we might find the dead valley and the icy fog. I looked at the sun; it was bright and clear, and all around insects were humming in the autumn air, and birds were darting to and fro. Surely there was no danger, not until nightfall at least; so I began to whistle, and with a rush mounted the last crest of brown hill.

"There lay the Dead Valley! A great oval basin, almost as smooth and regular as though made by man. On all sides the grass crept over the brink of the encircling hills, dusty green on the crests, then fading into ashy brown, and so to a deadly white, this last color forming a thin ring, running in a long line around the slope. And then? Nothing. Bare, brown, hard earth, glittering with grains of alkali, but otherwise dead and barren. Not a tuft of grass, not a stick of brushwood, not even a stone, but only the vast expanse of beaten clay.

"In the midst of the basin, perhaps a mile and a half away, the level expanse was broken by a great dead tree, rising leafless and gaunt into the air. Without a moment's hesitation I started down into the valley and made for this goal. Every particle of fear seemed to have left me, and even the valley itself did not look so very terrifying. At all events, I was driven by an overwhelming curiosity, and there seemed to be but one thing in the world to do,—to get to that Tree! As I trudged along over the hard earth, I noticed that the multitudinous voices of birds and insects had died away. No bee or butterfly hovered through the air, no insects leaped or crept over the dull earth. The very air itself was stagnant.

"As I drew near the skeleton tree, I noticed the glint of sunlight on a kind of white mound around its roots, and I wondered curiously. It was not until I had come close that I saw its nature.

"All around the roots and barkless trunk was heaped a wilderness of little bones. Tiny skulls of rodents and of birds, thousands of them, rising about the dead tree and streaming off for several yards in all directions, until the dreadful pile ended in isolated skulls and scattered skeletons. Here and there a larger bone appeared,—the thigh of a sheep, the hoofs of a horse, and to one side, grinning slowly, a human skull.

"I stood quite still, staring with all my eyes, when suddenly the dense silence was broken by a faint, forlorn cry high over my head. I looked up and saw a great falcon turning and sailing downward just over the tree. In a moment more she fell motionless on the bleaching bones.

"Horror struck me, and I rushed for home, my brain whirling, a strange numbness growing in me. I ran steadily, on and on. At last I glanced up. Where was the rise of hill? I looked around wildly. Close before me was the dead tree with its pile of bones. I had circled it round and round, and the valley wall was still a mile and a half away.

"I stood dazed and frozen. The sun was sinking, red and dull, towards the line of hills. In the east the dark was growing fast. Was there still time? *Time!* It was not *that* I wanted, it was *will*! My feet seemed clogged as in a nightmare. I could hardly drag them over the barren earth. And then I felt the slow chill creeping through me. I looked down. Out of the earth a thin mist was rising, collecting in little pools that grew ever larger until they joined here and there, their currents swirling slowly like thin blue smoke. The western hills halved the copper sun. When it was dark I should hear that shriek again, and then I should die. I knew that, and with every remaining atom of will I staggered towards the red west through the writhing mist that crept clammily around my ankles, retarding my steps.

"And as I fought my way off from the Tree, the horror grew, until at last I thought I was going to die. The silence pursued me like dumb ghosts, the still air held my breath, the hellish fog caught at my feet like cold hands.

"But I won! though not a moment too soon. As I crawled on my hands and knees up the brown slope, I heard, far away and high in the air, the cry that already had almost bereft me of reason. It was faint and vague, but unmistakable in its horrible intensity. I glanced behind. The fog was dense and pallid, heaving undulously up the brown slope. The sky was gold under the setting sun, but below was the ashy gray of death. I stood for a moment on the brink of this sea of hell, and then leaped down the slope. The sunset opened before me, the night closed behind, and as I crawled home weak and tired, darkness shut down on the Dead Valley."

The Devil of the Marsh

H. B. Marriott Watson

IT WAS NIGHT UPON DUSK WHEN I DREW CLOSE TO THE GREAT MARSH, AND ALREADY the white vapours were about, riding across the sunken levels like ghosts in a church-yard. Though I had set forth in a mood of wild delight, I had sobered in the lonely ride across the moor and was now uneasily alert. As my horse jerked down the grassy slope that fell away to the jaws of the swamp I could see thin streams of mist rise slowly, hover like wraiths above the long rustics, and then, turning gradually more material, go blowing heavily away across the flat. The appearance of the place at this desolate hour, so remote from human society and so darkly significant of evil presences, struck me with a certain wonder that she should have chosen this spot for our meeting. She was a familiar of the moors, where I had invariably encountered her; but it was like her arrogant caprice to test my devotion by some such dreary assignation. The wide and horrid prospect depressed me beyond reason, but the fact of her neighbourhood drew me on, and my spirits mounted at the thought that at last she was to put me in posses-sion of herself. Tethering my horse upon the verge of the swamp, I soon discovered the path that crossed it, and entering struck out boldly for the heart. The track could have been little used, for the reeds, which stood high above the level of my eyes upon either side, straggled everywhere across in low arches, through which I dodged, and broke my way with some inconvenience and much impatience. A full half-hour I was solitary in that wilderness, and when at last a sound other than my own footsteps broke the silence the dusk had fallen.

I was moving very slowly at the time, with a mind half disposed to turn from the melancholy expedition, which it seemed to me now must surely be a cruel jest she had played upon me. While some such reluctance held me, I was suddenly arrested by a hoarse croaking which broke out upon my left, sounding somewhere from the reeds in the black mire. A little further it came again from close at hand, and when I had passed on a few more steps in wonder and perplexity I heard it for the third time. I stopped and listened, but the marsh was as a grave, and so taking the noise for the signal of some raucous frog, I resumed my way. But in a little the croaking was repeated, and coming quickly to a stand I pushed the reeds aside and peered into the darkness. I could see nothing, but at the immediate moment of my pause I thought I detected the sound of some body trailing through the rushes. My distaste

for the adventure grew with this suspicion, and had it not been for my delirious infatu-
ation I had assuredly turned back and ridden home. The ghastly sound pursued me at
intervals along the track, until at last, irritated beyond endurance by the sense of this
persistent and invisible company, I broke into a sort of run. This, it seemed, the creature
(whatever it was) could not achieve, for I heard no more of it, and continued my way in
peace. My path at length ran out from among the reeds upon the smooth flat of which
she had spoken, and here my heart quickened, and the gloom of the dreadful place lifted:
The flat lay in the very centre of the marsh, and here and there in it a gaunt bush or
withered tree rose like a spectre against the white mists. At the further end I fancied
some kind of building loomed up; but the fog which had been gathering ever since my
entrance upon the passage sailed down upon me at that moment and the prospect went
out with suddenness. As I stood waiting for the cloud to pass, a voice cried to me out of
its centre, and I saw her next second with bands of mist swirling about her body, come
rushing to me from the darkness. She put her long arms about me, and, drawing her
close, I looked into her deep eyes. Far down in them, it seemed to me, I could discern a
mystic laughter dancing in the wells of light, and I had that ecstatic sense of nearness to
some spirit of fire which was wont to possess me at her contact.

"At last," she said, "at last, my beloved!" I caressed her.

"Why," said I, tingling at the nerves, "why have you put this dolorous journey
between us? And what mad freak is your presence in this swamp?" She uttered her
silver laugh, and nestled to me again.

"I am the creature of this place," she answered. "This is my home. I had sworn you
should behold me in my native sin ere you ravished me away."

"Come, then," said I; "I have seen; let there be an end of this. I know you, what you
are. This marsh chokes up my heart. God forbid you should spend more of your days
here. Come."

"You are in haste," she cried. "There is yet much to learn. Look, my friend," she
said, "you who know me, what I am. This is my prison, and I have inherited its proper-
ties. Have you no fear?"

For answer I pulled her to me, and her warm lips drove out the horrid humours of
the night; but the swift passage of a flickering mockery over her eyes struck me back as
a flash of lightning, and I grew chill again.

"I have the marsh in my blood," she whispered; "the marsh and the fog of it. Think
ere you vow to me, for I am the cloud in a starry night."

A lithe and lovely creature, palpable of warm flesh, she lifted her magic face to mine
and besought me plaintively with these words. The dews of the nightfall hung on her
lashes, and seemed to plead with me for her forlorn and solitary plight.

"Behold!" I cried, "witch or devil of the marsh, you shall come with me! I have known you on the moors, a roving apparition of beauty; nothing more I know, nothing more I ask. I care not what this dismal haunt means; nor what these strange and mystic eyes. You have powers and senses above me; your sphere and habits are as mysterious and incomprehensible as your beauty. But that," I said, "is mine, and the world that is mine shall be yours also."

She moved her head nearer to me with an antic gesture, and her gleaming eyes glanced up at me with a sudden flash, the similitude (great heavens!) of a hooded snake. Starting, I fell away, but at that moment she turned her face and set it fast towards the fog that came rolling in thick volumes over the flat. Noiselessly the great cloud crept down upon us, and all dazed and troubled I watched her watching it in silence. It was as if she awaited some omen of horror, and I too trembled in the fear of its coming.

Then suddenly out of the night issued the hoarse and hideous croaking I had heard upon my passage. I reached out my arm to take her hand, bur in an instant the mists broke over us, and I was groping in the vacancy. Something like panic took hold of me, and, beating through the blind obscurity, I rushed over the flat calling upon her. In a little the swirl went by, and I perceived her upon the margin of the swamp, her arm raised as in imperious command. I ran to her, but stopped, amazed and shaken by a fearful sight. Low by the dripping reeds crouched a small squat thing, in the likeness of a monstrous frog, coughing and choking in its throat. As I stared, the creature rose upon its legs and disclosed a horrid human resemblance. Its face was white and thin, with long black hair; its body gnarled, and twisted as with the ague of a thousand years. Shaking, it whined in a breathless voice, pointing a skeleton finger at the woman by my side.

"Your eyes were my guide," it quavered. "Do you think that after all these years I have no knowledge of your eyes? Lo, is there aught of evil in you I am not instructed in? This is the Hell you designed for me, and now you would leave me to a greater."

The wretch paused, and panting leaned upon a bush, while she stood silent, mocking him with her eyes, and soothing my terror with her soft touch.

"Hear!" he cried, turning to me, "hear the tale of this woman that you may know her as she is. She is the Presence of the marshes. Woman or Devil I know not, but only that the accursed marsh has crept into her soul and she herself is become its Evil Spirit; she herself, that lives and grows young and beautiful by it, has its full power to blight and chill and slay. I, who was once as you are, have this knowledge. What bones lie deep in this black swamp who can say but she? She has drained of health, she has drained of mind and of soul; what is between her and her desire that she should not drain also of life? She has made me a devil in her Hell, and now she would leave me to my solitary pain, and go search for another victim. But she shall not!" he screamed through his chattering teeth; "she shall not! My Hell is also hers! She shall not!"

Her smiling untroubled eyes left his face and turned to me; she put out her arms, swaying towards me, and so fervid and so great a light glowed in her face that, as one distraught of superhuman means, I took her into my embrace. And then the madness seized me.

"Woman or devil," I said, "I will go with you! Of what account this pitiful past? Blight me even as that wretch, so be only you are with me."

She laughed, and, disengaging herself, leaned, half-clinging to me, towards the coughing creature by the mire.

"Come," I cried, catching her by the waist. "Come!" She laughed again a silver-ringing laugh. She moved with me slowly across the flat to where the track started for the portals of the marsh. She laughed and clung to me.

But at the edge of the track I was startled by a shrill, hoarse screaming; and behold, from my very feet, that loathsome creature rose up and wound his long black arms about her, shrieking and crying in his pain. Stooping I pushed him from her skirts, and with one sweep of my arm drew her across the pathway; as her face passed mine her eyes were wide and smiling. Then of a sudden the still mist enveloped us once more; but ere it descended I had a glimpse of that contorted figure trembling on the margin, the white face drawn and full of desolate pain. At the sight, an icy shiver ran through me. And then through the yellow gloom the shadow of her darted past me to the further side. I heard the hoarse cough, the dim noise of a struggle, a swishing sound, a thin cry, and then the sucking of the slime over something in the rushes. I leapt forward and once again the fog thinned, and I beheld her, woman or devil, standing upon the verge, and peering with smiling eyes into the foul and sickly bog. With a sharp cry wrung from my nerveless soul, I turned and fled down the narrow way from that accursed spot; and as I ran the thickening fog closed round me, and I heard far off and lessening still the silver sound of her mocking laughter.

Dog or Demon?

Theo Gift

THE FOLLOWING PAGES CAME INTO MY HANDS SHORTLY AFTER THE WRITER'S DEATH. He was a brother officer of my own, had served under me with distinction in the last Afghan campaign, and was a young man of great spirit and promise. He left the army on the occasion of his marriage with a very beautiful girl, the daughter of a Leicestershire baronet; and I partially lost sight of him for some little time afterwards. I can, however, vouch for the accuracy of the principal facts herein narrated, and of the story generally; the sad fate of the family having made a profound impression, not only in the district in Ireland where the tragedy occurred, but throughout the country.

(Signed) WILLIAM J. PORLOCK,
Lieut.-Col.—Regt.
The Curragh, Co. Kildare.

At last she is dead!

It came to an end today: all that long agony, those heartrending cries and moans, the terrified shuddering of that poor, wasted body, the fixed and maddened glare, more awful for its very unconsciousness. Only this very day they faded out and died away one by one, as death crept at last up the tortured and emaciated limbs, and I stood over my wife's body, and tried to thank God for both our sakes that it was all over.

And yet it was I who had done it. I who killed her—not meaningly or of intent (I will swear that), not even so that the laws of this earth can punish me; but, truly, wilfully all the same; of my own brutal, thoughtless selfishness. I put it all down in my diary at the time. I tear out the pages that refer to it now, and insert them here, that when those few friends who still care for me hear of the end they may know how it came about.

June 10th, 1878. Castle Kilmoyle, Kerry.—Arrived here today with K. after a hard battle to get away from Lily, who couldn't bear my going, and tried all manner of arguments to keep me from leaving her.

"What have *you* to do with Lord Kilmoyle's tenants?" she would keep on asking. "They owe no rent to you. Oh, Harry, do let them alone and stay here. If you go with him you'll be sure to come in for some of the ill-feeling that already exists against himself; and I shall be so miserably anxious all the time. Pray don't go."

I told her, however, that I must; first, because I had promised, and men don't like to go back from their word without any cause; and secondly, because Kilmoyle would be desperately offended with me if I did. The fact is, I hadn't seen him for three years till we met at that tennis-party at the Fitz Herberts' last week; and when he asked me if I would like to run over for a week's fishing at his place in Ireland, and help him to enforce the eviction of a tenant who declined either to pay for the house he lived in or leave it, I accepted with effusion. It would be a spree. I had nothing to do, and I really wanted a little change and waking up. As for Lily, her condition naturally makes her rather nervous and fanciful at present, and to have me dancing attendance on her does her more harm than good. I told her so, and asked her, with half a dozen kisses, if she'd like to tie me to her apron-string altogether. She burst out crying, and said she would! There is no use in reasoning with the dear little girl at present. She is better with her sisters.

June 12th.—We have begun the campaign by giving the tenant twenty-four hours' notice to pay or quit. Kilmoyle and I rode down with the bailiff to the cottage, a well-built stone one in the loveliest glen ever dreamt of out of fairyland, to see it served ourselves. The door was shut and barred, and as no answer save a fierce barking from within responded to our knocks, we were beginning to think that the tenant had saved us the trouble of evicting him by decamping of his own accord, when, on crossing round to the side of the house where there was a small, unglazed window, we came in full view of him, seated as coolly as possible beside a bare hearthstone, with a pipe in his mouth and a big brown dog between his knees. His hair, which was snow-white, hung over his shoulders, and his face was browned to the colour of mahogany by exposure to sun and wind; but he might have been carved out of mahogany too for all the sign of attention that he gave while the bailiff repeated his messages, until Kilmoyle, losing patience, tossed a written copy of the notice in to him through the open window, with a threat that, unless he complied with it, he would be smoked out of the place like a rat: after which we rode off, followed by a perfect pandemonium of barks and howls from the dog, a lean and hideous mongrel, who seemed to be only held by force from flying at our throats.

We had a jolly canter over the hills afterwards; selected the bit of river that seemed most suitable for our fishing on the morrow; and wound up the day with a couple of bottles of champagne at dinner, after which Kilmoyle was warmed up into making me an offer which I accepted on the spot—*i.e.*, to let me have the identical cottage we had been visiting rent free, with right of shooting and fishing, for two years, on condition only of my putting and keeping it in order for that time. I wonder what Lily will say to the idea. She hates Ireland almost as much as Kilmoyle's tenants are supposed to hate him, but really it would cost mighty little to make a most picturesque little place of the cabin in question, and I believe we should both find it highly enjoyable to run down here for a couple of months' change in the autumn, after a certain and much-looked-forward-to event is well over.

June 19th.—The job is done, and the man out; and Kilmoyle and I shook hands laughing today over our victory as he handed me the key in token of my new ten-antship. It has been rather an exciting bit of work, however; for the fellow—an ill-conditioned old villain, who hasn't paid a stiver of rent for the last twelve months, and only a modicum for the three previous years—*wouldn't* quit; set all threats, persuasions, and warnings at defiance, and simply sat within his door with a loaded gun in his hand, and kept it pointed at anyone who tried to approach him. In the end, and to avoid bloodshed, we had to smoke him out. There was nothing else for it, for though we took care that none of the neighbours should come near the house with food, he was evidently prepared to starve where he was rather than budge an inch; and on the third day, Donovan, the bailiff, told Kilmoyle if he didn't want it to come to that, he must have in the help of either of the "peelers" or a bit of smoke.

Kilmoyle vowed he wouldn't have the peelers anyhow. He had said he'd put the man out himself, and he'd do it; and the end of it was, we first had the windows shuttered up from outside, a sod put on the chimney, and then the door taken off its hinges while the tenant's attention was momentarily distracted by the former operations. Next, a good big fire of damp weeds which had been piled up outside was set alight, and after that there was nothing to do but wait.

It didn't take long. The wind was blowing strongly in the direction of the house, and the dense volumes of thick, acrid smoke would have driven me out in about five minutes. As for the tenant, he was probably more hardened on the subject of atmosphere generally, for he managed to stand it for nearly half an hour, and until Kilmoyle and I were almost afraid to keep it up lest he should let himself be smothered out of sheer obstinacy. Just as I was debating, however, whether I wouldn't brave his gun, and make a rush in for him at all costs, nature or vindictiveness got the better of his perversity; a dark figure staggered through the stifling vapour to the door, fired wildly in the direction of Kilmoyle (without hitting him, thank God!), and then dropped, a miserable object, purple with suffocation and black with smoke, upon the threshold, whence one of the keepers dragged him out into the fresh air and poured a glass of whisky down his throat, just too late to prevent his fainting away.

Five minutes later the fire was out, the windows opened, and two stalwart Scotch keepers put in charge of the dwelling, while Kilmoyle and I went home to dinner, and the wretched old man, who had given us so much trouble for nothing, was conveyed in a handcart to the village by some of his neighbours, who had been looking on from a distance, and beguiling the time by hooting and groaning at us.

"Who wants the police in these cases?" said Kilmoyle triumphantly. "To my mind, Glennie, it's mere cowardice to send for those poor fellows to enforce orders we ought to be able to carry out for ourselves, and so get them into odium with the whole neighbourhood. We managed this capitally by ourselves"—and, upon my word, I couldn't help agreeing heartily with him. Indeed, the whole affair had gone off with only one trifling accident, and that was no one's fault but the tenant's.

It seems that for the last two days his abominable dog had been tied up in a miserable little pigsty a few yards from the house, Donovan having threatened him that if the brute flew at or bit anyone it would be shot instantly. Nobody was aware of this, however, and unfortunately, when the bonfire was at its height, a blazing twig fell on the roof of this little shelter and set it alight; the clouds of smoke which were blowing that way hiding what had happened until the wretched animal inside was past rescue; while even its howls attracted no attention, from the simple fact that not only it, but a score of other curs belonging to the neighbours round, had been making as much noise as they could from the commencement of the affair.

Now, of course, we hear that the evicted tenant goes about swearing that we deliberately and out of malice burnt his only friend alive, and calling down curses on our heads in consequence. I don't think we are much affected by them, however. Why didn't he untie the poor brute himself? * * *

June 22nd.—A letter from Lady Fitz Herbert, Lily's eldest sister, telling me she thinks I had better come back at once! L. not at all well, nervous about me, and made more, instead of less, so by my account of our successful raid. What a fool I was to write it! I thought she would be amused; but the only thing now is to get back as quickly as possible, and I started this morning, Kilmoyle driving me to the station. We were bowling along pretty fast, when, as we turned a bend in the road, the horse swerved suddenly to one side, and the off wheel of the trap went over something with that sickening sort of jolt, the meaning of which some of us know by experience, and which made Kilmoyle exclaim:

"Good heavens, we've run over something!"

Fortunately nothing to hurt! Nothing but the carcase of a dead dog, whose charred and blackened condition would have sufficiently identified it with the unlucky victim of Tuesday's bonfire, even if we had not now perceived its late owner seated among the heather near the roadside, and occupied in pouring forth a string of wailing sounds, which might have been either prayers or curses for aught we could tell; the while he waved his shaggy white head and brown claw-like hands to and fro in unison. I yelled at him to know why he had left his brute of a dog there to upset travellers, but he paid no attention, and did not seem to hear, and as we were in a hurry to catch the train we could not afford to waste words on him, but drove on. * * *

June 26th. Holly Lodge, West Kensington.—This day sees me the proud father of a son and heir, now just five hours old, and, though rather too red for beauty, a very sturdy youngster, with a fine pair of lungs of his own. Lily says she is too happy to live, and as the dread of losing her has been the one thought of the last twenty-four hours, it is a comfort to know from the doctor that this means she has got through it capitally, and is doing as well as can be expected. Thank God for all His mercies! * * *

July 17th.—Lily has had a nasty fright this evening, for which I hope she won't be any the worse. She was lying on a couch out in the veranda for the first time since her convalescence, and I had been reading to her till she fell asleep, when I closed the book, and, leaving the bell beside her in case she should want anything, went into my study to write letters. I hadn't been there for half an hour, however, when I was startled by a cry from Lily's voice and a sharp ringing of the bell, which made me fling open the study window and dart round to the veranda at the back of the house. It was empty, but in the drawing-room within Lily was standing upright, trembling with terror and clinging to her maid, while she tried to explain to her that there was *someone* hidden in the veranda or close by, though so incoherently, owing to the state of agitation she was in, that it was not till I and the manservant had searched veranda, garden, and outbuildings, and found nothing, that I was even able to understand what had frightened her.

It appeared then that she had been suddenly awakened from sleep by the pressure of a heavy hand on her shoulder, and a hot breath—so close, it seemed as if someone were about to whisper in her ear—upon her cheek. She started up, crying out, "Who's that? What is it?" but was only answered by a hasty withdrawal of the pressure, and the pit-pat of heavy but shoeless feet retreating through the dusk to the further end of the veranda. In a sudden access of ungovernable terror she screamed out, sprang to her feet, ringing the bell as she did so, and rushed into the drawing-room, where she was fortunately joined by her maid, who had been passing through the hall when the bell rang.

Well, as I said, we searched high and low, and not a trace of any intruder could we find; nay, not even a stray cat or dog, and we have none of our own. The garden isn't large, and there is neither tree nor shrub in it big enough to conceal a boy. The gate leading into the road was fastened inside, and the wall is too high for easy climbing; while the maid, having been in the hall, could certify that no one had passed out through the drawing-room. Finally I came to the conclusion that the whole affair was the outcome of one of those very vivid dreams which sometimes come to us in the semi-conscious moment between sleep and waking; and though Lily, of course, wouldn't hear of such an idea for a long while, I think even she began to give in to it after the doctor had been sent for, and had pronounced it the only rational one, and given her a composing draught before sending her off to bed. At present she is sleeping soundly, but it has been a disturbing evening, and I'm glad it's over. * * *

September 20th.—Have seen Dr. C—— today, and he agrees with me that there is nothing for it but change and bracing air. He declares that the fright Lily had in July must have been much more serious than we imagined, and that she has never got over it. She seemed to do so. She was out and about after her confinement as soon as other people; but I remember now her nerves seemed gone from the first. She was always starting, listening, and trembling without any cause, except that she appeared in constant alarm lest something should happen to the baby; and as I took that to be a common weakness with young mothers over their first child, I'm afraid I paid no attention to it. We've a very nice nurse for the boy, a young Irishwoman named Bridget McBean (not that she's ever seen Ireland herself, but her parents came from there, driven by poverty to earn their living elsewhere, and after faithfully sending over every farthing they could screw out of their own necessities to "the ould folks at home," died in the same poverty here). Bridget is devoted to the child, and as long as he is in her care Lily generally seems easy and peaceful. Otherwise (and some strange instinct tells me this is the case) she gets nervous at once, and is always restless and uneasy.

Once she awoke with a scream in the middle of the night, declaring, "Something was wrong with baby. Nurse had gone away and left it; she was sure of it!" To pacify her I threw on my dressing gown and ran up to the nursery to see; and, true enough, though the boy was all right and sound asleep, nurse was absent, having gone up to the cook's room to get something for her toothache. She came back the next moment, and I returned to satisfy Lily, but she would scarcely listen to me.

"Is it *gone?*" she asked. "Was the nursery door open? Oh, if it had been! Thank God, you were in time to drive the thing down. But how—how could it have got into the house?"

"*It?* What?" I repeated, staring.

"The dog you passed on the stairs. I saw it as it ran past the door—a *big black dog!*"

"My dear, you're dreaming. I passed no dog; nothing at all."

"Oh, Harry, didn't you see it then? I did, though it went by so quietly. Oh, is it in the house still?"

I seized the candle, went up and down stairs and searched the whole house thoroughly; but again found nothing. The fancied dog must have been a shadow on the wall only, and I told her so pretty sharply; yet on two subsequent occasions when, for some reason or another, she had the child's cot put beside her own bed at night, I was woke by finding her sitting up and shaking with fright, while she assured me that something—*some animal*—had been trying to get into the room. She could hear its breathing distinctly as it scratched at the door to open it! Dr. C—— is right. Her nerves are clearly all wrong, and a thorough change is the only thing for her. How glad I am that the builder writes me my Kerry shooting-box is finished! We'll run over there next week. * * *

September 26th, The Cabin, Kilmoyle Castle, Kerry.—Certainly this place is Paradise after London, and never did I imagine that by raising the roof so as to transform a garret into a large, bright attic, quite big enough for a nursery, throwing out a couple of bay windows in the two rooms below, and turning an adjoining barn into a kitchen and servants' room, this cottage could ever have been made into such a jolly little box. As for Lily, she's delighted with it, and looks ever so much better already. Am getting my guns in order for tomorrow, anticipating a pleasant day's shooting.

September 27th.—Here's an awful bother! Bridget has given warning and declares she will leave today! It seems she knew her mother came from Kerry, and this morning she has found out that the old man who lived in this very cottage was her own grandfather, and that he died of a broken heart within a week of his eviction, having first called down a solemn curse on Kilmoyle and me, and all belonging to us, in this world and the next. They say also that he managed to scoop out a grave for his dog, and bury it right in front of the cabin door, and now Bridget is alternately tearing her hair for ever having served under her "grandfather's murtherer," and weeping over the murderer's baby the while she packs her box for departure. That wouldn't matter so much, though it's awfully unpleasant, for the housekeeper at the Castle will send us someone to mind the boy till we get another nurse; but the disclosure seems to have driven Lily as frantic as Bridget. She entreated me with tears and sobs to give up the cabin, and take her and baby back to England before "the curse could fall upon us," and wept like one brokenhearted when I told her she must be mad even to suggest such a thing after all the expense I have been to. All the same, it's a horrid nuisance.

She has been crying all day, and if this fancy grows on her the change will do her no good, and I shan't know what to do. I'm sorry I was cross to her, poor child; but I was rather out of sorts myself, having been kept awake all night by the ceaseless, mournful howling of some unseen cur. Besides, I'm bothered about Kilmoyle. He arranged long ago to be here this week; but the bailiff says he has been ill and is travelling, and speaks in a mysterious way as if the illness were D.T. I hope not! I had no idea before that my old chum was even addicted to drink. Anyhow, I won't

be baulked of a few days' shooting, at all events, and perhaps by that time Lily will
have calmed down.

October 19th, The Castle.—It is weeks since I opened this, and I only do so now
before closing it forever. I shall never dare to look at it again after writing down what
I must today. I did go out for my shooting on the morning after my last entry, and my
wife, with the babe in her arms, stood at the cabin door to see me off. The sunlight
shone full on them—on the tear-stains still dark under her sweet blue eyes, and the
downy head and tiny face of the infant on her breast. But she smiled as I kissed my hand
to her. I shall never forget that—the last smile that *ever*. . . The woman we had brought
with us as servant told me the rest. She said her mistress went on playing with the child
in the sunshine till it fell asleep, and then laid it in its cot inside, and sat beside it rocking
it. By-and-by, however, the maid went in and asked her to come and look at something
that was wrong with the new kitchen arrangements, and Lily came out with her. They
were in the kitchen about ten minutes, when they heard a wail from the cabin, and both
ran out. Lily was first, and cried out:

"Oh, Heaven! Look! what's *that*—that great dog, *all black, and burnt-looking*, coming out of the house? Oh, my baby! My baby!"

The maid saw no dog, and stopped for an instant to look round for it, letting her
mistress run on. Then she heard one wild shriek from within—such a shriek as she had
never heard in all her life before—and followed. She found Lily lying senseless on the
floor, and in the cradle the child—stone dead! Its throat had been torn open by some
savage animal, and on the bed-clothes and the fresh white matting covering the floor
were the blood-stained imprints of a dog's feet!

That was three weeks ago. It was evening when I came back; came back to hear
my wife's delirious shrieks piercing the autumn twilight—those shrieks which, from
the moment of her being roused from the merciful insensibility which held her for the
first hours of her loss, she has never ceased to utter. We have moved her to the Castle
since then; but I can hear them now. She has never regained consciousness once. The
doctors fear she never will.

And she never did! That last entry in my diary was written two years ago. For
two years my young wife, the pretty girl who loved me so dearly, and whom I took from
such a happy home, has been a raving lunatic—obliged to be guarded, held down, and
confined behind high walls. They have been my own walls, and I have been her keeper.
The doctors wanted me to send her to an asylum; said it would be for her good, and on
that I consented; but she grew so much worse there, her frantic struggles and shrieks

for me to come to her, to "save her from the dog, to keep it off," were so incessant and heartrending that they sent for me; and I have never left her again. God only knows what that means; what the horror and agony of those two years, those ceaseless, piteous cries for her child, *our* child; those agonized entreaties to me "not to go with Kilmoyle; to take her away, away"; those—oh! how have I ever borne it! . . .

Today it is over. She is dead; and—I scarce dare leave her even yet! Never once in all this time have I been tempted to share the horrible delusion which, beginning in a weak state of health, and confirmed by the awful coincidence of our baby's death, upset my darling's brain; and yet now—now that it is over, I feel as if the madness which slew her were coming on me also. As she lay dying last night, and I watched by her alone, I seemed to hear a sound of snuffling and scratching at the door outside, as though some animal were there. Once, indeed, I strode to it and threw it open, but there was nothing—nothing but a dark, fleeting shadow seen for one moment, and the sound of soft, unshod feet going pit, pat, pit, pat, upon the stairs as they retreated downwards. It was but fancy, my own heart-beats, as I knew; and yet—yet if the women who turned me out an hour ago should have left her alone—if that sound *now*—

* * * * *

Here the writing came to an abrupt end, the pen lying in a blot across it. At the inquest held subsequently the footman deposed that he heard his master fling open the study door, and rush violently upstairs to the death-chamber above. A loud exclamation, and the report of a pistol-shot followed almost immediately; and on running to the rescue he found Captain Glennie standing inside the door, his face livid with horror, and the revolver in his outstretched hand still pointed at a corner of the room on the other side of the bier, the white covering on which had in one place been dragged off and torn. Before the man could speak, however, his master turned round to him, and exclaiming:

"Williams, *I have seen it!* It was there! *on her!* Better this than a madhouse! There is no other escape," put the revolver to his head, and fired. He was dead ere even the servant could catch him.

Dr. Pechal's Theory

Julian Hawthorne

Not long ago, the steamer *Ecliptic* brought to New York, among other passengers, a fat, frowzy man, rather short, and evidently a foreigner—though of what nationality, owing to his familiarity with languages, it was not easy to decide. He was not an engaging man, was supernaturally conceited, some said crazy. He wore a pair of unusually shiny spectacles—it was believed, to assist him in staring. His hair was long, tangled, and sandy, overhanging his coat-collar, and pushed back behind his ears. His luggage consisted of a ragged, black carpet-bag, which no one suspected of containing clothes.

The captain himself was not sacred from the intrusive impertinence of this man. The second day out, at dinner, he stared uninterruptedly for ten minutes at that officer, and then said:

"You must be a Scotchman!"

The captain's little hobby was, to be taken for an American; so he bowed somewhat stiffly, and continued his conversation with the American banker's wife at his right.

The frowzy foreigner drew from his pocket a greasy note-book, piloted his way through several pages with his dirty forefinger, till he arrived at a certain entry; then, with powerful assertativeness:

"You are forty-eight years old to-day!"

The captain was a young-looking man, perhaps not unwillingly so, especially in the eyes of his fair right-hand neighbor. So he looked up rather severely at the foreigner, and said, gruffly:

"Well, sir?"

"Of course," pursued the other, absorbed in his note-book—"all here, sir. I calculated your group some time ago; it comprises four, and possibly five. I met one last year in Turkey—a very pretty little girl. Whereabouts will you be seven weeks from to-day, captain?"

The captain's patience began to grow thin; but he commanded himself to reply, albeit somewhat testily:

"Give fair weather, off the southern coast of Ireland."

The frowzy foreigner was charmed. He bubbled over with an unclean smile; his teeth were dreadful.

"Right! quite right!" he exclaimed, rubbing his fat hands self-approvingly. "You will be drowned off that coast, sir; steamer founders, or you are washed overboard— cannot be sure which."

At this sally, every one, except the captain, either laughed or smiled. He, strange to say, turned pale and frowned slightly. The foreign lunatic calmly replaced his note-book, and resumed his dinner.

Could it have been a coincidence that, seven weeks from that day, in a heavy sea off the southern coast of Ireland, Captain McAlenny, of the *Ecliptic*, was washed over-board and lost? Curious, at all events! Moreover—though, what has this to do with it?—the little daughter of a prominent official in Constantinople died the same day, after the crisis of a long and painful fever.

The conceited foreigner was not, therefore, an agreeable companion. He was no respecter of persons; for he used up even a custom-house officer in this wise:

After transfixing him with an indignant and prolonged glare of his spectacles— "Why, you should have been dead two years ago. Your time expired in the summer of 1868. I saw one of your group condemned to be hanged for murder in June of that year, and I cannot be mistaken in you," said he, referring to his note-book.

The custom-house officer glared back in savage amazement. "Ef 'twarn't f' my wife 'nd child'n," he began, menacingly; but the fat foreigner's brow cleared up immedi-ately, as if his mind were relieved from an immense load of perplexity.

"My dear sir—to be sure! How could *I*, of all men, make such an oversight? And now I recollect—his sentence was commuted—imprisonment for life. Let me see— your wife? ah, yes! she belongs also with the young Frenchman; and that Jew, I think, must be a connection. Well, well, sir, you're safe for six years yet." And the maniac departed in total apparent unconsciousness of the black wrath distorting the custom-house officer's visage.

Landed in New York, he grasped his ragged, black carpet-bag, and walked to the South-Sea Hotel. On his way he stopped to purchase a directory, and barely escaped being knocked down by the salesman because he informed him the only safe thing in his case was to marry a certain African lady, a resident of Guinea. Arriving at the hotel, he engaged a room for three days, and registered his name as Dr. Pechal, from Belgium. He eyed the gentlemanly clerk searchingly.

"Your hair *must* be dyed, sir," said he at last, firmly.

The gentlemanly clerk drew himself up haughtily. The doctor glared, and shook his frowzy head.

"No use, sir; it won't save you. No immediate danger, however; your group remains till the next decade."

In short, Dr. Pechal was not merely disagreeable—he was awful.

He entered and locked his room-door, opened the black carpet-bag and poured the contents on the table—nothing but old books! There were a volume of logarithms, life-insurance reports, works on phrenology and physiology, metaphysical compilations, directories of various cities, and, at the very bottom of the bag, a large manuscript volume, whose contents only the doctor knew.

He placed these paraphernalia of research in a semicircle upon the table, seated himself in the concavity of the arc, and worked away steadily for at least three hours, concluding by writing down his results in the manuscript volume, and making an elimination thereof into the greasy note-book. Then he leaned back, ran his thick fingers into his hair, and ruminated. The manuscript book lay open on the table. It was entitled "Todes-Gesetz," which appellation, should it afford no enlightenment to the reader, places him on an equality with, let us say, nine people out of ten. It was filled with closely-written pages of mysterious and enigmatical import, in a dozen different languages, and, for the most part, unimportant to the present history. But the last entry, as transcribed into the greasy note-book, may possibly be of some assistance. Here it is:

> Group comprises four. Distribution—two to one each—in Belgium, America, possibly France, possibly Asia.
>
> Distribution as regards sex—male, two; female, two.
>
> Incidence of law (as calculated from table of logarithms, Natural Sine) — four days from date, subject to following impediments and exceptions:
>
> 1. Amalgamation to have occurred between two of this group; or—
>
> 2. Such amalgamation to take place within the next four days, provided that—
>
> Literal identity of surname exists between the two.
>
> Outside contracts no obstruction to law's course.

Besides this, there were sundry personal descriptions and data, and numerous references, citations, and comments, which may as well be passed over for the present. It will be more to the point, and quite as discreet, to listen to the doctor's ruminations:

"Poor prospects, Emil, very poor! Allowing thee every thing— that the person is in New York, is a woman, is unmarried, and is willing to marry thee—still are the chances as to literal identity an infinity against one. Ah, Emil! why didst thou shut thine eyes when Destiny offered thee all the most exact interpretation could require—sex, name, age, condition—all? And she loved thee, Emil. Yes, my friend; but that was twenty years ago! Hadst thou but known then what thou knowest now, thou hadst not then gone alone to seek thy fortune!

"And dost thou hope to find *her* here? As well that as another like her! Nay, even then, dost thou believe she would still care for thee, Emil?" exclaimed the doctor, rising and going to the dressing-table, on which was erected a small mirror. "Alas! thou art sadly changed! I fear she would find death more attractive than thee.

"But courage!" exclaimed Dr. Pechal, again arousing himself from his despondency. "Let us persevere to the end! One more attempt, friend Emil, ere we say farewell to each other! Let us use well the time that remains to us!" With which parting exhortations to the ample and lugubrious countenance in the mirror, the doctor turned away, replaced his library in his carpet-bag; and, it being already late, we will leave him in undisturbed possession of his room.

Next morning, having performed his arid toilet, this unpleasant and mysterious man appeared upon Broadway. The penetrating glare of his spectacles, as he shuffled onward, was ever and anon directed at some passing face, whenever it seemed to come within the range of his weird and preternatural intelligence. For himself, such attention as he received was not complimentary. What a turning of tables, could they have recognized in this uncouth individual the man who had reduced mortality to a working formula! But their non-appreciation troubled him not; he was perhaps used to it.

Having reached the Fifth-Avenue Hotel, the doctor paused, and looked about him somewhat wearily. What he sought was apparently no nearer than ever. For all that, his destiny was even then upon him; it was coming rapidly up the avenue in a spruce stage, with vivid medallions and golden scroll-work on a deep ultramarine background. Yet, so unconscious did the doctor appear that, were it not an established fact that Destiny never makes a mistake in her appointments, and is always punctual, it would seem a mere chance he did not miss her altogether.

The stage contained but one passenger—a charming young lady. To look at her was a refined and exquisite enjoyment. She was the flower of gentle breeding; and an indescribable, scarcely-perceptible aroma, peculiar to such flowers, hovered about her like an evanescent mist. The contrast between her very dark hazel eyes and straight, fine eyebrows, and the amber tint of her crisp and vigorous hair, made her beauty more striking than it would otherwise have been. Her complexion was clear and luminously pale, the skin drawn smoothly over the rounded flesh. All the refinement and fascination of her face seemed to culminate in a perfect little nose, with delicate nostrils and pointed tip. The curve of her lips might have seemed haughty, but that there hovered always about them the remembrance or the promise of a smile.

Swayed by I know not what mysterious impulse, this rare creature turned in her seat just as the stage was passing the upper corner of West Twenty-third Street, and looked straight at a foreign, ill-conditioned figure that happened at the moment to be standing there. The figure, at the same moment, raised a heavy and woe-begone countenance to the stage-window, and the shining spectacles and dark-hazel eyes met. Perhaps the extremes of human nature presented no wider contrast.

The young lady recoiled with a refined little shudder.

"What a dreadful thing!" Then she gave a startled little scream.

For the dreadful thing had suddenly frozen into an awful stare, rapidly shifting into an expression of wild delight. He had made a clumsy rush for the stage-door, wrenched it convulsively open, and flung himself, panting and perspiring, upon the opposite seat. Within the narrow limits of that Fifth-Avenue stage extremes had met at last!

And what did the high-bred lady do? First impulse—scream for help, or spring from the vehicle! But the next moment pride cast out fear—bullied it into submission, rather. Ten times more alarmed, by reason of her high-wrought organization, than any ordinary person could have been, no outward sign, save bloodless lips, betrayed it. She sat stern and motionless as a little statue, except that her heart beat so.

It was all thrown away on Dr. Pechal. He was at that moment too thoroughly impregnated with pleasurable emotions to admit of any other sensation. His first act, after recovering wind, was to draw forth the inevitable pocket note-book. From its pages to the pale little face and back again, he gazed with artless delight, as if comparing an excellent likeness with the original. One might detect, moreover, in his expression, the secret self-satisfaction of the successful artist. But, more skilful than his fellows, this man had drawn his portrait first, and by its means discovered the original afterward!

The comparison satisfactorily concluded, the artist pocketed his work, and surveyed his sitter complacently.

"How fortunate," he ejaculated, at last, "that you have turned out a woman! Had you been a man—" The doctor seemed loath to contemplate so fearful an alternative.

"Crazy!" thought the young lady, and an irrepressible shiver of horror ran through her.

"But being a woman," resumed the doctor, forcibly, "all may be well. Pray, take an interest in me! Believe me, I am no stranger to you, and our individual welfare depends exclusively upon each other."

"Do I understand you to say you are acquainted with me, sir?" demanded she, catching at the first hopeful straw.

"Ah, none better," replied the doctor. "You are not yet quite twenty—am I not fifty? You are rich—am I not poor? Your name is—" Here the doctor paused.

The young lady's hazel eyes were black with expectation.

"Caleph?" hazarded the doctor, with an insinuating grin, yet with an undertone of anxiety in his voice.

The young lady started, and blushed to the forehead. A moment she looked earnestly at the doctor with an indescribable expression; then burst forth into a most delicious little laugh.

"Well, now you *must* know me, though I don't remember you, I'm sure. And how strange that *he* never spoke of you either! But no," blushing again; "I'm not *that* yet—only Mabel Chapel still, if you please, sir," with ravishing severity.

"Chapel—Mabel Chapel," repeated the doctor, retiring behind his spectacles. It seemed to be all he heard, as it was certainly all he understood, of this remarkable little speech. "*Chapel*—ah, yes, yes; now, that certainly is wonderful!" And again a broad smile of delight disclosed those awful teeth.

Then he recovered himself, and turned to address his lovely companion once more. But the rattle of the wheels over the Fifth-Avenue pavement drowned the rest of the conversation for the present.

"Oh, nursie, he was so dreadful!" said Mabel, piteously, as old Christina, the time-honored domestic of the family, was combing out her hair that evening.

Christina had had the sole care of Mabel's amber hair ever since, twenty years ago, there had been any such hair to be cared for.

"Think not of him, my Mabelein," advised the old lady. "He was some crazy, runaway man."

"That's what I thought at first," rejoined Mabel. "But, nursie, he seemed to know all about me, even my engagement to Charlie, that *no* one knows, you know; why," said Mabel, blushing at the recollection, "he addressed me as Mrs. Caleph; and, when I told him I wasn't married yet, the horrid thing said I must marry *him*—and right-off, too, or we would both be dead! And then he went on and talked about all sorts of the strangest, most incomprehensible things, and read something to me out of a dirty note-book he had about groups and the law, and distributions, and literal identities, and I don't know what else. Wasn't it terrible?"

"But he is gone—he returns no more," said nursie, soothingly.

"Ah, but he does return," said Mabel, disconsolately. "He's coming here to-morrow night; he said he must come anyway to get my answer. Think of it! And I told him to come, then, because Charlie will be here, you know, and he can talk to him."

"What name has he, my Mabelein?" inquired Christina.

"Oh, some German name; I remember it reminded me somehow of your last name, nursie—'Lapech.' There was a 'pech' about it, and—oh, yes, I know, it was Pechal—Dr. Pechal."

Christina started so that, for almost the first time in her life, she pulled Mabel's hair.

"Ah!" screamed Mabel; then, catching sight of the old lady's face in the mirror, "why, nursie dear, what's the matter?"

"Nothing, my Liebchen, nothing; only that the name reminded old Christina of a time—long ago, before thou wast born, Mabelein—when she, too, was engaged to be married. Ah, that was a happy time!" sighed nursie.

"Tell me all about it, dear," said Mabel, persuasively; all matters of the heart were to her of paramount interest and importance.

"There is little to tell, Liebchen. He was stout, handsome, and brave; he wore a student's cap, and fought with the Schläger. He was wise, also; he knew more than all the professors. And he loved his Christinchen; and to me he was very dear," said the old lady, simply.

"But why didn't you marry him?" demanded Mabel.

"Ah, that is a sad history, Mabelein. Thou knowest we once were wealthy, and had rank. But a time came—we had lost our fortune—we were poor and unfortunate. But he was brave; he said: 'I will go, Christinchen, and see. I will make fortune for us all.' And he went, but I never after saw him, and I think he died, for I believe not he would ever forget his Christinchen."

"Poor, dear old nursie," said the tender-hearted Mabel, with tears standing in her sweet eyes. "And was this before you came to us?"

"Yes, Liebchen; your father and mother were then boarding at our house; and your dear mother, who is now dead, liked me and I her; so, when you went away, she took me to be nurse and to help her. I said: 'If he comes, I must leave you.' But he never came, and I am always here."

"Poor, dear, old nursie," thought Mabel, again, an hour later, as she lay with her cheek upon her hand, waiting for sleep. "And she never told me of it before! Well, some day perhaps he will come back and marry her, and then she will be as happy as—I shall be."

Do pleasant dreams always go by contraries?

"Do you mean to say, sir," demanded Charlie, who sat with Mabel's little trembling hand in his, "that you have evolved the law which regulates the time, place, and circumstances, of the death of every human being?"

"It is precisely that," replied Dr. Pechal, charmed at being so well understood. "Were the room not so dark, sir, I would ask you to look over my little book. All is explained there."

The doctor, calling late in the evening, had come upon Mabel and Charlie Caleph sitting together in the dusk; and, being a somewhat abrupt gentleman, he had entered upon his business at once, without waiting even for candles.

"But how do you know your law is true?" asked Mabel, defiantly.

"Is it not then logical?" said the doctor. "The insurance companies have gone so far as to establish the average age at which death comes: if a man die here at sixty, somewhere must die a boy of twelve, that the balance may be preserved. Is it probable that this balance should relate to age alone? Is there not also the balance of one sex against the other, of light against dark, of nation against nation, of temperament against temperament? Not even here can we draw the line; the farther we search, the more the conditions that arise: no trait, however subtle; no feature, however insignificant—but bears directly, however lightly, upon man's destiny. What could be more clear, more inevitable?"

Charlie and Mabel were silent; a strange chill seemed creeping around their hearts. The doctor's voice, all apparently remaining of him in the darkened room, sounded solemn and mysterious as he gave utterance to the thoughts which he had been all his life revolving. Wholly bound up in the contemplation of his awful theory, his words were not without an impressiveness even more powerful than ordinary eloquence.

"It is indeed strange," resumed he, "that mankind, continually prying after the mysteries of science and the laws of life, should never have set themselves to learn the most important and yet the simplest law which tells them when they are to die, and who shall die with them. For no man dies alone. There is a mysterious chain, formed of innumerable and invisible links, binding his life to that of others, be their number more or less. He is one of a group; and the breaking of that one chain is the dissolution of their common life."

"Can nothing hinder this law—if it be a law?" demanded Charlie.

"It is seldom possible," replied the doctor. "The only safety lies in marriage, which constitutes a new condition of things—annulling the old. But it must be no ordinary marriage. To be efficacious, the most exacting conditions have to be fulfilled. Of the many, it is only needful I should mention two: the husband and wife must belong to the same group, and their names must be composed of the same letters, differently arranged. And this," added the doctor, "bears upon my errand to-night."

Mabel shuddered, and drew nearer to Charlie, who passed his arm around her waist. Dr. Pechal proceeded:

"I have discovered, by the most exhaustive calculations, that before this hour to-morrow my death, and that of all my group, is destined to take place. My calculations also showed that one at least of the group must be a resident of this city. I knew there were but three besides myself: one, whom I was personally acquainted with"— the doctor cleared his throat—"was not to be thought of, though she once might have saved us all; of the two others remaining, one I knew to be a woman, and, trusting she might be the New-Yorker, I came here to seek her, and in the person of this young lady I have found her. She is a member of my group; and she, as her name proclaims her, is destined to save us both by uniting her destiny to mine. Analyze our names—you find them literally identical; and for the rest, the proofs are easy and irrefragable."

Here the doctor paused, and, holding out one of his fat hands, seemed duskily to summon Mabel from her lover's side. Charlie groaned, and removed his arm from her waist; but hers was around his neck in an instant, and her voice was clear and firm:

"Whether your hateful theory be a truth or a falsehood, neither it nor you shall ever part us. Do you suppose I care so much for my life here as to sell, for its sake, all that is most sacred and precious to me? You have much to learn, with all your wisdom. Did it never occur to you that there is a Life, somewhere, which no theory of yours can ever reach? And that very death, by which you seek to enslave me, shall be the means of my triumph over you!"

The doctor was awe-stricken and silent, and Charlie, who could scarce believe this to be the modest and tender little girl whom he had loved, and thought he knew, looked up at her with a reverence he had never felt before. "You are right, darling," he murmured, but sighing heavily. "Death is better than such a life as that."

"It is but an alternative of death," she answered, "one of the body, the other of the soul. But do not sigh, my love. What this man says is false; no divine law could authorize such a consummation. I do not believe his theory!"

At this, Dr. Pechal, who had been edging toward the door, advanced again into the room, and spoke with emphasis:

"You say you do not believe my theory? Very well! The proof is at any rate easy. Twenty-four hours will show; and I, at least, am ready to die in defence of what I have spent my life to verify."

As he turned to depart, the door opened, admitting a glare of light—Christina with two tall wax-candles. The doctor was dazzled, and shaded his face with his hand. Christina looked keenly at him as she placed the candles on the table.

"It is already so dark, Fräulein," said she, "and as the gentleman is here," turning to the doctor, "I thought the candles would be pleasant to you."

At the sound of her voice, Dr. Pechal started, and seemed strangely agitated. He peered earnestly at the speaker through his spectacles.

"You may go, Christina," said Mabel.

"Christina!" cried the doctor, in a tremulous voice, "Christina! Christina Lapech! can it be thou?" He stretched toward her his stumpy hands, which shook as if with an ague.

Christina gazed at him as if he were a ghost. At last she gave a low cry, pathetic and loving.

"Ah! Emil, my own Emil! after twenty years, hast thou come back to me?"

And what did these ridiculous old creatures proceed to do, but fall into each other's arms and blubber like two children; putting the younger lovers to the blush with the fervor of their emotion, bursting freshly through the cerements of a lifetime! . . . .

So the candles had at least as much to do with Dr. Pechal's destiny as the omnibus. Several other dusky points were also illuminated by their light. As soon as he had recovered himself, and things had begun to settle, the doctor recognized in Charlie Caleph the fourth member of the group.

"A remarkable coincidence!" and, after a moment's reflection, "Sir, I have not yet learned your name—except the first one. What is the last?"

"Why, Dr. Pechal!" exclaimed Mabel, in large-eyed wonderment, "how can you help knowing his name, when you addressed me in the omnibus as Mrs. Caleph?"

Upon which it transpired that the doctor had, in fact, known nothing either of her name or engagement; but had hazarded a name containing the same letters as his own, feeling that in case it turned out to be the correct one, he could lay a strong claim to the possession of her hand. The little game at cross-purposes which had ensued, ending in a solution which answered his purpose equally well, had banished his first guess from his mind. Now, as the reader has long ago divined, its appearance as the surname of our friend Charlie at once established *his* right to Mabel by the ruling of that very law which had at first seemed so adverse to their happiness.

And Dr. Pechal, it is needless to remark, was more than ready to forego his claim in one whom he already regarded with ridiculous awe, for the sake of her who, lost through so many years, he had long ago given up as married and done for. "And thou art rewarded for thy constancy, Christinchen," said the old hypocrite, sententiously; "for, hadst thou been married, and our union impossible, so also would have been the preservation of our lives." Charlie's eyes had a quiet twinkle in them; he was thinking what a constant man the doctor had been lately.

"The law has been very lenient to all of us," perorated the doctor; "seldom do all the members of a group possess the qualifications for intermarriage, or the opportunity to profit by the privilege if they have it."

"I'm afraid, doctor," said Charlie, "you'll never forgive those unfortunate candles for depriving you of the chance to prove your theory correct; though even yet, if you insist upon it, it is not too late."

"No, no!" said Dr. Pechal, rather gruffly; "after all, there would be no satisfaction in it; for not one of you would remain alive long enough to confess yourselves convinced."

And, as far as they are concerned, the theory still lacks confirmation.

"Dusty Death"

Violet M. Methley

"Dust—dust everywhere!" The whining, monotonous voice rose shrill. "It's impossible to keep things clean in this house, Mr. Corfield. The maids and I spend all our time in trying, and we *never* succeed! Ordinary London dirt is bad enough, but when it comes to antiques as well—"

"That's the penalty of marrying a scientist, Mrs. Marinder. The house is a regular museum."

"I hate them—the mummies, the curiosities, all of them." (The whine took a sharper note.) "The way they harbour dust . . . it's not natural. A human house isn't their right place."

Dr. Paul Marinder laughed softly.

"My wife, as you see, has a violent spite against my unfortunate mummies, Corfield!" he said, in his pleasant, gentle voice. "And, after all, the poor souls can't help the fact that they found 'the way to dusty death,' as Shakespeare calls it, so many centuries ago!"

"But *you* could help bringing them here and keeping them here!" Mrs. Marinder snapped. "They ought to be decently buried, I say."

"Well, perhaps they shall be some day, my dear."

Dr. Marinder spoke pacifically. He was a slim, upright man, under forty, with fair hair and a pink complexion—something, too, that was wistful and appealing in his blue eyes. The contrast to his wife was amazing. Mrs. Marinder was at least twenty years his senior, tall, gaunt, with a jaundiced skin and iron-grey hair. Her brown eyes were lustreless, and upon her upper lip was a large and disfiguring fleshy wart. Her dress was of the colour of coffeegrounds outlined in passementerie. Altogether, she was a woman, one would say, born to be a companion—but not to a man.

To Stephen Corfield, freshly home from South Africa, and meeting his friend's wife for the first time, the question why Marinder should have married her was quite unanswerable, until the solution was given by Mrs. Marinder herself.

"I really think I might have *some* say in the matter—considering that all the horrid things are bought with *my* money. . . ."

Dr. Marinder's colour deepened to crimson, but he spoke gently.

"And you'd far rather spend it on vacuum cleaners and linoleum, wouldn't you, Amelia? Never mind; you've enough for—anything."

Corfield noticed the tiny pause before the final word.

"Enough to buy *you*, body and soul, you poor devil!" he thought.

Mrs. Marinder whined on.

"There won't be much left at this rate," she nagged. "When you are talking about this new expedition to Egypt. . . . If you'd seen the state of the library last week, Mr. Corfield, after my husband had unwrapped a mummy hawk—the dust was inches thick—inches!"

Corfield rose at this point to take his leave. He felt that he could not endure that whining voice another minute.

"I'm afraid I must be off, Mrs. Marinder," he said. "But I shall see you next Sunday, then—at lunchtime—one o'clock."

Corfield was mistaken. He went to the gloomy house in Bloomsbury on the following Sunday, but he did not see Mrs. Marinder.

The servant who opened the door looked flurried and anxious. She answered his question doubtfully.

"Yes, sir—I suppose that Dr. Marinder will see you—"

"Why shouldn't he? He isn't ill, is he—or Mrs. Marinder?"

"No, sir—not as I know, sir—I'll inquire, sir."

As he waited Corfield glanced from object to object in the dingy, overcrowded hall, lined with antiquities. The servant returned.

"Dr. Marinder will see you, sir," she said.

In the library, lined with books and encased mummies, Corfield found Marinder pacing to and fro, his white face and fair hair gleaming through the foggy gloom. He burst into speech at once.

"Corfield, an awful thing has happened! My wife has disappeared—since yesterday morning, about lunchtime."

"Your wife?" Corfield stared at him in amazement. "Your *wife*? Oh, but she must have been called away somewhere. You'll hear tomorrow, of course, there is no post today."

Marinder shook his head.

"She wouldn't have gone like that. And she has no relations—no one likely to want her in a hurry. Something has happened, Corfield. There's been foul play. I feel it—I'm *sure* of it!" There was agonised conviction in Marinder's face and voice. Glancing at him, an amazing thought flashed through Corfield's mind: "Good God! He *cared* for her!"

"You don't think that she—that there was—" He broke off impotently. No! There could be no question of a man in *this* case. But there were hospitals—police stations—

"We've searched everywhere," said Marinder, helplessly. "We've asked everyone. And she was so devoted to her own home." His voice broke with an emotion which was obviously genuine. "I—I *know* she is dead."

Marinder's prophecy was verified. Many people may remember, more or less vaguely, the sensation which was caused by Mrs. Marinder's disappearance, the theories and counter-theories, the false trails ending in blind alleys. It was not for more than six months that Marinder himself gave up hope—or rather, gave up the search, for his hopelessness was plain from the first.

The two men were sitting together in the smoking-room of the club, where Marinder had taken up his abode temporarily, shutting up the Bloomsbury house. Leaning forward, he burst out suddenly:

"I can't stand England—I simply can't. I must go out to Egypt and get to work. It's the only thing left now. Nothing but want of funds brought me to a standstill before. Now that obstacle doesn't exist—" He broke off, sighing wearily and hopelessly.

Corfield felt a sudden pang of sympathy and self-reproach.

"I suppose there was something in her which I couldn't see," he thought. "There *must* have been—to make him feel like that."

"There's one thing I want to ask of you, Corfield," Marinder said. "Will you promise that, if anything happens to me—"

"Oh, come, Marinder! Don't be so pessimistic!"

"It's always possible. I've appointed you executor in my will. I want to be sure that all the antiques—all the mummies and their cases—go to the British Museum. It's what Amelia wished, too. You heard her say it—that they should go to a *proper* museum."

He smiled drearily, and Corfield gave the required promise.

He saw Marinder off at Victoria a few days later, and for the following six months received fairly regular letters from him, reporting progress in his researches. And then Corfield received a cablegram.

It informed him, curtly and baldly, that Dr. Marinder had been drowned in the Nile when bathing.

It was with an odd sense of taking part in a solemn religious ceremony that Corfield admitted himself, with Marinder's latchkey, into the Bloomsbury house, one morning some little time after he had received the news. He felt rather miserable, for Marinder's death hurt more than he had reckoned with, but at the same time a vague sense of relief filled him. After all, the poor chap had looked desperately unhappy. It didn't seem as though life had been much good to him since his wife's disappearance.

The big house was full of yellow, grimy fog—full of the stale smell of dust and closeness as Corfield entered the hall. From their perches the ape-faced, cat-faced deities grinned down at him more malignantly than usual. The very air seemed heavy with sinister meanings and knowledge.

The museum required a definite, detailed list of the objects in question, and Corfield set to work with notebook and pencil, steadily and methodically, starting with the crowded staircase and the overcrowded entrance-hall. It was not until some three or four hours later that he reached the study, where the most valuable part of the collection was kept. Here the mummies of various periods stood in their plain or ornate cases, with one or two unwrapped specimens in long glass coffins. Here were the shelves full of those costly works in a dozen languages which dealt with the processes of mummy-burial.

The first ardour of Corfield's industry was by this time blunted. He was dusty, tired, thirsty, heartily sick of the job, disposed to dawdle, to waste time in a lingering examination of the specimens.

He stopped before a large and elaborate mummy-case, outside which was painted the face of a beautiful woman, dark-eyed, warmly coloured, with hair rippled like ribbed, brown sand.

"I wonder if the mummy inside is still like her portrait outside," he thought. "Or whether there's any mummy left at all. Perhaps it's crumbled away entirely—perhaps it was never there in Marinder's time. . . . I suppose, by the way, that's one of the things I really ought to know, to put down in this blessed list."

He caught at the idea, tired of the monotonous business of inventory-making. He examined the case closely, and found that it could be prised open, with no particular difficulty, showing the plainer case within.

Laughing at himself for idle curiosity, yet with one side of his brain obstinately persuading itself that this was a legitimate part of his duty to Marinder and the Museum, Corfield lowered the long case to the ground and knelt beside it. He opened both coffers easily enough, and found within a thick layer of pungent-smelling dust.

He remembered poor Mrs. Marinder's bitterness on the subject, and laughed as he scraped away the soft powder. It covered a swathed shape, showing that the mummy itself was still there. When the dust was cleared away, Corfield came upon the folds of brownish linen, tucked round and about the stiff form beneath.

This removed, he saw at last the shrivelled, parchment-like face—a face which held no faintest trace of the beauty to be found in the dead woman's portrait upon the outer case.

And as Corfield looked at the face of the mummy, the linen which he was still holding fell from his limp clasp, and he knelt there—staring—staring.

His body was still, but his imagination moved actively. It seemed to him that there were others beside him in the library—a man and woman facing each other in anger. He heard again a nagging, querulous whine; heard complaints, abuse, reiterated vauntings of the possession of that money for which Marinder had sold himself, body and soul. He saw, in imagination, the clear pink-and-white of Marinder's skin turning to a dull crimson—that danger signal.

After that he could visualise no details. He was aware of a locked door, of a silent house, which held only one living thing—and one which was not alive. Marinder had known all that living man could know of the methods by which mummies were made. Here, in his library and laboratory, were gathered together the appliances, the chemicals, the spices. And the face of the mummy which lay in that inner case had, upon the upper-lip, a withered, fleshy wart.

THE DUTCH OFFICER'S STORY

CATHERINE CROWE

YOU KNOW THE BELGIAN REBELLION (HE ALWAYS CALLED IT SO) TOOK PLACE IN 1830. It broke out at Brussels on the 28th of August, and we immediately advanced with a considerable force to attack that city; but as the Prince of Orange hoped to bring the people to reason, without bloodshed, we encamped at Vilvorde, whilst he entered Brussels alone, to hold a conference with the armed people. I was a Lieutenant-Colonel then, and commanded the 20th foot, to which regiment I had been lately appointed.

We had been three or four days in cantonment, when I heard two of the men, who were digging a little drain at the back of my tent, talking of Jokel Falck, a private in my regiment, who was noted for his extraordinary disposition to somnolence, one of them remarked that he would certainly have got into trouble for being asleep on his post the previous night, if it had not been for Mungo. "I don't know how many times he has saved him," added he.

To which the other answered, that Mungo was a very valuable friend, and had saved many a man from punishment.

This was the first time I had ever heard of Mungo, and I rather wondered who it was they alluded to; but the conversation slipt from my mind and I never thought of asking any body.

Shortly after this I was going my rounds, being field-officer of the day, when I saw by the moonlight, the sentry at one of the outposts stretched upon the ground. I was some way off when I first perceived him; and I only knew what the object was from the situation, and because I saw the glitter of his accoutrements; but almost at the same moment that I discovered him, I observed a large black Newfoundland dog trotting towards him. The man rose as the dog approached, and had got upon his legs before I reached the spot. This occupied the space of about two minutes—perhaps, not so much.

"You were asleep on your post," I said; and turning to the mounted orderly that attended me, I told him to go back and bring a file of the guard to take him prisoner, and to send a sentry to relieve him.

"Non, mon colonel," said he, and from the way he spoke I perceived he was intoxicated, "it's all the fault of that *damné* Mungo. Il m'a manqué."

But I paid no attention to what he said and rode on, concluding *Mungo* was some slang term of the men for drink.

Some evenings after this, I was riding back from my brother's quarter—he was in the 15th, and was stationed about a mile from us—when I remarked the same dog I had seen before, trot up to a sentry who, with his legs crossed, was leaning against a wall. The man started, and began walking backwards and forwards on his beat. I recognised the dog by a large white streak on his side—all the rest of his coat being black.

When I came up to the man, I saw it was Jokel Falck, and although I could not have said he was asleep, I strongly suspected that that was the fact.

"You had better take care of yourself, my man," said I. "I have half a mind to have you relieved, and make a prisoner of you. I believe I should have found you asleep on your post, if that dog had not roused you."

Instead of looking penitent, as was usual on these occasions, I saw a half smile on the man's face, as he saluted me.

"Whose dog is that?" I asked my servant, as I rode away.

"Je ne sais pas mon, Colonel," he answered, smiling too.

On the same evening at mess, I heard one of the subalterns say to the officer who sat next him, "It's a fact, I assure you, and they call him Mungo."

"That's a new name they've got for Schnapps, isn't it?" I said.

"No, sir; it's the name of a dog," replied the young man, laughing.

"A black Newfoundland, with a large white streak on his flank?"

"Yes, sir, I believe that is the description," replied he, tittering still.

"I have seen that dog two or three times," said I. "I saw him this evening—who does he belong to?"

"Well, sir, that is a difficult question," answered the lad; and I heard his companion say, "To Old Nick, I should think."

"Do you mean to say you've really seen Mungo?" said somebody at the table.

"If Mungo is a large Newfoundland—black, with a white streak on its side—I saw him just now. Who does he belong to?"

By this time, the whole mess table was in a titter, with the exception of one old captain, a man who had been years in the regiment. He was of very humble extraction, and had risen by merit to his present position.

"I believe Captain T. is better acquainted with Mungo than anybody present," answered Major R., with a sneer. "Perhaps he can tell you who he belongs to."

The laughter increased, and I saw there was some joke, but not understanding what it meant, I said to Captain G., "Does the dog belong to Jokel Falck?'

"No, sir," he replied, "the dog belongs to nobody now. He once belonged to an officer called Joseph Atveld."

"Belonging to this regiment?"

"Yes, sir."

"He is dead, I suppose?"

"Yes, sir, he is."

"And the dog has attached himself to the regiment?"

"Yes, sir."

During this conversation, the suppressed laughter continued, and every eye was fixed on Captain T., who answered me shortly, but with the utmost gravity.

"In fact," said the major, contemptuously, "according to Captain T., Mungo is the ghost of a deceased dog."

This announcement was received with shouts of laughter, in which I confess I joined, whilst Captain T. still retained an unmoved gravity.

"It is easier to laugh at such a thing than to believe it, sir," said he. "*I* believe it, because I know it."

I smiled, and turned the conversation.

If anybody at the table except Captain T. had made such an assertion as this, I should have ridiculed them without mercy; but he was an old man, and from the circumstances I have mentioned regarding his origin, we were careful not to offend him; so no more was said about Mungo, and in the hurry of events that followed, I never thought of it again. We marched on to Brussels the next day; and after that, had enough to do till we went to Antwerp, where we were besieged by the French the following year.

During the siege, I sometimes heard the name of Mungo again; and, one night, when I was visiting the guards and sentries as grand rounds, I caught a glimpse of him, and I felt sure that the man he was approaching when I observed him, had been asleep; but he was screened by an angle of the bastion, and by the time I turned the corner, he was moving about.

This brought to my mind all I had heard about the dog; and as the circumstance was curious, in any point of view, I mentioned what I had seen to Captain T. the next day, saying, "I saw your friend Mungo, last night."

"Did you, sir?" said he. "It's a strange thing! No doubt, the man was asleep!"

"But do you seriously mean to say, that you believe this to be a visionary dog, and not a dog of flesh and blood?"

"I do, sir; I have been quizzed enough about it; and, once or twice, have nearly got into a quarrel, because people will persist in laughing at what they know nothing about; but as sure as that is a sword you hold in your hand, so sure is that dog a spectre, or ghost—if such a word is applicable to a four-footed beast!"

"But, it's impossible!" I said. "What reason have you for such an extraordinary belief!"

"Why, you know, sir, man-and-boy, I have been in the regiment all my life. I was born in it. My father was pay-serjeant of No. 3 company, when he died; and I have seen Mungo myself, perhaps twenty times, and known, positively, of others seeing him twice as many more."

"Very possibly; but that is no proof, that it is not some dog that has attached himself to the regiment."

"But I have seen and heard of the dog for fifty years, sir; and my father before me, had seen and heard of him as long!"

"Well, certainly, that is extraordinary,—if you are sure of it, and that it's the same dog!"

"It's a remarkable dog, sir. You won't see another like it with that large white streak on his flank. He won't let one of our sentries be found asleep, if he can help; unless, indeed, the fellow is drunk. He seems to have less care of drunkards, but Mungo has saved many a man from punishment. I was once, not a little indebted to him myself. My sister was married out of the regiment, and we had had a bit of a festivity, and drank rather too freely at the wedding, so that when I mounted guard that night—I wasn't to say, drunk, but my head was a little gone, or so; and I should have been caught nodding; but Mungo, knowing, I suppose, that I was not an habitual drunkard, woke me just in time."

"How did he wake you?" I asked.

"I was roused by a short, sharp bark, that sounded close to my ears. I started up, and had just time to catch a glimpse of Mungo before he vanished!"

"Is that the way he always wakes the men?"

"So they say; and, as they wake, he disappears."

I recollected now, that on each occasion when I had observed the dog, I had, somehow, lost sight of him in an instant; and, my curiosity being awakened, I asked Captain T., if ours were the only men he took charge of, or, whether he showed the same attention to those of other regiments?

"Only the 20th, sir; the tradition is, that after the battle of Fontenoy, a large black mastiff was found lying beside a dead officer. Although he had a dreadful wound from a sabre cut on his flank, and was much exhausted from loss of blood, he would not leave the body; and even after we buried it, he could not be enticed from the spot. The men, interested by the fidelity and attachment of the animal, bound up his wounds, and fed and tended him; and he became the dog of the regiment. It is said, that they had taught him to go his rounds before the guards and sentries were visited, and to wake any men that slept. How this may be, I cannot say; but he remained with the regiment till his death, and was buried with all the respect they could show him. Since that, he has shown his gratitude in the way I tell you, and of which you have seen some instances."

"I suppose the white streak is the mark of the sabre cut. I wonder you never fired at him."

"God forbid sir, I should do such a thing," said Captain T., looking sharp round at me. "It's said that a man did so once, and that he never had any luck afterwards; that may be a superstition, but I confess I wouldn't take a good deal to do it."

"If, as you believe, it's a spectre, it could not be hurt, you know; I imagine ghostly dogs are impervious to bullets."

"No doubt, sir; but I shouldn't like to try the experiment. Besides, it would be useless, as I am convinced already."

I pondered a good deal upon this conversation with the old captain. I had never for a moment entertained the idea that such a thing was possible. I should have as much expected to meet the minotaur or a flying dragon as a ghost of any sort, especially the ghost of a dog; but the evidence here was certainly startling. I had never observed anything like weakness and credulity about T.; moreover, he was a man of known courage, and very much respected in the regiment. In short, so much had his earnestness on the subject staggered me, that I resolved whenever it was my turn to visit the guards and sentries, that I would carry a pistol with me ready primed and loaded, in order to settle the question. If T. was right, there would be an interesting fact established, and no harm done; if, as I could not help suspecting, it was a cunning trick of the men, who had trained this dog to wake them, while they kept up the farce of the spectre, the animal would be well out of the way; since their reliance on him no doubt led them to give way to drowsiness when they would otherwise have struggled against it; indeed, though none of our men had been detected—thanks, perhaps, to Mungo—there had been so much negligence lately in the garrison that the general had issued very severe orders on the subject.

However, I carried my pistol in vain; I did not happen to fall in with Mungo; and some time afterwards, on hearing the thing alluded to at the mess-table, I mentioned what I had done, adding, "Mungo is too knowing, I fancy, to run the risk of getting a bullet in him."

"Well," said Major B., "I should like to have a shot at him, I confess. If I thought I had any chance of seeing him, I'd certainly try it; but I've never seen him at all."

"Your best chance," said another, "is when Jokel Falck is on duty. He is such a sleepy scoundrel, that the men say if it was not for Mungo he'd pass half his time in the guard house."

"If I could catch him I'd put an ounce of lead into him; that he may rely on."

"Into Jokel Falck, sir?" said one of the subs, laughing.

"No, sir," replied Major R.; "into Mungo—and I'll do it, too."

"Better not, sir," said Captain T., gravely; provoking thereby a general titter round the table.

Shortly after this, as I was one night going to my quarter, I saw a mounted orderly ride in and call out a file of the guard to take a prisoner.

"What's the matter?" I asked.

"One of the sentries asleep on his post, sir; I believe it's Jokel Falek."

"It will be the last time, whoever it is," I said; "for the general is determined to shoot the next man that's caught."

"I should have thought Mungo had stood Jokel Falck's friend, so often that he'd never have allowed him to be caught," said the adjutant. "Mungo has neglected his duty."

"No, sir," said the orderly, gravely. "Mungo would have waked him; but Major R. shot at him."

"And killed him," I said.

The man made no answer, but touched his cap and rode away.

I heard no more of the affair that night; but the next morning, at a very early hour, my servant woke me, saying that Major R. wished to speak to me. I desired he should be admitted, and the moment he entered the room, I saw by his countenance that something serious had occurred; of course, I thought the enemy had gained some unexpected advantage during the night, and sat up in bed inquiring eagerly what had happened.

To my surprise he pulled out his pocket-handkerchief and burst into tears. He had married a native of Antwerp, and his wife was in the city at this time. The first thing that occurred to me was, that she had met with some accident, and I mentioned her name.

"No, no," he said; "my son, my boy, my poor Fritz!"

You know that in our service, every officer first enters his regiment as a private soldier, and for a certain space of time does all the duties of that position. The major's son, Fritz, was thus in his noviciate. I concluded he had been killed by a stray shot, and for a minute or two I remained in this persuasion, the major's speech being choked by his sobs. The first words he uttered were—

"Would to God I had taken Captain T.'s advice!"

"About what?" I said. "What has happened to Fritz?"

"You know," said he, "yesterday I was field officer of the day; and when I was going my rounds last night, I happened to ask my orderly, who was assisting to put on my sash, what men we had told off for the guard. Amongst others, he named Jokel Falck, and remembering the conversation the other day at the mess table, I took one of my pistols out of the holster, and, after loading, put it in my pocket. I did not expect to see the dog, for I had never seen him; but as I had no doubt that the story of the spectre was some dodge of the men, I determined if ever I did, to have a shot at him. As I was going through the Place de Meyer, I fell in with the general, who joined me, and we rode on together, talking of the siege. I had forgotten all about the dog, but when we came to the rampart, above the Bastion du Matte, I suddenly saw exactly such an animal as the one described, trotting beneath us. I knew there must be a sentry immediately below where we rode, though I could not see him, and I had no doubt that the animal was making towards him; so without saying a word, I drew out my pistol and fired, at the same moment jumping off my horse, in order to look over the bastion, and get a sight of the man. Without comprehending what I was about, the general did the same, and there we saw the sentry lying on his face, fast asleep."

"And the body of the dog?" said I.

"Nowhere to be seen," he answered, "and yet I must have hit him—I fired bang into him. The general says it must have been a delusion, for he was looking exactly in the same direction, and saw no dog at all—but I am certain I saw him, so did the orderly."

"But Fritz?" I said.

"It was Fritz—Fritz was the sentry," said the major, with a fresh burst of grief. "The court-martial sits this morning, and my boy will be shot, unless interest can be made with the general to grant him a pardon."

I rose and drest myself immediately, but with little hope of success. Poor Fritz being the son of an officer, was against him rather than otherwise—it would have been considered an act of favouritism to spare him. He was shot; his poor mother died of a broken heart, and the major left the service immediately after the surrender of the city."

"And have you ever seen Mungo again?" said I.

"No," he replied; "but I have heard of others seeing him."

"And are you convinced that it was a spectre, and not a dog of flesh and blood?"

"I fancy I was then—but, of course, one can't believe—"

"Oh, no," I rejoined; "oh, no; never mind facts, if they don't fit into our theories."

The Effigy

G. Ranger Wormser

"Mr. Evans is upstairs in the library, ma'am." Genevieve Evans hurried through the hall and up the steps. She pulled off her gloves as she went. She rolled them into a hard, small ball and tucked them automatically in her muff.

She had hoped that she would get there before him. She had been thinking of that all during the quick rush home. She would have liked to have had a moment to pull herself together. After what she had been through she wondered if she could keep from going all to pieces. It could not be helped. She did not even know if she cared a lot about it. She was quite numbed. He was there ahead of her; there in the library. Of all the rooms in the house that he should have chosen the one so rarely used. The room she hated.

At the door of the library she paused breathless.

For a second she thought the long dark room empty.

Then she saw Ernest.

He was standing in one of the deep windows. A short squat figure black against the dim yellow of the velvet curtains. One hand held his cigarette; the fingers of the other hand tapped unevenly on the window glass.

She knew then that he must have seen her come into the house.

"Ernest."

He turned.

"I've been waiting for you," he told her with studied indifference. "Where've you been, Jenny?"

She took a step into the room.

"I'm sorry, Ernest. I didn't know you'd be home so early."

"It's late. Where've you been?"

She wondered why she should bother avoiding answering his question.

"Oh—out."

Her tone was vague.

"No," he scoffed. "I wouldn't have guessed it. Really, I wouldn't!"

She loosened the fur from her neck and tossed it onto the center table.

"Don't, Ernest."

"Don't what, Jenny?"

She sank down into the depths of the nearest chair.

"Oh—nothing." Her hands clinched themselves. "Nothing."

He came and stood quite close to her. He glanced quickly at her, puffing the while at his cigarette. She thought he looked wicked and pagan; hideous and yellow behind the rising smoke. His narrow eyes peered at her.

"Well, Jenny—out with it, my girl. Where've you been?"

She looked away from him. Her face was pale. In the twilight shadowed room he had seen how wide and strange her eyes were.

She made up her mind then that it was not worth bothering about. She would tell him the truth. She did not care how he took it.

"I've been to see—; to—see—father—"

She whispered the words. Her eyes wavered back to his face.

"Good heavens!" He laughed harshly. "After all you said?"

"Yes."

"Rather a joke, that."

"No. There wasn't anything funny about it."

"Well. Was the old man surprised?"

"No. He told me he knew I'd come—some time."

"Wise old beggar, Daniel Drare!"

Her breath came quickly; unevenly.

"He's a devil, Ernest! That's what he is—; he's—"

He interrupted her.

"Not so fast, Jenny. You went there to see him, you know."

"But, Ernest, I couldn't stand it any longer. I—simply—couldn't—"

He walked deliberately over to the screened fire-place and tossed his cigarette into it.

"Why d'you go to him?"

"You know why I went."

"Why!"

She had felt right along that he must be made to understand it. She could not see why he had not known before.

"Oh, don't pretend any more. I'm sick of it. You know I'm sick of it."

His brows drew together in an angry frown.

"Sick of what? Eh, Jenny?"

Her eyes crept away from his and went miserably about the room. They took no note of the rare old furniture; of the dark paneled walls; of the color mellowed tapestries. She sat looking at it all blindly. Then her eyes raised themselves a bit. She found herself staring at the picture hung just above the wood carved mantel. The famous picture. The work of the great artist. The picture before which she had stood and hated; and hated. The picture which was the pride and portrait of her father, Daniel Drare.

She got to her feet.

"I'm sick of you—"; she said it quite calmly. "And—I'm sick—of—him." She nodded her head in the direction of the portrait. "I'd do anything to get away from both of you—anything!"

He smiled.

"You'll not get away from me," he told her.

"You—!" The one word was contemptuous. "You don't really count."

"What d'you mean?"

He still smiled.

"I mean what I say." Her voice was tired. "You're nothing—; nothing but—oh, a kind of a henchman to him. That's all you are. Not that he needs you. He doesn't need any one. He's too unscrupulously powerful for that. He's never needed any one. Not you. Nor—me. He didn't even need my mother. He broke her heart and let her die because he didn't need her. I think you know he's like that. You're no different where he's concerned than the others."

"After all—I'm your husband!"

"That's the ghastly part of it. You—my—husband. You're only my husband because of him. You knew that when I married you, didn't you? You knew the lies he told me when he wanted me to marry you. You never contradicted them. And I was too silly, too young to know. I wanted to get away from it all; and from him. I couldn't guess that you—d'you think, Ernest, if it hadn't been for those lies I'd have married you? Do you?"

"Oh, I don't know. I usually get what I want, Jenny."

"And why do you get it? Why?"

"Perhaps because I want it."

She laughed harshly.

"Because Daniel Drare gets it for you. Because he's had everything all his life. Because he's behind you for the time being. That's why!"

"And what if it is?"

"My God!" She muttered. "I can't make you understand. I can't even talk to either of you."

"You went to see him!"

"I went to him to tell him I couldn't stand it any longer. I begged him to help me; just—this—once—I told him I couldn't go on this way. I told him I couldn't bear any more. I told him the truth; that I'd—I'd go mad."

"What did he say? Eh, Jenny?"

For a second her eyes closed.

"He laughed. Laughed—"

"Of course!"

"There's no 'of course' about it. I'm serious. Deadly serious."

"Don't be a fool, Jenny. If you ask me I'd say you were mighty well off. Your father gives you everything you want. Your husband gives you everything you want. There isn't a man in the whole city who has more power than Daniel Drare. Or more money for that matter. You ought to be jolly well satisfied."

She waited a full moment before speaking.

"Maybe I'm a fool, Ernest. Maybe I am. A weak, helpless kind of a fool. But I'm not happy, Ernest. I can't go this kind of a life any more. It's gotten unreal and horrible. And the kind of things you do to make money; the kind of things you're proud of. They prey on me, Ernest. There's nothing about all this that's clean. It's making me ill; the rottenness of this sort of living. I'm not happy. Doesn't that mean anything to you?"

"Nonsense. You've no reason for not being happy. The trouble with you, Jenny, is that you've too lively an imagination."

"Oh, no, Ernest. I've got to get away. Somewhere—anywhere. Just by myself. I don't love you, Ernest. You don't really love me. It's only because I'm Daniel Drare's daughter that you married me. It was just his wealth and his power and—and his unscrupulous self that fascinated you."

"You don't know what you're saying."

"I do, I do, Ernest! You'd like to be like him. But you can't. You are like him in a lot of ways. The little ways. But you're not big enough to be really like him. Let me go, Ernest. Before it's too late;—let me go!"

He came and put a hand on her shoulder.

"I'll never let you go," he said.

"You must!" She whispered. "You've got to let me. Just to get away from all this. I've never been away in all my life. He'd never let me go—either."

Unconsciously her eyes went up to the picture.

The full, red face with the hard lines in it. The thick, sensual lips. The small, cunning eyes that laughed. The ponderous, heavy set of the figure. The big, powerful hands.

His gaze followed after hers.

And very suddenly he left her side. He walked over to the mantel.

"Funny," he muttered to himself. "Jolly strange—that!"

Her fingers clutched at her breast.

"Ernest—! What're you doing?"

"Can you see anything wrong here, Jenny?"

He was looking up at the portrait.

"Wrong?" She said it beneath her breath. "Wrong—"

He reached up a hand. He drew his fingers across the canvas.

"By Jove!" His voice was excited. "So it is. Thought I wasn't crazy. When could it have happened, eh? Ever notice this, Jenny?"

She could not take her eyes from his hand that was going over and over the canvas along the arm of the painted figure.

"Can't you see it, Jenny?"

"I—I can't see anything."

She whispered it.

"Come over here—; where I am."

She hesitated.

"Ernest, what's the sense? How can you see in this light anyway, how—"

He did not let her finish.

"Come here!"

Slowly she went toward him.

"What is it, Ernest? What?"

"A crack?" His hand still worked across it. "In the paint—here along the arm. Or a cut, or something. How under the sun could it have happened? We've got to have it fixed somehow. Never heard of such a thing before. Old Daniel Drare'll be as sore as a crab if ever he gets wind of this. It'd be like hurting him to touch this portrait. He certainly does think the world of it! How could it have happened;— that's what I'd like to know."

"I—I don't know what you're talking about—I—!"

"Here! Can't you see it? It's as plain as the nose on your face. Along the arm. It's a cut. Right into the canvas. You can run your finger in it. Give me your hand."

She shrank back from him.

"No—no, Ernest."

He stared at her intently.

"You do look seedy. You'd better go up and lie down. I've got to dress for dinner, anyway. We'll have to have this fixed."

He started for the door.

She blocked his way.

"Will—you—let—me—go, Ernest?"

"Don't start that again."

"All right. I won't!"

"That's a sensible girl, Jenny. Even your father had to laugh at you when you told him the way you feel. It isn't natural. It's just nerves, I guess. You could stick it out with Daniel Drare. You can stick it out with me. Look here, Daniel Drare's a great old fellow, but I'm not as crude in some things as he is; am I, Jenny?"

"You would be if you could." Her voice was singsong. "You haven't his strength; that's all."

"I'm not as crude as he is."

"You haven't his strength," she droned.

"I've enough strength to keep you here; if that's what you mean."

"No, it's not what I mean." A puzzled look crept across her face. Her eyes were suddenly furtive. "Maybe I don't know what I mean. But I don't think it's you. I don't think you count. It's him. It's Daniel Drare! He's behind it all. I don't think I quite know what I'll do about it. I must do something! I mustn't be angry!"

He stared at her.

"You'd best come along if you're going to dress."

"I'll be up in a moment," she said.

When he was gone she went over to the window.

She stood there gazing out into the darkened quiet side-street. She was trembling in every limb. Now and again she would half turn. Her eyes would go slowly, warily toward the portrait hanging there over the mantel and then they would hurry away again.

She started nervously when the butler knocked at the door.

"What is it, Williams?"

"Mr. Drare's housekeeper, ma'am. She'd like to see you, ma'am. I said I'd ask."

"Show her in here, Williams."

The man left the room.

She walked over to the farther corner of the room and switched on the lights.

She heard footsteps in the hall.

She stood quite still; waiting.

Footsteps— Nearer—

A middle-aged woman very plainly dressed was in the doorway.

"Miss Genevieve—"

"Nannie!"

"Miss Genevieve. I wouldn't have come; only I've got to tell you."

"What, Nannie? Come and sit down, Nannie."

The woman came into the room. For a second she paused, and then hurriedly she closed the door behind her.

"No, Miss Genevieve. I'll not sit down. Thank you. I can't be staying long. He might want me. I wouldn't like him to know I was here."

The muscles on either side of Genevieve Evans' mouth pulled and twitched.

"So? You're frightened too, Nannie!"

She said the words to herself.

The woman heard her.

"That I am. Miss. And that I've got good reason to be; the same as you, my poor Miss Genevieve."

"Yes, yes, Nannie. What was it you wanted?"

The woman stood quite rigid.

"You was there. Miss—this afternoon?"

"Yes—"

"Did you notice anything. Miss?"

She drew a deep breath.

"What d'you mean, Nannie? Nannie, what?"

"It's him. Miss. It was last night—"

The woman broke off.

"Yes, Nannie"; Genevieve Evans urged.

"I don't rightly know how to tell it to you. Miss. It's hard to find the words to say it in. He'd kill me if he knew I come here and told you. But you got to know. I can't keep it to myself. He's been fierce of late. What with making so much more money. And the drinking, Miss. And the women. The women, they're there all hours, now."

"My mother's house!" Genevieve Evans said it uncertainly.

"Yes, Miss," the woman went on. "And it was almost as bad when she lived."

"I know, Nannie. I've always known!"

"But last night. Miss; after they'd gone. I was asleep. Miss Genevieve. It woke me. It was awful. Plain horrid. Miss."

"What—Nannie?"

"The scream. Miss— A shriek of pain."

"No,—no, Nannie!" Genevieve Evans interrupted wildly. "Don't say it! Don't!"

The woman looked at her wonderingly.

"Why, Miss Genevieve— Poor, little lamb."

"Nannie, Nannie." She made a tremendous effort to control herself. "What was it you were going to say?"

"The scream, Miss. In the night. I rushed down. I knocked at his door. He wouldn't let me in. He was moaning, Miss. And cursing. And moaning. He was swearing about a knife. I listened. Miss—at the keyhole. I was scared. He kept cursing and moaning about a knife; about his arm—"

"Nannie—"

She whispered the word beneath her breath.

"Yes, Miss. Cut in the arm. He would have it that way. And he wouldn't let me in. I waited for hours. And this morning I went into his room myself. He was in his shirt-sleeves. I pretended I wanted the linen for the wash. I was looking for blood, Miss. Not a drop did I find. Not a pin prick stain. But I seen him bandaging his arm; right in front of me he did it. And then I seen him rip the bandage off."

"Nannie—"

"It's his reason I fear for, Miss. He turns to me and asks me if I can see the cut."

"Yes? Yes, Nannie?"

"He shows me his arm. And, Miss—"

The woman stopped abruptly.

"Nannie—what? What?"

Genevieve Evans' hands had gone up to her throat.

"There wasn't a scratch;—not—a—scratch!"

"Oh—" She breathed.

"And that's why I came here. Miss. To ask if he'd said anything of it to you. Or if—if you'd noticed anything, Miss."

Genevieve Evans waited a full second before she answered:

"No, Nannie. He wouldn't have told me. I didn't notice anything. I wasn't there very long. You see I only went to ask him to let me get away. Out in the country—by myself. I wanted the money to go. He and—and Mr. Evans never give me money, Nannie. Just things—all the things, I want. Only I'm tired of things. I don't quite know what to do. When—I think about it I get very angry. I was very angry. Last night I was very angry! I've such funny ideas when I'm angry, Nannie. I mustn't get angry again. But I've got—to—get—away."

"I don't blame you, Miss Genevieve, for being angry. You've been an angel all your life; all your life pent up like—like a saint—with—with—devils."

"You—don't—blame—me—Nannie?"

"No, Lamb. Not your Nannie. Your Nannie knows what it's been like for you. I know him, Miss Genevieve. I know he didn't give you the money."

"No, Nannie. He laughed at me. Laughed—"

"He's a beast! That's what he is, Miss. He should have give it to you. And him going away himself. He was telling me only to-day. Into the country."

"What?"

"Oh, Miss. I hate to say such things to you. He's going with that black-haired woman;—the latest one, she is. He thinks she works too hard. He's taking her off for a rest. Is anything the matter? Aren't you well, darling?"

Genevieve Evans swayed dizzily for a second her one hand reaching out blindly before her.

The woman came quickly and took the hand between both of her hands and stroked it.

"Nannie, I'm sick—sick!"

"Nannie's darling—; Nannie's pet."

From somewhere in the house came the silvery, tinkling sound of a clock striking seven times.

"I've got to go, Miss Genevieve, dear."

"All right, Nannie."

The woman drew a chair up and pushed her gently into it.

"You'll not be telling him, Miss?"

"No, Nannie—; no—"

The woman started for the door.

"Thank you. Miss Genevieve."

"Nannie—; you said he was taking her—; the black-haired one—; away for a—a rest? Away into the country?"

With her hand on the door-knob the woman turned.

"Yes. Why—lamb!"

"Into the country." Genevieve Evans' voice was lifeless. "Into the country where everything is quiet and big—; and clean. You said that, Nannie?"

"I said the country, Miss Genevieve, dearie."

"Nannie—Nannie—"; her eyes were staring straight before her. "I—want—to—go!"

"Lamb—darling."

The woman stood undecided.

"But he wouldn't let me. He laughed at me. Nannie, he laughed."

The woman made up her mind.

"Will Nannie stop with you a bit, Miss Genevieve, dearie?"

"You said"; Genevieve Evans' lifeless, monotonous voice went on; "you said you wouldn't blame me for being angry. I get very angry, Nannie. Very angry. It brings all kinds of things to me when I get angry. His kind of things. Rotten things. And he's going to take her into the country; where everything's clean; and he won't let me—go. God!"

"Will I stay, Miss Genevieve?"

"No, Nannie—go! Go quickly! Go—now!"

"Yes, Miss Genevieve. He'll be wanting to know where I am."

"Go, Nannie!" She half rose from her chair. The door closed quietly behind the woman. "Go!" Genevieve Evans whispered. "He's going—into the country—; he's taking that woman. He wouldn't let me. He wants to keep me here. Just to feel his power—; his filthy power. He's not the only one." She was muttering now. "He's not the only one who can do things. Rotten—dirty things! His kind of things!"

She swayed to her feet. Her steps were short and uncertain. Her whole body reeled. Her face was blanched; drained of all color. Her fingers trembled wide spread at her sides. She was quivering from head to foot.

Only her eyes were steady; her eyes wide and dilated that were riveted on the portrait hanging there above the wood carved mantel.

She backed toward the door, her eyes glued to the picture.

Her shaking fingers, fumbling behind her, found the key and turned it.

Feeling her way with her hands, her distended eyes still fixed on that one thing, she got to the center table.

It took her a while to pull open the drawer.

Her breath came raspingly; as if she had been running.

The old Venetian dagger with the cracked jeweled handle was between her fingers.

Very slowly now she went toward the fire-place.

The electric light flared over the colored gems that studded the handle of the dagger, giving out small quick rays of blue and red and green.

"I'm angry"; she whispered hoarsely. "I—I'm very angry—with—you. You've no right—; no right—to—ruin—my—life—and laugh! You did—laugh—at—me!"

Her eyes stared up at the full, red face with the hard lines in it. Up at the thick, sensual lips. Up at the cunning eyes. At the ponderous, heavy-set figure. The powerful hands.

"Why—don't—you—laugh—now? You aren't afraid—are—you? You—aren't—afraid of—anything? Not of—me—are—you—Daniel Drare—? You've—done—your—best—to—keep—me—under—your—power—; you—stood—behind—Ernest—to keep—me under—your—power. You're—not—afraid—of—me? Why—don't—you—laugh—Daniel—Drare?"

Her right hand that held the dagger raised itself.

"Laugh, Daniel Drare! Laugh!"

She stood there under the portrait. Her left hand went stiffly out feeling over the long cut in the painted arm.

"Angry—last—night." She whispered. "And it—it—hurt—you, Daniel Drare—I—could—hurt—you!"

For a second her eyes went up to the dagger held there above her head; the dagger with the thousand colored gleams pointing from it.

She gave a quick choking laugh.

"I laugh—at—you—Daniel—Drare."

With all her strength she drove the dagger into the heart of the canvas.

She staggered back to the center of the room.

There was a gaping rent in the portrait.

She laughed again; stupidly. Her laughter trailed off and stopped.

She stood there waiting.

Once she thought some one paused outside the door.

Her hands were up across her eyes.

Motionless she waited.

Suddenly she gave a quick start.

Out there in the hall a telephone had rung.

She heard her husband answer it.

Her one distinct thought was that he must have been on his way out for dinner.

His unbelieving cry came to her.

"My God! it can't—"

Her fingers were pressed into her ears. She did not want to hear the rest. She knew it.

THE EMPIRE OF DEATH

ALICE BROWN

IT IS TRUE THAT THE MOST EXTRAORDINARY AND EXACT COINCIDENCES HAPPEN, as if pieces in the mosaic of life, made to fit together in some mysterious forecast of destiny, rush toward each other and are finally joined. The common motive of brother meeting brother or friend meeting friend from opposing ranks of a war is a not too crudely obvious one. It has happened over and over again, as if the two had been journeying toward each other by intent, and out of all the millions of men who accompany them, are unerringly accurate in their direction and their destiny of a poignant recognition or a last sickening sequel of wild warfare.

This story, told by an American for a time in the Foreign Legion and then disabled and, by noteworthy privilege, allowed to join an observation party in March of this year, 1917, is entirely true according to his psychology. I am ready to assert it is true also in a definite sense made to fit all outward facts as well.

"Let me go back," he said, that afternoon when I sat by his bedside while he talked to me and tried to explain the message he wanted to send to a girl in New Hampshire. "You've got to understand just what my connection was with Hugo and with her, too, before the war began. So I want to tell you the whole business. That's not to be repeated to her, mind you. Only that I saw Hugo, and that he's—'safe,' you can tell her. But I suppose I want, too, to pass over what happened—pass it over to somebody else. I'm tired of owning it alone and shutting it up inside me: for I don't know whether it's a treasure, you see, or only a strange secret. And anyway it's got to be shut up, unless you want to write it out, with a change of name, so that the people playing the old games—buying and selling and thinking the world will last their time and that going to church once a week and putting a check in the plate is enough to ensure their communication with the heavenly powers—so they'll get to wondering whether perhaps after all there isn't something between God and man that hasn't been entirely mapped out. And if there is, whether they'd better not explore a little before they're called on to take the unknown country at a dash and perhaps suffer terrors actual as hunger and thirst. For one thing I'm sure I've learned out of my own neck-and-crop pitch into futurity—that 'in my Father's house are many mansions.' And not all of the mansions are for the soul to inherit and take its ease in. Some of 'em are deserts full of torments; and they're none the less His mansions. And if you ask me why one man should be singled out for punishment when millions of men have committed the same offenses in his company, I tell you you don't know where those other millions are. For space—the 'mansions'—is illimitable, and every man that sins is pretty sure of getting a lonesome hell of his own.

"Now—Hugo and I were chums at Harvard. I'd never understood why he was there; when the rest of us were dying to get to Germany to study, he came from Germany here. His father was back and forth between us and Berlin, on vague business never quite defined. We assumed it was connected with imports; but before the war there was no particular curiosity about it. You won't have seen this, because you don't know his name; but the other day he was proved guilty of hostile propaganda and indubitable plotting at munition plants, and, according to the amiable, tolerant habit of our government, merely interned. But then, when Hugo and I were trotting round together, he was simply a beneficent deity, pocket full of money, always ready to blow it in for theatres and dinners, and simply the best comrade a set of fellows could find in a man of middle age. He sang German songs to admiration, and he never took the fatherly pose of 'you'll think so when you're older.' He was apparently one of us.

"When we came out of college, Hugo and I, we ran right along in the same groove. I wanted to write things—I've a kind of a gift of words—and I determined at the same time to be a farmer. Farming's in my blood. My grandfather was a farmer. He could graft trees and do all kinds of witch work with them. He anticipated this wave of growing improved apples by a good many years. While other people were rubbing along with old apple trees set out on side hills where you couldn't cultivate 'em and close to the stone wall where every apple that fell would get a nasty disfiguring bruise, he set out several acres with healthy little trees, and ploughed and fertilized and thinned the fruit, and pruned and scraped; and, if you'll believe me, it was that orchard that sent me to college. And better than that, I inherited the apple passion, and so, when I came out of college, I bought me a farm up in New Hampshire, and settled down there to write, and incidentally to grow fruit.

"And Hugo was with me. I don't think he wanted to be at first, but his father encouraged it in his big-voiced way, and bought some adjoining land for him and I've since fancied I saw why. We weren't so far from Canada, and I've guessed he wanted our little acreage for a base. Also, Hugo fell in love with Annie Mills. So did I. She was the daughter of the farmer next me, a quarter of a mile away, and kept house for him, and the first time we saw her—coming home from the woods she was, with her hands full of violets—well, I'm pretty sure each of us felt then what we kept on feeling till the war gripped us—and afterward. And when I say she was coming home with her hands full of violets you mustn't see any Sweet Lavender kind of girl in a pink sunbonnet and dialect on her tongue, ready to be awed by two college fellows. O Lord! you know, Annie'd had her course at a mighty good seminary, and she read her Greek for fun and because she liked it; whereas, if you asked me to translate at random, without context, I should be nowhere: not even come in by freight. So Hugo, having seen her, settled down with me and read books on forestry and his father encouraged it, and I wished the devil would fly away with him and not bring him back till I'd got Annie.

"Yes, give me a drink, but don't stop me. I'm going to keep right on till this story is told. If I get it off my chest I sha'n't do so much 'seeing things at night.'

"Annie was a discreet and level-headed little person, but she hadn't any eyes for me. It was all Hugo. Terrible nice to me, you understand, but in a sort of maze about him, hypnotized, you know, what's called being in love. Or, no. Sometimes I think she wasn't in love yet, only on the way to it. And Hugo's dad took up his share in the hypnotizing. He stayed with us from time to time, and sang German songs to her and made love in a kind of indirect fashion—nicely, you know, quite straight about it. Only, as an older man preparing the way for Hugo and turning the world upside down with the romance of everything as if he'd built a kind of palace with flowers to walk on and birds singing, for Hugo to lead her into and propose to her. Do you get me? I mean the whole atmosphere of our New England neighborhood, so far as we three were concerned, was back in some kind of super-civilization America hasn't a glimmer of, except through poetry and pictures, and Annie was being asked indirectly but in every way possible to accept the freedom of the city in a golden box.

"Her father? Annie's father? Oh, he didn't know what was happening. He was road commissioner, and he was sitting up nights figuring on harder roads for the automobiles, and over the motors—how to trap 'em better for over-speeding and so pay for the roads. And Annie was a wonder. She kept her gait. Only I could see her eyes grow big and black when she was pelted with the whole German Empire, and I had an idea if Hugo asked her right off the bat, she'd have to say 'yes.' You may think I was a fool not to ask her myself, but it was a fact I didn't dare to. I felt as if I stood for New Hampshire with her and the kind of person that would turn into a road commissioner some day, and I felt as if a joggle of the wheel might give me a chance to offer her some little glamour myself. It's no use saying I cherished any high-minded horseback determination to let Hugo have her because he was my chum. Not a bit of it. If I could have shipped him off to Siam I would, and 'father' and his German songs with him. Some days they got most infernally on my nerves, and I cursed myself for walking into the combination as I had or inviting it to walk over me.

"And then the turn of the wheel came, in August, 1914, and everything was different. In the first place father disappeared, lock, stock and barrel. Whether he said good-by to Hugo I don't know. He didn't say good-by to me, and I rather resented the unfriendliness of it and didn't ask about him. But Hugo had letters from him, and the post-mark was Canada. But straight off I found out things weren't the same between Hugo and me. He got rather strained and quiet; I can't tell you what effect it had after knowing him those last years when he was always banging round and whistling and singing. Now he was mum as a fish. He wouldn't talk about the war—not to me, though he did, I found out, talk to Annie. For she grew mum and white, to the same degree, and one day when I overtook her on the path through the Cathedral Woods she asked her question, right out from the shoulder. I'd gone into the woods to think things over, and so had she, and we were both just enough keyed up so she had to put her question.

"'Arnold,' said she, 'what do you think about Belgium?'

"It was just after that deviltry, you see, while we, the ones of us that see straight, and mean to act straight, were almost out of our minds with the helpless, mad desire to do something, and the others—well, the others it's better, to the end of time, to forget them. Don't you say so? What's the use of keeping on poisoning our own blood with the just contempt we've got to feel for 'em? Well, I told her what I thought, as well as I could, I don't know in what words. Maybe I didn't choose 'em for their academic flavor. About that time I was fed up with academic puddling. And I saw she thought she'd got it hot, but maybe no more than she expected, and the light, what little there was of it in her face, paled out and she walked along with her head bent.

"'Yes,' she said at last, 'that's the way I feel.' And then she lifted her head—she's a gallant girl, Annie—and she said, as if it might be a kind of challenge to me to understand she identified herself with him, 'But Hugo can't feel so.'

"'Can't he?' said I.

"I found myself mumbling. I'd spent what heat I had on Belgium.

"'No,' said she. 'There are all his traditions, you see. He has to be loyal to Germany.' He's German to the backbone.

"'Well!' said I.

"That was literally all I could say. I wanted to ask her if Hugo wasn't the son of a German who'd got himself naturalized in the United States, and whether he mightn't stiffen his own backbone accordingly. But I didn't. I felt as if I'd lost them all, Hugo and his father inevitably, and Annie, because, though she stood with me about Belgium, she seemed to have accepted their point of view, for them, which was, to my way of thinking, giving a kind of intangible aid and comfort to our spiritual enemies. But this I knew. If Hugo was even emotionally a citizen of Germany at this crisis—for that first crisis, you know, was like a great questioning fiat from a moral judgment seat—where did a man stand? And he that was not for the devil was against him—well, if Hugo was with the devil as he had been revealed walking abroad under a Prussian helmet—was he to sit at my table any more? Was I to break bread with him? I didn't say another word to Annie nor did she to me, and at the edge of the woods I left her and turned back into the Cathedral aisle. And, if you believe me, I stayed in the woods all night. I sent word to Hugo by a boy that came up through from fishing, not to expect me, that I was off trying to find a strayed calf—which was absurd, because we hadn't any cattle pastured and Hugo knew it. But I had an idea he wouldn't be enough interested in my movements to pin me down to facts. And perhaps he'd been as uneasy with me as I was with him. And when I did go back, next morning, dew-soaked and cold and sort of awkward about meeting him, he'd gone, and the housekeeper told me it was for good. He'd gone to the war.

"'And it's for Germany,' she kept saying. 'Mr. Grant, ain't it queer? he's goin' to fight for Germany.'

"And I told her it wasn't queer—quite natural, for he was a German. And I waited for her to tell me he'd left me something, a letter, of course, or if not that, some sort of message. But he hadn't, for she didn't say another word, and even before I had breakfast I went over the house hunting for his good-by—the living-room, his room, mine. Not a word did I find. He'd disappeared just as if his father'd given him the formula.

"That day I went to see Annie and her face told me he hadn't gone without saying good-by to her. She was as serious as we are after a sobering blow, not a girl now, a woman.

"I couldn't talk to her till she'd answered me one question.

"'Are you engaged to him?'

"I asked it plump and she answered as if it was a natural thing to ask and I'd every right to an answer.

"'No,' she said. 'I couldn't. I'm puzzled. I had to think things over. Belgium.'

"'Yes,' I said.

"And then I asked how long she was going to think things over, and she said:

"'I don't know. Till I can stop being puzzled, I guess.'

"'Well, Annie,' said I, 'I'm going, too. Only I shall fight on the other side.'

"And before she could think she put her hands together and the red ran into her face and she said:

"'Oh, bless you! bless you! I wish I could go, too.' And then she remembered the thing that was hurting her so, and she said, 'If you see him, won't you write me?'

"'I sha'n't see him,' I said, 'among ten million Germans. But I'll write you anyway.'

"And the next day I was off, up through Canada and over to the other side. The queer part of it was I hadn't thought of going till that minute facing Annie's eyes. It seemed as if she'd made me go. And maybe Hugo had, too. It was as if he'd challenged me and I'd got to make sure he didn't throw his little weight in for Germany without my throwing mine on the other side.

"Well, I'll skip all my dodges to get over, and what happened to me there and how I got my first wound—I've been sort of unlucky, you know—and then my good luck of getting a little pull, enough to put me into the observation party that followed along after the French when they banged the Germans into their 'strategic retreat' in March of this year. And you know what those same Germans that are bamboozling Russia now with their peace terms did when they retreated: how they blew up villages and poisoned wells and wrecked houses and destroyed fruit trees. Now that last is what I'm coming to—the destruction of the trees. I can forgive 'em my game leg, even if it never straightens out, and I can fancy in minutes I have sometimes when the sun's shining and it looks as if we'd got 'em on the run and somebody reminds me 'all's right with the world' that God may make a try at forgiving 'em for the houses and the gardens and the women—but I can't go into that. Honestly I haven't the nerve. Sometimes when it comes over me—the women I know about, the ghosts of children I've seen with my own eyes—well, I'm afraid I shall just go daffy lying here, with sheer mad. But—and this is what I've been coming to all this time—so long as I keep my brain to invent curses and my tongue to utter 'em, I never'll forgive the destruction of the trees. If my ticket for a comfortable hereafter depended on it I couldn't. 'Put me anywhere you like, Lord,' I should have to say, 'but that's a new crime. That's arboricide. You didn't mention it in the Decalogue but I've got it down in mine. And it proves there's more than one unpardonable sin among men.'

"Maybe it's my grandfather coming out in me. Anyway it's as strong as I am. Why, do you know what a tree represents, how slow it grows, what a push and urge it puts into its resurrection every spring and how it goes to sleep so pretty and stands there for all the winds of winter to buffet it and the rain to lash it in the face? And there it is in the spring ready again if you give it half a chance, gnarled maybe and brown and old, but with a bridal bloom no girl could ever equal—not even Annie. It's kind, a fruit tree is, it's beneficent, always offering you something, and even if you neglect it offering you a little still. As if it said, 'I'm poor, but I'll share with you.' Why, the relation between mankind and its fruit trees ought to be a never-ending alliance—protection on our part, generosity, kindness. Because on theirs they're always ready with an answer. Well, that's how I feel about fruit trees, and when I saw them by the hundred sawed two-thirds through and then broken down, split, mangled, murdered, how do you think I felt? And let me stop right here and say I found in a newspaper I got hold of the other day what a German military high joss said about their retreat:

"'Before our new positions runs, like a gigantic ribbon, an empire of death.'

"That describes it better than I could if I went into a day's talk of mine craters and gaping holes and what had been fruit trees with the life-blood in them standing there, bare, jagged spikes, pointing up to heaven. That idea rather got hold of me as I stared at them. There seemed to be something significant in it. They were pointing up to heaven.

"Well, we moved along, we of the observation party, and we found not only destruction of all the mechanism of life but the dead. Here and there were a few dead Boches. And one man, lying with two others quite safely off on their journey into some other planet, was a slender fellow, face downward, his hand stretched limp toward one of the others as if he had tried to touch him, get some comfort or give it, God knows which. And I knew that hand. I can't say now whether I actually did know it, the outward form of it, or whether some inside sense told me. But I knew. It was Hugo's, and I slid off my horse and told the others I'd overtake them, and I turned him over as gently as I could and his eyes opened and met mine—the strangest look, that was, as if he were relieved to see me and yet, too, as if he were too far away to have it count—and he said my name, and that one word that haunts the battlefield like a litany of torture: 'Water.' But with it he was gone, slipped away out of his body as if he'd been ready and only waiting for me to give him somehow his release, and I laid him down as easy as I could. Strange isn't it how we feel they can keep on being hurt, though we know their bodies are—as they are? And then I remembered I must see if he had anything I could send back to Annie, and as I put out my hand to him again something obliterated me and I'd got the earth behind me, too.

"Now you know how it was, how an apparently dead Boche at my left had come to himself and potted me, and you know of course I wasn't dead because I'm here now. But I did have a narrow squeak of it, as they'd tell you in hospital if they had time to remember also-rans like me. So far as this world goes, I was dead. I had gone out of my body and into some other state of existence, just as sure's you're here in this. I had a sensation of lightness, of rising, and of all my faculties being keener than they'd ever been. I seemed to be thinking of a dozen things at once and with a clearness, a power, that was even in itself a mode of action. Don't you see? I might not have my hands or feet or eyes to work with or a heart to beat, but I was perfectly conscious that I could do things. And I thought of Annie with a sort of regret that yet wasn't sad, even though now she'd lost us both and there was nobody but the road commissioner to stand between her and life—yes, I actually saw the road commissioner as I lay there on the field of France, with his pepper and salt suit and the gold tooth I always suspected him of being proud of—and above every stratum of feeling was the certainty that I'd got to hang on to Hugo till we could sit down and talk it over and somehow arrange things for her. And though I had that sensation of lightness, I was apparently there on the ground, only we were standing and we faced each other and I was the first to speak.

"'Well, old chap,' said I, 'how goes it?'

"And we seemed to shake hands, only I didn't feel the grip of his; but I knew he was tremendously glad to see me, and his voice sounded perfectly familiar when he answered.

"'I suppose,' said he, 'we're dead.'

"That was it. We were dead. It had been so far from my thoughts as anything I was likely to suffer, that particular day, that I actually hadn't known it. He began to peer round in exactly the way he used to when we were alive, and I laughed. Being dead wasn't going to be so bad if we were sufficiently ourselves to chum together in the old way. Though all the time I was conscious of something that tried to draw me away from him or him away from me. That's a commonplace, you know. I've heard lots of chaps speak of it that got knocked out and then had to come back. It was so strong that I felt breathless as I combated it, and gasped once or twice to get my breath, because I'd even thought of a little joke.

"'Evidently we're to be separated,' I said. 'I'm going to heaven. So you can draw your own conclusions.'

"How did it look round us? I forgot—I hadn't told you. Well, it simply didn't look any way at all, any more than it does at sea when the fogs shut down and the horn is groaning. And there wasn't any horn, not a sound in that eerie place unless we chose to speak. And Hugo did speak, and with such a relief in his voice that I knew he'd been as lost as I.

"'The fog is lifting,' he said.

"It was, or dispersing itself, thinner at first, then in little separate spirals like pipe smoke, and then, with a rush, it went. And we were in the most unbelievable place you ever saw—with your mind's eye, that is—for it was like no other place mapped out or charted. It was a place as big—I can't tell you how big, for it seemed illimitable. And that you must take my word for, because you can't see how we could get the idea of tremendous space when there were so many trees to break it. But they didn't break it. They just gave the impression of more and more miles and more and more trees.

"'Come,' said I, 'we've got to get somewhere out of this.'

"I spoke with the more decision because, mind you, I was determined not to leave Hugo, and I was conscious all the time of the force that was trying to pull me away from him.

"'Come,' it seemed to say, 'his way lies here. Yours doesn't. Break off and leave him.'

"And because I had an inward certainty that the phrase about leaving him might have been rounded out 'leave him to his fate' I was all the more determined not to go. It was partly because I was fond of him. The old days were pulling at me. And then I was morally bound not to fail Annie. Somehow or other I'd got to give him back to her, if we weren't both in here for keeps. I wanted Annie myself precisely as much as I ever had, but in that place something—I don't know what it was—fell away from me and I was ready to stand back and let the other man walk over me to his own. If he could: but there was something in the place that put a spell on you and decreed you should walk only its way. And when I said that last I told you, that we'd got to get out, he agreed with me, though I don't know whether he spoke, and we plunged into the undergrowth among the trees in a direction that seemed to lead to a kind of path. The air was green, oozy, damp, not exactly the air you find in tropical forests, but as if there was intention in it. You'll think I'm daffy, but it wasn't as if the trees were luxuriating naturally in that wet medium, but as if it were something they controlled and were breathing it out to choke and slay.

"And when my breath and my heart failed me and I stopped to wipe my dripping face, I looked round me and what I saw, though it ought to have been beautiful to me, was terrifying in the extreme. For they were fruit trees in full bloom. They were low-growing, so that their laced branches made a roof I could have touched by stretching up my arm, and their brown twigs were heavy with crowded petals, pink and white, and with hardly a leaf to break their blended continuity. And the fragrance of them, the heaviness of it that sickened you with its very sweetness and lay in your lungs like a drug! I looked at Hugo and I saw he was frightened. That is what he must have seen in me, pale fear reflected each to each.

"'Trees!' I said. My voice sounded faint and unfamiliar to me. It might have been 'death' I said or 'murder' or any of those words weighted with an awful inheritance from countless tragedies. (Am I talking rot? Maybe. You see I've thought for ever so long how I'd write this out if I could. But I can't. I can't. I lived it, once for all. That was my part. Anything I could say would sound like a penny whistle.) And Hugo, in the same kind of voice echoed back 'Trees!' and there we stood staring, as if there was no spell we could think of like that same word. And in a minute Hugo looked across me to one side where the light was growing a trifle brighter, and he gave a cry I never shall forget so long as I live. It was like a woman's scream, and a man's voice in a woman's scream is something to remember.

"'What's that?' said he, 'that over there—' Then he stopped and cried out again before he went on. 'It's like the road from Roye.'

"It was then I began to understand, and I cried out at him:

"'Were you one of the devils that cut down the trees?'

"And all the time my eyes, like his, were on that further space where there were no blossoms and no interlacing boughs: only maimed and mangled torsos such as I had seen that day. And then Hugo began to cry out in an awful abandonment, sobbing, too, as if he were beseeching something—as if he found himself helpless and the most terrific power that could be imagined stood over him with its most terrific weapon, and it was raised to fall. I never before realized what it is to see a man in every last nerve and sinew of him mad with fear. He began to beg, and justify himself all in one.

"'Why,' he said, 'what's a tree? If it were a man—they've all been killing men— the French and English, look at them! they've killed *me*. And I've killed, too. I know I have. But you don't punish me for that. You punish me for sawing down a tree or two. I had to, don't you see? It was orders, and common sense, too. What's the crime of sawing down a tree?'

"And I understood. He was in hell, a hell of trees, and I was with him because I wouldn't let him go. For all the time, mind you, the power that forbade me to stay with him was tugging at me and beating in my ears, 'Give him up, give him up.' And I wouldn't give him up, and gripped tighter on his hand. By this time he had gone to pieces, over his entire body, and fallen to his knees and still I held his hand and tried to drag him up by it. And he did get up and turned about obliquely toward the naked torsos of the ruined wood and took a step miserably and then another and I took mine with him.

"'I've got to go,' he kept saying, and now he sobbed without any restraint or shame. 'That's the way I've got to go.'

"And as we stumbled on in that thick sweet air—oh, a million apple trees in bloom shut up like concentrated poison in a flask couldn't have been stronger—I understood that the trees were unfriendly to us. That broke my heart. Trees! the patient, generous friend of man—they were unfriendly. I felt as if God Himself had forsaken me. And another delicately exquisite bit of torture piled up on this last. The trees were moving, too. They ran beside us, they pursued us, they waved their branches—it was their own volition, mind you—there was no wind—they outran us and beckoned us on, they pelted us with blooms that hurt like ice-pellets and suffocated like wool. It seemed millions of years that we were running—for we ran fast now, as if we spurned the undergrowth, ran through the air—but never, never could we outrun the racing trees. And one fear in me was stronger than all other fears—would they, somehow, at last speak in some arboreal fashion? Would they charge Hugo with his crime and me for my unfriendliness to them and all my inherited past in staying with him? And finally the maimed victims neared us, as if they might be running to meet us, and Hugo spoke with that small sobbing breath he had:

"'It is the road from Roye. That's the way I've got to go.'

"How far had he got to go? And where would the road of torment lead him at the last? And now he stopped short and looked at me. In that minute, from that look of his, I knew he loved me, that he saw what I'd been trying to do. The trees stopped, too. I had a foolish fancy they were giving him an instant's breathing space just for that look, that look of human kindliness and sacrifice. And he spoke precisely as he might have spoken in those first days in New Hampshire or in Cambridge, when we sat with a table between us and smoked and rearranged the world.

"'Good-by, old chap,' said he. 'Good-by.'

"'But I'm with you,' I called out to him as if there'd already begun to be widening space between us. 'I won't go.'

"And with a quick pull, as if he'd got to do it that way or not at all, because I'd grip the harder if he did it otherwise, he snatched his hand out of mine, and it was dark before me, and something kind—oh you don't know what beneficent destinies there are till you've been where Hugo and I were—it seemed to lift me and carry me to where there was breath and light.

"And to go back a minute, to the kind destinies. You know the Furies have another name. And I can't help thinking that when they'd got done scourging him through his wilderness of murdered trees, he'd see their other faces and call that name, and they'd answer him and smile."

"And you," said I. "You were in hospital?"

"Yes. I was in hospital. And you tell Annie I saw Hugo, saw him die, quickly, without pain, and that—yes, you say it!—that he's safe."

THE ENGLISHMAN

GUY DE MAUPASSANT

THEY MADE A CIRCLE AROUND JUDGE BERMUTIER, WHO WAS GIVING HIS OPINION OF the mysterious affair that had happened at Saint-Cloud. For a month Paris had doted on this inexplicable crime. No one could understand it at all.

M. Bermutier, standing with his back to the chimney, talked about it, discussed the divers opinions, but came to no conclusions.

Many women had risen and come nearer, remaining standing, with eyes fixed upon the shaven mouth of the magistrate, whence issued these grave words. They shivered and vibrated, crisp through their curious fear, through that eager, insatiable need of terror which haunts their soul, torturing them like a hunger.

One of them, paler than the others, after a silence, said:

"It is frightful. It touches the supernatural. We shall never know anything about it."

The magistrate turned toward her, saying:

"Yes, Madame, it is probable that we never shall know anything about it. As for the word 'supernatural,' when you come to use that, it has no place here. We are in the presence of a crime skillfully conceived, very skillfully executed, and so well enveloped in mystery that we cannot separate the impenetrable circumstances which surround it. But, once in my life, I had to follow an affair which seemed truly to be mixed up with something very unusual. However, it was necessary to give it up, as there was no means of explaining it."

Many of the ladies called out at the same time, so quickly that their voices sounded as one:

"Oh! tell us about it."

M. Bermutier smiled gravely, as judges should, and replied:

"You must not suppose, for an instant, that I, at least, believed there was anything superhuman in the adventure. I believe only in normal causes. And, if in place of using the word 'supernatural' to express what we cannot comprehend we should simply use the word 'inexplicable,' it would be much better. In any case, the surrounding circumstances in the affair I am going to relate to you, as well as the preparatory circumstances, have affected me much. Here are the facts:

"I was then judge of Instruction at Ajaccio, a little white town lying on the border of an admirable gulf that was surrounded on all sides by high mountains.

"What I particularly had to look after there was the affairs of *vendetta*. Some of them were superb; as dramatic as possible, ferocious, and heroic. We find there the most beautiful subjects of vengeance that one could dream of, hatred a century old, appeased for a moment but never extinguished, abominable plots, assassinations becoming massacres and almost glorious battles. For two years I heard of nothing but the price of blood, of the terribly prejudiced Corsican who is bound to avenge all injury upon the person of him who is the cause of it, or upon his nearest descendants. I saw old men and infants, cousins, with their throats cut, and my head was full of these stories.

"One day we learned that an Englishman had rented for some years a little villa at the end of the Gulf. He had brought with him a French domestic, picked up at Marseilles on the way.

"Soon everybody was occupied with this singular person, who lived alone in his house, only going out to hunt and fish. He spoke to no one, never came to the town, and, every morning, practiced shooting with a pistol and a rifle for an hour or two.

"Some legends about him were abroad. They pretended that he was a high personage fled from his own country for political reasons; then they affirmed that he was concealing himself after having committed a frightful crime. They even cited some of the particularly horrible details.

"In my capacity of judge, I wished to get some information about this man. But it was impossible to learn anything. He called himself Sir John Rowell.

"I contented myself with watching him closely; although, in reality, there seemed nothing to suspect regarding him.

"Nevertheless, as rumors on his account continued, grew, and became general, I resolved to try and see this stranger myself, and for this purpose began to hunt regularly in the neighborhood of his property.

"I waited long for an occasion. It finally came in the form of a partridge which I shot and killed before the very nose of the Englishman. My dog brought it to me; but, immediately taking it I went and begged Sir John Rowell to accept the dead bird, excusing myself for intrusion.

"He was a tall man with red hair and red beard, very large, a sort of placid, polite Hercules. He had none of the so-called British haughtiness, and heartily thanked me for the delicacy in French, with a beyond-the-Channel accent. At the end of a month we had chatted together five or six times.

"Finally, one evening, as I was passing by his door, I perceived him astride a chair in the garden, smoking his pipe. I saluted him and he asked me in to have a glass of beer. It was not necessary for him to repeat before I accepted.

"He received me with the fastidious courtesy of the English, spoke in praise of France and of Corsica, and declared that he loved that country and that shore.

"Then, with great precaution in the form of a lively interest, I put some questions to him about his life and his projects. He responded without embarrassment, told me that he had traveled much, in Africa, in the Indies, and in America. He added, laughing:

"'I have had many adventures, oh! yes.'

"I began to talk about hunting, and he gave me many curious details of hunting the hippopotamus, the tiger, the elephant, and even of hunting the gorilla.

"I said: 'All these animals are very formidable.'

"He laughed: 'Oh! no. The worst animal is man.' Then he began to laugh, with the hearty laugh of a big contented Englishman. He continued:

"'I have often hunted man, also.'

"He spoke of weapons and asked me to go into his house to see his guns of various makes and kinds.

"His drawing-room was hung in black, in black silk embroidered with gold. There were great yellow flowers running over the somber stuff, shining like fire.

"'It is Japanese cloth,' he said.

"But in the middle of a large panel, a strange thing attracted my eye. Upon a square of red velvet, a black object was attached. I approached and found it was a hand, the hand of a man. Not a skeleton hand, white and characteristic, but a black, desiccated hand, with yellow joints with the muscles bare and on them traces of old blood, of blood that seemed like a scale, over the bones sharply cut off at about the middle of the fore-arm, as with a blow of a hatchet. About the wrist was an enormous iron chain, riveted, soldered to this unclean member, attaching it to the wall by a ring sufficiently strong to hold an elephant.

"I asked: 'What is that?'

"The Englishman responded tranquilly:

"'It belonged to my worst enemy. It came from America. It was broken with a saber, cut off with a sharp stone, and dried in the sun for eight days. Oh, very good for me, that was!'

"I touched the human relic, which must have belonged to a colossus. The fingers were immoderately long and attached by enormous tendons that held the straps of skin in place. This dried hand was frightful to see, making one think, naturally, of the vengeance of a savage.

"I said: 'This man must have been very strong.'

"With gentleness the Englishman answered:

"'Oh! yes; but I was stronger than he. I put this chain on him to hold him.'

"I thought he spoke in jest and replied:

"'The chain is useless now that the hand cannot escape.'

"Sir John Rowell replied gravely: 'It always wishes to escape. The chain is necessary.'

"With a rapid, questioning glance, I asked myself: 'Is he mad, or is that an unpleasant joke?'

"But the face remained impenetrable, tranquil, and friendly. I spoke of other things and admired the guns.

"Nevertheless, I noticed three loaded revolvers on the pieces of furniture, as if this man lived in constant fear of attack.

"I went there many times after that; then for some time I did not go. We had become accustomed to his presence; he had become indifferent to us.

"A whole year slipped away. Then, one morning, toward the end of November, my domestic awoke me with the announcement that Sir John Rowell had been assassinated in the night.

"A half hour later, I entered the Englishman's house with the central Commissary and the Captain of Police. The servant, lost in despair, was weeping at the door. I suspected him at first, but afterward found that he was innocent.

"The guilty one could never be found.

"Upon entering Sir John's drawing-room, I perceived his dead body stretched out upon its back, in the middle of the room. His waistcoat was torn, a sleeve was hanging, and it was evident that a terrible struggle had taken place.

"The Englishman had been strangled! His frightfully black and swollen face seemed to express an abominable fear; he held something between his set teeth; and his neck, pierced with five holes apparently done with a pointed iron, was covered with blood.

"A doctor joined us. He examined closely the prints of fingers in the flesh and pronounced these strange words:

"'One would think he had been strangled by a skeleton.'

"A shiver ran down my back and I cast my eyes to the place on the wall where I had seen the horrible, torn-off hand. It was no longer there. The chain was broken and hanging.

"Then I bent over the dead man and found in his mouth a piece of one of the fingers of the missing hand, cut off, or rather sawed off by the teeth exactly at the second joint.

"Then they tried to collect evidence. They could find nothing. No door had been forced, no window opened, or piece of furniture moved. The two watchdogs on the premises had not been aroused.

"Here, in a few words, is the deposition of the servant:

"For a month, his master had seemed agitated. He had received many letters which he had burned immediately. Often, taking a whip, in anger which seemed like dementia, he had struck in fury, this dried hand, fastened to the wall and taken, one knew not how, at the moment of a crime.

"He had retired late and shut himself in with care. He always carried arms. Often in the night he talked out loud, as if he were quarreling with some one. On that night, however, there had been no noise, and it was only on coming to open the windows that the servant had found Sir John assassinated. He suspected no one.

"I communicated what I knew of the death to the magistrates and public officers, and they made minute inquiries upon the whole island. They discovered nothing.

"One night, three months after the crime, I had a frightful nightmare. It seemed to me that I saw that hand, that horrible hand, running like a scorpion or a spider along my curtains and my walls. Three times I awoke, three times I fell asleep and again saw that hideous relic galloping about my room, moving its fingers like paws.

"The next day they brought it to me, found in the cemetery upon the tomb where Sir John Rowell was interred—for they had not been able to find his family. The index finger was missing.

"This, ladies, is my story. I know no more about it."

The ladies were terrified, pale, and shivering. One of them cried:

"But that is not the end, for there was no explanation! We cannot sleep if you do not tell us what was your idea of the reason of it all."

The magistrate smiled with severity, and answered:

"Oh! certainly, ladies, but it will spoil all your terrible dreams. I simply think that the legitimate proprietor of the hand was not dead and that he came for it with the one that remained to him. But I was never able to find out how he did it. It was one kind of revenge."

One of the women murmured:

"No, it could not be thus."

And the Judge of Information, smiling still, concluded:

"I told you in the beginning that my explanation would not satisfy you."

The Escape

George W. Nixon

The Professor sat down at the breakfast table. He slipped his serviette from the ring and spread it carefully across his knees. Then he folded the morning paper in a neat oblong, placed it to the left of his plate, and read as he ate. A delicate precision characterised all his movements. His slim, white fingers held the knife and fork as though they might be soiled in the contact, and his highly polished nails gleamed in the morning sun.

There was, indeed, nothing about the man to suggest a scientist of European reputation. He had an air of feminine daintiness, though cruelty seemed to lie in his thin lips, in his white snapping teeth, and in his cautious eyes—often half-closed. His smooth, silky hair, his neat shoes and socks, like his well-manicured hands, showed him as vain of his appearance as a woman. And, strangely enough, he had an irrational antipathy to mice.

Once while a student the Professor spent a night of agony in his bathroom, tottering in the dawn to his room pale and sweating. He had been about to enter the bath when a slight rustle drew his quick attention. Turning, he saw a mouse emerge from a hole in a corner of the room and make its way with a sidling movement along the wall. The Professor dropped cautiously to his knees, and at the sound the rodent paused. He held his breath, and the mouse ambled across the room to within a few inches of him. An unnameable repugnance seized the watcher, and at his exclamation of disgust the mouse scuttled back to its hole. The Professor sat with fearful eyes fixed upon the tiny aperture through which the mouse had disappeared, waiting for its return. What seemed interminable hours passed before the soft rustle again broke the stillness. In the pale light not one, but a dozen small grey shapes were discernible, creeping and scampering about the room. The wretched watcher mounted a chair, peering and trembling, held yet disgusted, by the sight. So he remained until the coming of the daylight and the vanishing of the mice.

Every morning the Professor read his paper well through before addressing any kind of remark to his wife. She sat this morning, as she had done for years, at the opposite end of the table with her back to the light. Her position in the house which, together with a small income she had brought as a marriage dowry, was pathetically negative. Her husband was not actually cruel to her; that is, he did not lay hands on her—he just ignored her. She scarcely existed for him. She did not matter. Never very attractive in her best days, the years had done their worst with her, and the Professor recognised with the detached criticism of a stranger that she was decidedly plain.

This morning he had occasion to refold his paper, and in so doing his glance fell on his wife. As he did so, a strange quiver ran from his head to his very toes. He felt himself draw in his breath while his eyes remained fixed on the figure opposite. A visitor coming into the room would have seen merely a round-shouldered woman sitting at the table crumbling a piece of bread and nibbling furtively. The Professor, a man never given to delusions, saw the outline of an enormous mouse. The hair scraped tightly back from the forehead left the pointed ears exposed. They stood out slightly from the head, and the sun shone through them, tingeing them pink. The grey face, with its long nose and quickly munching mouth, the weak chin lost in the shadow, the sloping shoulders, and the nervous fingers curled over the bread, completed the startling illusion. It was a monstrous mouse, and not a woman.

A passing cloud obscured the sun, and the impression lost its vividness. The Professor felt sick, almost disappointed, that he could not sit and gaze longer at his discovery. Odd that he had never seen it before!

During the days that followed he could not forget. He tried to lose himself in his work; he spent hours in his laboratory, but the memory would not go. He found himself watching his wife stealthily. He even took to creeping in on her unawares. She would be sewing or writing, and at his entrance, it seemed to him, she would crouch lower and turn her head quickly, while her bright pleading eyes might have belonged to a mouse itself.

In his own room the Professor tossed and turned at night and thought over all the little tricks he had discovered in her. The way her head sank back on her shoulders, her sidelong glances, and her shrinking body. He went to a doctor, who examined him and told him he was never in better form. He read feverishly, but all to no purpose.

It was with feelings of mingled relief and disappointment that he received his wife's announcement that she was going to spend a fortnight with her sister. During her absence he slept better, and since he never encouraged her to write when away from home there was nothing to remind him of his experience. As time went on, he was able to feel amused at the whole business, and was inclined to attribute his former condition, despite the doctor's verdict, to an attack of nerves. True, he had not suffered with nerves before, but that did not prove his immunity.

On the day appointed for his wife's return, however, the same sweeping shiver that had passed over him on the memorable morning at breakfast visited him again. Her attitude then came vividly back to his mind.

He tried to remember her under other circumstances, before this loathsome impression was borne in upon him. When he first met her! When they were married. Ah! There had always been this resemblance. No matter how he recalled her picture there it was, the huddled, furtive, nauseating caricature of a mouse.

The sight of his wife when she came back was almost unbearable. More than ever was he repelled and yet mysteriously attracted.

The ensuing days were torture to him, and at last he decided to take a long walk and solve the situation once and for all. He set out soon after lunch and took a road leading across quiet country. Late in the evening he set his face homewards, his brain sick with imaginings, and his mind still unresolved. Was it really unresolved, or was he convinced that there was but one way of deliverance?

As he turned in at the gate he met the maid coming down the short drive. He saluted her and reflected that this was her evening off. Perhaps it was as well. The house was quiet when he got in. He looked in at the drawing-room. His wife was not there. On the balcony, perhaps. No! Already having dinner maybe. He crept to the dining-room. It was empty. He *must* find her. A frenzy possessed him. He went up to her room and pushed the door open. Empty!

She had never been out like this before. But he would find the wretched creature. He sped from room to room until he reached his study. His eyes, dry and burning, fell on a letter propped against the clock. He seized it in his shaking fingers and read the following letter from his wife:

> I have gone for good. By the time you get this I shall be many miles away. Nothing will induce me to return, and I do not flatter myself you will try to make me.
>
> I am aware it will sound mad, but for some weeks past I have been unable to rid myself of the idea that you are a cat in human guise. It first came over me one morning at breakfast when I looked up and saw you glaring at me. The shape of your head, the expression of your mouth were a cat's, your hands were cat's paws. I tried to dismiss the notion, but could not. You crept about and seemed to be ceaselessly watching me. My life was untold torture. The fortnight away did no real good. I thought the hallucination would pass. It seemed to be worse, and I grew so mortally afraid that I am afraid to be near you. I have enough to live on. Goodbye.

The Feather Pillow

Horacio Quiroga

Alicia's entire honeymoon gave her hot and cold shivers. A blonde, angelic, and timid young girl, the childhood fancies she had dreamed about being a bride had been chilled by her husband's rough character. She loved him very much, nonetheless, although sometimes she gave a light shudder when, as they returned home through the streets together at night, she cast furtive glances at the impressive stature of her Jordan, who had been silent for an hour. He, for his part, loved her profoundly but never let it be seen.

For three months—they had been married in April—they lived in a special kind of bliss. Doubtless she would have wished less severity in the rigorous sky of love, more expansive and less cautious tenderness, but her husband's impassive manner always restrained her.

The house in which they lived influenced her chills and shuddering to no small degree. The whiteness of the silent patio—friezes, columns, and marble statues—produced the wintry impression of an enchanted palace. Inside the glacial brilliance of stucco, the completely bare walls, affirmed the sensation of unpleasant coldness. As one crossed from one room to another, the echo of his steps reverberated throughout the house, as if long abandonment had sensitized its resonance.

Alicia passed the autumn in this strange love nest. She had determined, however, to cast a veil over her former dreams and live like a sleeping beauty in the hostile house, trying not to think about anything till her husband arrived each evening.

It is not strange that she grew thin. She had a light attack of influenza that dragged on insidiously for days and days: after that Alicia's health never returned. Finally one afternoon she was able to go into the garden, supported on her husband's arm. She looked around listlessly. Suddenly Jordan, with deep tenderness, ran his hand very slowly over her head, and Alicia instantly burst into sobs, throwing her arms around his neck. For a long time she cried out all the fears she had kept silent, redoubling her weeping at Jordan's slightest caress. Then her sobs subsided, and she stood a long while, her face hidden in the hollow of his neck, not moving or speaking a word.

This was the last day Alicia was well enough to be up. The following day she awakened feeling faint. Jordan's doctor examined her with minute attention, prescribing calm and absolute rest.

"I don't know," he said to Jordan at the street door. "She has a great weakness that I am unable to explain. And with no vomiting, nothing . . . if she wakes tomorrow as she did today, call me at once."

When she awakened the following day, Alicia was worse. There was a consultation. It was agreed there was an anaemia of incredible progression, completely inexplicable. Alicia had no more fainting spells but she was visibly moving towards death. The lights were lighted all day long in her bedroom, and there was complete silence. Hours went by without the slightest sound. Alicia dozed. Jordan virtually lived in the drawing-room, which was also always lighted. With tireless persistence he paced ceaselessly from one end of the room to the other. The carpet swallowed his steps. At times he entered the bedroom and continued his silent pacing back and forth alongside the bed, stopping for an instant at each end to regard his wife.

Suddenly Alicia began to have hallucinations, vague images, at first seeming to float in the air, then descending to floor level. Her eyes excessively wide, she stared continuously at the carpet on either side of the head of her bed. One night she suddenly focused on one spot. Then she opened her mouth to scream, and pearls of sweat suddenly beaded her nose and lips.

"Jordan! Jordan!" she clamoured, rigid with fright, still staring at the carpet.

Jordan ran to the bedroom, and, when she saw him appear, Alicia screamed with terror. "It's I, Alicia, it's I!"

Alicia looked at him confusedly; she looked at the carpet; she looked at him once again; and after a long moment of stupefied confrontation she regained her senses. She smiled and took her husband's hand in hers, caressing it, trembling, for half an hour.

Among her most persistent hallucinations was that of an anthropoid poised on his fingertips on the carpet, staring at her.

The doctors returned, but to no avail. They saw before them a diminishing life, a life bleeding away day by day, hour by hour, absolutely without their knowing why. During the last consultation Alicia lay in a stupor while they took her pulse, passing her inert wrist from one to another. They observed her a long time in silence and then moved into the dining room.

"Phew . . ." The discouraged chief physician shrugged his shoulders. "It's an inexplicable case. There is little we can do . . ."

"That's my last hope," Jordan groaned. And he staggered blindly against the table.

Alicia's life was fading away in the subdelirium of anaemia, a delirium which grew worse throughout the evening hours but which let up somewhat after dawn. The illness never worsened during the daytime, but each morning she awakened pale as death, almost in a swoon. It seemed only at night that her life drained out of her in new waves of blood. Always when she awakened she had the sensation of lying collapsed in the bed with a million-pound weight on top of her. Following the third day of this relapse she never left her bed again. She could scarcely move her head. She did not want her bed to be touched, not even to have her bedcovers arranged. Her crepuscular terrors advanced now in the form of monsters that dragged themselves toward the bed and laboriously climbed upon the bedspread.

Then she lost consciousness. The final two days she raved ceaselessly in a weak voice. The lights funereally illuminated the bedroom and drawing room. In the deathly silence of the house the only sound was the monotonous delirium from the bedroom and the dull echoes of Jordan's eternal pacing.

Finally, Alicia died. The servant, when she came in afterward to strip the now empty bed, stared wonderingly for a moment at the pillow.

"Sir!" she called to Jordan in a low voice. "There are stains on the pillow that look like blood."

Jordan approached rapidly and bent over the pillow. Truly, on the case, on both sides of the hollow left by Alicia's head, were two small dark spots.

"They look like punctures," the servant murmured after a moment of motionless observation.

"Hold it up to the light," Jordan told her.

The servant raised the pillow but immediately dropped it and stood staring at it, livid and trembling. Without knowing why, Jordan felt the hair rise on the back of his neck.

"What is it?" he murmured in a hoarse voice.

"It's very heavy," the servant whispered, still trembling.

Jordan picked it up; it was extraordinarily heavy. He carried it out of the room, and on the dining room table he ripped open the case and the ticking with a slash. The top feathers floated away, and the servant, her mouth opened wide, gave a scream of horror and covered her face with clenched fists: in the bottom of the pillow case, among the feathers, slowly moving its hairy legs, was a monstrous animal, a living, viscous ball. It was so swollen one could barely make out its mouth.

Night after night, since Alicia had taken to her bed, this abomination had stealthily applied its mouth—its proboscis one might better say—to the girl's temples, sucking her blood. The puncture was scarcely perceptible. The daily plumping of the pillow had doubtlessly at first impeded its progress, but as soon as the girl could no longer move, the suction became vertiginous. In five days, in five nights, the monster had drained Alicia's life away.

These parasites of feathered creatures, diminutive in their habitual environment, reach enormous proportions under certain conditions. Human blood seems particularly favourable to them, and it is not rare to encounter them in feather pillows.

THE FIGURE IN THE MIRAGE

ROBERT S. HICHENS

ON A WINDY NIGHT OF SPRING I SAT BY A GREAT FIRE THAT HAD BEEN BUILT BY Moors on a plain of Morocco under the shadow of a white city, and talked with a fellow-countryman, stranger to me till that day. We had met in the morning in a filthy alley of the town, and had forgathered. He was a wanderer for pleasure like myself, and, learning that he was staying in a dreary hostelry haunted by fever, I invited him to dine in my camp, and to pass the night in one of the small peaked tents that served me and my Moorish attendants as home. He consented gladly. Dinner was over—no bad one, for Moors can cook, can even make delicious caramel pudding in desert places—and Mohammed, my stalwart *valet de chambre*, had given us most excellent coffee. Now we smoked by the great fire, looked up at the marvellously bright stars, and told, as is the way of travellers, tales of our wanderings. My companion, whom I took at first to be a rather ironic, sceptical, and by nature unimaginative globe-trotter—he was a hard-looking, iron-grey man of middle-age—related the usual tiger story, the time-honoured elephant anecdote, and a couple of snake yarns of no special value, and I was beginning to fear that I should get little entertainment from so prosaic a sportsman, when I chanced to mention the desert.

"Ah!" said my guest, taking his pipe from his mouth, "the desert is the strangest thing in nature, as woman is the strangest thing in human nature. And when you get them together—desert and woman—by Jove!"

He paused, then he shot a keen glance at me.

"Ever been in the Sahara?" he said.

I replied in the affirmative, but added that I had as yet only seen the fringe of it.

"Biskra, I suppose," he rejoined, "and the nearest oasis, Sidi-Okba, and so on?"

I nodded. I saw I was in for another tale, and anticipated some history of shooting exploits under the salt mountain of El Outaya.

"Well," he continued, "I know the Sahara pretty fairly, and about the oddest thing I ever could believe in I heard of and believed in there."

"Something about gazelle?" I queried.

"Gazelle? No—a woman!" he replied.

As he spoke a Moor glided out of the windy darkness, and threw an armful of dry reeds on the fire. The flames flared up vehemently, and I saw that the face of my companion had changed. The hardness of it was smoothed away. Some memory, that held its romance, sat with him.

"A woman," he repeated, knocking the ashes out of his pipe almost sentimentally— "more than that, a French woman of Paris, with the nameless charm, the *chic*, the— But I'll tell you. Some years ago three Parisians—a man, his wife, and her unmarried sister, a girl of eighteen, with an angel and a devil in her dark beauty—came to a great resolve. They decided that they were tired of the Francais, sick of the Bois, bored to death with the boulevards, that they wanted to see for themselves the famous French colonies which were for ever being talked about in the Chamber. They determined to travel. No sooner was the determination come to than they were off. Hôtel des Colonies, Marseilles; steamboat, *Le Général Chanzy*; five o'clock on a splendid, sunny afternoon—Algiers, with its terraces, its white villas, its palm-trees, and its Spahis!"

"But—" I began.

He foresaw my objection.

"There were Spahis, and that's a point of my story. Some fête was on in the town while our Parisians were there. All the African troops were out—Zouaves, chasseurs, tirailleurs. The Governor went in procession to perform some ceremony, and in front of his carriage rode sixteen Spahis—probably got in from that desert camp of theirs near El Outaya. All this was long before the Tsar visited Paris, and our Parisians had never before seen the dashing Spahis, had only heard of them, of their magnificent horses, their turbans and flowing Arab robes, their gorgeous figures, lustrous eyes, and diabolic horse-manship. You know how they ride? No cavalry to touch them—not even the Cossacks! Well, our French friends were struck. The unmarried sister, more especially, was *boule-versée* by these glorious demons. As they caracoled beneath the balcony on which she was leaning she clapped her little hands, in their white kid gloves, and threw down a shower of roses. The falling flowers frightened the horses. They pranced, bucked, reared. One Spahi—a great fellow, eyes like a desert eagle, grand aquiline profile—on whom three roses had dropped, looked up, saw mademoiselle—call her Valérie—gazing down with her great, bright eyes—they were deuced fine eyes, by Jove!—"

"You've seen her?" I asked.

"— and flashed a smile at her with his white teeth. It was his last day in the ser-vice. He was in grand spirits. '*Mon Dieu! Mais quelles dents!*' she sang out. Her people laughed at her. The Spahi looked at her again—not smiling. She shrank back on the balcony. Then his place was taken by the Governor—small imperial, *chapeau de forme*, evening dress, landau and pair. Mademoiselle was *désolée*. Why couldn't civilised men look like Spahis? Why were all Parisians commonplace? Why—why? Her sister and brother-in-law called her the savage worshipper, and took her down to the café on the terrace to dine. And all through dinner mademoiselle talked of the *beaux* Spahis—in the plural, with a secret reservation in her heart. After Algiers our Parisians went by way of Constantine to Biskra. Now they saw desert for the first time—the curious iron-grey, velvety-brown, and rose-pink mountains; the nomadic Arabs camping in their earth-coloured tents patched with rags; the camels against the skyline; the everlasting sands, broken here and there by the deep green shadows of distant oases, where the close-growing palms, seen from far off, give to the desert almost the effect that clouds give to Cornish waters. At Biskra mademoiselle—oh! what she must have looked like under the mimosa-trees before the Hôtel de l'Oasis!—"

"Then you've seen her," I began.

"—mademoiselle became enthusiastic again, and, almost before they knew it, her sister and brother-in-law were committed to a desert expedition, were fitted out with a dragoman, tents, mules—the whole show, in fact—and one blazing hot day found themselves out in that sunshine—you know it—with Biskra a green shadow on that sea, the mountains behind the sulphur springs turning from bronze to black-brown in the distance, and the table flatness of the desert stretching ahead of them to the limits of the world and the judgment day."

My companion paused, took a flaming reed from the fire, put it to his pipe bowl, pulled hard at his pipe—all the time staring straight before him, as if, among the glowing logs, he saw the caravan of the Parisians winding onward across the desert sands. Then he turned to me, sighed, and said:

"You've seen mirage?"

"Yes," I answered.

"Have you noticed that in mirage the things one fancies one sees generally appear in large numbers—buildings crowded as in towns, trees growing together as in woods, men shoulder to shoulder in large companies?"

My experience of mirage in the desert was so, and I acknowledged it.

"Have you ever seen in a mirage a solitary figure?" he continued.

I thought for a moment. Then I replied in the negative.

"No more have I," he said. "And I believe it's a very rare occurrence. Now mark the mirage that showed itself to mademoiselle on the first day of the desert journey of the Parisians. She saw it on the northern verge of the oasis of Sidi-Okba, late in the afternoon. As they journeyed Tahar, their dragoman—he had applied for the post, and got it by the desire of mademoiselle, who admired his lithe bearing and gorgeous aplomb—Tahar suddenly pulled up his mule, pointed with his brown hand to the horizon, and said in French:

"'There is mirage! Look! There is the mirage of the great desert!'

"Our Parisians, filled with excitement, gazed above the pointed ears of their beasts, over the shimmering waste. There, beyond the palms of the oasis, wrapped in a mysterious haze, lay the mirage. They looked at it in silence. Then Mademoiselle cried, in her little bird's clear voice:

"'Mirage! But surely he's real?'

"'What does mademoiselle see?' asked Tahar quickly.

"'Why, a sort of faint landscape, through which a man—an Arab, I suppose—is riding, towards Sidi—what is it?—Sidi-Okba! He's got something in front of him, hanging across his saddle.'

"Her relations looked at her in amazement.

"'I only see houses standing on the edge of water,' said her sister.

"'And I!' cried the husband.

"'Houses and water,' assented Tahar. 'It is always so in the mirage of Sidi-Okba.'

"'I see no houses, no water,' cried mademoiselle, straining her eyes. 'The Arab rides fast, like the wind. He is in a hurry. One would think he was being pursued. Why, now he's gone!'

"She turned to her companions. They saw still the fairy houses of the mirage standing in the haze on the edge of the fairy water.

"'But,' mademoiselle said impatiently, 'there's nothing at all now—only sand.'

"'Mademoiselle dreams,' said Tahar. 'The mirage is always there.'

"They rode forward. That night they camped near Sidi-Okba. At dinner, while the stars came out, they talked of the mirage, and mademoiselle still insisted that it was a mirage of a horseman bearing something before him on his saddle-bow, and riding as if for life. And Tahar said again:

"'Mademoiselle dreams!'

"As he spoke he looked at her with a mysterious intentness, which she noticed. That night, in her little camp-bed, round which the desert winds blew mildly, she did indeed dream. And her dream was of the magic forms that ride on magic horses through mirage.

"The next day, at dawn, the caravan of the Parisians went on its way, winding farther into the desert. In leaving Sidi-Okba they left behind them the last traces of civilisation—the French man and woman who keep the auberge in the orange garden there. To-day, as they journeyed, a sense of deep mystery flowed upon the heart of mademoiselle. She felt that she was a little cockle-shell of a boat which, accustomed hitherto only to the Seine, now set sail upon a mighty ocean. The fear of the Sahara came upon her."

My companion paused. His face was grave, almost stern.

"And her relations?" I asked. "Did they feel—"

"Haven't an idea what they felt," he answered curtly.

"But how do you know that mademoiselle—"

"You'll understand at the end of the story. As they journeyed in the sun across the endless flats—for the mountains had vanished now, and nothing broke the level of the sand—mademoiselle's gaiety went from her. Silent was the lively, chattering tongue that knew the jargon of cities, the gossip of the Plage. She was oppressed. Tahar rode close at her side. He seemed to have taken her under his special protection. Far before them rode the attendants, chanting deep love songs in the sun. The sound of those songs seemed like the sound of the great desert singing of its wild and savage love to the heart of mademoiselle. At first her brother-in-law and sister bantered her on her silence, but Tahar stopped them, with a curious authority.

"'The desert speaks to mademoiselle,' he said in her hearing. 'Let her listen.'

"He watched her continually with his huge eyes, and she did not mind his glance, though she began to feel irritated and restless under the observation of her relations.

"Towards noon Tahar again described mirage. As he pointed it out he stared fixedly at mademoiselle.

"The two other Parisians exclaimed that they saw forest trees, a running stream, a veritable oasis, where they longed to rest and eat their *déjeuner*.

"'And mademoiselle?' said Tahar. 'What does she see?'

"She was gazing into the distance. Her face was very pale, and for a moment she did not answer. Then she said:

"'I see again the Arab bearing the burden before him on the saddle. He is much clearer than yesterday. I can almost see his face—'

"She paused. She was trembling.

"'But I cannot see what he carries. It seems to float on the wind, like a robe, or a woman's dress. Ah! *mon Dieu!* how fast he rides!'

"She stared before her as if fascinated, and following with her eyes some rapidly-moving object. Suddenly she shut her eyes.

"'He's gone!' she said.

"'And now—mademoiselle sees?' said Tahar.

"She opened her eyes.

"'Nothing.'

"'Yet the mirage is still there,' he said.

"'Valérie,' cried her sister, 'are you mad that you see what no one else can see, and cannot see what all else see?'

"'Am I mad, Tahar?' she said gravely, almost timidly, to the dragoman.

"And the fear of the Sahara came again upon her.

"'Mademoiselle sees what she must,' he answered. 'The desert speaks to the heart of mademoiselle.'

"That night there was moon. Mademoiselle could not sleep. She lay in her narrow bed and thought of the figure in the mirage, while the moonbeams stole in between the tent pegs to keep her company. She thought of second sight, of phantoms, and of wraiths. Was this riding Arab, whom she alone could see, a phantom of the Sahara, mysteriously accompanying the caravan, and revealing himself to her through the medium of the mirage as if in a magic mirror? She turned restlessly upon her pillow, saw the naughty moonbeams, got up, and went softly to the tent door. All the desert was bathed in light. She gazed out as a mariner gazes out over the sea. She heard jackals yelping in the distance, peevish in their insomnia, and fancied their voices were the voices of desert demons. As she stood there she thought of the figure in the mirage, and wondered if mirage ever rises at night—if, by chance, she might see it now. And, while she stood wondering, far away across the sand there floated up a silvery haze, like a veil of spangled tissue—exquisite for a ball robe, she said long after!—and in this haze she saw again the phantom Arab galloping upon his horse. But now he was clear in the moon. Furiously he rode, like a thing demented in a dream, and as he rode he looked back over his shoulder, as if he feared pursuit. Mademoiselle could see his fierce eyes, like the eyes of a desert eagle that stares unwinking at the glaring African sun. He urged on his fleet horse. She could hear now the ceaseless thud of its hoofs upon the hard sand as it drew nearer and nearer. She could see the white foam upon its steaming flanks, and now at last she knew that the burden which the Arab bore across his saddle and supported with his arms was a woman. Her robe flew out upon the wind; her dark, loose hair streamed over the breast of the horseman; her face was hidden against his heart; but mademoiselle saw his face, uttered a cry, and shrank back against the canvas of the tent.

"For it was the face of the Spahi who had ridden in the procession of the Governor— of the Spahi to whom she had thrown the roses from the balcony of Algiers.

"As she cried out the mirage faded, the Arab vanished, the thud of the horse's hoofs died in her ears, and Tahar, the dragoman, glided round the tent, and stood before her. His eyes gleamed in the moonlight like ebon jewels.

"'Hush!' he whispered, 'mademoiselle sees the mirage?'

"Mademoiselle could not speak. She stared into the eyes of Tahar, and hers were dilated with wonder."

He drew nearer to her.

"'Mademoiselle has seen again the horseman and his burden.'

"She bowed her head. All things seemed dream-like to her. Tahar's voice was low and monotonous, and sounded far away.

"'It is fate,' he said. He paused, gazing upon her.

"'In the tents they all sleep,' he murmured. 'Even the watchman sleeps, for I have given him a powder of hashish, and hashish gives long dreams—long dreams.'

"From beneath his robe he drew a small box, opened it, and showed to mademoiselle a dark brown powder, which he shook into a tiny cup of water.

"'Mademoiselle shall drink, as the watchman has drunk,' he said—'shall drink and dream.'

"He held the cup to her lips, and she, fascinated by his eyes, as by the eyes of a mesmerist, could not disobey him. She swallowed the hashish, swayed, and fell forward into his arms.

"A moment later, across the spaces of the desert, whitened by the moon, rode the figure mademoiselle had seen in the mirage. Upon his saddle he bore a dreaming woman. And in the ears of the woman through all the night beat the thunderous music of a horse's hoofs spurning the desert sand. Mademoiselle had taken her place in the vision which she no longer saw."

My companion paused. His pipe had gone out. He did not relight it, but sat looking at me in silence.

"The Spahi?" I asked.

"Had claimed the giver of the roses."

"And Tahar?"

"The shots he fired after the Spahi missed fire. Yet Tahar was a notable shot."

"A strange tale," I said. "How did you come to hear it?"

"A year ago I penetrated very far into the Sahara on a sporting expedition. One day I came upon an encampment of nomads. The story was told me by one of them as we sat in the low doorway of an earth-coloured tent and watched the sun go down."

"Told you by an Arab?"

He shook his head.

"By whom, then?"

"By a woman with a clear little bird's voice, with an angel and a devil in her dark beauty, a woman with the gesture of Paris—the grace, the *diablerie* of Paris."

Light broke on me.

"By mademoiselle!" I exclaimed.

"Pardon," he answered; "by madame."

"She was married?"

"To the figure in the mirage; and she was content."

"Content!" I cried.

"Content with her two little dark children dancing before her in the twilight, content when the figure of the mirage galloped at evening across the plain, shouting an Eastern love song, with a gazelle—instead of a woman—slung across his saddle-bow. Did I not say that, as the desert is the strangest thing in nature, so a woman is the strangest thing in human nature? Which heart is most mysterious?"

"Its heart?" I said.

"Or the heart of mademoiselle?"

"I give the palm to the latter."

"And I," he answered, taking off his wide-brimmed hat—"I gave it when I saluted her as madame before the tent door, out there in the great desert."

The First Comer

B. M. Croker

"Making night hideous."
—*Hamlet*

I AM AN OLD MAID, AND AM NOT THE LEAST ASHAMED OF THE CIRCUMSTANCE. PRAY, why should women not be allowed the benefit of the doubt like men, and be supposed to remain single from choice?

I can assure you that it is not from want of *offers* that I am Miss Janet MacTavish, spinster. I could tell—but no matter. It is not to set down a list of proposals that I have taken pen in hand, but to relate a very mysterious occurrence that happened in our house last spring.

My sister Matilda and I are a well-to-do couple of maiden ladies, having no poor relatives, and a comfortable private fortune. We keep four servants (all female), and occupy a large detached house in a fashionable part of Edinburgh, and the circle in which we move is most exclusive and genteel.

Matilda is a good deal older than I am (though we dress alike), and is somewhat of an invalid.

Our east winds are certainly trying, and last March she had a very sharp attack of bronchitis, brought on (between ourselves) by her own rash imprudence. Though I may not say this to her face, I may say it here.

She does not approve of fiction, though, goodness knows, what I am going to set down is not fiction, but fact; but any literary work in a gay paper cover (of course, I don't mean tracts), such as novels and magazines, is an abomination in her eyes, and "reading such-like trash" she considers sinful waste of time.

So, even if this falls into her hands by an odd chance, she will never read it, and I am quite safe in writing out everything that happened, as I dare not do if I thought that Mattie was coming after me and picking holes in every sentence.

Matilda is terribly particular about grammar and orthography, and reads over all my letters before I venture to close them.

Dear me, how I have wandered away from my point! I'm sure that no one will care to know that I am a little in awe of my elder, that she treats me sometimes as if I were still in my teens. But people may like to hear of the queer thing that happened to me, and I am really and truly coming to it at last.

Matilda was ill with bronchitis, very ill. Bella (that's our sewing-maid and general factotum, who has been with us twelve years this term) and I took it in turns to sit up with her at night. It happened to be my night, and I was sitting over the fire in a half-kind of doze, when Matilda woke up, and nothing would serve her but a cup of tea of all things, at two o'clock in the morning—the kitchen fire out, no hot water, and every one in the house in their beds, except myself.

I had some nice beef-tea in a little pan beside the hob, and I coaxed her hard to try some of that, but not a bit of it. Nothing would serve her but real tea, and I knew that once she had taken the notion in her head, I might just as well do her bidding first as last. So I opened the door and went out, thinking to take the small lamp, for, of course, all the gas was out, and turned off at the meter—as it ought to be in every decent house.

"You'll no do that!" she said, quite cross. Mattie speaks broad when she is vexed, and we had had a bit of argument about the tea. "You'll no do that, and leave me here without the light! Just go down and infuse me a cup of tea as quick as ever you can, for I know I'll be awfully the better of it!"

So there was just nothing else for it, and down I went in the pitch-black darkness, not liking the job at all.

It was not that I was afraid. Not I. But the notion of having to rake up and make the kitchen fire, and boil the kettle, was an errand that went rather against the grain, especially as I'm a terrible bad hand at lighting a fire.

I was thinking of this and wondering where were the wood and the matches to be found, when, just as I reached the head of the stairs, I was delighted to hear a great raking out of cinders below in the kitchen. Such a raking and poking and banging of coals and knocking about of the range I never did hear, and I said to myself—

"This is fine; it's washing morning" (we do our washing at home) "and later than I thought; and the servants are up, so it's all right"; and I ran down the kitchen stairs, quite inspirited like by the idea. As I passed the door of the servants' room (where cook and housemaid slept), Harris, that's the housemaid, called out—

"Who's that?"

I went to the door and said—

"It's I, Miss Janet. I want a cup of tea for Miss MacTavish."

In a moment Harris had thrown on some clothes and was out in the passage. She was always a quick, willing girl, and very obliging. She said (it was black dark, and I could not see her)—

"Never you mind, Miss Janet; I'll light the fire and boil up the kettle in no time."

"You need not do that," said I, "for there's some one at the fire already—cook, I suppose."

"Not me, ma'am," said a sleepy voice from the interior of the bedroom. "I'm in my bed."

"Then who can it be?" I asked, for the banging and raking had become still more tremendous, and the thunder of the poker was just awful!

"It must be Bella," said Harris, feeling her way to the kitchen door and pushing it open, followed by me.

We stood for full half a minute in the dark, whilst she felt about and groped for the matches, and still the noise continued.

"Bella," I said crossly, "what on earth—"

But at this instant the match was struck, and dimly lit up the kitchen. I strained my eyes into the darkness, whilst Harris composedly lit a candle. I looked, and looked, and looked again, but there was no one in the kitchen but ourselves.

I was just petrified, I can tell you, and I staggered against the dresser, and gaped at the now silent fireplace. The coals and cinders and ashes were exactly as they had gone out, not a bit disturbed; any one could see that they had never been stirred.

"In the name of goodness, Harris," I said in a whisper, "where is the person that was poking that fire? You heard them yourself!"

"I heard a noise, sure enough, Miss Janet," she said, not a bit daunted; "and if I was a body that believed in ghosts and such-like clavers, I'd say it was them," putting firewood in the grate as she spoke. "It's queer, certainly. Miss MacTavish will be wearying for her tea," she added. "I know well what it is to have a kind of longing for a good cup. Save us! what a cold air there is in this kitchen. I wonder where cook put the bellows."

Seeing that Harris was taking the matter so coolly, for very shame I was forced to do the like; so I did not say a word about my misgivings, nor the odd queer thrill I had felt as we stood in the pitch darkness and listened to the furious raking of the kitchen grate.

How icy cold the kitchen had been! just like a vault, and with the same damp, earthy smell!

I was in a mighty hurry to get back upstairs, believe me, and did all in my power to speed the fire and the kettle, and in due time we wended our way above, Harris bearing the tea on a tray, and walking last.

I left her to administer the refreshment, whilst I went into Bella's room, which was close by, candle in hand.

"You are awake, I see, Bella," I remarked, putting it down as I spoke (I felt that I must unbosom myself to some one, or never close an eye that night). "Tell me, did you hear a great raking of the kitchen fire just now?"

"Yes, miss, of course. Why, it woke me. I suppose you had occasion to go down for something, Miss Janet; but why did you not call me?"

"It was not I who woke you, Bella," I rejoined quickly. "I was on my way downstairs when I heard that noise below, and I thought it was cook or Harris, but when I got down Harris came out of the bedroom. Cook was in bed. Maggie, you know, is up above you, and we went into the kitchen, thinking it might be you or her, and lit a candle; but I give you my word of honour that, although the noise was really terrible till we struck a light, when we looked about us not a soul was to be seen!"

At this, Bella started up in bed, and became of a livid, chalky kind of colour.

"No one, Miss Janet?" she gasped out.

"Not a soul!" I replied solemnly.

"Then, oh!" she exclaimed, now jumping bodily out on the floor, and looking quite wild and distracted, "tell me, in Heaven's name, which of you went into the kitchen first, you or Harris?" She was so agitated, she seemed scarcely able to bring out the words, and her eyes rested upon mine with a strange, frightened look, that made me fancy she had taken temporary leave of her wits.

"Harris went first," I answered shortly.

"Thank Heaven for that!" she returned, now collapsing on the edge of her bed. "But poor Kate Harris is a dead woman!"

I stared hard at Bella, as well I might. Was she talking in her sleep? or was I dreaming? "What do you mean, Bella Cameron?" I cried. "Are you gone crazy? Are you gone clean daft?"

"It was a warning," she replied, in a low and awe-struck voice. "We Highlanders understand the like well! It was a warning of death! Kate Harris's hour has come."

"If you are going to talk such wicked nonsense, Bella," I said, "I'm not going to stop to listen. Whatever you do, don't let Matilda hear you going on with such foolishness. The house would not hold her, and you know that well."

"All right, Miss Janet; you heard the commotion yourself—you will allow that; and you will see that the kitchen grate is never raked out for nothing. I only wish, from the bottom of my heart, that what I've told you may not come true; but, bad as it was, I'm thankful that you were not first in the kitchen."

A few more indignant expostulations on my part, and lamentations on Bella's, and then I went back to Matilda, and it being now near three o'clock, and she inclined to be drowsy, I lay down on the sofa, and got a couple of hours' sleep.

A day or two afterwards I was suddenly struck with a strange thrill of apprehension by noticing how very, very ill Kate Harris looked. I taxed her with not feeling well, and she admitted that she had not been herself, and could not say what ailed her. She had no actual pain, but she felt weak all over, and could scarcely drag herself about the house, "It would go off. She would not see a doctor—No, no, no!—It was only just a kind of cold feeling in her bones, and a sort of notion that a hand was gripping her throat. It was all fancy; and Dr. Henderson (our doctor) would make fine game of her if he saw her by way of being a patient. She would be all right in a day or two." Vain hope! In a day or two she was much worse. She was obliged to give in—to take to her bed. I sent for Dr. Henderson—indeed he called daily to visit Mattie—so I had only to pilot him down below to see Kate. He came out to me presently with a very grave face, and said—

"Has she any friends ?"—pointing towards Kate's door with his thumb.

"Friends! To be sure," I answered. "She has a sister married to a tram conductor in Wickham Street."

"Send for her at once; and you had better have her moved. She can't last a week."

"Do you mean that she is going to die?" I gasped, clutching the balusters, for we were standing in the lower hall.

"I am sorry to say the case is hopeless. Nothing can save her, and the sooner she is with her own people the better."

I was, I need scarcely tell you, greatly shocked—terribly shocked—and presently, when I had recovered myself, I sent off, post-haste, for Kate's sister.

I went in to see her. She, poor creature, was all curiosity to know what the doctor had said.

"He would tell me nothing, miss," she observed smilingly. "Only felt my pulse, and tried my heart with a stethoscope, and my temperature with that queer little tube. I only feel a bit tired and out of breath; but you'll find I'll be all right in a day or two. I'm only sorry I'm giving all this trouble, and Bella and Mary having to do my work. However, I'll be fit to clean the plate on Saturday."

Poor soul, little did she dream that her work in this world was done!

And I, as I sat beside the bed and looked at her always pale face, her now livid lips and hollow eyes, told myself that already I could see the hand of Death on her countenance. I was obliged to tell her sister what the doctor had said; and how she cried—and so did I—and who was to tell Kate? We wished to keep her with us undisturbed—Matilda and I—but her people would not hear of it, and so we had an ambulance from the hospital and sent her home.

She just lived a week, and, strange to say, she had always the greatest craving for me to be with her, for me to sit beside her, and read to her, and hold her hand. She showed far more anxiety for *my* company than for that of any of her own people.

Bella alone, of all the household, expressed no astonishment when she heard the doctor's startling verdict. Being in Mattie's room at the time, she merely looked over at me gravely, and significantly shook her head.

One evening Bella and I were with her; she had lain silent for a long time, and then she said to me quite suddenly—

"Miss Janet, you'll remember the morning you came downstairs looking for Miss MacTavish's tea?" (Did I not recollect it, only too well!) "Somehow, I got a queer kind of chill then; I felt it at the time, to the very marrow of my bones. I have never been warm since. It was just this day fortnight. I remember it well, because it was washing Monday."

That night Kate Harris died. She passed away, as it were, in her sleep, with her hand in mine. As she was with me on that mysterious night, so I was now with her.

Call me a superstitious old imbecile, or what you like, but I firmly believe that, had I entered that kitchen first, it would have been Janet MacTavish, and not Kate Harris, who was lying in her coffin!

Of course Matilda knows nothing of this, nor ever will. Perhaps—for she is one of your strong-minded folk—she would scout at the idea, and at me, for a daft, silly body, and try to explain it all away quite reasonable like. I only wish she could!

FOOTPRINTS

A. M. BURRAGE

SIR ARNOLD SOMBY AND HIS SON REGGIE HAD GONE INTO THE BILLIARD-ROOM after dinner. The butler brought them coffee, and noticed that they ceased speaking when he entered the room. Sir Arnold hummed a tune as he helped himself to sugar, a sure sign that he was keeping a tight hold on his temper. Mr. Reggie, the servant observed, seemed out of sorts—the cup and saucer rattled in his hand as he took them.

Barlow left the billiard-room with a distinct impression that there was something wrong.

Sir Arnold Somby was stout, red-faced, well-preserved, standing over six feet high in his low-heeled evening shoes. He had lived hard, ridden hard, and drunk hard all his life, and now that age was approaching, gout and a hobnailed liver were enforcing the debts he owed to Nature. A big, blatant blackguard of a man, this, boastful of the evil he had done, looking back with relish on a life full of vicious memories.

His son Reggie took after his dead mother in most things.

He was a tall, slim young man of three-and-twenty, with a girlish face. He stood in mortal dread of his father, who treated him with ill-disguised contempt. He was reading for the Bar, with very little chance of being called, and no chance at all of making a living for himself if he were.

When the butler had gone, Sir Arnold turned sharply towards his son, who was searching in the pockets of the table for chalk.

"Now Reggie," he said sharply, "what's the matter with you? Let's hear what you've got to say. You've been throwing out hints all day long. Why the deuce can't you speak straight out, and have done with it?"

Reggie turned and leaned against the table, one arm along the cushion. His fingers moved nervously, tapping and stroking the cloth. What he had to say required all his courage, and the look on his father's face seemed to baulk him of speech.

"I want to get married, sir," he said at length, with an obvious effort. He spoke quickly lest his resolution should fail him before the sentence was completed, and the words seemed to jostle one another as they fell from his lips. Sir Arnold's deep-throated chuckle of genuine amusement almost reassured him.

"Then why the devil couldn't you have said so before, instead of beating about the bush all day?" the baronet demanded. "Dash it, man, I thought you'd been cheating at cards or something from the way you'd been going on. I didn't say you couldn't marry if you can find a girl fool enough to have you, did I? If the girl's all right I don't mind allowing both of you enough to live on until you step into my shoes. Is it that Wharton girl?"

"No, sir," Reggie answered, flushing, and then added as he saw another question framing itself on his father's lips: "It's—it's no one you know. I—I met her in town."

"I see," Sir Arnold chuckled. "Some little trap your Aunt Polly let you in for, I'll wager. Well, tell me all about her."

The young man began to stammer. He drew away from the table so that he stood outside the radii of the shaded lights.

"I didn't meet her at Aunt Polly's," he confessed. "She's—she's a shop-girl."

He hung his head and waited for the torrent of his father's wrath to be loosened. But there was a profound silence for nearly a minute, broken only by the garrulous ticking of a little clock. It seemed to mimic his own hurried uneven tones.

"Is this a joke, Reggie?" Sir Arnold said at last.

"Good heavens, no, sir!" The words seemed to be jerked out of the young man. "Do you think I should joke on such a subject?"

"No," Sir Arnold echoed, pursing his lips. "No, I'm very much afraid you think you mean it. Good Lord! and you're my son! Didn't you know me better than to come to me with such a tale, eh, you fool?"

"But father—"

"Look here, my boy," the baronet continued rapidly, with an odd kindliness in his tone, "I don't want to be hard on you. Just be a bit sensible, and you won't regret it. I had a good time myself when I was young, and I don't want to stint you. You shall have an extra hundred tomorrow. I shan't grumble at increasing your allowance, and I don't care a hang what you do so long as you keep outside the registry office. When I was a young man—"

Reggie flushed like a girl.

"You don't understand!" he exclaimed. "I want to be fair to her—I want to marry her."

Sir Arnold did not storm—such was not the way with him when he was deeply moved. It was only on trivial occasions that he displayed a broad and catholic taste in oaths. He merely shrugged his shoulders.

"Well," he said, "I can stop you. You are of age, you know. Will you pardon my curiosity if I inquire how you mean to live?"

The younger man did not answer.

"You've been counting on me, I suppose? Well, you've made a miscalculation. Did you think I was going to pay for the honour of having some aitchless little guttersnipe in my family? *Did* you? Reggie, you're the biggest fool that ever breathed! And you're my son!—my son!"

"I thought," Reggie faltered, "you might. I've never given you any trouble yet, sir, and she's quite presentable—or nearly."

The baronet threw what remained of his small stock of patience to the winds.

"Do you imagine that I'm going to put up with a daughter-in-law who's *nearly* presentable?" he demanded, "when half the girls in the county would jump at the chance of one day becoming Lady Somby. Why on earth are you such a fool, Reggie? Why can't you chuck her, if only for your own sake?"

"Because I love her, sir."

The words were spoken haltingly; but with a note of defiance which did not escape Sir Arnold, who sighed.

"I was afraid that was coming," he said. "If you were a boy of sixteen I could understand it, and be amused. But you're too old now for me to laugh at you."

"Whatever you say," Reggie muttered, "I *must* marry her."

"Why *must* you?"

Reggie licked his dry lips and lowered his eyes, after glancing once at his father's fierce, red face. Slowly the truth dawned on Sir Arnold's not very active imagination.

"You don't mean!" he gasped, drawing a long breath, "you don't mean that—that—"

"Yes." The young man took up his cup and began to stir the dregs of his coffee. "Now you see why it's necessary for me to—"

Sir Arnold seated himself on the edge of the table and regarded his carefully-manicured nails.

"I don't see your point of view at all," he said. "Perhaps she is only trying to blackmail you."

"No, she's not that sort," the son answered. "She's a respectable girl—her people are respectable."

"Of course," Sir Arnold sneered. "They always are. Parson's daughter, isn't she? Offer her a couple of hundred without prejudice. I'll write you out a cheque tomorrow."

The younger man passed a hot hand across his forehead.

"I can't do that!" he cried. "My responsibility doesn't end there, and you know it! She expects me to marry her. It is the only thing left for me to do."

"It's not your duty to sacrifice your career for her. Your duty to the family comes first. The woman must pay. That is one of the first laws of society."

"But she won't pay all!" the other cried. "Neither shall I. The guiltless one will suffer—suffer a whole lifetime. It's not fair!—it's not right!"

Sir Arnold shrugged his shoulders.

"You are talking like a fool!" he said. "All of us have to pay for our existence by inheriting something from our parents that we would sooner be without. I inherited gout from mine. You can see that your child has a fair start in life."

"But——"

"The subject of marriage is closed," said Sir Arnold firmly. "I can see what's worrying you. Well, I'll take all the responsibility in the sight of heaven——a little more or less won't make any difference. But mind, if you dare to disobey me you can go to the devil! You won't get another ha'penny from me while I live."

Reggie turned away with a sob in his throat.

"All right," he muttered. "You know I can't afford to quarrel with you. I hope you're satisfied now that your infernal money has bought your son's honour."

The passage of nearly three years had left its traces on Reginald Somby. In many ways he had approached nearer to his father's ideal. He followed the hounds with extraordinary fortitude, considering that his heart seemed to turn to ice at every jump. He had acquired an average taste for strong liquors, and a capacity for holding them like a gentleman. Sir Arnold was pleased to note a growing breadth of view and fewer signs of what he called a "dame-school sense of honour." Moreover, Reginald was engaged to marry the daughter of a neighbouring family, a lady whose deficiencies were well screened by her undisputed social position and roseate expectations. In a word, Reginald was doing the right thing by his people.

To look at him on that December evening, however, did not suggest that he was at peace with the world. The shivering tout who held open for him the door of the taxi, and took his sixpence, pitied him. His face was pale and haggard, his eyes sunken and dull. Damocles, sitting at the banquet under the suspended sword, might have looked less ghastly.

The motor-cab drew up before the entrance to a block of small flats in St. John's Wood. Reggie alighted and paid the man, and, as the cab drove away, walked cautiously up the steps and passed through under the great lamp.

Inside it was dark and cold and cheerless. Stone steps led from floor to floor, and these were slippery with snow, caked and melting, which many pairs of feet had brought in from the cheerless streets. There were footprints in which Reggie took a morbid, half-conscious interest, and caught himself speculating as to which were the doctor's.

He knocked at a door on the second floor, and a woman came and opened it. A single bulb of electric light burned in the passage behind her, but even in the dimness, which concealed so much, her face was not pleasant to gaze upon.

To Reggie's surprise she had not been crying—or, at least, her face bore no traces of tears. Her eyes, slightly protruding, shone as if they reflected the light of a fierce fire. There was an expression in them which the man could not fathom, but in that instant he realised with a sudden painful shock the meaning of the word "horror." He almost recoiled from her.

"Come in!" was all she said.

He entered, feeling his way in spite of the light. As the door closed behind him he turned and faced her. He now saw that her face was drawn and haggard, and that her high cheek-bones stood out in unwonted prominence. She looked like a *passée* woman of five-and-thirty, whereas she was not yet twenty-two. He read in her face all that he had feared, so that the question he put was almost superfluous.

"Yes," she answered in a colourless voice, "the child is dead!"

He did not ask any further questions. He coughed, and struggled with an unfamiliar sensation in his eyes and throat. The woman saw tears glisten on his lashes, and some of the hardness left her face. Her own eyes grew wet, and suddenly she came to him, resting her head on his shoulder and twining her fingers behind his neck.

"Reggie!" she sobbed. "Reggie! Reggie!"

He muttered something, but neither knew what he said. He no longer loved her, but a great pity was choking him. His thoughts, for the most part, centred themselves on the dead child—*his* child. He had seen it once or twice, and loved it in spite of himself. Nature implants parental affection even among the animals, who neither marry nor give in marriage. His life was not lightened of a burden—he had lost a son!

"Ah, I loved him, too!" the woman whispered presently. "Dear God, if he only had a name to die with!—a name to be written in the registry of heaven!"

Her face quivered with passion.

"I wish that scoundrel was here to hear me curse him!" she panted. "Your precious father who made a coward of you and robbed our boy of birthright, father, and honour! Your father, with his sneer and his light regard for virtue! He who was to be responsible, on his own wishing, in the light of heaven! I wish—"

Her voice rose to a high pitch and cracked. Further speech was stifled by sobs that racked her body. The man did his utmost to soothe her—half-awed, half-irritated by her violent grief. Presently she recovered the use of her voice.

"I know what you're thinking!" she exclaimed violently. "You're thinking that a real lady wouldn't go on like this. I don't care. I—oh, don't mind what I'm saying, Reggie." Her voice suddenly sank into a whisper. "Would you like to see him?" she asked tremulously.

He nodded, and she led the way into a dimly-lit bedroom, pausing by the switch to turn on another light. Reggie tiptoed across the thin carpet until he stood in the middle of the room, where he remained stationary. The dead child lay in a cot, drawn up close beside a big brass bedstead. He did not approach any nearer.

Now that the child was dead a vague, unreasoning fear of it came over him. He was not squeamish of death itself, but he knew that somewhere, in some world, a soul was wandering—a soul as powerful as his own. It was not a child any longer, it had become a Being.

The woman came and stood beside him. She turned her face towards that of the dead child, and, as she gazed upon it, all the softness that remained in her expression faded away. Her eyes blazed suddenly with the malevolence of a demon, and she went over to the cot and lifted the dead child in her arms.

Reggie fidgeted and looked away. There was something weird about the woman—something subtly repulsive. He heard the soft sound of impassioned whispering, and his heart began to flutter. It is not nice to hear a woman whispering to her dead.

Presently the sound ceased, and Reggie looked up. The woman's wild eyes met his across the room.

"My son has heard me," she said in a hushed voice.

"Mabel!" he pleaded, "don't!"

"My son has heard me," she repeated. "I had a message. Sir Arnold shall stand by the words he spoke so lightly. My son shall take his hand and lead him to the Judgement Seat. A child shall lead him—a little child—my son."

Her voice died away into an unintelligible muttering, her eyes closed in a swoon. Reggie was at her side just in time to save her from falling.

Early on the following morning Reggie received a telegram. It was from Barlow, and to the effect that Sir Arnold had died suddenly on the previous night. When the new baronet had partly recovered from the shock—but not from the haunting sense of horror that accompanied it—he drove straight to King's Cross and took the first train home.

Barlow greeted him as the hired fly from the station drew up before the hall door. The old man's face was as white as the snow that lay like a cloak over the land. The sudden death of his old master seemed to have affected him more than the dead man's son.

"I'm glad you managed to come down so quick, sir," he said.

"How did it happen?" was Reggie's first question.

"He died sitting in his chair in the library last night," Barlow whispered, as he took his master's hat and coat. "We left him there until you came, sir." The old man's lips twisted and straightened again. "Dr. MacVeitch has been in, sir. Says it was heart-failure caused by a shock."

Reggie took a step in the direction of a chair. A feeling of weakness and nausea had come over him.

"What sort of shock?" he asked, in a voice that was unlike his own.

"Nobody quite knows, sir," Barlow muttered hoarsely.

The new Baronet gathered together all his courage.

"Take me to him, Barlow," he commanded.

They climbed the stairs together. The library was on the first floor. It was originally intended for a bedroom, but Sir Arnold had made the alteration to suit his own convenience. Together they entered the chamber of death.

The dead man sat upright in a cane-backed chair before a small table, on which were a glass, a decanter of whisky, a syphon, and a box of cigars. A cigar had burned itself out between his fingers.

His eyes were wide open, and his gaze was directed low down towards the door. They were eyes that seemed to see something even in death—something not to be mentioned, scarcely to be thought of. There was a whole inferno of terror concentrated in that gaze. Reggie uttered a low cry and reeled, but the strong arm of Barlow held him up.

He took only one glance at his father and looked away—saw the wide-open, terror-stricken eyes, the parted lips, the head thrust forward to the full extent of the neck.

"Barlow!" he gasped, "tell me how it happened."

"How am I to know, sir?"

"You know something," the other insisted. "For God's sake tell me!'

"Yes, sir, I do know—something." The voice was hushed and quavering.

"But I covered up the tracks—trod them out one by one—and nobody'll ever know but me and you. I saw them, sir, when I went out after the doctor, when James had woke me up and told me what had happened." He paused for breath. Each man could hear his own heart beating quickly and irregularly.

"There's no snow under the fir plantation, sir," Barlow continued in a strained voice, "and the footprints commenced just on the edge. They went across into the drive, and up the drive to the front door. There was a print on every step, sir. There was wet prints in the hall, and just dabs here and there on the stairs. The last one was on the polished boards just inside the library, sir—just over there by the door, where I'm pointin'. I wiped 'em up, sir, with my own hands, and kicked snow over the ones outside."

He held his young master more firmly by the arm. When he continued speaking his voice had sunk so that it was almost inaudible.

"Mr. Reggie—sir—they was the naked footprints of a little child!"

THE FORTUNES OF
SIR ROBERT ARDAGH

J. SHERIDAN LE FANU

The earth hath bubbles as the water hath—
And these are of them.

IN THE SOUTH OF IRELAND, AND ON THE BORDERS OF THE COUNTY OF LIMERICK, there lies a district of two or three miles in length, which is rendered interesting by the fact that it is one of the very few spots throughout this country in which some vestiges of aboriginal forests still remain. It has little or none of the lordly character of the American forest, for the axe has felled its oldest and its grandest trees; but in the close wood which survives live all the wild and pleasing peculiarities of nature: its complete irregularity, its vistas, in whose perspective the quiet cattle are browsing; its refreshing glades, where the grey rocks arise from amid the nodding fern; the silvery shafts of the old birch-trees; the knotted trunks of the hoary oak, the grotesque but graceful branches which never shed their honours under the tyrant pruning-hook; the soft green sward; the chequered light and shade; the wild luxuriant weeds; the lichen and the moss—all are beautiful alike in the green freshness of spring or in the sadness and sere of autumn. Their beauty is of that kind which makes the heart full with joy—appealing to the affections with a power which belongs to nature only. This wood runs up, from below the base, to the ridge of a long line of irregular hills, having perhaps, in primitive times, formed but the skirting of some mighty forest which occupied the level below.

But now, alas! whither have we drifted? whither has the tide of civilization borne us? It has passed over a land unprepared for it—it has left nakedness behind it; we have lost our forests, but our marauders remain; we have destroyed all that is picturesque, while we have retained everything that is revolting in barbarism. Through the midst of this woodland there runs a deep gully or glen, where the stillness of the scene is broken in upon by the brawling of a mountain-stream, which, however, in the winter season, swells into a rapid and formidable torrent.

There is one point at which the glen becomes extremely deep and narrow; the sides descend to the depth of some hundred feet, and are so steep as to be nearly perpendicular. The wild trees which have taken root in the crannies and chasms of the rock are so intersected and entangled, that one can with difficulty catch a glimpse of the stream which wheels, flashes, and foams below, as if exulting in the surrounding silence and solitude.

This spot was not unwisely chosen, as a point of no ordinary strength, for the erection of a massive square tower or keep, one side of which rises as if in continuation of the precipitous cliff on which it is based. Originally, the only mode of ingress was by a narrow portal in the very wall which overtopped the precipice, opening upon a ledge of rock which afforded a precarious pathway, cautiously intersected, however, by a deep trench cut out with great labour in the living rock; so that, in its pristine state, and before the introduction of artillery into the art of war, this tower might have been pronounced, and that not presumptuously, impregnable.

The progress of improvement and the increasing security of the times had, however, tempted its successive proprietors, if not to adorn, at least to enlarge their premises, and about the middle of the last century, when the castle was last inhabited, the original square tower formed but a small part of the edifice.

The castle, and a wide tract of the surrounding country, had from time immemorial belonged to a family which, for distinctness, we shall call by the name of Ardagh; and owing to the associations which, in Ireland, almost always attach to scenes which have long witnessed alike the exercise of stern feudal authority, and of that savage hospitality which distinguished the good old times, this building has become the subject and the scene of many wild and extraordinary traditions. One of them I have been enabled, by a personal acquaintance with an eye-witness of the events, to trace to its origin; and yet it is hard to say whether the events which I am about to record appear more strange and improbable as seen through the distorting medium of tradition, or in the appalling dimness of uncertainty which surrounds the reality.

Tradition says that, sometime in the last century, Sir Robert Ardagh, a young man, and the last heir of that family, went abroad and served in foreign armies; and that, having acquired considerable honour and emolument, he settled at Castle Ardagh, the building we have just now attempted to describe. He was what the country people call a *dark* man; that is, he was considered morose, reserved, and ill-tempered; and, as it was supposed from the utter solitude of his life, was upon no terms of cordiality with the other members of his family.

The only occasion upon which he broke through the solitary monotony of his life was during the continuance of the racing season, and immediately subsequent to it; at which time he was to be seen among the busiest upon the course, betting deeply and unhesitatingly, and invariably with success. Sir Robert was, however, too well known as a man of honour, and of too high a family, to be suspected of any unfair dealing. He was, moreover, a soldier, and a man of intrepid as well as of a haughty character; and no one cared to hazard a surmise, the consequences of which would be felt most probably by its originator only.

Gossip, however, was not silent; it was remarked that Sir Robert never appeared at the race-ground, which was the only place of public resort which he frequented, except in company with a certain strange-looking person, who was never seen elsewhere, or under other circumstances. It was remarked, too, that this man, whose relation to Sir Robert was never distinctly ascertained, was the only person to whom he seemed to speak unnecessarily; it was observed that while with the country gentry he exchanged no further communication than what was unavoidable in arranging his sporting transactions, with this person he would converse earnestly and frequently. Tradition asserts that, to enhance the curiosity which this unaccountable and exclusive preference excited, the stranger possessed some striking and unpleasant peculiarities of person and of garb—though it is not stated, however, what these were—but they, in conjunction with Sir Robert's secluded habits and extraordinary run of luck—a success which was supposed to result from the suggestions and immediate advice of the unknown—were sufficient to warrant report in pronouncing that there was something *queer* in the wind, and in surmising that Sir Robert was playing a fearful and a hazardous game, and that, in short, his strange companion was little better than the Devil himself.

Years rolled quietly away, and nothing very novel occurred in the arrangements of Castle Ardagh, excepting that Sir Robert parted with his odd companion, but as nobody could tell whence he came, so nobody could say whither he had gone. Sir Robert's habits, however, underwent no consequent change; he continued regularly to frequent the race meetings, without mixing at all in the convivialities of the gentry, and immediately afterwards to relapse into the secluded monotony of his ordinary life.

It was said that he had accumulated vast sums of money—and, as his bets were always successful and always large, such must have been the case. He did not suffer the acquisition of wealth, however, to influence his hospitality or his house-keeping—he neither purchased land, nor extended his establishment; and his mode of enjoying his money must have been altogether that of the miser—consisting merely in the pleasure of touching and telling his gold, and in the consciousness of wealth.

Sir Robert's temper, so far from improving, became more than ever gloomy and morose. He sometimes carried the indulgence of his evil dispositions to such a height that it bordered upon insanity. During these paroxysms he would neither eat, drink, nor sleep. On such occasions he insisted on perfect privacy, even from the intrusion of

his most trusted servants; his voice was frequently heard, sometimes in earnest supplication, sometimes raised, as if in loud and angry altercation with some unknown
visitant. Sometimes he would for hours together walk to and fro throughout the long
oak-wainscoted apartment which he generally occupied, with wild gesticulations and
agitated pace, in the manner of one who has been roused to a state of unnatural excitement by some sudden and appalling intimation.

These paroxysms of apparent lunacy were so frightful, that during their continuance even his oldest and most faithful domestics dared not approach him; consequently
his hours of agony were never intruded upon, and the mysterious causes of his sufferings appeared likely to remain hidden for ever.

On one occasion a fit of this kind continued for an unusual time; the ordinary
term of their duration—about two days—had been long past, and the old servant
who generally waited upon Sir Robert after these visitations, having in vain listened
for the well-known tinkle of his master's hand-bell, began to feel extremely anxious; he feared that his master might have died from sheer exhaustion, or perhaps put
an end to his own existence during his miserable depression. These fears at length
became so strong, that having in vain urged some of his brother servants to accompany him, he determined to go up alone, and himself see whether any accident had
befallen Sir Robert.

He traversed the several passages which conducted from the new to the more
ancient parts of the mansion, and having arrived in the old hall of the castle, the utter
silence of the hour—for it was very late in the night—the idea of the nature of the
enterprise in which he was engaging himself, a sensation of remoteness from anything
like human companionship, but, more than all, the vivid but undefined anticipation of
something horrible, came upon him with such oppressive weight that he hesitated as to
whether he should proceed. Real uneasiness, however, respecting the fate of his master, for whom he felt that kind of attachment which the force of habitual intercourse
not unfrequently engenders respecting objects not in themselves amiable, and also
a latent unwillingness to expose his weakness to the ridicule of his fellow-servants,
combined to overcome his reluctance; and he had just placed his foot upon the first
step of the staircase which conducted to his master's chamber, when his attention was
arrested by a low but distinct knocking at the hall-door. Not, perhaps, very sorry at
finding thus an excuse even for deferring his intended expedition, he placed the candle
upon a stone block which lay in the hall and approached the door, uncertain whether
his ears had not deceived him. This doubt was justified by the circumstance that the
hall entrance had been for nearly fifty years disused as a mode of ingress to the castle.
The situation of this gate also, which we have endeavoured to describe, opening upon

a narrow ledge of rock which overhangs a perilous cliff, rendered it at all times, but particularly at night, a dangerous entrance. This shelving platform of rock, which formed the only avenue to the door, was divided, as I have already stated, by a broad chasm, the planks across which had long disappeared, by decay or otherwise; so that it seemed at least highly improbable that any man could have found his way across the passage in safety to the door, more particularly on a night like this, of singular darkness. The old man, therefore, listened attentively, to ascertain whether the first application should be followed by another. He had not long to wait. The same low but singularly distinct knocking was repeated; so low that it seemed as if the applicant had employed no harder or heavier instrument than his hand, and yet, despite the immense thickness of the door, with such strength that the sound was distinctly audible.

The knock was repeated a third time, without any increase of loudness; and the old man, obeying an impulse for which to his dying hour he could never account, proceeded to remove, one by one, the three great oaken bars which secured the door. Time and damp had effectually corroded the iron chambers of the lock, so that it afforded little resistance. With some effort, as he believed, assisted from without, the old servant succeeded in opening the door; and a low, square-built figure, apparently that of a man wrapped in a large black cloak, entered the hall. The servant could not see much of this visitor with any distinctness; his dress appeared foreign, the skirt of his ample cloak was thrown over one shoulder; he wore a large felt hat, with a very heavy leaf, from under which escaped what appeared to be a mass of long sooty-black hair; his feet were cased in heavy riding-boots. Such were the few particulars which the servant had time and light to observe. The stranger desired him to let his master know instantly that a friend had come, by appointment, to settle some business with him. The servant hesitated, but a slight motion on the part of his visitor, as if to possess himself of the candle, determined him; so, taking it in his hand, he ascended the castle stairs, leaving the guest in the hall.

On reaching the apartment which opened upon the oak-chamber he was surprised to observe the door of that room partly open, and the room itself lit up. He paused, but there was no sound; he looked in, and saw Sir Robert, his head and the upper part of his body reclining on a table, upon which two candles burned; his arms were stretched forward on either side, and perfectly motionless; it appeared that, having been sitting at the table, he had thus sunk forward, either dead or in a swoon. There was no sound of breathing; all was silent, except the sharp ticking of a watch, which lay beside the lamp. The servant coughed twice or thrice, but with no effect; his fears now almost amounted to certainty, and he was approaching the table on which his master partly lay, to satisfy himself of his death, when Sir Robert slowly raised his head, and, throwing himself back in his chair, fixed his eyes in a ghastly and uncertain gaze upon his attendant. At length he said, slowly and painfully, as if he dreaded the answer,—

"In God's name, what are you?"

"Sir," said the servant, "a strange gentleman wants to see you below."

At this intimation Sir Robert, starting to his feet and tossing his arms wildly upwards, uttered a shriek of such appalling and despairing terror that it was almost too fearful for human endurance; and long after the sound had ceased it seemed to the terrified imagination of the old servant to roll through the deserted passages in bursts of unnatural laughter. After a few moments Sir Robert said,—

"Can't you send him away? Why does he come so soon? O Merciful Powers! let him leave me for an hour; a little time. I can't see him now; try to get him away. You see I can't go down now; I have not strength. O God! O God! let him come back in an hour; it is not long to wait. He cannot lose anything by it; nothing, nothing, nothing. Tell him that! Say anything to him."

The servant went down. In his own words, he did not feel the stairs under him till he got to the hall. The figure stood exactly as he had left it. He delivered his master's message as coherently as he could. The stranger replied in a careless tone:

"If Sir Robert will not come down to me; I must go up to him."

The man returned, and to his surprise he found his master much more composed in manner. He listened to the message, and though the cold perspiration rose in drops upon his forehead faster than he could wipe it away, his manner had lost the dreadful agitation which had marked it before. He rose feebly, and casting a last look of agony behind him, passed from the room to the lobby, where he signed to his attendant not to follow him. The man moved as far as the head of the staircase, from whence he had a tolerably distinct view of the hall, which was imperfectly lighted by the candle he had left there.

He saw his master reel, rather than walk, down the stairs, clinging all the way to the banisters. He walked on, as if about to sink every moment from weakness. The figure advanced as if to meet him, and in passing struck down the light. The servant could see no more; but there was a sound of struggling, renewed at intervals with silent but fearful energy. It was evident, however, that the parties were approaching the door, for he heard the solid oak sound twice or thrice, as the feet of the combatants, in shuffling hither and thither over the floor, struck upon it. After a slight pause, he heard the door thrown open with such violence that the leaf seemed to strike the side-wall of the hall, for it was so dark without that this could only be surmised by the sound. The struggle was renewed with an agony and intenseness of energy that betrayed itself in deep-drawn gasps. One desperate effort, which terminated in the breaking of some part of the door, producing a sound as if the door-post was wrenched from its position, was followed by another wrestle, evidently upon the narrow ledge which ran outside the door, overtopping the precipice. This proved to be the final struggle; it was followed by a crashing sound as if some heavy body had fallen over, and was rushing down the precipice through the light boughs that crossed near the top. All then became still as the grave, except when the moan of the night-wind sighed up the wooded glen.

The old servant had not nerve to return through the hall, and to him the darkness seemed all but endless; but morning at length came, and with it the disclosure of the events of the night. Near the door, upon the ground, lay Sir Robert's sword-belt, which had given way in the scuffle. A huge splinter from the massive door-post had been wrenched off by an almost superhuman effort—one which nothing but the gripe of the despairing man could have severed—and on the rocks outside were left the marks of the slipping and sliding of feet. At the foot of the precipice, not immediately under the castle, but dragged some way up the glen, were found the remains of Sir Robert, with hardly a vestige of a limb or feature left distinguishable. The right hand, however, was uninjured, and in its fingers were clutched, with the fixedness of death, a long lock of coarse sooty hair—the only direct circumstantial evidence of the presence of a second person.

THE GARDEN THAT
WAS DESOLATE

ULRIC DAUBENY

THE COUNTRY TO THE SOUTH OF BIRDLIP, A COTSWOLD EYRIE CLOSE ON ROMAN Ermine Street, is, if scarcely wild, at least bleak, austere, and sparsely populated. It is a region of prehistoric burial mounds, of straggling British trackways, of Roman roads, Norman churches, ancient farm buildings, ruinous cottages; a dry-wall country, sharply undulating, its bleak downs relieved by occasional secretive woods of larch or beech. In striking contrast is the Cotswold "Edge," precipitous drop of several hundred feet into the fertile Severn Valley, where a kaleidoscopic vista of irregularly shaped and parti-coloured fields spreads out in a level tract, for a distance of some thirty miles. Close to Birdlip, the high-road skirts this "edge," and there, for the space of several minutes, Philip Cranham lingered, watching the play of sunlight over the jagged chine of Malvern, pale and beautiful in the shimmering distance.

"What a position for a house!" he mused, turning reluctantly, and continuing at a brisk walk, for the air on these heights is chilly, even towards the end of June. His way bore to the southwest, in the direction of the forgotten town of Painswick, which was to be the last stage of his tour.

A lover of the unconventional in walking, Philip deserted the usual high road through the woods, striking across a strip of common, and over several fields, until he met a narrow lane, which promised to lead him in the right direction. Deeply rutted by former traffic, it was long since grass-grown, scattered with mossy boulders, and enclosed on either side by a straggling bramble hedge. A veritable picture of desolation, thought Philip, glancing uneasily at the approaching heavy clouds, for the tremulous mutter of thunder had assailed his ears, and he looked in vain for a place of shelter. This was an upper rampart of the Cotswolds, a ridge bleak and desolate, set apart from all things hospitable, where there was no course but to throw one's weight against the wind, and face the threatened downpour. The lane, overgrown and serrulated, continued for some distance until, quite unexpectedly, the hedge was succeeded by a wall, dry-built as is the custom of the district, and strengthened by a massive cornice. Philip marvelled at its height, for it stood at least twelve feet; it looked to be of recent building, and still retained that bright, cream colour, peculiar to the local limestone, when freshly dug. Near the middle, the wall was broken by a gateway, flanked by massive pillars, on which hung double doors, palpably amateurish in construction. One of these had been unhooked, and dragged into the enclosure, where an elderly man was busy strengthening it with pieces of rough timber.

" 'Afternoon!" he volunteered, after a nervous scrutiny of Philip, who had come to a halt before the gateway. "Going to have a storm!"

He needed to be no prophet, for already great, bloated drops of rain were falling, heralded by a resounding clap of thunder. Philip cast an apprehensive glance skywards, and commenced to unstrap his mackintosh.

"Yes. We are in for it," he agreed, with the pointed addition, "Unpleasantly exposed, up here. Not even a decently thick hedge to shelter under!"

There was a noticeable hesitation before the stranger answered, and when he did, it was with a certain shy reluctance.

"Come inside. You can shelter in my room, until the rain stops."

Philip required no second bidding. Half-a-dozen steps, and he was viewing an extensive garden, consisting first of a rough lawn, backed by currant and gooseberry bushes, young fruit trees, a yew hedge industriously trimmed, and then divers beds and footpaths, disappearing over the sloping hillside. Signs of any habitable building, there were none.

"Come along!" enjoined the stranger, advancing hastily across the spacious lawn. "I live over there, in the look-out post."

For the first time, Philip noticed, built against and forming part of the left-hand boundary wall, a kind of miniature watch-tower, with pyramidal stone roof, terminated by a central chimney. A flight of steps led them to the doorway, for the place was built upon a mound, with floor-level half way up, and sloping roof considerably above the wall. Within there was a single room, possibly twelve feet square, having a fireplace in one corner, a narrow window cut through the outer wall, and another, a very large one, facing down the garden, and over the lovely Vale of Severn.

"What a glorious view!" exclaimed Philip, despite himself.

"Damned view! Damned view! Wish I had never set eyes upon it!"

Philip turned in open mouthed astonishment, but his companion paid no heed, though he continued in a quieter tone.

"I am a slave to that view. I can sit, and look at it for hours. I worship it—yet all the while I hate it! . . . Like to hear the story of all this?"

With rather an abandoned gesture, he swept his hand about, to indicate the tiny house, the garden, and the towering outer walls.

"I should like to know why there are immensely high walls on three sides—or rather, two, for the third is incomplete and yet—"

"To keep out undesirables, my dear Sir; to keep out undesirables!" interrupted the stranger, with uncontrolled impatience. "The walls and the tall gates, which I am busy strengthening."

"But—excuse me," continued Philip, obstinately bent on satisfying his curiosity, "the third wall, as I say, is but partially built, while no barrier of any kind protects the bottom of the garden!"

A long silence ensued, broken only by the drumming of the rain upon the unceiled roof, and an occasional echoing burst of thunder. Philip lounged thoughtfully near the open window, while his companion stood irresolute, chewing at his moustache, and with close knit brows, as if striving to recapture some elusive or forgotten memory. Presently his expression cleared, and as quickly changed to one of crafty eagerness.

"Come, come, Sir. Come, come! You cannot expect everything, *all* at once! Do you know, every stone of those walls—yes, even of this house—built myself?"

Philip nodded encouragingly. At times the man seemed sane enough, and yet he was decidedly peculiar.

"The reason for all this," he continued, repeating the gesture which embraced the whole of the surroundings, and ended with the larger window. "The reason of it all, is that. The view. More than seven years ago, I camped here, while on a holiday from London. After all the noise and smoke and racket, this place seemed like Paradise; and the view—I simply could not tear myself away! It ended in my purchasing the land, for I had determined to erect a house here. There was some trouble with a woman, who held part as an allotment, and claimed the place as hers, but she could produce no legal title, so the lawyer and I bundled her out, between us. Vindictive old harridan, she was—"

He ceased abruptly, creeping across to the rickety door, which he slowly opened, and after a stealthy glance around, closed, with an exclamation of relief. Philip watched narrowly. The manner was so ridiculously furtive as to point without a doubt to lunacy; it was becoming distinctly creepy, this sheltering from a thunderstorm, in the cottage of a maniac!

"Where was I?" the man resumed, seating himself by the empty fireplace. "What? Ah, yes! I had determined, as you say, to build a house here. Seven years ago, it was, this very day, that half-adozen labourers commenced to turn the sods, for the foundations. A month later I was all alone. Nobody would work for me, though I had men up from Stroud, Gloucester, Cheltenham, finally from London. Will you credit me, when I tell you that the beastly old hag who claimed the place had frightened 'em all away? I admit that there were several distressing accidents. The first day, a man was bitten by an adder, and another crushed beneath a heavy stone-cart. The Cheltenham foreman tripped up in a rabbit hole, and broke a leg, and his successor suddenly went mad, but— Fools! Idiots! They actually believed the crude tales of the country folk, who said that the ranting old woman was a witch! They took to their heels, and ran, the dirty cowards!"

"What happened after that?"

"They left me, to build the house as best I might; and build it, I swore I would, in face of Beelzebub! Witch or no witch, she did not frighten me, though often enough she came and threatened; yes, cursed and threatened. . . . So I started right away, to build the highest wall I could, to keep her out!"

"Has it taken seven years to do all this?"

"Yes. I could only build at intervals, for the garden had to be planted, and I practically live on its contents. In two years' time, I hope to have the defensive walls completed, and then the illomened old faggot will be shut out from my property for ever!"

"But, pardon me once more," insisted Philip, bent on settling the question of the stranger's sanity, "Why did you not run up a medium wall all round, sufficient to exclude unwelcome visitors, and then raise and strengthen it at your leisure?"

The recluse made no reply. Instead, he sprang towards the door, tore it open, and halted on the threshold, quivering with rage. Facing him was a wizened, bent old woman, clad in an assortment of dirty rags, leaning heavily upon a stick. Her face was stained and wrinkled like a winter walnut, and inexpressibly malignant was the look that shot from beneath the overhanging eyebrows.

"What is it, you old devil?" choked the man, his voice pitched high in apprehension. "Why do you stand gibbering at me like that?"

She made no immediate answer, but pointing a skinny talon, uttered a husky chuckle.

"Ha, ha! Ralf Cook! What did I tell 'ee? What did I tell 'ee, these seven years agone?"

"Stand back there. Stand back. Don't you dare to molest me, woman!"

"Why don't ye answer, Ralf Cook? Is it that ye are afeard, or can it be that ye don't remember? Seven years I gev thee; seven years, I said, and then— Are ye leavin', Ralf Cook, leavin' here this very day?"

"No, you old fool! You won't frighten me by your threats and curses. I bought this land, and paid for it, and—by glory!—I mean to stay here, in face of you or anybody!"

"Then, Ralf Cook, by all the Powers—"

Her arms were raised in vehement imprecation, but before the words could leave her lips, the man had dealt her a smashing blow across the face. She swayed helplessly for a moment, and then staggered backwards, falling heavily to the ground. A sudden vivid flash of lightning transfixed the two men, but as the echoes of the thunder died away, Philip pushed through the open doorway, and bounded down the steps. One glance was sufficient to convince him that the old woman's neck was broken. Awe stricken by the sight, he looked back, to meet a pair of fiend's eyes, madman's eyes—homicidal maniac's eyes. Then blank, unreasoning panic overtook him; he fled blindly, in his terror taking what appeared to be a different route across the garden. Here the grass grew rank, a yew hedge was pitifully unkempt, the fruit trees were old and straggling, the pathway all but indistinguishable. At last the boundary wall: but it was stained by the flight of many winters, and near a crumbling gateway lay one wooden door, rotting amid the weeds, while the other hung perilously upon its rusted hinges. When at last he checked his pace, Philip found himself in the grass-grown lane, and on looking back, felt relieved that the walls of the accursed garden were no longer visible.

With the memory so fresh upon him, Philip's judgment lost its normal balance. To witness, perhaps in some measure to be a mute accomplice in the murder of an old woman by a maniac, might well upset the strongest nerves, and he could not forget that his own life must have hung in fearful jeopardy. So alarming was the thought of giving evidence in the witness-box, that by the time Philip had reached Painswick, he was fully determined to say no word to the police. Instead, he gave himself to headlong flight, catching the late motor bus to Stroud, and the evening train to London. Months went by, but although he kept in anxious touch with local news, no hint came that the murder had been detected. At times Philip suffered considerable pangs of conscience, and on more than one occasion he was on the point of going to the police, only to be deterred by the anticipation of considerable official censure, for so long concealing knowledge of the crime. Later, his engagement, and then the happiness of marriage put a period to further vain recriminations, but the memory of that awful afternoon, a secret even from his wife, was seldom from him.

Two years passed before he again set foot in Cotswold, this time with his wife and sister, viewing the romantic beauty of the district from a comfortable motor. It had been entirely Philip's proposition, this re-visiting of scenes with which he had been familiar since his youth, and if the suggestion had not entirely sprung from sentiment, the other reason was such that he refused to admit it, even to himself.

It fell out that they stayed a while at Painswick, and then it was that Philip, throwing further self-deception to the winds, determined to satisfy his pent-up curiosity. Explaining that he wished to make enquiries of an old acquaintance, they one day motored over, approaching the garden from the direction by which he had so precipitately left it. A passable road led past the entrance to the grass-grown lane, and there, near a cottage, they drew up. Philip, in a happy moment of inspiration, crossed to the cottage, with a view to making some discreet enquiries.

A typical Cotswold woman answered to his knock, tanned and healthy, but prematurely grey.

"Good afternoon," he greeted her. "Can you tell me anything about the house— that is, the garden up the lane? Mr. Ralf Cook, I think, was the owner's name," he added, seeing that the woman preserved a stolid silence.

"I'll ask father to come," she answered, regarding him with questioning eyes. "Will you step inside, Sir?"

Philip followed into the neatly furnished parlour, and was presently joined by a corduroyed rustic, very old and lame.

"Ralf Cook?" repeated the latter, on becoming acquainted with the business. "Yes, zur, I can tell 'ee zummat about he, to be zure I can. Ralf Cook, o' Cook's Folly, we called un; ay, and fule he were right 'nough, when he tried to be upsides o' Mother Gaskin! 'T'were a bad day for he when he went up theere, zur, an' no mistake, not but what I allus said as how——"

"Is the building complete?" ventured Philip, breaking in upon the old fellow's ponderous garrulity. "Are the walls finished?"

"Nowe, o' coourse not. *She* seed to that, bless ye! Why, I can yet mind the day, zur, when he began a-buildin'. Six men he brought wi' un, and what o' that? One were crushed beneath a waggin, 'nother broke his leg, the foreman——"

"Yes. Yes. I know about that. What I really wanted to ask was, of Mr. Cook himself. Is he still living there?"

The old man glared at Philip in open-mouthed astonishment.

"*Still theere?*" he at last gasped. "Lor' sakes, an' he old 'nough to be my own feyther when he came, more'n forty years back!"

"What do you mean? Forty years! Mr. Cook told me that he had been there about seven."

"He——he *towld* you?"

"Yes. Don't you understand? I was here the summer before last, and had a long conversation with him."

Instead of making a direct reply, the old man shuffled to the door, and called his daughter. His voice was distinctly tremulous, when he began to question her.

"Polly. Can ye mind the time when Ralf Cook were a-livin' up at the Folly?"

"Why, no, father," she replied, obviously puzzled. "You know, I wasn't born then. Not till several years later."

"Ah, ye be thirty-vour, now, baint ye? This here gen'leman—but no matter, Polly. Ye can run along!"

Left alone, the two men regarded each other in moody silence. "What became of him?" asked Philip presently.

"Hung 'isself—leastways so t'were said, but people do hold as how Mother Gaskin did it vur un. She allus was a rum un, was Mother Gaskin. Folks don't rightly know what became o' her, though some vows she went off a-ridin' upon her broomstick, and got took up inter the moon. O' course that bain't rightly possible, leastways, not to my way o' thinkin'."

There was no more to be learnt, so Philip, curiously unconvinced, hurried back towards the motor. This was empty, and realizing that the girls had wandered off alone, he decided to seize the opportunity, and put an end to further doubt by private personal investigation. Accordingly he set off up the lane, ruminating all the while on the extraordinary tales he had just heard. Could the old man have been weak-witted, and was he backed up by his daughter merely to preserve appearances before a stranger? It seemed quite probable, more probable than that he must disbelieve the evidence of his own senses. Yes, of course how could he have doubted! There, ahead of him, stood the garden wall, bright and new looking, and the massive, dry-built gateway, with one door still unhooked! A few steps more, and he had come to a stand-still before the familiar entrance.

" 'Afternoon!" greeted an elderly man, who was at work mending the dismantled gate with pieces of odd timber. "Going to have a storm!"

A heavy echo of thunder came, as if to confirm his supposition, and then the rain began to fall, in isolated, swollen drops.

"Yes, we are in for it!" Philip found himself repeating, as a person in a dream. "Unpleasantly exposed up here. Not even—"

Then he was running, racing madly away from the accursed spot. Horror in its most primitive form pursued him, and he fled until, soaked with perspiration and painfully short of breath, he found himself clambering on board the waiting motor. Presently his wife and sister came into view, approaching from the entrance to the grass-grown lane. Both were somewhat breathless, and a trifle pale.

"Oh, Philip!" the former panted, as soon as they had reached the motor. "We've found such a horrid place! Joyce suggested walking up that lane, just to see where it led, and we came across a kind of deserted garden, surrounded by enormous walls. They looked old and dilapidated, and there was a tumbled-down gateway— Oh, all so sad and dreary. Everything inside was wild, and overgrown, and there was a curious little house, built against the wall, which looked as if it had not been touched for years.

"Suddenly, as we were wandering around, we both had an impression that some-body was watching us. I don't know why, but it quite gave us the horrors, and we simply had to run—What is the matter, dear? You look quite ill!"

"Oh, nothing. Perhaps the thunder. It was quite a heavy clap."

"When? We heard nothing! Have you seen your friend?"

"Yes—No, I mean. He has left this neighbourhood. Shall we be making a move homewards?"

GAVON'S EVE

E. F. BENSON

IT IS ONLY THE LARGEST KIND OF ORDNANCE MAP THAT RECORDS THE EXISTENCE OF the village of Gavon, in the shire of Sutherland, and it is perhaps surprising that any map on whatever scale should mark so small and huddled a group of huts, set on a bare, bleak headland between moor and sea, and, so one would have thought, of no import at all to any who did not happen to live there. But the river Gavon, on the right bank of which stand this half-dozen of chimneyless and wind-swept habitations, is a geographical fact of far greater interest to outsiders, for the salmon there are heavy fish, the mouth of the river is clear of nets, and all the way up to Gavon Loch, some six miles inland, the coffee-coloured water lies in pool after deep pool, which verge, if the river is in order and the angler moderately sanguine, on a fishing probability amounting almost to a certainty. In any case during the first fortnight of September last I had no blank day on those delectable waters, and up till the 15th of that month there was no day on which some one at the lodge in which I was stopping did not land a fish out of the famous Picts' pool. But after the 15th that pool was not fished again. The reason why is here set forward.

The river at this point, after some hundred yards of rapid, makes a sudden turn round a rocky angle, and plunges madly into the pool itself. Very deep water lies at the head of it, but deeper still further down on the east side, where a portion of the stream flicks back again in a swift dark backwater towards the top of the pool again. It is fishable only from the western bank, for to the east, above this backwater, a great wall of black and basaltic rock, heaved up no doubt by some fault in strata, rises sheer from the river to the height of some sixty feet. It is in fact nearly precipitous on both sides, heavily serrated at the top, and of so curious a thinness, that at about the middle of it where a fissure breaks its topmost edge, and some twenty feet from the top, there exists a long hole, a sort of lancet window, one would say, right through the rock, so that a slit of daylight can be seen through it. Since, therefore, no one would care to cast his line standing perched on that razor-edged eminence, the pool must needs be fished from the western bank. A decent fly, however, will cover it all.

It is on the western bank that there stand the remains of that which gave its title to the pool, namely, the ruins of a Pict castle, built out of rough and scarcely hewn masonry, unmortared but on a certain large and impressive scale, and in a very well-preserved condition considering its extreme antiquity. It is circular in shape and measures some twenty yards of diameter in its internal span. A staircase of large blocks with a rise of at least a foot leads up to the main gate, and opposite this on the side towards the river is another smaller postern through which down a rather hazardously steep slope a scrambling path, where progress demands both caution and activity, conducts to the head of the pool which lies immediately beneath it. A gate-chamber still roofed over exists in the solid wall: inside there are foundation indications of three rooms, and in the centre of all a very deep hole, probably a well. Finally, just outside the postern leading to the river is a small artificially levelled platform, some twenty feet across, as if made to support some super-incumbent edifice. Certain stone slabs and blocks are dispersed over it.

Brora, the post-town of Gavon, lies some six miles to the south-west, and from it a track over the moor leads to the rapids immediately above the Picts' pool, across which by somewhat extravagant striding from boulder to boulder a man can pass dry-foot when the river is low, and make his way up a steep path to the north of the basaltic rock, and so to the village. But this transit demands a steady head, and at the best is a somewhat giddy passage. Otherwise the road between it and Brora lies in a long detour higher up the moor, passing by the gates of Gavon Lodge, where I was stopping. For some vague and ill-defined reason the pool itself and the Picts' Castle had an uneasy reputation on the country side, and several times trudging back from a day's fishing I have known my gillie take a longish circuit, though heavy with fish, rather than make this short cut in the dusk by the castle. On the first occasion when Sandy, a strapping yellow-bearded viking of twenty-five, did this he gave as a reason that the ground round about the castle was "mossy," though as a God-fearing man, he must have known he lied. But on another occasion he was more frank, and said that the Picts' pool was "no canny" after sunset. I am now inclined to agree with him, though, when he lied about it, I think it was because as a God-fearing man he feared the devil also.

It was on the evening of September 14 that I was walking back with my host, Hugh Graham, from the forest beyond the lodge. It had been a day unseasonably hot for the time of year, and the hills were blanketed with soft, furry clouds. Sandy, the gillie of whom I have spoken, was behind with the ponies, and, idly enough, I told Hugh about his strange distaste for the Picts' pool after sunset. He listened, frowning a little.

"That's curious," he said. "I know there is some dim local superstition about the place, but last year certainly Sandy used to laugh at it. I remember asking him what ailed the place, and he said he thought nothing about the rubbish folk talked. But this year you say he avoids it."

"On several occasions with me he has done so."

Hugh smoked a while in silence, striding noiselessly over the dusky fragrant heather.

"Poor chap," he said, "I don't know what to do about him. He's becoming useless."

"Drink?" I asked.

"Yes, drink in a secondary manner. But trouble led to drink, and trouble, I am afraid, is leading him to worse than drink."

"The only thing worse than drink is the devil," I remarked.

"Precisely. That's where he is going. He goes there often."

"What on earth do you mean?" I asked.

"Well, it's rather curious," said Hugh. "You know I dabble a bit in folklore and local superstition, and I believe I am on the track of something odder than odd. Just wait a moment."

We stood there in the gathering dusk till the ponies laboured up the hillside to us, Sandy with his six feet of lithe strength strolling easily beside them up the steep brae, as if his long day's trudging had but served to half awaken his dormant powers of limb.

"Going to see Mistress Macpherson again tonight?" asked Hugh.

"Aye, puir body," said Sandy. "She's auld, and she's lone."

"Very kind of you, Sandy," said Hugh, and we walked on.

"What then?" I asked when the ponies had fallen behind again.

"Why, superstition lingers here," said Hugh, "and it's supposed she's a witch. To be quite candid with you, the thing interests me a good deal. Supposing you asked me, on oath, whether I believed in witches, I should say 'No.' But if you asked me again, on oath, whether I suspected I believed in them, I should, I think, say 'Yes.' And the fifteenth of this month—to-morrow—is Gavon's Eve."

"And what in Heaven's name is that?" I asked. "And who is Gavon? And what's the trouble?"

"Well, Gavon is the person, I suppose, not saint, who is what we should call the eponymous hero of this district. And the trouble is Sandy's trouble. Rather a long story. But there's a long mile in front of us yet, if you care to be told."

During that mile I heard. Sandy had been engaged a year ago to a girl of Gavon who was in service at Inverness. In March last he had gone, without giving notice, to see her, and as he walked up the street in which her mistress' house stood, had met her suddenly face to face, in company with a man whose clipped speech betrayed him English, whose manner a kind of gentleman. He had a flourish of his hat for Sandy, pleasure to see him, and scarcely any need of explanation as to how he came to be walking with Catrine. It was the most natural thing possible, for a city like Inverness boasted its innocent urbanities, and a girl could stroll with a man. And for the time, since also Catrine was so frankly pleased to see him, Sandy was satisfied. But after his return to

Gavon, suspicion, fungus-like, grew rank in his mind, with the result that a month ago he had, with infinite pains and blottings, written a letter to Catrine, urging her return and immediate marriage. Thereafter it was known that she had left Inverness; it was known that she had arrived by train at Brora. From Brora she had started to walk across the moor by the path leading just above the Picts' Castle, crossing the rapids to Gavon, leaving her box to be sent by the carrier. But at Gavon she had never arrived. Also it was said that, though it was a hot afternoon, she wore a big cloak.

By this time we had come to the lodge, the lights of which showed dim and blurred through the thick hill-mists that had streamed sullenly down from the higher ground.

"And the rest," said Hugh, "which is as fantastic as this is sober fact, I will tell you later."

Now, a fruit-bearing determination to go to bed is, to my mind, as difficult to ripen as a fruit-bearing determination to get up, and in spite of our long day, I was glad when Hugh (the rest of the men having yawned themselves out of the smoking-room) came back from the hospitable dispensing of bedroom candlesticks with a briskness that denoted that, as far as he was concerned, the distressing determination was not imminent.

"As regards Sandy," I suggested.

"Ah, I also was thinking of that," he said. "Well, Catrine Gordon left Brora, and never arrived here. That is fact. Now for what remains. Have you any remembrance of a woman always alone walking about the moor by the loch? I think I once called your attention to her."

"Yes, I remember," I said. "Not Catrine, surely; a very old woman, awful to look at. Moustache, whiskers, and muttering to herself. Always looking at the ground, too."

"Yes, that is she—not Catrine. Catrine! My word, a May morning! But the other—it is Mrs. Macpherson, reputed witch. Well, Sandy trudges there, a mile and more away, every night to see her. You know Sandy: Adonis of the north. Now, can you account by any natural explanation for that fact? That he goes off after a long day to see an old hag in the hills?"

"It would seem unlikely," said I.

"Unlikely! Well, yes, unlikely."

Hugh got up from his chair and crossed the room to where a bookcase of rather fusty-looking volumes stood between windows. He took a small morocco-backed book from a top shelf.

"Superstitions of Sutherlandshire," he said, as he handed it to me. "Turn to page 128, and read."

I obeyed, and read.

"September 15 appears to have been the date of what we may call this devil festival. On the night of that day the powers of darkness held pre-eminent dominion, and over-rode for any who were abroad that night and invoked their aid, the protective Providence of Almighty God. Witches, therefore, above all, were peculiarly potent. On this night any witch could entice to herself the heart and the love of any young man who consulted her on matters of philtre or love charm, with the result that on any night in succeeding years of the same date, he, though he was lawfully affianced and wedded, would for that night be hers. If, however, he should call on the name of God through any sudden grace of the Spirit, her charm would be of no avail. On this night, too, all witches had the power by certain dreadful incantations and indescribable profanities, to raise from the dead those who had committed suicide."

"Top of the next page," said Hugh. "Leave out this next paragraph; it does not bear on this last."

"Near a small village in this country," I read, "called Gavon, the moon at midnight is said to shine through a certain gap or fissure in a wall of rock close beside the river on to the ruins of a Pict castle, so that the light of its beams falls on to a large flat stone erected there near the gate, and supposed by some to be an ancient and pagan altar. At that moment, so the superstition still lingers in the country side, the evil and malignant spirits which hold sway on Gavon's Eve, are at the zenith of their powers, and those who invoke their aid at this moment and in this place, will, though with infinite peril to their immortal souls, get all that they desire of them."

The paragraph on the subject ended here, and I shut the book.

"Well?" I asked.

"Under favourable circumstances two and two make four," said Hugh.

"And four means—"

"This. Sandy is certainly in consultation with a woman who is supposed to be a witch, whose path no crofter will cross after nightfall. He wants to learn, at whatever cost, poor devil, what happened to Catrine. Thus I think it more than possible that to-morrow, at midnight, there will be folk by the Picts' pool. There is another curious thing. I was fishing there yesterday, and just opposite the river gate of the castle, someone has set up a great flat stone, which has been dragged (for I noticed the crushed grass) from the débris at the bottom of the slope."

"You mean that the old hag is going to try to raise the body of Catrine, if she is dead?"

"Yes, and I mean to see myself what happens. Come too."

The next day Hugh and I fished down the river from the lodge, taking with us not Sandy, but another gillie, and ate our lunch on the slope of the Picts' Castle after landing a couple of fish there. Even as Hugh had said, a great flat slab of stone had been dragged on to the platform outside the river gate of the castle, where it rested on certain rude supports, which, now that it was in place, seemed certainly designed to receive it. It was also exactly opposite that lancet window in the basaltic rock across the pool, so that if the moon at midnight did shine through it, the light would fall on the stone. This then was the almost certain scene of the incantations.

Below the platform, as I have said, the ground fell rapidly away to the level of the pool, which owing to rain on the hills was running very high, and, streaked with lines of greyish bubbles, poured down in amazing and ear-filling volume. But directly underneath the steep escarpment of rock on the far side of the pool it lay foamless and black, a still backwater of greath depth. Above the altar-like erection again the ground rose up seven rough-hewn steps to the gate itself, on each side of which, to the height of about four feet, ran the circular wall of the castle. Inside again were the remains of partition walls between the three chambers, and it was in the one nearest to the river gate that we determined to conceal ourselves that night. From there, should the witch and Sandy keep tryst at the altar, any sound of movement would reach us, and through the aperture of the gate itself we could see, concealed in the shadow of the wall, whatever took place at the altar or down below at the pool. The lodge, finally, was but a short ten minutes away, if one went in the direct line, so that by starting at a quarter to twelve that night, we could enter the Picts' Castle by the gate away from the river, thus not betraying our presence to those who might be waiting for the moment when the moon should shine through the lancet window in the wall of rock on to the altar in front of the river gate.

Night fell very still and windless, and when not long before midnight we let ourselves silently out of the lodge, though to the east the sky was clear, a black continent of cloud was creeping up from the west, and had now nearly reached the zenith. Out of the remote fringes of it occasional lightning winked, and the growl of very distant thunder sounded drowsily at long intervals after. But it seemed to me as if another storm hung over our heads, ready every moment to burst, for the oppression in the air was of a far heavier quality than so distant a disturbance could have accounted for. To the east, however, the sky was still luminously clear; the curiously hard edges of the western cloud were star-embroidered, and by the dove-coloured light in the east it was evident that the moonrise over the moor was imminent. And though I did not in my heart believe that our expedition would end in anything but yawns, I was conscious of an extreme tension and rawness of nerves, which I set down to the thunder-charged air.

For noiselessness of footstep we had both put on india-rubber soled shoes, and all the way down to the pool we heard nothing but the distant thunder and our own padded tread. Very silently and cautiously we ascended the steps of the gate away from the river, and keeping close to the wall inside, sidled round to the river gate and peered out. For the first moment I could see nothing, so black lay the shadow of the rock-wall opposite across the pool, but by degrees I made out the lumps and line of the glimmering foam which streaked the water. High as the river was running this morning it was infinitely more voluminous and turbulent now, and the sound of it filled and bewildered the ear with its sonorous roaring. Only under the very base of the rock opposite it ran quite black and unflecked by foam: there lay the deep still surface of the backwater. Then suddenly I saw something black move in the dimness in front of me, and against the grey foam rose up first the head, then the shoulders, and finally the whole figure of a woman coming towards us up the bank. Behind her walked another, a man, and the two came to where the altar of stone had been newly erected and stood there side by side silhouetted against the churned white of the stream. Hugh had seen too, and touched me on the arm to call my attention. So far then he was right: there was no mistaking the stalwart proportions of Sandy.

Suddenly across the gloom shot a tiny spear of light, and momentarily as we watched, it grew larger and longer, till a tall beam, as from some window cut in the rock opposite, was shed on the bank below us. It moved slowly, imperceptibly to the left till it struck full between the two black figures standing there, and shone with a curious bluish gleam on the flat stone in front of them. Then the roar of the river was suddenly overscored by a dreadful screaming voice, the voice of a woman, and from her side her arms shot up and out as if in invocation of some power. At first I could catch none of the words, but soon from repetition they began to convey an intelligible message to my brain, and I was listening as in the paralytic horror of nightmare to a bellowing of the most hideous and un-nameable profanity. What I heard I cannot bring myself to record; suffice it to say that Satan was invoked by every adoring and reverent name, that cursing and unspeakable malediction was poured forth on Him whom we hold most holy. Then the yelling voice ceased as suddenly as it had begun, and for a moment there was silence again, but for the reverberating river.

Then once more that horror of sound was uplifted.

"So, Catrine Gordon," it cried, "I bid ye in the name of my master and yours to rise from where ye lie. Up with ye—up!"

Once more there was silence; then I heard Hugh at my elbow draw a quick sobbing breath, and his finger pointed unsteadily to the dead black water below the rock. And I too looked and saw.

Right under the rock there appeared a pale subaqueous light, which waved and quivered in the stream. At first it was very small and dim, but as we looked it seemed to swim upwards from remote depths and grew larger till I suppose the space of some square yard was illuminated by it. Then the surface of the water was broken, and a head, the head of a girl, dead-white and with long, flowing hair, appeared above the stream. Her eyes were shut, the corners of her mouth drooped as in sleep, and the moving water stood in a frill round her neck. Higher and higher rose the figure out of the tide, till at last it stood, luminous in itself, so it appeared, up to the middle. The head was bent down over the breast, and the hands clasped together. As it emerged from the water it seemed to get nearer, and was by now half-way across the pool, moving quietly and steadily against the great flood of the hurrying river.

Then I heard a man's voice crying out in a sort of strangled agony.

"Catrine!" it cried; "Catrine! In God's name; in God's name!"

In two strides Sandy had rushed down the steep bank, and hurled himself out into that mad swirl of waters. For one moment I saw his arms flung up into the sky, the next he had altogether gone. And on the utterance of that name the unholy vision had vanished too, while simultaneously there burst in front of us a light so blinding, followed by a crack of thunder so appalling to the senses, that I know I just hid my face in my hands. At once, as if the flood-gates of the sky had been opened, the deluge was on us, not like rain, but like one sheet of solid water, so that we cowered under it. Any hope or attempt to rescue Sandy was out of the question; to dive into that whirlpool of mad water meant instant death, and even had it been possible for any swimmer to live there, in the blackness of the night there was absolutely no chance of finding him. Besides, even if it had been possible to save him, I doubt whether I was sufficiently master of my flesh and blood as to endure to plunge where that apparition had risen.

Then, as we lay there, another horror filled and possessed my mind. Somewhere close to us in the darkness was that woman whose yelling voice just now had made my blood run ice-cold, while it brought the streaming sweat to my forehead. At that moment I turned to Hugh.

"I cannot stop here," I said.

"I must run, run right away. Where is she?"

"Did you not see?" he asked.

"No. What happened?"

"The lightning struck the stone within a few inches of where she was standing. We—we must go and look for her."

I followed him down the slope, shaking as if I had the palsy, and groping with my hands on the ground in front of me, in deadly terror of encountering something human. The thunder-clouds had in the last few minutes spread over the moon, so that no ray from the window in the rock guided our search. But up and down the bank from the stone that lay shattered there to the edge of the pool we groped and stumbled, but found nothing. At length we gave it up: it seemed morally certain that she, too, had rolled down the bank after the lightning stroke, and lay somewhere deep in the pool from which she had called the dead.

None fished the pool next day, but men with drag-nets came from Brora. Right under the rock in the backwater lay two bodies, close together, Sandy and the dead girl. Of the other they found nothing.

It would seem, then, that Catrine Gordon, in answer to Sandy's letter, left Inverness in heavy trouble. What happened afterwards can only be conjectured, but it seems likely she took the short cut to Gavon, meaning to cross the river on the boulders above the Picts' pool. But whether she slipped accidentally in her passage, and so was drawn down by the hungry water, or whether, unable to face the future, she had thrown herself into the pool, we can only guess. In any case they sleep together now in the bleak, wind-swept graveyard at Brora, in obedience to the inscrutable designs of God.

A Gentle Ghost

Mary E. Wilkins Freeman

Out in front of the cemetery stood a white horse and a covered wagon. The horse was not tied, but she stood quite still, her four feet widely and ponderously planted, her meek white head hanging. Shadows of leaves danced on her back. There were many trees about the cemetery, and the foliage was unusually luxuriant for May. The four women who had come in the covered wagon remarked it. "I never saw the trees so forward as they are this year, seems to me," said one, gazing up at some magnificent gold-green branches over her head.

"I was sayin' so to Mary this mornin'," rejoined another. "They're uncommon forward, I think."

They loitered along the narrow lanes between the lots—four homely, middle-aged women, with decorous and subdued enjoyment in their worn faces. They read with peaceful curiosity and interest the inscriptions on the stones; they turned aside to look at the tender, newly blossomed spring bushes—the flowering almonds and the bridal wreaths. Once in a while they came to a new stone, which they immediately surrounded with eager criticism. There was a solemn hush when they reached a lot where some relatives of one of the party were buried. She put a bunch of flowers on a grave, then she stood looking at it with red eyes. The others grouped themselves deferentially aloof.

They did not meet anyone in the cemetery until just before they left. When they had reached the rear and oldest portion of the yard, and were thinking of retracing their steps, they became suddenly aware of a child sitting in a lot at their right. The lot held seven old, leaning stones, dark and mossy, their inscriptions dimly traceable. The child sat close to one, and she looked up at the staring knot of women with a kind of innocent keenness, like a baby. Her face was small and fair and pinched. The women stood eying her.

"What's your name, little girl?" asked one. She had a bright flower in her bonnet and a smart lift to her chin, and seemed the natural spokeswoman of the party. Her name was Holmes. The child turned her head sideways and murmured something.

"What? We can't hear. Speak up; don't be afraid! What's your name?" The woman nodded the bright flower over her, and spoke with sharp pleasantness.

"Nancy Wren," said the child, with a timid catch of her breath.

"Wren?"

The child nodded. She kept her little pink, curving mouth parted.

"It's nobody I know," remarked the questioner, reflectively. "I guess she comes from—over there." She made a significant motion of her head towards the right. "Where do you live, Nancy?" she asked.

The child also motioned towards the right.

"I thought so," said the woman. "How old are you?"

"Ten."

The women exchanged glances. "Are you sure you're tellin' the truth?"

The child nodded.

"I never saw a girl so small for her age if she is," said one woman to another.

"Yes," said Mrs. Holmes, looking at her critically; "she is dreadful small. She's considerable smaller than my Mary was. Is there any of your folks buried in this lot?" said she, fairly hovering with affability and determined graciousness.

The child's upturned face suddenly kindled. She began speaking with a soft volubility that was an odd contrast to her previous hesitation.

"That's mother," said she, pointing to one of the stones, "an' that's father, an' there's John, an' Marg'ret, an' Mary, an' Susan, an' the baby, and here's—Jane."

The women stared at her in amazement. "Was it your—" began Mrs. Holmes; but another woman stepped forward, stoutly impetuous.

"Land! it's the Blake lot!" said she. "This child can't be any relation to 'em. You hadn't ought to talk so, Nancy."

"It's so," said the child, shyly persistent. She evidently hardly grasped the force of the woman's remark.

They eyed her with increased bewilderment. "It can't be," said the woman to the others. "Every one of them Blakes died years ago."

"I've seen Jane," volunteered the child, with a candid smile in their faces.

Then the stout woman sank down on her knees beside Jane's stone, and peered hard at it.

"She died forty year ago this May," said she, with a gasp. "I used to know her when I was a child. She was ten years old when she died. You ain't ever seen her. You hadn't ought to tell such stories."

"I ain't seen her for a long time," said the little girl.

"What made you say you'd seen her at all?" said Mrs. Holmes, sharply, thinking this was capitulation.

"I did use to see her a long time ago, an' she used to wear a white dress, an' a wreath on her head. She used to come here an' play with me."

The women looked at each other with pale, shocked faces; one nervous; one shivered. "She ain't quite right," she whispered. "Let's go." The women began filing away. Mrs. Holmes, who came last, stood about for a parting word to the child.

"You can't have seen her," said she, severely, "an' you are a wicked girl to tell such stories. You mustn't do it again, remember."

Nancy stood with her hand on Jane's stone, looking at her. "She did," she repeated, with mild obstinacy.

"There's somethin' wrong about her, I guess," whispered Mrs. Holmes, rustling on after the others.

"I see she looked kind of queer the minute I set eyes on her," said the nervous woman.

When the four reached the front of the cemetery they sat down to rest for a few minutes. It was warm, and they had still quite a walk, nearly the whole width of the yard, to the other front corner where the horse and wagon were.

They sat down in a row on a bank; the stout woman wiped her face; Mrs. Holmes straightened her bonnet. Directly opposite across the street stood two houses, so close to each other that their walls almost touched. One was a large square building, glossily white, with green blinds; the other was low, with a facing of whitewashed stone-work reaching to its lower windows, which somehow gave it a disgraced and menial air; there were, moreover, no blinds.

At the side of the low building stretched a wide ploughed field, where several halting old figures were moving about planting. There was none of the brave hope of the sower about them. Even across the road one could see the feeble stiffness of their attitudes, the half-palsied fling of their arms.

"I declare I shouldn't think them old men over there would ever get that field planted," said Mrs. Holmes, energetically watchful. In the front door of the square white house sat a girl with bright hair. The yard was full of green light from two tall maple-trees, and the girl's hair made a brilliant spot of color in the midst of it.

"That's Flora Dunn over there on the door-step, ain't it?" said the stout woman.

"Yes. I should think you could tell her by her red hair."

"I knew it. I should have thought Mr. Dunn would have hated to have had their house so near the poor-house. I declare I should!"

"Oh, he wouldn't mind," said Mrs. Holmes; "he's as easy as old Tilly. It wouldn't have troubled him any if they'd set it right in his front yard. But I guess she minded some. I heard she did. John said there wa'n't any need of it. The town wouldn't have set it so near, if Mr. Dunn had set his foot down he wouldn't have it there. I s'pose they wanted to keep that big field on the side clear; but they would have moved it along a little if he'd made a fuss. I tell you what 'tis, I've 'bout made up my mind—I dun know as it's Scripture, but I can't help it—if folks don't make a fuss they won't get their rights in this world. If you jest lay still an' don't rise up, you're goin' to get stepped on. If people like to be, they can; I don't."

"I should have thought he'd have hated to have the poor-house quite so close," murmured the stout woman.

Suddenly Mrs. Holmes leaned forward and poked her head among the other three. She sat on the end of the row. "Say," said she, in a mysterious whisper, "I want to know if you've heard the stories 'bout the Dunn house?"

"No; what?" chorussed the other women, eagerly. They bent over towards her till the four faces were in a knot.

"Well," said Mrs. Holmes, cautiously, with a glance at the bright-headed girl across the way—"I heard it pretty straight—they say the house is haunted."

The stout woman sniffed and straightened herself. "Haunted!" repeated she.

"They say that ever since Jenny died there's been queer noises 'round the house that they can't account for. You see that front chamber over there, the one next to the poorhouse; well, that's the room, they say."

The women all turned and looked at the chamber windows, where some ruffled white curtains were fluttering.

"That's the chamber where Jenny used to sleep, you know," Mrs. Holmes went on; "an' she died there. Well, they said that before Jenny died, Flora had always slept there with her, but she felt kind of bad about goin' back there, so she thought she'd take another room. Well, there was the awfulest moanin' an' takin' on up in Jenny's room, when she did, that Flora went back there to sleep."

"I shouldn't thought she could," whispered the nervous woman, who was quite pale.

"The moanin' stopped jest as soon as she got in there with a light. You see Jenny was always terrible timid an' afraid to sleep alone, an' had a lamp burnin' all night, an' it seemed to them jest as if it really was her, I s'pose."

"I don't believe one word of it," said the stout woman, getting up. "It makes me all out of patience to hear people talk such stuff, jest because the Dunns happen to live opposite a graveyard."

"I told it jest as I heard it," said Mrs. Holmes, stiffly.

"Oh, I ain't blamin' you; it's the folks that start such stories that I ain't got any patience with. Think of that dear, pretty little sixteen-year-old girl hauntin' a house!"

"Well, I've told it jest as I heard it," repeated Mrs. Holmes, still in a tone of slight umbrage. "I don't ever take much stock in such things myself."

The four women strolled along to the covered wagon and climbed in. "I declare," said the stout woman, conciliatingly, "I dun know when I've had such an outin'. I feel as if it had done me good. I've been wantin' to come down to the cemetery for a long time, but it's most more'n I want to walk. I feel real obliged to you, Mis' Holmes."

The others climbed in. Mrs. Holmes disclaimed all obligations gracefully, established herself on the front seat, and shook the reins over the white horse. Then the party jogged along the road to the village, past outlying farmhouses and rich green meadows, all freckled gold with dandelions. Dandelions were in their height; the buttercups had not yet come.

Flora Dunn, the girl on the door-step, glanced up when they started down the street; then she turned her eyes on her work; she was sewing with nervous haste.

"Who were those folks, did you see, Flora?" called her mother, out of the sitting-room.

"I didn't notice," replied Flora, absently.

Just then the girl whom the women had met came lingeringly out of the cemetery and crossed the street.

"There's that poor little Wren girl," remarked the voice in the sitting-room.

"Yes," assented Flora. After a while she got up and entered the house. Her mother looked anxiously at her when she came into the room.

"I'm all out of patience with you, Flora," said she. "You're jest as white as a sheet. You'll make yourself sick. You're actin' dreadful foolish."

Flora sank into a chair and sat staring straight ahead with a strained, pitiful gaze. "I can't help it; I can't do any different," said she. "I shouldn't think you'd scold me, mother."

"Scold you; I ain't scoldin' you, child; but there ain't any sense in your doin' so. You'll make yourself sick, an' you're all I've got left. I can't have anything happen to you, Flora." Suddenly Mrs. Dunn burst out in a low wail, hiding her face in her hands.

"I don't see as you're much better yourself, mother," said Flora, heavily.

"I don't know as I am," sobbed her mother; "but I've got you to worry about besides—everything else. Oh, dear! oh, dear, dear!"

"I don't see any need of your worrying about me." Flora did not cry, but her face seemed to darken visibly with a gathering melancholy like a cloud. Her hair was beautiful, and she had a charming delicacy of complexion; but she was not handsome, her features were too sharp, her expression too intense and nervous. Her mother looked like her as to the expression; the features were widely different. It was as if both had passed through one corroding element which had given them the similarity of scars. Certainly a stranger would at once have noticed the strong resemblance between Mrs. Dunn's large, heavy-featured face and her daughter's thin, delicately outlined one—a resemblance which three months ago had not been perceptible.

"I see, if you don't," returned the mother. "I ain't blind."

"I don't see what you are blaming me for."

"I ain't blamin' you, but it seems to me that you might jest as well let me go up there an' sleep as you."

Suddenly the girl also broke out into a wild cry. "I ain't going to leave her. Poor little Jenny! poor little Jenny! You needn't try to make me, mother; I won't!"

"Flora, don't!"

"I won't! I won't! I won't! Poor little Jenny! Oh, dear! oh, dear!"

"What if it is so? What if it is—*her*? Ain't she got me as well as you? Can't her mother go to her?"

"I won't leave her. I won't! I won't!"

Suddenly Mrs. Dunn's calmness seemed to come uppermost, raised in the scale by the weighty impetus of the other's distress. "Flora," said she, with mournful solemnity, "you mustn't do so; it's wrong. You mustn't wear yourself all out over something that maybe you'll find out wasn't so some time or other."

"Mother, don't you think it is—don't you?"

"I don't know what to think, Flora." Just then a door shut somewhere in the back part of the house. "There's father," said Mrs. Dunn, getting up; "an' the fire ain't made."

Flora rose also, and went about helping her mother to get supper. Both suddenly settled into a rigidity of composure; their eyes were red, but their lips were steady. There was a resolute vein in their characters; they managed themselves with wrenches, and could be hard even with their grief. They got tea ready for Mr. Dunn and his two hired men; then cleared it away, and sat down in the front room with their needlework. Mr. Dunn, a kindly, dull old man, was in there too, over his newspaper. Mrs. Dunn and Flora sewed intently, never taking their eyes from their work. Out in the next room stood a tall clock, which ticked loudly; just before it struck the hours it made always a curious grating noise. When it announced in this way the striking of nine, Mrs. Dunn and Flora exchanged glances; the girl was pale, and her eyes looked larger. She began folding up her work. Suddenly a low moaning cry sounded through the house, seemingly from the room overhead. "There it is!" shrieked Flora. She caught up a lamp and ran. Mrs. Dunn was following, when her husband, sitting near the door, caught hold of her dress with a bewildered air; he had been dozing. "What's the matter?" said he, vaguely.

"Don't you hear it? Didn't you hear it, father?"

The old man let go of her dress suddenly. "I didn't hear nothin'," said he.

"Hark!"

But the cry, in fact, had ceased. Flora could be heard moving about in the room overhead, and that was all. In a moment Mrs. Dunn ran up-stairs after her. The old man sat staring. "It's all dum foolishness," he muttered, under his breath. Presently he fell to dozing again, and his vacantly smiling face lopped forward. Mr. Dunn, slow-brained, patient, and unimaginative, had had his evening naps interrupted after this manner for the last three months, and there was as yet no cessation of his bewilderment. He dealt with the simple, broad lights of life; the shadows were beyond his speculation. For his consciousness his daughter Jenny had died and gone to heaven; he was not capable of listening for her ghostly moans in her little chamber overhead, much less of hearing them with any credulity.

When his wife came down-stairs finally she looked at him, sleeping there, with a bitter feeling. She felt as if set about by an icy wind of loneliness. Her daughter, who was after her own kind, was all the one to whom she could look for sympathy and under-standing in this subtle perplexity which had come upon her. And she would rather have dispensed with that sympathy, and heard alone those piteous, uncanny cries, for she was wild with anxiety about Flora. The girl had never been very strong. She looked at her distressfully when she came down the next morning.

"Did you sleep any last night?" said she.

"Some," answered Flora.

Soon after breakfast they noticed the little Wren girl stealing across the road to the cemetery again. "She goes over there all the time," remarked Mrs. Dunn. "I b'lieve she runs away. See her look behind her."

"Yes," said Flora, apathetically.

It was nearly noon when they heard a voice from the next house calling, "Nancy! Nancy! Nancy Wren!" The voice was loud and imperious, but slow and evenly modu-lated. It indicated well its owner. A woman who could regulate her own angry voice could regulate other people. Mrs. Dunn and Flora heard it understandingly.

"That poor little thing will catch it when she gets home," said Mrs. Dunn.

"Nancy! Nancy! Nancy Wren!" called the voice again.

"I pity the child if Mrs. Gregg has to go after her. Mebbe she's fell asleep over there. Flora, why don't you run over there an' get her?"

The voice rang out again. Flora got her hat and stole across the street a little below the house, so the calling woman should not see her. When she got into the cemetery she called in her turn, letting out her thin sweet voice cautiously. Finally she came directly upon the child. She was in the Blake lot, her little slender body, in its dingy cotton dress, curled up on the ground close to one of the graves. No one but Nature tended those old graves now, and she seemed to be lapsing them gently back to her own lines, at her own will. Of the garden shrubs which had been planted about them not one was left but an old low-spraying white rose-bush, which had just gotten its new leaves. The

Blake lot was at the very rear of the yard, where it verged upon a light wood, which was silently stealing its way over its own proper boundaries. At the back of the lot stood a thicket of little thin trees, with silvery twinkling leaves. The ground was quite blue with houstonias.

The child raised her little fair head and stared at Flora, as if just awakened from sleep. She held her little pink mouth open, her innocent blue eyes had a surprised look, as if she were suddenly gazing upon a new scene.

"Where's she gone?" asked she, in her sweet, feeble pipe.

"Where's who gone?"

"Jane."

"I don't know what you mean. Come, Nancy, you must go home now."

"Didn't you see her?"

"I didn't see anybody," answered Flora, impatiently. "Come!"

"She was right here."

"What *do* you mean?"

"Jane was standin' right here. An' she had her white dress on, an' her wreath."

Flora shivered, and looked around her fearfully. The fancy of the child was overlapping her own nature. "There wasn't a soul here. You've been dreaming, child. Come!"

"No, I wasn't. I've seen them blue flowers an' the leaves winkin' all the time. Jane stood right there." The child pointed with her tiny finger to a spot at her side. "She hadn't come for a long time before," she added. "She's stayed down there." She pointed at the grave nearest her."You mustn't talk so," said Flora, with tremulous severity. "You must get right up and come home. Mrs. Gregg has been calling you and calling you. She won't like it."

Nancy turned quite pale around her little mouth, and sprang to her feet. "Is Mis' Gregg comin'?"

"She will come if you don't hurry."

The child said not another word. She flew along ahead through the narrow paths, and was in the almshouse door before Flora crossed the street.

"She's terrible afraid of Mrs. Gregg," she told her mother when she got home. Nancy had disturbed her own brooding a little, and she spoke more like herself.

"Poor little thing! I pity her," said Mrs. Dunn. Mrs. Dunn did not like Mrs. Gregg.

Flora rarely told a story until she had ruminated awhile over it herself. It was afternoon, and the two were in the front room at their sewing, before she told her mother about "Jane."

"Of course she must have been dreaming," Flora said.

"She must have been," rejoined her mother.

But the two looked at each other, and their eyes said more than their tongues. Here was a new marvel, new evidence of a kind which they had heretofore scented at, these two rigidly walking New England souls; yet walking, after all, upon narrow paths through dark meadows of mysticism. If they never lost their footing, the steaming damp of the meadows might come in their faces.

This fancy, delusion, superstition, whichever one might name it, of theirs had lasted now three months—ever since young Jenny Dunn had died. There was apparently no reason why it should not last much longer, if delusion it were; the temperaments of these two women, naturally nervous and imaginative, overwrought now by long care and sorrow, would perpetuate it.

If it were not delusion, pray what exorcism, what spell of book and bell, could lay the ghost of a little timid child who was afraid alone in the dark?

The days went on, and Flora still hurried up to her chamber at the stroke of nine. If she were a moment late, sometimes if she were not, that pitiful low wail sounded through the house.

The strange story spread gradually through the village. Mrs. Dunn and Flora were silent about it, but Gossip is herself of a ghostly nature, and minds not keys nor bars.

There was quite an excitement over it. People affected with morbid curiosity and sympathy came to the house. One afternoon the minister came and offered a prayer. Mrs. Dunn and Flora received them all with a certain reticence: they did not concur in their wishes to remain and hear the mysterious noises for themselves. People called them "dreadful close." They got more satisfaction out of Mr. Dunn, who was perfectly ready to impart all the information in his power and his own theories in the matter.

"I never heard a thing but once," said he, "an' then it sounded more like a cat to me than anything. I guess mother and Flora air kinder nervous."

The spring was waxing late when Flora went up-stairs one night with the oil low in her lamp. She had neglected filling it that day. She did not notice it until she was undressed; then she thought to herself that she must blow it out. She always kept a lamp burning all night, as she had in timid little Jenny's day. Flora herself was timid now.

So she blew the light out. She had barely laid her head upon the pillow when the low moaning wail sounded through the room. Flora sat up in bed and listened, her hands clinched. The moan gathered strength and volume; little broken words and sentences, the piteous ejaculations of terror and distress, began to shape themselves out of it.

Flora sprang out of bed, and stumbled towards her west window—the one on the almshouse side. She leaned her head out, listening a moment. Then she called her mother with wild vehemence. But her mother was already at the door with a lamp. When she entered, the moans ceased.

"Mother," shrieked Flora, "it ain't Jenny. It's somebody over there—at the poor-house. Put the lamp out in the entry, and come back here and listen."

Mrs. Dunn set out the lamp and came back, closing the door. It was a few minutes first, but presently the cries recommenced.

"I'm goin' right over there," said Mrs. Dunn. "I'm goin' to dress myself an' go over there. I'm goin' to have this affair sifted now."

"I'm going too," said Flora.

It was only half-past nine when the two stole into the almshouse yard. The light was not out in the room on the ground-floor, which the overseer's family used for a sitting-room. When they entered, the overseer was there asleep in his chair, his wife sewing at the table, and an old woman in a pink cotton dress, apparently doing nothing. They all started, and stared at the intruders.

"Good-evenin'," said Mrs. Dunn, trying to speak composedly. "We thought we'd come in; we got kind of started. Oh, there 'tis now! What is it, Mis' Gregg?"

In fact, at that moment, the wail, louder and more distinct, was heard.

"Why, it's Nancy," replied Mrs. Gregg, with dignified surprise. She was a large woman, with a masterly placidity about her. "I heard her a few minutes ago," she went on; "an' I was goin' up there to see to her if she hadn't stopped."

Mr. Gregg, a heavy, saturnine old man, with a broad bristling face, sat staring stupidly. The old woman in pink calico surveyed them all with an impersonal grin.

"Nancy!" repeated Mrs. Dunn, looking at Mrs. Gregg. She had not fancied this woman very much, and the two had not fraternized, although they were such near neighbors. Indeed, Mrs. Gregg was not of a sociable nature, and associated very little with anything but her own duties.

"Yes; Nancy Wren," she said, with gathering amazement. "She cries out this way 'most every night. She's ten years old, but she's as afraid of the dark as a baby. She's a queer child. I guess mebbe she's nervous. I don't know but she's got notions into her head, stayin' over in the graveyard so much. She runs away over there every chance she can get, an' she goes over a queer rigmarole about playin' with Jane, and her bein' dressed in white an' a wreath. I found out she meant Jane Blake, that's buried in the Blake lot. I knew there wa'n't any children round here, an' I thought I'd look into it. You know it says 'Our Father,' an' 'Our Mother,' on the old folks' stones. An' there she was, callin' them father an' mother. You'd thought they was right there. I've got 'most out o 'patience with the child. I don't know nothin' about such kind of folks." The wail continued. "I'll go right up there," said Mrs. Gregg, determinately, taking a lamp.

Mrs. Dunn and Flora followed. When they entered the chamber to which she led them they saw little Nancy sitting up in bed, her face pale and convulsed, her blue eyes streaming with tears, her little pink mouth quivering.

"Nancy—" began Mrs. Gregg, in a weighty tone. But Mrs. Dunn sprang forward and threw her arms around the child.

"You got frightened, didn't you?" whispered she; and Nancy clung to her as if for life.

A great wave of joyful tenderness rolled up in the heart of the bereaved woman. It was not, after all, the lonely and fearfully wandering little spirit of her dear Jenny; she was peaceful and blessed, beyond all her girlish tumults and terrors; but it was this little living girl. She saw it all plainly now. Afterwards it seemed to her that any one but a woman with her nerves strained, and her imagination unhealthily keen through watching and sorrow, would have seen it before.

She held Nancy tight, and soothed her. She felt almost as if she held her own Jenny. "I guess I'll take her home with me, if you don't care," she said to Mrs. Gregg.

"Why, I don't know as I've got any objections, if you want to," answered Mrs. Gregg, with cold stateliness. "Nancy Wren has had everything done for her that I was able to do," she added, when Mrs. Dunn had wrapped up the child, and they were all on the stairs. "I ain't coaxed an' cuddled her, because it ain't my way. I never did with my own children."

"Oh, I know you've done all you could," said Mrs. Dunn, with abstracted apology. "I jest thought I'd like to take her home to-night. Don't you think I'm blamin' you, Mis' Gregg." She bent down and kissed the little tearful face on her shoulder: she was carrying Nancy like a baby. Flora had hold of one of her little dangling hands.

"You shall go right upstairs an' sleep with Flora," Mrs. Dunn whispered in the child's ear, when they were going across the yard; "an' you shall have the lamp burnin' all night, an' I'll give you a piece of cake before you go."

It was the custom of the Dunns to visit the cemetery and carry flowers to Jenny's grave every Sunday afternoon. Next Sunday little Nancy went with them. She followed happily along, and did not seem to think of the Blake lot. That pitiful fancy, if fancy it were, which had peopled her empty childish world with ghostly kindred, which had led into it an angel playmate in white robe and crown, might lie at rest now. There was no more need for it. She had found her place in a nest of living hearts, and she was getting her natural food of human love.

They had dressed Nancy in one of the little white frocks which Jenny had worn in her childhood, and her hat was trimmed with some ribbon and rose-buds which had adorned one of the dead young girl's years before.

It was a beautiful Sunday. After they left the cemetery they strolled a little way down the road. The road lay between deep green meadows and cottage yards. It was not quite time for the roses, and the lilacs were turning gray. The buttercups in the meadows had blossomed out, but the dandelions had lost their yellow crowns, and their filmy skulls appeared. They stood like ghosts among crowds of golden buttercups; but none of the family thought of that; their ghosts were laid in peace.

The Giant Wistaria

Charlotte Perkins Gilman

"Meddle not with my new vine, child! See! Thou hast already broken the tender shoot! Never needle or distaff for thee, and yet thou wilt not be quiet!"

The nervous fingers wavered, clutched at a small carnelian cross that hung from her neck, then fell despairingly.

"Give me my child, mother, and then I will be quiet!"

"Hush! hush! thou fool—some one might be near! See—there is thy father coming, even now! Get in quickly! She raised her eyes to her mother's face, weary eyes that yet had a flickering, uncertain blaze in their shaded depths.

"Art thou a mother and hast no pity on me, a mother? Give me my child!"

Her voice rose in a strange, low cry, broken by her father's hand upon her mouth.

"Shameless!" said he, with set teeth. "Get to thy chamber, and be not seen again to-night, or I will have thee bound!"

She went at that, and a hard-faced serving woman followed, and presently returned, bringing a key to her mistress.

"Is all well with her,—and the child also?"

"She is quiet, Mistress Dwining, well for the night, be sure. The child fretteth endlessly, but save for that it thriveth with me."

The parents were left alone together on the high square porch with its great pillars, and the rising moon began to make faint shadows of the young vine leaves that shot up luxuriantly around them; moving shadows, like little stretching fingers, on the broad and heavy planks of the oaken floor.

"It groweth well, this vine thou broughtest me in the ship, my husband."

"Aye," he broke in bitterly, "and so doth the shame I brought thee! Had I known of it I would sooner have had the ship founder beneath us, and have seen our child cleanly drowned, than live to this end!"

"Thou art very hard, Samuel, art thou not afeard for her life? She grieveth sore for the child, aye, and for the green fields to walk in!"

"Nay," said he grimly, "I fear not. She hath lost already what is more than life; and she shall have air enough soon. To-morrow the ship is ready, and we return to England. None knoweth of our stain here, not one, and if the town hath a child unaccounted for to rear in decent ways—why, it is not the first, even here. It will be well enough cared for! And truly we have matter for thankfulness, that her cousin is yet willing to marry her."

"Hast thou told him?"

"Aye! Thinkest thou I would cast shame into another man's house, unknowing it? He hath always desired her, but she would none of him, the stubborn! She hath small choice now!"

"Will he be kind, Samuel? can he—"

"Kind? What call'st thou it to take such as she to wife? Kind! How many men would take her, an' she had double the fortune? and being of the family already, he is glad to hide the blot forever."

"An' if she would not? He is but a coarse fellow, and she ever shunned him."

"Art thou mad, woman? She weddeth him ere we sail to-morrow, or she stayeth ever in that chamber. The girl is not so sheer a fool! He maketh an honest woman of her, and saveth our house from open shame. What other hope for her than a new life to cover the old? Let her have an honest child, an' she so longeth for one!"

He strode heavily across the porch, till the loose planks creaked again, strode back and forth, with his arms folded and his brows fiercely knit above his iron mouth.

Overhead the shadows flickered mockingly across a white face among the leaves, with eyes of wasted fire.

"O, George, what a house! what a lovely house! I am sure it's haunted! Let us get that house to live in this summer! We will have Kate and Jack and Susy and Jim of course, and a splendid time of it!"

Young husbands are indulgent, but still they have to recognize facts.

"My dear, the house may not be to rent; and it may also not be habitable."

"There is surely somebody in it. I am going to inquire!"

The great central gate was rusted off its hinges, and the long drive had trees in it, but a little footpath showed signs of steady usage, and up that Mrs. Jenny went, followed by her obedient George. The front windows of the old mansion were blank, but in a wing at the back they found white curtains and open doors. Outside, in the clear May sunshine, a woman was washing. She was polite and friendly, and evidently glad of visitors in that lonely place. She "guessed it could be rented—didn't know." The heirs were in Europe, but "there was a lawyer in New York had the lettin' of it." There had been folks there years ago, but not in her time. She and her husband had the rent of their part for taking care of the place. Not that they took much care on't either, "but keepin' robbers out." It was furnished throughout, old-fashioned enough, but good; and "if they took it she could do the work for 'em herself, she guessed—if *he* was willin'!"

Never was a crazy scheme more easily arranged. George knew that lawyer in New York; the rent was not alarming; and the nearness to a rising sea-shore resort made it a still pleasanter place to spend the summer.

Kate and Jack and Susy and Jim cheerfully accepted, and the June moon found them all sitting on the high front porch.

They had explored the house from top to bottom, from the great room in the garret, with nothing in it but a rickety cradle, to the well in the cellar without a curb and with a rusty chain going down to unknown blackness below. They had explored the grounds, once beautiful with rare trees and shrubs, but now a gloomy wilderness of tangled shade.

The old lilacs and laburnums, the spirea and syringa, nodded against the second-story windows. What garden plants survived were great ragged bushes or great shapeless beds. A huge wistaria vine covered the whole front of the house. The trunk, it was too large to call a stem, rose at the corner of the porch by the high steps, and had once climbed its pillars; but now the pillars were wrenched from their places and held rigid and helpless by the tightly wound and knotted arms.

It fenced in all the upper story of the porch with a knitted wall of stem and leaf; it ran along the eaves, holding up the gutter that had once supported it; it shaded every window with heavy green; and the drooping, fragrant blossoms made a waving sheet of purple from roof to ground.

"Did you ever see such a wistaria!" cried ecstatic Mrs. Jenny. "It is worth the rent just to sit under such a vine,—a fig tree beside it would be sheer superfluity and wicked extravagance!"

"Jenny makes much of her wistaria," said George, "because she's so disappointed about the ghosts. She made up her mind at first sight to have ghosts in the house, and she can't find even a ghost story!"

"No," Jenny assented mournfully; "I pumped poor Mrs. Pepperill for three days, but could get nothing out of her. But I'm convinced there is a story, if we could only find it. You need not tell me that a house like this, with a garden like this, and a cellar like this, isn't haunted!"

"I agree with you," said Jack. Jack was a reporter on a New York daily, and engaged to Mrs. Jenny's pretty sister. "And if we don't find a real ghost, you may be very sure I shall make one. It's too good an opportunity to lose!"

The pretty sister, who sat next him, resented. "You shan't do anything of the sort, Jack! This is a *real* ghostly place, and I won't have you make fun of it! Look at that group of trees out there in the long grass—it looks for all the world like a crouching, hunted figure!"

"It looks to me like a woman picking huckleberries," said Jim, who was married to George's pretty sister.

"Be still, Jim!" said that fair young woman. "I believe in Jenny's ghost as much as she does. Such a place! Just look at this great wistaria trunk crawling up by the steps here! It looks for all the world like a writhing body—cringing—beseeching!"

"Yes," answered the subdued Jim, "it does, Susy. See its waist,—about two yards of it, and twisted at that! A waste of good material!"

"Don't be so horrid, boys! Go off and smoke somewhere if you can't be congenial!"

"We can! We will! We'll be as ghostly as you please." And forthwith they began to see bloodstains and crouching figures so plentifully that the most delightful shivers multiplied, and the fair enthusiasts started for bed, declaring they should never sleep a wink.

"We shall all surely dream," cried Mrs. Jenny, "and we must all tell our dreams in the morning!"

"There's another thing certain," said George, catching Susy as she tripped over a loose plank; "and that is that you frisky creatures must use the side door till I get this Eiffel tower of a portico fixed, or we shall have some fresh ghosts on our hands! We found a plank here that yawns like a trap-door—big enough to swallow you,—and I believe the bottom of the thing is in China!"

The next morning found them all alive, and eating a substantial New England breakfast, to the accompaniment of saws and hammers on the porch, where carpenters of quite miraculous promptness were tearing things to pieces generally.

"It's got to come down mostly," they had said. "These timbers are clean rotted through, what ain't pulled out o' line by this great creeper. That's about all that holds the thing up."

There was clear reason in what they said, and with a caution from anxious Mrs. Jenny not to hurt the wistaria, they were left to demolish and repair at leisure.

"How about ghosts?" asked Jack after a fourth griddle cake. "I had one, and it's taken away my appetite!"

Mrs. Jenny gave a little shriek and dropped her knife and fork.

"Oh, so had I! I had the most awful—well, not dream exactly, but feeling. I had forgotten all about it!"

"Must have been awful," said Jack, taking another cake. "Do tell us about the feeling. My ghost will wait."

"It makes me creep to think of it even now," she said. "I woke up, all at once, with that dreadful feeling as if something were going to happen, you know! I was wide awake, and hearing every little sound for miles around, it seemed to me. There are so many strange little noises in the country for all it is so still. Millions of crickets and things outside, and all kinds of rustles in the trees! There wasn't much wind, and the moonlight came through in my three great windows in three white squares on the black old floor, and those fingery wistaria leaves we were talking of last night just seemed to crawl all over them. And—O, girls, you know that dreadful well in the cellar?"

A most gratifying impression was made by this, and Jenny proceeded cheerfully:

"Well, while it was so horridly still, and I lay there trying not to wake George, I heard as plainly as if it were right in the room, that old chain down there rattle and creak over the stones!"

"Bravo!" cried Jack. "That's fine! I'll put it in the Sunday edition!"

"Be still!" said Kate. "What was it, Jenny? Did you really see anything?"

"No, I didn't, I'm sorry to say. But just then I didn't want to. I woke George, and made such a fuss that he gave me bromide, and said he'd go and look, and that's the last I thought of it till Jack reminded me,—the bromide worked so well."

"Now, Jack, give us yours," said Jim. "Maybe, it will dovetail in somehow. Thirsty ghost, I imagine; maybe they had prohibition here even then!"

Jack folded his napkin, and leaned back in his most impressive manner.

"It was striking twelve by the great hall clock—" he began.

"There isn't any hall clock!"

"O hush, Jim, you spoil the current! It was just one o'clock then, by my old-fashioned repeater."

"Waterbury! Never mind what time it was!"

"Well, honestly, I woke up sharp, like our beloved hostess, and tried to go to sleep again, but couldn't. I experienced all those moonlight and grasshopper sensations, just like Jenny, and was wondering what could have been the matter with the supper, when in came my ghost, and I knew it was all a dream! It was a female ghost, and I imagine she was young and handsome, but all those crouching, hunted figures of last evening ran riot in my brain, and this poor creature looked just like them. She was all wrapped up in a shawl, and had a big bundle under her arm,—dear me, I am spoiling the story! With the air and gait of one in frantic haste and terror, the muffled figure glided to a dark old bureau, and seemed taking things from the drawers. As she turned, the moonlight shone full on a little red cross that hung from her neck by a thin gold chain—I saw it glitter as she crept noiselessly from the room! That's all."

"O Jack, don't be so horrid! Did you really? Is that all? What do you think it was?"

"I am not horrid by nature, only professionally. I really did. That was all. And I am fully convinced it was the genuine, legitimate ghost of an eloping chambermaid with kleptomania!"

"You are too bad, Jack!" cried Jenny. "You take all the horror out of it. There isn't a 'creep' left among us."

"It's no time for creeps at nine-thirty A.M., with sunlight and carpenters outside! However, if you can't wait till twilight for your creeps, I think I can furnish one or two," said George. "I went down cellar after Jenny's ghost!"

There was a delighted chorus of female voices, and Jenny cast upon her lord a glance of genuine gratitude.

"It's all very well to lie in bed and see ghosts, or hear them," he went on. "But the young householder suspecteth burglars, even though as a medical man he knoweth nerves, and after Jenny dropped off I started on a voyage of discovery. I never will again, I promise you!"

"Why, what *was* it?"

"Oh, George!"

"I got a candle—"

"Good mark for the burglars," murmured Jack.

"And went all over the house, gradually working down to the cellar and the well."

"Well?" said Jack.

"Now you can laugh; but that cellar is no joke by daylight, and a candle there at night is about as inspiring as a lightning-bug in the Mammoth Cave. I went along with the light, trying not to fall into the well prematurely; got to it all at once; held the light down and *then* I saw, right under my feet—(I nearly fell over her, or walked through her, perhaps),—a woman, hunched up under a shawl! She had hold of the chain, and the candle shone on her hands—white, thin hands,—on a little red cross that hung from her neck—*vide* Jack! I'm no believer in ghosts, and I firmly object to unknown parties in the house at night; so I spoke to her rather fiercely. She didn't seem to notice that, and I reached down to take hold of her,—then I came upstairs!"

"What for?"

"What happened?"

"What was the matter?"

"Well, nothing happened. Only she wasn't there! May have been indigestion, of course, but as a physician I don't advise any one to court indigestion alone at midnight in a cellar!"

"This is the most interesting and peripatetic and evasive ghost I ever heard of!" said Jack. "It's my belief she has no end of silver tankards, and jewels galore, at the bottom of that well, and I move we go and see!"

"To the bottom of the well, Jack?"

"To the bottom of the mystery. Come on!"

There was unanimous assent, and the fresh cambrics and pretty boots were gallantly escorted below by gentlemen whose jokes were so frequent that many of them were a little forced.

The deep old cellar was so dark that they had to bring lights, and the well so gloomy in its blackness that the ladies recoiled.

"That well is enough to scare even a ghost. It's my opinion you'd better let well enough alone!" quoth Jim.

"Truth lies hid in a well, and we must get her out," said George. "Bear a hand with the chain?"

Jim pulled away on the chain, George turned the creaking windlass, and Jack was chorus.

"A wet sheet for this ghost, if not a flowing sea," said he. "Seems to be hard work raising spirits! I suppose he kicked the bucket when he went down!"

As the chain lightened and shortened there grew a strained silence among them; and when at length the bucket appeared, rising slowly through the dark water, there was an eager, half reluctant peering, and a natural drawing back. They poked the gloomy contents. "Only water."

"Nothing but mud."

"Something—"

They emptied the bucket up on the dark earth, and then the girls all went out into the air, into the bright warm sunshine in front of the house, where was the sound of saw and hammer, and the smell of new wood. There was nothing said until the men joined them, and then Jenny timidly asked:

"How old should you think it was, George?"

"All of a century," he answered. "That water is a preservative,—lime in it. Oh!—you mean?—Not more than a month; a very little baby!"

There was another silence at this, broken by a cry from the workmen. They had removed the floor and the side walls of the old porch, so that the sunshine poured down to the dark stones of the cellar bottom. And there, in the strangling grasp of the roots of the great wistaria, lay the bones of a woman, from whose neck still hung a tiny scarlet cross on a thin chain of gold.

THE GRAY MAN

SARAH ORNE JEWETT

HIGH ON THE SOUTHERN SLOPE OF AGAMENTICUS THERE MAY STILL BE SEEN the remnant of an old farm. Frost-shaken stone walls surround a fast-narrowing expanse of smooth turf which the forest is overgrowing on every side. The cellar is nearly filled up, never having been either wide or deep, and the fruit of a few mossy apple-trees drops ungathered to the ground. Along one side of the forsaken garden is a thicket of seedling cherry-trees to which the shouting robins come year after year in busy flights; the caterpillars' nests are unassailed and populous in this untended hedge. At night, perhaps, when summer twilights are late in drawing their brown curtain of dusk over the great rural scene,—at night an owl may sit in the hemlocks near by and hoot and shriek until the far echoes answer back again. As for the few men and women who pass this deserted spot, most will be repulsed by such loneliness, will even grow impatient with those mistaken fellow-beings who choose to live in solitude, away from neighbors and from schools,—yes, even from gossip and petty care of self or knowledge of the trivial fashions of a narrow life.

Now and then one looks out from this eyrie, across the wide-spread country, who turns to look at the sea or toward the shining foreheads of the mountains that guard the inland horizon, who will remember the place long afterward. A peaceful vision will come, full of rest and benediction into busy and troubled hours, to those who understand why some one came to live in this place so near the sky, so silent, so full of sweet air and woodland fragrance; so beaten and buffeted by winter storms and garlanded with summer greenery; where the birds are nearest neighbors and a clear spring the only wine-cellar, and trees of the forest a choir of singers who rejoice and sing aloud by day and night as the winds sweep over. Under the cherry thicket or at the edge of the woods you may find a stray-away blossom, some half-savage, slender grandchild of the old flower-plots, that you gather gladly to take away, and every year in June a red rose blooms toward which the wild pink roses and the pale sweet briars turn wondering faces as if a queen had shown her noble face suddenly at a peasant's festival.

There is everywhere a token of remembrance, of silence and secrecy. Some stronger nature once ruled these neglected trees and this fallow ground. They will wait the return of their master as long as roots can creep through mould, and the mould make way for them. The stories of strange lives have been whispered to the earth, their thoughts have burned themselves into the cold rocks. As one looks from the lower country toward the long slope of the great hillside, this old abiding-place marks the dark covering of trees like a scar. There is nothing to hide either the sunrise or the sunset. The low lands reach out of sight into the west and the sea fills all the east.

The first owner of the farm was a seafaring man who had through freak or fancy come ashore and cast himself upon the bounty of nature for support in his later years, though tradition keeps a suspicion of buried treasure and of a dark history. He cleared his land and built his house, but save the fact that he was a Scotsman no one knew to whom he belonged, and when he died the state inherited the unclaimed property. The only piece of woodland that was worth anything was sold and added to another farm, and the dwelling-place was left to the sunshine and the rain, to the birds that built their nests in the chimney or under the eaves. Sometimes a strolling company of country boys would find themselves near the house on a holiday after-noon, but the more dilapidated the small structure became, the more they believed that some uncanny existence possessed the lonely place, and the path that led toward the clearing at last became almost impassable.

Once a number of officers and men in the employ of the Coast Survey were encamped at the top of the mountain, and they smoothed the rough track that led down to the spring that bubbled from under a sheltering edge. One day a laughing fellow, not content with peering in at the small windows of the house, put his shoul-der against the rain-blackened door and broke the simple fastening. He hardly knew that he was afraid as he first stood within the single spacious room, so complete a curiosity took possession of him. The place was clean and bare, the empty cupboard doors stood open, and yet the sound of his companions' voices outside seemed far away, and an awful sense that some unseen inhabitant followed his footsteps made him hurry out again pale and breathless to the fresh air and sunshine. Was this really a dwelling-place of spirits, as had been already hinted? The story grew more fearful, and spread quickly like a mist of terror among the lowland farms. For years the tale of the coast-surveyor's adventure in the haunted house was slowly magni-fied and told to strangers or to wide-eyed children by the dim firelight. The former owner was supposed to linger still about his old home, and was held accountable for deep offense in choosing for the scene of his unsuccessful husbandry a place that escaped the proprieties and restraints of life upon lower levels. His grave was concealed by the new growth of oaks and beeches, and many a lad and full-grown man beside has taken to his heels at the flicker of light from across a swamp or under a decaying tree in that neighborhood. As the world in some respects grew wiser, the good people near the mountain understood less and less the causes of these simple effects, and as they became familiar with the visible world, grew more shy of the unseen and more sensitive to unexplained foreboding.

One day a stranger was noticed in the town, as a stranger is sure to be who goes his way with quick, furtive steps straight through a small village or along a country road. This man was tall and had just passed middle age. He was well made and vigorous, but there was an unusual pallor in his face, a grayish look, as if he had been startled by bad news. His clothes were somewhat peculiar, as if they had been made in another country, yet they suited the chilly weather, being homespun of undyed wools, just the color of his hair, and only a little darker than his face or hands. Some one observed in one brief glance as he and this gray man met and passed each other, that his eyes had a strange faded look; they might, however, flash and be coal-black in a moment of rage. Two or three persons stepped forward to watch the wayfarer as he went along the road with long, even strides, like one taking a journey on foot, but he quickly reached a turn of the way and was out of sight. They wondered who he was; one recalled some recent advertisement of an escaped criminal, and another the appearance of a native of the town who was supposed to be long ago lost at sea, but one surmiser knew as little as the next. If they had followed fast enough they might have tracked the mysterious man straight across the country, threading the by-ways, the shorter paths that led across the fields where the road was roundabout and hindering. At last he disappeared in the leaf-less, trackless woods that skirted the mountain.

That night there was for the first time in many years a twinkling light in the window of the haunted house, high on the hill's great shoulder; one farmer's wife and another looked up curiously, while they wondered what daring human being had chosen that awesome spot of all others for his home or for even a transient shelter. The sky was already heavy with snow; he might be a fugitive from justice, and the startled people looked to the fastening of their doors unwontedly that night, and waked often from a troubled sleep.

An instinctive curiosity and alarm possessed the country men and women for a while, but soon faded out and disappeared. The newcomer was by no means a hermit; he tried to be friendly, and inclined toward a certain kindliness and familiarity. He bought a comfortable store of winter provisions from his new acquaintances, giving every one his price, and spoke more at length, as time went on, of current events, of politics and the weather, and the town's own news and concerns. There was a sober cheerfulness about the man, as if he had known trouble and perplexity, and was fulfilling some mission that gave him pain; yet he saw some gain and reward beyond; therefore he could be contented with his life and such strange surroundings. He was more and more eager to form brotherly relations with the farmers near his home. There was almost a pleading look in his kind face at times, as if he feared the later prejudice of his associates. Surely this was no common or uneducated person, for in every way he left the stamp of his character and influence upon men and things. His reasonable words of advice and warning are current as sterling coins in that region yet; to one man he taught a new rotation of crops, to another he gave some priceless cures for devastating diseases of cattle. The lonely women of those remote country homes learned of him how to achieve their household toil with less labor and drudgery, and here and there he singled out promising children and kept watch of their growth, giving freely a most affectionate companionship, and a fair start in the journey of life. He taught those who were guardians of such children to recognize and further the true directions and purposes of existence; and the easily warped natures grew strong and well-established under his thoughtful care. No wonder that some people were filled with amazement, and thought his wisdom supernatural, from so many proofs that his horizon was wider than their own.

Perhaps some envious soul, or one aggrieved by being caught in treachery or deception, was the first to find fault with the stranger. The prejudice against his dwelling-place, and the superstition which had become linked to him in consequence, may have led back to the first suspicious attitude of the community. The whisper of distrust soon started on an evil way. If he were not a criminal, his past was surely a hidden one, and shocking to his remembrance, but the true foundation of all dislike was the fact that the gray man who went to and fro, living his simple, harmless life among them, *never was seen to smile*. Persons who remember him speak of this with a shudder, for nothing is more evident than that his peculiarity became at length intolerable to those whose minds lent themselves readily to suspicion. At first, blinded by the gentle good fellowship of the stranger, the changeless expression of his face was scarcely observed, but as the winter wore away he was watched with renewed disbelief and dismay.

After the first few attempts at gayety nobody tried to tell a merry story in his presence. The most conspicuous of a joker's audience does a deep-rankling injustice if he sits with unconscious, unamused face at the receipt of raillery. What a chilling moment when the gray man softly opened the door of a farmhouse kitchen, and seated himself like a skeleton at the feast of walnuts and roasted apples beside the glowing fire! The children whom he treated so lovingly, to whom he ever gave his best, though they were won at first by his gentleness, when they began to prattle and play with him would raise their innocent eyes to his face and hush their voices and creep away out of his sight. Once only he was bidden to a wedding, but never afterward, for a gloom was quickly spread through the boisterous company; the man who never smiled had no place at such a festival. The wedding guests looked over their shoulders again and again in strange foreboding, while he was in the house, and were burdened with a sense of coming woe for the newly-married pair. As one caught sight of his, among the faces of the rural folk, the gray man was like a sombre mask, and at last the bridegroom flung open the door with a meaning gesture, and the stranger went out like a hunted creature, into the bitter coldness and silence of the winter night.

Through the long days of the next summer the outcast of the wedding, forbidden, at length, all the once-proffered hospitality, was hardly seen from one week's end to another's. He cultivated his poor estate with patient care, and the successive crops of his small garden, the fruits and berries of the wilderness, were food enough. He seemed unchangeable, and was always ready when he even guessed at a chance to be of use. If he were repulsed, he only turned away and went back to his solitary home. Those persons who by chance visited him there tell wonderful tales of the wild birds which had been tamed to come at his call and cluster about him, of the orderliness and delicacy of his simple life. The once-neglected house was covered with vines that he had brought from the woods, and planted about the splintering, decaying walls. There were three or four books in worn bindings on a shelf above the fire-place; one longs to know what volumes this mysterious exile had chosen to keep him company!

There may have been a deeper reason for the withdrawal of friendliness; there are vague rumors of the gray man's possession of strange powers. Some say that he was gifted with amazing strength, and once when some belated hunters found shelter at his fireside, they told eager listeners afterward that he did not sleep but sat by the fire reading gravely while they slumbered uneasily on his own bed of boughs. And in the dead of night an empty chair glided silently toward him across the floor as he softly turned his pages in the flickering light.

But such stories are too vague, and in that neighborhood too common to weigh against the true dignity and bravery of the man. At the beginning of the war of the rebellion he seemed strangely troubled and disturbed, and presently disappeared, leaving his house key with a neighbor as if for a few days' absence. He was last seen striding rapidly through the village a few miles away, going back along the road by which he had come a year or two before. No, not last seen either; for in one of the first battles of the war, as the smoke suddenly lifted, a farmer's boy, reared in the shadow of the mountain, opened his languid pain-dulled eyes as he lay among the wounded, and saw the gray man riding by on a tall horse. At that moment the poor lad thought in his faintness and fear that Death himself rode by in the gray man's likeness; unsmiling Death who tries to teach and serve mankind so that he may at the last win welcome as a faithful friend!

The Haunted Dragoon

Arthur Quiller-Couch

Besides the Plymouth road, as it plunges downhill past Ruan Lanihale church toward Ruan Cove, and ten paces beyond the lych-gate—where the graves lie level with the coping, and the horseman can decipher their inscriptions in passing, at the risk of a twisted neck—the base of the churchyard wall is pierced with a low archway, festooned with toad-flax and fringed with the hart's-tongue fern. Within the archway bubbles a well, the water of which was once used for all baptisms in the parish, for no child sprinkled with it could ever be hanged with hemp. But this belief is discredited now, and the well neglected; and the events which led to this are still a winter's tale in the neighbourhood. I set them down as they were told me, across the blue glow of a wreck-wood fire, by Sam Tregear, the parish bedman. Sam himself had borne an inconspicuous share in them; and because of them Sam's father had carried a white face to his grave.

My father and mother (said Sam) married late in life, for his trade was what mine is, and 'twasn't till her fortieth year that my mother could bring herself to kiss a gravedigger. That accounts, maybe, for my being born rickety and with other drawbacks that only made father the fonder. Weather permitting, he'd carry me off to churchyard, set me upon a flat stone, with his coat folded under, and talk to me while he delved. I can mind, now, the way he'd settle lower and lower, till his head played hidey-peep with me over the grave's edge, and at last he'd be clean swallowed up, but still discussing or calling up how he'd come upon wonderful towns and kingdoms down underground, and how all the kings and queens there, in dyed garments, was offering him meat for his dinner every day of the week if he'd only stop and hobbynob with them—and all such gammut. He prettily doted on me—the poor old ancient!

But there came a day—a dry afternoon in the late wheat harvest—when we were up in the churchyard together, and though father had his tools beside him, not a tint did he work, but kept travishing back and forth, one time shading his eyes and gazing out to sea, and then looking far along the Plymouth road for minutes at a time. Out by Bradden Point there stood a little dandy-rigged craft, tacking lazily to and fro, with her mains'le all shiny-yellow in the sunset. Though I didn't know it then, she was the Preventive boat, and her business was to watch the Hauen: for there had been a brush between her and the *Unity* lugger, a fortnight back, and a Preventive man shot through the breast-bone and my mother's brother Philip was hiding down in the town. I minded, later, how that the men across the vale, in Farmer Tresidder's wheat-field, paused every now and then, as they pitched the sheaves, to give a look up toward the churchyard, and the gleaners moved about in small knots, causeying and glancing over their shoulders at the cutter out in the bay; and how, when all the field was carried, they waited round the last load, no man offering to cry the *Neck*, as the fashion was, but lingering till sun was near down behind the slope, and the long shadows stretching across the stubble.

"Sha'n't thee go underground to-day, Father?" says I, at last.

He turned slowly round, and says he, "No, sonny. Reckon us'll climb skywards for a change."

And with that, he took my hand, and pushing abroad the belfry door began to climb the stairway. Up and up, round and round we went, in a sort of blind-man's-holiday full of little glints of light and whiffs of wind where the open windows came; and at last stepped out upon the leads of the tower and drew breath.

"There's two-an'-twenty parishes to be witnessed from where we're standin', sonny—if ye've got eyes," says my father.

Well, first I looked down toward the harvesters and laughed to see them so small: and then I fell to counting the church-towers dotted across the high-lands, and seeing if I could make out two-and-twenty. 'Twas the prettiest sight—all the country round looking as if 'twas dusted with gold, and the Plymouth road winding away over the hills like a long white tape. I had counted thirteen churches, when my father pointed his hand out along this road and called to me:

"Look 'ee out yonder, honey, an' say what ye see!"

"I see dust," says I.

"Nothin' else? Sonny, boy, use your eyes, for mine be dim."

"I see dust," says I again, "an' suthin' twinklin' in it, like a tin can—"

"Dragooners!" shouts my father; and then, running to the side of the tower facing the harvest-field, he put both hands to his mouth and called:

"*What have 'ee? What have 'ee?*"—very loud and long.

"*A neck—a neck!*" came back from the field, like as if all shouted at once—dear, the sweet sound! And then a gun was fired, and craning forward over the coping I saw a dozen men running across the stubble and out into the road toward the Hauen; and they called as they ran, "*A neck—a neck!*"

"Iss," says my father, "'tis a neck, sure 'nuff. Pray God they save en! Come, sonny—"

But we dallied up there till the horsemen were plain to see, and their scarlet coats and armor blazing in the dust as they came. And when they drew near within a mile,

and our limbs ached with crouching—for fear they should spy us against the sky—
father took me by the hand and pulled hot foot down the stairs. Before they rode by he
had picked up his shovel and was shovelling out a grave for his life.

Forty valiant horsemen they were, riding two-and-two (by reason of the narrowness of
the road) and a captain beside them—men broad and long, with hairy top-lips, and all clad
in scarlet jackets and white breeches that showed bravely against their black war-horses,
and jet-black holsters, thick as they were wi' dust. Each man had a golden helmet, and a
scabbard flapping by his side, and a piece of metal like a half-moon jingling from his horse's
cheek-strap; 12 D was the number on every saddle, meaning the Twelfth Dragoons.

Tramp, tramp! they rode by, talking and joking, and taking no more heed of me—
that sat upon the wall, with my heels dangling above them—than if I'd been a sprig
of stonecrop. But the captain, who carried a drawn sword, and mopped his face with
a handkerchief so that the dust ran across it in streaks, drew rein, and looked over my
shoulder to where father was digging.

"Sergeant!" he calls back, turning with a hand upon his crupper; "didn't we see a
figger like this a-top o' the tower, some way back?"

The sergeant pricked his horse forward and saluted. He was the tallest, straightest
man in the troop, and the muscles on his arm filled out his sleeve with the three stripes
upon it—a handsome, red-faced fellow, with curly black hair.

Says he, "That we did, sir—a man with sloping shoulders, and a boy with a goose
neck." Saying this, he looked up at me with a grin.

"I'll bear it in mind," answered the officer, and the troop rode on in a cloud of
dust, the sergeant looking back and smiling, as if 'twas a joke that he shared with
us. Well, to be short, they rode down into the town as night fell. But 'twas too late,
Uncle Philip having had fair warning and plenty of time to flee up toward the little
secret hold under Mabel Down, where none but two families knew how to find him.
All the town, though, knew he was safe, and lashins of women and children turned
out to see the comely soldiers hunt in vain till ten o'clock at night.

The next thing was to billet the warriors. The captain of the troop, by this,
was pesky cross-tempered, and flounced off to The Jolly Pilchards in a huff.
"Sergeant," says he, "here's an inn, though a damned bad 'un, an' here I means to
stop. Somewheres about there's a farm called Constantine, where I am told the men
can be accommodated. Find out the place, if you can, an' do your best: an' don't let
me see yer face till to-morra," says he.

So Sergeant Basket—that was his name—gave the salute, and rode his troop
up the street, where—for his manners were mighty winning, notwithstanding the
dirty nature of his errand—he soon found plenty to direct him to Farmer Noy's of

Constantine; and up the coombe they rode into the darkness, a dozen or more going along with them to show the way, being won by their martial bearing as well as the sergeant's very friendly way of speech.

Farmer Noy was in bed—a pock-marked, lantern-jawed old gaffer of sixty-five; and the most remarkable point about him was the wife he had married two years before—a young slip of a girl but just husband-high. Money did it, I reckon; but if so, 'twas a bad bargain for her. He was noted for stinginess to such a degree that they said his wife wore a brass wedding-ring, weekdays, to save the genuine article from wearing out. She was a Ruan woman, too, and therefore ought to have known all about him. But woman's ways be past finding out.

Hearing the hoofs in his yard and the sergeant's *stram-a-ram* upon the door, down comes the old curmudgeon with a candle held high above his head. "What the devil's here?" he calls out.

Sergeant Basket looks over the old man's shoulder; and there, halfway up the stairs, stood Madam Noy in her night rail—a high-colored ripe girl, languishing for love, her red lips parted and neck all lily-white against a loosened pile of dark brown hair.

"Be cussed if I turn back!" said the sergeant to himself; and added out loud:

"Forty souldjers, in the King's name!"

"Forty devils!" says Old Noy.

"They've devils to eat," answered the sergeant, in the most friendly manner; "an', begad, ye must feed an' bed 'em this night—or else I'll search your cellars. Ye are a loyal man—eh, farmer? An' your stables are big, I'm told."

"Sarah," calls out the old man, following the sergeant's bold glance, "go back an' dress yersel' dacently this instant! These here honest souldjers—forty damned honest gormandisin' souldjers—be come in his majesty's name, forty strong, to protect honest folks' rights in the intervals of eatin' 'em out o' house an' home. Sergeant, ye be very welcome i' the King's name. Cheese an' cider ye shall have, an' I pray the mixture may turn your forty stomachs."

In a dozen minutes he had fetched out his stable-boys and farm hands, and, lantern in hand, was helping the sergeant to picket the horses and stow the men about on clean straw in the outhouses. They were turning back to the house, and the old man was turning over in his mind that the sergeant hadn't yet said a word about where he was to sleep, when by the door they found Madam Noy waiting, in her wedding gown, and with her hair freshly braided.

Now, the farmer was mortally afraid of the sergeant, knowing he had thirty ankers and more of contraband liquor in his cellars, and minding the sergeant's threat. None the less his jealousy got the upper hand.

"Woman," he cries out, "to thy bed!"

"I was waiting," said she, "to say the Cap'n's bed—"

"Sergeant's," says the dragoon, correcting her.

"—was laid i' the spare room."

"Madam," replies Sergeant Basket, looking into her eyes and bowing, "a soldier with my responsibility sleeps but little. In the first place, I must see that my men sup."

"The maids be now cuttin' the bread an' cheese and drawin' the cider."

"Then, Madam, leave me but possession of the parlor, and let me have a chair to sleep in."

By this they were in the passage together, and her gaze devouring his regimentals. The old man stood a pace off, looking sourly. The sergeant fed his eyes upon her, and Satan got hold of him.

"Now if only," said he, "one of you could play cards!"

"But I must go to bed," she answered; "though l can play cribbage, if only you stay another night."

For she saw the glint in the farmer's eye; and so Sergeant Basket slept bolt upright that night in an armchair by the parlor fender. Next day the dragooners searched the town again, and were billeted all about among the cottages. But the sergeant returned to Constantine, and before going to bed—this time in the spare room—played a game of cribbage with Madam Noy, the farmer smoking sulkily in his armchair.

"Two for his heels!" said the rosy woman suddenly, half-way through the game. "Sergeant, you're cheatin' yoursel' an' forgettin' to mark. Gi'e me the board; I'll mark for both."

She put out her hand upon the board, and Sergeant Basket closed upon it. 'Tis true he had forgot to mark; and feeling the hot pulse in her wrist, and beholding the hunger in her eyes, 'tis to be supposed he'd have forgot his own soul.

He rode away next day with his troop; but my uncle Philip not being caught yet, and the Government set on making an example of him, we hadn't seen the last of these dragoons. 'Twas a time of fear down in the town. At the dead of night or at noonday they came on us—six times in all: and for two months the crew of the *Unity* couldn't call their souls their own, but lived from day to day in secret closets and wandered the county by night, hiding in hedges and straw-houses. All that time the revenue men watched the Hauen, night and day, like dogs before a rat-hole.

But one November morning 'twas whispered abroad that Uncle Philip had made his way to Falmouth, and slipped across to Guernsey. Time passed on, and the dragooners were seen no more, nor the handsome devil-may-care face of Sergeant Basket. Up at Constantine, where he had always contrived to billet himself, 'tis to be thought pretty

Madam Noy pined to see him again, kicking his spurs in the porch and smiling out of his gay brown eyes: for her face fell away from its plump condition, and the hunger in her eyes grew and grew. But a more remarkable fact was that her old husband—who wouldn't have yearned after the dragoon ye'd have thought—began to dwindle and fall away too. By the New Year he was a dying man, and carried his doom on his face. And on New Year's Day he straddled his mare for the last time, and rode over to Looe, to Doctor Gale's.

"Goody-losh!" cried the doctor, taken aback by his appearance—"What's come to ye, Noy?"

"Death!" says Noy. "Doctor, I bain't come for advice, for before this day week I'll be a clay-cold corpse. I come to ax a favor. When they summon ye, before lookin' at my body—that'll be past help—go you to the little left-top corner drawer o' my wife's bureau, an' there ye'll find a packet. You're my executor," says he, "and I leaves ye to deal wi' that packet as ye thinks fit."

With that, the farmer rode away home-along, and the very day week he went dead.

The doctor, when called over, minded what the old chap had said, and sending Madam Noy on some pretense to the kitchen, went over and unlocked the little drawer with a duplicate key, that the farmer had unhitched from his watch-chain and given him. There was no parcel of letters, as he looked to find, but only a small packet crumpled away in the corner. He pulled it out and gave a look, and a sniff, and another look; then shut the drawer, locked it, strode straight downstairs to his horse, and galloped away.

In three hours' time, pretty Madam Noy was in the constables' hands upon the charge of murdering her husband by poison.

They tried her, next Spring Assize, at Bodmin, before the Lord Chief Justice. There wasn't evidence enough to put Sergeant Basket in the dock alongside of her—though 'twas freely guessed he knew more than anyone (saving the prisoner herself) about the arsenic that was found in the little drawer and inside the old man's body. He was subpoena'd from Plymouth, and cross-examined by a great hulking King's Counsel for three-quarters of an hour. But they got nothing out of him. All through the examination the prisoner looked at him and nodded her white face, every now and then, at his answers, as much as to say, "That's right—that's right: they shan't harm thee, my dear." And the love-light shone in her eyes for all the court to see. But the sergeant never let his look meet it. When he stepped down at last she gave a sob of joy, and fainted bang-off.

They roused her up, after this, to hear the verdict of *Guilty* and her doom spoken by the judge. "Pris'ner at the bar," said the Clerk of Arraigns, "have ye anything to say why this court should not pass sentence o' death?"

She held tight of the rail before her, and spoke out loud and clear:

"My lord and gentleman all, I be a guilty woman; an' I be ready to die at once for my sin. But if ye kill me now, ye kill the child in my body—an' he is innocent."

Well, 'twas found she spoke the truth; and the hanging was put off till after the time of her delivery. She was led back to prison, and there, about the end of June, her child was born, and died before he was six hours old. But the mother recovered, and quietly abode the time of her hanging.

I can mind her execution very well; for father and mother had determined it would be an excellent thing for my rickets to take me into Bodmin that day, and get a touch of the dead woman's hand, which in those times was considered an unfailing remedy. So we borrowed the parson's manure-cart, and cleaned it thoroughly, and drove in together.

The place of the hangings, then, was a little door in the prison wall, looking over the bank where the railway now goes, and a dismal piece of water called Jail-pool, where the townsfolk drowned most of the dogs and cats they'd no further use for. All the bank under the gallows was that thick with people you could almost walk upon their heads; and my ribs were squeezed by the crowd so that I couldn't breathe freely for a month after. Back across the pool, the fields along the side of the valley were lined with booths and sweet-stalls and standings—a perfect Whitsun-fair; and a din going up that cracked your ears.

But there was the stillness of death when the woman came forth, with the sheriff and the chaplain reading in his book, and the unnamed man behind—all from the little door. She wore a straight black gown, and a white kerchief about her neck—a lovely woman, young and white and tearless.

She ran her eye over the crowd and stepped forward a pace, as if to speak; but lifted a finger and beckoned instead: and out of the people a man fought his way to the foot of the scaffold. 'Twas the dashing sergeant, that was here upon sick-leave. Sick he was, I believe. His face above his shining regimentals was gray as a slate; for he had committed perjury to save his skin, and on the face of the perjured no sun will ever shine.

"Have you got it?" the doomed woman said, many hearing the words.

He tried to reach, but the scaffold was too high, so he tossed up what was in his hand, and the woman caught it—a little screw of tissue-paper.

"I must see that, please!" said the sheriff, laying a hand upon her arm.

"'Tis but a weddin'-ring, sir,"—and she slipped it over her finger. Then she kissed it once, under the beam, and, lookin' into the dragoon's eyes, spoke very slow:

"Husband, our child shall go wi' you; an' when I want you he shall fetch you."

And with that turned to the sheriff, saying: "I be ready, sir."

The sheriff wouldn't give father and mother leave for me to touch the dead woman's hand; so they drove back that evening grumbling a good bit. 'Tis a sixteen-mile drive, and the ostler in at Bodmin had swindled the poor old horse out of his feed, I believe; for he crawled like a slug. But they were so taken up with discussing the day's doings, and what a mort of people had been present, and how the sheriff might have used milder language in refusing my father, that they forgot to use the whip. The moon was up before we got halfway home, and a star to be seen here and there; and still we never mended our pace.

'Twas in the middle of the lane leading down to Hendra Bottom, where for more than a mile two carts can't pass each other, that my father pricks up his ears and looks back.

"Hullo!" says he; "there's somebody gallopin' behind us."

Far back in the night we heard the noise of a horse's hoofs, pounding furiously on the road and drawing nearer and nearer.

"Save us!" cries father; "whoever 'tis, he's comin' down th' lane!" And in a minute's time the clatter was close on us and someone shouting behind.

"Hurry that crawlin' worm o' yourn—or draw aside in God's name, an' let me by!" the rider yelled.

"What's up?" asked my father, quartering as well as he could. "Why! Hullo! Farmer Hugo, be that you?"

"There's a mad devil o' a man behind, ridin' down all he comes across. A 's blazin' drunk, I reckon—but 'tisn' *that*—'tis the horrible voice that goes wi' en—Hark! Lord protect us, he's turn'd into the lane!"

Sure enough, the clatter of a second horse was coming down upon us, out of the night—and with it the most ghastly sounds that ever creamed a man's flesh. Farmer Hugo pushed past us and sent a shower of mud in our faces as his horse leapt off again, and 'way-to-go down the hill. My father stood up and lashed our old grey with the reins, and down we went too, bumpity-bump for our lives, the poor beast being taken suddenly like one possessed. For the screaming behind was like nothing on earth but the wailing and sobbing of a little child—only tenfold louder. 'Twas just as you'd fancy a baby might wail if his little limbs was being twisted to death.

At the hill's foot, as you know, a stream crosses the lane—that widens out there a bit, and narrows again as it goes up t'other side of the valley. Knowing we must be overtaken further on—for the screams and clatter seemed at our very backs by this—father jumped out here into the stream and backed the cart well to one side; and not a second too soon.

The next moment, like a wind, this thing went by us in the moonlight—a man upon a black horse that splashed the stream all over us as he dashed through it and up the hill. 'Twas the scarlet dragoon with his ashen face; and behind him, holding to his cross-belt, rode a little shape, that tugged and wailed and raved. As I stand here, sir, 'twas the shape of a naked babe!

Well, I won't go on to tell how my father dropped upon his knees in the water, or how my mother fainted off. The thing was gone, and from that moment for eight years nothing was seen or heard of Sergeant Basket. The fright killed my mother. Before next spring she fell into a decline, and early next fall the old man—for he was an old man now—had to delve her grave. After this he went feebly about his work, but held on, being wishful for me to step into his shoon, which I began to do as soon as I was fourteen, having outgrown the rickets by that time.

But one cool evening in September month, father was up digging in the yard alone; for 'twas a small child's grave, and in the loosest soil, and I was off on a day's work, thatching Farmer Tresidder's stacks. He was digging away slowly when he heard a rattle at the lych-gate, and looking over the edge of the grave, saw in the dusk a man hitching his horse there by the bridle.

'Twas a coal-black horse, and the man wore a scarlet coat all powdered with pilm; and as he opened the gate and came over the graves, father saw that 'twas the dashing dragoon. His face was still a slaty-grey, and clammy with sweat, and; when he spoke, his voice was all of a whisper, with a shiver therein.

"Bedman," says he, "go to the hedge, and look down the road, and tell me what you see."

My father went, with his knees shaking, and came back again.

"I see a woman," says he, "not fifty yards down the road. She is dressed in black, an' has a veil over her face, an' she's comin' this way."

"Bedman," answers the dragoon, "go to the gate an' look back along the Plymouth road, an' tell me what you see."

"I see," says my father, coming back with his teeth chattering, "I see, twenty yards back, a naked child comin'. He looks to be callin', but he makes no sound."

"Because his voice is wearied out," says the dragoon. And with that he faced about, and walked to the gate slowly.

"Bedman, come wi' me an' see the rest," he says over his shoulder.

He opened the gate, unhitched the bridle, and swung himself heavily up in the saddle.

Now from the gate the bank goes down pretty steep into the road, and at the foot of the bank my father saw two figures waiting. 'Twas the woman and the child, hand in hand, and their eyes burned up like coals; and the woman's veil was lifted, and her throat bare.

As the horse went down the bank toward these two, they reached out and took each a stirrup and climbed upon his back, the child before the dragoon and the woman behind. The man's face was set like a stone. Not a word did either speak, and in this fashion they rode down the hill toward Ruan sands. All that my father could mind, beyond, was that the woman's hands were passed round the man's neck, where the rope had passed round her own. No more could he tell, being a stricken man from that hour. But Aunt Polgrain, the housekeeper up to Constantine, saw them, an hour later, go along the road below the town-place; and Jacobs, the smith, saw them pass his forge toward Bodmin about midnight. So the tale's true enough. But since that night no man has set eyes on horse or riders.

The Haunted Landscape

Greye La Spina

I

Only once in my life did I experience contact with the supernatural, and the incident is still inexplicable, looked at from the materialistic standpoint. It happened in connection with the death of a close friend of mine, Jack Lindsay, the artist.

Jack was possessed of a stubbornly determined nature; he never gave up anything once begun, no matter how difficult the circumstances in connection with it. He was especially determined in regard to his painting; he often remarked, with a touch of quite natural melancholy in character with the observation, that death alone would stop him from reaching the highest point in his artistic career before he was thirty. He was about twenty-seven when he said that.

In discussing Jack's dogged grit with a common friend, Doctor Wilmott, the latter said: "If Jack lives to be forty, he will already have become famous." When I replied that Jack had declared it his intention to make a name for himself by the time he was thirty, our friend assented thoughtfully. "I believe he will make the attempt," he granted; "but he has no time to lose."

The last time I saw Jack was just before he went away on one of his frequent sketching trips. When he mentioned his itinerary, I found he was passing within a few miles of a city where a cousin of mine was living, and I penciled a few words of informal introduction on the reverse of one of my cards, which, however, as afterward transpired, he never presented. He left me, apparently in high spirits, and although I heard nothing from him for a couple of months, I thought nothing of it because he was a notoriously poor correspondent.

Then I received a notice that shocked me to the soul. The police of a certain small town had found a dead body, presumably his, in the woods, where it had lain for weeks. Their supposition was that the young artist had taken his own life, as there were no marks of violence upon the body, and apparently nothing had been removed from the pockets. My card had served to identify him. His sketching paraphernalia in its entirety had been located at the home of a farmer of the neighborhood, Pete Grimstead, one of those "poor but honest" countrymen in which America abounds.

The farmer declared that several weeks back the artist had stopped at the house for something to eat; that after lunch he asked permission to leave his sketching outfit, as he wished to take a stroll through the woods without it. Grimstead had put the things into the "front room," which, as any one who is at all acquainted with country people knows, is rarely used by them. Naturally they had forgotten all about the things until the hue and cry was made upon the discovery of the artist's body, when they had immediately notified the police and given up the dead man's effects.

Both the farmer and his wife had declared that they were glad to get rid of the things. Asked why, they said they didn't know, but they felt there was something queer about them. And they did seem relieved to have the last vestige of the unfortunate man's visit removed from their house.

I did not like the idea of Jack's having committed suicide on the verge of a promising career; it was quite out of character with what I knew of him. But Grimstead and his wife were well regarded in their vicinity, and there seemed no reason to suspect that anything other than suicide or an accident of some kind had happened to poor Jack. However, the thought clung to me and persisted in obtruding itself the rest of the day when I was back at the country hotel, that there was much more back of the affair than appeared on the surface. The coroner persisted in his belief that it was a case of suicide, although I begged him to let it go down on the records as death by accident.

You know how it is when you suddenly feel an antipathy to a person without the slightest foundation for your feelings. Well, I simply "felt" that Grimstead and his wife knew more about Jack's tragic death than they had related, and the more I thought it over, the more strongly was I convinced in my intuition. There was something I didn't like about the hanging head of the farmer; something shifty in the wife's eyes and unpleasant in the constant restless rubbing and twisting of her thin, gnarled hands. I determined to ferret out the secret hidden back of their apparently simple story.

Jack's effects were turned over to me, in lieu of relatives, and I put them in my room at the hotel. That night I set up the easel and 0put the landscape on it; I wanted to look at my friend's last piece of work while I strove to untangle the threads of thought which threatened to become hopelessly knotted. I lit my pipe and sat back comfortably, reflecting sadly on poor Jack's sudden and tragic death, the while my eyes took in the salient features of the landscape before me.

It was a carelessly executed bit of work, quite unfinished as yet on the right-hand side. The left side showed a bit of country with woods beyond and plowed fields toward the center. At the right appeared the roughly sketched-in outlines of a house. And it was upon this house that my attention became fixed as I smoked and reflected. Perhaps I grew drowsy; perhaps it was a case of auto-suggestion; perhaps it was the powerful will of my friend projected no one knows how. Whatever it was, the longer I looked at that house the clearer the outlines grew. Such is the magic of the imagination that it seemed to me that an invisible brush was working over the house, dashing in a bit of color here, a touch there, until the whole house stood out clearly before my eyes.

I realized that I was hardly normal; that my long reflection on my friend's death had resulted in my becoming half drowsy, half languid; but I dreamily contemplated the picture, watching it come up, as it were, under my intent gaze, from a mere sketch into a finished piece of work. All that I saw I attributed to the vivid working of an overstimulated imagination, but at last something happened in that picture which by no means could have been attributed to imagination. A light sprang up within the house and shone through one of the windows!

II

I rubbed my eyes, leaned forward, taking my pipe from my lips, and looked intently, incredulously. There was no mistake about it; there was an actual flicker of light from behind one of the half-closed shutters of a window toward the rear of the house. I pinched myself vigorously and felt the pain with waking nerves, but the light did not fade away; it shone steadily on.

I whipped the picture from the easel and turned it over. It was an ordinary canvas, such as Jack had always used. A cold chill began to play down my spinal column as I returned the picture to the easel. I realized that there was in truth something unearthly about my friend's landscape; the farmer and his wife had been correct in their assertions that there was something supernatural and queer about it. I did not blame them for wishing to be rid of such a strange and unusual painting.

As for myself, I felt certain that there was something more than appeared upon the surface of this supernatural manifestation. I held myself rigidly alert, watching that strange and weird lighting of a painted landscape. I was aware that there was a Presence in the room with me and that there was something, some message, which it desired to impart; but while I held myself open for the intuitional reception of such a message, I could not restrain the cold shiver that went over me at the realization of the propinquity of the discarnate, although I realized that my old friend could mean no harm to me.

I kept my eyes upon that mysteriously lighted window. As I watched, suddenly the door of the house seemed to open, and the light from within streamed out along the path before it. Simultaneously a shadow fell across the shaft of light, projected by moving figures within, and there appeared in the doorway a dark mass that, as it issued, could be distinguished as three figures. I strained my eyes to see the better. Good heavens, it was the figures of a man and a woman, carrying between them the limp body of another human being! As the significance of this flashed through my mind, they stopped on the threshold to close the door, shutting out the stream of light from the path. But as they passed the lighted window, where the path wound past it to the front gate, I saw, outlined against it in a broken but unmistakably familiar silhouette, the face of the honest farmer who had last seen my poor friend alive!

In my excitement I cried aloud. "You shall have justice, Jack!" I exclaimed.

The light in the window faded slowly away, but the outlines of the house remained, as did all the color work invisible hands had brushed in before my startled eyes. And the painting remained as it is today, a finished picture, the last gift of my dead friend to me. I sat back, filled with unutterable awe at what I had witnessed. I knew that my friend had not died by his own hand; nor had he fallen and injured himself mortally in the woods. I knew that he had been foully done to death by hands which I could, and would, identify. I cannot say that I was afraid during the period of that marvelous manifestation; no, it was fury I felt that my friend must lie under the accusation of suicide when he had in reality been the victim of a sordid crime. I knew that he had come back to me to justify himself and to point out his murderers. I determined that they should be brought to justice. But how?

III

The rest of the night I sat smoking pipe after pipe, going over all the circumstances of Jack's death as they had been presented to me by the police and by Grimstead and his wife. There was no flaw in the story of the latter couple; it was probable enough for the country constables to credit it readily. They had known Pete Grimstead and his wife for years, and had never seen anything to their discredit, save that they were poor and had a hard struggle for existence.

But—poverty is frequently the motive for crime. Yet what could have tempted them to kill a poor artist, who certainly had not carried on his person more than a few dollars? And the small amount found upon his body might have been all in his possession at that time. What else could he have shown them that they might have envied? His watch? It was a dollar watch, the fob a knotted black silk cord. Nothing tempting about that. Moreover, it had been found upon his body. His cuff links? Plain white buttons.

The body had been fully clothed when found. Stop! I did not remember having seen his hat. There had been no hat, and Jack had always worn—it was his only extravagance—a superfine Panama. His hat! Perhaps here was the clew to the mystery. It was not until dawn that I finally retired to sleep brokenly, sure in my heart that I had found a clew that would eventually unfold the motive and the mystery of the crime. It could not be that my poor friend had been murdered, at the threshold of a promising career, for the sake of a Panama hat! But that the hat was closely connected with the real story of his death I was fully persuaded. I was filled with impotent fury, but I determined to get a good sleep and then to make a visit to Pete Grimstead's farm. I did not wish to present myself there with my brain stupid after a sleepless night.

It was late that afternoon when I walked up the path to the house I had seen pictured so strangely in poor friend's last painting. I had asked the local constable to drive me out, and I recognized it immediately as the scene of the crime. He sat waiting outside in the wagon until I should have completed my questioning. I felt as though I were in a dream as I stood upon the threshold from which I had seen, the night before, that guilty pair issuing. I knocked strongly.

It was the woman who answered. She opened the door slowly, and, as it appeared to me, cautiously. When she saw who it was, she uttered a single choked exclamation, and shut the door sharply in my face. I heard her hurried footsteps retreating in the hall, and then the sound of her voice calling her husband from the back door.

I kept up an occasional sharp knocking. The constable, who had not seen the door opened, called out that I'd better go to the back door, so I stepped down to the path. As I turned the corner, I saw the woman on the doorstep, her face absolutely gray in the soft afternoon light, her eyes straining anxiously toward the barn, from whence came the gruff call of her husband. When she heard my footsteps she turned abruptly, threw out her hands as if to ward off something, made as though to re-enter the house, and crumpled up in a heap on the door stone.

I stood rooted to the spot, torn by conflicting emotions. She was a woman, an elderly woman, and I should have gone to her assistance. She was a woman—but perhaps her hands had been stained in the blood of my dearest friend! I stood coldly aloof, awaiting events.

It was her husband who lifted her from the ground, shooting a vindictive glance at me as he bent over her. I could see that he had been suffering mentally; yet I felt nothing but fierce pleasure at the sight. He was a murderer, and it was meet that he should experience mental torture until such time as he suffered the legal punishment that was his just due.

He carried the limp form into the house and laid her down on a horsehair sofa in the front room. I followed him. The chill of that room penetrated my bones with a horrid suggestion of what had taken place there so short a time ago. He turned upon me with a sudden bracing of his shoulders and a tossing back of his head that reminded me against my will of a gallant stag driven at bay.

"Well, what do you want?" he asked, with such hopelessness in his tones that I could have felt pity for him in his plight had I not steeled my heart for what I had to do.

"I want to ask you a few more questions about the—the manner of my friend's death," I replied tensely, bending a piercing gaze upon him.

He took an involuntary step backward against the sofa where lay the unconscious partner of his guilt. The movement displaced a crudely decorated sofa pillow, one of two propped against either arm of the sofa. It slipped, and would have gone to the floor had he not thrown himself upon it with a desperate effort that seemed out of all proportion to the trifling incident.

"Well," he shot at me, but in an agitated manner, "what is it you want to know?"

He remained before the sofa, his attitude that of one who hides a secret or protects something helpless. Flashing through my mind came the subconscious memory of a glint of white under the pillow. With a quick movement I sprang to the sofa, and although the farmer flung himself simultaneously against me, he was too late. I pulled the cushion away with determined hand and disclosed—Jack Lindsay's Panama hat!

IV

I looked at Grimstead with stern accusation. He regarded me with horror written large upon his weather-beaten countenance. His eyes were stricken; his shoulders, so courageously braced back a moment since in an assumption of innocence, sank in and stooped over. He was the very picture of confounded guilt.

Stepping to the door, I hallooed to the constable, who clambered out, secured the horse, and came hurrying up the path. Wordlessly I pointed to the hanging head of the guilty man and to the Panama hat, crushed up against the arm of the sofa. The officer stood with dropped jaw and straining eyes.

From the sofa came the moaning cry of the woman. "Tell them the truth, Pete! Oh, I told you it would have been better to have told it in the beginning! Such things are always found out."

The constable looked horror-stricken at me, and I looked triumphantly back at him. I had located the murderer when no one had so much as suspected a murder; I had vindicated my poor friend from the charge of suicide, under which his noble spirit had been unable to rest in peace.

The woman's voice went on weakly. "He came in here to get something to eat," she wailed. "We gave him his lunch. When he got up to go he put his hands suddenly to his heart, opened his mouth as if he were going to speak, and then fell right down on the floor. He was dead! Oh, believe it or not, he was dead! We didn't lay a hand on him. But he was dead, in our house, and we were afraid. We are poor. We were afraid of what people might think, because that very morning Pete plowed up the bag of coins he had lost thirty years ago. We wouldn't dare spend it. We were afraid we'd be accused of killing and robbing!" Her voice rose in a shrieking crescendo of agony: "Oh, believe it or not, it is true—every word I'm telling you is God's own truth!"

Her husband threw himself down beside her, hiding his face in his toil-worn hands.

"What did you do then?" I managed to ask, my head whirling.

Grimstead lifted a defiant face. "I don't suppose you will believe us," he said shortly and without bitterness, "but what my wife says is quite true. After he dropped and we found he was dead, we talked it over. We were afraid of what people might think. We decided to carry his body away to a distance and say he had left here for a walk and had never returned. I wish now," he added dejectedly, "that we had come out with the truth in the beginning. I suppose it looks worse for us now than it would've looked then."

The constable's eyes questioned me appealingly.

I touched the Panama hat. "And this?" I questioned.

"It fell off when we were carrying him away," said Grimstead dully. "We found it on the path when we came back, and we didn't dare go out there with it, so we hid it here."

"Why didn't you burn it?" queried the constable, astonished that this incriminating evidence should have been left in such a conspicuous hiding place.

Grimstead shrugged his shoulders. "We weren't guilty of anything. Why should we burn it? We never thought anyone would come looking here. We'd have given it up with the other things, only it might have looked queer if we'd had his hat."

He looked directly at my companion then. "Well, why don't you arrest me?" he demanded.

Again the constable and I exchanged glances. By common consent we stepped out of the chilling atmosphere of the room into the soft light of summer afternoon.

"I must tell you," said the constable, "that I remember hearing, when I was a young fellow, that Pete Grimstead had the money ready to pay off the mortgage on his farm and lost it somewhere as he was plowing his fields. Hunt as he might, he could never lay hands on it again. There's never been anything against the Grimsteads, in all the time I can remember, except that they are poor and hard working, and that isn't really a crime. Of course, sir, if you feel that you want to go further in the matter," his voice died away, and his eyes questioned mine.

I thought hard and fast. Perhaps, after all, my poor friend's spirit had come to me not to bring murderers to justice, but merely to vindicate his own reputation, he who had always intended to fight it out to the end, he who had determined to become famous before death cut short his career. As I came to this conclusion I felt a lightness of heart that convinced me I had arrived at the correct significance of Jack's manifestation.

At the expression on my face the man drew a long sigh of relief.

"I'm glad you aren't going to pile up troubles for them." He jerked his thumb toward the house. "I'm sure the story is just as they told it. Did your friend ever mention his having any heart trouble, now?"

Into my mind flashed Doctor Wilmott's words. "If he lives to be forty he will be a famous man," he had said.

As I recollected more or less distinctly, there had been a faint accentuation upon the word "lives."

"I believe they've told us the truth," I said heartily, meeting the other man's eyes frankly. "The only thing I want now is to have the record of suicide cleared up positively once and for all. I'm sure it can be done without implicating those poor unhappy people further."

The constable stepped to the door. "Better give me that hat," he suggested, his cheerful, matter-of-fact voice affecting both the stricken man and his wife with sudden hope. "I'm sure you don't want to be reminded of the affair any longer," and he put out his hand for the Panama, which he passed on to me. Then he stretched out his right hand wordlessly to Grimstead.

The farmer took it wonderingly, his expression incredulous. So much had he suffered from his own fears for weeks that he could hardly believe the matter entirely cleared up. Not so Mrs. Grimstead. With happy tears streaming down her cheeks, she said brokenly: "God bless you both for believing us!"

The records in town were changed when the constable returned, so that my unfortunate friend was no longer charged with suicide; his death was entered as heart failure. But no mention was made of the Grimsteads. The story they had given in the beginning stood in the records as true; only the constable, the coroner, and myself knew the real facts.

Upon my return to my home city I satisfied myself that Doctor Wilmott had indeed accented the word "lives"; he had examined Jack, and had told him that only with the utmost care could he expect to live longer than five or six years and that even this time might be cut short without a moment's notice.

As for the haunted landscape, it hangs on the walls of my room, one of the best examples of my dead friend's masterly art. There seems to be nothing mysterious about it now, for although I have often sat late, smoking, watching the half-closed shutters of the house, never again have I seen light streaming from the windows upon the pathway before the door.

His Unconquerable Enemy

W. C. Morrow

I was summoned from Calcutta to the heart of India to perform a difficult surgical operation on one of the women of a great rajah's household. I found the rajah a man of a noble character, but possessed, as I afterwards discovered, of a sense of cruelty purely Oriental and in contrast to the indolence of his disposition. He was so grateful for the success that attended my mission that he urged me to remain a guest at the palace as long as it might please me to stay, and I thankfully accepted the invitation.

One of the male servants early attracted my notice for his marvellous capacity of malice. His name was Neranya, and I am certain that there must have been a large proportion of Malay blood in his veins, for, unlike the Indians (from whom he differed also in complexion), he was extremely alert, active, nervous, and sensitive. A redeeming circumstance was his love for his master. Once his violent temper led him to the commission of an atrocious crime,—the fatal stabbing of a dwarf. In punishment for this the rajah ordered that Neranya's right arm (the offending one) be severed from his body. The sentence was executed in a bungling fashion by a stupid fellow armed with an axe, and I, being a surgeon, was compelled, in order to save Neranya's life, to perform an amputation of the stump, leaving not a vestige of the limb remaining.

After this he developed an augmented fiendishness. His love for the rajah was changed to hate, and in his mad anger he flung discretion to the winds. Driven once to frenzy by the rajah's scornful treatment, he sprang upon the rajah with a knife, but, fortunately, was seized and disarmed. To his unspeakable dismay the rajah sentenced him for this offence to suffer amputation of the remaining arm. It was done as in the former instance. This had the effect of putting a temporary curb on Neranya's spirit, or, rather, of changing the outward manifestations of his diabolism. Being armless, he was at first largely at the mercy of those who ministered to his needs,—a duty which I undertook to see was properly discharged, for I felt an interest in this strangely distorted nature. His sense of helplessness, combined with a damnable scheme for revenge which he had secretly formed, caused Neranya to change his fierce, impetuous, and unruly conduct into a smooth, quiet, insinuating bearing, which he carried so artfully as to deceive those with whom he was brought in contact, including the rajah himself.

Neranya, being exceedingly quick, intelligent, and dexterous, and having an unconquerable will, turned his attention to the cultivating of an enlarged usefulness of his legs, feet, and toes, with so excellent effect that in time he was able to perform wonderful feats with those members. Thus his capability, especially for destructive mischief, was considerably restored.

One morning the rajah's only son, a young man of an uncommonly amiable and noble disposition, was found dead in bed. His murder was a most atrocious one, his body being mutilated in a shocking manner, but in my eyes the most significant of all the mutilations was the entire removal and disappearance of the young prince's arms.

The death of the young man nearly brought the rajah to the grave. It was not, therefore, until I had nursed him back to health that I began a systematic inquiry into the murder. I said nothing of my own discoveries and conclusions until after the rajah and his officers had failed and my work had been done; then I submitted to him a written report, making a close analysis of all the circumstances and closing by charging the crime to Neranya. The rajah, convinced by my proof and argument, at once ordered Neranya to be put to death, this to be accomplished slowly and with frightful tortures. The sentence was so cruel and revolting that it filled me with horror, and I implored that the wretch be shot. Finally, through a sense of gratitude to me, the rajah relaxed. When Neranya was charged with the crime he denied it, of course, but, seeing that the rajah was convinced, he threw aside all restraint, and, dancing, laughing, and shrieking in the most horrible manner, confessed his guilt, gloated over it, and reviled the rajah to his teeth,—this, knowing that some fearful death awaited him.

The rajah decided upon the details of the matter that night, and in the morning he informed me of his decision. It was that Neranya's life should be spared, but that both of his legs should be broken with hammers, and that then I should amputate the limbs at the trunk! Appended to this horrible sentence was a provision that the maimed wretch should be kept and tortured at regular intervals by such means as afterwards might be devised.

Sickened to the heart by the awful duty set out for me, I nevertheless performed it with success, and I care to say nothing more about that part of the tragedy. Neranya escaped death very narrowly and was a long time in recovering his wonted vitality. During all these weeks the rajah neither saw him nor made inquiries concerning him, but when, as in duty bound, I made official report that the man had recovered his strength, the rajah's eyes brightened, and he emerged with deadly activity from the stupor into which he so long had been plunged.

The rajah's palace was a noble structure, but it is necessary here to describe only the grand hall. It was an immense chamber, with a floor of polished, inlaid stone and a lofty, arched ceiling. A soft light stole into it through stained glass set in the roof and in high windows on one side. In the middle of the room was a rich fountain, which threw up a tall, slender column of water, with smaller and shorter jets grouped around it. Across one end of the hall, half-way to the ceiling, was a balcony, which communicated with the upper story of a wing, and from which a flight of stone stairs descended to the floor of the hall. During the hot summers this room was delightfully cool; it was the rajah's favorite lounging-place, and when the nights were hot he had his cot taken thither, and there he slept.

This hall was chosen for Neranya's permanent prison; here was he to stay so long as he might live, with never a glimpse of the shining world or the glorious heavens. To one of his nervous, discontented nature such confinement was worse than death. At the rajah's order there was constructed for him a small pen of open iron-work, circular, and about four feet in diameter, elevated on four slender iron posts, ten feet above the floor, and placed between the balcony and the fountain. Such was Neranya's prison. The pen was about four feet in depth, and the pen-top was left open for the convenience of the servants whose duty it should be to care for him. These precautions for his safe confinement were taken at my suggestion, for, although the man was now deprived of all four of his limbs, I still feared that he might develop some extraordinary, unheard-of power for mischief. It was provided that the attendants should reach his cage by means of a movable ladder.

All these arrangements having been made and Neranya hoisted into his cage, the rajah emerged upon the balcony to see him for the first time since the last amputation. Neranya had been lying panting and helpless on the floor of his cage, but when his quick ear caught the sound of the rajah's footfall he squirmed about until he had brought the back of his head against the railing, elevating his eyes above his chest, and enabling him to peer through the open-work of the cage. Thus the two deadly enemies faced each other. The rajah's stern face paled at sight of the hideous, shapeless thing which met his gaze; but he soon recovered, and the old hard, cruel, sinister look returned. Neranya's black hair and beard had grown long, and they added to the natural ferocity of his aspect. His eyes blazed upon the rajah with a terrible light, his lips parted, and he gasped for breath; his face was ashen with rage and despair, and his thin, distended nostrils quivered.

The rajah folded his arms and gazed down from the balcony upon the frightful wreck that he had made. Oh, the dreadful pathos of that picture; the inhumanity of it; the deep and dismal tragedy of it! Who might look into the wild, despairing heart of the prisoner and see and understand the frightful turmoil there; the surging, choking passion; unbridled but impotent ferocity; frantic thirst for a vengeance that should be deeper than hell! Neranya gazed, his shapeless body heaving, his eyes aflame; and then, in a strong, clear voice, which rang throughout the great hall, with rapid speech he hurled at the rajah the most insulting defiance, the most awful curses. He cursed the womb that had conceived him, the food that should nourish him, the wealth that had brought him power; cursed him in the name of Buddha and all the wise men; cursed by the sun, the moon, and the stars; by the continents, mountains, oceans, and rivers; by all things living; cursed his head, his heart, his entrails; cursed in a whirlwind of unmentionable words; heaped unimaginable insults and contumely upon him; called him a knave, a beast, a fool, a liar, an infamous and unspeakable coward.

The rajah heard it all calmly, without the movement of a muscle, without the slightest change of countenance; and when the poor wretch had exhausted his strength and fallen helpless and silent to the floor, the rajah, with a grim, cold smile, turned and strode away.

The days passed. The rajah, not deterred by Neranya's curses often heaped upon him, spent even more time than formerly in the great hall, and slept there oftener at night; and finally Neranya wearied of cursing and defying him, and fell into a sullen silence. The man was a study for me, and I observed every change in his fleeting moods. Generally his condition was that of miserable despair, which he attempted bravely to conceal. Even the boon of suicide had been denied him, for when he would wriggle into an erect position the rail of his pen was a foot above his head, so that he could not clamber over and break his skull on the stone floor beneath; and when he had tried to starve himself the attendants forced food down his throat; so that he abandoned such attempts. At times his eyes would blaze and his breath would come in gasps, for imaginary vengeance was working within him; but steadily he became quieter and more tractable, and was pleasant and responsive when I would converse with him. Whatever might have been the tortures which the rajah had decided on, none as yet had been ordered; and although Neranya knew that they were in contemplation, he never referred to them or complained of his lot.

The awful climax of this situation was reached one night, and even after this lapse of years I cannot approach its description without a shudder.

It was a hot night, and the rajah had gone to sleep in the great hall, lying on a high cot placed on the main floor just underneath the edge of the balcony. I had been unable to sleep in my own apartment, and so I had stolen into the great hall through the heavily curtained entrance at the end farthest from the balcony. As I entered I heard a peculiar, soft sound above the patter of the fountain. Neranya's cage was partly concealed from my view by the spraying water, but I suspected that the unusual sound came from him. Stealing a little to one side, and crouching against the dark hangings of the wall, I could see him in the faint light which dimly illuminated the hall, and then I discovered that my surmise was correct—Neranya was quietly at work. Curious to learn more, and knowing that only mischief could have been inspiring him, I sank into a thick robe on the floor and watched him.

To my great astonishment Neranya was tearing off with his teeth the bag which served as his outer garment. He did it cautiously, casting sharp glances frequently at the rajah, who, sleeping soundly on his cot below, breathed heavily. After starting a strip with his teeth, Neranya, by the same means, would attach it to the railing of his cage and then wriggle away, much after the manner of a caterpillar's crawling, and this would cause the strip to be torn out the full length of his garment. He repeated this operation with incredible patience and skill until his entire garment had been torn into strips. Two or three of these he tied end to end with his teeth, lips, and tongue, tightening the knots by placing one end of the strip under his body and drawing the other taut with his teeth. In this way he made a line several feet long, one end of which he made fast to the rail with his mouth. It then began to dawn upon me that he was going to make an insane attempt—impossible of achievement without hands, feet, arms, or legs—to escape from his cage! For what purpose? The rajah was asleep in the hall—ah! I caught my breath. Oh, the desperate, insane thirst for revenge which could have unhinged so clear and firm a mind! Even though he should accomplish the impossible feat of climbing over the railing of his cage that he might fall to the floor below (for how could he slide down the rope?), he would be in all probability killed or stunned; and even if he should escape these dangers it would be impossible for him to clamber upon the cot without rousing the rajah, and impossible even though the rajah were dead! Amazed at the man's daring, and convinced that his sufferings and brooding had destroyed his reason, nevertheless I watched him with breathless interest.

With other strips tied together he made a short swing across one side of his cage. He caught the long line in his teeth at a point not far from the rail; then, wriggling with great effort to an upright position, his back braced against the rail, he put his chin over the swing and worked toward one end. He tightened the grasp of his chin on the swing, and with tremendous exertion, working the lower end of his spine against the railing, he began gradually to ascend the side of his cage. The labor was so great that he was compelled to pause at intervals, and his breathing was hard and painful; and even while thus resting he was in a position of terrible strain, and his pushing against the swing caused it to press hard against his windpipe and nearly strangle him.

After amazing effort he had elevated the lower end of his body until it protruded above the railing, the top of which was now across the lower end of his abdomen. Gradually he worked his body over, going backward, until there was sufficient excess of weight on the outer side of the rail; and then, with a quick lurch, he raised his head and shoulders and swung into a horizontal position on top of the rail. Of course, he would have fallen to the floor below had it not been for the line which he held in his teeth. With so great nicety had he estimated the distance between his mouth and the point where the rope was fastened to the rail, that the line tightened and checked him just as he reached the horizontal position on the rail. If one had told me beforehand that such a feat as I had just seen this man accomplish was possible, I should have thought him a fool.

Neranya was now balanced on his stomach across the top of the rail, and he eased his position by bending his spine and hanging down on either side as much as possible. Having rested thus for some minutes, he began cautiously to slide off backward, slowly paying out the line through his teeth, finding almost a fatal difficulty in passing the knots. Now, it is quite possible that the line would have escaped altogether from his teeth laterally when he would slightly relax his hold to let it slip, had it not been for a very ingenious plan to which he had resorted. This consisted in his having made a turn of the line around his neck before he attacked the swing, thus securing a threefold control of the line,—one by his teeth, another by friction against his neck, and a third by his ability to compress it between his cheek and shoulder. It was quite evident now that the minutest details of a most elaborate plan had been carefully worked out by him before beginning the task, and that possibly weeks of difficult theoretical study had been consumed in the mental preparation. As I observed him I was reminded of certain hitherto unaccountable things which he had been doing for some weeks past—going through certain hitherto inexplicable motions, undoubtedly for the purpose of training his muscles for the immeasurably arduous labor which he was now performing.

A stupendous and seemingly impossible part of his task had been accomplished. Could he reach the floor in safety? Gradually he worked himself backward over the rail, in imminent danger of falling; but his nerve never wavered, and I could see a wonderful light in his eyes. With something of a lurch, his body fell against the outer side of the railing, to which he was hanging by his chin, the line still held firmly in his teeth. Slowly he slipped his chin from the rail, and then hung suspended by the line in his teeth. By almost imperceptible degrees, with infinite caution, he descended the line, and, finally, his unwieldy body rolled upon the floor, safe and unhurt!

What miracle would this superhuman monster next accomplish? I was quick and strong, and was ready and able to intercept any dangerous act; but not until danger appeared would I interfere with this extraordinary scene.

I must confess to astonishment upon having observed that Neranya, instead of proceeding directly toward the sleeping rajah, took quite another direction. Then it was only escape, after all, that the wretch contemplated, and not the murder of the rajah. But how could he escape? The only possible way to reach the outer air without great risk was by ascending the stairs to the balcony and leaving by the corridor which opened upon it, and thus fall into the hands of some British soldiers quartered thereabout, who might conceive the idea of hiding him; but surely it was impossible for Neranya to ascend that long flight of stairs! Nevertheless, he made directly for them, his method of progression this: He lay upon his back, with the lower end of his body toward the stairs; then bowed his spine upward, thus drawing his head and shoulders a little forward; straightened, and then pushed the lower end of his body forward a space equal to that through which he had drawn his head; repeating this again and again, each time, while bending his spine, preventing his head from slipping by pressing it against the floor. His progress was laborious and slow, but sensible; and, finally, he arrived at the foot of the stairs.

It was manifest that his insane purpose was to ascend them. The desire for freedom must have been strong within him! Wriggling to an upright position against the newel-post, he looked up at the great height which he had to climb and sighed; but there was no dimming of the light in his eyes. How could he accomplish the impossible task?

His solution of the problem was very simple, though daring and perilous as all the rest. While leaning against the newel-post he let himself fall diagonally upon the bottom step, where he lay partly hanging over, but safe, on his side. Turning upon his back, he wriggled forward along the step to the rail and raised himself to an upright position against it as he had against the newel-post, fell as before, and landed on the second step. In this manner, with inconceivable labor, he accomplished the ascent of the entire flight of stairs.

It being apparent to me that the rajah was not the object of Neranya's movements, the anxiety which I had felt on that account was now entirely dissipated. The things which already he had accomplished were entirely beyond the nimblest imagination. The sympathy which I had always felt for the wretched man was now greatly quickened; and as infinitesimally small as I knew his chances for escape to be, I nevertheless hoped that he would succeed. Any assistance from me, however, was out of the question; and it never should be known that I had witnessed the escape.

Neranya was now upon the balcony, and I could dimly see him wriggling along toward the door which led out upon the balcony. Finally he stopped and wriggled to an upright position against the rail, which had wide openings between the balusters. His back was toward me, but he slowly turned and faced me and the hall. At that great distance I could not distinguish his features, but the slowness with which he had worked, even before he had fully accomplished the ascent of the stairs, was evidence all too eloquent of his extreme exhaustion. Nothing but a most desperate resolution could have sustained him thus far, but he had drawn upon the last remnant of his strength.

He looked around the hall with a sweeping glance, and then down upon the rajah, who was sleeping immediately beneath him, over twenty feet below. He looked long and earnestly, sinking lower, and lower, and lower upon the rail. Suddenly, to my inconceivable astonishment and dismay, he toppled through and shot downward from his lofty height! I held my breath, expecting to see him crushed upon the stone floor beneath; but instead of that he fell full upon the rajah's breast, driving him through the cot to the floor. I sprang forward with a loud cry for help, and was instantly at the scene of the catastrophe. With indescribable horror I saw that Neranya's teeth were buried in the rajah's throat! I tore the wretch away, but the blood was pouring from the rajah's arteries, his chest was crushed in, and he was gasping in the agony of death. People came running in, terrified. I turned to Neranya. He lay upon his back, his face hideously smeared with blood. Murder, and not escape, had been his intentions from the beginning; and he had employed the only method by which there was ever a possibility of accomplishing it. I knelt beside him, and saw that he too was dying; his back had been broken by the fall. He smiled sweetly into my face, and a triumphant look of accomplished revenge sat upon his face even in death.

The Hollow of
the Three Hills

Nathaniel Hawthorne

In those strange old times, when fantastic dreams and madmen's reveries were realized among the actual circumstances of life, two persons met together at an appointed hour and place. One was a lady, graceful in form and fair of feature, though pale and troubled, and smitten with an untimely blight in what should have been the fullest bloom of her years; the other was an ancient and meanly-dressed woman, of ill-favored aspect, and so withered, shrunken, and decrepit, that even the space since she began to decay must have exceeded the ordinary term of human existence. In the spot where they encountered, no mortal could observe them. Three little hills stood near each other, and down in the midst of them sunk a hollow basin, almost mathematically circular, two or three hundred feet in breadth, and of such depth that a stately cedar might but just be visible above the sides. Dwarf pines were numerous upon the hills, and partly fringed the outer verge of the intermediate hollow; within which there was nothing but the brown grass of October, and here and there a tree trunk, that had fallen long ago, and lay mouldering with no green successor from its roots. One of these masses of decaying wood, formerly a majestic oak, rested close beside a pool of green and sluggish water at the bottom of the basin. Such scenes as this (so gray tradition tells) were once the resort of the Power of Evil and his plighted subjects; and here, at midnight or on the dim verge of evening, they were said to stand round the mantling pool, disturbing its putrid waters in the performance of an impious baptismal rite. The chill beauty of an autumnal sunset was now gilding the three hill tops, whence a paler tint stole down their sides into the hollow.

"Here is our pleasant meeting come to pass," said the aged crone, "according as thou hast desired. Say quickly what thou wouldst have of me, for there is but a short hour that we may tarry here."

As the old withered woman spoke, a smile glimmered on her countenance, like lamplight on the wall of a sepulchre. The lady trembled, and cast her eyes upward to the verge of the basin, as if meditating to return with her purpose unaccomplished. But it was not so ordained.

"I am a stranger in this land, as you know," said she at length. "Whence I come it matters not; but I have left those behind me with whom my fate was intimately bound, and from whom I am cut off forever. There is a weight in my bosom that I cannot away with, and I have come hither to inquire of their welfare."

"And who is there by this green pool, that can bring thee news from the ends of the earth?" cried the old woman, peering into the lady's face. "Not from my lips mayst thou hear these tidings; yet, be thou bold, and the daylight shall not pass away from yonder hill top, before thy wish be granted."

"I will do your bidding though I die," replied the lady desperately.

The old woman seated herself on the trunk of the fallen tree, threw aside the hood that shrouded her gray locks, and beckoned her companion to draw near.

"Kneel down," she said, "and lay your forehead on my knees."

She hesitated a moment, but the anxiety, that had long been kindling, burned fiercely up within her. As she knelt down, the border of her garment was dipped into the pool; she laid her forehead on the old woman's knees, and the latter drew a cloak about the lady's face, so that she was in darkness. Then she heard the muttered words of prayer, in the midst of which she started, and would have arisen.

"Let me flee,—let me flee and hide myself, that they may not look upon me!" she cried. But, with returning recollection, she hushed herself, and was still as death.

For it seemed as if other voices—familiar in infancy, and unforgotten through many wanderings, and in all the vicissitudes of her heart and fortune—were mingling with the accents of the prayer. At first the words were faint and indistinct, not rendered so by distance, but rather resembling the dim pages of a book which we strive to read by an imperfect and gradually brightening light. In such a manner, as the prayer proceeded, did those voices strengthen upon the ear; till at length the petition ended, and the conversation of an aged man, and of a woman broken and decayed like himself, became distinctly audible to the lady as she knelt. But those strangers appeared not to stand in the hollow depth between the three hills. Their voices were encompassed and reëchoed by the walls of a chamber, the windows of which were rattling in the breeze; the regular vibration of a clock, the crackling of a fire, and the tinkling of the embers as they fell among the ashes, rendered the scene almost as vivid as if painted to the eye. By a melancholy hearth sat these two old people, the man calmly despondent, the woman querulous and tearful, and their words were all of sorrow. They spoke of a daughter, a wanderer they knew not where, bearing dishonor along with her, and leaving shame and affliction to bring their gray heads to the grave. They alluded also to other and more recent woe, but in the midst of their talk, their voices seemed to melt into the sound of the wind sweeping mournfully among the autumn leaves; and when the lady lifted her eyes, there was she kneeling in the hollow between three hills.

"A weary and lonesome time yonder old couple have of it," remarked the old woman, smiling in the lady's face.

"And did you also hear them?" exclaimed she, a sense of intolerable humiliation triumphing over her agony and fear.

"Yea; and we have yet more to hear," replied the old woman. "Wherefore, cover thy face quickly."

Again the withered hag poured forth the monotonous words of a prayer that was not meant to be acceptable in Heaven; and soon, in the pauses of her breath, strange murmurings began to thicken, gradually increasing so as to drown and overpower the charm by which they grew. Shrieks pierced through the obscurity of sound, and were succeeded by the singing of sweet female voices, which in their turn gave way to a wild roar of laughter, broken suddenly by groanings and sobs, forming altogether a ghastly confusion of terror and mourning and mirth. Chains were rattling, fierce and stern voices uttered threats, and the scourge resounded at their command. All these noises deepened and became substantial to the listener's ear, till she could distinguish every soft and dreamy accent of the love songs, that died causelessly into funeral hymns. She shuddered at the unprovoked wrath which blazed up like the spontaneous kindling of flame, and she grew faint at the fearful merriment, raging miserably around her. In the midst of this wild scene, where unbound passions jostled each other in a drunken career, there was one solemn voice of a man, and a manly and melodious voice it might once have been. He went to and fro continually, and his feet sounded upon the floor. In each member of that frenzied company, whose own burning thoughts had become their exclusive world, he sought an auditor for the story of his individual wrong, and interpreted their laughter and tears as his reward of scorn or pity. He spoke of woman's perfidy, of a wife who had broken her holiest vows, of a home and heart made desolate. Even as he went on, the shout, the laugh, the shriek, the sob, rose up in unison, till they changed into the hollow, fitful, and uneven sound of the wind, as it fought among the pine trees on those three lonely hills. The lady looked up, and there was the withered woman smiling in her face.

"Couldst thou have thought there were such merry times in a madhouse?" inquired the latter.

"True, true," said the lady to herself; "there is mirth within its walls, but misery, misery without."

"Wouldst thou hear more?" demanded the old woman.

"There is one other voice I would fain listen to again," replied the lady, faintly.

"Then, lay down thy head speedily upon my knees, that thou mayst get thee hence before the hour be past."

The golden skirts of day were yet lingering upon the hills, but deep shades obscured the hollow and the pool, as if sombre night were rising thence to overspread the world. Again that evil woman began to weave her spell. Long did it proceed unanswered, till the knolling of a bell stole in among the intervals of her words, like a clang that had travelled far over valley and rising ground, and was just ready to die in the air. The lady shook upon her companion's knees, as she heard that boding sound. Stronger it grew and sadder, and deepened into the tone of a death bell, knolling dolefully from some ivy-mantled tower, and bearing tidings of mortality and woe to the cottage, to the hall, and to the solitary wayfarer, that all might weep for the doom appointed in turn to them. Then came a measured tread, passing slowly, slowly on, as of mourners with a coffin, their garments trailing on the ground, so that the ear could measure the length of their melancholy array. Before them went the priest, reading the burial service, while the leaves of his book were rustling in the breeze. And though no voice but his was heard to speak aloud, still there were revilings and anathemas, whispered but distinct, from women and from men, breathed against the daughter who had wrung the aged hearts of her parents,—the wife who had betrayed the trusting fondness of her husband,—the mother who had sinned against natural affection, and left her child to die. The sweeping sound of the funeral train faded away like a thin vapor, and the wind, that just before had seemed to shake the coffin pall, moaned sadly round the verge of the Hollow between three Hills. But when the old woman stirred the kneeling lady, she lifted not her head.

"Here has been a sweet hour's sport!" said the withered crone, chuckling to herself.

HOP-FROG

EDGAR ALLAN POE

I NEVER KNEW ANY ONE SO KEENLY ALIVE TO A JOKE AS THE KING WAS. HE SEEMED to live only for joking. To tell a good story of the joke kind, and to tell it well, was the surest road to his favor. Thus it happened that his seven ministers were all noted for their accomplishments as jokers. They all took after the king, too, in being large, corpulent, oily men, as well as inimitable jokers. Whether people grow fat by joking, or whether there is something in fat itself which predisposes to a joke, I have never been quite able to determine; but certain it is that a lean joker is a *rara avis in terris*.

About the refinements, or, as he called them, the "ghosts" of wit, the king troubled himself very little. He had an especial admiration for *breadth* in a jest, and would often put up with *length*, for the sake of it. Over-niceties wearied him. He would have preferred Rabelais's "Gargantua," to the "Zadig" of Voltaire: and, upon the whole, practical jokes suited his taste far better than verbal ones.

At the date of my narrative, professing jesters had not altogether gone out of fashion at court. Several of the great continental "powers" still retained their "fools," who wore motley, with caps and bells, and who were expected to be always ready with sharp witticisms, at a moment's notice, in consideration of the crumbs that fell from the royal table.

Our king, as a matter of course, retained his "fool." The fact is, he *required* something in the way of folly—if only to counterbalance the heavy wisdom of the seven wise men who were his ministers—not to mention himself.

His fool, or professional jester, was not *only* a fool, however. His value was trebled in the eyes of the king, by the fact of his being also a dwarf and a cripple. Dwarfs were as common at court, in those days, as fools; and many monarchs would have found it difficult to get through their days (days are rather longer at court than elsewhere) without both a jester to laugh *with*, and a dwarf to laugh *at*. But, as I have already observed, your jesters, in ninety-nine cases out of a hundred, are fat, round and unwieldy—so that it was no small source of self-gratulation with our king that, in Hop-Frog (this was the fool's name,) he possessed a triplicate treasure in one person.

I believe the name "Hop-Frog" was *not* that given to the dwarf by his sponsors at baptism, but it was conferred upon him, by general consent of the several ministers, on account of his inability to walk as other men do. In fact, Hop-Frog could only get along by a sort of interjectional gait—something between a leap and a wriggle—a movement that afforded illimitable amusement, and of course consolation, to the king, for (notwithstanding the protuberance of his stomach and a constitutional swelling of the head) the king, by his whole court, was accounted a capital figure.

But although Hop-Frog, through the distortion of his legs, could move only with great pain and difficulty along a road or floor, the prodigious muscular power which nature seemed to have bestowed upon his arms, by way of compensation for deficiency in the lower limbs, enabled him to perform many feats of wonderful dexterity, where trees or ropes were in question, or anything else to climb. At such exercises he certainly much more resembled a squirrel, or a small monkey, than a frog.

I am not able to say, with precision, from what country Hop-Frog originally came. It was from some barbarous region, however, that no person ever heard of—a vast distance from the court of our king. Hop-Frog, and a young girl very little less dwarf-ish than himself (although of exquisite proportions, and a marvellous dancer,) had been forcibly carried off from their respective homes in adjoining provinces, and sent as presents to the king, by one of his ever-victorious generals.

Under these circumstances, it is not to be wondered at that a close intimacy arose between the two little captives. Indeed, they soon became sworn friends. Hop-Frog, who, although he made a great deal of sport, was by no means popular, had it not in his power to render Trippetta many services; but *she*, on account of her grace and exquisite beauty (although a dwarf,) was universally admired and petted: so she possessed much influence; and never failed to use it, whenever she could, for the benefit of Hop-Frog.

On some grand state occasion—I forgot what—the king determined to have a masquerade, and whenever a masquerade or anything of that kind, occurred at our court, then the talents both of Hop-Frog and Trippetta were sure to be called in play. Hop-Frog, in especial, was so inventive in the way of getting up pageants, suggesting novel characters, and arranging costume, for masked balls, that nothing could be done, it seems, without his assistance.

The night appointed for the *fête* had arrived. A gorgeous hall had been fitted up, under Trippetta's eye, with every kind of device which could possibly give *éclat* to a masquerade. The whole court was in a fever of expectation. As for costumes and characters, it might well be supposed that everybody had come to a decision on such points. Many had made up their minds (as to what *rôles* they should assume) a week, or even a month, in advance; and, in fact, there was not a particle of indecision any-where—except in the case of the king and his seven minsters. Why *they* hesitated I never could tell, unless they did it by way of a joke. More probably, they found it dif-ficult, on account of being so fat, to make up their minds. At all events, time flew; and, as a last resource, they sent for Trippetta and Hop-Frog.

When the two little friends obeyed the summons of the king, they found him sitting at his wine with the seven members of his cabinet council; but the monarch appeared to be in a very ill humor. He knew that Hop-Frog was not fond of wine; for it excited the poor cripple almost to madness; and madness is no comfortable feeling. But the king loved his practical jokes, and took pleasure in forcing Hop-Frog to drink and (as the king called it) "to be merry."

"Come here, Hop-Frog," said he, as the jester and his friend entered the room: "swallow this bumper to the health of your absent friends [here Hop-Frog sighed,] and then let us have the benefit of your invention. We want characters—*characters*, man—something novel—out of the way. We are wearied with this everlasting sameness. Come, drink! the wine will brighten your wits."

Hop-Frog endeavored, as usual, to get up a jest in reply to these advances from the king; but the effort was too much. It happened to be the poor dwarf's birthday, and the command to drink to his "absent friends" forced the tears to his eyes. Many large, bitter drops fell into the goblet as he took it, humbly, from the hand of the tyrant.

"Ah! ha! ha! ha!" roared the latter, as the dwarf reluctantly drained the beaker. "See what a glass of good wine can do! Why, your eyes are shining already!"

Poor fellow! his large eyes *gleamed*, rather than shone; for the effect of wine on his excitable brain was not more powerful than instantaneous. He placed the goblet nervously on the table, and looked round upon the company with a half-insane stare. They all seemed highly amused at the success of the king's "*joke*."

"And now to business," said the prime minister, a *very* fat man.

"Yes," said the King; "come, Hop-Frog, lend us your assistance. Characters, my fine fellow; we stand in need of characters—all of us—ha! ha! ha!" and as this was seriously meant for a joke, his laugh was chorused by the seven.

Hop-Frog also laughed, although feebly and somewhat vacantly.

"Come, come," said the king, impatiently, "have you nothing to suggest?"

"I am endeavoring to think of something *novel*," replied the dwarf, abstractedly, for he was quite bewildered by the wine.

"Endeavoring!" cried the tyrant, fiercely; "what do you mean by *that*? Ah, I perceive. You are sulky, and want more wine. Here, drink this!" and he poured out another goblet full and offered it to the cripple, who merely gazed at it, gasping for breath.

"Drink, I say!" shouted the monster, "or by the fiends —"

The dwarf hesitated. The king grew purple with rage. The courtiers smirked. Trippetta, pale as a corpse, advanced to the monarch's seat, and, falling on her knees before him, implored him to spare her friend.

The tyrant regarded her, for some moments, in evident wonder at her audacity. He seemed quite at a loss what to do or say—how most becomingly to express his indignation. At last, without uttering a syllable, he pushed her violently from him, and threw the contents of the brimming goblet in her face.

The poor girl got up as best she could, and, not daring even to sigh, resumed her position at the foot of the table.

There was a dead silence for about half a minute, during which the falling of a leaf, or of a feather, might have been heard. It was interrupted by a low, but harsh and protracted *grating* sound which seemed to come at once from every corner of the room.

"What—what—*what* are you making that noise for?" demanded the king, turning furiously to the dwarf.

The latter seemed to have recovered, in great measure, from his intoxication, and looking fixedly but quietly into the tyrant's face, merely ejaculated:

"I—I? How could it have been me?"

"The sound appeared to come from without," observed one of the courtiers. "I fancy it was the parrot at the window, whetting his bill upon his cage-wires."

"True," replied the monarch, as if much relieved by the suggestion; "but, on the honor of a knight, I could have sworn that it was the gritting of this vagabond's teeth."

Hereupon the dwarf laughed (the king was too confirmed a joker to object to any one's laughing), and displayed a set of large, powerful, and very repulsive teeth. Moreover, he avowed his perfect willingness to swallow as much wine as desired. The monarch was pacified; and having drained another bumper with no very perceptible ill effect, Hop-Frog entered at once, and with spirit, into the plans for the masquerade.

"I cannot tell what was the association of idea," observed he, very tranquilly, and as if he had never tasted wine in his life, "but *just after* your majesty had struck the girl and thrown the wine in her face—*just after* your majesty had done this, and while the parrot was making that odd noise outside the window, there came into my mind a capital diversion—one of my own country frolics—often enacted among us, at our masquerades: but here it will be new altogether. Unfortunately, however, it requires a company of eight persons, and—"

"Here we *are!*" cried the king, laughing at his acute discovery of the coincidence; "eight to a fraction—I and my seven ministers. Come! what is the diversion?"

"We call it," replied the cripple, "the Eight Chained Ourang-Outangs, and it really is excellent sport if well enacted."

"*We* will enact it," remarked the king, drawing himself up, and lowering his eyelids.

"The beauty of the game," continued Hop-Frog, "lies in the fright it occasions among the women."

"Capital!" roared in chorus the monarch and his ministry.

"*I* will equip you as ourang-outangs," proceeded the dwarf; "leave all that to me. The resemblance shall be so striking, that the company of masqueraders will take you for real beasts—and of course, they will be as much terrified as astonished."

"O, this is exquisite!" exclaimed the king. "Hop-Frog! I will make a man of you."

"The chains are for the purpose of increasing the confusion by their jangling. You are supposed to have escaped, *en masse*, from your keepers. Your majesty cannot conceive the *effect* produced, at a masquerade, by eight chained ourang-outangs, imagined to be real ones by most of the company; and rushing in with savage cries, among the crowd of delicately and gorgeously habited men and women. The *contrast* is inimitable."

"It *must* be," said the king: and the council arose hurriedly (as it was growing late), to put in execution the scheme of Hop-Frog.

His mode of equipping the party as ourang-outangs was very simple, but effective enough for his purposes. The animals in question had, at the epoch of my story, very rarely been seen in any part of the civilized world; and as the imitations made by the dwarf were sufficiently beast-like and more than sufficiently hideous, their truthfulness to nature was thus thought to be secured.

The king and his ministers were first encased in tight-fitting stockinet shirts and drawers. They were then saturated with tar. At this stage of the process, some one of the party suggested feathers; but the suggestion was at once overruled by the dwarf, who soon convinced the eight, by ocular demonstration, that the hair of such a brute as the ourang-outang was much more efficiently represented by *flax*. A thick coating of the latter was accordingly plastered upon the coating of tar. A long chain was now procured. First, it was passed about the waist of the king, *and tied*; then about another of the party, and also tied; then about all successively, in the same manner. When this chaining arrangement was complete, and the party stood as far apart from each other as possible, they formed a circle; and to make all things appear natural, Hop-Frog passed the residue of the chain, in two diameters, at right angles, across the circle, after the fashion adopted, at the present day, by those who capture Chimpanzees, or other large apes, in Borneo.

The grand saloon in which the masquerade was to take place, was a circular room, very lofty, and receiving the light of the sun only through a single window at top. At night (the season for which the apartment was especially designed,) it was illuminated principally by a large chandelier, depending by a chain from the centre of the sky-light, and lowered, or elevated, by means of a counter-balance as usual; but (in order not to look unsightly) this latter passed outside the cupola and over the roof.

The arrangements of the room had been left to Trippetta's superintendence; but, in some particulars, it seems, she had been guided by the calmer judgment of her friend the dwarf. At his suggestion it was that, on this occasion, the chandelier was removed. Its waxen drippings (which, in weather so warm, it was quite impossible to prevent,) would have been seriously detrimental to the rich dresses of the guests, who, on account of the crowded state of the saloon, could not *all* be expected to keep from out its centre—that is to say, from under the chandelier. Additional sconces were set in various parts of the hall, out of the way; and a flambeau, emitting sweet odor, was placed in the right hand of each of the Caryatides that stood against the wall—some fifty or sixty altogether.

The eight ourang-outangs, taking Hop-Frog's advice, waited patiently until midnight (when the room was thoroughly filled with masqueraders) before making their appearance. No sooner had the clock ceased striking, however, than they rushed, or rather rolled in, all together—for the impediment of their chains caused most of the party to fall, and all to stumble as they entered.

The excitement among the masqueraders was prodigious, and filled the heart of the king with glee. As had been anticipated, there were not a few of the guests who supposed the ferocious-looking creatures to be beasts of *some* kind in reality, if not precisely ourang-outangs. Many of the women swooned with affright; and had not the king taken the precaution to exclude all weapons from the saloon, his party might soon have expiated their frolic in their blood. As it was, a general rush was made for the doors; but the king had ordered them to be locked immediately upon his entrance; and, at the dwarf's suggestion, the keys had been deposited with *him*.

While the tumult was at its height, and each masquerader attentive only to his own safety—(for, in fact, there was much *real* danger from the pressure of the excited crowd,)—the chain by which the chandelier ordinarily hung, and which had been drawn up on its removal, might have been seen very gradually to descend, until its hooked extremity came within three feet of the floor.

Soon after this, the king and his seven friends, having reeled about the hall in all directions, found themselves, at length, in its centre, and, of course, in immediate contact with the chain. While they were thus situated, the dwarf, who had followed closely at their heels, inciting them to keep up the commotion, took hold of their own chain at the intersection of the two portions which crossed the circle diametrically and at right angles. Here, with the rapidity of thought, he inserted the hook from which the chandelier had been wont to depend; and, in an instant, by some unseen agency, the chandelier-chain was drawn so far upward as to take the hook out of reach, and, as an inevitable consequence, to drag the ourang-outangs together in close connection, and face to face.

The masqueraders, by this time, had recovered, in some measure, from their alarm; and, beginning to regard the whole matter as a well-contrived pleasantry, set up a loud shout of laughter at the predicament of the apes.

"Leave them to *me!*" now screamed Hop-Frog, his shrill voice making itself easily heard through all the din. "Leave them to *me*. I fancy *I* know them. If I can only get a good look at them, *I* can soon tell who they are."

Here, scrambling over the heads of the crowd, he managed to get to the wall; when, seizing a flambeau from one of the Caryatides, he returned, as he went, to the centre of the room—leaped, with the agility of a monkey, upon the king's head—and thence clambered a few feet up the chain—holding down the torch to examine the group of ourang-outangs, and still screaming, "*I* shall soon find out who they are!"

And now, while the whole assembly (the apes included) were convulsed with laughter, the jester suddenly uttered a shrill whistle; when the chain flew violently up for about thirty feet—dragging with it the dismayed and struggling ourang-outangs, and leaving them suspended in mid-air between the sky-light and the floor. Hop-Frog, clinging to the chain as it rose, still maintained his relative position in respect to the eight maskers, and still (as if nothing were the matter) continued to thrust his torch down towards them, as though endeavoring to discover who they were.

So thoroughly astonished were the whole company at this ascent, that a dead silence, of about a minute's duration, ensued. It was broken by just such a low, harsh, *grating* sound, as had before attracted the attention of the king and his councillors, when the former threw the wine in the face of Trippetta. But, on the present occasion, there could be no question as to *whence* the sound issued. It came from the fang-like teeth of the dwarf, who ground them and gnashed them as he foamed at the mouth, and glared, with an expression of maniacal rage, into the upturned countenances of the king and his seven companions.

"Ah, ha!" said at length the infuriated jester. "Ah, ha! I begin to see who these people *are*, now!" Here, pretending to scrutinize the king more closely, he held the flambeau to the flaxen coat which enveloped him, and which instantly burst into a sheet of vivid flame. In less than half a minute the whole eight ourang-outangs were blazing fiercely, amid the shrieks of the multitude who gazed at them from below, horror-stricken, and without the power to render them the slightest assistance.

At length the flames, suddenly increasing in virulence, forced the jester to climb higher up the chain, to be out of their reach; and, as he made this movement, the crowd again sank, for a brief instant, into silence. The dwarf seized his opportunity, and once more spoke:

"I now see *distinctly*," he said, "what manner of people these maskers are. They are a great king and his seven privy-councillors—a king who does not scruple to strike a defenceless girl, and his seven councillors who abet him in the outrage. As for myself, I am simply Hop-Frog, the jester—and *this is my last jest.*"

Owing to the high combustibility of both the flax and the tar to which it adhered, the dwarf had scarcely made an end of his brief speech before the work of vengeance was complete. The eight corpses swung in their chains, a fetid, blackened, hideous, and indistinguishable mass. The cripple hurled his torch at them, clambered leisurely to the ceiling, and disappeared through the sky-light.

It is supposed that Trippetta, stationed on the roof of the saloon, had been the accomplice of her friend in his fiery revenge, and that, together, they effected their escape to their own country: for neither was seen again.

THE HOUSE OF SILENCE

E. NESBIT

THE THIEF STOOD CLOSE UNDER THE HIGH WALL, AND LOOKED TO RIGHT AND LEFT. To the right the road wound white and sinuous, lying like a twisted ribbon over the broad grey shoulder of the hill; to the left the road turned sharply down towards the river; beyond the ford the road went away slowly in a curve, prolonged for miles through the green marshes.

No least black fly of a figure stirred on it. There were no travellers at such an hour on such a road.

The thief looked across the valley, at the top of the mountain flushed with sunset, and at the grey-green of the olives about its base. The terraces of olives were already dusk with twilight, but his keen eyes could not have missed the smallest variance or shifting of their lights and shadows. Nothing stirred there. He was alone.

Then, turning, he looked again at the wall behind him. The face of it was grey and sombre, but all along the top of it, in the crannies of the coping stones, orange wall-flowers and sulphur-coloured snapdragons shone among the haze of feathery-flowered grasses. He looked again at the place where some of the stones had fallen from the coping—had fallen within the wall, for none lay in the road without. The bough of a mighty tree covered the gap with its green mantle from the eyes of any chance way-farer; but the thief was no chance wayfarer, and he had surprised the only infidelity of the great wall to its trust.

To the chance wayfarer, too, the wall's denial had seemed absolute, unanswerable. Its solid stone, close knit by mortar hardly less solid, showed not only a defence, it offered a defiance—a menace. But the thief had learnt his trade; he saw that the mortar might be loosened a little here, broken a little there, and now the crumbs of it fell rustling on to the dry, dusty grass of the roadside. He drew back, took two quick steps forward, and, with a spring, sudden and agile as a cat's, grasped the wall where the gap showed, and drew himself up. Then he rubbed his hands on his knees, because his hands were bloody from the sudden grasping of the rough stones, and sat astride on the wall.

He parted the leafy boughs and looked down; below him lay the stones that had fallen from the wall—already grass was growing upon the mound they made. As he ventured his head beyond the green leafage, the level light of the sinking sun struck him in the eyes. It was like a blow. He dropped softly from the wall and stood in the shadow of the tree—looking, listening.

Before him stretched the park—wide and still; dotted here and there with trees, and overlaid with gold poured from the west. He held his breath and listened. There was no wind to stir the leaves to those rustlings which may deceive and disconcert the keenest and the boldest; only the sleepy twitter of birds, and the little sudden soft movements of them in the dusky privacy of the thick-leaved branches. There was in all the broad park no sign of any other living thing.

The thief trod softly along under the wall where the trees were thickest, and at every step he paused to look and listen.

It was quite suddenly that he came upon the little lodge near the great gates of wrought iron with the marble gate-posts bearing upon them the two gaunt griffins, the cognisance of the noble house whose lands these were. The thief drew back into the shadow and stood still, only his heart beat thickly. He stood still as the tree trunk beside him, looking, listening. He told himself that he heard nothing—saw nothing—yet he became aware of things. That the door of the lodge was not closed, that some of its windows were broken, and that into its little garden straw and litter had drifted from the open door: and that between the stone step and the threshold grass was growing inches high. When he was aware of this he stepped forward and entered the lodge. All the sordid sadness of a little deserted home met him here—broken crocks and bent pans, straw, old rags, and a brooding, dusty stillness.

"There has been no one here since the old keeper died. They told the truth," said the thief; and he made haste to leave the lodge, for there was nothing in it now that any man need covet—only desolation and the memory of death.

So he went slowly among the trees, and by devious ways drew a little nearer to the great house that stood in its walled garden in the middle of the park. From very far off, above the green wave of trees that broke round it, he could see the towers of it rising black against the sunset; and between the trees came glimpses of its marble white where the faint grey light touched it from the east.

Moving slowly—vigilant, alert, with eyes turning always to right and to left, with ears which felt the intense silence more acutely than they could have felt any tumult— the thief reached the low wall of the garden, at the western side. The last redness of the sunset's reflection had lighted all the many windows, and the vast place blazed at him for an instant before the light dipped behind the black bar of the trees, and left him face to face with a pale house, whose windows now were black and hollow, and seemed like eyes that watched him. Every window was closed; the lower ones were guarded by jalousies; through the glass of the ones above he could see the set painted faces of the shutters.

From far off he had heard, and known, the plash-plash of fountains, and now he saw their white changing columns rise and fall against the background of the terrace. The garden was full of rose bushes trailing and unpruned; and the heavy, happy scent of the roses, still warm from the sun, breathed through the place, exaggerating the sadness of its tangled desolation. Strange figures gleamed in the deepening dusk, but they were too white to be feared. He crept into a corner where Psyche drooped in marble, and, behind her pedestal, crouched. He took food from his pockets and ate and drank. And between the mouthfuls he listened and watched.

The moon rose, and struck a pale fire from the face of the house and from the marble limbs of the statues, and the gleaming water of the fountains drew the moonbeams into the unchanging change of its rise and fall.

Something rustled and stirred among the roses. The thief grew rigid: his heart seemed suddenly hollow; he held his breath. Through the deepening shadows something gleamed white; and not marble, for it moved, it came towards him. Then the silence of the night was shattered by a scream, as the white shape glided into the moonlight. The thief resumed his munching, and another shape glimmered after the first. "Curse the beasts!" he said, and took another draught from his bottle, as the white peacocks were blotted out by the shadows of the trees, and the stillness of the night grew more intense.

In the moonlight the thief went round and about the house, pushing through the trailing briers that clung to him—and now grown bolder he looked closely at doors and windows. But all were fast barred as the doors of a tomb. And the silence deepened as the moonlight waxed.

There was one little window, high up, that showed no shutter. He looked at it; measured its distance from the ground and from the nearest of the great chestnut trees. Then he walked along under the avenue of chestnuts with head thrown back and eyes fixed on the mystery of their interlacing branches.

At the fifth tree he stopped; leaped to the lowest bough, missed it; leaped again, caught it, and drew up his body. Then climbing, creeping, swinging, while the leaves, agitated by his progress, rustled to the bending of the boughs, he passed to that tree, to the next—swift, assured, unhesitating. And so from tree to tree, till he was at the last tree—and on the bough that stretched to touch the little window with its leaves.

He swung from this. The bough bent and cracked, and would have broken, but that at the only possible instant the thief swung forward, felt the edge of the window with his feet, loosed the bough, sprang, and stood, flattened against the mouldings, clutching the carved drip-stone with his hands. He thrust his knee through the window, waiting for the tinkle of the falling glass to settle into quietness, opened the window, and crept in. He found himself in a corridor: he could see the long line of its white windows, and the bars of moonlight falling across the inlaid wood of its floor.

He took out his thief's lantern—high and slender like a tall cup—lighted it, and crept softly along the corridor, listening between his steps till the silence grew to be like a humming in his ears.

And slowly, stealthily, he opened door after door; the rooms were spacious and empty—his lantern's yellow light flashing into their corners told him this. Some poor, plain furniture he discerned, a curtain or a bench here and there, but not what he sought. So large was the house, that presently it seemed to the thief that for many hours he had been wandering along its galleries, creeping down its wide stairs, opening the grudging doors of the dark, empty rooms, whose silence spoke ever more insistently in his ears.

"But it is as he told me," he said inwardly: "no living soul in all the place. The old man—a servant of this great house—he told me; he knew, and I have found all even as he said."

Then the thief turned away from the arched emptiness of the grand staircase, and in a far corner of the hall he found himself speaking in a whisper because now it seemed to him that nothing would serve but that this clamorous silence should be stilled by a human voice.

"The old man said it would be thus—all emptiness, and not profit to a man; and he died, and I tended him. Dear Jesus! How our good deeds come home to us! And he told me how the last of the great family had gone away none knew whither. And the tales I heard in the town—how the great man had not gone, but lived here in hiding—it is not possible. There is the silence of death in this house."

He moistened his lips with his tongue. The stillness of the place seemed to press upon him like a solid thing. "It is like a dead man on one's shoulders," thought the thief, and he straightened himself up and whispered again: "The old man said, 'The door with the carved griffin, and the roses enwreathed, and the seventh rose holds the secret in its heart.'"

With that the thief set forth again, creeping softly across the bars of moonlight down the corridor.

And after much seeking he found at last, under the angle of the great stone staircase behind a mouldering tapestry wrought with peacocks and pines, a door, and on it carved a griffin, wreathed about with roses. He pressed his finger into the deep heart of each carven rose, and when he pressed the rose that was seventh in number from the griffin, he felt the inmost part of it move beneath his finger as though it sought to escape. So he pressed more strongly, leaning against the door till it swung open, and he passed through it, looking behind him to see that nothing followed. The door he closed as he entered.

And now he was, as it seemed, in some other house. The chambers were large and lofty as those whose hushed emptiness he had explored—but these rooms seemed warm with life, yet held no threat, no terror. To the dim yellow flicker from the lantern came out of the darkness hints of a crowded magnificence, a lavish profusion of beautiful objects such as he had never in his life dreamed of, though all that life had been one dream of the lovely treasures which rich men hoard, and which, by the thief's skill and craft, may come to be his.

He passed through the rooms, turning the light of his lantern this way and that, and ever the darkness withheld more than the light revealed. He knew that thick tapestries hung from the walls, velvet curtains masked the windows; his hand, exploring eagerly, felt the rich carving of chairs and presses; the great beds were hung with silken cloth wrought in gold thread with glimmering strange starry devices. Broad sideboards flashed back to his lantern's questionings the faint white laugh of silver; the tall cabinets could not, with all their reserve, suppress the confession of wrought gold, and, from the caskets into whose depths he flashed the light, came the trembling avowal of rich jewels. And now, at last, that carved door closed between him and the poignant silence of the deserted corridors, the thief felt a sudden gaiety of heart, a sense of escape, of security. He was alone, yet warmed and companioned. The silence here was no longer a horror, but a consoler, a friend.

And, indeed, now he was not alone. The ample splendours about him, the spoils which long centuries had yielded to the grasp of a noble family—these were companions after his own heart.

He flung open the shade of his lantern and held it high above his head. The room still kept half its secrets. The discretion of the darkness should be broken down. He must see more of this splendour—not in unsatisfying dim detail, but in the lit gorgeous mass of it. The narrow bar of the lantern's light chafed him. He sprang on to the dining-table, and began to light the half-burnt chandelier. There were a hundred candles, and he lighted all, so that the chandelier swung like a vast living jewel in the centre of the hall. Then, as he turned, all the colour in the room leapt out at him. The purple of the couches, the green gleam of the delicate glass, the blue of the tapestries, and the vivid scarlet of the velvet hangings, and with the colour sprang the gleams of white from the silver, of yellow from the gold, of many-coloured fire from strange inlaid work and jewelled caskets, till the thief stood aghast with rapture in the strange, sudden revelation of this concentrated splendour.

He went along the walls with a lighted candle in his hand—the wax dripped warm over his fingers as he went—lighting one after another, the tapers in the sconces of the silver-framed glasses. In the state bedchamber he drew back suddenly, face to face with a death-white countenance in which black eyes blazed at him with triumph and delight. Then he laughed aloud. He had not known his own face in the strange depths of this mirror. It had no sconces like the others, or he would have known it for what it was. It was framed in Venice glass—wonderful, gleaming, iridescent.

The thief dropped the candle and threw his arms wide with a gesture of supreme longing.

"If I could carry it all away! All, all! Every beautiful thing! To sell some—the less beautiful, and to live with the others all my days!"

And now a madness came over the thief. So little a part of all these things could he bear away with him; yet all were his—his for the taking—even the huge carved presses and the enormous vases of solid silver, too heavy for him to lift—even these were his: had he not found them—he, by his own skill and cunning? He went about in the rooms, touching one after the other the beautiful, rare things. He caressed the gold and the jewels. He threw his arms round the great silver vases; he wound round himself the heavy red velvet of the curtain where the griffins gleamed in embossed gold, and shivered with pleasure at the soft clinging of its embrace. He found, in a tall cupboard, curiously-shaped flasks of wine, such wine as he had never tasted, and he drank of it slowly—in little sips—from a silver goblet and from a green Venice glass, and from a cup of rare pink china, knowing that any one of his drinking vessels was worth enough to keep him in idleness for a long year. For the thief had learnt his trade, and it is a part of a thief's trade to know the value of things.

He threw himself on the rich couches, sat in the stately carved chairs, leaned his elbows on the ebony tables. He buried his hot face in the chill, smooth linen of the great bed, and wondered to find it still scented delicately as though some sweet woman had lain there but last night. He went hither and thither laughing with pure pleasure, and making to himself an unbridled carnival of the joys of possession.

In this wise the night wore on, and with the night his madness wore away. So presently he went about among the treasures—no more with the eyes of a lover, but with the eyes of a Jew—and he chose those precious stones which he knew for the most precious, and put them in the bag he had brought, and with them some fine-wrought goldsmith's work and the goblet out of which he had drunk the wine. Though it was but of silver, he would not leave it. The green Venice glass he broke and the cup, for he said: "No man less fortunate than I, to-night, shall ever again drink from them." But he harmed nothing else of all the beautiful things, because he loved them.

Then, leaving the low, uneven ends of the candles still alight, he turned to the door by which he had come in. There were two doors, side by side, carved with straight lilies, and between them a panel wrought with the griffin and the seven roses enwreathed. He pressed his finger in the heart of the seventh rose, hardly hoping that the panel would move, and indeed it did not; and he was about to seek for a secret spring among the lilies, when he perceived that one of the doors wrought with these had opened itself a little. So he passed through it and closed it after him.

"I must guard my treasures," he said. But when he had passed through the door and closed it, and put out his hand to raise the tattered tapestry that covered it from without, his hand met the empty air, and he knew that he had not come out by the door through which he had entered.

When the lantern was lighted, it showed him a vaulted passage, whose floor and whose walls were stone, and there was a damp air and a mouldering scent in it, as of a cellar long unopened. He was cold now, and the room with the wine and the treasures seemed long ago and far away, though but a door and a moment divided him from it, and though some of the wine was in his body, and some of the treasure in his hands. He set about to find the way to the quiet night outside, for this seemed to him a haven and a safeguard since, with the closing of that door, he had shut away warmth, and light, and companionship. He was enclosed in walls once more, and once more menaced by the invading silence that was almost a presence. Once more it seemed to him that he must creep softly, must hold his breath before he ventured to turn a corner—for always he felt that he was not alone, that near him was something, and that its breath, too, was held.

So he went by many passages and stairways, and could find no way out; and after a long time of searching he crept by another way back to come unawares on the door which shut him off from the room where the many lights were, and the wine and the treasure. Then terror leaped out upon him from the dark hush of the place, and he beat on the door with his hands and cried aloud, till the echo of his cry in the groined roof cowed him back into silence.

Again he crept stealthily by strange passages, and again could find no way except, after much wandering, back to the door where he had begun.

And now the fear of death beat in his brain with blows like a hammer. To die here like a rat in a trap, never to see the sun alight again, never to climb in at a window, or see brave jewels shine under his lantern, but to wander, and wander, and wander between these inexorable walls till he died, and the rats, admitting him to their brother-hood, swarmed round the dead body of him.

"I had better have been born a fool," said the thief.

Then once more he went through the damp and the blackness of the vaulted pas-sages, tremulously searching for some outlet, but in vain.

Only at last, in a corner behind a pillar, he found a very little door and a stair that led down. So he followed it, to wander among other corridors and cellars, with the silence heavy about him, and despair growing thick and cold like a fungus about his heart, and in his brain the fear of death beating like a hammer.

It was quite suddenly in his wanderings, which had grown into an aimless frenzy, having now less of search in it than of flight from the insistent silence, that he saw at last a light—and it was the light of day coming through an open door. He stood at the door and breathed the air of the morning. The sun had risen and touched the tops of the towers of the house with white radiance; the birds were singing loudly. It was morning, then, and he was a free man.

He looked about him for a way to come at the park, and thence to the broken wall and the white road, which he had come by a very long time before. For this door opened on an inner enclosed courtyard, still in damp shadow, though the sun above struck level across it—a courtyard where tall weeds grew thick and dank. The dew of the night was heavy on them.

As he stood and looked, he was aware of a low, buzzing sound that came from the other side of the courtyard. He pushed through the weeds towards it; and the sense of a presence in the silence came upon him more than ever it had done in the darkened house, though now it was day, and the birds sang all gaily, and the good sun shone so bravely overhead.

As he thrust aside the weeds which grew waist-high, he trod on something that seemed to writhe under his feet like a snake. He started back and looked down. It was the long, firm, heavy plait of a woman's hair. And just beyond lay the green gown of a woman, and a woman's hands, and her golden head, and her eyes; all about the place where she lay was the thick buzzing of flies, and the black swarming of them.

The thief saw, and he turned and he fled back to his doorway, and down the steps and through the maze of vaulted passages—fled in the dark, and empty-handed, because when he had come into the presence that informed that house with silence, he had dropped lantern and treasure, and fled wildly, the horror in his soul driving him before it. Now fear is more wise than cunning, so, whereas he had sought for hours with his lantern and with all his thief's craft to find the way out, and had sought in vain, he now, in the dark and blindly, without thought or will, without pause or let, found the one way that led to a door, shot back the bolts, and fled through the awakened rose garden and across the dewy park.

He dropped from the wall into the road, and stood there looking eagerly to right and left. To the right the road wound white and sinuous, like a twisted ribbon over the great, grey shoulder of the hill; to the left the road curved down towards the river. No least black fly of a figure stirred on it. There are no travellers on such a road at such an hour.

THE IMAGE

VERNON LEE

À MME LOUIS ORMAND.

"I believe that's the last bit of *bric*-à-*brac* I shall ever buy in my life," she said, closing the Renaissance casket—"that and the Chinese dessert set we have just been using. The passion seems to have left me utterly. And I think I can guess why. At the same time as the plates and the little coffer I bought a thing—I scarcely know whether I ought to call it a thing—which put me out of conceit with ferreting about among dead people's effects. I have often wanted to tell you all about it, and stopped for fear of seeming an idiot. But it weighs upon me sometimes like a secret; so, silly or not silly, I think I should like to tell you the story. There, ring for some more logs, and put that screen before the lamp.

"It was two years ago, in the autumn, at Foligno, in Umbria. I was alone at the inn, for you know my husband is too busy for my *bric*-à-*brac* journeys, and the friend who was to have met me fell ill and came on only later. Foligno isn't what people call an interesting place, but I liked it. There are a lot of picturesque little towns all round; and great savage mountains of pink stone, covered with ilex, where they roll fagots down into the torrent beds, within a drive. There's a full, rushing little river round one side of the walls, which are covered with ivy; and there are fifteenth-century frescoes, which I dare say you know all about. But, what of course I care for most, there are a number of fine old palaces, with gateways carved in that pink stone, and courts with pillars, and beautiful window gratings, mostly in good enough repair, for Foligno is a market town and a junction, and altogether a kind of metropolis down in the valley. Also, and principally, I liked Foligno because I discovered a delightful curiosity-dealer. I don't mean delightful curiosity shop, for he had nothing worth twenty francs to sell; but a delightful, enchanting old man. His Christian name was Orestes, and that was enough for me. He had a long white beard and such kind brown eyes, and beautiful hands; and he always carried an earthenware brazier under his cloak. He had taken to the curiosity business from a passion for beautiful things, and for the past of his native place, after having been a master mason. He knew all the old chronicles, lent me thereof Matarazzo, and knew exactly where everything had happened for the last six hundred years. He spoke of the Trincis, who had been local despots, and of St. Angela, who is the local saint, and of the Baglionis and Caesar Borgia and Julius II, as if he had known them; he showed me the place where St. Francis preached to the birds, and the place where Propertius—was it Propertius or Tibullus?—had had his farm; and when he accompanied me on my rambles in search of *bric-à-brac* he would stop at corners and under arches and say, 'This, you see, is where they carried off those nuns I told you about; that's where the cardinal was stabbed. That's the place where they razed the palace after the massacre, and passed the ploughshare through the ground and sowed salt.' And all with a vague, far-off, melancholy look, as if he lived in those days and not these. Also he helped me to get that little velvet coffer with the iron clasps, which is really one of the best things we have in the house. So I was very happy at Foligno, driving and prowling about all day, reading the chronicles Orestes lent me in the evening, and I didn't mind waiting so long for my friend who never turned up. That is to say, I was perfectly happy until within three days of my departure. And now comes the story of my strange purchase.

"Orestes, with considerable shrugging of shoulders, came one morning with the information that a certain noble person of Foligno wanted to sell me a set of Chinese plates. 'Some of them are cracked,' he said; 'but at all events you will see the inside of one of our finest palaces, with all its rooms as they used to be—nothing valuable, but I know that the signora appreciates the past wherever it has been let alone.'

"The palace, by way of exception, was of the late seventeenth century, and looked like a barracks among the neat little carved Renaissance houses. It had immense lions' heads over all the windows, a gateway in which two coaches could have met, a yard where a hundred might have waited, and a colossal staircase with stucco virtues on the vaultings. There was a cobbler in the lodge and a soap factory on the ground floor, and at the end of the colonnaded court a garden with ragged yellow vines and dead sunflowers. 'Grandiose, but very coarse—almost eighteenth-century,' said Orestes as we went up the sounding, low-stepped stairs. Some of the dessert set had been placed, ready for my inspection, on a great gold console in the immense escutcheoned anteroom. I looked at it, and told them to prepare the rest for me to see the next day. The owner, a very noble person, but half ruined—I should have thought entirely ruined, judging by the state of the house—was residing in the country, and the only occupant of the palace was an old woman, just like those who raise the curtains for you at church doors.

"The palace was very grand. There was a ball-room as big as a church, and a number of reception rooms, with dirty floors and eighteenth-century furniture, all tarnished and tattered, and a gala room, all yellow satin and gold, where some emperor had slept; and there were horrible racks of faded photographs on the walls, and twopenny screens, and Berlin wool cushions, attesting the existence of more modern occupants.

"I let the old woman unbar one painted and gilded shutter after another, and open window after window, each filled with little greenish panes of glass, and followed her about passively, quite happy, because I was wandering among the ghosts of dead people. 'There is the library at the end here,' said the old woman, 'if the signora does not mind passing through my room and the ironing-room; it's quicker than going back by the big hall.' I nodded, and prepared to pass as quickly as possible through an untidy-looking back room, when I suddenly stepped back. There was a woman in 1820 costume seated opposite, quite motionless. It was a huge doll. She had a sort of Canova classic face, like the pictures of Mme. Pasta and Lady Blessington. She sat with her hands folded on her lap and stared fixedly.

"'It is the first wife of the Count's grandfather,' said the old woman. 'We took her out of her closet this morning to give her a little dusting.'

"The doll was dressed to the utmost detail. She had on open-work silk stockings, with sandal shoes, and long silk embroidered mittens. The hair was merely painted, in flat bands narrowing the forehead into a triangle. There was a big hole in the back her head, showing it was cardboard.

"'Ah,' said Orestes, musingly, 'the image of the beautiful Countess! I had forgotten all about it. I hadn't seen it since I was a lad,' and he wiped some cobweb off the folded hands with his red handkerchief, infinitely gently. 'She used still to be kept in her own boudoir.'

"'That was before my time,' answered the housekeeper. 'I've always seen her in the cupboard, and I've been here thirty years. Will the signora care to see the old Count's collection of medals?'

"Orestes was very pensive as he accompanied me home.

"'That was a very beautiful lady,' he said, shyly, as we came within sight of my inn; 'I mean the first wife of the grandfather of the present Count. She died after they had been married a couple of years. The old Count, they say, went half crazy. He had the image made from a picture, and kept it in the poor lady's room, and spent several hours in it every day with her. But he ended by marrying a woman he had in the house, a laundress, by whom he had had a daughter.'

"'What a curious story!' I said, and thought no more about it.

"But the doll returned to my thoughts, she and her folded hands, and wide open eyes, and the fact of her husband's having ended by marrying the laundress. And next day, when we returned to the palace to see the complete set of old Chinese plates, I suddenly experienced an odd wish to see the doll once more. I took advantage of Orestes, and the old woman, and the Count's lawyer being busy deciding whether a certain dish cover which my maid had dropped, had or had not been previously chipped, to slip off and make my way to the ironing-room.

"The doll was still there, sure enough, and they hadn't found time to dust her yet. Her white satin frock, with little *ruches* at the hem, and her short bodice, had turned grey with engrained dirt; and her black fringed kerchief was almost red. The poor white silk mittens and white silk stockings were, on the other hand, almost black. A newspaper had fallen from an adjacent table on to her knees, or been thrown there by some one, and she looked as if she were holding it. It came home to me then that the clothes which she wore were the real clothes of her poor dead original. And when I found on the table a dusty, unkempt wig, with straight bands in front and an elaborate jug handle of curls behind, I knew at once that it was made of the poor lady's real hair.

"'It is very well made,' I said shyly, when the old woman, of course, came creaking after me.

"She had no thought except that of humouring whatever caprice might bring her a tip. So she smirked horribly, and, to show me that the image was really worthy of my attention, she proceeded in a ghastly way to bend the articulated arms, and to cross one leg over the other beneath the white satin skirt.

"'Please, please, don't do that!' I cried to the old witch. But one of the poor feet, in its sandalled shoe, continued dangling and wagging dreadfully.

"I was afraid lest my maid should find me staring at the doll. I felt I couldn't stand my maid's remarks about her. So, though fascinated by the fixed dark stare in her Canova goddess or Ingres Madonna face, I tore myself away and returned to the inspection of the dessert set.

"I don't know what that doll had done to me; but I found that I was thinking of her all day long. It was as if I had just made a new acquaintance of a painfully interesting kind, rushed into a sudden friendship with a woman whose secret I had surprised, as sometimes happens, by some mere accident. For I somehow knew everything about her, and the first items of information which I gained from Orestes—I ought to say that I was irresistibly impelled to talk about her to him—did not enlighten me in the least, but merely confirmed what I was aware of.

"The image—for I made no distinction between the portrait and the original—had been married straight out of the convent, and, during her brief wedded life, been kept secluded from the world by her husband's mad love for her, so that she had remained a mere shy, proud, inexperienced child.

"Had she loved him? She did not tell me that at once. But gradually I became aware that in a deep, inarticulate way she had really cared for him more than he cared for her. She did not know what answer to make to his easy, overflowing, garrulous, demonstrative affection; he could not be silent about his love for two minutes, and she could never find a word to express hers, fully though she longed to do so. Not that he wanted it; he a brilliant, will-less, lyrical sort of person, who knew nothing the feelings of others and cared only to welter and dissolve in his own. In those two years of ecstatic, talkative, all-absorbing love for her he not only forswore all society and utterly neglected his affairs, but he never made an attempt to train this raw young creature into a companion, or showed any curiosity as to whether his idol might have a mind or a character of her own. This difference she explained by her own stupid, inconceivable incapacity for expressing her feelings; how should he guess her longing to know, to understand, when she could not even tell him how much she loved him? At last the spell seemed broken: the words and the power of saying them came; but it was on her death-bed. The poor young creature died in childbirth, scarcely more than a child herself.

"There now! I knew even you would think it all silliness. I know what people are—what we all are—how impossible it is ever *really* to make others feel in the same way as ourselves about anything. Do you suppose I could have ever told all this about the doll to my husband? Yet I tell him everything about myself; and I know he would have been quite kind and respectful. It was silly of me ever to embark on the story of the doll with any one; it ought to have remained a secret between me and Orestes. *He*, I really think, would have understood all about the poor lady's feelings, or known it already as well as I. Well, having begun, I must go on, I suppose.

"I knew all about the doll when she was alive—I mean about the lady—and I got to know, in the same way, all about her after she was dead. Only I don't think I'll tell you. *Basta*. The husband had the image made, and dressed it in her clothes, and placed it in her boudoir, where not a thing was moved from how it had been at the moment of her death. He allowed no one to go in, and cleaned and dusted it all himself, and spent hours every day weeping and moaning before the image. Then, gradually, he began to look at his collection of medals, and to resume his rides; but he never went into society, and never neglected spending an hour in the boudoir with the image. Then came the business with the laundress. And then he sent the image into a cupboard? Oh, no; he wasn't that sort of man. He was an idealising, sentimental, feeble sort of person, and the amour with the laundress grew up quite gradually in the shadow of the inconsolable passion for the wife. He would never have married another woman of his own rank, given *her* son a stepmother (the son was sent to a distant school and went to the bad); and when he *did* marry the laundress it was almost in his dotage, and because she and the priests bullied him so fearfully about legitimating that other child. He went on paying visits to the image for a long time, while the laundress idyl went on quite peaceably. Then, as he grew old and lazy, he went less often; other people were sent to dust the image, and finally she was not dusted at all. Then he died, having quarrelled with his son and got to live like a feeble old boor, mostly in the kitchen. The son—the image's son—having gone to the bad, married a rich widow. It was she who refurnished the boudoir and sent the image away. The daughter of the laundress, the illegitimate child, who had become a kind of housekeeper in her half-brother's palace, nourished a lingering regard for the image, partly because the old Count had made such a fuss about it, partly because it must have cost a lot of money, and partly because the lady had been a *real* lady. So when the boudoir was refurnished she emptied out a closet and put the image to live there; and she occasionally had it brought out to be dusted.

"Well, while all these things were being borne in upon me there came a telegram saying my friend was not coming on to Foligno, and asking me to meet her at Perugia. The little Renaissance coffer had been sent to London; Orestes and my maid and myself had carefully packed every one of the Chinese plates and fruit dishes in baskets of hay. I had ordered a set of the 'Archivio Storico' as a parting gift for dear old Orestes—I could never have dreamed of offering him money, or cravat pins, or things like that—and there was no excuse for staying one hour more at Foligno. Also I had got into low spirits of late—I suppose we poor women cannot stay alone six days in an inn, even with *bric-à-brac* and chronicles and devoted maids—and I knew I should not get better till I was out of the place. Still I found it difficult, nay, impossible, to go. I will confess it outright: I couldn't abandon the image. I couldn't leave her, with the hole in her poor cardboard head, with the Ingres Madonna features gathering dust in that filthy old woman's ironing-room. It was just impossible. Still go I must. So I sent for Orestes. I knew exactly what I wanted; but it seemed impossible, and I was afraid, somehow, of asking him. I gathered up my courage, and, as if it were the most natural thing in the world, I said—

"'Dear Signer Oreste, I want you to help me to make one last purchase. I want the Count to sell me the—the portrait of his grandmother; I mean the doll.'

"I had prepared a speech to the effect that Orestes would easily understand that a life-size figure so completely dressed in the original costume of a past epoch would soon possess the highest historical interest, &c. But I felt that I neither needed nor ventured to say any of it. Orestes, who was seated opposite me at table—he would only accept a glass of wine and a morsel of bread, although I had asked him to share my hotel dinner—Orestes nodded slowly, then opened his eyes out wide, and seemed to frame the whole of me in them. It wasn't surprise. He was weighing me and my question.

"'Would it be very difficult?' I asked. 'I should have thought that the Count—'

"'The Count,' answered Orestes drily, 'would sell his soul, if he had one, let alone his grandmother, for the price of a new trotting pony.'

"Then I understood.

"'Signor Oreste,' I replied, feeling like a child under the dear old man's glance, 'we have not known one another long, so I cannot expect you to trust me yet in many things. Perhaps also buying furniture out of dead people's houses to stick it in one's own is not a great recommendation of one's character. But I want to tell you that I am an honest woman according to my lights, and I want you to trust me in this matter.'

"Orestes bowed. 'I will try to induce the Count to sell you the image,' he said.

"I had her sent in a closed carriage to the house of Orestes. He had, behind his shop, a garden which extended into a little vineyard, whence you could see the circle of great Umbrian mountains; and on this I had had my eye.

"'Signor Oreste,' I said, 'will you be very kind, and have some fagots—I have seen some beautiful fagots of myrtle and bay in your kitchen—brought out into the vineyard; and may I pluck some of your chrysanthemums?' I added.

"We stacked the fagots at the end of the vineyard, and placed the image in the midst of them, and the chrysanthemums on her knees. She sat there in her white satin Empire frock, which, in the bright November sunshine, seemed white once more, and sparkling. Her black fixed eyes stared as in wonder on the yellow vines and reddening peach trees, the sparkling dewy grass of the vineyard, upon the blue morning sunshine, the misty blue amphitheatre of mountains all round.

"Orestes struck a match and slowly lit a pine cone with it; when the cone was blazing he handed it silently to me. The dry bay and myrtle blazed up crackling, with a fresh resinous odour; the image was veiled in flame and smoke. In a few seconds the flame sank, the smouldering fagots crumbled. The image was gone. Only, where she had been, there remained in the embers something small and shiny. Orestes raked it out and handed it to me. It was a wedding ring of old-fashioned shape, which had been hidden under the silk mitten. 'Keep it, signora,' said Orestes; 'you have put an end to her sorrows.'"

In Articulo Mortis

Roger Pater

"You must not attach too much importance to my unusual faculty," said the old priest to me some days later, when I was pressing him for other stories of his strange experiences. "There are times, even now, when I think the 'direct speech' is all imagination, a product of my highly strung nature acted upon by circumstances of an unusual kind."

"That doesn't seem to me sufficient explanation," I answered; "besides, in the cases you have told me of, the circumstances were not specially unusual, at any rate not so far as you could tell before the event took place."

"True," said he, "but in a good many instances the circumstances were more out of the common, more calculated to excite the imagination and prepare it for self-deception. But I must own that, although at times I doubt if the whole thing be not subjective, still in the end I always come back to the opinion that such an explanation is quite inadequate. In fact, I only mentioned it because I thought you were inclined to take it all too seriously. For my part I refuse to attach any special meaning or value to the phenomena. I know that my account of them is as truthful and exact as I can make it, and if you ask me for an explanation, all I have to say is that I seem to possess a certain kind of spiritual perception in an unusual degree; but it does not follow that what I hear is of any particular importance, any more than the possession of exceptional long sight by one man would render a thing important, because he could see it while it was beyond the range of his companions' vision."

He paused for a few moments and I kept silent, hoping he might develop his views on the subject more fully, but instead he proposed to give me another instance of his curious gift.

"Let me tell you another story," he began, "one of the kind I mentioned just now, in which the circumstances themselves were calculated to excite the imagination." I begged him to do so and he continued:

"While I was in Rome, at the Accademia, I became very intimate with one of my fellow-students. He was an Austrian and a member of one of the most ancient families in the empire, but if you do not mind I will not give you his name. We chanced to attend the same set of lectures, and the acquaintance thus begun ripened rapidly, so that we were soon on terms of real friendship, and in the vacation time we made several excursions together to various parts of Italy.

"He was ordained at the Advent Ordination, and left Rome at once, so as to celebrate his first Mass at his old home, a famous castle in Austria, but before leaving, he made me promise that I would go and stay at his home for a little while on my return journey to England, after my own ordination. That event took place some three months later, on Holy Saturday, and a fortnight afterwards I left the Accademia and set my face homewards.

"The journey was a leisurely one, and it must have been the beginning of June when I crossed over the Brenner Pass and entered Austrian territory; but that done I went straight on to the station nearest my friend's home. Even this place was twelve leagues away from the castle, but a diligence ran the rest of the way, and I took a seat in it, glad to be quit of the train. I put up for the night at an inn where the diligence had stopped about an hour before sunset.

"After taking my room and arranging for supper, I walked across the way to see the parish priest and get permission to say Mass next morning. The good man proved to be very unwell, but on learning from his housekeeper that a strange priest wished to say Mass next day, he sent down a message begging me to come upstairs and see him. I found him in bed, apparently suffering from fever, but he assured me that my coming was as good as medicine to him.

"'It is certainly our holy Mother who has sent you,' he exclaimed, 'for tomorrow is a feast day with us, and it would be dreadful if there were no Mass in the church; yet the Herr Doctor has forbidden me to attempt it. Now you are here and will say Mass for my good people, will you not?'

"Of course I said that I would do anything I could, and he explained that he had special permission from the bishop of the diocese to grant faculties to any priest who came to help him during his illness, so that I could hear confessions if anyone wished to go.

"By the time I left him, it was quite dark, and my dinner was waiting for me. Soon after ten o'clock, when I was just thinking of going to bed, a knock came at the door and the landlord entered.

"'Your pardon, Herr Priest,' said he, 'but there is a gentleman below who wishes to speak with you.'

"'Impossible,' I exclaimed, 'there must be some mistake; I do not know anyone in the neighborhood.'

"'But it is true, *mein Herr*,' replied the man, 'the Pastor, so he says, told him to come across and ask for you.'

"'That is another matter, of course,' said I; 'I will come down with you,' and we went together to the large room on the ground floor where I had dined.

"At the door the landlord bowed me in before him and then retired, leaving me alone with a tall, distinguished-looking stranger. He was obviously an Austrian noble, but to my surprise he addressed me in excellent English: put shortly, his story was this. He was Count A——, who lived with his younger brother at their family castle, some leagues distant. Neither his brother nor himself were what could be called devout Catholics, and, moreover, they had quarrelled with the local priest. The previous evening his brother had been taken seriously ill, and now wished to see a priest. He had, therefore, come himself to the town to beg the Pastor to go back with him and see his brother, but as the good man was himself so unwell, this was impossible, and the only alternative seemed to be to come and appeal to me to go instead. He knew it was a very unusual thing to ask of a stranger on a journey, but his brother was dying, of that the doctor left no doubt, and his soul was in danger. I was a priest and, he understood, an English noble. He begged I would not refuse his appeal.

"It was certainly a most inconvenient occurrence, and my first impulse was to refuse, or rather to point out difficulties which made my acquiescence impossible. I was a stranger, had no faculties, was on a journey, and must be off by tomorrow's diligence, had promised to say Mass for the Pastor next morning, and anything else I could think of in the way of objections. The Count waited until I had finished, and then said quietly, 'My Father, it is a question of saving a soul, surely you cannot refuse?'

"I was silent for a moment, wondering what I ought to do, and then, as if in answer, I heard a voice whispering in my ear say 'Go.' I looked up quickly at the Count, wondering if he had spoken, and he began to plead with me once more. 'Go with him,' came the voice again in my ears. It could not be the Count, for he was speaking at the moment; and I felt somehow convinced that my duty was to go. Just as he paused the voice came again as if to reassure me, 'Go without doubting, for I am with thee,' and half-dazed I said to him, 'Yes, I will go.'

"As we went through the hall to the door of the inn I chanced to look at the clock. It was just half-past ten, and I remember thinking to myself, 'I shall not get to bed before midnight at the earliest.' At the door stood a carriage, its four horses restlessly pawing the ground, and anxious to be on the move. As the Count opened the door and motioned to me to enter, I stopped in surprise. 'Surely,' I said, 'you wish me to bring the blessed Sacrament. I must go over to the church and obtain it.'

"'No, no,' said he, somewhat nervously, I thought; 'we must not delay even for that. You understand it is unlikely my brother will be in a condition to receive Communion.'

"Amazed at this, I began to expostulate with him—what good could I do compared with what our Lord would do in the Holy Viaticum—but even as I spoke the voice came again in my ears, 'Go at once, delay no longer,' and alarmed I stepped into the carriage.

"With a look of relief my companion called out an order to the driver and stepped in after me, the horses at once starting off at a great pace. The carriage was of the old-fashioned, traveling type quite unknown nowadays, with deep comfortable seats, and curtains to the windows. My companion was proceeding to close the windows and draw the curtains, and it was only after some difficulty that I got him to leave the window on my side a little open, with its curtain not drawn. This gave me some fresh air, but the night was very dark, and there was a candle alight in a swinging candlestick within the carriage, so that I could make out nothing of the country through which we were passing.

"I felt some anxiety about the Mass I had promised to say for the Pastor next morning, and asked the Count how far it was to his castle, and at what time I could get back. 'Several leagues,' was all I got out of him as, ignoring my second question, he lay back in the carriage and closed his eyes as if tired out. Then all at once it struck me that I was behaving very selfishly. The poor man's only brother was dying, and here was I worrying him about needless details; so I too kept silence, and taking my rosary from my pocket, leaned back in my seat and closed my eyes.

"I think I must have fallen into a doze, for I had no idea how long we had been driving, when I was suddenly awakened by the noise of the horses' hoofs striking loudly on a wooden bridge. I sat up abruptly and looked out of the window. The moon must have risen by now, for I could see quite plainly, as we passed under an arched gateway and halted in a stone-paved courtyard.

"The castle loomed up, huge and uncertain in the dim light, the buttresses casting deep shadows across the walls that stood out white in the moonlight. But I had no time to survey the building for Count A—— quickly alighted and helped me out of the carriage. Before us, at an open door, stood a man-servant holding a lantern, and I was hurried in, through an outer room and across a huge hall, into a smaller one fitted as a library with dark carved bookcases, and a bright log fire in a deep, old-fashioned fireplace. Here the Count stopped, begging me to warm myself—though the night was not cold—and to take a glass of wine, while he went to find out if his brother was able and ready to see me. As I was uncertain of the time I took no wine, since I had to say Mass in the morning, but stood by the fire, glad to stretch my limbs after the long drive. Not more than two or three minutes elapsed before a servant entered with a message from Count A——, begging me to go with the messenger, who would show the way to his brother's room, where all was ready for me.

"I went at once, preceded by the servant with a light. We went down a long corridor and up some steep stairs, but I took no special notice of the way, and cannot say if we had ascended one flight or two, when we finally passed through a 'passage-room,' and stopped at a door before which there hung a deep red curtain. Drawing this aside my guide knocked at the door, and a voice within answered clearly in German. The servant then opened the door and stepped back, holding the red portière aside for me to enter. As I did so the door was shut behind me, and I heard a dull thud as the weighted curtain fell back into position behind it.

"Now all this, no doubt, sounds very ordinary and natural, but somehow I had a growing feeling that something was wrong. The non-return of Count A—— to the library, the deserted condition of the whole place, the absence of anything suggesting illness, no sign of doctor, nurse, etc., had surprised me, and my feeling of uneasiness was increased enormously by what I now saw. I found myself in a room, not a bedroom as I had expected, but a large apartment panelled in oak or some other dark wood, with a heavily carved cornice and elaborate plaster ceiling decorated in gold and colour. Some handsome old-fashioned chairs were ranged stiffly along the walls, which bore several portraits; a wood fire burned in the deep, open fireplace, above which was a lofty overmantel reaching to the ceiling, and carved with classic figures. In the centre of the room stood a large table, with a litter of playing-cards and a dice box on it, beside some lighted candles in tall silver candlesticks. Beyond this was seated a young man, not more than twenty-five years old at most, and apparently in perfect health.

"He looked up quickly as I entered, but said nothing, and with some hesitation I began to apologise, as best I could in German, for intruding upon him. The servant must have made some mistake. I was a priest, a stranger, and had been brought in great haste to see the brother of Count A—— who was ill—in fact, was not expected to live till morning. At this the young man rose and came towards me.

"'There is no mistake, my Father,' he said, speaking in German, 'it is I whom you were brought to see; I shall be a dead man before sunrise.'

"At this my previous misgivings were increased a hundredfold, and I felt thoroughly alarmed; my fears being oddly coupled with annoyance at the way I had been tricked. Crushing down the angry words which were rushing up for utterance, I repeated as calmly as I could that there was evidently some mistake. That Count A—— had told me definitely that my services as a priest were needed by his brother, who was very seriously ill and not likely to live till morning; whereas he appeared to be perfectly well. The stranger waited in silence until I had finished.

"'It is not to be wondered at,' said he, 'that you are surprised and annoyed; indeed, the Count seems to have misled you in some details, but the main fact is perfectly true. I am his brother, I shall be dead before morning, and it is to hear my confession that we have brought you all this long journey. You will not refuse me, surely, now that you have come?'

"My first inclination was to protest angrily against the way I had been treated, when the recollection of the voice I had heard at the inn came back to my mind. After all it was not the Count's story which had brought me, but the strange command, three times repeated, and I was as sure as ever that Count A—— had not spoken the words which impelled me to go with him.

"Taking my silence for consent the young man motioned me to a recess, apparently a window but with shutters drawn, in which there stood a prie-dieu with a chair beside it. Almost unconsciously I obeyed his gesture, walking beside him to the prie-dieu, where he knelt down as I seated myself at his side. Even now I am not clear if I did wrong in hearing his confession, and you will understand I had to decide without any time for deliberation. I had only been a priest for a few weeks only, and had not heard a dozen confessions in all. The Pastor certainly had given me faculties, and Count A—— had mentioned that his castle was in the same diocese when I raised this point as an obstacle to my coming. Then too there was the memory of the voice I had heard, commanding me to go without fear. Automatically I gave the stranger my blessing, and he began his confession.

"What he told me, under the seal, I cannot, of course, repeat to you—indeed, I scarcely understood it all myself, what with the turmoil in my mind and the strange language, for my knowledge of German was, and is, far from perfect. But this I may say, that no sufficient explanation of his position was offered, nor did my questions elicit anything more than that his death before morning was quite certain and utterly unavoidable, and that he desired most earnestly to make his peace with God before he should stand at His judgement seat. In the end I abandoned all efforts to break down his reserve, and with many misgivings imparted absolution. As I finished he rose and thanked me, adding in the most earnest manner, 'Let me beg you, my Father, not to inquire further into this matter. No harm whatever will come to you, and no inquiries you may make will bring you any nearer its solution.' With that he rang a small hand bell, which stood upon the table, and the servant who had brought me to the room appeared almost immediately.

"I tried to speak, but not a word would come; indeed, my one idea was to escape, for I was rapidly becoming unnerved. Accordingly I allowed myself to be conducted from the room, through the ante-chamber and down a flight of stairs, where the servant showed me into a room which I had not entered before. Here he left me, saying that Count A—— would be with me very shortly. Left to myself, my mind ran riot as to the meaning of the strange adventure I had just gone through. Doubts if I had done right in hearing the confession and giving absolution, mingled with vague notions of a secret society, and, I must own, no small amount of fear for my own safety. All at once the last prevailed, and I ran quickly to the window and opened it, thinking I might perhaps escape unnoticed.

"The casement opened inwards, and outside were strong iron bars fixed in the masonry, which prevented my leaning out of it, much less climbing through the opening. However, the cool night air revived and calmed me, and I stood looking out into the moonlight. Below was the castle moat, still as glass and reflecting the cold, silvery light, save where the dark shadow of the building fell across it. This shadow stopped in a hard, straight line some few yards to the right of my window, showing me that my room was near a corner of the building; and I found that by pressing my face against the bars, I could just see the angle of the retaining wall which formed the outer side of the moat as it too turned round the corner.

"I do not suppose I had stood there more than four or five minutes, when I heard the noise of a window being opened somewhere overhead, and apparently round the corner of the building. I listened intently, and could just catch the sound of a voice speaking in a rapid low tone, as if giving some directions; and then, to my amazement, there came a sound like something falling, followed by a loud splash in the moat beneath. My heart was in my mouth, but not another sound came. Then, a few seconds later, a series of little waves broke the calm surface of the moat, as they flowed round the angle of the wall. Soon they sank into mere rings, and in a minute or two the water was a mirror once more. I gazed, fascinated, until the last of the rings disappeared, and then the thirst for safety seized me again. I closed the window and walked quickly to the door. Opening it I found the servant who had brought me there standing, as if listening, at the foot of the stairs. I called to him in German, saying I could wait no longer, but must return at once whence I had come.

"'But surely the Herr Priest will wait and see my master the Count?' asked the man in some surprise.

"'No, no,' I said. 'I must get back immediately; I have to say the Mass for the people tomorrow morning.'

"'It is *this* morning now, *mein Herr*,' replied the man, 'and indeed if that is so, you will need to start at once, if you wish to get any sleep at all'; and he led the way downstairs, going before me with a light.

"We crossed the same large hall and ante-chamber, and the man opened the door into the courtyard. To my relief the carriage was waiting at the door, so, telling him to make my excuses to his master, I entered it and drove off with a feeling of intense relief. The drive back must have taken a full hour or more, and I was surprised to find the innkeeper waiting for me on my arrival. As I passed upstairs I looked at the clock again, it was ten minutes to two! Fortunately the Mass was to be at a fairly late hour, as it was a feast day, but it seemed as if I had scarcely slept at all, when I was awakened and told it was half-past eight.

"After the Mass, when I returned to the inn, I found to my surprise that there was a letter waiting for me. It was from my friend, telling me that he had been called to Vienna, where his mother was lying ill, but begging me to go on to his home all the same, where he would join me as soon as he could leave his mother. Of course I did nothing of the kind, but came straight home to England; and it was some ten years before we met by chance in Rome, when I told him my strange experience. He made me give him every detail I could remember about the buildings and everything connected with the place, and then said, 'There is one castle in the neighbourhood and only one which fits in with your description,' and he named a place I had never heard of.

"'And its owner,' I asked, 'who is he?' The name was as strange to me as that of the castle, but the answer to my next question was significant.

"'What sort of a man is he?' I asked, and my friend hesitated a little before replying.

"'Well,' said he at length, 'I scarcely know; he is quite a recluse nowadays—in fact, I have only seen him once. People say that he was very wild in his youth, and the story goes that he quarrelled with his younger brother about a beautiful peasant girl who lived in the neighbourhood. He is supposed to have circulated a false report that she was dead, and a few days later his brother was found drowned in the castle moat. The official view was that he had committed suicide, but many people suspected foul play, though no evidence of it was ever forthcoming. It must be ten years now since the affair took place, and it is becoming a mere legend even in the neighbourhood. All the same, if I were you, I should not publish your story in Austria, at any rate so long as the Count is living.'"

In the Séance Room

Lettice Galbraith

Dr. Valentine Burke sat alone by the fire. He had finished his rounds, and no patient had disturbed his post-prandial reflections. The house was very quiet, for the servants had gone to bed, and only the occasional rattle of a passing cab and the light patter of the rain on the window-panes broke the silence of the night. The cheerful glow of the fire and the soft light from the yellow-shaded lamp contrasted pleasantly with the dreary fog which filled the street outside. There were spirit-decanters on the table, flanked by a siphon and a box of choice cigars. Valentine Burke liked his creature comforts. The world and the flesh held full measure of attraction for him, but he did not care about working for his *menus plaisirs*.

The ordinary routine of his profession bored him. That he might eventually succeed as a ladies' doctor was tolerably certain. For a young man with little influence and less money, he was doing remarkably well; but Burke was ambitious, and he had a line of his own. He dabbled in psychics, and had written an article on the future of hypnotism, which had attracted considerable attention. He was a strong magnetiser, and offered no objection to semi-private exhibitions of his powers. In many drawing-rooms he was already regarded as the apostle of the coming revolution which is to substitute disintegration of matter and cerebral precipitation for the present system of the parcels mail and telegraphic communication. In that section of society which interests itself in occultism Burke saw his way to making a big success.

Meanwhile, as man cannot live on adulation alone, the doctor had a living to get, and he had no intention whatever of getting it by the labour of his hands. He was an astute young man, who knew how to invest his capital to the best advantage. His good looks were his capital, and he was about to invest them in a wealthy marriage. The fates had certainly been propitious when they brought Miss Elma Lang into the charmed circle of the Society for the Revival of Eastern Mysticism. Miss Lang was an orphan. She had full control of her fortune of thirty thousand pounds. She was sufficiently pretty, and extremely susceptible. Burke saw his chance, and went for it, to such good purpose that before a month had passed his engagement to the heiress was announced, and the wedding-day within measurable distance. There were several other candidates for Miss Lang's hand, but it soon became evident that the doctor was first favourite. The gentlemen who devoted themselves to occultism for the most part despised physical attractions; their garments were fearfully and wonderfully made. They were careless as to the arrangement of their hair. Beside them, Valentine Burke, handsome, well set up, and admirably turned out, showed to the very greatest advantage. Elma Lang adored him. She was never tired of admiring him. She was lavish of pretty tokens of her regard. Her photographs, in costly frames, were scattered about his room, and on his hand glittered the single-stone diamond ring which had been her betrothal gift.

He smiled pleasantly as he watched the firelight glinting from the many-coloured facets. "I have been lucky," he said aloud; "I pulled that through very neatly. Just in time, too, for my credit would not stand another year. I ought to be all right now if—" He broke off abruptly, and the smile died away. "If it were not for that other unfortunate affair! What a fool—what a damned fool I was not to let the girl alone, and what a fool she was to trust me! Why could she not have taken better care of herself? Why could not the old man have looked after her? He made row enough over shutting the stable-door when the horse was gone. It was cleverly managed though. I think even *ce cher papa* exonerates me from any participation in her disappearance; and fate seems to be playing into my hand too. That body turning up just now is a stroke of luck. I wonder who the poor devil really is?"

He felt for his pocket-book, and took out a newspaper cutting. It was headed in large type,

MYSTERIOUS DISAPPEARANCE OF A YOUNG LADY

The body found yesterday by the police in Muddlesham Harbour is believed to be that of Miss Katharine Greaves, whose mysterious disappearance in January last created so great a sensation. It will be remembered that Miss Greaves, who was a daughter of a well-known physician of Templeford, Worcestershire, had gone to Muddlesham on a visit to her married sister, from whose house she suddenly disappeared. Despite the most strenuous efforts on the part of her distracted family, backed by the assistance of able detectives, her fate has up to the present remained enshrouded in mystery. On the recovery of the body yesterday the Muddlesham police at once communicated with the relations of Miss Greaves, by whom the clothing was identified. It is now supposed that the unhappy girl threw herself into the harbour during a fit of temporary insanity, resulting, it is believed, from an unfortunate love affair.

Valentine Burke read the paragraph through carefully, and replaced it in the pocket-book with a cynical smile.

"How exquisitely credulous are the police, and the relatives, and the noble British public. Poor Kitty is practically dead—to the world. What a pity—" He hesitated, and stared into the blazing coals. "It would save so much trouble," he went on after a pause, "and I hate trouble."

His fingers were playing absently with a letter from which he had taken the slip of printed paper—an untidy letter, blotted and smeared, and hastily written on poor, thin paper. He looked at it once or twice and tossed it into the fire. The note-sheet shrivelled and curled over, dropping on to the hearth, where it lay smouldering. A hot cinder had fallen out of the grate, and the doctor, stretching out his foot, kicked the letter close to the live coal. Little red sparks crept like glow-worms along the scorched edges, flickered and died out. The paper would not ignite; it was damp—damp with a woman's tears. "I was a fool," he murmured, with conviction. "It was not good enough, and it might have ruined me." He turned to the spirit-stand and replenished his glass, measuring the brandy carefully. "I don't know that I am out of the wood yet," he went on, as he filled up the tumbler with soda-water. "The money is running short, and women are so damned inconsiderate. If Kitty were to take it into her head to turn up here it would be the—" The sentence remained unfinished, cut short by a sound from below. Someone had rung the night-bell.

Burke set down the glass and bent forward, listening intently. The ring, timid, almost deprecating, was utterly unlike the usual imperative summons for medical aid. Following immediately on his outspoken thoughts, it created an uncomfortable impression of coming danger. He felt certain that it was not a patient; and if it were not a patient, who was it? There was a balcony to the window. He stepped quietly out and leaned over the railing. By the irregular flicker of the street-lamp he could make out the dark figure of a woman on the steps beneath, and through the patter of the falling rain he fancied he caught the sound of a suppressed sob. With a quick glance, to assure himself that no one was in sight, the doctor ran downstairs and opened the door. A swirl of rain blew into the lighted hall. The woman was leaning against one of the pillars, apparently unconscious. Burke touched her shoulder. "What are you doing here?" he asked sharply. At the sound of his voice she uttered a little cry and made a sudden step forward, stumbling over the threshold, and falling heavily against him.

"Val, Val," she cried, despairingly. "I thought I should never find you. Take me home, take me home. I am so tired—and, oh, so frightened!"

The last word died away in a wailing sob, then her hands relaxed their clinging hold and dropped nervelessly at her side.

In an emergency Dr. Burke acted promptly. He shut the outer door, and gathering up the fainting girl in his arms, carried her into the consulting-room, and laid her on the sofa. There was no touch of tenderness in his handling of the unconscious form. He had never cared much about her, when at her best, dainty in figure and fair of face; he had made love to her, pour passer le temps, in the dullness of a small country town. She had met him more than half way, and almost before his caprice was gratified he was weary of her. Her very devotion nauseated him. He looked at her now with a shudder of repulsion. The gaslight flared coldly on the white face, drawn by pain and misery. All its pretty youthfulness had vanished. The short hair, uncurled by the damp night air, straggled over the thin forehead. There were lines about the closed eyes and the drooping corners of the mouth. The skin was strained tightly over the cheek-bones and looked yellow, like discoloured wax. His eyes noted every defect of face and figure, as he stood wondering what he should do with her.

He knew, no one better, how quickly the breath of scandal can injure a professional man. Once let the real story of his relations with Katharine Greaves get wind and his career would be practically ruined. He began to realise the gravity of the situation. Two futures lay before him. The one, bright with the sunshine of love and prosperity; the other darkened by poverty and disgrace. He pictured himself the husband of Elma Lang, with all the advantages accruing to the possessor of a charming wife and a large fortune, and he cursed fate which had sent this wreck of womanhood to stand between him and happiness. By this time she had partially recovered, and her eyes opened with the painful upward roll common to nervous patients when regaining consciousness. With her dishevelled hair and rain-soaked garments, she had all the appearance of a dead body. The sight, horrible as it was, fascinated Burke. He turned up the gas, twisting the chandelier so as to throw a full light on the girl's face.

"She looks as though she were drowned," he thought. "When she is really dead she will look like that." The idea took possession of his mind. "If she were dead, if only she were dead!"

Who can trust the discretion of a wronged and forsaken woman, but—the dead tell no tales. If only she were dead! The words repeated themselves again and again, beating into his brain like the heavy strokes of a hammer. Why should she not die? Her life was over, a spoiled, ruined thing. There was nothing before her but shame and misery. She would be better dead. Why (he laughed suddenly a hard, mirthless laugh), she *was* dead already. Her body had been found by the police, identified by her own relations. She was supposed to be drowned, so why not make the supposition a reality? A curious light flashed into the doctor's handsome face. A woman seeing him at that moment would have hesitated before trusting her life in his hands. He looked at his unwelcome visitor with an evil smile.

She had come round now and was crouched in the corner of the sofa sobbing and shivering.

"Don't be angry with me, Val, please don't be angry. I waited till I had only just enough money for my ticket, and I dare not stay there any longer. It is so lonely, and you never come to see me now. It is ten weeks since you were down, and you won't answer my letters. I was so frightened all alone. I began to think you were getting tired of me. Of course I know it is all nonsense. You love me as much as you ever did. It is only that you are so busy and hate writing letters." She paused, waiting for some reassuring words, but he did not answer, only watched her with cold, steady eyes.

"Did you see the papers," she went on, with chattering teeth. "They think I am dead. Ever since I read it I have had such dreadful thoughts. I keep seeing myself drowned; I believe I am going to die, Val—and I don't want to die. I am so—so frightened. I thought you would take me in your arms and comfort me like you used to do, and I should feel safe. Oh, why don't you speak to me? Why do you look at me like that? Val, dear, don't do it, *don't* do it, I cannot bear it."

Her great terrified eyes were fixed on his, fascinated by his steady, unflinching gaze. She was trembling violently. Her words came with difficulty, in short gasps.

"You have never said you were glad to see me. It is true, then, that you don't love me any more? You are tired of me, and you will not marry me now. What shall I do? What shall I do? No one cares for me, no one wants me, and there is nothing left for me but to die."

Still no answer. There was a long silence while their eyes met in that fixed stare—his cold, steady, dominating, hers flinching and striving vainly to withstand the power of the stronger will. In a few moments the unequal struggle had ended. The girl sat stiff and erect, her hand grasping the arm of the sofa. The light of consciousness had died out of the blue eyes, leaving them fixed and glassy. Burke crossed the floor and stood in front of her.

"Where is your luggage?" he asked, authoritatively.

She answered in a dull, mechanical way, "At the station."

"Have you kept anything marked with your own name—any of my letters?"

"No, nothing—there."

"You *have* kept some of my letters. Where are they?"

"Here." Her hand sought vaguely for her pocket.

"Give them to me—all of them."

Mechanically she obeyed him, holding out three envelopes, after separating them carefully from her purse and handkerchief.

"Give me the other things." He opened the purse. Besides a few shillings, it contained only a visiting-card, on which an address had been written in pencil. The doctor tore the card across and tossed it into the fireplace. Then his eyes fastened on those of the girl before him. Very slowly he bent forward and whispered a few words in her ear, repeating them again and again. The abject terror visible in her face would have touched any heart but that of the man in whose path she stood. No living soul, save the "sensitive" on whom he was experimenting, heard those words, but they were registered by a higher power than that of the criminal court, damning evidence to be produced one day against the man who had prostituted his spiritual gift to mean and selfish ends.

In the grey light of the chilly November morning a park-keeper, near the Regent's Canal, was startled by a sudden, piercing shriek. Hurrying in the direction of the sound, he saw, through leafless branches, a figure struggling in the black water. The park-keeper was a plucky fellow, whose courage had gained more than one recognition from the Humane Society, and he began to run towards the spot where the dark form had been, but before he had covered ten yards of ground rapid footsteps gained on his and a man shot past him. "Someone in the canal," he shouted as he ran. "I think it is a woman. You had better get help."

"He was a good plucky one," the park-keeper averred, when a few days later he retailed the story to a select circle of friends at the bar of the "Regent's Arms," where the inquest had been held. "Not that I'd have been behindhand, but my wind ain't what it was, and he might have been shot out of a catapult. He was off with his coat and into the water before you could say Jack Robinson. Twice I thought he had her safe enough, and twice she pulled him under; the third time, blest if I thought they were coming up at all. Then the doctor chap, he comes to the surface dead-beat, but the girl in his arms."

"'I'm afraid she's gone,' he says, when I took her from him, 'but we won't lose time,' and he set to and carried out all the instructions for recovering the apparently drowned while I went for some brandy. It wasn't a bit of use. The young woman were as dead as a door-nail. 'If she'd only have kept quiet, I might have saved her,' he says, quite sorrowful like, 'but she struggled so,' and sure enough his hands were regularly torn and bruised where she'd gripped him."

Dr. Burke and the park-keeper were the chief witnesses at the inquest. There were no means of identifying the dead woman. The jury returned a verdict of *felo-de-se*, and the coroner complimented the doctor on his courageous attempt to rescue the poor outcast.

The newspapers, too, gave him a nice little paragraph, headed, "Determined Suicide in Regent's Park. Gallant conduct of a well-known physician"; and Elma Lang's dark eyes filled with fond and happy tears as she read her lover's praises.

"You are so brave, Val, so good," she cried, "and I am so proud of you; but you ran a horrible risk."

"Yes," he answered, gravely, "I thought once it was all up with me. That poor girl nearly succeeded in drowning the pair of us. Still, there wasn't much in it, you know; any other fellow would have done the same."

"No, they would not. It is no use trying to pretend you are not a hero, Val, because you are. How awful it must have been when she clung to you so desperately. It might have cost you your life."

"It cost me my ring," he replied, ruefully. "It is lying at the bottom of the canal at this moment, unless some adventurous fish has swallowed it—your first gift."

"What does it matter," she answered, impulsively, "I can give you another tomorrow. What does anything matter since you are safe?"

Burke took her in his arms, and kissed the pretty upturned face. She was his now, bought with the price of another woman's life. Bah! he wanted to forget the clutch of those stiffening fingers and the glazed awful stare of the dead eyes through the water.

"Let us drop the subject," he said, gently. "It is not a pleasant one, and, as you say, nothing matters since I am safe"—he added under his breath, "quite safe *now*."

The carriage stood at the door. In the drawing-room Mrs. Burke was waiting for her husband. She had often waited for the doctor during the four years which had elapsed since their marriage. Those four years had seen to a great extent the fulfilment of Burke's ambition. He had money. He was popular, sought after, an acknowledged leader of the new school of Philosophy, an authority on psychic phenomena, and the idol of the "smart" women who played with the fashionable theories and talked glibly on subjects the very A B C of which was far beyond their feeble comprehension. Socially, Dr. Burke was an immense success. If, as a husband, he fell short of Elma's expectations, she never admitted the fact. She made an admirable wife, interesting herself in his studies, and assisting him materially in his literary work. Outwardly, they were a devoted couple. The world knew nothing of the indefinable barrier which held husband and wife apart; of a certain vague distrust which had crept into the woman's heart, bred of an instinctive feeling that her husband was not what he seemed to be. Something, she knew not what, lay between them. Her quick perceptions told her that he was always acting a part. She held in her hand a little sheaf of papers, notes that she had prepared for him on the series of *séances*, which for a month past had been the talk of the town. A medium of extraordinary power had flashed like a meteor into the firmament of London society. Phenomena of the most startling kind had baffled alike the explanations of both scientist and occultist. Spiritualism was triumphant. A test committee had been formed, of which Dr. Burke was unanimously elected president, but so far the attempts to expose the alleged frauds had not been attended with any success.

It was to Mme. Delphine's house that the Burkes were going tonight. The *séance* commenced at ten, and the hands of the clock already pointed to a quarter to that hour, when the doctor hurried into the room.

"Ready?" he said. "Come along then. Where are the notes?"

He glanced hastily through them as he went downstairs.

"Falconer and I have been there all afternoon," he explained as they drove off. "I had only just time to get something to eat at the club before I dressed. We have taken the most elaborate precautions. If something cannot be proved tonight——" He paused.

"Well?" she said, anxiously.

"We shall be the laughing-stock of London," he concluded, emphatically.

"What do you really think of it?"

"Humbug, of course; but the difficulty is to prove it."

"Mrs. Thirlwall declares that the fifth appearance last night was undoubtedly her husband. I saw her today; she was quite overcome."

"Mrs. Thirlwall is a hysterical fool."

"But your theory admitted the possibility of materialising the intense mental——"

Burke leaned back in the carriage, laughing softly.

"My dear child, I had to say something."

"Valentine," she cried, sorrowfully, "is there no truth in anything you say or write? Do you believe in nothing?"

"Certainly. I believe in matter and myself, also that the many fools exist for the benefit of a minority with brains. When I see any reason to alter my belief, I shall not hesitate to do so. If, for instance, I am convinced that I see with my material eyes a person whom I know to be dead, I will become a convert to spiritualism. But I shall never see it."

The drawing-room was filled when they arrived at Mme. Delphine's. Seats had been kept for the doctor and his wife. There was a short whispered consultation between Burke and his colleagues, the usual warning from the medium that the audience must conform to the rules of the *séance*, and the business of the evening began in the customary style. Musical instruments sounded in different parts of the room, light fingers touched the faces of the sitters. Questions written on slips of paper and placed in a sealed cabinet received answers from the spirit world, which the inquirers admitted to be correct. The medium's assistant handed one of these blank slips to Burke, requesting him to fill it up.

It struck the doctor that if he were to ask some question the answer to which he did not himself know, but could afterwards verify, he would guard against the possibility of playing into the hands of an adroit thought-reader. He accordingly wrote on the paper, "What was I doing this time four years ago? Give the initials of my companion, if any."

He had not the vaguest idea as to where exactly he had been on the date in question, but a reference to the rough diary he always kept would verify or disprove the answer.

The folded slip was sealed and placed in the cabinet. In due time the medium declared the replies were ready. The cabinet was opened, and the slips, numbered in the order in which they had been given in, were returned to their owners. Burke noticed that there were no fresh folds in his paper, and the seal was of course unbroken. He opened it, and as his eye fell on the writing he gave a slight start, and glanced sharply at the medium. Beneath his query was written in ink that was scarcely yet dry: "On Wednesday, November, 17, 1885, you were at No. 63, Abbey Road. Only I was with you. You hypnotised me.—K. G." The handwriting was that of Katharine Greaves.

The doctor was staggered. In the multiplied interests and distractions of his daily life he had completely forgotten the date of that tragic visit. He tried to recall the exact day of the month and week. He remembered now that it was on a Wednesday, and this was Monday. Calculating the odd days for the leap year, 1888, that would bring it to Monday—Monday, the 17th. Four years ago tonight Kitty had been alive. She was dead now, and yet here before him was a page written in her hand. He sat staring at the characters, lost in thought. The familiar writing brought back with irresistible force the memory of that painful interview. It suggested another and very serious danger. Burke did not believe for a moment that the answer to his question had been dictated by the disembodied spirit of his victim. He was racking his brains to discover how his secret might possibly have leaked out, who this woman could be who knew, and traded on her knowledge, of that dark passage in his life which he had believed to be hidden from all the world. Was it merely a bow drawn at a venture, which had chanced to strike the one weak place in his armour, or was it deliberately planned with a view to extorting money?

So deeply was he wrapped in his reflections, that the manifestations went on around him unheeded. The dark curtain which screened off a portion of the room divided, and a white-robed child stepped out. It was instantly recognised by one of the sitters— a nervous, highly-strung woman, whose passionate entreaties that her dead darling would return to earth fairly harrowed the feelings of the listeners. Other manifestations followed. The audience were becoming greatly excited. Burke sat indifferent to it all, his eyes fixed on the writing before him, till his wife touched him gently.

"What is the matter, Val?" she whispered, trying to read the paper over his shoulder. "Is your answer correct?"

He turned on her sharply, crushing the message in his hand. "No," he said audibly. "It is a gross imposture. There was no such person."

"Hush." She laid a restraining hand on his arm. "Do not speak so loudly. That is a point in our favour, anyway. Mr. Falconer has proposed a fresh test. He has asked if a material object, something that had been lost at any time, you know, can be restored by the spirits. Madame returned a favourable answer. Mr. Falconer could not think of anything at the moment, but I had a brilliant inspiration. I told him to ask for your diamond ring—the ring you lost when you tried to save that poor girl's life."

Burke rose to his feet, then recollecting himself, sat down again and tried to pull himself together. There was nothing in it. If this Madame Delphine really was acquainted with the facts of his relations with Katharine Greaves she could not know its ghastly termination. He tried to reassure himself, but vainly. His nerve was deserting him, and his eyes roved vacantly round the semi-darkened room, as if in search of something. A sudden silence had fallen on the audience. A cold chill, like a draught of icy air, swept through the *séance* chamber. Mrs. Burke shivered from head to foot, and drew closer to her husband. Suddenly the stillness was broken by a shriek of horror. It issued from the lips of the medium, who, like a second Witch of Endor, saw more than she expected, and crouched terror-stricken in the chair to which she was secured by cords adjusted by the test committee. The presence which had appeared before the black curtain was no white-clad denizen of "summer-land," but a woman in dark, clinging garments—a woman with wide-opened, glassy eyes, fixed in an unalterable stony stare. It was a ghastly sight. All the concentrated agony of a violent death was stamped on that awful face.

Of the twenty people who looked upon it, not one had power to move or speak.

Slowly the terrible thing glided forward, hardly touching the ground, one hand outstretched, and on the open palm a small, glittering object—a diamond ring!

It moved very slowly, and the second or so during which it traversed the space between the curtain and the seats of the audience seemed hours to the man who knew for whom it came.

Valentine Burke sat rigid. He was oblivious to the presence of spectators, hardly conscious of his own existence. Everything was swallowed up in a suspense too agonising for words, the fearful expectancy of what was about to happen. Nearer and nearer "it" came. Now it was close to him. He could feel the deathly dampness of its breath; those awful eyes were looking into his. The distorted lips parted—formed a single word. Was it the voice of a guilty conscience, or did that word really ring through and through the room—"Murderer!"

For a full minute the agony lasted, then something fell with a sharp click on the carpet-less floor. The sound recalled the petrified audience to a consciousness of mundane things. They became aware that "it" was gone.

They moved furtively, glanced at each other—at last someone spoke. It was Mrs. Burke. She had vainly tried to attract her husband's attention, and now turned to Falconer, who sat next to her.

"Help me get him away," she said.

The doctor alone had not stirred; his eyes were fixed as though he were still confronted by that unearthly presence.

Someone had turned up the gas. Two of the committee were releasing the medium, who was half-dead with fright. Falconer unfastened the door, and sent a servant whom he met in the hall for a hansom.

When he returned to the *séance* room the doctor was still in the same position. It was some moments before he could be roused, but when once they succeeded in their efforts Burke's senses seemed to return. He rose directly, and prepared to accompany his wife. As they quitted their seats, Falconer's eyes fell on the diamond ring which lay unnoticed on the ground. He was going to pick it up, but someone caught his hand and stopped him.

"Leave it alone," said Mrs. Burke, in a horrified whisper. "For God's sake, don't touch it."

Husband and wife drove home in silence. Silently the doctor dismissed the cab and opened the hall-door. The gas was burning brightly in the study. The servant had left on the side-table a tray with sandwiches, wine, and spirits. Burke poured out some brandy and tossed it off neat. His face was still rather white, otherwise he had quite recovered his usual composure.

Mrs. Burke loosened her cloak and dropped wearily into a chair by the fire. A hopeless despondency was visible in every line of her attitude. Once or twice the doctor looked at her, and opened his lips to speak. Then he thought better of it, and kept silent. Half an hour passed in this way. At last Burke lighted a candle and left the room. When he returned he carried in his hand a small bottle. He had completely regained his self-possession as he came over to his wife and scrutinised her troubled face.

"Have some wine," he said, "and then you had better go to bed. You look thoroughly done up."

"What is that?" She pointed to the bottle in his hand.

"A sleeping-draught. Merely a little morphia and bromide. I should advise you to take one, too. Frankly, tonight's performance was enough to try the strongest nerves. Mine require steadying by a good night's rest, and I do not intend risking an attack of insomnia."

She rose suddenly from her chair and clasped her hands on his arm.

"Val," she cried, piteously, "don't try to deceive me. Dear, I can bear anything if you will only trust me and tell me the truth. What is this thing which stands between us? What was the meaning of that awful sight?"

For a moment he hesitated; then he pulled himself together and answered lightly—

"My dear girl, you are unnerved, and I do not wonder at it. Let us forget it."

"I cannot, I cannot," she interrupted wildly. "I must know what it meant. I have always felt there was something. Valentine, I beseech you, by everything you hold sacred, tell me the truth now before it is too late. I could forgive you almost—almost anything, if you will tell me bravely; but do not leave me to find it out for myself."

"There is nothing to tell."

"You will not trust me?"

"I tell you there is nothing."

"That is your final answer?"

"Yes."

Without a word she left the room and went upstairs. Burke soon followed her. His nerves had been sufficiently shaken to make solitude undesirable. He smoked a cigar in his dressing-room, and took the sleeping-draught before going to bed. The effects of the opiate lasted for several hours. It was broad daylight when the doctor awoke. He felt weak and used up, and his head was splitting. He lay for a short time in that drowsy condition which is the borderland between sleeping and waking. Then he became conscious that his wife was not in the room. He looked at his watch, and saw that it was half-past nine. He waited a few minutes, expecting her to return, but she did not come. Presently he got up and drew back the window-curtains. As the full light streamed in, he was struck by a certain change in the appearance of the room. At first he was uncertain in what the change consisted, but gradually he realised that it lay in the absence of the usual feminine impedimenta. The dressing-table was shorn of its silver toilet accessories. One or two drawers were open and emptied of their contents. The writing-table was cleared, and his wife's dressing case had disappeared from its usual place. Burke's first impulse was to ring for a servant and make inquiries, but as he stretched out his hand to the bell his eyes fell on a letter, conspicuously placed on the centre of a small table. It was addressed in Elma's handwriting. From that moment Burke knew that something had happened, and he was prepared for the worst. The letter was not long. It was written firmly, though pale-blue stains here and there indicated where the wet ink had been splashed by falling tears.

"When you read this," she wrote, "I shall have left you for ever. The only reparation in your power is to refrain from any attempt to follow me; indeed, you will hardly desire to do so, when I tell you that I know all. I said last night I could not endure the torture of uncertainty. My fears were so terrible that I felt I must know the truth or die. I implored you to trust me. You put me off with a lie. Was I to blame if I used against you a power which you yourself had taught me? In the last four hours I have heard from your own lips the whole story of Katharine Greaves. Every detail of that horrible tragedy you confessed unconsciously in your sleep, and I who loved you—Heaven knows how dearly!—have to endure the agony of knowing my husband to be a murderer, and that my wretched fortune supplied the motive for the crime. Thank God that I have no child to bear the curse of your sin, to inherit its father's nature! I hardly know what I am writing. The very ground seems to be cut away from under my feet. On every side I can see nothing but dense darkness, and the only thing that is left to us is death.—Your wretched wife, ELMA."

From the moment he opened the letter, Burke's decision was made. He possessed the exact admixture of physical courage and moral cowardice which induces a man worsted in the battle of life to end the conflict by removing himself from the arena. He had taken the best of the world's gifts, and there was nothing left worth having. His belief in a future life was too vague to cause him any uneasiness, and physically, fear was a word he did not understand. He quietly lighted his wife's litter with a match, and threw it into the fireless grate. He smoked a cigar while he watched it burn, and carefully hid the charred ashes among the cinders. Then he fetched from his dressing-room a small polished box, unlocked it, and took out the revolver. It was loaded in all six chambers.

Burke leisurely finished his cigarette, and tossed the end away. He never hesitated a moment. He had no regret for the life he was leaving. As Elma had said, there was only one thing left for him to do, and—he did it.

The Kennel

Maurice Level

As ten o'clock struck, M. de Hartevel emptied a last tankard of beer, folded his newspaper, stretched himself, yawned, and slowly rose.

The hanging-lamp cast a bright light on the table-cloth, over which were scattered piles of shot and cartridge wads. Near the fireplace, in the shadow, a woman lay back in a deep armchair.

Outside the wind blew violently against the windows, the rain beat noisily on the glass, and from time to time deep bayings came from the kennel where the hounds had struggled and strained since morning.

There were forty of them: big mastiffs with ugly fangs, stiff-haired griffons of Vendée, that flung themselves with ferocity on the wild boar on hunting days. During the night their sullen bayings disturbed the country-side, evoking response from all the dogs in the neighborhood.

M. de Hartevel lifted a curtain and looked out into the darkness of the park. The wet branches shone like steel blades; the autumn leaves were blown about like whirligigs and flattened against the walls. He grumbled.

"Dirty weather!"

He walked a few steps, his hands in his pockets, stopped before the fireplace, and with a kick broke a half-consumed log. Red embers fell on the ashes; a flame rose, straight and pointed.

Madame de Hartevel did not move. The light of the fire played on her face, touching her hair with gold, throwing a rosy glow on her pale cheeks and, dancing about her, cast fugitive shadows on her forehead, her eyelids, her lips.

The hounds, quiet for a moment, began to growl again; and their bayings, the roaring of the wind and the hiss of the rain on the trees made the quiet room seem warmer, the presence of the silent woman more intimate.

Subconsciously this influenced M. de Hartevel. Desires stimulated by those of the beasts and by the warmth of the room crept through his veins. He touched his wife's shoulders.

"It is ten o'clock. Are you going to bed?"

She said "yes," and left her chair, as if regretfully.

"Would you like me to come with you?"

"No— thank you—"

Frowning, he bowed.

"As you like."

His shoulders against the mantelshelf, his legs apart, he watched her go. She walked with a graceful, undulating movement, the train of her dress moving on the carpet like a little flat wave. A surge of anger stiffened his muscles.

In this chateau where he had her all to himself he had in bygone days imagined a wife who would like living in seclusion with him, attentive to his wishes, smiling acquiesence to all his desires. She would welcome him with gay words when he came back from a day's hunting, his hands blue with cold, his strong body tired, bringing with him the freshness of the fields and moors, the smell of horses, of game and of hounds, would lift eager lips to meet his own. Then, after the long ride in the wind, the rain, the snow, after the intoxication of the crisp air, the heavy walking in the furrows, or the gallop under branches that almost caught his beard, there would have been long nights of love, orgies of caresses of which the thrill would be mutual.

The difference between the dream and the reality!

When the door had shut and the sound of steps died away in the corridor, he went to his room, lay down, took a book and tried to read.

The rain hissed louder than ever. The wind roared in the chimney; out in the park, branches were snapping from the trees; the hounds bayed without ceasing, their howlings sounded through the creaking of the trees, dominating the roar of the storm; the door of the kennel strained under their weight.

He opened the window and shouted:

"Down!"

For some seconds they were quiet. He waited. The wind that drove the rain on his face refreshed him. The barkings began again. He banged his fist against the shutter, threatening:

"Quiet, you devils!"

There was a singing in his ears, a whistling, a ringing; a desire to strike, to ransact, to feel flesh quiver under his fists took possession of him. He roared: "Wait a moment!" slammed the window, seized a whip, and went out.

He strode along the corridors with no thought of the sleeping house till he got near his wife's room, when he walked slowly and quietly, fearing to disturb her sleep. But a ray of light from under her door caught his lowered eyes, and there was a sound of hurried footsteps that the carpet did not deaden. He listened. The noise ceased, the light went out. . . . He stood motionless, and suddenly, impelled by a suspicion, he called softly:

"Marie Thérèse . . ."

No reply. He called louder. Curiosity, a doubt that he dared not formulate, held him breathless. He gave two sharp little taps on the door; a voice inside asked:

"Who is there?"

"I—open the door—"

A whiff of warm air laden with various perfumes and a suspicion of other odors passed over his face.

The voice asked:

"What is it?"

He walked in without replying. He felt his wife standing close in front of him; her breath was on him, the lace of her dress touched his chest. He felt in his pocket for matches. Not finding any, he ordered:

"Light the lamp!"

She obeyed, and as his eyes ran over the room he saw the curtains drawn closely, a shawl on the carpet, the open bed, white and very large; and in a corner, near the fireplace, a man lying across a long rest-chair, his collar unfastened, his head drooping, his arms hanging loosely, his eyes shut.

He gripped his wife's wrist:

"Ah, you . . . filth! . . . Then this is why you turn your back on me!" . . .

She did not shrink from him, did not move. No shadow of fear passed over her pallid face.

She only raised her head, murmuring:

"You are hurting me!—"

He let her go, and bending over the inert body, his fist raised, cried:

"A lover in my wife's bedroom! . . . And . . . what a lover! A friend . . . Almost a son . . . Whore!—"

She interrupted him:

"He is not my lover . . ."

He burst into a laugh.

"Ah! Ah! You expect me to believe that!"

He seized the collar of the recumbent man, and lifted him up towards him. But when he saw the livid face, the half-opened mouth showing the teeth and gums, when he felt the strange chill of the flesh that touched his hands, he started and let go. The body fell back heavily on the cushions, the forehead beating twice against a chair. His fury turned upon his wife.

"What have you to say? . . . Explain! . . ."

"It is very simple," she said. "I was just going to bed when I heard the sound of footsteps in the corridor . . . uncertain steps . . . faltering . . . and a voice begging, 'Open the door . . . open the door' . . . I thought you might be ill. I opened the door. Then he came, or rather, fell into the room. . . I knew he was subject to heart-attacks. . . I laid him there . . . I was just going to bring you when you knocked . . . That's all . . ."

Bending over the body, and apparently quite calm again, he asked, every word pronounced distinctly:

"And it does not surprise you that no one heard him come in? . . ."

"The hounds bayed . . ."

"And why should he come here at this hour of the night?"

She made a vague gesture:

"It does seem strange . . . But . . . I can only suppose that he felt ill and that . . . quite alone in his own house . . . he was afraid to stay there . . . came here to beg for help . . . In any case, when he is better . . . as soon as he is able to speak . . . he will be able to explain . . ."

M. de Hartevel drew himself up to his full height, and looked into his wife's eyes.

"It appears we shall have to accept your supposition, and that we shall never know exactly what underlies his being here to-night . . . for he is dead."

She held out her hands and stammered, her teeth chattering:

"It's not possible . . . He is . . ."

"Yes—dead . . ."

He seemed to be lost in thought for a moment, then went on in an easier voice:

"After all, the more I think of it, the more natural it seems . . . Both his father and his uncle died like this, suddenly . . . Heart disease is hereditary in his family . . . A shock . . . a violent emotion . . . too keen a sensation . . . a great joy . . . We are weak creatures at best . . ."

He drew an arm-chair to the fire, sat down, and, his hands stretched out to the flames, continued:

"But however simple and natural the event in itself may be, nothing can alter the fact that a man has died in your bedroom during the night . . . Is that not so?"

She hid her face in her hands and made no reply.

"And if your explanation satisfies me, I am not able to make others accept it. The servants will have their own ideas, will talk . . . That will be dishonor for you, for me, for my family . . . That is not possible. . . We must find a way out of it . . . and I have already found it . . . With the exception of you and me, no one knows, no one will ever know what has happened in this room . . . No one saw him come in . . . Take the lamp and come with me . . ."

He seized the body in his arms and ordered:

"Walk on first . . ."

She hesitated as they went out at the door.

"What are you going to do? . . ."

"Leave it to me . . . Go on . . ."

Slowly and very quietly they went towards the staircase, she holding high the lamp, its light flickering on the walls, he carefully placing his feet on stair after stair. When they got to the door that led to the garden, he said:

"Open it without a sound."

A gust of wind made the light flare up. Beaten on by the rain, the glass burst and fell in pieces on the threshold. She placed the extinguished lamp on the soil. They went into the park. The gravel crunched under their steps and the rain beat upon them. He asked:

"Can you see the walk? . . . Yes? . . . Then come close to me . . . hold the legs . . . the body is heavy . . ."

They went forward in silence. M. de Hartevel stopped near a low door, saying:

"Feel in my right-hand pocket . . . There is a key there . . . That's it . . . Give it to me . . . Now let the legs go . . . It is as dark as a grave . . . Feel about till you find the key-hole . . . Have you got it?—Turn . . ."

Excited by the noise, the hounds began to bay. Madame de Hartevel started back.

"You are frightened? . . . Nonsense . . . Another turn . . . That's it!—Stand out of the way . . ."

With a thrust from his knee he pushed open the door. Believing themselves free, the hounds bounded against his legs. Pushing them back with a kick, suddenly, with one great effort, he raised the body above his head, balanced it there a moment, flung it into the kennel, and shut the door violently behind him.

Baying at full voice, the beasts fell on their prey. A frightful death-rattle: "Help!" pierced their clamor, a terrible cry, superhuman. It was followed by violent growlings.

An unspeakable horror took possession of Madame de Hartevel; a quick flash of understanding dominated her fear, and, her eyes wild, she flung herself on her husband, digging her nails in his face as she shrieked:

"Fiend! . . . He wasn't dead! . . ."

M. de Hartevel pushed her off with the back of his hand, and standing straight up before her, jeered:

"Did you think he was!"

THE KIT-BAG

ALGERNON BLACKWOOD

WHEN THE WORDS "NOT GUILTY" SOUNDED THROUGH THE CROWDED COURT-ROOM
that dark December afternoon, Arthur Wilbraham, the great criminal K.C., and leader
for the triumphant defence, was represented by his junior; but Johnson, his private secretary, carried the verdict across to his chambers like lightning.

"It's what we expected, I think," said the barrister, without emotion; "and, personally, I am glad the case is over." There was no particular sign of pleasure that his
defence of John Turk, the murderer, on a plea of insanity, had been successful, for no
doubt he felt, as everybody who had watched the case felt, that no man had ever better
deserved the gallows.

"I'm glad too," said Johnson. He had sat in the court for ten days watching the face
of the man who had carried out with callous detail one of the most brutal and cold-
blooded murders of recent years.

The counsel glanced up at his secretary. They were more than employer and
employed; for family and other reasons, they were friends. "Ah, I remember; yes," he
said with a kind smile, "and you want to get away for Christmas? You're going to skate
and ski in the Alps, aren't you? If I was your age I'd come with you."

Johnson laughed shortly. He was a young man of twenty-six, with a delicate face
like a girl's. "I can catch the morning boat now," he said; "but that's not the reason I'm
glad the trial is over. I'm glad it's over because I've seen the last of that man's dreadful
face. It positively haunted me. That white skin, with the black hair brushed low over
the forehead, is a thing I shall never forget, and the description of the way the dismembered body was crammed and packed with lime into that—"

"Don't dwell on it, my dear fellow," interrupted the other, looking at him curiously
out of his keen eyes, "don't think about it. Such pictures have a trick of coming back
when one least wants them." He paused a moment. "Now go," he added presently, "and
enjoy your holiday. I shall want all your energy for my Parliamentary work when you
get back. And don't break your neck skiing."

Johnson shook hands and took his leave. At the door he turned suddenly.

"I knew there was something I wanted to ask you," he said. "Would you mind lending me one of your kit-bags? It's too late to get one tonight, and I leave in the morning
before the shops are open."

"Of course; I'll send Henry over with it to your rooms. You shall have it the moment I get home."

"I promise to take great care of it," said Johnson gratefully, delighted to think that within thirty hours he would be nearing the brilliant sunshine of the high Alps in winter. The thought of that criminal court was like an evil dream in his mind.

He dined at his club and went on to Bloomsbury, where he occupied the top floor in one of those old, gaunt houses in which the rooms are large and lofty. The floor below his own was vacant and unfurnished, and below that were other lodgers whom he did not know. It was cheerless, and he looked forward heartily to a change. The night was even more cheerless: it was miserable, and few people were about. A cold, sleety rain was driving down the streets before the keenest east wind he had ever felt. It howled dismally among the big, gloomy houses of the great squares, and when he reached his rooms he heard it whistling and shouting over the world of black roofs beyond his windows.

In the hall he met his landlady, shading a candle from the draughts with her thin hand. "This come by a man from Mr. Wilbr'im's, sir."

She pointed to what was evidently the kit-bag, and Johnson thanked her and took it upstairs with him. "I shall be going abroad in the morning for ten days, Mrs. Monks," he said. "I'll leave an address for letters."

"And I hope you'll 'ave a merry Christmas, sir," she said, in a raucous, wheezy voice that suggested spirits, "and better weather than this."

"I hope so too," replied her lodger, shuddering a little as the wind went roaring down the street outside.

When he got upstairs he heard the sleet volleying against the window-panes. He put his kettle on to make a cup of hot coffee, and then set about putting a few things in order for his absence. "And now I must pack—such as my packing is," he laughed to himself, and set to work at once.

He liked the packing, for it brought the snow mountains so vividly before him, and made him forget the unpleasant scenes of the past ten days. Besides, it was not elaborate in nature. His friend had lent him the very thing—a stout canvas kit-bag, sack-shaped, with holes round the neck for the brass bar and padlock. It was a bit shapeless, true, and not much to look at, but its capacity was unlimited, and there was no need to pack carefully. He shoved in his waterproof coat, his fur cap and gloves, his skates and climbing boots, his sweaters, snow-boots, and ear-caps; and then on the top of these he piled his woollen shirts and underwear, his thick socks, puttees, and knickerbockers. The dress suit came next, in case the hotel people dressed for dinner, and then, thinking of the best way to pack his white shirts, he paused a moment to reflect. "That's the worst of these kit-bags," he mused vaguely, standing in the centre of the sitting-room, where he had come to fetch some string.

It was after ten o'clock. A furious gust of wind rattled the windows as though to hurry him up, and he thought with pity of the poor Londoners whose Christmas would be spent in such a climate, whilst he was skimming over snowy slopes in bright sunshine, and dancing in the evening with rosy-cheeked girls— Ah! that reminded him; he must put in his dancing-pumps and evening socks. He crossed over from his sitting-room to the cupboard on the landing where he kept his linen.

And as he did so he heard some one coming softly up the stairs.

He stood still a moment on the landing to listen. It was Mrs. Monks's step, he thought; she must be coming up with the last post. But then the steps ceased suddenly, and he heard no more. They were at least two flights down, and he came to the conclusion they were too heavy to be those of his bibulous landlady. No doubt they belonged to a late lodger who had mistaken his floor. He went into his bedroom and packed his pumps and dress-shirts as best he could.

The kit-bag by this time was two-thirds full, and stood upright on its own base like a sack of flour. For the first time he noticed that it was old and dirty, the canvas faded and worn, and that it had obviously been subjected to rather rough treatment. It was not a very nice bag to have sent him—certainly not a new one, or one that his chief valued. He gave the matter a passing thought, and went on with his packing. Once or twice, however, he caught himself wondering who it could have been wandering down below, for Mrs. Monks had not come up with letters, and the floor was empty and unfurnished. From time to time, moreover, he was almost certain he heard a soft tread of someone padding about over the bare boards—cautiously, stealthily, as silently as possible—and, further, that the sounds had been lately coming distinctly nearer.

For the first time in his life he began to feel a little creepy. Then, as though to emphasize this feeling, an odd thing happened: as he left the bedroom, having just packed his recalcitrant white shirts, he noticed that the top of the kit-bag lopped over towards him with an extraordinary resemblance to a human face. The canvas fell into a fold like a nose and forehead, and the brass rings for the padlock just filled the position of the eyes. A shadow—or was it a travel stain? for he could not tell exactly—looked like hair. It gave him rather a turn, for it was so absurdly, so outrageously, like the face of John Turk, the murderer.

He laughed, and went into the front room, where the light was stronger.

"That horrid case has got on my mind," he thought; "I shall be glad of a change of scene and air." In the sitting-room, however, he was not pleased to hear again that stealthy tread upon the stairs, and to realize that it was much closer than before, as well as unmistakably real. And this time he got up and went out to see who it could be creeping about on the upper staircase at so late an hour.

But the sound ceased; there was no one visible on the stairs. He went to the floor below, not without trepidation, and turned on the electric light to make sure that no one was hiding in the empty rooms of the unoccupied suite. There was not a stick of furniture large enough to hide a dog. Then he called over the banisters to Mrs. Monks, but there was no answer, and his voice echoed down into the dark vault of the house, and was lost in the roar of the gale that howled outside. Everyone was in bed and asleep—everyone except himself and the owner of this soft and stealthy tread.

"My absurd imagination, I suppose," he thought. "It must have been the wind after all, although—it seemed so *very* real and close, I thought." He went back to his packing. It was by this time getting on towards midnight. He drank his coffee up and lit another pipe—the last before turning in.

It is difficult to say exactly at what point fear begins, when the causes of that fear are not plainly before the eyes. Impressions gather on the surface of the mind, film by film, as ice gathers upon the surface of still water, but often so lightly that they claim no definite recognition from the consciousness. Then a point is reached where the accumulated impressions become a definite emotion, and the mind realizes that something has happened. With something of a start, Johnson suddenly recognized that he felt nervous—oddly nervous; also, that for some time past the causes of this feeling had been gathering slowly in his mind, but that he had only just reached the point where he was forced to acknowledge them.

It was a singular and curious malaise that had come over him, and he hardly knew what to make of it. He felt as though he were doing something that was strongly objected to by another person, another person, moreover, who had some right to object. It was a most disturbing and disagreeable feeling, not unlike the persistent promptings of conscience: almost, in fact, as if he were doing something he knew to be wrong. Yet, though he searched vigorously and honestly in his mind, he could nowhere lay his finger upon the secret of this growing uneasiness, and it perplexed him. More, it distressed and frightened him.

"Pure nerves, I suppose," he said aloud with a forced laugh. "Mountain air will cure all that! Ah," he added, still speaking to himself, "and that reminds me—my snow-glasses."

He was standing by the door of the bedroom during this brief soliloquy, and as he passed quickly towards the sitting-room to fetch them from the cupboard he saw out of the corner of his eye the indistinct outline of a figure standing on the stairs, a few feet from the top. It was someone in a stooping position, with one hand on the banisters, and the face peering up towards the landing. And at the same moment he heard a shuffling footstep. The person who had been creeping about below all this time had at last come up to his own floor. Who in the world could it be? And what in the name of Heaven did he want?

Johnson caught his breath sharply and stood stock still. Then, after a few seconds' hesitation, he found his courage, and turned to investigate. The stairs, he saw to his utter amazement, were empty; there was no one. He felt a series of cold shivers run over him, and something about the muscles of his legs gave a little and grew weak. For the space of several minutes he peered steadily into the shadows that congregated about the top of the staircase where he had seen the figure, and then he walked fast—almost ran, in fact—into the light of the front room; but hardly had he passed inside the doorway when he heard some one come up the stairs behind him with a quick bound and go swiftly into his bedroom. It was a heavy, but at the same time a stealthy footstep—the tread of somebody who did not wish to be seen. And it was at this precise moment that the nervousness he had hitherto experienced leaped the boundary line, and entered the state of fear, almost of acute, unreasoning fear. Before it turned into terror there was a further boundary to cross, and beyond that again lay the region of pure horror. Johnson's position was an unenviable one.

"By Jove! That *was* someone on the stairs, then," he muttered, his flesh crawling all over; "and whoever it was has now gone into my bedroom." His delicate, pale face turned absolutely white, and for some minutes he hardly knew what to think or do. Then he realized intuitively that delay only set a premium upon fear; and he crossed the landing boldly and went straight into the other room, where, a few seconds before, the steps had disappeared.

"Who's there? Is that you, Mrs. Monks?" he called aloud, as he went, and heard the first half of his words echo down the empty stairs, while the second half fell dead against the curtains in a room that apparently held no other human figure than his own.

"Who's there?" he called again, in a voice unnecessarily loud and that only just held firm. "What do you want here?"

The curtains swayed very slightly, and, as he saw it, his heart felt as if it almost missed a beat; yet he dashed forward and drew them aside with a rush. A window, streaming with rain, was all that met his gaze. He continued his search, but in vain; the cupboards held nothing but rows of clothes, hanging motionless; and under the bed there was no sign of any one hiding. He stepped backwards into the middle of the room, and, as he did so, something all but tripped him up. Turning with a sudden spring of alarm he saw—the kit-bag.

"Odd!" he thought. "That's not where I left it!" A few moments before it had surely been on his right, between the bed and the bath; he did not remember having moved it. It was very curious. What in the world was the matter with everything? Were all his senses gone queer? A terrific gust of wind tore at the windows, dashing the sleet against the glass with the force of small gun-shot, and then fled away howling dismally over the waste of Bloomsbury roofs. A sudden vision of the Channel next day rose in his mind and recalled him sharply to realities.

"There's no one here at any rate; that's quite clear!" he exclaimed aloud. Yet at the time he uttered them he knew perfectly well that his words were not true and that he did not believe them himself. He felt exactly as though someone was hiding close about him, watching all his movements, trying to hinder his packing in some way. "And two of my senses," he added, keeping up the pretence, "have played me the most absurd tricks: the steps I heard and the figure I saw were both entirely imaginary."

He went back to the front room, poked the fire into a blaze, and sat down before it to think. What impressed him more than anything else was the fact that the kit-bag was no longer where he had left it. It had been dragged nearer to the door.

What happened afterwards that night happened, of course, to a man already excited by fear, and was perceived by a mind that had not the full and proper control, therefore, of the senses. Outwardly, Johnson remained calm and master of himself to the end, pretending to the very last that everything he witnessed had a natural explanation, or was merely delusions of his tired nerves. But inwardly, in his very heart, he knew all along that someone had been hiding downstairs in the empty suite when he came in, that this person had watched his opportunity and then stealthily made his way up to the bedroom, and that all he saw and heard afterwards, from the moving of the kit-bag to—well, to the other things this story has to tell—were caused directly by the presence of this invisible person.

And it was here, just when he most desired to keep his mind and thoughts controlled, that the vivid pictures received day after day upon the mental plates exposed in the courtroom of the Old Bailey, came strongly to light and developed themselves in the dark room of his inner vision. Unpleasant, haunting memories have a way of coming to life again just when the mind least desires them—in the silent watches of the night, on sleepless pillows, during the lonely hours spent by sick and dying beds. And so now, in the same way, Johnson saw nothing but the dreadful face of John Turk, the murderer, lowering at him from every corner of his mental field of vision; the white skin, the evil eyes, and the fringe of black hair low over the forehead. All the pictures of those ten days in court crowded back into his mind unbidden, and very vivid.

"This is all rubbish and nerves," he exclaimed at length, springing with sudden energy from his chair. "I shall finish my packing and go to bed. I'm overwrought, overtired. No doubt, at this rate I shall hear steps and things all night!"

But his face was deadly white all the same. He snatched up his field-glasses and walked across to the bedroom, humming a music-hall song as he went—a trifle too loud to be natural; and the instant he crossed the threshold and stood within the room something turned cold about his heart, and he felt that every hair on his head stood up.

The kit-bag lay close in front of him, several feet nearer to the door than he had left it, and just over its crumpled top he saw a head and face slowly sinking down out of sight as though someone were crouching behind it to hide, and at the same moment a sound like a long-drawn sigh was distinctly audible in the still air about him between the gusts of the storm outside.

Johnson had more courage and will-power than the girlish indecision of his face indi-cated; but at first such a wave of terror came over him that for some seconds he could do nothing but stand and stare. A violent trembling ran down his back and legs, and he was conscious of a foolish, almost a hysterical, impulse to scream aloud. That sigh seemed in his very ear, and the air still quivered with it. It was unmistakably a human sigh.

"Who's there?" he said at length, finding his voice; but though he meant to speak with loud decision, the tones came out instead in a faint whisper, for he had partly lost the control of his tongue and lips.

He stepped forward, so that he could see all round and over the kit-bag. Of course there was nothing there, nothing but the faded carpet and the bulging canvas sides. He put out his hands and threw open the mouth of the sack where it had fallen over, being only three parts full, and then he saw for the first time that round the inside, some six inches from the top, there ran a broad smear of dull crimson. It was an old and faded blood stain. He uttered a scream, and drew back his hands as if they had been burnt. At the same moment the kit-bag gave a faint, but unmistakable, lurch forward towards the door.

Johnson collapsed backwards, searching with his hands for the support of some-thing solid, and the door, being further behind him than he realized, received his weight just in time to prevent his falling, and shut to with a resounding bang. At the same moment the swinging of his left arm accidentally touched the electric switch, and the light in the room went out.

It was an awkward and disagreeable predicament, and if Johnson had not been pos-sessed of real pluck he might have done all manner of foolish things. As it was, however, he pulled himself together, and groped furiously for the little brass knob to turn the light on again. But the rapid closing of the door had set the coats hanging on it a-swinging, and his fingers became entangled in a confusion of sleeves and pockets, so that it was some moments before he found the switch. And in those few moments of bewilderment and terror two things happened that sent him beyond recall over the boundary into the region of genuine horror—he distinctly heard the kit-bag shuffling heavily across the floor in jerks, and close in front of his face sounded once again the sigh of a human being.

In his anguished efforts to find the brass button on the wall he nearly scraped the nails from his fingers, but even then, in those frenzied moments of alarm—so swift and alert are the impressions of a mind keyed-up by a vivid emotion—he had time to realize that he dreaded the return of the light, and that it might be better for him to stay hidden in the merciful screen of darkness. It was but the impulse of a moment, however, and before he had time to act upon it he had yielded automatically to the original desire, and the room was flooded again with light.

But the second instinct had been right. It would have been better for him to have stayed in the shelter of the kind darkness. For there, close before him, bending over the half-packed kit-bag, clear as life in the merciless glare of the electric light, stood the figure of John Turk, the murderer. Not three feet from him the man stood, the fringe of black hair marked plainly against the pallor of the forehead, the whole horrible presentment of the scoundrel, as vivid as he had seen him day after day in the Old Bailey, when he stood there in the dock, cynical and callous, under the very shadow of the gallows.

In a flash Johnson realized what it all meant: the dirty and much-used bag; the smear of crimson within the top; the dreadful stretched condition of the bulging sides. He remembered how the victim's body had been stuffed into a canvas bag for burial, the ghastly, dismembered fragments forced with lime into this very bag; and the bag itself produced as evidence— It all came back to him as clear as day. . . .

Very softly and stealthily his hand groped behind him for the handle of the door, but before he could actually turn it the very thing that he most of all dreaded came about, and John Turk lifted his devil's face and looked at him. At the same moment that heavy sigh passed through the air of the room, formulated somehow into words: "It's my bag. And I want it."

Johnson just remembered clawing the door open, and then falling in a heap upon the floor of the landing, as he tried frantically to make his way into the front room.

He remained unconscious for a long time, and it was still dark when he opened his eyes and realized that he was lying, stiff and bruised, on the cold boards. Then the memory of what he had seen rushed back into his mind, and he promptly fainted again. When he woke the second time the wintry dawn was just beginning to peep in at the windows, painting the stairs a cheerless, dismal grey, and he managed to crawl into the front room, and cover himself with an overcoat in the armchair, where at length he fell asleep.

A great clamour woke him. He recognized Mrs. Monks's voice, loud and voluble.

"What! You ain't been to bed, sir! Are you ill, or has anything 'appened? And there's an urgent gentleman to see you, though it ain't seven o'clock yet, and——"

"Who is it?" he stammered. "I'm all right, thanks. Fell asleep in my chair, I suppose."

"Some one from Mr. Wilb'rim's, and he says he ought to see you quick before you go abroad, and I told him——"

"Show him up, please, at once," said Johnson, whose head was whirling, and his mind was still full of dreadful visions.

Mr. Wilbraham's man came in with many apologies, and explained briefly and quickly that an absurd mistake had been made, and that the wrong kit-bag had been sent over the night before.

"Henry somehow got hold of the one that came over from the court-room, and Mr. Wilbraham only discovered it when he saw his own lying in his room, and asked why it had not gone to you," the man said.

"Oh!" said Johnson stupidly.

"And he must have brought you the one from the murder case instead, sir, I'm afraid," the man continued, without the ghost of an expression on his face. "The one John Turk packed the dead body in. Mr. Wilbraham's awful upset about it, sir, and told me to come over first thing this morning with the right one, as you were leaving by the boat."

He pointed to a clean-looking kit-bag on the floor, which he had just brought. "And I was to bring the other one back, sir," he added casually.

For some minutes Johnson could not find his voice. At last he pointed in the direction of his bedroom. "Perhaps you would kindly unpack it for me. Just empty the things out on the floor."

The man disappeared into the other room, and was gone for five minutes. Johnson heard the shifting to and fro of the bag, and the rattle of the skates and boots being unpacked.

"Thank you, sir," the man said, returning with the bag folded over his arm. "And can I do anything more to help you, sir?"

"What is it?" asked Johnson, seeing that he still had something he wished to say.

The man shuffled and looked mysterious. "Beg pardon, sir, but knowing your interest in the Turk case, I thought you'd maybe like to know what's happened——"

"Yes."

"John Turk killed hisself last night with poison immediately on getting his release, and he left a note for Mr. Wilbraham saying as he'd be much obliged if they'd have him put away, same as the woman he murdered, in the old kit-bag."

"What time—did he do it?" asked Johnson.

"Ten o'clock last night, sir, the warder says."

LADY GREEN-SLEEVES

ALICE AND CLAUDE ASKEW

"As you're not fishing—this being the Sabbath Day—would you like to walk as far as the pine woods with me, Dexter, and I'll tell you the story of Lady Green-Sleeves—that is, if you're not getting bored with my yarns?"

Aylmer Vance smiled, his quiet, wise smile, as he addressed me. He had just wandered into the quaint old-fashioned garden of the Magpie Inn, and had found me lounging in a basket chair—basking in the sunshine, for the rainy night had been followed by a glorious morning, and, needless to say, I sprang to my feet at once, for the two queer tales that Vance had already told me had made me very curious to hear about Lady Green-Sleeves, and I said as much to my friend.

"So you're quite ready to wander to the pine woods with me, and you'd like to be told about my little ghost—the daintiest ghost a man could ever have the pleasure of meeting. There's nothing dreadful or tragic in this tale—'tis sheer romance; you'll enjoy it, Dexter—you'll enjoy it."

Vance slipped his arm familiarly through mine, then he laughed softly.

"You're such a surprising person, Dexter. Who, to look at you, would imagine for one instant that you are a dreamer of dreams—a firm believer in spooks? You are such a typical barrister, as far as appearances go; yet here I am pouring out all my adventures to you—every uncanny adventure I have ever had—for you do believe in my stories. There's nothing of the sniffing sceptic about you; that's why I am able to talk so freely—to open out my heart."

"I couldn't fail to believe your stories," I answered slowly; "no one could who watched your face whilst you are relating them—heard your voice; and now I am impatient—most impatient—to hear all about Lady Green-Sleeves."

"Wait till we reach the pine woods. I'll throw myself down on a bed of pine needles, close my eyes, and you shall have the whole story as it occurred. It may tax your credulity more than the other tales, though; it's so dreamy and so unexplainable."

Vance lowered his voice. I could feel the nervous trembling of his thin, sensitive fingers as he clutched my arm, and I was more than ever conscious of the strange sympathy that existed between us. I knew—something seemed to tell me—that we were going to be friends, firm friends, for the rest of our lives, and I hoped that Vance would ask me to be his companion during some of his future expeditions to haunted houses.

It took us about ten minutes to walk to the woods. The spicy scent of the pines filled the air; hot sunshine poured down upon a world that was literally a riot of green this morning, and I felt—I could not help feeling—how good it was to be alive. I said as much to Vance, and he laughed; I confess I was extremely puzzled by his laughter at times, but I understood why he had laughed after he told me his story—I understood quite well.

Vance threw himself down on a great heap of pine needles, just as he had said he would—a soft, scented heap, and I made myself a similar couch. We both lay luxuriating in the brilliant sunshine for a minute or two, then Vance bent towards me. His face looked much softer than I had ever seen it, a vague smile played about his mouth.

"Now I will tell you all about my Lady Green-Sleeves. I met her about twelve years ago, and the evening we spent together stands out with startling distinctness in my memory—such a rose-scented evening."

"The evening you spent together?" I raised myself on my elbow and stared hard at Vance, wondering if I had heard aright. "Why, did Lady Green-Sleeves' ghost pay the world such a long visit as all that? I thought ghosts only appeared for a few seconds and then vanished?"

Vance nodded his head.

"So did I; but I was wrong, it appeared—quite wrong; and now, with your leave, my good friend, I will continue my narrative."

Vance paused. He had thrown himself down on his back. He was gazing straight up into a dazzlingly blue sky, and I knew he saw far more than I could see—that he was conjuring up the ghost of a little dead and gone lady—recalling a romantic episode.

"Well, Dexter, I must commence my story by explaining to you that I had not the least idea that my Lady Green-Sleeves was a ghost till she had made me her pretty curtsy and departed. I took her for a masquerader first of all—a dainty rogue of a masquerader; for, you see, I met her at a fancy dress ball, a big dance given by some very rich people in Yorkshire—a dance to which I had been taken by friends."

Vance closed his eyes. His voice sounded very rich and musical; the dreamy smile still played about his lips.

"How well I remember that night, Dexter. It was a cold December evening, and we had to drive over nine miles to Arden Hall, for that was the name of the house where the dance was taking place. I felt very cross at being taken to the ball; I was not particularly fond of dancing, and I hated—as so many men do—the bother of having to go to it in fancy dress. I wore a Georgian suit; the coat was of plum-coloured satin, I recollect, with a white brocade waistcoat sprigged with silver, and my hostess had been pleased to compliment me on my appearance—I was ten years younger than I am now."

Aylmer Vance paused. Looking at him as he lay on the ground, it was not difficult to guess that with his long, well-knit limbs he would cut a fine figure in Georgian costume, and that a white peruke would prove very becoming. There was certainly an old-world dignity about him, a polished refinement.

"Continue your story!" I exclaimed. "I want to hear when you first caught sight of Lady Green-Sleeves. Your plum-coloured coat was very beautiful, I expect; but let us get to the lady."

"I caught sight of her the moment I entered the all. There was a great balcony running round it, and she was bending over the oak balcony gazing down into the hall below, watching the guests arrive, so I imagined she must be one of the house-party. Our eyes met, and I can tell you, Dexter, a thrill ran through me; my heart suddenly began beating wildly. I made up my mind I'd contrive to get introduced to Lady Green-Sleeves that evening, for that was the name I gave her to myself— Lady Green-Sleeves."

Vance raised himself suddenly to a sitting position. His eyes were wide open now, but he did not look at me; he gazed straight ahead, and I knew who he was gazing at, for his smile deepened; he had forgotten me for the moment—he had conjured up a memory.

"Was Lady Green-Sleeves very pretty?"

I put the question rather diffidently. I hated to arouse Vance from his reverie, yet I longed to hear the rest of the story.

"Pretty! That's a poor word to describe Lady Green-Sleeves. She was adorable; but I think it was her daintiness that most appealed to me—her delicious daintiness. She had a sweet face, a roguish smile; her eyes were as violet and velvety as purple pansies. Her brown curls, innocent of powder, clustered becomingly about a pure low forehead, peep-ing from under a lace hood, a hood fastened under Lady Green-Sleeves' soft little chin with a rosebud. She was very young—barely seventeen, I thought—a sweet child, who would blossom presently into a delightful woman; and I suddenly found myself wishing that I was a few years younger—more of an age with this brown-haired beauty."

Vance played idly with a handful of fir cones; a longing look had come over his face; then he sighed heavily.

"I hardly know how to describe what Lady Green-Sleeves had on. Her dress struck me as being distinctly fantastic, but I suppose it belonged to the Georgian period, like my own. Her hooped petticoat was of fine creamy silk, and over this petticoat she wore a sort of looped-up green mantle, with long wide sleeves. As far as I can recollect, her bodice was of the same creamy stuff as her petticoat, fastened in front with a green lace. She wore a small bunch of pink roses at her breast, and her green mantle was looped up with a slightly bigger bunch of the same roses.

"Her shoes—such tiny little shoes to fit such tiny little feet—had high red heels, and she wore dainty white silk mittens on her small, exquisitely-shaped hands. Oh! I tell you there wasn't another girl at the dance to match Lady Green-Sleeves for looks; I knew that directly I caught sight of her bending over the wide balustrade. Besides, there was something about her that set her apart from all other women—a delicate, ineffable charm, a distinctive daintiness, a curious elusiveness. The extraordinary thing was—at least, I thought it extraordinary first of all—that no one else seemed to see her bending over the balcony rail, for I remember turning to one of the other men of the party and asking him if he knew who Lady Green-Sleeves was, but he shook his head and looked at me queerly.

"'I don't see anyone on the balcony,' he said, peering up. 'It's quite deserted.' And as he spoke Lady Green-Sleeves disappeared.

"I couldn't make out what in the world had become of her, how she had managed to flit away so quickly; but I caught sight of her about a quarter of an hour later standing alone and partnerless in a corner of the ballroom. The band was playing 'The Choristers' Waltz,' playing it well, and I thought what a shame it was that such a bewitching little lady should not be dancing—I couldn't think what all the men were about. I expect my partner, a plump, unattractive girl, dressed as a Swiss peasant, found me uncommonly dull and distrait during the rest of our waltz—I kept watching Lady Green-Sleeves, I remember. Presently I lost sight of her; she disappeared just as suddenly as she had vanished from the balcony, and I couldn't for the life of me imagine what had become of her. I determined to ask my hostess for an introduction to Lady Green-Sleeves, however; so after I had sat out with my Swiss girl, given her an ice, and handed her over thankfully to her next partner, I made my way up to Mrs. Latham—for that was my hostess's name—and asked her if she would very kindly introduce me to the girl who was wearing a green silk mantle, a creamy silk petticoat, and a little white lace cap, and who did not appear to be dancing very much.

"Mrs. Latham looked distinctly puzzled.

"'I am awfully sorry, Mr. Vance,' she answered, 'but I don't seem to know the girl whom you want to be introduced to, or to recognise her from your description. It's very stupid of me, I know, but so many people have brought friends with them tonight, that perhaps I have not noticed the lady who is wearing a green silk mantle. If you can only find her, I will introduce you to her at once, with the greatest pleasure.'

"I gazed helplessly round the ballroom, and as I did so I suddenly caught sight of Lady Green-Sleeves. She was standing by the raised daïs on which the band were playing; she was still alone and unattended.

"'There she is!' I cried, turning to Mrs. Latham. 'There's Lady Green-Sleeves by the daïs.'

"Mrs. Latham looked straight across the room at Lady Green Sleeves. As she did so her eyes opened—opened wide.

"'How extraordinary!' she exclaimed. 'To think that I never caught sjght of that girl before—noticed her! Why, she ought to be the belle of the ball; and she's paid us such a pretty compliment, Mr. Vance; she has copied the dress of one of our ances-tresses—copied it exactly. The portrait hangs in the long gallery, and now I come to think of it, she's strikingly like poor Mistress Latham's portrait—yes, there really is an extraordinary resemblance.'

"Mrs. Latham rose from her chair. She was a tall, dignified woman—one of those slow, quiet women whom it is impossible to hurry. I wished she would hasten her pace as she made her leisurely way round the ballroom towards the band-stand—I was so afraid that Lady Green-Sleeves would disappear again; and my fears were not ill-founded. We had to wait for a second to allow a couple who were dancing to pass us, and during that brief second Lady Green-Sleeves had disappeared. When we reached the band-stand she had gone.

"Mrs. Latham looked at me in a puzzled sort of way.

"'Dear me, Mr. Vance, how very annoying,' she remarked, 'and how singular.' I could see she looked vaguely troubled—a little bewildered.

"'It's all right, Mrs. Latham,' I assured her. 'Don't you worry about me. I will con-trive to get introduced to Lady Green-Sleeves somehow, even if I have to introduce myself, for after all it's a fancy dress ball; we are none of us ourselves tonight, our staid, decorous, conventional selves.'

"Mrs. Latham hesitated, then she suddenly put a hand upon my arm.

"'If you do get introduced to Lady Green-Sleeves, if you do manage to speak to her, I wish you would bring her round to me, Mr. Vance; I should like to compliment her upon her dress.'

"'I shall be delighted,' I answered.

"Some other guest came up at that moment and claimed Mrs. Latham's attention, and so set me free to go searching for Lady Green-Sleeves, but it was a long search. She was not to be found in any of the rooms given over to the sitting-out couples, neither could I discover her in the refreshment-room. When the music sounded for the next dance she did not come back to the ballroom; just as I was giving up heart, I caught sight of her bending over the gallery balustrade again. She looked a little tired, I thought, vaguely disappointed, and she was still alone."

Aylmer Vance paused, then he suddenly turned to me.

"You can imagine how fast I ran up those wide oak stairs, can you not, Dexter? I suppose you have been in love in your time; and I don't mind confessing to you that this was a case of love at first sight on my part. I had absolutely lost my head over Lady Green-Sleeves. I might have been a callow youth of eighteen instead of a man of thirty, and my heart beat like a boy's heart—it did indeed—when Lady Green-Sleeves suddenly turned her head and looked at me when I reached the gallery; and then, without waiting for me to speak, she dropped me a formal curtsy, the most graceful, dipping, sweeping curtsy that you could imagine; she seemed to touch the floor and then to rise again in a vast billow of silk, and her voice, when she addressed me, was extraordinarily soft and sweet.

"'Your servant, sir.'

"That was all she said, but the pretty conceit of the words pleased me; here was a masquerader who was clearly acting up to her part.

"I made my very best bow.

"'Will you accord me the pleasure of a dance, madam?' I requested. 'I have my hostess's permission to introduce myself to you. My name is Aylmer Vance.'

"'I should be delighted for you to lead me out in a dance, Mr. Vance,' the little lady answered, 'but unfortunately I know none of these modern dances; they are after my time.'

"A faint note of regret tinged Lady Green-Sleeves' voice as she spoke. The corners of her mouth drooped a little.

"'Oh! You know how to dance the waltz, madam,' I protested. 'It is true that it is a dance that does not accord with our costume, but still—'

"I bowed, and offered my arm, but she declined it with a faint shake of her head.

"'I am afraid I could not venture on that dance, sir. The very music to which the dancers revolve has an unfamiliar sound to me, and yet it is tuneful music—very tuneful.'

"'May I have the honour of taking you in to supper? I believe supper is to be served at twelve o'clock, and it is a quarter to twelve now.'

"'I never take supper, sir.' Lady Green-Sleeves folded her little hands together, the little hands that I longed to hold in my own; then she suddenly looked at me from under her long lashes, her face dimpled into smiles. 'You will think me vastly uncivil. I declined your invitation to dance with you and to have supper, but I'll tell you what I will do, sir; I will take you into my own parlour, and we will sit and converse there together till midnight strikes.'

"'I should like nothing better,' I answered; but as I said the words I felt puzzled—distinctly puzzled, for my hostess had told me that she did not know who the girl in the green mantle was, and yet Lady Green-Sleeves must be staying here—she must be one of the house-party. It was all rather mysterious, to say the least of it.

"'I will take you to my parlour at once. To confess the truth, I shall not be sorry to rest there a few minutes. I find this gay scene a little confusing, and the music is very strident.'

"Lady Green-Sleeves glanced slowly about her. She appeared to be trying to remember something, then her brow suddenly cleared.

"'Ah! I recollect; this is the way to the oak parlour.'

"She led me along a balcony, stopping in front of a closed door. She gazed at me silently, as though asking me to open the door.

"I obeyed that glance. I turned the handle and held the door open. Lady Green-Sleeves gave a happy little cry when she found herself in the parlour; her eyes roved round the queer little three-cornered room, a soft smile played on her lips.

"'My own parlour—I bid you welcome to it.'

"She sat down on a big chair. She folded her small mittened hands in her lap; she glanced about the room with eager interest.

"'Hardly anything has been changed; the parlour is very much as I left it. The curtains have been altered, and my spinet has gone. The old mirror still hangs over the mantelpiece, however; 'tis over a hundred and fifty years since that glass reflected my face.'

"I laughed—this was pretty fooling, then I gazed round the oakpanelled room in my turn. It was full of quaint old furniture; there was a beautiful apple-green tea set in a high china cupboard, a big bowl full of sweet-scented purple violets stood on a gate-leg table; the air was quite heavy with the perfume of the flowers—oppressively heavy.

"'It is so strange to come back again.'

"Lady Green-Sleeves spoke in soft, reflectful tones. She seemed to have forgotten me for the moment and to be talking to herself.

"'Where have you been?' I asked. 'Abroad?'

"She started and smiled—a faint, curious smile.

"'Very far away, and I found it difficult to come back—exceedingly difficult; but, indeed, I wanted to see what the world is like nowadays. I protest it has greatly changed.' She gave an airy wave of her little hands. 'I was so young when my time came—barely seventeen; an' 'twas hard to say farewell to this world. I would gladly have remained here longer. I was the toast of the country, and my worshipful parents made my days one long delight; but I fell into decline suddenly.'

"'Am I to understand that I am conversing with a ghost?'

"I put the question laughingly to Lady Green-Sleeves, never doubting that the pretty little masquerader, as I took her to be, would laugh back; but instead of laughing she gazed at me reproachfully.

"'Why, indeed, sir, I thought you knew that. Oh! 'twas a foolish thought of mine to return to my old home tonight. This world belongs to another generation than mine, and I feel I am a stranger in my father's house—a flitting guest.'

"She paused. A tear trembled on one of her long eyelashes.

"'I do not understand modern ways. Everything is unfamiliar to me—strange; and the glamour has departed. Once it would have pleased me vastly to dance till the dawn stole into the ballroom, but it would be no such great pleasure now; I have tasted deeper joys, known far more exquisite pleasures.'

"She spoke with intense gravity, intense simplicity, but I still thought that Lady Green-Sleeves was playing a part. I could not believe that it was really an apparition from another world who was addressing me; but I knew one thing—I knew that I had lost my heart to the girl in the green silk mantle—lost it irretrievably.

"'Dear Lady Green-Sleeves!' I threw myself on my knees at her feet. 'Now that you have come back to this world, won't you stay here—consent to remain in it? Will you be angry with me when I tell you that I have dared to fall in love with you?'

"'What! You have fallen in love with me?' She clasped her little hands tightly together; she gave the low, delighted laugh of an innocent coquette. 'Oh, la! Sir, what a romance! But indeed'—her laugh was suddenly followed by a sigh, a short, sweet sigh—'I may not listen to lovers' vows; it would not be right, it would not be fair to you. My time for love is over. I told you, did I not, that I died when I was barely seventeen?'

"'Oh! Lady Green-Sleeves, Lady Green-Sleeves, don't tease me any longer pretending to be a ghost. Don't you realise that I am speaking to you seriously—that I am in earnest? I tell you that I love you—that I have fallen in love at first sight, and I want to know your name; I want to be allowed to call you and see you, to woo you, to win you.'

"She rose to her feet, her silk skirts rustling heavily, the laces fluttering at her breast, but she was not angry with me—oh, no, she was not angry.

"'Sir, believe me, I am very sorry that I have got to leave you. I wish that we had met a hundred and fifty years ago, that we could have danced together, for indeed, sir, none of the suitors who wooed me in the past took my fancy as greatly as you have done, and yet they were brave gentlemen in their day—brave gentlemen.'

"She paused a second. She fixed her big blue eyes upon me. Her voice was like the sweetest and most exquisite music, but it seemed to come from a long way off.

"'This may not be farewell, sir. It is quite likely that in the future we shall meet again, but not in this world—oh, no, not in this world—indeed, it is more than likely.' She hesitated. 'Shall we say "Au revoir" instead of "Goodbye"?'

"She swept me another of her long sweeping curtsies, and I realised that she was on the eve of taking her departure. I begged her passionately to stay with me, but she shook her head.

"'Indeed, sir, you must not ask that of me. I had a foolish fancy to come back to this world, as I told you. I remembered it as such a brave place, but now that I have returned—now that I can contrast it with another land that I know—why, I would not remain here if I could.' She gave a gentle little wave of her hands. 'I wish I could make you see the truth as plainly as I see it, sir. This world lacks reality, and the men and women who inhabit it are but as changing shadows; here today, they will be gone tomorrow. There is nothing in this world that endures except—except love.'

"She looked at me straight in the eyes as she said the last words. I remember that I opened my arms, and would have drawn her into my embrace, only she stepped back.

"'No, sir—no!' she rebuked me. 'Your lips may not touch mine any more than my lips may touch yours. Now I am going back from whence I came.'

"'Where are you going?' I cried passionately. 'Do you prefer the grave to my arms, Lady Green-Sleeves—to my love?'

"She shook her head.

"'The grave—what have I to do with the grave? I said farewell to my mortal body over a hundred years ago; I have merely clothed myself in my old semblance to come here. I am a spirit—an immortal spirit—and it is not to the grave I am returning, but life—life!'

"She smiled. There was such wisdom in her smile, such infinite knowledge; and then, before my eyes, she slowly faded away—vanished. I found myself alone in the oak parlour, most tragically, most sombrely alone. I could hear the violins playing wild gipsy music in the ballroom, I could hear the rhythmical swing of the dancers' feet, and 'tip-tap' down the passage sounded like the click of the little red-heeled shoes; but I knew—something seemed to tell me—that even if I went out on to the balcony I should not see her. I realised that no one on this earth would ever catch a glimpse of Lady Green-Sleeves again; her home was in a better country."

Aylmer Vance paused. He put up his hands to his eyes and he sighed—sighed heavily.

"Ah, me—it might have been! Still, it's no use to cherish foolish fancies, is it, Dexter—to dream day and night about a little sweet-eyed ghost—a little lady who will never re-visit this dusty old world again. It's better to be practical and sensible—and to forget."

I looked at him very gravely.

"You will never be able to forget her," I said slowly, "to really forget Lady Green-Sleeves; and you will meet her one day, Vance—you know you will."

"How can I tell?" He shrugged his shoulders. "It may all have been hallucination on my part; and yet Mrs. Latham saw Lady Green-Sleeves too—or thought she did; but, of course, I may have conveyed the impression to her—it may only have been a case of thought transference. Still, for me Lady Green-Sleeves exists—will always exist."

He rose slowly to his feet. He stretched himself, and stood up a tall, lean figure in the sunshine.

"She said 'Au revoir'—not 'Goodbye,' mark you; I like to remember that—that she only said 'Au revoir.'"

Legend of the Engulphed Convent

Washington Irving

At the dark and melancholy period when Don Roderick the Goth and his chivalry were overthrown on the banks of the Guadalete, and all Spain was overrun by the Moors, great was the devastation of churches and convents throughout that pious kingdom. The miraculous fate of one of those holy piles is thus recorded in an authentic legend of those days.

On the summit of a hill, not very distant from the capital city of Toledo, stood an ancient convent and chapel, dedicated to the invocation of Saint Benedict, and inhabited by a sisterhood of Benedictine nuns. This holy asylum was confined to females of noble lineage. The younger sisters of the highest families were here given in religious marriage to their Saviour, in order that the portions of their elder sisters might be increased, and they enabled to make suitable matches on earth; or that the family wealth might go undivided to elder brothers, and the dignity of their ancient houses be protected from decay. The convent was renowned, therefore, for enshrining within its walls a sisterhood of the purest blood, the most immaculate virtue, and most resplendent beauty, of all Gothic Spain.

When the Moors overran the kingdom, there was nothing that more excited their hostility, than these virgin asylums. The very sight of a convent-spire was sufficient to set their Moslem blood in a foment, and they sacked it with as fierce a zeal as though the sacking of a nunnery were a sure passport to Elysium.

Tidings of such outrages, committed in various parts of the kingdom, reached this noble sanctuary, and filled it with dismay. The danger came nearer and nearer; the infidel hosts were spreading all over the country; Toledo itself was captured; there was no flying from the convent, and no security within its walls.

In the midst of this agitation, the alarm was given one day, that a great band of Saracens were spurring across the plain. In an instant the whole convent was a scene of confusion. Some of the nuns wrung their fair hands at the windows; others waved their veils, and uttered shrieks, from the tops of the towers, vainly hoping to draw relief from a country overrun by the foe. The sight of these innocent doves thus fluttering about their dove-cote, but increased the zealot fury of the whiskered Moors.

They thundered at the portal, and at every blow the ponderous gates trembled on their hinges.

The nuns now crowded round the abbess. They had been accustomed to look up to her as all-powerful, and they now implored her protection. The mother abbess looked with a rueful eye upon the treasures of beauty and vestal virtue exposed to such imminent peril. Alas! how was she to protect them from the spoiler! She had, it is true, experienced many signal interpositions of Providence in her individual favor. Her early days had been passed amid the temptations of a court, where her virtue had been purified by repeated trials, from none of which had she escaped but by miracle. But were miracles never to cease? Could she hope that the marvellous protection shown to herself, would be extended to a whole sisterhood? There was no other resource. The Moors were at the threshold; a few moments more, and the convent would be at their mercy. Summoning her nuns to follow her, she hurried into the chapel, and throwing herself on her knees before the image of the blessed Mary, "Oh, holy Lady!" exclaimed she, "oh, most pure and immaculate of virgins! thou seest our extremity. The ravager is at the gate, and there is none on earth to help us! Look down with pity, and grant that the earth may gape and swallow us, rather than that our cloister vows should suffer violation!"

The Moors redoubled their assault upon the portal; the gates gave way, with a tremendous crash; a savage yell of exultation arose; when of a sudden the earth yawned; down sank the convent, with its cloisters, its dormitories, and all its nuns. The chapel tower was the last that sank, the bell ringing forth a peal of triumph in the very teeth of the infidels.

Forty years had passed and gone, since the period of this miracle. The subjugation of Spain was complete. The Moors lorded it over city and country; and such of the Christian population as remained, and were permitted to exercise their religion, did it in humble resignation to the Moslem sway.

At this time, a Christian cavalier, of Cordova, hearing that a patriotic band of his countrymen had raised the standard of the cross in the mountains of the Asturias, resolved to join them, and unite in breaking the yoke of bondage. Secretly arming himself, and caparisoning his steed, he set forth from Cordova, and pursued his course by unfrequented mule-paths, and along the dry channels made by winter torrents. His spirit burned with indignation, whenever, on commanding a view over a long sweeping plain, he beheld the mosque swelling in the distance, and the Arab horsemen careering about, as if the rightful lords of the soil. Many a deep-drawn sigh, and heavy groan, also, did the good cavalier utter, on passing the ruins of churches and convents desolated by the conquerors.

It was on a sultry midsummer evening, that this wandering cavalier, in skirting a hill thickly covered with forest, heard the faint tones of a vesper bell sounding melodiously in the air, and seeming to come from the summit of the hill. The cavalier crossed himself with wonder, at this unwonted and Christian sound. He supposed it to proceed from one of those humble chapels and hermitages permitted to exist through the indulgence of the Moslem conquerors. Turning his steed up a narrow path of the forest, he sought this sanctuary, in hopes of finding a hospitable shelter for the night. As he advanced, the trees threw a deep gloom around him, and the bat flitted across his path. The bell ceased to toll, and all was silence.

Presently a choir of female voices came stealing sweetly through the forest, chanting the evening service, to the solemn accompaniment of an organ. The heart of the good cavalier melted at the sound, for it recalled the happier days of his country. Urging forward his weary steed, he at length arrived at a broad grassy area, on the summit of the hill, surrounded by the forest. Here the melodious voices rose in full chorus, like the swelling of the breeze; but whence they came, he could not tell. Sometimes they were before, sometimes behind him; sometimes in the air, sometimes as if from within the bosom of the earth. At length they died away, and a holy stillness settled on the place.

The cavalier gazed around with bewildered eye. There was neither chapel nor convent, nor humble hermitage, to be seen; nothing but a moss-grown stone pinnacle, rising out of the centre of the area, surmounted by a cross. The green sward appeared to have been sacred from the tread of man or beast, and the surrounding trees bent toward the cross, as if in adoration.

The cavalier felt a sensation of holy awe. He alighted, and tethered his steed on the skirts of the forest, where he might crop the tender herbage; then approaching the cross, he knelt and poured forth his evening prayers before this relic of the Christian days of Spain. His orisons being concluded, he laid himself down at the foot of the pinnacle, and reclining his head against one of its stones, fell into a deep sleep.

About midnight, he was awakened by the tolling of a bell, and found himself lying before the gate of an ancient convent. A train of nuns passed by, each bearing a taper. He rose and followed them into the chapel; in the centre was a bier, on which lay the corpse of an aged nun. The organ performed a solemn requiem, the nuns joining in chorus. When the funeral service was finished, a melodious voice chanted, "*Requiescat in pace!*"—"May she rest in peace!" The lights immediately vanished; the whole passed away as a dream; and the cavalier found himself at the foot of the cross, and beheld, by the faint rays of the rising moon, his steed quietly grazing near him.

When the day dawned, he descended the hill, and following the course of a small brook, came to a cave, at the entrance of which was seated an ancient man, in hermit's garb, with rosary and cross, and a beard that descended to his girdle. He was one of those holy anchorites permitted by the Moors to live unmolested in the dens and caves, and humble hermitages, and even to practise the rites of their religion. The cavalier, dismounting, knelt and craved a benediction. He then related all that had befallen him in the night, and besought the hermit to explain the mystery.

"What thou hast heard and seen, my son," replied the other, "is but a type and shadow of the woes of Spain."

He then related the foregoing story of the miraculous deliverance of the convent.

"Forty years," added the holy man, "have elapsed since this event, yet the bells of that sacred edifice are still heard, from time to time, sounding from underground, together with the pealing of the organ, and the chanting of the choir. The Moors avoid this neighborhood, as haunted ground, and the whole place, as thou mayest perceive, has become covered with a thick and lonely forest."

The cavalier listened with wonder to the story. For three days and nights did he keep vigils with the holy man beside the cross; but nothing more was to be seen of nun or convent. It is supposed that, forty years having elapsed, the natural lives of all the nuns were finished, and the cavalier had beheld the obsequies of the last. Certain it is, that from that time, bell, and organ, and choral chant, have never more been heard.

The mouldering pinnacle, surmounted by the cross, remains an object of pious pilgrimage. Some say that it anciently stood in front of the convent, but others that it was the spire which remained above ground, when the main body of the building sank, like the topmast of some tall ship that has foundered. These pious believers maintain, that the convent is miraculously preserved entire in the centre of the mountain, where, if proper excavations were made, it would be found, with all its treasures, and monuments, and shrines, and relics, and the tombs of its virgin nuns.

Should any one doubt the truth of this marvellous interposition of the Virgin, to protect the vestal purity of her votaries let him read the excellent work entitled "España Triumphante," written by Fray Antonio de Sancta Maria, a barefoot friar of the Carmelite order, and he will doubt no longer.

THE LONG CHAMBER

OLIVIA HOWARD DUNBAR

THERE WAS PERHAPS NO WARRANT FOR THE VAGUELY SWELLING DISQUIET THAT possessed me from the moment that, late in the sultry August afternoon, there arrived the delayed telegram that announced the immediate coming of Beatrice Vesper.

. . . Beatrice Vesper abruptly on her way to me, and alone—it was the most strangely unlikely news. Yet I had no cause for real concern. She would find ready conveyance over the three steep miles from the railroad—our pleasantly decaying village being unlinked with the contemporary world. And, as the others reminded me, it wasn't as though the redundant spaciousness of Burleigh House didn't seem to invite, almost to select and compel, unaccustomed guests; or as though the Long Chamber, our supreme source of pride, hadn't that morning received the final touches that consecrated it to the utmost hospitality we could offer. As for Beatrice, she would delight in the survival of Burleigh House as unfailingly as she herself would prove its most harmonious ornament. And that matter of ornament wasn't one that David and I could be said to have taken at all lightly. How prodigally, how passionately, we had spent our love and labor on the precious house, in the months since it had so unexpectedly fallen into our hands—only to admit to each other, at the end of it all, in almost hysterical dismay, that the stately interiors seemed always empty, however vociferously we strove to be at home in them. There were void, waiting spaces that not the sum of all our alien, cheerful presences could fill. We had achieved a background, but a background for brilliant life; and it was as though we, living in terms of the palest prose, defiled past it almost invisibly. The truth was that we had established no spiritual tenancy, and that we didn't, ourselves, belong there. But though I was far from guessing with what mysterious tentacles the past would seize her, I knew that Beatrice Vesper would belong.

It was plain enough, however, from the first sight of my old friend, that she had come to me in no unhappy stress. Her secure and unvexed air was for an instant disconcerting; I had, in my panic, so prepared myself for haggard pathos. And indeed it was almost incredible that the hurrying, untender years should not have bruised so delicate a creature. With swiftly relaxing nerves I surrendered to the flattery of her explanation that when, only the day before, her husband had been summoned to Europe by cable—she herself being kept behind by the important final proof-reading of a technical work of Dr. Vesper's, to be published in the early autumn—she had from all her social resources chosen Burleigh House as her temporary refuge. . . . So that, after all, it seemed stupid to have taken fright. Beatrice and I had been the closest companions in earlier days. And doubtless I had exaggerated those conditions of her life which, for years past, had led her friends into the way of speaking of her ruefully, reminiscently, almost as if she were dead.

It was in this latter spirit that I had been speaking of her to David, only the day before, picturing her as the only woman I knew whose marriage had been complete self-immolation. Those of us who wore our fetters with a more modern jauntiness had resented, from our ill-informed distance, what seemed to be her slavish submission. She might as well have been chained in a cave—the rest of the world had not a glimpse of her. Dr. Vesper—a mild enough tyrant in appearance—did not care for society, so they had literally no visitors. There prevailed a legend that he was the most miserable of dyspeptics; and that Beatrice devoted most of her time to preparing the unheard-of substances that fed him. His financial concerns—for important mining interests had sprung from the geological work in which he had become famous—kept him in the city throughout the year, and Beatrice had never left him for a day, even in torrid midsummer.

But David, who is sturdily unmodern, refused to be astonished. "Why not, if she's in love with him?" he asked.

"But she's not," I insisted "or—she wasn't. It's her husband who's in love, and with the most unheard-of concentration. He has cared for her ever since she was a child, so the thing hung over her—though I suppose that's not a romantic way of putting it—for years before they were married. So isn't it rather extreme for her to relinquish everything else in the world for the sake of the man she merely—likes?"

David may have submitted a discreet version of this to our old friend Anthony Lloyd, who had been with us all that summer, and I imagine that in consequence both men looked to find in Beatrice Vesper the dull, heavy-domestic type. So when, an hour after her arrival, they saw her vivid smile and smooth black hair and her young, slim figure in its mulberry-colored taffeta against the dark panels of our candle-lighted dining-room, they both bore very definite evidence of response to her loveliness. Anthony even betrayed his admiration a shade too markedly, for he had rather an assured way of paying court to women who attracted him. But his advance was deftly and unmistakably cut off. Beatrice Vesper's wifely attitude remained true, I saw, to its severely classic pattern.

However, pitfalls of this order were easily avoided, teased as we all were by the irresistible topic of our dazzling inheritance. And David was shortly embarked upon his familiar contention that we cared much more for the place than if he had been the direct heir and we had been able to anticipate the glory of ownership.

"Oh, we're very humble," David conceded, "but we do claim credit as resuscitators. That's what we've really felt ourselves to be doing for months—breathing life into a beautiful thing that had been left for dead. And it has begun to live again, don't you think, in a feeble way? But it's as showmen that we're so shockingly deficient. You see a house that Judge Timothy Burleigh built in 1723 and that was continuously lived in until they deserted it a generation ago, must—well, must have its secrets. But we have to admit we don't know them."

"Oh, do you think you *can* live here without knowing?" Beatrice broke out with an intensity that surprised us all. "You'll divine them, if you learn them in no other way. Family traditions can never be smothered, you know—they cling too imperishably!"

"But the legend famine has already been relieved," Anthony announced, "or we assume that it has. At least, we've found a group of old trunks, filled with papers, and they've all been assigned to me, to dig secrets from. I'm going to begin in the morning."

"It's not that Molly and I haven't longed to dig for ourselves," David hastily defended us, "but we haven't had time. And as for divination—our imaginations lack the necessary point of departure because our cousins have kept all the portraits. That's the really serious gap, you'll notice, in our conscientious furnishing—that apparently we've sprung from the soil, that we haven't an ancestor. Though of course we have seen the old pictures, long ago, or I have."

"Oh, what were they—" Beatrice began.

"Mrs. Vesper, need you ask?" Anthony interrupted. "Wigged men with heavy, hawk-nosed faces—"

"And meek-eyed women," David assented, laughing. "Yes, they do look like that, mostly. The Burleighs were a formidable race and their wives must have been unnaturally submissive."

"But that's according to the Colonial portrait-painter's conventions," Anthony argued. "The very earliest of your portraits must have been painted less than two hundred years ago. Well, that's time enough for fashions in portraits to change; but do human beings alter essentially? The old Burleighs cannot have been so different, inside their Colonial purple and fine linen, from you and Molly. Your hawk-nosed grandfathers must have enjoyed a joke, now and then, and those meek-eyed Patiences and Charities—mustn't they have had their emotions?"

"There must be conditions so harsh that emotions remain latent," I suggested, carelessly.

But Anthony never missed an occasion to dogmatize, after his own fashion: "I admit there are temperaments that cannot love, for instance. But to those that can the opportunity doesn't fail."

"But surely," he roused me to protest, "there is a type of woman who never learns her own capacity, who remains ingenuous, undeveloped—"

"Only until her appointed time," Anthony extravagantly persisted.

"What you are trying to express," David flouted, "is the old-fashioned schoolgirlish belief in predestined lovers. And perhaps it has remained for you to explain what happens in case the predestined lover dies!"

"In that case he'll come back from the dead to teach her!" But this point was made amid a shout of laughter, and we all conceded that the subject had been carried as far as it could be.

Almost immediately after dinner, Beatrice confessing that she was very tired, I rather self-consciously took a pewter candlestick from its stand in the lower hall and guided her up-stairs. And I found myself weakly unable to bid her good night without a fond proprietary emphasis on the treasures of the Long Chamber, its ancient oaken chests and still more ancient powdering-table, its carved bed and woven counterpane, even the long mirror, faintly time-blurred, in which we had been told that Anne Burleigh, the first mistress of the house, used once to contemplate her charming face and towering head-dress.

"Then, of course, it contains her image still." Beatrice's smiling, confident glance seemed to penetrate with singular ease the delicate clouds with which two centuries had lightly flecked the glass. "I shall see it, of course, after she gets used to me. I wonder if this was her room?"

"That is one of the thousand things we don't know," I lamented. "But it may well have been. It is the finest, we think, of all the rooms. Judge Timothy's lovely young wife should have had it!"

"Don't you think it's almost heartless to have preserved her mere possessions," Beatrice admonished me, "and yet allow the memories of her life to be so scattered? We must gather them up and piece them together!"

"Reconstruction ought not to be too difficult in her case," I laughed. "I imagine she was a simple creature."

It was our household custom to breakfast in our rooms, and after that to pursue our independent occupations throughout the greater part of the day. But Beatrice's proof-sheets and documents, which were of the most inordinate bulk, and which further depressingly renewed themselves by express every few days, often consumed her evenings likewise. It had struck me that we might achieve an arid semblance of friendly intercourse if she would assign to me some clerkly and mechanical part of her labors. But I saw from her look that it was as though I had asked a priestess to delegate to me her hieratic function. Her fealty to her dingy religion of ink and paper and chemical symbols was inflexible. And unreasoning, I thought, since it had cost her the look of freshness and vigor she had worn on coming to us. The thing was consuming her—her altered face told the story. Two weeks, indeed, after she had come, I realized that we had not yet had a comfortable talk together. What, after all, did I know of this new Beatrice, except that her highly decorative presence justified our otherwise empty splendor, and that for her own part she was working herself into an illness. She had come to us, she said, for rest and country peace and a season of friendship, but it was patent to the point of irony that she was profiting by none of these. And I did confess to myself, I remember, a secret hurt that there were so many days when she was unable, or ostensibly so, to join us at the hour of frank idleness when we took our tea under the oak-tree on the lawn, and when we always, sooner or later, fell to talking of our somewhat shadowy guest.

"Is it I whom Mrs. Vesper is avoiding?" Anthony asked, rather wistfully, one afternoon. "I'll admit I didn't seize her tone directly she arrived, but I have it now—completely! She would find me irreproachable if she would only mingle with us a little. How comforting it would be if she had a human liking for tennis and riding!"

"My dear Anthony, I don't think she knows you are under the same roof, except when she sees you at dinner," I assured him. "But she's under the thrall of an inhuman husband who is overworking her from the other end of the world and practically denying us any share in her."

"Are you so sure it's overwork," David demanded, "and not the beginning of typhoid? She does look downright ill, you know. My own impulse would be to send for a doctor. Could there be anything unwholesome about the house—any eighteenth-century germ that has escaped our scourings?"

We all brooded for a moment on the possibility this opened.

"Do you think distraction would help her?" Anthony asked. "Because I have it here!"—he tapped his breast-pocket, triumphantly. "I've patched together in the last few days a good part of the history of Burleigh House. I had meant not to tell you yet, but secrecy is consuming me."

"Dole the stories out to us one at a time," David lazily suggested, his interest half-paralyzed by the sheer weight of the August atmosphere. "We'll inaugurate a series of Nights—if not a Thousand and One, then as many as you please. And you'll begin to-night, of course. Can you go as far back as Judge Timothy?"

"Yes—if you would rather begin there. Though I hadn't planned—"

"Then it's settled," I interrupted. And this was indeed so precisely what we had all been thirstily waiting for that I thought it a sufficient pretext for disturbing Beatrice on the spot. Moreover, David's hints had freshly stimulated my own smoldering anxiety in regard to my friend. I had been too passive—I should have forced her to spare herself. The unnamable fears that I had felt on the day of her arrival recurred and pierced me.

In the Long Chamber I found her rather wearily putting away her work for the day. She stood by her table, a slender, drooping figure with a sheaf of fluttering papers in her hand, and faced me—still without the look of affectionate welcome I had so missed of late; merely with a sweet patience and courtesy. I should perhaps have approached my end by gentle, gradual arts, but my concern for her abruptly overflowed in unconsidered words. I begged her to admit to me that she wasn't well, that I might insist on proper care for her. I blamed bitterly my own laxity in allowing her to wear herself out as she had done. The publication of her husband's book on a certain day could not, I urged, be a matter so imperative that she must sacrifice her youth, her life, to it. By every obligation of our old friendship I implored her to intrust herself to me—and I laid especial stress on my responsibility to her absent husband.

"You were all vigor and loveliness when you came to us," I reminded her. "And now—now—you are so changed!"

She looked at me in a half-startled fashion as I said this, and a dim, ambiguous smile trembled on her lips.

"Yes—he will find me changed." She spoke thoughtfully, but quite without emphasis. "But that is something I must face alone."

If she had said no more than this she would have left me with the impression that the distant Dr. Vesper was a subtler Bluebeard. And indeed a look of secrecy and dread that I now for the first time caught flowing darkly over her candid face was wretchedly that of the wife who has opened the forbidden door and is haunted by the intolerable knowledge that must shortly betray her. Could it, after all, be a worse than physical suffering that was draining her eyes of their look of life? She had begun to move uneasily about, and I felt that she would have been glad to have me leave her. But unable longer to endure the intervening shield, I made a desperate effort to demolish it, to force her reluctant confidence; and with hot cheeks and trembling voice I stammered crude, disconnected sentences on the frequent failure of men to understand women and situations, . . . on the indulgence with which we were forced to regard many masculine traits. . . .

"Oh, you have thought that?" she interrupted me, almost shrilly—"that my husband caused me suffering? Why, Molly, I supposed you knew, that *everybody* knew, how utterly, stainlessly good he is. It is I, oh, always I, who fall short." She took my hand gently. "You must not go until I have told you how it is." And we sat down together.

Much of what she then told me I did indeed already know, but under a different complexion from that with which she now invested it—how at nineteen she had married Edward Vesper almost frivolously, with no sense of sacredness, lightly assuming—though this was, of course, true enough—that she was bestowing a blessing by becoming the wife of the man for whom she felt a merely childlike affection. How, afterward, she had discovered that the marriage had been urged, hurried, by her poor, desperate mother, who, with four younger children, was at the end of everything; and how Dr. Vesper's money had supported them all ever since. . . .

"Then I saw," Beatrice slowly went on, after a little, though I saw what the words were costing her, "how narrowly my own foolish ignorance had saved me from baseness. I had married for my own advantage a man who gave me perfect love. Facing this, I saw that from that moment I was bound to give more than I had ever dreamed of giving. And that, if I couldn't love my husband as he so wonderfully loved me, I must at least offer him the most sedulous counterfeit I could muster. That the least abatement of unremitting devotion would be treachery. . . . Well, that has been my life, and always, until now, I have known that no woman could do more—"

She would have gone on, the momentum of an impulsive confidence is so great, but at that point the maid came in search of me, announcing dinner. So, after a violent flurry of dressing, Beatrice and I contrived, ten minutes later, to be with the others in the dining-room. The disclosure she had made to me, with its intensely characteristic light on the apparent enigmas of her marriage, seemed for the time to have loosed a painful restraint. She talked with gentle gaiety, exchanging swift jests with the imperturbable Anthony, for whom I knew she had come to have a genuine liking, and seeming humanly at home with all of us, rather than driven, as one could fancy her latterly to have been, by some invisible harriers.

It even seemed natural and expected when, after dinner, Beatrice, who had so often spent her evenings alone, chose to seat herself at the old spinet and coax from it a few dim spectral chords.

"There's the prelude for your story, Anthony," David remarked when she had finished.

"It's a perfect one," Anthony declared. "Those are, of course, the very sounds with which Anne Burleigh beguiled her solemn days."

I had caught a note in his voice that awed me a little. "Anne Burleigh—you're to tell us of her! Then it won't, of course, be a cheerful story. Why is it that it has always been she, rather than any of the others, for whom our hearts have vaguely ached?"

"Cheerful? But of course not," Anthony rejoined with energy. "It can't be that you wanted me to discover simple tales of domestic lethargy. That isn't the sort of thing that leaves its impress on a family—and a house. That wouldn't be a story."

Then, as we urged him to begin, he altered his tone and turned to David a serious face. "You'll have to understand," he said, "that I'm taking a great liberty—with you and with your ancestors. This story that I've made out and that I'll repeat to you is, as a matter of fact, very largely—inferred. It's by no means an explicit tradition. But the inference seems to me so plain—and after living here in the house it is, oddly, so credible—and, well, you must forgive me if, after all, you prefer to leave the inference unformulated."

None of us spoke; and I let my sewing drop in my lap.

"As you know," Anthony began, "Judge Timothy Burleigh married Anne Steele when she was seventeen. A year or two afterward, when they were living in this new and splendid Burleigh House, Sophia Steele, the young wife's sister, came to pay a visit. In this young girl's diary, which tells so much else, and which I've had the astonishing fortune to discover, she records her impression of her sister, who looked 'very maidenly, though the wife of so great a man and the mistress of so fine a house.' But I won't read you her crabbed little sentences—you can see them for yourselves later; I'll simply try to make a connected story. . . . "

"Judge Timothy does not appear to have markedly played the lover to his charming little bride, but Sophia heard him praise her for her obedience, saying that it was the prime virtue in a wife. I had supposed that the housewives of that day had exacting responsibilities, but possibly because it was so fine a thing to be the Judge's wife, or else because her youth exempted her, little Mistress Burleigh seems to have had abundant leisure. She would play the spinet for hours at a time or she would sit with her baby boy—"

"The boy must have been Colonel Jonathan," David, who has always been rather too fond of facts, interposed. "Anne Burleigh had but one child."

"You see her, don't you, as I do," Anthony went on, "forlorn little Maeterlinckian heroine, treated as a child by her husband and practising rigidly the submission he exacted of her? It must have been a dull household, in spite of the splendid entertaining that took place at intervals, or sister Sophia wouldn't have had so much leisure to write in her diary. And it must have been an unnatural one, or—the climax wouldn't have flamed so suddenly. Something had to happen in such a house—and it did happen, as I make out, when a young relative of the Burleighs from Virginia came North to seek advancement in the law through his distinguished relative, the Judge. This young man, Brian Calvert, was asked to Burleigh House as a guest. It is very plain that he was keenly admired from the first by little sister Sophia, who meticulously describes his height and beauty and 'merry manners.' The Judge, I imagine, did not diffuse much merriment through the house. But the Virginian probably didn't see little Sophia; his attention was too completely and frankly absorbed. So she stayed apart, a sad, involuntary little spy, not critical or even fully comprehending, but vaguely and innocently envious, I gather, of an unknown mysterious thing with which the air about her had suddenly become surcharged. Anne Burleigh herself, poor child, was doubtless almost as far from understanding what had befallen her. At all events, there seems to have been no concealment. Anne and Calvert spent long days together, sitting under the trees in the garden. No one knows whether he said a word of love to her—I could almost believe that he did not. But the young, innocent creatures were none the less firmly in the grasp of the elemental force that was about to shatter them. It may have been love of the kind that absolutely cannot yield to reason, and that could never adapt itself to a slow cooling and decline—"

"Of course, they had to die," Beatrice Vesper broke in. "One cannot love like that—and live."

Her voice held somber secrets. It was as though she were speaking of something intimately real. I tried to see her face, but the shadow veiled it. Anthony paused for a moment as though he, too, were amazed at her interruption. "Yes," he said, "there had to be a tragic issue. . . . The happenings of a certain day were told long after, but vaguely, in Sophia's journal. Perhaps the child herself only suspected. . . . One day Brian Calvert was ill and remained in his room. When evening came Anne suggested taking some supper to him. The Judge reminded her, and rather ungently, that such an errand was for a servant to perform. . . . An hour later she burst into her sister's bedroom in a passion of fear. She had for the first time eluded and disobeyed her husband, taking to Calvert's room a porringer of gruel that she had made herself. The Judge, whom she doubtless supposed busy with his books, heard her step, followed her, and, entering the room a moment later, discovered her in Calvert's arms. I am sure they had never kissed before, but to her husband this was no extenuation. The Judge forced Anne from the room. Listening outside, she heard the sound of swords—and more— and worse. . . . Brian Calvert was never seen again. Anne Burleigh herself fell ill, and a few months later she died."

I felt that we had heard as much as we could bear, but David did not understand my signal, and advanced his literal and perfectly reasonable inquiry:

"Are you sure that Calvert was killed?"

"Entirely sure," Anthony said, a little dryly, "though there isn't a shadow of proof. Can you imagine such a husband hesitating or failing of his purpose?"

"You believe that they fought each other in this house?" David went on, in his solemn effort to realize the thing. "And there is no record of it? But where can it have been? You don't know that, of course?"

"Yes, I know," Anthony admitted, slowly. "It was in the guest-room. They called it the Long Chamber."

"The Long Chamber!" David repeated. And he turned toward Beatrice his honest, unperceiving eyes.

Beatrice had been sitting motionless. Now she rose hastily. "Why should you feel it tragic that he died?" she demanded, almost with brusqueness, but without looking at any one of us. "He would have chosen it. It was no unwilling death—that much I know." Her voice, usually so calm, was roughened with agitation. "I have stayed too long," she added. "I am very tired and should have gone earlier. But the story held us so."

She was gone before I had found words to detain her, and we all sat silent. Then Anthony said:

"I felt it before I had half finished the story. I know it now. *She has seen Calvert's ghost!*"

"That's preposterous!" David exclaimed.

"Because you haven't seen it yourself?" our friend inquired, quietly. "But, my dear David, have you ever slept in that room? And in any case what would the ghost of that young lover have to say to you?"

"Or to Beatrice Vesper, for that matter?" I added.

Anthony shrugged his shoulders. "Who knows?" he said. "I admit that if it were the usual family specter, I can't conceive her risking a second encounter. But Calvert's apparition—that might perhaps be less formidable. . . . Still, it's all much queerer than I like—and I'm not even sure I want her to tell."

David began to be troubled. "Molly, you know her. We don't. Is she so infernally secretive? Could she see a ghost in our house without telling us? And why shouldn't she tell?"

I sat brooding, conscious that I was trembling a response to every lightest breath of air. There were secrets about; the troubled atmosphere was heavy with them. Something had happened to Beatrice, as any one but my dear dull David could have seen. But since we three were so blindly in the dark, how and whence could it have come? Anthony was, of course, uncommonly astute, yet I had no curiosity as to the guesses I saw him shrewdly elaborating. He did not know Beatrice's sound, unassailable simplicity as I knew it.

We were all, indeed, unnaturally alert, tensely awaiting we knew not what, so that when the door-bell rang we all started as though the sound had some portentous significance—holding our breath, fairly, until the maid came in with an envelope which she said was for Mrs. Vesper.

"It's a cable," I said. "I'll take it up to her."

A half-hour must have passed since she had gone up-stairs, yet when I knocked she came to her door fully dressed. When she saw the envelope she asked me to stay until she had read the message—which was, she told me, a moment later, from her husband. He was sailing and would arrive in a week.

With a sense of relief that was almost disloyal I welcomed this definite, prosaic event. At least it would dissipate the vapors that had gathered.

"Can't we send for him to come directly here?" I suggested. "Must you meet him in New York when it is so hot and you're not really well?"

She laid her hand gently on my arm, instinctively trying to soften the harsh abruptness of what she was about to say.

"Why shouldn't I tell you? I shall never see him again."

The words sounded so unreasoning that I felt myself growing literally cold. "But, dear Beatrice—it was such a little time ago—in this very room—that you told me—"

"Of his goodness and his love. And of the obligations they imposed on me. But now—if I can't fully meet them—if I'm not the same—"

Her phrases were still without meaning to me. I tried vaguely to protest. "But your courage—"

"Oh, I had courage—for a lifetime. But I was mercifully blindfolded. Now, when I *know*—"

Anthony's confident statement recurred to me, precipitating dim suspicions, intimations, of my own.

"Beatrice, what is it that you have learned to know?" I demanded, firmly. "What is it that you have—seen?"

She cast a quick glance toward the old mirror, dull-rimmed, garlanded, in which she had gaily told me that she expected to see Anne Burleigh's childlike face. "Seen?" she repeated. "Oh, dear Molly, it's not alone what I have *seen*. . . . But there is something that lives on here, in this room, of which I merely knew the name. . . . I have felt it almost from the first moment. And there have been hours when I have so shared in it—when I have lived with an intensity I had never dreamed of—"

"Beatrice,"—I pressed her for something more definite—"you have seen Anne Burleigh?"

"Oh, it's not she who has left the deathless element," Beatrice said. "It's the man who loved her, who loved so well that he did not need to live. You see his love was so complete that it gained an earthly immortality of its own. It is here—now. I did not know such things could be. And, oh, Molly, I have tried *not* to know! You have seen how I have struggled to fill up my time and thought with work. I have not welcomed this other new thing, I have shrunk from it. But it has seized me and stripped my eyes and dazzled them—and I know what love can be."

"Brian Calvert has taught you!" I could not help the words. And, in spite of me, they sounded like an accusation.

"If it were only a lesson I could unlearn," she answered, quietly. "If I could only forget the sweet terror of it all."

"The terror of dreams and visions? But, dear Beatrice, that fades and vanishes."

"It is already vanished. But not before it has changed me past all helping. You can see how, after this, I can never—*pretend* to love."

I did not try to press her further, for I hoped that the next day, when Anthony's story would be less vivid to us all, I could prevail on the desperation of her attitude. I did insist, however, that she should not spend the night alone, and she consented, after a little, that I should sleep with her. Or so, at least, we termed it. But my patient vigil told me plainly enough that poor Beatrice slept no more than I. It is true that I assumed—though how could I be sure?—that I had dispelled her disturbing phantasms. I did not, though I lay there expectant at her side, feel the clutch at my own heart of Brian Calvert's strangely inextinguishable love; and though in the first few pale moments of dawn I saw Beatrice's strained eyes bent steadily on Anne Burleigh's garlanded mirror, to me its unrevealing surface presented merely a reticent blur.

It did not surprise me when, an hour later, Beatrice told me that she must leave Burleigh House that morning. And indeed it seemed that to let her go—out of the reach of the ghostliness that had so preyed upon her sensitive spirit—was, at that critical moment, the best that I could do for her. Yet, strangely, even after all that she had told me, I did not guess into what utter darkness she was going. Immune as I then believed myself to spectral invasions of my own serenity, I did not know at that time, nor until long after, how the reverberations of spent lives may sometimes sound so loud as to muffle the merely human cry. All that Beatrice Vesper saw and felt as she sat in the Long Chamber and battled ineffectually with the insistent presence, or presences, that may have abided within the distances of the dim, garlanded mirror, is still, I know, beyond my vain conjecture. And there are certain bare and almost intolerable facts that seem indeed to close the door on such imaginings. . . . For Edward Vesper never saw his wife again, and a month after Beatrice's going word came to me that she was dead. We have closed the Long Chamber for all time.

THE MAN-EATING TREE

PHIL ROBINSON

PEREGRINE ORIEL, MY MATERNAL UNCLE, WAS A GREAT TRAVELLER, AS HIS prophetical sponsors at the font seemed to have guessed he would be. Indeed he had rummaged in the garrets and cellars of the earth with something more than ordinary diligence. But in the narrative of his travels he did not, unfortunately, preserve the judicious caution of Xenophon between the thing seen and the thing heard, and thus it came about that the town-councillors of Brunsbüttel (to whom he had shown a duck-billed platypus, caught alive by him in Australia, and who had him posted for an importer of artificial vermin) were not alone in their scepticism of some of the old man's tales.

Thus, for instance, who could hear and believe the tale of the man-sucking tree from which he had barely escaped with life? He called it himself *more terrible than the Upas*.

Such was his summing up of the plant; and the other day, looking it up in a botanical dictionary, I find that there is really known to naturalists a family of carnivorous plants; but I see that they are most of them very small, and prey upon little insects only. My maternal uncle, however, knew nothing of this, for he died before the days of the discovery of the sundew and pitcher plants; and grounding his knowledge of the man-sucking tree simply on his own terrible experience of it, explained its existence by theories of his own. Denying the fixity of all the laws of nature except one, that the stronger shall endeavour to consume the weaker, and holding even this fixity to be itself only a means to a greater general changefulness, he argued that—since any partial distribution of the faculty of self-defence would presume an unworthy partiality in the Creator, and since the sensual instincts of beast and vegetable are manifestly analogous—the world must be as percipient as sentient throughout. Carrying on his theory (for it was something more than hypothesis with him) a stage or two further, he arrived at the belief that, given the necessity of any imminent danger or urgent self-interest, every animal or vegetable could eventually revolutionise its nature, the wolf feeding on grass or nesting in trees, and the violet arming herself with thorns or entrapping insects.

"Many years ago," said my uncle, "I turned my restless steps towards Central Africa, and made the journey from where the Senegal empties itself into the Atlantic to the Nile, skirting the Great Desert, and reaching Nubia on my way to the eastern coast. I had with me then three native attendants—two of them brothers, the third, Otona, a young savage from the Gaboon uplands, a mere lad in his teens; and one day, leaving my mule with the two men, who were pitching my tent for the night, I went on with my gun, the boy accompanying me, towards a fern brake, which I saw in the near distance. As I approached it I found the brake was cut into two by a wide glade; and seeing a small herd of the common antelope, an excellent beast in the pot, browsing their way along the shaded side, I crept after them. Though ignorant of their real danger the herd were suspicious, and, slowly trotting along before me, enticed me for a mile or more along the verge of the fern growths. Turning a corner I suddenly became aware of a solitary tree growing in the middle of the glade—one tree alone. It struck me at once that I had never seen a tree exactly like it before; but, being intent upon venison for my supper, I looked at it only long enough to satisfy my first surprise at seeing a single plant of such rich growth flourishing luxuriantly in a spot where only the harsh fern-canes seemed to thrive.

"The deer, meanwhile, were midway between me and the tree, and looking at them I saw they were going to cross the glade. Exactly opposite them was an opening in the forest, in which I should certainly have lost my supper; so I fired into the middle of the party as they were filing before me. I hit a young fawn, and the rest of the herd, wheeling round in their sudden terror, made off in the direction of the tree, leaving the fawn struggling on the ground. Otona, the boy, ran forward at my order to secure it, but the little creature seeing him coming, attempted to follow its comrades, and at a slow pace held on their course. The herd had meanwhile reached the tree, but suddenly, instead of passing under it, they swerved in their career, and swept round it at some yards distance.

"*Was I mad, or did the plant really try to catch the deer?* On a sudden I saw, or thought I saw, the tree violently agitated, and while the ferns all round were standing motionless in the dead evening air, its boughs were swayed by some sudden gust towards the herd, and swept, in the force of their impulse, almost to the ground. I drew my hand across my eyes, closed them for a moment, and looked again. The tree was as motionless as myself!

"Towards it, and now close to it, the boy was running in excited pursuit of the fawn. He stretched out his hands to catch it. It bounded from his eager grasp. Again he reached forward, and again it escaped him. There was another rush forward, and the next instant boy and deer were beneath the tree.

"*And now there was no mistaking what I saw.*

"The tree was convulsed with motion, leaned forward, swept its thick foliaged boughs to the ground, and enveloped from my sight the pursuer and the pursued. I was within a hundred yards, and the cry of Otona from the midst of the tree came to me in all the clearness of its agony. There was then one stifled, strangling scream, and except for the agitation of the leaves where they had closed upon the boy, there was not a sign of life!

"I called out 'Otona!' No answer came. I tried to call out again, but my utterance was like that of some wild beast smitten at once with sudden terror and its death wound. I stood there, changed from all semblance of a human being. Not all the terrors of earth together could have made me take my eye from the awful plant, or my foot off the ground. I must have stood thus for at least an hour, for the shadows had crept out from the forest half across the glade before that hideous possession of fear left me. My first impulse then was to creep stealthily away lest the tree should perceive me, but my returning reason bade me approach it. The boy might have fallen into the lair of some beast of prey, or perhaps the terrible life in the tree was that of some great serpent among its branches. Preparing to defend myself I approached the silent tree,—the harsh grass crisping beneath my feet with a strange loudness, the cicadas in the canes shrilling till the air seemed throbbing round me with waves of sound. The terrible truth was soon before me in all its awful novelty.

"The vegetable first discovered my presence at about fifty yards distance. I then became aware of a stealthy motion among the thick-lipped leaves, reminding me of some wild beast slowly gathering itself up from long sleep, a vast coil of snakes in restless motion. Have you ever seen bees hanging from a bough—a great cluster of bodies, bee clinging to bee—and by striking the bough, or agitating the air, caused that massed life to begin sulkily to disintegrate, each insect asserting its individual right to move? And do you remember how without one bee leaving the pensile cluster, the whole became gradually instinct with sullen life and horrid with a multitudinous motion?

"I came within twenty yards of it. The tree was quivering through every bough, muttering for blood, and, helpless with rooted feet, yearning with every branch towards me. It was that terror of the deep sea which the men of the northern fiords dread, and which, anchored upon some sunken rock, stretches into vain space its longing arms, pellucid as the sea itself, and as relentless—maimed Polypheme groping for his victims.

"Each separate leaf was agitated and hungry. Like hands they fumbled together, their fleshy palms curling upon themselves and again unfolding, closing on each other and falling apart again—thick, helpless, fingerless hands (rather lips or tongues than hands) dimpled closely with little cup-like hollows. I approached nearer and nearer, step by step, till I saw that these soft horrors were all of them in motion, opening and closing incessantly.

"I was now within ten yards of the farthest reaching bough. Every part of it was hysterical with excitement. The agitation of its members was awful—sickening yet fascinating. In an ecstacy of eagerness for the food so near them, the leaves turned upon each other. Two meeting would suck together face to face, with a force that compressed their joint thickness to a half, thinning the two leaves into one, now grappling in a volute like a double shell, writhing like some green worm, and at last, faint with the violence of the paroxysm, would slowly separate, falling apart as leeches gorged drop off the limbs. A sticky dew glistened in the dimples, welled over, and trickled down the leaf. The sound of it dripping from leaf to leaf made it seem as if the tree was muttering to itself. The beautiful golden fruit as they swung here and there were clutched now by one leaf and now by another, held for a moment close enfolded from the sight, and then as suddenly released. Here a large leaf, vampire-like, had sucked out the juices of a smaller one. It hung limp and bloodless, like a carcass of which the weasel has tired.

"I watched the terrible struggle till my starting eyes, strained by intense attention, refused their office, and I can hardly say what I saw. But the tree before me seemed to have become a live beast. Above me I felt conscious was a great limb, and each of its thousand clammy hands reached downwards towards me, fumbling. It strained, shivered, rocked, and heaved. It flung itself about in despair. The boughs, tantalised to madness with the presence of flesh, were tossed to this side and to that, in the agony of a frantic desire. The leaves were wrung together as the hands of one driven to madness by sudden misery. I felt the vile dew spurting from the tense veins fall upon me. My clothes began to give out a strange odour. The ground I stood on glistened with animal juices.

"Was I bewildered by terror? Had my senses abandoned me in my need? I know not—but the tree seemed to me to be alive. Leaning over towards me, it seemed to be pulling up its roots from the softened ground, and to be moving towards me. A mountainous monster, with myriad lips, mumbling together for my life, was upon me!

"Like one who desperately defends himself from imminent death, I made an effort for life, and fired my gun at the approaching horror. To my dizzied senses the sound seemed far off, but the shock of the recoil partially recalled me to myself, and starting back I reloaded. The shot had torn their way into the soft body of the great thing. The trunk as it received the wound shuddered, and the whole tree was struck with a sudden quiver. A fruit fell down—slipping from the leaves, now rigid with swollen veins, as from carven foliage. Then I saw a large arm slowly droop, and without a sound it was severed from the juice-fattened bole, and sank down softly, noiselessly, through the glistening leaves. I fired again, and another vile fragment was powerless—*dead*. At each discharge the terrible vegetable yielded a life. Piecemeal I attacked it, killing here a leaf and there a branch. My fury increased with the slaughter till, when my ammunition was exhausted, the splendid giant was left a wreck—as if some hurricane had torn through it. On the ground lay heaped together the fragments, struggling, rising and falling, gasping. Over them drooped in dying languor a few stricken boughs, while upright in the midst stood, dripping at every joint, the glistening trunk.

"My continued firing had brought up one of my men on my mule. He dared not, so he told me, come near me, thinking me mad. I had now drawn my hunting-knife, and with this was fighting—with the leaves. Yes—but each leaf was instinct with a horrid life; and more than once I felt my hand entangled for a moment and seized as if by sharp lips. Ignorant of the presence of my companion I made a rush forward over the fallen foliage, and with a last paroxysm of frenzy drove my knife up to the handle into the soft bole, and, slipping on the fast congealing sap, fell exhausted and unconscious, among the still panting leaves.

"My companion carried me back to the camp, and after vainly searching for Otona awaited my return to consciousness. Two or three hours elapsed before I could speak, and several days before I could approach the terrible thing. My men would not go near it. It was quite dead; for as we came up a great-billed bird with gaudy plumage that had been securely feasting on the decaying fruit, flew up from the wreck. We removed the rotting foliage, and there among the dead leaves still limp with juices, and piled round the roots, we found the ghastly relics of many former meals, and—its last nourishment—the corpse of little Otona. To have removed the leaves would have taken too long, so we buried the body as it was with a hundred vampire leaves still clinging to it."

Such, as nearly as I remember it, was my uncle's story of the man-eating tree.

The Man with the Roller

E. G. Swain

On the edge of that vast tract of East Anglia, which retains its ancient name of the Fens, there may be found, by those who know where to seek it, a certain village called Stoneground. It was once a picturesque village. Today it is not to be called either a village, or picturesque. Man dwells not in one "house of clay," but in two, and the material of the second is drawn from the earth upon which this and the neighbouring villages stood. The unlovely signs of the industry have changed the place alike in aspect and in population. Many who have seen the fossil skeletons of great saurians brought out of the clay in which they have lain from pre-historic times, have thought that the inhabitants of the place have not since changed for the better. The chief habitations, however, have their foundations not upon clay, but upon a bed of gravel which anciently gave to the place its name, and upon the highest part of this gravel stands, and has stood for many centuries, the Parish Church, dominating the landscape for miles around.

Stoneground, however, is no longer the inaccessible village, which in the middle ages stood out above a waste of waters. Occasional floods serve to indicate what was once its ordinary outlook, but in more recent times the construction of roads and railways, and the drainage of the Fens, have given it freedom of communication with the world from which it was formerly isolated.

The Vicarage of Stoneground stands hard by the Church, and is renowned for its spacious garden, part of which, and that (as might be expected) the part nearest the house, is of ancient date. To the original plot successive Vicars have added adjacent lands, so that the garden has gradually acquired the state in which it now appears.

The Vicars have been many in number. Since Henry de Greville was instituted in the year 1140 there have been 30, all of whom have lived, and most of whom have died, in successive vicarage houses upon the present site.

The present incumbent, Mr. Batchel, is a solitary man of somewhat studious habits, but is not too much enamoured of his solitude to receive visits, from time to time, from schoolboys and such. In the summer of the year 1906 he entertained two, who are the occasion of this narrative, though still unconscious of their part in it, for one of the two, celebrating his 15th birthday during his visit to Stoneground, was presented by Mr. Batchel with a new camera, with which he proceeded to photograph, with considerable skill, the surroundings of the house.

One of these photographs Mr. Batchel thought particularly pleasing. It was a view of the house with the lawn in the foreground. A few small copies, such as the boy's camera was capable of producing, were sent to him by his young friend, some weeks after the visit, and again Mr. Batchel was so much pleased with the picture, that he begged for the negative, with the intention of having the view enlarged.

The boy met the request with what seemed a needlessly modest plea. There were two negatives, he replied, but each of them had, in the same part of the picture, a small blur for which there was no accounting otherwise than by carelessness. His desire, therefore, was to discard these films, and to produce something more worthy of enlargement, upon a subsequent visit.

Mr. Batchel, however, persisted in his request, and upon receipt of the negative, examined it with a lens. He was just able to detect the blur alluded to; an examination under a powerful glass, in fact revealed something more than he had at first detected. The blur was like the nucleus of a comet as one sees it represented in pictures, and seemed to be connected with a faint streak which extended across the negative. It was, however, so inconsiderable a defect that Mr. Batchel resolved to disregard it. He had a neighbour whose favourite pastime was photography, one who was notably skilled in everything that pertained to the art, and to him he sent the negative, with the request for an enlargement, reminding him of a long-standing promise to do any such service, when as had now happened, his friend might see fit to ask it.

This neighbour who had acquired such skill in photography was one Mr. Groves, a young clergyman, residing in the Precincts of the Minster near at hand, which was visible from Mr. Batchel's garden. He lodged with a Mrs. Rumney, a superannuated servant of the Palace, and a strong-minded vigorous woman still, exactly such a one as Mr. Groves needed to have about him. For he was a constant trial to Mrs. Rumney, and but for the wholesome fear she begot in him, would have converted his rooms into a mere den. Her carpets and tablecloths were continually bespattered with chemicals; her chimney-piece ornaments had been unceremoniously stowed away and replaced by labelled bottles; even the bed of Mr. Groves was, by day, strewn with drying films and mounts, and her old and favourite cat had a bald patch on his flank, the result of a mishap with the pyrogallic acid.

Mrs. Rumney's lodger, however, was a great favourite with her, as such helpless men are apt to be with motherly women, and she took no small pride in his work. A life-size portrait of herself, originally a peace-offering, hung in her parlour, and had long excited the envy of every friend who took tea with her.

"Mr. Groves," she was wont to say, "is a nice gentleman, AND a gentleman; and chemical though he may be, I'd rather wait on him for nothing than what I would on anyone else for twice the money."

Every new piece of photographic work was of interest to Mrs. Rumney, and she expected to be allowed both to admire and to criticise. The view of Stoneground Vicarage, therefore, was shewn to her upon its arrival. "Well may it want enlarging," she remarked, "and it no bigger than a postage stamp; it looks more like a doll's house than a vicarage," and with this she went about her work, while Mr. Groves retired to his dark room with the film, to see what he could make of the task assigned to him.

Two days later, after repeated visits to his darkroom, he had made something considerable; and when Mrs. Rumney brought him his chop for luncheon, she was lost in admiration. A large but unfinished print stood upon his easel, and such a picture of Stoneground Vicarage was in the making as was calculated to delight both the young photographer and the Vicar.

Mr. Groves spent only his mornings, as a rule, in photography. His afternoons he gave to pastoral work, and the work upon this enlargement was over for the day. It required little more than "touching up," but it was this "touching up" which made the difference between the enlargements of Mr. Groves and those of other men. The print, therefore, was to be left upon the easel until the morrow, when it was to be finished. Mrs. Rumney and he, together, gave it an admiring inspection as she was carrying away the tray, and what they agreed in admiring most particularly was the smooth and open stretch of lawn, which made so excellent a foreground for the picture. "It looks," said Mrs. Rumney, who had once been young, "as if it was waiting for someone to come and dance on it."

Mr. Groves left his lodgings—we must now be particular about the hours—at half-past two, with the intention of returning, as usual, at five. "As reg'lar as a clock," Mrs. Rumney was wont to say, "and a sight more reg'lar than some clocks I knows of."

Upon this day he was, nevertheless, somewhat late, some visit had detained him unexpectedly, and it was a quarter-past five when he inserted his latch-key in Mrs. Rumney's door.

Hardly had he entered, when his landlady, obviously awaiting him, appeared in the passage: her face, usually florid, was of the colour of parchment, and, breathing hurriedly and shortly, she pointed at the door of Mr. Groves' room.

In some alarm at her condition, Mr. Groves hastily questioned her; all she could say was: "The photograph! the photograph!" Mr. Groves could only suppose that his enlargement had met with some mishap for which Mrs. Rumney was responsible. Perhaps she had allowed it to flutter into the fire. He turned towards his room in order to discover the worst, but at this Mrs. Rumney laid a trembling hand upon his arm, and held him back. "Don't go in," she said, "have your tea in the parlour."

"Nonsense," said Mr. Groves, "if that is gone we can easily do another."

"Gone," said his landlady, "I wish to Heaven it was."

The ensuing conversation shall not detain us. It will suffice to say that after a considerable time Mr. Groves succeeded in quieting his landlady, so much so that she consented, still trembling violently, to enter the room with him. To speak truth, she was as much concerned for him as for herself, and she was not by nature a timid woman.

The room, so far from disclosing to Mr. Groves any cause for excitement, appeared wholly unchanged. In its usual place stood every article of his stained and ill-used furniture, on the easel stood the photograph, precisely where he had left it; and except that his tea was not upon the table, everything was in its usual state and place.

But Mrs. Rumney again became excited and tremulous. "It's there," she cried. "Look at the lawn."

Mr. Groves stepped quickly forward and looked at the photograph. Then he turned as pale as Mrs. Eumney herself.

There was a man, a man with an indescribably horrible suffering face, rolling the lawn with a large roller.

Mr. Groves retreated in amazement to where Mrs. Rumney had remained standing. "Has anyone been in here?" he asked.

"Not a soul," was the reply, "I came in to make up the fire, and turned to have another look at the picture, when I saw that dead-alive face at the edge. It gave me the creeps," she said, "particularly from not having noticed it before. If that's any-one in Stoneground, I said to myself, I wonder the Vicar has him in the garden with that awful face. It took that hold of me I thought I must come and look at it again, and at five o'clock I brought your tea in. And then I saw him moved along right in front, with a roller dragging behind him, like you see."

Mr. Groves was greatly puzzled. Mrs. Rumney's story, of course, was incredible, but this strange evil-faced man had appeared in the photograph somehow. That he had not been there when the print was made was quite certain.

The problem soon ceased to alarm Mr. Groves; in his mind it was investing itself with a scientific interest. He began to think of suspended chemical action, and other possible avenues of investigation. At Mrs. Rumney's urgent entreaty, however, he turned the photograph upon the easel, and with only its white back presented to the room, he sat down and ordered tea to be brought in.

He did not look again at the picture. The face of the man had about it something unnaturally painful: he could remember, and still see, as it were, the drawn features, and the look of the man had unaccountably distressed him.

He finished his slight meal, and having lit a pipe, began to brood over the scientific possibilities of the problem. Had any other photograph upon the original film become involved in the one he had enlarged? Had the image of any other face, distorted by the enlarging lens, become a part of this picture? For the space of two hours he debated this possibility, and that, only to reject them all. His optical knowledge told him that no conceivable accident could have brought into his picture a man with a roller. No negative of his had ever contained such a man; if it had, no natural causes would suffice to leave him, as it were, hovering about the apparatus.

His repugnance to the actual thing had by this time lost its freshness, and he determined to end his scientific musings with another inspection of the object. So he approached the easel and turned the photograph round again. His horror returned, and with good cause. The man with the roller had now advanced to the middle of the lawn. The face was stricken still with the same indescribable look of suffering. The man seemed to be appealing to the spectator for some kind of help. Almost, he spoke.

Mr. Groves was naturally reduced to a condition of extreme nervous excitement. Although not by nature what is called a nervous man, he trembled from head to foot. With a sudden effort, he turned away his head, took hold of the picture with his outstretched hand, and opening a drawer in his sideboard thrust the thing underneath a folded tablecloth which was lying there. Then he closed the drawer and took up an entertaining book to distract his thoughts from the whole matter.

In this he succeeded very ill. Yet somehow the rest of the evening passed, and as it wore away, he lost something of his alarm. At ten o'clock, Mrs. Rumney, knocking and receiving answer twice, lest by any chance she should find herself alone in the room, brought in the cocoa usually taken by her lodger at that hour. A hasty glance at the easel showed her that it stood empty, and her face betrayed her relief. She made no comment, and Mr. Groves invited none.

The latter, however, could not make up his mind to go to bed. The face he had seen was taking firm hold upon his imagination, and seemed to fascinate him and repel him at the same time. Before long, he found himself wholly unable to resist the impulse to look at it once more. He took it again, with some indecision, from the drawer and laid it under the lamp.

The man with the roller had now passed completely over the lawn, and was near the left of the picture.

The shock to Mr. Groves was again considerable. He stood facing the fire, trembling with excitement which refused to be suppressed. In this state his eye lighted upon the calendar hanging before him, and it furnished him with some distraction. The next day was his mother's birthday. Never did he omit to write a letter which should lie upon her breakfast-table, and the preoccupation of this evening had made him wholly forgetful of the matter. There was a collection of letters, however, from the pillar-box near at hand, at a quarter before midnight, so he turned to his desk, wrote a letter which would at least serve to convey his affectionate greetings, and having written it, went out into the night and posted it.

The clocks were striking midnight as he returned to his room. We may be sure that he did not resist the desire to glance at the photograph he had left on his table. But the results of that glance, he, at any rate, had not anticipated. The man with the roller had disappeared. The lawn lay as smooth and clear as at first, "looking," as Mrs. Rumney had said, "as if it was waiting for someone to come and dance on it."

The photograph, after this, remained a photograph and nothing more. Mr. Groves would have liked to persuade himself that it had never undergone these changes which he had witnessed, and which we have endeavoured to describe, but his sense of their reality was too insistent. He kept the print lying for a week upon his easel. Mrs. Rumney, although she had ceased to dread it, was obviously relieved at its disappearance, when it was carried to Stoneground to be delivered to Mr. Batchel. Mr. Groves said nothing of the man with the roller, but gave the enlargement, without comment, into his friend's hands. The work of enlargement had been skilfully done, and was deservedly praised.

Mr. Groves, making some modest disclaimer, observed that the view, with its spacious foreground of lawn, was such as could not have failed to enlarge well. And this lawn, he added, as they sat looking out of the Vicar's study, looks as well from within your house as from without. It must give you a sense of responsibility, he added, reflectively, to be sitting where your predecessors have sat for so many centuries and to be continuing their peaceful work. The mere presence before your window, of the turf upon which good men have walked, is an inspiration.

The Vicar made no reply to these somewhat sententious remarks. For a moment he seemed as if he would speak some words of conventional assent. Then he abruptly left the room, to return in a few minutes with a parchment book.

"Your remark, Groves," he said as he seated himself again, "recalled to me a curious bit of history: I went up to the old library to get the book. This is the journal of William Longue who was Vicar here up to the year 1602. What you said about the lawn will give you an interest in a certain portion of the journal. I will read it."

Aug. 1, 1600.—I am now returned in haste from a journey to
Brightelmstone whither I had gone with full intention to remain about
the space of two months. Master Josiah Wilburton, of my dear College
of Emmanuel, having consented to assume the charge of my parish of
Stoneground in the meantime. But I had intelligence, after 12 days' absence,
by a messenger from the Churchwardens, that Master Wilburton had disappeared last Monday sennight, and had been no more seen. So here I am
again in my study to the entire frustration of my plans, and can do nothing in my perplexity but sit and look out from my window, before which
Andrew Birch rolleth the grass with much persistence. Andrew passeth so
many times over the same place with his roller that I have just now stepped
without to demand why he so wasteth his labour, and upon this he hath
pointed out a place which is not levelled, and hath continued his rolling.

Aug. 2.—There is a change in Andrew Birch since my absence, who hath
indeed the aspect of one in great depression, which is noteworthy of so
chearful a man. He haply shares our common trouble in respect of Master
Wilburton, of whom we remain without tidings. Having made part of
a sermon upon the seventh Chapter of the former Epistle of St. Paul to
the Corinthians and the 27th verse, I found Andrew again at his task,
and bade him desist and saddle my horse, being minded to ride forth and
take counsel with my good friend John Palmer at the Deanery, who bore
Master Wilburton great affection.

Aug. 2 continued.—Dire news awaiteth me upon my return. The Sheriff's
men have disinterred the body of poor Master W. from beneath the grass
Andrew was rolling, and have arrested him on the charge of being his
cause of death.

Aug. 10.—Alas! Andrew Birch hath been hanged, the Justice having
mercifully ordered that he should hang by the neck until he should be
dead, and not sooner molested. May the Lord have mercy on his soul. He
made full confession before me, that he had slain Master Wilburton in
heat upon his threatening to make me privy to certain peculation of which
I should not have suspected so old a servant. The poor man bemoaned his
evil temper in great contrition, and beat his breast, saying that he knew
himself doomed for ever to roll the grass in the place where he had tried
to conceal his wicked fact.

"Thank you," said Mr. Groves. "Has that little negative got the date upon it?" Yes,
replied Mr. Batchel, as he examined it with his glass. The boy has marked it August 10.

The Vicar seemed not to remark the coincidence with the date of Birch's execution. Needless to say that it did not escape Mr. Groves. But he kept silence about the man with the roller, who has been no more seen to this day.

Doubtless there is more in our photography than we yet know of. The camera sees more than the eye, and chemicals in a freshly prepared and active state, have a power which they afterwards lose. Our units of time, adopted for the convenience of persons dealing with the ordinary movements of material objects, are of course conventional. Those who turn the instruments of science upon nature will always be in danger of seeing more than they looked for. There is such a disaster as that of knowing too much, and at some time or another it may overtake each of us. May we then be as wise as Mr. Groves in our reticence, if our turn should come.

Many Waters
Cannot Quench Love

Louisa Baldwin

DID I NOT KNOW MY OLD FRIEND JOHN HORTON TO BE AS TRUTHFUL AS HE IS
devoid of imagination, I should have believed that he was romancing or dreaming
when he told me of a circumstance that happened to him some thirty years ago. He
was at that time a bachelor, living in London and practising as a solicitor in Bedford
Row. He was not a strong man, though neither nervous nor excitable, and as I said
before singularly unimaginative.

If Horton told you a fact, you might be certain that it had occurred in the precise
manner he stated. If he told it you a hundred times, he would not vary it in the repetition. This literal and conscientious habit of mind, made his testimony of value, and
when he told me a fact that I should have disbelieved from any other man, from my
friend I was obliged to accept it as truth.

It was during the long vacation in the autumn of 1857, that Horton determined
to take a few weeks' holiday in the country. He was such an inveterate Londoner he
had not been able to tear himself away from town for more than a few days at a time
for many years past. But at length he felt the necessity for quiet and pure air, only
he would not go far to seek them. It was easier then than it is now to find a lodging
that would meet his requirements, a place in the country yet close to the town, and it
was near Wandsworth that Horton found what he sought, rooms for a single gentleman in an old farmhouse. He read the advertisement of the lodgings in the paper
at luncheon, and went that very afternoon to see if they answered to the tempting
description given. He had some little difficulty in finding Maitland's Farm. It was
not easy to find his way through country lanes that to his town eyes looked precisely
alike, and with nothing to indicate whether he had taken a right or wrong turning.
The railway now runs shrieking over what were then green fields, lanes have been
transformed into gas-lighted streets, and Maitland's Farm, the old red brick house
standing in its high walled garden, has been pulled down long ago. The last time
Horton went to look at the old place it was changed beyond recognition, and the
orchard in which he gathered pears and apples during his stay at the farm, was now
the site of a public house and a dissenting chapel.

It was on a hot afternoon early in September when Horton opened the big iron gates and walked up the path bordered with dahlias and hollyhocks leading to the front door, and rang for admittance at Maitland's Farm. The bell echoed in a distant part of the empty house and died away into silence, but no one came to answer its summons. As Horton stood waiting he took the opportunity of thoroughly examining the outside of the house. Though it was called a farm it had not been built for one originally. It was a substantial, four-storey brick house of Queen Anne's period, with five tall sash windows on each floor, and dormer windows in the tiled roof. The front door was approached by a shallow flight of stone steps, and above the fan-light projected a penthouse of solidly carved wood-work. On either side were brackets of wrought iron, supporting extinguishers that had quenched the torch of many a late returning reveller a century ago. Only the windows to right and left of the door had blinds or curtains, or betrayed any sign of habitation. "Those are the rooms to be let, I wonder which is the bedroom," thought my friend as he rang the bell for the second time. Presently he heard within the sound of approaching footsteps, there was a great drawing of bolts and after a final struggle with the rusty lock, the door was opened by an old woman of severe and cheerless aspect. Horton was the first to speak.

"I have called to see the rooms advertised to be let in this house." The old woman eyed him from head to foot without making any reply, then opening the door wider, nodded to him to enter. He did so and found himself in a large paved hall lighted from the fan-light over the door, and by a high narrow window facing him at the top of a short flight of oak stairs. The air was musty and damp as that of an old church.

"A hall this size should have a fire in it," said Horton, glancing at the empty rusty grate.

"Farmers and folks that work out of doors keep themselves warm without fires," said the old woman sharply.

"This house was never built for a farm, why is it called one?" enquired Horton of his taciturn guide as she opened the door of the sitting-room.

"Because it was one," was the blunt reply. "When I was a girl it was the Manor House, and may be called that again for all I know, but thirty years since, a man named Maitland took it on a lease and farmed the land, and folks forgot the old name, and called it Maitland's Farm."

"When did Maitland leave?"

"About two months ago."

"Why did he go away from a nice place like this?"

"You are fond of asking questions," remarked the old woman drily. "He went for two good reasons, his lease was up, and his family was a big one. Nine children he had, from a girl of two-and-twenty down to a little lad of four years old. His wife and him thought it best to take 'em out to Australia, where there's room for all. They were glad to go, all but the eldest, Esther, and she nearly broke her heart over it. But then she had to leave her sweetheart behind her. He's a young man on a dairy farm near here, and though he's to follow her out and marry her in twelve months, she did nothing but mourn, same as if she was leaving him altogether."

"Ah, indeed!" said Horton, who could not readily enter into details about people whom he did not know. "So this is the sitting-room; it's large and airy, and has as much furniture in it as a man needs by himself. Now show me the bedroom, if you please."

"Follow me upstairs, sir," and the old woman preceded him slowly up the oak staircase, and opened the door of the back room on the first floor.

"Then the bedroom that you let is not over the sitting-room?"

"No, the front room is mine, and the room next to it is my son's. He's out all day at his work, but he sleeps here, and mostly keeps me company of an evening. I'm alone here all day looking after the place, and if you take the rooms I shall cook for you and wait on you myself."

Horton liked the look of the bedroom. It was large and airy, with little furniture in it beyond a bed and a chest of drawers. But it was delicately clean, and silent as the grave. How a tired man might sleep here! The walls were decorated with old prints in black frames of the "Rake's Progress" and "Marriage à la Mode," and above the high carved mantelpiece hung an engraving of the famous portrait of Charles the First, on a prancing brown horse.

"Those things were on the walls when the Maitlands took the place, and they had to leave 'em where they found 'em," said the old woman. "And they found that sword too," she added, pointing to a rusty cutlass that hung from a nail by the head of the bed; "but I think they'd have done no great harm if they'd sold it for old iron."

Horton took down the weapon and examined it. It was an ordinary cutlass, such as was worn by the marines in George the Third's reign, not old enough to be of antiquarian interest, nor of sufficient beauty of workmanship to make it of artistic value. He replaced it, and stepped to the windows and looked into the garden below. It was bounded by a high wall enclosing a row of poplars, and beyond lay the open country, visible for miles in the clear air, a sight to rest and fascinate the eye of a Londoner.

Horton made his bargain with the old woman whom the landlord had put into the house as caretaker, pending his decision about the disposition of the property. She was allowed to take a lodger for her own profit, and as soon as Mrs. Belt found that the stranger agreed to her terms, she assured him that everything should be comfortably arranged for his reception by the following Wednesday.

Horton arrived at Maitland's Farm on the evening of the appointed day. A stormy autumnal sunset was casting an angry glow on the windows of the house, the rising wind filled the air with mournful sounds, and the poplars swayed against a background of lurid sky.

Mrs. Belt was expecting her lodger, and promptly opened the door, candle in hand, when she heard the wheels stopping at the gate. The driver of the fly carried Horton's portmanteau into the hall, was paid his fare, and drove away thinking the darkening lanes more cheerful than the glimpse he had had of the inside of Maitland's Farm.

Horton was thoroughly pleased with his country quarters. The intense quiet of the almost empty house, that might have made another man melancholy, soothed and rested him. In the day time he wandered about the country, or amused himself in the garden and orchard, and he spent the long evenings alone, reading and smoking in his sitting-room. Mrs. Belt brought in supper at nine o'clock, and usually stayed to have a chat with her lodger, and many a long story she related of her neighbours, and the Maitland family, while she waited upon him at his evening meal.

On several occasions she told him that Esther Maitland's sweetheart, Michael Winn, had come to talk with her about the Maitlands, or to bring her a newspaper containing tidings that their ship had reached some point on its long voyage in safety.

"You see the *Petrel* is a sailing vessel, sir, and there's no saying how long she'll take getting to Australia. The last news Michael had, she'd got as far as some islands with an outlandish name, and he's had a letter from Esther posted at a place called Madeira. And now he gives himself no peace till he can hear that the ship's safe as far as—somewhere, I think he said, in Africa."

"It would be the Cape, Mrs. Belt."

"That's the name, sir, the Cape, and he werrits all the time for fear of storms and shipwrecks. But I tell him the world's a wide place, and the sea wider than all, and very likely when the chimney pots is flying about our heads in a gale here, the *Petrel*'s lying becalmed somewhere. And then he takes up my thought and turns it against me. 'Yes,' he says, 'and when it's a dead calm here on shore, the ship may be sinking in a storm, and my Esther being drowned.'"

"Michael Winn must be a very nervous young man."

"That's where it is, sir, and I tell him when he follows the Maitlands it's a good job that he leaves no one behind him that'll werrit after him, the same as he's werrited after Esther."

It was the middle of October, and Horton had been a month at the farm. The weather was now cold and wet, and he began to think it was time he returned to his snug London home, for the autumn rain made everything at Maitland's Farm damp and mouldy. It had blown half a gale all day, and the rain had fallen in torrents, keeping him a prisoner indoors. But he occupied himself in writing letters, and reading some legal documents his clerk had brought out to him, and the time passed rapidly. Indeed the evening flew by so quickly he had no idea it was nine o'clock, when Mrs. Belt entered the room to lay the cloth for supper.

"It's stopped raining now, sir," she said, as she poked the fire into a cheerful blaze, "and a good job too, for Michael Winn brings me word the Wandle's risen fearful since morning, and it's out in places more than it's been for years. But there's a full moon tonight, so no one need walk into the water unless they've a mind to."

Horton's head was too full of a knotty legal point to pay much heed to Mrs. Belt, and the old woman, seeing that he was not in a mood for conversation, said nothing further. At half-past ten she brought her lodger some spirits and hot water, and his bedroom candle, and wished him good night. Horton sat reading for some time, and then made an entry in his diary concerning a day of which there was absolutely nothing to record, lighted his candle, and went upstairs. I am familiar with the precise order of each trifling circumstance. My friend has so often told me the events of that night, and never with the slightest addition or omission in the telling. It was his habit, the last thing at night, to draw up the blinds. He looked out of the window, and though the moon was at the full, the clouds had not yet dispersed, and her light was fitful and obscure. It was twenty minutes to twelve as he extinguished the candle by his bedside. Everything was propitious for rest. He was weary, and the house profoundly silent. The rain had stopped, the wind fallen to a sigh, and it seemed to him that as soon as his head pressed the pillow he sank into a dreamless slumber.

Shortly after two o'clock Horton awoke suddenly, passing instantaneously from deep sleep to the possession of every faculty in a heightened degree, and with an insupportable sense of fear weighing upon him like a thousand nightmares. He started up and looked around him. The perspiration poured from his brow, and his heart beat to suffocation. He was convinced that he had been waked by some strange and terrible noise, that had thrilled through the depths of sleep, and he dreaded the repetition of it inexpressibly. The room was flooded with moonlight streaming through the narrow windows, lying like sheets of molten silver on the floor, and the poplars in the garden cast tremulous shadows on the ceiling.

Then Horton heard through the silence of the house a sound that was not the moan of the wind, nor the rustling of trees, nor any sound he had heard before. Clear and distinct, as though it were in the room with him, he heard a voice of weeping and lamentation, with more than human sorrow in the cry, so that it seemed to him as though he listened to the mourning of a lost soul. He leaped up, struck a match, and lighted the candle, and seizing the cutlass that hung by the bed, unlocked the door, and opened it to listen.

So far as all ordinary sounds were concerned, the house was silent as death, and the moonlight streamed through the staircase window in a flood of pale light. But the unearthly sound of weeping, thrilling through heart and soul, came from the hall below, and Horton walked downstairs to the landing at the top of the first flight. There, on the lowest step, a woman was seated with bowed head, her face hidden in her hands, rocking to and fro in extremity of grief. The moonlight fell full on her, and he saw that she was only partly clothed, and her dark hair lay in confusion on her bare shoulders.

"Who are you, and what is the matter with you?" said Horton, and his trembling voice echoed in the silent house. But she neither stirred nor spoke, nor abated her weeping. Slowly he descended the moonlit staircase till there were but four steps between him and the woman. A mortal fear was growing upon him.

"Speak! if you are a living being!" he cried. The figure rose to its full height, turned and faced him for a moment that seemed an eternity, and rushed full on the point of the cutlass Horton involuntarily presented. As the impalpable form glided up the blade of the weapon, a cold wave seemed to break over him, and he fell in a dead faint on the stairs.

How long he remained insensible he could not tell. When he came to himself and opened his eyes, the moon had set, and he groped his way in darkness to his room, where the candle had burnt itself out.

When Horton came down to breakfast, he looked as though he had been ill for a month, and his hands trembled like a drunkard's. At any other time Mrs. Belt would have been struck by his appearance, but this morning she was too much excited by some bad news she had heard, to notice whether her lodger was looking well or ill. Horton asked her how she had slept, for if she had not heard the terrible sounds that waked him, it still seemed impossible she should not have heard his heavy fall on the stairs. Mrs. Belt replied, with some astonishment at her lodger's concern for her welfare, that she had never had a better night, it was so quiet after the wind fell.

"But did your son think the house was quiet, did he sleep too?" asked Horton with feverish eagerness.

Mrs. Belt was yearning to impart her bad news to her lodger, and remarking that she had something else to do than ask folks how they slept o' nights, she said a neighbour had just told her that Michael Winn had fallen into the Wandle during the night—no one knew how—and was drowned, and they were carrying his body home then.

"What a terrible blow for his sweetheart," said Horton, greatly shocked.

"Aye! there's a pretty piece of news to send her, when she's expecting to see poor Michael himself soon."

"Mrs. Belt, have you any portrait of Esther Maitland you could show me? I've heard the girl's name so often I'm curious to know what she is like." And the old woman retired to hunt among her treasures for a small photograph on glass, that Esther had given her before she went away. Presently Mrs. Belt returned, polishing the picture with her apron.

"It's but a poor affair, sir, taken in a caravan on the Common, yet it's like the girl, it's very like."

It was a miserable production, a cheap and early effort in photography, and Horton rose from the table with the picture in his hand to examine it at the window. And there, surrounded by the thin brass frame, he recognised the face of all faces that had dismayed him, the face he beheld in the vision of the preceding night. He suppressed a groan, and turned from the window with a face so white, that, as he handed the picture back to Mrs. Belt, she said, "You're not feeling well this morning, sir?"

"No, I'm feeling very ill. I must get back to town today to be near to my own doctor. You shall be no loser by my leaving you so suddenly, but if I am going to be ill, I am best in my own home." For Horton could not have stayed another night at Maitland's Farm to save his life.

He was at his office in Bedford Row by noon, and his clerks thought that he looked ten years older for his visit to the country.

A little more than three weeks after Horton returned to town, when his nerves were beginning to recover their accustomed tone, his attention was unexpectedly recalled to the abhorrent subject of the apparition he had seen. He read in his daily paper that the mail from the Cape had brought news of the wreck of the sailing vessel *Petrel* bound for Australia, with loss of all on board, in a violent storm off the coast, shortly before the steamer left for England. By a careful comparison of dates, allowing for the variation of time, the conviction was forced upon John Horton that the ill-fated ship foundered at the very hour in which he beheld the wraith of Esther Maitland. She and her lover, divided by thousands of miles, both perished by drowning at the same time—Michael Winn in the little river at home, and Esther Maitland in the depths of a distant ocean.

The Moon-Slave

Barry Pain

The Princess Viola had, even in her childhood, an inevitable submission to the dance; a rhythmical madness in her blood answered hotly to the dance music, swaying her, as the wind sways trees, to movements of perfect sympathy and grace.

For the rest, she had her beauty and her long hair, that reached to her knees, and was thought lovable; but she was never very fervent and vivid unless she was dancing; at other times there almost seemed to be a touch of lethargy upon her. Now, when she was sixteen years old, she was betrothed to the Prince Hugo. With others the betrothal was merely a question of state. With her it was merely a question of obedience to the wishes of authority; it had been arranged; Hugo was *comme ci, comme* ça—no god in her eyes; it did not matter. But with Hugo it was quite different—he loved her.

The betrothal was celebrated by a banquet, and afterwards by a dance in the great hall of the palace. From this dance the Princess soon made her escape, quite discontented, and went to the furthest part of the palace gardens, where she could no longer hear the music calling her.

"They are all right," she said to herself as she thought of the men she had left, "but they cannot dance. Mechanically they are all right; they have learned it and don't make childish mistakes; but they are only one-two-three machines. They haven't the inspiration of dancing. It is so different when I dance alone."

She wandered on until she reached an old forsaken maze. It had been planned by a former king. All round it was a high crumbling wall with foxgloves growing on it. The maze itself had all its paths bordered with high opaque hedges; in the very centre was a circular open space with tall pine-trees growing round it. Many years ago the clue to the maze had been lost; it was but rarely now that anyone entered it. Its gravel paths were green with weeds, and in some places the hedges, spreading beyond their borders, had made the way almost impassable.

For a moment or two Viola stood peering in at the gate—a narrow gate with curiously twisted bars of wrought iron surmounted by a heraldic device. Then the whim seized her to enter the maze and try to find the space in the centre. She opened the gate and went in.

Outside everything was uncannily visible in the light of the full moon, but here in the dark shaded alleys the night was conscious of itself. She soon forgot her purpose, and wandered about quite aimlessly, sometimes forcing her way where the brambles had flung a laced barrier across her path, and a dragging mass of convolvulus struck wet and cool upon her cheek. As chance would have it she suddenly found herself standing under the tall pines, and looking at the open space that formed the goal of the maze. She was pleased that she had got there. Here the ground was carpeted with sand, fine and, as it seemed, beaten hard. From the summer night sky immediately above, the moonlight, unobstructed here, streamed straight down upon the scene.

Viola began to think about dancing. Over the dry, smooth sand her little satin shoes moved easily, stepping and gliding, circling and stepping, as she hummed the tune to which they moved. In the centre of the space she paused, looked at the wall of dark trees all round, at the shining stretches of silvery sand and at the moon above.

"My beautiful, moonlit, lonely, old dancing-room, why did I never find you before?" she cried; "but," she added, "you need music—there must be music here."

In her fantastic mood she stretched her soft, clasped hands upwards towards the moon.

"Sweet moon," she said in a kind of mock prayer, "make your white light come down in music into my dancing-room here, and I will dance most deliciously for you to see." She flung her head backward and let her hands fall; her eyes were half closed, and her mouth was a kissing mouth. "Ah! sweet moon," she whispered, "do this for me, and I will be your slave; I will be what you will."

Quite suddenly the air was filled with the sound of a grand invisible orchestra. Viola did not stop to wonder. To the music of a slow saraband she swayed and postured. In the music there was the regular beat of small drums and a perpetual drone. The air seemed to be filled with the perfume of some bitter spice. Viola could fancy almost that she saw a smouldering camp-fire and heard far off the roar of some desolate wild beast. She let her long hair fall, raising the heavy strands of it in either hand as she moved slowly to the laden music. Slowly her body swayed with drowsy grace, slowly her satin shoes slid over the silver sand.

The music ceased with a clash of cymbals. Viola rubbed her eyes. She fastened her hair up carefully again. Suddenly she looked up, almost imperiously.

"Music! more music!" she cried.

Once more the music came. This time it was a dance of caprice, pelting along over the violin-strings, leaping, laughing, wanton. Again an illusion seemed to cross her eyes. An old king was watching her, a king with the sordid history of the exhaustion of pleasure written on his flaccid face. A hook-nosed courtier by his side settled the ruffles at his wrists and mumbled, "Ravissant! Quel malheur que la vieil-lesse!" It was a strange illusion. Faster and faster she sped to the music, stepping, spinning, pirouetting; the dance was light as thistle-down, fierce as fire, smooth as a rapid stream.

The moment that the music ceased Viola became horribly afraid. She turned and fled away from the moonlit space, through the trees, down the dark alleys of the maze, not heeding in the least which turn she took, and yet she found herself soon at the outside iron gate. From thence she ran through the palace garden, hardly ever pausing to take breath, until she reached the palace itself. In the eastern sky the first signs of dawn were showing; in the palace the festivities were drawing to an end. As she stood alone in the outer hall Prince Hugo came towards her.

"Where have you been, Viola?" he said sternly. "What have you been doing?"

She stamped her little foot.

"I will not be questioned," she replied angrily.

"I have some right to question," he said.

She laughed a little.

"For the first time in my life," she said, "I have been dancing."

He turned away in hopeless silence.

The months passed away. Slowly a great fear came over Viola, a fear that would hardly ever leave her. For every month at the full moon, whether she would or no, she found herself driven to the maze, through its mysterious walks into that strange dancing-room. And when she was there the music began once more, and once more she danced most deliciously for the moon to see. The second time that this happened she had merely thought that it was a recurrence of her own whim, and that the music was but a trick that the imagination had chosen to repeat. The third time frightened her, and she knew that the force that sways the tides had strange power over her. The fear grew as the year fell, for each month the music went on for a longer time—each month some of the pleasure had gone from the dance. On bitter nights in winter the moon called her and she came, when the breath was vapour, and the trees that circled her dancing- room were black bare skeletons, and the frost was cruel. She dared not tell anyone, and yet it was with difficulty that she kept her secret. Somehow chance seemed to favour her, and she always found a way to return from her midnight dance to her own room without being observed. Each month the summons seemed to be more imperious and urgent. Once when she was alone on her knees before the lighted altar in the private chapel of the palace she suddenly felt that the words of the familiar Latin prayer had gone from her memory. She rose to her feet, she sobbed bitterly, but the call had come and she could not resist it. She passed out of the chapel and down the palace-gardens. How madly she danced that night!

She was to be married in the spring. She began to be more gentle with Hugo now. She had a blind hope that when they were married she might be able to tell him about it, and he might be able to protect her, for she had always known him to be fearless. She could not love him, but she tried to be good to him. One day he mentioned to her that he had tried to find his way to the centre of the maze, and had failed. She smiled faintly. If only she could fail! But she never did.

On the night before the wedding day she had gone to bed and slept peacefully, thinking with her last waking moments of Hugo. Overhead the full moon came up the sky. Quite suddenly Viola was wakened with the impulse to fly to the dancing-room. It seemed to bid her hasten with breathless speed. She flung a cloak around her, slipped her naked feet into her dancing-shoes, and hurried forth. No one saw her or heard her—on the marble staircase of the palace, on down the terraces of the garden, she ran as fast as she could. A thorn-plant caught in her cloak, but she sped on, tearing it free; a sharp stone cut through the satin of one shoe, and her foot was wounded and bleeding, but she sped on. As the pebble that is flung from the cliff must fall until it reaches the sea, as the white ghost-moth must come in from cool hedges and scented darkness to a burning death in the lamp by which you sit so late—so Viola had no choice. The moon called her. The moon drew her to that circle of hard, bright sand and the pitiless music.

It was brilliant, rapid music tonight. Viola threw off her cloak and danced. As she did so, she saw that a shadow lay over a fragment of the moon's edge. It was the night of a total eclipse. She heeded it not. The intoxication of the dance was on her. She was all in white; even her face was pale in the moonlight. Every movement was full of poetry and grace.

The music would not stop. She had grown deathly weary. It seemed to her that she had been dancing for hours, and the shadow had nearly covered the moon's face, so that it was almost dark. She could hardly see the trees around her. She went on dancing, stepping, spinning, pirouetting, held by the merciless music.

It stopped at last, just when the shadow had quite covered the moon's face, and all was dark. But it stopped only for a moment, and then began again. This time it was a slow, passionate waltz. It was useless to resist; she began to dance once more. As she did so she uttered a sudden shrill scream of horror, for in the dead darkness a hot hand had caught her own and whirled her round, *and she was no longer dancing alone.*

* * * * *

The search for the missing Princess lasted during the whole of the following day. In the evening Prince Hugo, his face anxious and firmly set, passed in his search the iron gate of the maze, and noticed on the stones beside it the stain of a drop of blood. Within the gate was another stain. He followed this clue, which had been left by Viola's wounded foot, until he reached that open space in the centre that had served Viola for her dancing-room. It was quite empty. He noticed that the sand round the edges was all worn down, as though someone had danced there, round and round, for a long time. But no separate footprint was distinguishable there. Just outside this track, however, he saw two footprints clearly defined close together: one was the print of a tiny satin shoe; the other was the print of a large naked foot—a cloven foot.

MUJINA

LAFCADIO HEARN

ON THE AKASAKA ROAD, IN TŌKYŌ, THERE IS A SLOPE CALLED KII-NO-KUNI-ZAKA,— which means the Slope of the Province of Kii. I do not know why it is called the Slope of the Province of Kii. On one side of this slope you see an ancient moat, deep and very wide, with high green banks rising up to some place of gardens;—and on the other side of the road extend the long and lofty walls of an imperial palace. Before the era of street-lamps and jinrikishas, this neighbourhood was very lonesome after dark; and belated pedestrians would go miles out of their way rather than mount the Kii-no-kuni-zaka, alone, after sunset.

All because of a Mujina that used to walk there.

The last man who saw the Mujina was an old merchant of the Kyōbashi quarter, who died about thirty years ago. This is the story, as he told it:—

One night, at a late hour, he was hurrying up the Kii-no-kuni-zaka, when he perceived a woman crouching by the moat, all alone, and weeping bitterly. Fearing that she intended to drown herself, he stopped to offer her any assistance or consolation in his power. She appeared to be a slight and graceful person, handsomely dressed; and her hair was arranged like that of a young girl of good family. "O-jochu⁻,"1 he exclaimed, approaching her,—"O-jochu⁻, do not cry like that! . . . Tell me what the trouble is; and if there be any way to help you, I shall be glad to help you." (He really meant what he said; for he was a very kind man.) But she continued to weep,—hiding her face from him with one of her long sleeves. "O-jochu⁻," he said again, as gently as he could,—"please, please listen to me! . . . This is no place for a young lady at night! Do not cry, I implore you!—only tell me how I may be of some help to you!" Slowly she rose up, but turned her back to him, and continued to moan and sob behind her sleeve. He laid his hand lightly upon her shoulder, and pleaded:— "O-jochu⁻!—O-jochu⁻!—O-jochu⁻! . . . Listen to me, just for one little moment! . . . O-jochu⁻—O-jochu⁻!" . . . Then that O-jochu⁻ turned round, and dropped her sleeve, and stroked her face with her hand;—and the man saw that she had no eyes or nose or mouth,—and he screamed and ran away.

---

1. O-jochū ("honourable damsel"),—a polite form of address used in speaking to a young lady whom one does not know.

Up Kii-no-kuni-zaka he ran and ran; and all was black and empty before him. On and on he ran, never daring to look back; and at last he saw a lantern, so far away that it looked like the gleam of a firefly; and he made for it. It proved to be only the lantern of an itinerant *soba*-seller,[2] who had set down his stand by the road-side; but any light and any human companionship was good after that experience; and he flung himself down at the feet of the *soba-seller*, crying out, "Aa!—aa!!—*aa!!!*"

"*Koré! koré!*" roughly exclaimed the soba-man. "Here! what is the matter with you? Anybody hurt you?"

"No—nobody hurt me," panted the other,—"only . . . *Aa!—aa!*" . . .

"—Only scared you?" queried the pedlar, unsympathetically. "Robbers?"

"Not robbers,—not robbers," gasped the terrified man. . . . "I saw . . . I saw a woman—by the moat;—and she showed me . . . *Aa!* I cannot tell you what she showed me!" . . .

"*Hé!* Was it anything like THIS that she showed you?" cried the soba-man, stroking his own face—which therewith became like unto an Egg. . . . And, simultaneously, the light went out.

---

2. *Soba* is a preparation of buckwheat, somewhat resembling vermicelli.

THE MUSIC OF ERICH ZANN

H. P. LOVECRAFT

I HAVE EXAMINED MAPS OF THE CITY WITH THE GREATEST CARE, YET HAVE NEVER again found the Rue d'Auseil. These maps have not been modern maps alone, for I know that names change. I have, on the contrary, delved deeply into all the antiquities of the place; and have personally explored every region, of whatever name, which could possibly answer to the street I knew as the Rue d'Auseil. But despite all I have done it remains an humiliating fact that I cannot find the house, the street, or even the locality, where, during the last months of my impoverished life as a student of metaphysics at the university, I heard the music of Erich Zann.

That my memory is broken, I do not wonder; for my health, physical and mental, was gravely disturbed throughout the period of my residence in the Rue d'Auseil, and I recall that I took none of my few acquaintances there. But that I cannot find the place again is both singular and perplexing; for it was within a half-hour's walk of the university and was distinguished by peculiarities which could hardly be forgotten by anyone who had been there. I have never met a person who has seen the Rue d'Auseil.

The Rue d'Auseil lay across a dark river bordered by precipitous brick blear-windowed warehouses and spanned by a ponderous bridge of dark stone. It was always shadowy along that river, as if the smoke of neighbouring factories shut out the sun perpetually. The river was also odorous with evil stenches which I have never smelled elsewhere, and which may some day help me to find it, since I should recognise them at once. Beyond the bridge were narrow cobbled streets with rails; and then came the ascent, at first gradual, but incredibly steep as the Rue d'Auseil was reached.

I have never seen another street as narrow and steep as the Rue d'Auseil. It was almost a cliff, closed to all vehicles, consisting in several places of flights of steps, and ending at the top in a lofty ivied wall. Its paving was irregular, sometimes stone slabs, sometimes cobblestones, and sometimes bare earth with struggling greenish-grey vegetation. The houses were tall, peaked-roofed, incredibly old, and crazily leaning backward, forward, and sidewise. Occasionally an opposite pair, both leaning forward, almost met across the street like an arch; and certainly they kept most of the light from the ground below. There were a few overhead bridges from house to house across the street.

The inhabitants of that street impressed me peculiarly. At first I thought it was because they were all silent and reticent; but later decided it was because they were all very old. I do not know how I came to live on such a street, but I was not myself when I moved there. I had been living in many poor places, always evicted for want of money; until at last I came upon that tottering house in the Rue d'Auseil, kept by the paralytic Blandot. It was the third house from the top of the street, and by far the tallest of them all.

My room was on the fifth story; the only inhabited room there, since the house was almost empty. On the night I arrived I heard strange music from the peaked garret overhead, and the next day asked old Blandot about it. He told me it was an old German viol-player, a strange dumb man who signed his name as Erich Zann, and who played evenings in a cheap theatre orchestra; adding that Zann's desire to play in the night after his return from the theatre was the reason he had chosen this lofty and isolated garret room, whose single gable window was the only point on the street from which one could look over the terminating wall at the declivity and panorama beyond. Thereafter I heard Zann every night, and although he kept me awake, I was haunted by the weirdness of his music. Knowing little of the art myself, I was yet certain that none of his harmonies had any relation to music I had heard before; and concluded that he was a composer of highly original genius. The longer I listened, the more I was fascinated, until after a week I resolved to make the old man's acquaintance.

One night, as he was returning from his work, I intercepted Zann in the hallway and told him that I would like to know him and be with him when he played. He was a small, lean, bent person, with shabby clothes, blue eyes, grotesque, satyr-like face, and nearly bald head; and at my first words seemed both angered and frightened. My obvious friendliness, however, finally melted him; and he grudgingly motioned to me to follow him up the dark, creaking, and rickety attic stairs. His room, one of only two in the steeply pitched garret, was on the west side, toward the high wall that formed the upper end of the street. Its size was very great, and seemed the greater because of its extraordinary bareness and neglect. Of furniture there was only a narrow iron bedstead, a dingy washstand, a small table, a large bookcase, an iron music-rack, and three old-fashioned chairs. Sheets of music were piled in disorder about the floor. The walls were of bare boards, and had probably never known plaster; whilst the abundance of dust and cobwebs made the place seem more deserted than inhabited. Evidently Erich Zann's world of beauty lay in some far cosmos of the imagination.

Motioning me to sit down, the dumb man closed the door, turned the large wooden bolt, and lighted a candle to augment the one he had brought with him. He now removed his viol from its moth-eaten covering, and taking it, seated himself in the least uncomfortable of the chairs. He did not employ the music-rack, but offering no choice and playing from memory, enchanted me for over an hour with strains I had never heard before; strains which must have been of his own devising. To describe their exact nature is impossible for one unversed in music. They were a kind of fugue, with recurrent passages of the most captivating quality, but to me were notable for the absence of any of the weird notes I had overheard from my room below on other occasions.

Those haunting notes I had remembered, and had often hummed and whistled inaccurately to myself; so when the player at length laid down his bow I asked him if he would render some of them. As I began my request the wrinkled satyr-like face lost the bored placidity it had possessed during the playing, and seemed to shew the same curious mixture of anger and fright which I had noticed when first I accosted the old man. For a moment I was inclined to use persuasion, regarding rather lightly the whims of senility; and even tried to awaken my host's weirder mood by whistling a few of the strains to which I had listened the night before. But I did not pursue this course for more than a moment; for when the dumb musician recognised the whistled air his face grew suddenly distorted with an expression wholly beyond analysis, and his long, cold, bony right hand reached out to stop my mouth and silence the crude imitation. As he did this he further demonstrated his eccentricity by casting a startled glance toward the lone curtained window, as if fearful of some intruder—a glance doubly absurd, since the garret stood high and inaccessible above all the adjacent roofs, this window being the only point on the steep street, as the concierge had told me, from which one could see over the wall at the summit. The old man's glance brought Blandot's remark to my mind, and with a certain capriciousness I felt a wish to look out over the wide and dizzying panorama of moonlit roofs and city lights beyond the hill-top, which of all the dwellers in the Rue d'Auseil only this crabbed musician could see. I moved toward the window and would have drawn aside the nondescript curtains, when with a frightened rage even greater than before the dumb lodger was upon me again; this time motioning with his head toward the door as he nervously strove to drag me thither with both hands. Now thoroughly disgusted with my host, I ordered him to release me, and told him I would go at once. His clutch relaxed, and as he saw my disgust and offence his own anger seemed to subside. He tightened his relaxing grip, but this time in a friendly manner; forcing me into a chair, then with an appearance of wistfulness crossing to the littered table, where he wrote many words with a pencil in the laboured French of a foreigner. The note which he finally handed me was an appeal for tolerance and forgiveness. Zann said that he was old, lonely, and afflicted with strange fears and nervous disorders connected with his music and with other things. He had enjoyed my listening to his music, and wished I would come again and not mind his eccentricities. But he could not play to another his weird harmonies, and could not bear hearing them from another; nor could he bear having anything in his room touched by another. He had not known until our hallway conversation that I could overhear his playing in my room, and now asked me if I would arrange with Blandot to take a lower room where I could not hear him in the night. He would, he wrote, defray the difference in rent. As I sat deciphering the execrable French I felt more lenient toward the old man. He was a victim of physical and nervous suffering, as was I; and my metaphysical studies had taught me kindness. In the silence there came a slight sound from the window— the shutter must have rattled in the night-wind—and for some reason I started almost as violently as did Erich Zann. So when I had finished reading I shook my host by the hand, and departed as a friend. The next day Blandot gave me a more expensive room on the third floor, between the apartments of an aged money-lender and the room of a respectable upholsterer. There was no one on the fourth floor.

It was not long before I found that Zann's eagerness for my company was not as great as it had seemed while he was persuading me to move down from the fifth story. He did not ask me to call on him, and when I did call he appeared uneasy and played listlessly. This was always at night—in the day he slept and would admit no one. My liking for him did not grow, though the attic room and the weird music seemed to hold an odd fascination for me. I had a curious desire to look out of that window, over the wall and down the unseen slope at the glittering roofs and spires which must lie outspread there. Once I went up to the garret during theatre hours, when Zann was away, but the door was locked.

What I did succeed in doing was to overhear the nocturnal playing of the dumb old man. At first I would tiptoe up to my old fifth floor, then I grew bold enough to climb the last creaking staircase to the peaked garret. There in the narrow hall, outside the bolted door with the covered keyhole, I often heard sounds which filled me with an indefinable dread—the dread of vague wonder and brooding mystery. It was not that the sounds were hideous, for they were not; but that they held vibrations suggesting nothing on this globe of earth, and that at certain intervals they assumed a symphonic quality which I could hardly conceive as produced by one player. Certainly, Erich Zann was a genius of wild power. As the weeks passed, the playing grew wilder, whilst the old musician acquired an increasing haggardness and furtiveness pitiful to behold. He now refused to admit me at any time, and shunned me whenever we met on the stairs.

Then one night as I listened at the door I heard the shrieking viol swell into a chaotic babel of sound; a pandemonium which would have led me to doubt my own shaking sanity had there not come from behind that barred portal a piteous proof that the horror was real—the awful, inarticulate cry which only a mute can utter, and which rises only in moments of the most terrible fear or anguish. I knocked repeatedly at the door, but received no response. Afterward I waited in the black hallway, shivering with cold and fear, till I heard the poor musician's feeble effort to rise from the floor by the aid of a chair. Believing him just conscious after a fainting fit, I renewed my rapping, at the same time calling out my name reassuringly. I heard Zann stumble to the window and close both shutter and sash, then stumble to the door, which he falteringly unfastened to admit me. This time his delight at having me present was real; for his distorted face gleamed with relief while he clutched at my coat as a child clutches at its mother's skirts. Shaking pathetically, the old man forced me into a chair whilst he sank into another, beside which his viol and bow lay carelessly on the floor. He sat for some time inactive, nodding oddly, but having a paradoxical suggestion of intense and frightened listening. Subsequently he seemed to be satisfied, and crossing to a chair by the table wrote a brief note, handed it to me, and returned to the table, where he began to write rapidly and incessantly. The note implored me in the name of mercy, and for the sake of my own curiosity, to wait where I was while he prepared a full account in German of all the marvels and terrors which beset him. I waited, and the dumb man's pencil flew. It was perhaps an hour later, while I still waited and while the old musician's feverishly written sheets still continued to pile up, that I saw Zann start as from the hint of a horrible shock. Unmistakably he was looking at the curtained window and listening shudderingly. Then I half fancied I heard a sound myself; though it was not a horrible sound, but rather an exquisitely low and infinitely distant musical note, suggesting a player in one of the neighbouring houses, or in some abode beyond the lofty wall over which I had never been able to look. Upon Zann the effect was terrible, for dropping his pencil suddenly he rose, seized his viol, and commenced to rend the night with the wildest playing I had ever heard from his bow save when listening at the barred door. It would be useless to describe the playing of Erich Zann on that dreadful night. It was more horrible than anything I had ever overheard, because I could now see the expression of his face, and could realise that this time the motive was stark fear. He was trying to make a noise; to ward something off or drown something out—what, I could not imagine, awesome though I felt it must be. The playing grew fantastic, delirious, and hysterical, yet kept to the last the qualities of supreme genius which I knew this strange old man possessed. I recognised the air—it was a wild Hungarian dance popular in the theatres, and I reflected for a moment that this was the first time I had ever heard Zann play the work of another composer. Louder and louder, wilder and wilder, mounted the shrieking and whining of that desperate viol. The player was dripping with an uncanny perspiration and twisted like a monkey, always looking frantically at the curtained window. In

his frenzied strains I could almost see shadowy satyrs and Bacchanals dancing and whirling insanely through seething abysses of clouds and smoke and
lightning. And then I thought I heard a shriller, steadier note that was not from
the viol; a calm, deliberate, purposeful, mocking note from far away in the west.
At this juncture the shutter began to rattle in a howling night-wind which had sprung
up outside as if in answer to the mad playing within. Zann's screaming viol now outdid
itself, emitting sounds I had never thought a viol could emit. The shutter rattled more
loudly, unfastened, and commenced slamming against the window. Then the glass
broke shiveringly under the persistent impacts, and the chill wind rushed in, making
the candles sputter and rustling the sheets of paper on the table where Zann had begun
to write out his horrible secret. I looked at Zann, and saw that he was past conscious
observation. His blue eyes were bulging, glassy, and sightless, and the frantic playing
had become a blind, mechanical, unrecognisable orgy that no pen could even suggest.
A sudden gust, stronger than the others, caught up the manuscript and bore it toward the
window. I followed the flying sheets in desperation, but they were gone before I reached
the demolished panes. Then I remembered my old wish to gaze from this window, the
only window in the Rue d'Auseil from which one might see the slope beyond the wall,
and the city outspread beneath. It was very dark, but the city's lights always burned,
and I expected to see them there amidst the rain and wind. Yet when I looked from that
highest of all gable windows, looked while the candles sputtered and the insane viol
howled with the night-wind, I saw no city spread below, and no friendly lights gleaming from remembered streets, but only the blackness of space illimitable; unimagined
space alive with motion and music, and having no semblance to anything on earth. And
as I stood there looking in terror, the wind blew out both the candles in that ancient
peaked garret, leaving me in savage and impenetrable darkness with chaos and pandemonium before me, and the daemon madness of that night-baying viol behind me.
I staggered back in the dark, without the means of striking a light, crashing against
the table, overturning a chair, and finally groping my way to the place where the
blackness screamed with shocking music. To save myself and Erich Zann I could
at least try, whatever the powers opposed to me. Once I thought some chill thing
brushed me, and I screamed, but my scream could not be heard above that hideous viol. Suddenly out of the blackness the madly sawing bow struck me, and
I knew I was close to the player. I felt ahead, touched the back of Zann's chair,
and then found and shook his shoulder in an effort to bring him to his senses.
He did not respond, and still the viol shrieked on without slackening. I moved my
hand to his head, whose mechanical nodding I was able to stop, and shouted in his
ear that we must both flee from the unknown things of the night. But he neither

answered me nor abated the frenzy of his unutterable music, while all through the garret strange currents of wind seemed to dance in the darkness and babel. When my hand touched his ear I shuddered, though I knew not why—knew not why till I felt of the still face; the ice-cold, stiffened, unbreathing face whose glassy eyes bulged uselessly into the void. And then, by some miracle finding the door and the large wooden bolt, I plunged wildly away from that glassy-eyed thing in the dark, and from the ghoulish howling of that accursed viol whose fury increased even as I plunged. Leaping, floating, flying down those endless stairs through the dark house; racing mindlessly out into the narrow, steep, and ancient street of steps and tottering houses; clattering down steps and over cobbles to the lower streets and the putrid canyon-walled river; panting across the great dark bridge to the broader, healthier streets and boulevards we know; all these are terrible impressions that linger with me. And I recall that there was no wind, and that the moon was out, and that all the lights of the city twinkled. Despite my most careful searches and investigations, I have never since been able to find the Rue d'Auseil. But I am not wholly sorry; either for this or for the loss in undreamable abysses of the closely written sheets which alone could have explained the music of Erich Zann.

THE NECROMANCER

ARTHUR GRAY

THIS IS A STORY OF JESUS COLLEGE, AND IT RELATES TO THE YEAR 1643. IN THAT year Cambridge town was garrisoned for the Parliament by Colonel Cromwell and the troops of the Eastern Counties' Association. Soldiers were billeted in all the colleges, and contemporary records testify to their violent behavior and the damage they committed in the chambers that they occupied. In the previous year the Master of Jesus College, Doctor Sterne, was arrested by Cromwell when he was leaving the chapel, conveyed to London, and there imprisoned in the Tower. Before the summer of 1643 fourteen of the sixteen Fellows were expelled, and during the whole of that year there were, besides the soldiers, only some ten or twelve occupants of the college. The names of the two Fellows who were not ejected were John Boyleston and Thomas Allen.

With Mr. Boyleston this history is only concerned for the part which he took on the occasion of the visit to the college of the notorious fanatic, William Dowsing. Dowsing came to Cambridge in December, 1642, armed with powers to put in execution the ordinance of Parliament for the reformation of churches and chapels. Among the devastations committed by this ignorant clown, and faithfully recorded by him in his diary, it stands on record that on December 28, in the presence and perhaps with the approval of John Boyleston, he "digg'd up the steps (*i.e.* of the altar) and brake down Superstitions and Angels, 120 at the least." Dowsing's account of his proceedings is supplemented by the Latin History of the college, written in the reign of Charles II by one of the Fellows, a certain Doctor John Sherman. Sherman records, but Dowsing does not, that there was a second witness of the desecration—Thomas Allen. Of the two he somewhat enigmatically remarks: "The one (*i.e.* Boyleston) stood behind a curtain to witness the evil work: the other, afflicted to behold the exequies of his Alma Mater, made his life a filial offering at her grave, and, to escape the hands of wicked rebels, laid violent hands on himself."

That Thomas Allen committed suicide seems a fairly certain fact: and that remorse for the part he had unwillingly taken in the sacrilege of December 28 prompted his act we may accept on the testimony of Sherman. But there is something more to tell that Sherman either did not know or did not think fit to record. His book deals only with the college and its society. He had no occasion to remember Adoniram Byfield.

Byfield was a chaplain attached to the Parliamentary forces in Cambridge, and quarters were assigned to him in Jesus College, in the first floor room above the gate of entrance. Below his chamber was the Porter's lodge, which at that time served as the armoury of the troopers who occupied the college. Above it, on the highest floor of the gate-tower "kept" Thomas Allen. These were the only rooms on the staircase. At the beginning of the Long Vacation of 1643 Allen was the only member of the college who continued to reside.

Some light is thrown on the character of Byfield and his connection with this story by a pudgy volume of old sermons of the Commonwealth period that is contained in the library of the college. Among the sermons which are bound up in it is one that bears the date 1643 and is designated on the title page:

> A faithful admonicion of the Baalite sin of *Enchanters & Stargazers*, preacht to the Colonel Cromwell's Souldiers in Saint Pulcher's (*i.e.* Saint Sepulchre's) church, in Cambridge, by the fruitfull Minister, Adoniram Byfield, late departed unto God, in the yeare 1643, touching that of *Acts* the seventh, verse 43, *Ye tooke up the Tabernacle of Moloch, the Star of your god Remphan, figures which ye made to worship them; & I will carrie you away beyond Babylon.*

The discourse, in its title as in its contents, reveals its author as one of the fanatics who wrought on the ignorance and prejudice against "carnal" learning which actuated the Cromwellian soldiers in their brutal usage of the University "scholars" in 1643. All Byfield's learning was contained in one book—*the* Book. For him the revelation that gave it sufficed for its interpretation. What needed Greek to the man who spoke mysteries in unknown tongues, or the light of comment to him who was carried in the spirit into the radiance of the third heaven?

Now Allen, too, was an enthusiast, lost in mystic speculation. His speculation was in the then novel science of mathematics and astronomy. Even to minds not darkened by the religious mania that possessed Byfield that science was clouded with suspicion in the middle of the seventeenth century. Anglican, Puritan, and Catholic were agreed in regarding its great exponent, Descartes, as an atheist. Mathematicians were looked upon as necromancers, and Thomas Hobbes says that in his days at Oxford the study was considered to be "smutched with the black art," and fathers, from an apprehension of its malign influence, refrained from sending their sons to that University. How deep the prejudice had sunk into the soul of Adoniram his sermon shows. The occasion that suggested it was this. A pious cornet, leaving a prayer-meeting at night, fell down one of the steep, unlighted staircases of the college and broke his neck. Two or three of the troopers were taken with a dangerous attack of dysentery. There was talk of these misadventures among the soldiers, who somehow connected them with Allen and his studies. The floating gossip gathered into a settled conviction in the mind of Adoniram.

For Allen was a mysterious person. Whether it was because he was engrossed in his studies, or that he shrank from exposing himself to the insults of the soldiers, he seldom showed himself outside of his chamber. Perhaps he was tied to it by the melancholy to which Sherman ascribed his violent end. In his three months' sojourn on Allen's staircase Byfield had not seen him a dozen times, and the mystery of his closed door awakened the most fantastic speculations in the chaplain's mind. For hours together, in the room above, he could hear the mumbled tones of Allen's voice, rising and falling in ceaseless flow. No answer came, and no word that the listener could catch conveyed to his mind any intelligible sense. Once the voice was raised in a high key and Byfield distinctly heard the ominous ejaculation "Avaunt, Sathanas, avaunt!" Once through his partly open door he had caught sight of him standing before a board chalked with figures and symbols which the imagination of Byfield interpreted as magical. At night, from the court below, he would watch the astrologer's lighted window, and when Allen turned his perspective glass upon the stars the conviction became rooted in his watcher's mind that he was living in perilous neighborhood to one of the peeping and muttering wizards of whom the Holy Book spoke.

An unusual occurrence strengthened the suspicions of Byfield. One night he heard Allen creep softly down the staircase past his room; and opening his door, he saw him disappear round the staircase foot, candle in hand. Silently, in the dark, Byfield followed him and saw him pass into the Porter's lodge. The soldiers were in bed and the armoury was unguarded. Through the lighted pane he saw Allen take down a horse-pistol from a rack on the wall. He examined it closely, tried the lock, poised it as if to take aim, then replaced it and, leaving the lodge, disappeared up the staircase with his candle. A world of suspicions rushed on Byfield's mind, and they were not allayed when the soldiers reported in the morning that the pistols were intact. But one of the sick soldiers died that week.

Brooding on this incident Adoniram became more than ever convinced of the Satanic purposes and powers of his neighbour, and his suspicions were confirmed by another mysterious circumstance. As the weeks passed he became aware that at a late hour of night Allen's door was quietly opened. There followed a patter of scampering feet down the staircase, succeeded by silence. In an hour or two the sound came back. The patter went up the stairs to Allen's chamber, and then the door was closed. To lie awake waiting for this ghostly sound became a horror to Byfield's diseased imagination. In his bed he prayed and sang psalms to be relieved of it. Then he abandoned thoughts of sleep and would sit up waiting if he might surprise and detect this walking terror of the night. At first in the darkness of the stairs it eluded him. One night, light in hand, he managed to get a glimpse of it as it disappeared at the foot of the stairs. It was shaped like a large black cat.

Far from allaying his terrors, the discovery awakened new questionings in the heart of Byfield. Quietly he made his way up to Allen's door. It stood open and a candle burnt within. From where he stood he could see each corner of the room. There was the board scribbled with hieroglyphs: there were the magical books open on the table: there were the necromancer's instruments of unknown purpose. But there was no live thing in the room, and no sound save the rustling of papers disturbed by the night air from the open window.

A horrible certitude seized on the chaplain's mind. This Thing that he had caught sight of was no cat. It was the Evil One himself, or it was the wizard translated into animal shape. On what foul errand was he bent? Who was to be his new victim? With a flash there came upon his mind the story how Phinehas had executed judgment on the men that were joined to Baal-peor, and had stayed the plague from the congregation of Israel. He would be the minister of the Lord's vengeance on the wicked one, and it should be counted unto him for righteousness unto all generations for evermore.

He went down to the armory in the Porter's lodge. Six pistols, he knew, were in the rack on the wall. Strange that tonight there were only five—a fresh proof of the justice of his fears. One of the five he selected, primed, loaded, and cocked it in readiness for the wizard's return. He took his stand in the shadow of the wall, at the entrance of the staircase. That his aim might be surer he left his candle burning at the stair-foot.

In solemn stillness the minutes drew themselves out into hours while Adoniram waited and prayed to himself. Then in the poring darkness he became sensible of a moving presence, noiseless and unseen. For a moment it appeared in the light of the candle, not two paces distant. It was the returning cat. A triumphant exclamation sprang to Byfield's lips, "God shall shoot at them, suddenly they be wounded"—and he fired.

With the report of the pistol there rang through the court a dismal outcry, not human or animal, but resembling, as it seemed to the excited imagination of the chaplain, that of a lost soul in torment. With a scurry the creature disappeared in the darkness of the court, and Byfield did not pursue it. The deed was done—that he felt sure of—and as he replaced the pistol in the rack a gush of religious exaltation filled his heart. That night there was no return of the pattering steps outside his door, and he slept well.

* * * * *

Next day the body of Thomas Allen was discovered in the grove which girds the college—his breast pierced by a bullet. It was surmised that he had dragged himself thither from the court. There were tracks of blood from the staircase foot, where it was conjectured that he had shot himself, and a pistol was missing from the armoury. Some of the inmates of the court had been aroused by the discharge of the weapon. The general conclusion was that recorded by Sherman—that the fatal act was prompted by brooding melancholy.

Of his part in the night's transactions Byfield said nothing. The grim intelligence, succeeding the religious excitation of the night, brought to him questioning dread, horror. Whatever others might surmise, he was fatally convinced that it was by his hand that Allen had died. Pity for the dead man had no place in the dark cabin of his soul. But how was it with himself? How should this action be weighed before the awful Throne? His lurid thought pictured the Great Judgment as already begun, the Book opened, the Accuser of the Brethren standing to resist him, and the dreadful sentence of Cain pronounced upon him, "Now art thou cursed from the earth."

In the evening he heard them bring the dead man to the chamber above his own. They laid him on his bed, and, closing the door, left him and descended the stairs. The sound of their footsteps died away and left a dreadful silence. As the darkness grew the horror of the stillness became insupportable. How he yearned that he might hear again the familiar muffled voice in the room above! And in an excess of fervour he prayed aloud that the terrible present might pass from him, that the hours might go back, as on the dial of Ahaz, and all might be as yesterday.

Suddenly, as the prayer died on his lips, the silence was broken. He could not be mistaken. Very quietly he heard Allen's door open, and the old pattering steps crept softly down the stairs. They passed his door. They were gone before he could rise from his knees to open it. A momentary flash lighted the gloom in Byfield's soul. What if his prayer was heard, if Allen was not dead, if the events of the past twenty-four hours were only a dream and a delusion of the Wicked One? Then the horror returned intensified. Allen was assuredly dead. This creeping Thing—what might it be?

For an hour in his room Byfield sat in agonised dread. The thought of the open door possessed him like a nightmare. Somehow it must be closed before the foul Thing returned. Somehow the mangled shape within must be barred up from the wicked powers that might possess it. The fancy gripped and stuck to his delirious mind. It was horrible, but it must be done. In a cold terror he opened his door and looked out.

A flickering light played on the landing above. Byfield hesitated. But the thought that the cat might return at any moment gave him a desperate courage. He mounted the stairs to Allen's door. Precisely as yesternight it stood wide open. Inside the room the books, the instruments, the magical figures were unchanged, and a candle, exposed to the night wind from the casement, threw wavering shadows on the walls and floor. At a glance he saw it all, and he saw the bed where, a few hours ago, the poor remains of Allen had been laid. The coverlet lay smooth upon it. The dead necromancer was not there.

Then as he stood footbound, at the door a wandering breath from the window caught the taper, and with a gasp the flame went out. In the black silence he became conscious of a moving sound. Nearer, up the stairs, they drew—the soft creeping steps—and in panic he shrank backward into Allen's room before their advance. Already they were on the last flight of the stairs; and then in the doorway the darkness parted and Byfield saw. In a ring of pallid light that seemed to emanate from its body he beheld the cat— horrible, gory, its foreparts hanging in ragged collops from its neck. Slowly it crept into the room, and its eyes, smoking with dull malevolence, were fastened on Byfield. Further he backed into the room, to the corner where the bed was laid. The creature followed. It crouched to spring upon him. He dropped in a sitting posture on the bed and as he saw it launch itself upon him, he closed his eyes and found speech in a gush of prayer, "O my God, make haste for my help." In an agony he collapsed upon the couch and clutched its covering with both hands. Beneath it he gripped the stiffened limbs of the dead necromancer, and, when he opened his eyes, the darkness had returned and the spectral cat was gone.

THE NEW PASS

AMELIA B. EDWARDS

THE CIRCUMSTANCES I AM ABOUT TO RELATE HAPPENED JUST FOUR AUTUMNS AGO, when I was travelling in Switzerland with my old school and college friend, Egerton Wolfe.

Before going further, however, I wish to observe that this is no dressed-up narrative. I am a plain, prosaic man; by name Francis Legrice; by profession a barrister; and I think it would be difficult to find many persons less given to look upon life from a romantic or imaginative point of view. By my enemies, and sometimes, perhaps, by my friends, I am supposed to push my habit of incredulity to the verge of universal scepticism; and indeed I admit that I believe in very little that I do not hear and see for myself. But for these things that I am going to relate, I can vouch; and in so far as mine is a personal narrative, I am responsible for its truth. What I saw, I saw with my own eyes in the broad daylight. I offer nothing, therefore, in the shape of a story; but simply a plain statement of facts, as they happened to myself.

I was travelling, then, in Switzerland with Egerton Wolfe. It was not our first joint long-vacation tour by a good many, but it promised to be our last; for Wolfe was engaged to be married the following spring to a very beautiful and charming girl, the daughter of a north-country baronet.

He was a handsome fellow, tall, graceful, dark-haired, dark-eyed; a poet, a dreamer, an artist—as thoroughly unlike myself, in short, as one man having arms, legs, and a head, can be unlike another. And yet we suited each other capitally, and were the fastest friends and best travelling companions in the world.

We had begun our holiday on this occasion with a week's idleness at a place which I will call Oberbrunn—a delightful place, wholly Swiss, consisting of one huge wooden building, half water-cure establishment, half hotel; two smaller buildings called *Dépendances*; a tiny church with a bulbous steeple painted green; and a handful of village—all perched together on a breezy mountain-plateau, some three thousand feet above the lake and valley. Here, far from the haunts of the British tourist and the Alpine club-man, we read, smoked, climbed, rose with the dawn, rubbed up our rusty German, and got ourselves into training for the knapsack work to follow.

At length, our week being up, we started—rather later on the whole than was prudent, for we had a thirty-miles' walk before us, and the sun was already high.

It was a glorious morning, however; the sky flooded with light, and a cool breeze blowing. I see the bright scene now, just as it lay before us when we came down the hotel steps and found our guide waiting for us outside. There were the water-drinkers gathered round the fountain on the lawn; the usual crowd of itinerant vendors of stag-horn ornaments and carved toys in wood and ivory squatted in a semi-circle about the door; some half-dozen barefooted little mountain children running to and fro with wild raspberries for sale; the valley so far below, dotted with hamlets and traversed by a winding stream, like a thread of flashing silver; the black pine-wood, half-way down the slope; the frosted peaks glittering on the horizon.

"*Bon voyage!*" said our good host, Dr. Steigl, with a last hearty shake of the hand.

"*Bon voyage!*" echoed the waiters and miscellaneous hangers-on.

Some three or four of the water-drinkers at the fountain raised their hats—the ragged children pursued us with their wild fruits as far as the gate—and so we departed.

For some distance our path lay along the mountain side, through pine-woods and by cultivated slopes where the Indian corn was ripening to gold, and the late hay-harvest was waiting for the mower. Then the path wound gradually downwards—for the valley lay between us and the pass we had laid out for our day's work—and then, through a succession of soft green slopes and ruddy apple orchards, we came to a blue lake fringed with rushes, where we hired a boat with a striped awning, like the boats on Lago Maggiore, and were rowed across by a boatman who rested on his oars and sang a *jodel*-song when we were half way across.

Being landed on the opposite bank, we found our road at once begin to trend upwards; and here, as the guide informed us, the ascent of the Höhenhorn might be said to begin.

"This, however, *meine Herren*," said he, "is only part of the old pass. It is ill-kept; for none but country folks and travellers from Oberbrunn come this way now. But we shall strike the New Pass higher up. A grand road, *meine Herren*—as fine a road as the Simplon, and good for carriages all the way. It has only been open since the spring."

"The old pass is good enough for me, anyhow!" said Egerton, crowding a hand-ful of wild forget-me-nots, under the ribbon of his hat. "It's like a stray fragment of Arcadia."

And in truth it was wonderfully lovely and secluded—a mere rugged path wind-ing steeply upwards in a soft green shade, among large forest trees and moss-grown rocks covered with patches of velvety lichen. A little streamlet ran singing beside it all the way—now gurgling deep in ferns and grasses; now feeding a rude trough made of a hollow trunk; now crossing our road like a broken flash of sunlight; now breaking away in a tiny fall and foaming out of sight, only to reappear a few steps further on.

Then overhead, through the close roof of leaves, we saw patches of blue sky and golden shafts of sunshine, and small brown squirrels leaping from bough to bough; and in the deep rich grass on either hand, thick ferns, and red and golden mosses, and blue campanulas, and now and then a little wild strawberry, ruby red. By-and-by, when we had been following this path for nearly an hour, we came upon a patch of clearing, in the midst of which stood a rough upright monolith, antique, weather-stained, covered with rude carvings like a Runic monument—the primitive boundary-stone between the Cantons of Uri and Unterwalden.

"Let us rest here!" cries Egerton, flinging himself at full length on the grass. "*Eheu fugaces!*—and the hours are shorter than the years. Why not enjoy them?"

But the guide, whose name is Peter Kauffmann, interposes after the manner of guides in general, and will by no means let us have our own way. There is a mountain inn, he urges, now only five minutes distant—"an excellent little inn, where they sell good red wine." So we yield to fate and Peter Kauffmann and pursue our upward way, coming presently, as he promised and predicted, upon a bright open space and a brown châlet on a shelf of plateau overhanging a giddy precipice. Here, sitting under a vine-covered trellis built out on the very brink of the cliff, we find three mountaineers discussing a flask of the good red wine aforesaid.

In this picturesque eyrie we made our mid-day halt. A smiling *Mädchen* brought us coffee, brown bread, and goats'-milk cheese; while our guide, pulling out a huge lump of the dry black bread from his wallet, fraternised with the mountaineers over a half-flask of his favourite vintage.

The men chattered merrily in their half-intelligible patois. We sat silent, looking down into the deep misty valley and across to the great amethyst mountains, streaked here and there with faint blue threads of slender waterfalls.

"There must surely be moments," said Egerton Wolfe after awhile, "when even such men as you, Frank—men of the world, and lovers of it—feel within them some stirrings of the primitive Adam; some vague longing for that idyllic life of the woods and fields that we dreamers are still, in our inmost souls, insane enough to sigh after as the highest good."

"You mean, don't I sometimes wish to be a Swiss peasant-farmer, with *sabots*; a goître; a wife without form as regards her person, and void as regards her head; and a cretin grandfather a hundred and three years old? Why, no. I prefer myself as I am."

My friend smiled, and shock his head.

"Why take it for granted," said he, "that no man can cultivate his brains and his paternal acres at the same time? Horace, with none of the adjuncts you name, loved a country life and turned it to immortal poetry."

"The world has gone round once or twice since then, my dear fellow," I replied, philosophically. "The best poetry comes out of cities now-a-days."

"And the worst. Do you see those avalanches over yonder?"

Following the direction of his eyes, I saw something like a tiny puff of white smoke gliding over the shoulder of a huge mountain on the opposite side of the valley. It was followed by another and another. We could neither see whence they came nor whither they went. We were too far away to hear the sullen thunder of their fall. Silently they flashed into sight, and as silently they vanished.

Wolfe sighed heavily.

"Poor Lawrence!" said he. "Switzerland was his dream. He longed for the Alps as ardently as other men long for money or power."

Lawrence was a younger brother of his, whom I had never seen—a lad of great promise, whose health had broken down at Addiscombe some ten or twelve years before, and who had soon after died of rapid consumption at Torquay.

"And he never had that longing gratified, had he?"

"Ah, no—he was never out of England. They prescribe bracing climates now, I am told, for lung disease; but not so then. Poor dear fellow! I sometimes fancy he might have lived, if only he had had his heart's desire."

"I would not let such a painful thought enter my head, if I were you," said I, hastily.

"But I can't help it! My mind has been running on poor Lawrence all the morning; and, somehow, the grander the scenery gets, the more I keep thinking how he would have exulted in it. Do you remember those lines by Coleridge, written in the Valley of Chamouni? He knew them by heart. 'Twas the sight of yonder avalanches that reminded me— Well! I will try not to think of these things. Let us change the subject."

Just at this moment, the landlord of the châlet came out—a bright eyed voluble young mountaineer about five- or six-and-twenty, with a sprig of Edelweiss in his hat.

"Good day, *meine Herren*," he said, including all alike in his salute, but addressing himself especially to Wolfe and myself. "Fine weather for travelling—fine weather for the grapes. These *Herren* are going on by the New Pass? *Ach, Herr Gott!* a grand work! a wonderful work!—and all begun and completed in less than three years. These *Herren* see it today for the first time? Good. They have probably been over the Tête Noir? No! Over the Splügen? Good—good. If these *Herren* have been over the Splügen, they can form an idea of the New Pass. The New Pass is very like the Splügen. It has a gallery tunneled in the solid rock, just like the gallery on the Via Mala, with this difference that the gallery in the New Pass is much longer, and lighted by loop-holes at regular intervals. These *Herren* will please to observe the view looking both up and down the pass, before entering the mouth of the tunnel—there is not a finer view in all Switzerland."

"It must be a great advantage to the people hereabouts, having so good a road carried from valley to valley," said I, smiling at his enthusiasm.

"Oh, it is a fine thing for us, *mein Herr!*" he replied. "And a fine thing for all this part of the Canton. It will bring visitors—floods of visitors! By-the-way, these *Herren* must not omit to look out for the waterfall above the gallery. Holy St. Nicholas! the way in which that waterfall has been arranged!"

"Arranged!" echoed Wolfe, who was as much amused as myself. "*Diavolo!* Do you arrange the waterfalls in your country?"

"It was the Herr Becker," said the landlord, unconscious of banter; "the eminent engineer who planned the New Pass. The waterfall, you see, *meine Herren*, could not be suffered to follow its old course down the face of the rock through which the gallery is tunneled, or it would have flowed in at the loopholes and flooded the road. What, therefore, did the Herr Becker do?"

"Turned the course of the fall, and brought it down a hundred yards further on," said I somewhat impatiently.

"Not so, *mein Herr*—not so! The Herr Becker attempts nothing so expensive. He permits the fall to keep its old couloir and come down its old way—but instead of letting it wash the outside of the gallery, he pierces the rock in another direction—vertically—behind the tunnel; constructs an artificial shoot, or conduit in the heart of the rock; and brings the fall out *below* the gallery, just where the cliff overhangs the valley. Now what do the English *Herren* say to that?"

"That it must certainly be a clever piece of engineering," replied Wolfe.

"And that, having rested long enough, we will push on and see it," added I, glad to cut short the thread of our host's native eloquence.

So we paid our reckoning; took a last look at the view; and, plunging back into the woods, went on our way refreshed.

The path still continued to ascend, till we suddenly came upon a burst of daylight and found ourselves on a magnificent high road some thirty feet in breadth, with the forest and the telegraph wires on the one hand, and the precipice on the other. Massive granite posts at close intervals protected the edge of the road; and the *cantonniers* were still at work here and there, breaking and laying fresh stones, and clearing *débris*. We did not need to be informed that this was the New Pass.

Always ascending, we continued now to follow the road which at every turn commanded finer and finer views across the valley. Then by degrees the forest dwindled, and was at last left far below; and the giddy precipices to our left grew steeper; and the mountain slopes above became more and more barren, till the last Alp-roses vanished and there remained only a carpet of brown and tan moss scattered over here and there with great boulders—some freshly broken away from the heights above—others thickly coated with lichen, as if they might have been lying there for centuries.

We seemed here to have reached the highest point of the New Pass, for our road continued at this barren level for several miles. An immense panorama of peaks, snow-fields, and glaciers lay outstretched before us to the left, with an unfathomable gulf of misty valley between. The hot air simmered in the sun. The heat and silence were intense. Once, and once only, we came upon a party of travellers. They were three in number, lying at full length in the shade of a huge fragment of fallen rock, their heads comfortably pillowed on their knapsacks, and all fast asleep.

And now the grey rock began to crop out in larger masses close beside our path, encroaching nearer and nearer, till at last the splintered cliffs towered straight above our heads, and the road became a mere broad shelf, along the face of the precipice. Presently, on turning a sharp angle of rock, we saw before us a vista of road, cliff, and valley—the road now perceptibly on the decline, and vanishing about a mile ahead into the mouth of a small cavernous opening (no bigger, as it seemed from that distance, than a good-sized rabbit-hole) pierced through a huge projecting spur, or buttress, of the mountain.

"Behold the famous gallery!" said I. "Mine host was right—it *is* something like the Splügen, barring the much greater altitude of the road, and the still greater width of the valley. But where is the waterfall?"

"Well, it's not much of a waterfall," said Wolfe. "I can just see it—a tiny thread of mist wavering down the cliff a long way on, beyond the mouth of the tunnel."

"Ay; I see it now—a sort of inferior Staubbach. Heavens! what power the sun has up here! At what time did Kauffmann say we should get to Schwartzenfelden?"

"Not before seven, at the earliest—and it is now nearly four."

"Humph! three hours more—say three and a half. Well, that will be a pretty good first day's pedestrianising, heat and all considered!"

Here the conversation dropped, and we plodded on again in silence.

Meanwhile the sun blazed in the heavens, and the light, struck back from white rock and whiter road, was almost blinding. And still the hot air danced and simmered before us; and a windless stillness, as of death, lay upon all the scene.

Suddenly, quite suddenly—as if he had started out of the rock—I saw a man coming towards us with rapid and eager gesticulations. He seemed to be waving us back; but I was so startled for the moment by the unexplained way in which he made his appearance, that I scarcely took in the meaning of his gestures.

"How odd!" I exclaimed, coming to a halt. "How did he get there?"

"How did who get there?" said Wolfe.

"Why, that fellow yonder. Did you see where he came from?"

"What fellow, my dear boy? I see no one but ourselves." And he stared vaguely round, while all the time the man between us and the gallery was waving his right arm above his head, and running on to meet us.

"Good heavens! Egerton," I said impatiently, "where are your eyes? Here—straight before us—not a quarter of a mile off—making signs as hard as he can. Perhaps we had better wait till he comes up."

My friend drew his race-glass from its case, adjusted it carefully, and took a long, steady look down the road. Seeing him do this, the man stood still; but kept his right hand up all the same.

"You see him now, surely?" said I.

"*No.*"

I turned and looked him in the face. I could not believe my ears.

"Upon my honour, Frank," he said earnestly, "I see only the empty road, and the mouth of the tunnel beyond. Here, Kauffmann!"

Kauffmann, who was standing close by, stepped up and touched his cap.

"Look down the road," said Wolfe.

The guide shaded his eyes with his hand, and looked.

"What do you see?"

"I see the entrance to the gallery, *mein Herr.*"

"Nothing else?"

"Nothing else, *mein Herr.*"

And still the man stood there in the road—even came a step or two nearer! Was I mad?

"You still think you see some one yonder?" said Egerton, looking at me very seriously.

"I *know* that I do."

He handed me his race-glass.

"Look through that," he said, "and tell me if you still see him."

"I see him more plainly than before."

"What is he like?"

"Very tall—very slender—fair—quite young—not more, I should say, than fifteen or sixteen—evidently an Englishman."

"How is he dressed?"

"In a grey suit—his collar open, and his throat bare. Wears a Scotch cap with a silver badge in it. He takes his cap off, and waves it! He has a whitish scar on his right temple. I can see the motion of his lips—he seems to say, 'Go back!—go back!' Look for yourself—you *must* see him!"

I turned to give him the glass, but he pushed it away.

"No, no," he said, hoarsely. "It's of no use. Go on looking. . . . What more, for God's sake?"

I looked again—the glass all but dropped from my hand.

"Gracious heavens!" I exclaimed breathlessly, "he is gone!"

"Gone!"

Ay, gone. Gone as suddenly as he came—gone as though he had never been! I could not believe it. I rubbed my eyes, rubbed the glass on my sleeve. I looked, and looked again; and still, though I looked, I doubted.

At this moment, with a wild, unearthly cry, and a strange sound as of some heavy projectile cleaving the stagnant air, an eagle plunged past us upon mighty wings, and swooped down into the valley.

"*Ein adler! ein adler!*" shouted the guide, flinging up his cap and running to the brink of the precipice.

Wolfe laid his hand upon my arm, and drew a deep breath.

"Legrice," he said very calmly, but with a white, awestruck look in his face, "you described my brother Lawrence—age, height, dress, everything; even to the Scotch cap he always wore, and the silver badge my uncle Horace gave him on his birthday. He got that scar in a cricket-match at Harrowgate."

"Your brother Lawrence?" I faltered.

"Why you should be the one permitted to see him is strange," he went on, speaking more to himself than to me. "Very strange! I wish . . . but there! perhaps I should not have believed my own eyes. I *must* believe yours."

"I will never believe that my eyes saw your brother Lawrence," I said resolutely.

"We must turn back, of course," he went on, taking no notice of my answer. "Look here, Kauffmann—can we get to Schwartzenfelden tonight by the old pass, if we turn back at once?"

"Turn back!" I interrupted. "My dear Egerton, you are not serious?"

"I was never more serious in my life," he said, gravely.

"If these *Herren* wish to take the old pass," said the astonished guide, "we cannot possibly get to Schwartzenfelden before midnight. We have already come seven miles out of the way, and the old pass is twelve miles further round."

"Twelve and fourteen are twenty-six," said I. "We cannot add twenty-six miles to our original thirty. It is out of the question."

"These *Herren* can sleep at the châlet where we halted," suggested the guide.

"True—I had not thought of that," said Wolfe. "We can sleep at the châlet, and go on as soon as it is day."

"Turn back, sleep at the châlet, go on in the morning, and lose full half a day, with one of the finest passes in Switzerland before us, and our journey two-thirds done!" I cried. "The idea is too absurd."

"Nothing shall induce me to go on, in defiance of a warning from the dead," said Wolfe, hastily.

"And nothing," I replied, "shall induce me to believe that we have received any such warning. I either saw that man, or I laboured under some kind of optical illusion. But ghosts I do not believe in."

"As you please. You can go on if you prefer it, and take Kauffmann with you. I know my way back."

"Agreed—except as regards Kauffmann. Let him take his choice."

Kauffmann, having the matter explained to him, elected at once to go back with Egerton Wolfe.

"If the Herr Englishman has been warned in a vision," he said, crossing himself devoutly, "it is suicide to go on. Obey the blessed spirit, *mein Herr*!"

But nothing now would have induced me to turn back, even if I had felt inclined to do so; so, agreeing to meet next day at Schwartzenfelden, my friend and I said goodbye.

"God grant you may come to no harm, dear old fellow," said Wolfe, as he turned away.

"I don't feel like harm, I assure you," I replied, laughing.

And so we parted.

I stood still and watched them till they were out of sight. At the turn of the road they paused and looked back. When Wolfe waved his hand for the last time, and finally disappeared, I could not repress a sudden thrill—he looked so like the figure of my illusion!

For that it was an illusion, I did not doubt for a moment. Such phenomena, though not common, are by no means unheard of. I had talked with more than one eminent physician on this very subject, and I remembered that each had spoken of cases within his own experience. Besides, there was the famous case of Nicolai, the bookseller of Berlin; not to mention many others, equally well attested. That I must have been temporarily in the condition of persons so affected, I took for granted; and yet I felt well—never better; my head cool—my mind clear—my pulse regular. Well—I would never disbelieve in hallucinations again. To that I made up my mind; but as for ghosts . . . pshaw! how could any sane man, above all, such a man as Egerton Wolfe, believe in ghosts?

Reasoning thus, and smiling to myself, I tightened the shoulder-straps of my knapsack, took a pull at my wine-flask, and set off towards the tunnel.

It was still half a mile distant; for I had stopped on first sight of the figure, before we were half across the space that lay between that dark opening and the turn of the road above. And now, plodding steadily towards it, I examined the ground at every step (especially on the side of the precipice) for any path or rocky projection of which a man could possibly have availed himself for retreat or shelter; but the smooth upright wall of solid limestone on the one hand, and the sheer, inaccessible, giddy depths on the other, made all such explanation impossible. Thrown back thus on the illusion theory, I paused once or twice, and tried to conjure up the figure before my eyes, but in vain.

And now, with every step that I took the mouth of the tunnel grew larger, and the depth of shade within it blacker and more mysterious. I was by this time near enough to see that it was faced with brickwork—that it spanned the full width of the road—and that it was more than lofty enough for an old-fashioned, top-heavy diligence to pass under it. The next moment, being within half a dozen yards of it, I distinctly heard the cool murmur of the more distant waterfall (now hidden by the great mountain spur through which the gallery was carried); and the next moment after that, I had plunged into the tunnel.

It was like the transition from an orchid-house to an ice-house—from mid-day to midnight. The darkness was profound, and so intense the sudden chill, that for the first second it almost took my breath away.

The roof and sides of the gallery, and the road beneath my feet, were all hewn in the solid rock. A sharp, arrowy gleam of light, shooting athwart the gloom about fifty yards ahead, marked the position of the first loop-hole. A second, a third, a fourth, as many perhaps as eight or ten, gleamed faintly in the distance. The tiny blue speck which showed where the gallery opened out again upon the day, looked at least a mile away. The path underfoot was wet and slippery; and as I went on, and my eyes became accustomed to the darkness, I saw that every part of the tunnel was streaming with moisture.

I pushed on rapidly. The first and second loop-holes were soon left behind, but at the third I paused for a moment to breathe the outer air. Then, for the first time, I observed that every rut in the road beneath my feet was filled with running water.

I hurried on faster and faster. I shivered. I felt the cold seizing me. The arched entrance through which I had just passed had dwindled already to a shining patch no bigger than my hand, while the tiny blue speck on ahead seemed far off as ever. Meanwhile the tunnel was dripping like a shower-bath.

All at once, my attention was arrested by a sound—a strange indescribable sound—heavy, muffled, as of mighty forces at work in the heart of the mountain. I stood still—I held my breath—I fancied I felt the solid rock vibrate beneath my feet! Then it flashed upon me that I must now be approaching that part of the gallery behind which the waterfall was conducted, and that what I heard was the muffled roar of its descent. At the same moment, chancing to look down at my feet, I saw that the road was an inch deep in running water from wall to wall.

Now, lawyer as I am, and ignorant of the first principles of civil engineering, I felt sure that this much-praised Herr Becker should at least have made his tunnel water-tight. That it leaked somewhere was plain, and that it should be suffered to go on leaking to the discomfort of travellers was simply intolerable. An inch of water, for instance, was more than—an inch did I say? Gracious heavens! since the moment I looked, it had risen to three—it was closing over my boots—it was becoming a rushing torrent!

In that instant a great horror fell upon me—the horror of darkness and sudden death. I turned, flung away my Alpenstock, and fled for my life. Fled blindly, breathlessly, wildly, with the horrible grinding sound of the imprisoned waterfall in my ears, and the gathering torrent at my heels!

Never while I live shall I forget the agony of those next few seconds—the icy numbness seizing on my limbs—the sudden, frightful sense of impeded respiration—the water rising, eddying, clamouring, pursuing me, passing me—the swirl of it, as it flashed past each loop-hole in succession—the rush with which (as I strained on to the mouth of the gallery, now not a dozen yards distant) it leaped out into the sunlight like a living thing, and dashed to the edge of the precipice!

At that supreme instant, just as I had darted out through the echoing arch and staggered a few paces up the road, a deafening report, crackling, hurried, tremendous, like the explosion of a mine, rent the air and roused a hundred echoes. It was followed by a moment of strange and terrible suspense. Then, with a deep and sullen roar, audible above all the rolling thunders of the mountains round, a mighty wave—smooth, solid, glassy, like an Atlantic wave on an English western coast—came gleaming up the mouth of the tunnel, paused, as it were, upon the threshold, reared its majestic crest, curved, trembled, burst in a cataract of foam, flooded the road for yards beyond the spot where I was clinging to the rock like a limpet, and rushing back again, as the wave rushes down the beach, hurled itself over the cliff, and vanished in a cloud of mist.

After this, the imprisoned flood came pouring out tumultuously for several minutes, bringing with it fragments of rock and masonry, and filling the road with *débris*; but even this disturbance presently subsided, and almost as soon as the last echoes of the explosion had died away, the liberated waters were rippling pleasantly along their new bed, sparkling out into the sunshine as they emerged from the gallery, and gliding in a smooth continuous stream over the brink of the precipice, thence to fall, in multitudinous wavy folds and wreaths of prismatic mist, into the valley two thousand feet below.

For myself, drenched to the skin as I was, I could do nothing but turn back and follow meekly in the track of Egerton Wolfe and Peter Kauffmann. How I did so, dripping and weary, and minus my Alpenstock; how I arrived at the châlet about sunset, shivering and hungry, just in time to claim my share of a capital omelette and a dish of mountain trout; how the Swiss press rang with my escape for at least nine days after the event; how the Herr Becker was liberally censured for his defective engineering; and how Egerton Wolfe believes to this day that his brother Lawrence came back from the dead to save us from utter destruction, are matters upon which it were needless to dwell in these pages. Enough that I narrowly escaped with my life, and that had we gone on, as we doubtless should have gone on but for the delay consequent upon my illusion, we should most probably have been in the heart of the tunnel at the time of the explosion, and not one left to tell the tale.

Nevertheless, my dear friends, I do not believe, and I have made up my mind never to believe—in ghosts.

No Eye-Witnesses

Henry S. Whitehead

There were blood stains on Everard Simon's shoes. . . .

Simon's father had given up his country house in Rye when his wife died, and moved into an apartment in Flatbush among the rising apartment houses which were steadily replacing the original rural atmosphere of that residential section of swelling Brooklyn.

Blood stains—and forest mold—on his shoes!

The younger Simon—he was thirty-seven, his father getting on toward seventy—always spent his winters in the West Indies, returning in the spring, going back again in October. He was a popular writer of informative magazine articles. As soon as his various visits for week-ends and odd days were concluded, he would move his trunks into the Flatbush apartment and spend a week or two, sometimes longer, with his father. There was a room for him in the apartment, and this he would occupy until it was time for him to leave for his summer camp in the Adirondacks. Early in September he would repeat the process, always ending his autumn stay in the United States with his father until it was time to sail back to St. Thomas or Martinique or wherever he imagined he could write best for that particular winter.

There was only one drawback in this arrangement. This was the long ride in the subway necessitated by his dropping in to his New York club every day. The club was his real American headquarters. There he received his mail. There he usually lunched and often dined as well. It was at the club that he received his visitors and his telephone calls. The club was on Forty-Fourth Street, and to get there from the apartment he walked to the Church Avenue subway station, changed at De Kalb Avenue, and then took a Times Square express train over the Manhattan Bridge. The time consumed between the door of the apartment and the door of the club was exactly three-quarters of an hour, barring delays. For the older man the arrangement was ideal. He could be in his office, he boasted, in twenty minutes.

To avoid the annoyances of rush hours in the subway. Mr. Simon senior commonly left home quite early in the morning, about seven o'clock. He was a methodical person, always leaving before seven in the morning, and getting his breakfast in a downtown restaurant near the office. Everard Simon rarely left the apartment until after nine, thus avoiding the morning rush-hour at its other end. During the five or six weeks every year that they lived together the two men really saw little of each other, although strong bonds of understanding, affection, and respect bound them together. Sometimes the older man would awaken his son early in the morning for a brief conversation. Occasionally the two would have a meal together, evenings, or on Sundays; now and then an evening would be spent in each other's company. They had little to converse about. During the day they would sometimes call each other up and speak together briefly on the telephone from club to office or office to club. On the day when Everard Simon sailed south, his father and he always took a farewell luncheon together somewhere downtown. On the day of his return seven months later, his father always made it a point to meet him at the dock. These arrangements had prevailed for eleven years. He must get that blood wiped off. Blood! How——?

During that period, the neighborhood of the apartment had changed out of all recognition. Open lots, community tennis-courts, and many of the older one-family houses had disappeared, to be replaced by the ubiquitous apartment houses. In 1928 the neighborhood which had been almost rural when the older Simon had taken up his abode "twenty minutes from his Wall Street office" was solidly built up except for an occasional, and now incongruous, frame house standing lonely and dwarfed in its own grounds among the towering apartment houses, like a lost child in a preoccupied crowd of adults whose business caused them to look over the child's head.

One evening, not long before the end of his autumn sojourn in Flatbush, Everard Simon, having dined alone in his club, started for the Times Square subway station about a quarter before nine. Doubled together lengthwise, and pressing the pocket of his coat out of shape, was a magazine, out that day, which contained one of his articles. He stepped on board a waiting Sea Beach express train, in the rearmost car, sat down, and opened the magazine, looking down the table of contents to find his article. The train started after the ringing of the warning bell and the automatic closing of the side doors, while he was putting on his reading-spectacles. He began on the article.

He was dimly conscious of the slight bustle of incoming passengers at Broadway and Canal Street, and again when the train ran out on the Manhattan Bridge because of the change in the light, but his closing of the magazine with a page-corner turned down, and the replacing of the spectacles in his inside pocket when the train drew in to De Kalb Avenue, were almost entirely mechanical. He could make that change almost without thought. He had to cross the platform here at De Kalb Avenue, get into a Brighton Beach local train. The Brighton Beach expresses ran only in rush hours and he almost never travelled during those periods.

He got into his train, found a seat, and resumed his reading. He paid no attention to the stations—Atlantic and Seventh Avenues. The next stop after that, Prospect Park, would give him one of his mechanical signals, like coming out on the bridge. The train emerged from its tunnel at Prospect Park, only to re-enter it again at Parkside Avenue, the next following station. After that came Church Avenue, where he got out every evening.

As the train drew in to that station, he repeated the mechanics of turning down a page in the magazine, replacing his spectacles in their case and putting the case in his inside pocket. His mind entirely on the article, he got up, left the train, walked back toward the Caton Avenue exit, started to mount the stairs.

A few moments later he was walking, his mind still entirely occupied with his article, in the long-familiar direction of his father's apartment.

The first matter which reminded him of his surroundings was the contrast in his breathing after the somewhat stuffy air of the subway train. Consciously he drew in a deep breath of the fresh, sweet outdoor air. There was a spicy odor of wet leaves about it somehow. It seemed, as he noticed his environment with the edge of his mind, darker than usual. The crossing of Church and Caton Avenues was a brightly lighted corner. Possibly something was temporarily wrong with the lighting system. He looked up. Great trees nodded above his head. He could see the stars twinkling above their lofty tops. The sickle edge of a moon cut sharply against black branches moving gently in a fresh wind from the sea.

He walked on several steps before he paused, slackened his gait, then stopped dead, his mind responding in a note of quiet wonderment.

Great trees stood all about him. From some distance ahead a joyous song in a manly bass, slightly muffled by the wood of the thick trees, came to his ears. It was a song new to him. He found himself listening to it eagerly. The song was entirely strange to him, the words unfamiliar. He listened intently. The singer came nearer. He caught various words, English words. He distinguished "merry," and "heart," and "repine."

It seemed entirely natural to be here, and yet, as he glanced down at his brown clothes, his highly polished shoes, felt the magazine bulging his pocket, the edge of his mind caught a note of incongruity. He remembered with a smile that strange drawing of Aubrey Beardsley's, of a lady playing an upright cottage pianoforte in the midst of a field of daisies! He stood, he perceived, in a kind of rough path worn by long usage. The ground was damp underfoot. Already his polished shoes were soiled with mold.

The singer came nearer and nearer. Obviously, as the fresh voice indicated, it was a young man. Just as the voice presaged that before many seconds the singer must come out of the screening array of tree boles, Everard Simon was startled by a crashing, quite near by, at his right. The singer paused in the middle of a note, and for an instant there was a primeval silence undisturbed by the rustle of a single leaf.

Then a huge timber wolf burst through the underbrush to the right, paused, crouched, and sprang, in a direction diagonal to that in which Everard Simon was facing, toward the singer.

Startled into a frigid immobility, Simon stood as though petrified. He heard an exclamation, in the singer's voice, a quick "heh"; then the sound of a struggle. The great wolf, apparently, had failed to knock down his quarry. Then without warning, the two figures, man and wolf, came into plain sight; the singer, for so Simon thought of him, a tall, robust fellow, in fringed deerskin, slashing desperately with a hunting-knife, the beast crouching now, snapping with a tearing motion of a great punishing jaw. Short-breathed "heh's" came from the man, as he parried dexterously the lashing snaps of the wicked jaws.

The two, revolving about each other, came very close. Everard Simon watched the struggle, fascinated, motionless. Suddenly the animal shifted its tactics. It backed away stealthily, preparing for another spring. The young woodsman abruptly dropped his knife, reached for the great pistol which depended from his belt in a rough leather holster. There was a blinding flash, and the wolf slithered down, its legs giving under it. A great cloud of acrid smoke drifted about Everard Simon, cutting off his vision; choking smoke which made him cough.

But through it, he saw the look of horrified wonderment on the face of the young woodsman; saw the pistol drop on the damp ground as the knife had dropped; followed with his eyes, through the dimming medium of the hanging smoke, the fascinated, round-eyed stare of the man who had fired the pistol.

There, a few feet away from him, he saw an eldritch change passing over the beast, shivering now in its death-struggle. He saw the hair of the great paws dissolve, the jaws shorten and shrink, the lithe body buckle and heave strangely. He closed his eyes, and when he opened them, he saw the figure in deerskins standing mutely over the body of a man, lying prone across tree-roots, a pool of blood spreading, spreading, from the concealed face, mingling with the damp earth under the tree-roots.

Then the strange spell of quiescence which had held him in its weird thrall was dissolved, and, moved by a nameless terror, he ran, wildly, straight down the narrow path between the trees. . . .

It seemed to him that he had been running only a short distance when something, the moon above the trees, perhaps, began to increase in size, to give a more brilliant light. He slackened his pace. The ground now felt firm underfoot, no longer damp, slippery. Other lights joined that of the moon. Things became brighter all about him, and as this brilliance increased, the great trees all about him turned dim and pale. The ground was now quite hard underfoot. He looked up. A brick wall faced him. It was pierced with windows. He looked down. He stood on pavement. Overhead a streetlight swung lightly in the late September breeze. A faint smell of wet leaves was in the air, mingled now with the fresh wind from the sea. The magazine was clutched tightly in his left hand. He had, it appeared, drawn it from his pocket. He looked at it curiously, put it back into the pocket.

He stepped along over familiar pavement, past well-known façades. The entrance to his father's apartment loomed before him. Mechanically he thrust his left hand into his trousers pocket. He took out his key, opened the door, traversed the familiar hallway with its rugs and marble walls and bracket side-wall light-clusters. He mounted the stairs, one flight, turned the corner, reached the door of the apartment, let himself in with his key.

It was half-past nine and his father had already retired. They talked through the old man's bedroom door, monosyllabically. The conversation ended with the request from his father that he close the bedroom door. He did so, after wishing the old man good-night.

He sat down in an armchair in the living-room, passed a hand over his forehead, bemused. He sat for fifteen minutes. Then he reached into his pocket for a cigarette. They were all gone. Then he remembered that he had meant to buy a fresh supply on his way to the apartment. He had meant to get the cigarettes from the drug-store between the Church Avenue subway station and the apartment! He looked about the room for one. His father's supply, too, seemed depleted.

He rose, walked into the entry, put on his hat, stepped out again into the hallway, descended the one flight, went out into the street. He walked into an unwonted atmosphere of excitement. People were conversing as they passed, in excited tones; about the drug-store entrance a crowd was gathered. Slightly puzzled, he walked toward it, paused, blocked, on the outer edge.

"What's happened?" he inquired of a young man he found standing just beside him, a little to the fore.

"It's a shooting of some kind," the young man explained. "I only just got here myself. The fellow that got bumped off is inside the drug-store—what's left of him. Some gang-war stuff, I guess."

He walked away, skirting the rounded edge of the clustering crowd of curiosity-mongers, proceeded down the street, procured the cigarettes elsewhere. He passed the now enlarged crowd on the other side of the street on his way back, returned to the apartment, where he sat, smoking and thinking, until eleven, when he retired. Curious—a man shot; just at the time, or about the time, he had let that imagination of his get the better of him—those trees!

His father awakened him about five minutes before seven. The old man held a newspaper in his hand. He pointed to a scare-head on the front page.

"This must have happened about the time you came in," remarked Mr. Simon.

"Yes—the crowd was around the drugstore when I went out to get some cigarettes," replied Everard Simon, stretching and yawning.

When his father was gone and he had finished with his bath, he sat down, in a bathrobe, to glance over the newspaper account. A phrase arrested him:

" . . . the body was identified as that of 'Jerry the Wolf,' a notorious gangster with a long prison record." Then, lower down, when he had resumed his reading:

" . . . a large-caliber bullet which, entering the lower jaw, penetrated the base of the brain . . . no eye-witnesses. . . ."

Everard Simon sat for a long time after he had finished the account, the newspaper on the floor by his chair. "No eyewitnesses!" He must, really, keep that imagination of his within bounds, within his control.

Slowly and reflectively, this good resolution uppermost, he went back to the bathroom and prepared for his morning shave.

Putting on his shoes, in his room, he observed something amiss. He picked up a shoe, examined it carefully. The soles of the shoes were caked with black mold, precisely like the mold from the woodpaths about his Adirondack camp. Little withered leaves and dried pine-needles clung to the mold. And on the side of the right shoe were brownish stains, exactly like freshly dried bloodstains. He shuddered as he carried the shoes into the bathroom, wiped them clean with a damp towel, then rinsed out the towel. He put them on, and shortly afterward, before he entered the subway to go over to the club for the day, he had them polished.

The bootblack spoke of the killing on that corner the night before. The bootblack noticed nothing amiss with the shoes, and when he had finished, there was no trace of any stains.

Simon did not change at De Kalb Avenue that morning. An idea had occurred to him between Church Avenue and De Kalb, and he stayed on the Brighton local, secured a seat after the emptying process which took place at De Kalb, and went on through the East River tunnel.

He sent in his name to Forrest, a college acquaintance, now in the district attorney's office, and Forrest received him after a brief delay.

"I wanted to ask a detail about this gangster who was killed in Flatbush last night," said Simon. "I suppose you have his record, haven't you?"

"Yes, we know pretty well all about him. What particular thing did you want to know?"

"About his name," replied Simon. "Why was he called 'Jerry the Wolf'—that is, why 'The Wolf' particularly?"

"That's the very queer thing, Simon. Such a name is not, really, uncommon. There was that fellow Goddard, you remember? They called him 'The Wolf of Wall Street.' There was the fiction criminal known as 'The Lone Wolf.' There have been plenty of 'wolves' among criminal 'monikers.' But this fellow, Jerry Goraffsky, was a Hungarian, really. He was called 'The Wolf,' queerly enough, because there were those in his gang who believed he was one of those birds who could change himself into a wolf! It's a queer combination, isn't it?—for a New York gangster?"

"Yes," said Everard Simon, "it is, very queer, when you come to think of it. I'm much obliged to you for telling me. I was curious about it somehow."

"That isn't the only queer aspect of this case, however," resumed Forrest. A light frown suddenly showing on his keen face. "In fact that wolf-thing isn't a part of the case—doesn't concern us, of course, here in the district attorney's office. That's nothing but blah. Gangsters are as superstitious as sailors; more so, in fact!

"No. The real mystery in this affair is—the bullet, Simon. Want to see it?"

"Why—yes; of course—if you like, Forrest. What's wrong with the bullet?"

Forrest stepped out of the room, returned at once, laid a large, round ball on his desk. Both men bent over it curiously.

"Notice that diameter, Simon," said Forrest. "It's a hand-molded round ball—belongs in a collection of curios, not in any gangster's gat! Why, man, it's like the slugs they used to hunt the bison before the old Sharps rifle was invented. It's the kind of a ball Fenimore Cooper's people used—'Deerslayer!' It would take a young cannon to throw that thing. Smashed in the whole front of Jerry's ugly mug. The inside works of his head were spilled all over the sidewalk! It's what the newspapers always call a 'clue.' Who do you suppose resurrected the horse-pistol—or the ship's blunderbuss—to do that job on Jerry? Clever, in a way. Hooked it out of some dime museum, perhaps. There are still a few of those old 'pitches' still operating, you know, at the old stand—along East Fourteenth Street."

"A flintlock, single-shot horse-pistol, I'd imagine," said Everard Simon, laying the ounce lead ball back on the mahogany desk. He knew something of weapons, new and old. As a writer of informational articles that was part of his permanent equipment.

"Very likely," mused the assistant district attorney. "Glad you came in, old man."

And Everard Simon went on uptown to his club.

Not to Be Taken at Bedtime

Rosa Mulholland

This is the legend of a house called the Devil's Inn, standing in the heather on the top of the Connemara mountains, in a shallow valley hollowed between five peaks. Tourists sometimes come in sight of it on September evenings; a crazy and weather-stained apparition, with the sun glaring at it angrily between the hills, and striking its shattered window-panes. Guides are known to shun it, however.

The house was built by a stranger, who came no one knew whence, and whom the people nicknamed Coll Dhu (Black Coll), because of his sullen bearing and solitary habits. His dwelling they called the Devil's Inn, because no tired traveller had ever been asked to rest under its roof, nor friend known to cross its threshold. No one bore him company in his retreat but a wizen-faced old man, who shunned the good-morrow of the trudging peasant when he made occasional excursions to the nearest village for provisions for himself and master, and who was as secret as a stone concerning all the antecedents of both.

For the first year of their residence in the country, there had been much speculation as to who they were, and what they did with themselves up there among the clouds and eagles. Some said that Coll Dhu was a scion of the old family from whose hands the surrounding lands had passed; and that, embittered by poverty and pride, he had come to bury himself in solitude, and brood over his misfortunes. Others hinted of crime, and flight from another country; others again whispered of those who were cursed from their birth, and could never smile, nor yet make friends with a fellow-creature till the day of their death. But when two years had passed, the wonder had somewhat died out, and Coll Dhu was little thought of, except when a herd looking for sheep crossed the track of a big dark man walking the mountains gun in hand, to whom he did not dare say "Lord save you!" or when a housewife rocking her cradle of a winter's night, crossed herself as a gust of storm thundered over her cabin-roof, with the exclamation, "Oh, then, it's Coll Dhu that has enough o' the fresh air about his head up there this night, the crature!"

Coll Dhu had lived thus in his solitude for some years, when it became known that Colonel Blake, the new lord of the soil, was coming to visit the country. By climbing one of the peaks encircling his eyrie, Coll could look sheer down a mountain-side, and see in miniature beneath him, a grey old dwelling with ivied chimneys and weather-slated walls, standing amongst straggling trees and grim warlike rocks, that gave it the look of a fortress, gazing out to the Atlantic for ever with the eager eyes of all its windows, as if demanding perpetually, "What tidings from the New World?"

He could see now masons and carpenters crawling about below, like ants in the sun, over-running the old house from base to chimney, daubing here and knocking there, tumbling down walls that looked to Coll, up among the clouds, like a handful of jackstones, and building up others that looked like the toy fences in a child's Farm. Throughout several months he must have watched the busy ants at their task of breaking and mending again, disfiguring and beautifying; but when all was done he had not the curiosity to stride down and admire the handsome paneling of the new billiard-room, nor yet the fine view which the enlarged bay-window in the drawing-room commanded of the watery highway to Newfoundland.

Deep summer was melting into autumn, and the amber streaks of decay were beginning to creep out and trail over the ripe purple of moor and mountain, when Colonel Blake, his only daughter, and a party of friends, arrived in the country. The grey house below was alive with gaiety, but Coll Dhu no longer found an interest in observing it from his eyrie. When he watched the sun rise or set, he chose to ascend some crag that looked on no human habitation. When he sallied forth on his excursions, gun in hand, he set his face towards the most isolated wastes, dipping into the loneliest valleys, and scaling the nakedest ridges. When he came by chance within call of other excursionists, gun in hand he plunged into the shade of some hollow, and avoided an encounter. Yet it was fated, for all that, that he and Colonel Blake should meet.

Towards the evening of one bright September day, the wind changed, and in half an hour the mountains were wrapped in a thick blinding mist. Coll Dhu was far from his den, but so well had he searched these mountains, and inured himself to their climate, that neither storm, rain, nor fog, had power to disturb him. But while he stalked on his way, a faint and agonised cry from a human voice reached him through the smothering mist. He quickly tracked the sound, and gained the side of a man who was stumbling along in danger of death at every step.

"Follow me!" said Coll Dhu to this man, and, in an hour's time, brought him safely to the lowlands, and up to the walls of the eager-eyed mansion.

"I am Colonel Blake," said the frank soldier, when, having left the fog behind him, they stood in the starlight under the lighted windows. "Pray tell me quickly to whom I owe my life."

As he spoke, he glanced up at his benefactor, a large man with a sombre sun-burned face.

"Colonel Blake," said Coll Dhu, after a strange pause, "your father suggested to my father to stake his estates at the gaming table. They were staked, and the tempter won. Both are dead; but you and I live, and I have sworn to injure you."

The colonel laughed good humouredly at the uneasy face above him.

"And you began to keep your oath tonight by saving my life?" said he. "Come! I am a soldier, and know how to meet an enemy; but I had far rather meet a friend. I shall not be happy till you have eaten my salt. We have merry-making to-night in honour of my daughter's birthday. Come in and join us?"

Coll Dhu looked at the earth doggedly.

"I have told you," he said, "who and what I am, and I will not cross your threshold."

But at this moment (so runs my story) a French window opened among the flower-erbeds by which they were standing, and a vision appeared which stayed the words on Coll's tongue. A stately girl, clad in white satin, stood framed in the ivied window, with the warm light from within streaming around her richly-moulded figure into the night. Her face was as pale as her gown, her eyes were swimming in tears, but a firm smile sat on her lips as she held out both hands to her father. The light behind her, touched the glistening folds of her dress—the lustrous pearls round her throat—the coronet of blood-red roses which encircled the knotted braids at the back of her head. Satin, pearls, and roses—had Coll Dhu, of the Devil's Inn, never set eyes upon such things before?

Evleen Blake was no nervous tearful miss. A few quick words—"Thank God! you're safe; the rest have been home an hour"—and a tight pressure of her father's fingers between her own jewelled hands, were all that betrayed the uneasiness she had suffered.

"Faith, my love, I owe my life to this brave gentleman!" said the blithe colonel. "Press him to come in and be our guest, Evleen. He wants to retreat to his mountains, and lose himself again in the fog where I found him; or, rather, where he found me! Come, sir" (to Coll), "you must surrender to this fair besieger."

An introduction followed. "Coll Dhu!" murmured Evleen Blake, for she had heard the common tales of him; but with a frank welcome she invited her father's preserver to taste the hospitality of that father's house.

"I beg you to come in, sir," she said; "but for you our gaiety must have been turned into mourning. A shadow will be upon our mirth if our benefactor disdains to join in it."

With a sweet grace, mingled with a certain hauteur from which she was never free, she extended her white hand to the tall looming figure outside the window; to have it grasped and wrung in a way that made the proud girl's eye's flash their amazement, and the same little hand clench itself in displeasure, when it had hid itself like an outraged thing among the shining folds of her gown. Was this Coll Dhu mad, or rude?

The guest no longer refused to enter, but followed the white figure into a little study where a lamp burned; and the gloomy stranger, the bluff colonel, and the young mistress of the house, were fully discovered to each other's eyes. Evleen glanced at the new comer's dark face, and shuddered with a feeling of indescribable dread and dislike; then, to her father, accounted for the shudder after a popular fashion, saying lightly: "There is some one walking over my grave."

So Coll Dhu was present at Evleen Blake's birthday ball. Here he was, under a roof which ought to have been his own, a stranger, known only by a nickname, shunned and solitary. Here he was, who had lived among the eagles and foxes, lying in wait with a fell purpose, to be revenged on the son of his father's foe for poverty and disgrace, for the broken heart of a dead mother, for the loss of a self-slaughtered father, for the dreary scattering of brothers and sisters. Here he stood, a Samson shorn of his strength; and all because a haughty girl had melting eyes, a winning mouth, and looked radiant in satin and roses.

Peerless where many were lovely, she moved among her friends, trying to be unconscious of the gloomy fire of those strange eyes which followed her unweariedly wherever she went. And when her father begged her to be gracious to the unsocial guest whom he would fain conciliate, she courteously conducted him to see the new picture-gallery adjoining the drawing-rooms; explained under what odd circumstances the colonel had picked up this little painting or that; using every delicate art her pride would allow to achieve her father's purpose, whilst maintaining at the same time her own personal reserve; trying to divert the guest's oppressive attention from herself to the objects for which she claimed his notice. Coll Dhu followed his conductress and listened to her voice, but what she said mattered nothing; nor did she wring many words of comment or reply from his lips, until they paused in a retired corner where the light was dim, before a window from which the curtain was withdrawn. The sashes were open, and nothing was visible but water; the night Atlantic, with the full moon riding high above a bank of clouds, making silvery tracks outward towards the distance of infinite mystery dividing two worlds. Here the following little scene is said to have been enacted.

"This window of my father's own planning, is it not creditable to his taste?" said the young hostess, as she stood, herself glittering like a dream of beauty, looking on the moonlight.

Coll Dhu made no answer; but suddenly, it is said, asked her for a rose from a cluster of flowers that nestled in the lace on her bosom.

For the second time that night Evleen Blake's eyes flashed with no gentle light. But this man was the saviour of her father. She broke off a blossom, and with such good grace, and also with such queen-like dignity as she might assume, presented it to him. Whereupon, not only was the rose seized, but also the hand that gave it, which was hastily covered with kisses.

Then her anger burst upon him.

"Sir," she cried, "if you are a gentleman you must be mad! If you are not mad, then you are not a gentleman!"

"Be merciful," said Coll Dhu; "I love you. My God, I never loved a woman before! Ah!" he cried, as a look of disgust crept over her face, "you hate me. You shuddered the first time your eyes met mine. I love you, and you hate me!"

"I do," cried Evleen, vehemently, forgetting everything but her indignation. "Your presence is like something evil to me. Love me?—your looks poison me. Pray, sir, talk no more to me in this strain."

"I will trouble you no longer," said Coll Dhu. And, stalking to the window, he placed one powerful hand upon the sash, and vaulted from it out of her sight.

Bare-headed as he was, Coll Dhu strode off to the mountains, but not towards his own home. All the remaining dark hours of that night he is believed to have walked the labyrinths of the hills, until dawn began to scatter the clouds with a high wind. Fasting, and on foot from sunrise the morning before, he was then glad enough to see a cabin right in his way. Walking in, he asked for water to drink, and a corner where he might throw himself to rest.

There was a wake in the house, and the kitchen was full of people, all wearied out with the night's watch; old men were dozing over their pipes in the chimney-corner, and here and there a woman was fast asleep with her head on a neighbour's knee. All who were awake crossed themselves when Coll Dhu's figure darkened the door, because of his evil name; but an old man of the house invited him in, and offering him milk, and promising him a roasted potato by-and-by, conducted him to a small room off the kitchen, one end of which was strewed with heather, and where there were only two women sitting gossiping over a fire.

"A thraveller," said the old man, nodding his head at the women, who nodded back, as if to say "he has the traveller's right." And Coll Dhu flung himself on the heather, in the furthest corner of the narrow room.

The women suspended their talk for a while; but presently, guessing the intruder to be asleep, resumed it in voices above a whisper. There was but a patch of window with the grey dawn behind it, but Coll could see the figures by the firelight over which they bent: an old woman sitting forward with her withered hands extended to the embers, and a girl reclining against the hearth wall, with her healthy face, bright eyes, and crimson draperies, glowing by turns in the flickering blaze.

"I do' know," said the girl, "but it's the quarest marriage iver I h'ard of. Sure it's not three weeks since he tould right an' left that he hated her like poison!"

"Whist, asthoreen!" said the colliagh, bending forward confidentially; "throth an' we all know that o' him. But what could he do, the crature! When she put the burragh-bos on him!"

"The *what?*" asked the girl.

"Then the burragh-bos machree-o? That's the spanchel o' death, avourneen; an' well she has him tethered to her now, bad luck to her!"

The old woman rocked herself and stifled the Irish cry breaking from her wrinkled lips by burying her face in her cloak.

"But what is it?" asked the girl, eagerly. "What's the burragh-bos, anyways, an' where did she get it?"

"Och, och! it's not fit for comin' over to young ears, but cuggir (whisper), acushla! It's a sthrip o' the skin o' a corpse, peeled from the crown o' the head to the heel, without crack or split, or the charrm's broke; an' that, rowled up, an' put on a sthring roun' the neck o' the wan that's cowld by the wan that wants to be loved. An' sure enough it puts the fire in their hearts, hot an' sthrong, afore twenty-four hours is gone."

The girl had started from her lazy attitude, and gazed at her companion with eyes dilated by horror.

"Marciful Saviour!" she cried. "Not a sowl on airth would bring the curse out o' heaven by sich a black doin'!"

"Aisy, Biddeen alanna! an' there's wan that does it, an' isn't the divil. Arrah, asthoreen, did ye niver hear tell o' Pexie na Pishrogie, that lives betune two hills o' Maam Turk?"

"I h'ard o' her," said the girl, breathlessly.

"Well, sorra bit lie, but it's hersel' that does it. She'll do it for money any day. Sure they hunted her from the graveyard o' Salruck, where she had the dead raised; an' glory be to God! they would ha' murthered her, only they missed her thracks, an' couldn't bring it home to her afther."

"Whist, a-wauher" (my mother), said the girl; "here's the thraveller gettin' up to set off on his road again! Och, then, it's the short rest he tuk, the sowl!"

It was enough for Coll, however. He had got up, and now went back to the kitchen, where the old man had caused a dish of potatoes to be roasted, and earnestly pressed his visitor to sit down and eat of them. This Coll did readily; having recruited his strength by a meal, he betook himself to the mountains again, just as the rising sun was flashing among the waterfalls, and sending the night mists drifting down the glens. By sundown the same evening he was striding over the hills of Maam Turk, asking of herds his way to the cabin of one Pexie na Pishrogie.

In a hovel on a brown desolate heath, with scared-looking hills flying off into the distance on every side, he found Pexie: a yellow-faced hag, dressed in a dark-red blanket, with elflocks of coarse black hair protruding from under an orange kerchief swathed round her wrinkled jaws. She was bending over a pot upon her fire, where herbs were simmering, and she looked up with an evil glance when Coll Dhu darkened her door.

"The burragh-bos is it her honour wants?" she asked, when he had made known his errand. "Ay, ay; but the arighad, the arighad (money) for Pexie. The burragh-bos is ill to get."

"I will pay," said Coll Dhu, laying a sovereign on the bench before her.

The witch sprang upon it, and chuckling, bestowed on her visitor a glance which made even Coll Dhu shudder.

"Her honour is a fine king," she said, "an' her is fit to get the burragh-bos. Ha! ha! her sall get the burragh-bos from Pexie. But the arighad is not enough. More, more!"

She stretched out her claw-like hand, and Coll dropped another sovereign into it. Whereupon she fell into more horrible convulsions of delight.

"Hark ye!" cried Coll. "I have paid you well, but if your infernal charm does not work, I will have you hunted for a witch!"

"Work!" cried Pexie, rolling up her eyes. "If Pexie's charrm not work, then her honour come back here an' carry these bits o' mountain away on her back. Ay, her will work. If the colleen hate her honour like the old diaoul hersel', still an' withal her will love her honour like her own white sowl afore the sun sets or rises. That, (with a furtive leer), or the colleen dhas go wild mad afore wan hour."

"Hag!" returned Coll Dhu; "the last part is a hellish invention of your own. I heard nothing of madness. If you want more money, speak out, but play none of your hideous tricks on me."

The witch fixed her cunning eyes on him, and took her cue at once from his passion.

"Her honour guess thrue," she simpered; "it is only the little bit more arighad poor Pexie want."

Again the skinny hand was extended. Coll Dhu shrank from touching it, and threw his gold upon the table.

"King, king!" chuckled Pexie. "Her honour is a grand king. Her honour is fit to get the burragh-bos. The colleen dhas sall love her like her own white sowl. Ha, ha!"

"When shall I get it?" asked Coll Dhu, impatiently.

"Her honour sall come back to Pexie in so many days, do-deag (twelve), so many days, fur that the burragh-bos is hard to get. The lonely graveyard is far away, an' the dead man is hard to raise—"

"Silence!" cried Coll Dhu; "not a word more. I will have your hideous charm, but what it is, or where you get it, I will not know."

Then, promising to come back in twelve days, he took his departure. Turning to look back when a little way across the heath, he saw Pexie gazing after him, standing on her black hill in relief against the lurid flames of the dawn, seeming to his dark imagination like a fury with all hell at her back.

At the appointed time Coll Dhu got the promised charm. He sewed it with perfumes into a cover of cloth of gold, and slung it to a fine-wrought chain. Lying in a casket which had once held the jewels of Coll's brokenhearted mother, it looked a glittering bauble enough. Meantime the people of the mountains were cursing over their cabin fires, because there had been another unholy raid upon their graveyard, and were banding themselves to hunt the criminal down.

A fortnight passed. How or where could Coll Dhu find an opportunity to put the charm round the neck of the colonel's proud daughter? More gold was dropped into Pexie's greedy claw, and then she promised to assist him in his dilemma.

Next morning the witch dressed herself in decent garb, smoothed her elf-locks under a snowy cap, smoothed the evil wrinkles out of her face, and with a basket on her arm locked the door of the hovel, and took her way to the lowlands. Pexie seemed to have given up her disreputable calling for that of a simple mushroom-gatherer. The housekeeper at the grey house bought poor Muireade's mushrooms of her every morning. Every morning she left unfailingly a nosegay of wild flowers for Miss Evleen Blake, "God bless her! She had never seen the darling young lady with her own two longing eyes, but sure hadn't she heard tell of her sweet purty face, miles away!" And at last, one morning, whom should she meet but Miss Evleen herself returning alone from a ramble. Whereupon poor Muireade "made bold" to present her flowers in person.

"Ah," said Evleen, "it is you who leave me the flowers every morning? They are very sweet."

Muireade had sought her only for a look at her beautiful face. And now that she had seen it, as bright as the sun, and as fair as the lily, she would take up her basket and go away contented. Yet she lingered a little longer.

"My lady never walk up big mountain?" said Pexie.

"No," Evleen said, laughing; she feared she could not walk up a mountain.

"Ah yes; my lady ought to go, with more gran' ladies an' gentlemen, ridin' on purty little donkeys, up the big mountain. Oh, gran' things up big mountain for my lady to see!"

Thus she set to work, and kept her listener enchained for an hour, while she related wonderful stories of those upper regions. And as Evleen looked up to the burly crowns of the hills, perhaps she thought there might be sense in this wild old woman's suggestion. It ought to be a grand world up yonder.

Be that as it may, it was not long after this when Coll Dhu got notice that a party from the grey house would explore the mountains next day; that Evleen Blake would be of the number; and that he, Coll, must prepare to house and refresh a crowd of weary people, who in the evening should be brought, hungry and faint, to his door. The simple mushroom gatherer should be discovered laying in her humble stock among the green places between the hills, should volunteer to act as guide to the party, should lead them far out of their way through the mountains and up and down the most toilsome ascents and across dangerous places; to escape safely from which, the servants should be told to throw away the baskets of provisions which they carried.

Coll Dhu was not idle. Such a feast was set forth, as had never been spread so near the clouds before. We are told of wonderful dishes furnished by unwholesome agency, and from a place believed much hotter than is necessary for purposes of cookery. We are told also how Coll Dhu's barren chambers were suddenly hung with curtains of velvet, and with fringes of gold; how the blank white walls glowed with delicate colours and gilding; how gems of pictures sprang into sight between the panels; how the tables blazed with plate and gold, and glittered with the rarest glass; how such wines flowed, as the guests had never tasted; how servants in the richest livery, amongst whom the wizen-faced old man was a mere nonentity, appeared, and stood ready to carry in the wonderful dishes, at whose extraordinary fragrance the eagles came pecking to the windows, and the foxes drew near the walls, snuffing. Sure enough, in all good time, the weary party came within sight of the Devil's Inn, and Coll Dhu sallied forth to invite them across his lonely threshold. Colonel Blake (to whom Evleen, in her delicacy, had said no word of the solitary's strange behaviour to herself) hailed his appearance with delight, and the whole party sat down to Coll's banquet in high good humour. Also, it is said, in much amazement at the magnificence of the mountain recluse.

All went in to Coll's feast, save Evleen Blake, who remained standing on the threshold of the outer door; weary, but unwilling to rest there; hungry, but unwilling to eat there. Her white cambric dress was gathered on her arms, crushed and sullied with the toils of the day; her bright cheek was a little sun-burned; her small dark head with its braids a little tossed, was bared to the mountain air and the glory of the sinking sun; her hands were loosely tangled in the strings of her hat; and her foot sometimes tapped the threshold stone. So she was seen.

The peasants tell that Coll Dhu and her father came praying her to enter, and that the magnificent servants brought viands to the threshold; but no step would she move inward, no morsel would she taste.

"Poison, poison!" she murmured, and threw the food in handfuls to the foxes, who were snuffing on the heath.

But it was different when Muireade, the kindly old woman, the simple mushroom-gatherer, with all the wicked wrinkles smoothed out of her face, came to the side of the hungry girl, and coaxingly presented a savoury mess of her own sweet mushrooms, served on a common earthen platter.

"An' darlin', my lady, poor Muireade her cook them hersel', an' no thing o' this house touch them or look at poor Muireade's mushrooms."

Then Evleen took the platter and ate a delicious meal. Scarcely was it finished when a heavy drowsiness fell upon her, and, unable to sustain herself on her feet, she presently sat down upon the door-stone. Leaning her head against the framework of the door, she was soon in a deep sleep, or trance. So she was found.

"Whimsical, obstinate little girl!" said the colonel, putting his hand on the beautiful slumbering head. And taking her in his arms, he carried her into a chamber which had been (say the story-tellers) nothing but a bare and sorry closet in the morning, but which was now fitted up with Oriental splendour. And here on a luxurious couch she was laid, with a crimson coverlet wrapping her feet. And here in the tempered light coming through jewelled glass, where yesterday had been a coarse rough-hung window, her father looked his last upon her lovely face.

The colonel returned to his host and friends, and by-and-by the whole party sallied forth to see the after-glare of a fierce sunset swathing the hills in flames. It was not until they had gone some distance that Coll Dhu remembered to go back and fetch his telescope. He was not long absent. But he was absent long enough to enter that glowing chamber with a stealthy step, to throw a light chain around the neck of the sleeping girl, and to slip among the folds of her dress the hideous glittering burragh-bos.

After he had gone away again, Pexie came stealing to the door, and, opening it a little, sat down on the mat outside, with her cloak wrapped round her. An hour passed, and Evleen Blake still slept, her breathing scarcely stirring the deadly bauble on her breast. After that, she began to murmur and moan, and Pexie pricked up her ears. Presently a sound in the room told that the victim was awake and had risen. Then Pexie put her face to the aperture of the door and looked in, gave a howl of dismay, and fled from the house, to be seen in that country no more.

The light was fading among the hills, and the ramblers were returning towards the Devil's Inn, when a group of ladies who were considerably in advance of the rest, met Evleen Blake advancing towards them on the heath, with her hair disordered as by sleep, and no covering on her head. They noticed something bright, like gold, shifting and glancing with the motion of her figure. There had been some jesting among them about Evleen's fancy for falling asleep on the door-step instead of coming in to dinner, and they advanced laughing, to rally her on the subject. But she stared at them in a strange way, as if she did not know them, and passed on. Her friends were rather offended, and commented on her fantastic humour; only one looked after her, and got laughed at by her companions for expressing uneasiness on the wilful young lady's account.

So they kept their way, and the solitary figure went fluttering on, the white robe blushing, and the fatal burragh-bos glittering in the reflexion from the sky. A hare crossed her path, and she laughed out loudly, and clapping her hands, sprang after it. Then she stopped and asked questions of the stones, striking them with her open palm because they would not answer. (An amazed little herd sitting behind a rock, witnessed these strange proceedings.) By-and-by she began to call after the birds, in a wild shrill way, startling the echoes of the hills as she went along. A party of gentlemen returning by a dangerous path, heard the unusual sound and stopped to listen.

"What is that?" asked one.

"A young eagle," said Coll Dhu, whose face had become livid; "they often give such cries."

"It was uncommonly like a woman's voice!" was the reply; and immediately another wild note rang towards them from the rocks above: a bare saw-like ridge, shelving away to some distance ahead, and projecting one hungry tooth over an abyss. A few more moments and they saw Evleen Blake's light figure fluttering out towards this dizzy point.

"My Evleen!" cried the colonel, recognising his daughter, "she is mad to venture on such a spot!"

"Mad!" repeated Coll Dhu. And then dashed off to the rescue with all the might and swiftness of his powerful limbs.

When he drew near her, Evleen had almost reached the verge of the terrible rock. Very cautiously he approached her, his object being to seize her in his strong arms before she was aware of his presence, and carry her many yards away from the spot of danger. But in a fatal moment Evleen turned her head and saw him. One wild ringing cry of hate and horror, which startled the very eagles and scattered a flight of curlews above her head, broke from her lips. A step backward brought her within a foot of death.

One desperate though wary stride, and she was struggling in Coll's embrace. One glance in her eyes, and he saw that he was striving with a mad woman. Back, back, she dragged him, and he had nothing to grasp by. The rock was slippery and his shod feet would not cling to it. Back, back! A hoarse panting, a dire swinging to and fro; and then the rock was standing naked against the sky, no one was there, and Coll Dhu and Evleen Blake lay shattered far below.

ON THE LEADS

SABINE BARING GOULD

HAVING REALISED A COMPETENCE IN AUSTRALIA, AND HAVING A HANKERING after country life for the remainder of my days in the old home, on my return to England I went to an agent with the object of renting a house with shooting attached, over at least three thousand acres, with the option of a purchase should the place suit me. I was no more intending to buy a country seat without having tried what it was like, than is a king disposed to go to war without knowing something of the force that can be brought against him. I was rather taken with photographs of a manor called Fernwood, and I was still further engaged when I saw the place itself on a beautiful October day, when St. Luke's summer was turning the country into a world of rainbow tints under a warm sun, and a soft vaporous blue haze tinted all shadows cobalt, and gave to the hills a stateliness that made them look like mountains. Fernwood was an old house, built in the shape of the letter H, and therefore, presumably, dating from the time of the early Tudor monarchs. The porch opened into the hall which was on the left of the cross-stroke, and the drawing-room was on the right. There was one inconvenience about the house; it had a staircase at each extremity of the cross-stroke, and there was no upstair communication between the two wings of the mansion. But, as a practical man, I saw how this might be remedied. The front door faced the south, and the hall was windowless on the north. Nothing easier than to run a corridor along at the back, giving communication both upstairs and downstairs, without passing through the hall. The whole thing could be done for, at the outside, two hundred pounds, and would be no disfigurement to the place. I agreed to become tenant of Fernwood for a twelvemonth, in which time I should be able to judge whether the place would suit me, the neighbours be pleasant, and the climate agree with my wife. We went down to Fernwood at once, and settled ourselves comfortably in by the first week in November.

The house was furnished; it was the property of an elderly gentleman, a bachelor named Framett, who lived in rooms in town, and spent most of his time at the club. He was supposed to have been jilted by his intended, after which he eschewed female society, and remained unmarried.

I called on him before taking up our residence at Fernwood, and found him a somewhat blasé, languid, cold-blooded creature, not at all proud of having a noble manor-house that had belonged to his family for four centuries; very willing to sell it, so as to spite a cousin who calculated on coming in for the estate, and whom Mr. Framett, with the malignity that is sometimes found in old people, was particularly desirous of disappointing.

"The house has been let before, I suppose?" said I.

"Oh, yes," he replied indifferently, "I believe so, several times."

"For long?"

"No—o. I believe, not for long."

"Have the tenants had any particular reasons for not remaining on there—if I may be so bold as to inquire?"

"All people have reasons to offer, but what they offer you are not supposed to receive as genuine."

I could get no more from him than this. "I think, sir, if I were you I would not go down to Fernwood till after November was out."

"But," said I, "I want the shooting."

"Ah, to be sure—the shooting, ah! I should have preferred if you could have waited till December began."

"That would not suit me," I said, and so the matter ended.

When we were settled in, we occupied the right wing of the house. The left or west wing was but scantily furnished and looked cheerless, as though rarely tenanted. We were not a large family, my wife and myself alone; there was consequently ample accommodation in the east wing for us. The servants were placed above the kitchen, in a portion of the house I have not yet described. It was a half-wing, if I may so describe it, built on the north side parallel with the upper arm of the western limb of the hall and the H. This block had a gable to the north like the wings, and a broad lead valley was between them, that, as I learned from the agent, had to be attended to after the fall of the leaf, and in times of snow, to clear it.

Access to this valley could be had from within by means of a little window in the roof, formed as a dormer. A short ladder allowed anyone to ascend from the passage to this window and open or shut it. The western staircase gave access to this passage, from which the servants' rooms in the new block were reached, as also the untenanted apartments in the old wing. And as there were no windows in the extremities of this passage that ran due north and south, it derived all its light from the aforementioned dormer window.

One night, after we had been in the house about a week, I was sitting up smoking, with a little whisky-and-water at my elbow, reading a review of an absurd, ignorantly written book on New South Wales, when I heard a tap at the door, and the parlourmaid came in, and said in a nervous tone of voice: "Beg your pardon, sir, but cook nor I, nor none of us dare go to bed."

"Why not?" I asked, looking up in surprise.

"Please, sir, we dursn't go into the passage to get to our rooms."

"Whatever is the matter with the passage?"

"Oh, nothing, sir, with the passage. Would you mind, sir, just coming to see? We don't know what to make of it."

I put down my review with a grunt of dissatisfaction, laid my pipe aside, and followed the maid.

She led me through the hall, and up the staircase at the western extremity.

On reaching the upper landing I saw all the maids there in a cluster, and all evidently much scared.

"Whatever is all this nonsense about?" I asked.

"Please, sir, will you look? We can't say."

The parlourmaid pointed to an oblong patch of moonlight on the wall of the passage. The night was cloudless, and the full moon shone slanting in through the dormer and painted a brilliant silver strip on the wall opposite. The window being on the side of the roof to the east, we could not see that, but did see the light thrown through it against the wall. This patch of reflected light was about seven feet above the floor.

The window itself was some ten feet up, and the passage was but four feet wide. I enter into these particulars for reasons that will presently appear.

The window was divided into three parts by wooden mullions, and was composed of four panes of glass in each compartment.

Now I could distinctly see the reflection of the moon through the window with the black bars up and down, and the division of the panes. But I saw more than that: I saw the shadow of a lean arm with a hand and thin, lengthy fingers across a portion of the window, apparently groping at where was the latch by which the casement could be opened.

My impression at the moment was that there was a burglar on the leads trying to enter the house by means of this dormer.

Without a minute's hesitation I ran into the passage and looked up at the window, but could see only a portion of it, as in shape it was low, though broad, and, as already stated, was set at a great height. But at that moment something fluttered past it, like a rush of flapping draperies obscuring the light.

I had placed the ladder, which I found hooked up to the wall, in position, and planted my foot on the lowest rung, when my wife arrived. She had been alarmed by the housemaid, and now she clung to me, and protested that I was not to ascend without my pistol.

To satisfy her I got my Colt's revolver that I always kept loaded, and then, but only hesitatingly, did she allow me to mount. I ascended to the casement, unhasped it, and looked out. I could see nothing. The ladder was over-short, and it required an effort to heave oneself from it through the casement on to the leads. I am stout, and not so nimble as I was when younger. After one or two efforts, and after presenting from below an appearance that would have provoked laughter at any other time, I succeeded in getting through and upon the leads.

I looked up and down the valley—there was absolutely nothing to be seen except an accumulation of leaves carried there from the trees that were shedding their foliage.

The situation was vastly puzzling. As far as I could judge there was no way off the roof, no other window opening into the valley; I did not go along upon the leads, as it was night, and moonlight is treacherous. Moreover, I was wholly unacquainted with the arrangement of the roof, and had no wish to risk a fall.

I descended from the window with my feet groping for the upper rung of the ladder in a manner even more grotesque than my ascent through the casement, but neither my wife—usually extremely alive to anything ridiculous in my appearance—nor the domestics were in a mood to make merry. I fastened the window after me, and had hardly reached the bottom of the ladder before again a shadow flickered across the patch of moonlight.

I was fairly perplexed, and stood musing. Then I recalled that immediately behind the house the ground rose; that, in fact, the house lay under a considerable hill. It was just possible by ascending the slope to reach the level of the gutter and rake the leads from one extremity to the other with my eye.

I mentioned this to my wife, and at once the whole set of maids trailed down the stairs after us. They were afraid to remain in the passage, and they were curious to see if there was really some person on the leads.

We went out at the back of the house, and ascended the bank till we were on a level with the broad gutter between the gables. I now saw that this gutter did not run through, but stopped against the hall roof; consequently, unless there were some opening of which I knew nothing, the person on the leads could not leave the place, save by the dormer window, when open, or by swarming down the fall pipe.

It at once occurred to me that if what I had seen were the shadow of a burglar, he might have mounted by means of the rain-water pipe. But if so—how had he vanished the moment my head was protruded through the window? and how was it that I had seen the shadow flicker past the light immediately after I had descended the ladder? It was conceivable that the man had concealed himself in the shadow of the hall roof, and had taken advantage of my withdrawal to run past the window so as to reach the fall pipe, and let himself down by that.

I could, however, see no one running away, as I must have done, going outside so soon after his supposed descent.

But the whole affair became more perplexing when, looking towards the leads, I saw in the moonlight something with fluttering garments running up and down them.

There could be no mistake—the object was a woman, and her garments were mere tatters. We could not hear a sound.

I looked round at my wife and the servants,—they saw this weird object as distinctly as myself. It was more like a gigantic bat than a human being, and yet, that it was a woman we could not doubt, for the arms were now and then thrown above the head in wild gesticulation, and at moments a profile was presented, and then we saw, or thought we saw, long flapping hair, unbound.

"I must go back to the ladder," said I; "you remain where you are, watching."

"Oh, Edward! not alone," pleaded my wife.

"My dear, who is to go with me?"

I went. I had left the back door unlocked, and I ascended the staircase and entered the passage. Again I saw the shadow flicker past the moonlit patch on the wall opposite the window.

I ascended the ladder and opened the casement.

Then I heard the clock in the hall strike one.

I heaved myself up to the sill with great labour, and I endeavoured to thrust my short body through the window, when I heard feet on the stairs, and next moment my wife's voice from below, at the foot of the ladder. "Oh, Edward, Edward! please do not go out there again. It has vanished. All at once. There is nothing there now to be seen."

I returned, touched the ladder tentatively with my feet, refastened the window, and descended—perhaps inelegantly. I then went down with my wife, and with her returned up the bank, to the spot where stood clustered our servants.

They had seen nothing further; and although I remained on the spot watching for half an hour, I also saw nothing more.

The maids were too frightened to go to bed, and so agreed to sit up in the kitchen for the rest of the night by a good fire, and I gave them a bottle of sherry to mull, and make themselves comfortable upon, and to help them to recover their courage.

Although I went to bed, I could not sleep. I was completely baffled by what I had seen. I could in no way explain what the object was and how it had left the leads.

Next day I sent for the village mason and asked him to set a long ladder against the well-head of the fall pipe, and examine the valley between the gables.

At the same time I would mount to the little window and contemplate proceedings through that.

The man had to send for a ladder sufficiently long, and that occupied some time. However, at length he had it planted, and then mounted. When he approached the dormer window—

"Give me a hand," said I, "and haul me up; I would like to satisfy myself with my own eyes that there is no other means of getting upon or leaving the leads."

He took me under both shoulders and heaved me out, and I stood with him in the broad lead gutter.

"There's no other opening whatever," said he, "and, Lord love you, sir, I believe that what you saw was no more than this," and he pointed to a branch of a noble cedar that grew hard by the west side of the house.

"I warrant, sir," said he, "that what you saw was this here bough as has been carried by a storm and thrown here, and the wind last night swept it up and down the leads."

"But was there any wind?" I asked. "I do not remember that there was."

"I can't say," said he; "before twelve o'clock I was fast asleep, and it might have blown a gale and I hear nothing of it."

"I suppose there must have been some wind," said I, "and that I was too surprised and the women too frightened to observe it," I laughed. "So this marvellous spectral phenomenon receives a very prosaic and natural explanation. Mason, throw down the bough and we will burn it to-night."

The branch was cast over the edge, and fell at the back of the house. I left the leads, descended, and going out picked up the cedar branch, brought it into the hall, summoned the servants, and said derisively: "Here is an illustration of the way in which weak-minded women get scared. Now we will burn the burglar or ghost that we saw. It turns out to be nothing but this branch, blown up and down the leads by the wind."

"But, Edward," said my wife, "there was not a breath stirring."

"There must have been. Only where we were we were sheltered and did not observe it. Aloft, it blew across the roofs, and formed an eddy that caught the broken bough, lifted it, carried it first one way, then spun it round and carried it the reverse way. In fact, the wind between the two roofs assumed a spiral movement. I hope now you are all satisfied. I am."

So the bough was burned, and our fears—I mean those of the females— were allayed.

In the evening, after dinner, as I sat with my wife, she said to me: "Half a bottle would have been enough, Edward. Indeed, I think half a bottle would be too much; you should not give the girls a liking for sherry, it may lead to bad results. If it had been elderberry wine, that would have been different."

"But there is no elderberry wine in the house," I objected.

"Well, I hope no harm will come of it, but I greatly mistrust——"

"Please, sir, it is there again."

The parlourmaid, with a blanched face, was at the door.

"Nonsense," said I, "we burnt it."

"This comes of the sherry," observed my wife. "They will be seeing ghosts every night."

"But, my dear, you saw it as well as myself!"

I rose, my wife followed, and we went to the landing as before, and, sure enough, against the patch of moonlight cast through the window in the roof, was the arm again, and then a flutter of shadows, as if cast by garments.

"It was not the bough," said my wife. "If this had been seen immediately after the sherry I should not have been surprised, but—as it is now it is most extraordinary."

"I'll have this part of the house shut up," said I. Then I bade the maids once more spend the night in the kitchen, "and make yourselves lively on tea," I said—for I knew my wife would not allow another bottle of sherry to be given them. "To-morrow your beds shall be moved to the east wing."

"Beg pardon," said the cook, "I speaks in the name of all. We don't think we can remain in the house, but must leave the situation."

"That comes of the tea," said I to my wife. "Now," to the cook, "as you have had another fright, I will let you have a bottle of mulled port to-night."

"Sir," said the cook, "if you can get rid of the ghost, we don't want to leave so good a master. We withdraw the notice."

Next day I had all the servants' goods transferred to the east wing, and rooms were fitted up for them to sleep in. As their portion of the house was completely cut off from the west wing, the alarm of the domestics died away.

A heavy, stormy rain came on next week, the first token of winter misery.

I then found that, whether caused by the cedar bough, or by the nailed boots of the mason, I cannot say, but the lead of the valley between the roofs was torn, and water came in, streaming down the walls, and threatening to severely damage the ceilings. I had to send for a plumber as soon as the weather mended. At the same time I started for town to see Mr. Framett. I had made up my mind that Fernwood was not suitable, and by the terms of my agreement I might be off my bargain if I gave notice the first month, and then my tenancy would be for the six months only. I found the squire at his club.

"Ah!" said he, "I told you not to go there in November. No one likes Fernwood in November; it is all right at other times."

"What do you mean?"

"There is no bother except in November."

"Why should there be bother, as you term it, then?"

Mr. Framett shrugged his shoulders. "How the deuce can I tell you? I've never been a spirit, and all that sort of thing. Mme. Blavatsky might possibly tell you. I can't. But it is a fact."

"What is a fact?"

"Why, that there is no apparition at any other time. It is only in November, when she met with a little misfortune. That is when she is seen."

"Who is seen?"

"My aunt Eliza—I mean my great-aunt."

"You speak mysteries."

"I don't know much about it, and care less," said Mr. Framett, and called for a lemon squash. "It was this: I had a great-aunt who was deranged. The family kept it quiet, and did not send her to an asylum, but fastened her in a room in the west wing. You see, that part of the house is partially separated from the rest. I believe she was rather shabbily treated, but she was difficult to manage, and tore her clothes to pieces. Somehow, she succeeded in getting out on the roof, and would race up and down there. They allowed her to do so, as by that means she obtained fresh air. But one night in November she scrambled up and, I believe, tumbled over. It was hushed up. Sorry you went there in November. I should have liked you to buy the place. I am sick of it."

I did buy Fernwood. What decided me was this: the plumbers, in mending the leads, with that ingenuity to do mischief which they sometimes display, succeeded in setting fire to the roof, and the result was that the west wing was burnt down. Happily, a wall so completely separated the wing from the rest of the house, that the fire was arrested. The wing was not rebuilt, and I, thinking that with the disappearance of the leads I should be freed from the apparition that haunted them, purchased Fernwood. I am happy to say we have been undisturbed since.

THE OTHER ROOM

MARY HEATON VORSE

IT WAS AFTER JOHN MACFARLAND WAS CAPTAIN OF BLACK BAR LIFE-SAVING Station for nearly twenty years. Every summer evening all that time I would see him and Mis' MacFarland driving along to the station, for in the summer the crew is off for two months and only the Captain stays there from sundown to sunup.

I never saw her drive past without thinking how she hated to look at the sea. She never sat where she could see salt water. She had been going out to Black Bar all these years and never once had seen the boat-drill. This was because she knew, on account of her husband's being a life-saver, what the sea does to the vessels and the men in them.

When Mis' MacFarland's married daughter died and her little granddaughter Moira came to live with her, I would see all of them, the Captain, Mis' MacFarland and Moira, driving to the station summer evenings, Moira's head peeping out between them like a little bird. And I would always think how Mis' MacFarland hated the sea, and I'd be real glad that the blowing of the sand grinds the station windows white till you can't see through them.

Then John MacFarland died all of a sudden just at the end of the summer. He had been building a yawl out there at the station for nearly two years, and she was just ready to la'nch. I remember meeting him on the boardwalk and him telling me about that boat of his, and thinking what a fine figure of a man he was for over sixty. And next I heard he was dead.

Then Mis' MacFarland had a spell of sickness, and that is how I came to be house-keeper to her and Moira. And I remember how she struck me the first day, for there she was sitting looking out over the bay watching the boats as though the sight of them gave her pleasure. I was so surprised I spoke right out:

"Why, Mis' MacFarland," says I, "I thought you couldn't abide the look of salt water."

"I don't seem to feel there's the difference between land and sea I used to," she says in her gentle, smiling way. "We learn."

I wanted to ask her how we learned what I saw she'd learned, for, if you can understand me, *she seemed to have gotten beyond grief*, but before I could speak Moira came running in and it seemed as if the joy in her heart shone out of her so the place was all lighted up. Her face was tanned so brown that her blue eyes looked strange, and against her skin the fair hair around her forehead looked almost silver.

"Where you been," I said, "to have so much fun?"

"In the back country," says she. "I'm always happy when I come from in back."

"Were you alone?" She stopped a minute before she answered.

"Yes—I suppose so," as if she didn't quite know. It was a funny answer but there was a funny, secret, joyful look on her face that suddenly made me take her in my arms and kiss her, and quite surprised to find myself doing it.

Then she sat down and I went around getting supper; first I thought she was reading, she was so still. Then my eyes happened to fall on her and I saw she was *listening*; then suddenly it was like she *heard*. She had the stillest, shiningest look. All this don't sound like much, I know, but I won't forget how Moira and Mis' MacFarland struck me that first day, not till I die.

When I went to bed I couldn't get 'em out of my mind and I found myself saying out loud:

"There's joy and peace in this house!"

It was quite a time before I sensed what had happened to Mis' MacFarland and what made her change so toward the sea. She'd sit by the window, a Bible in her hands and praying, and you would catch the words of her prayer, and she was praying for those she loved—for the living and the dead. That was only natural—but what I got to understand was that *she didn't feel any different about them*. Not a bit different did she feel about the living and the dead!

They were all there in her heart, the dead and the living, and not divided off at all like in most folks' minds.

I used to wonder about Moira, too, when she'd have these quiet spells—like she was *listening*, but not to any sounds. Then next you'd feel as if she was gladder than anything you'd ever known, sitting there so still with that listening look on her face—only now like I told you, as if she'd *heard*. She'd be so happy inside that you'd like to be near her, as if there was a light in her heart so you could warm yourself by it.

It's hard to tell just how I came to feel this. I suppose just by living with folks you get to know all sorts of things about them. It's not the things they say that matters. I knew a woman once, a pleasant-spoken body, yet she'd pizen the air about her by the unspoken thoughts of her heart. Sometimes these thoughts would burst out in awful fits of anger—but you'd know how she was inside, if she spoke to you always as gentle as a dove.

I'd like to be near Moira those times and yet it made me uneasy, too, her sitting so still, listening, and Mis' MacFarland, as you might say, always looking over the edge of eternity. It was all right for *her* but I'd wonder about Moira. I wondered so hard I took it up with Mis' MacFarland.

"Do you think you're doing right by that child?" I asked her right out plain.

"Why, how do you mean?" she says in her calm way.

"Teaching her things that's all right for us older people to know but that don't seem to me are for young things."

"Teaching her things!" says Mis' MacFarland. "I haven't taught Moira nothing. If you mean them still, quiet, happy spells of hers, she's always had 'em. *She* taught *me*. It was watching her when she was little that taught me—"

"Taught you what?" I asked her when she wouldn't go on.

"It's hard to say it in words—taught me how near all the rest is."

I didn't get her, so I asked what she meant by "the rest."

"The rest of creation!" says she. "Some folks is born in the world feeling and knowing it in their hearts that creation don't stop where the sight of the eyes stop, and the thinner the veil is the better, and something in them sickens when the veil gets too thick."

"You talk like you believed in spooks and God knows what," I says, but more to make myself comfortable than anything else.

"You know what I mean, Jane McQuarry," says she. "There's very few folks, especially older ones, who haven't sometimes felt the veil get thinner and thinner until you could see the light shining through. But we've been brought up to think such ideas are silly and to be ashamed of 'em and only to believe in what we can touch and taste and, in spite of stars shining every night over our heads, to think creation stops with heavy things like us. And how anyone who's ever seen a fish swimming in the water can think that—I don't know. What do they know of us and how can they imagine folks on legs walking around and breathing the air that makes 'em die? So why aren't there creatures, all kind of 'em, we can no more see than a fish can us?"

I couldn't answer that, so I went back to Moira.

"She'll get queer going on like this," I said. "Thin veils and light shining through and creatures that feel about us like we do about fishes are all right for old folks who've lived their lives. She's got to live hers and live it the way ordinary folks do."

"Ain't she happy?" asked Mis' MacFarland. "Don't she like rolling a hoop and playing with the other children? Didn't you say only yesterday her mischief would drive you out of your senses?"

I couldn't deny this. Unless you'd seen her as I had, she was just like any other happy little girl, only happier maybe. Like, I said, you could see her heart shine some days, she was so happy. About that time I found out more how she felt. One still night, for no reason, I got out of my bed and went into Moira's room and there she was sitting up in her bed, her eyes like starlight.

"What are you doing?" I asked.

"Why—I—don't know—I'm waiting for something!"

"Waiting! At this time of the night! How you talk! You lie right down, Moira Anderson, and go to sleep," says I, sharp.

"I can't yet," she says, turning to me. "I haven't been able to find it for two days now. I've not been good inside and I drove it away."

"For mercy's sake, speak plain! What did you drive away?"

"Why, don't you know?" says she. "You lose your good when you're unkind or anything."

"Your *good*!" I says. "Where do you get it from?" For she spoke as though she were talking of something that was outside herself and that came and went.

"It comes from out there," she says, surprised that I didn't know.

"From out there?"

"Oh, out there where all the things are you can *feel* but can't see. There's lots of things out there."

I sat quiet, for all of a sudden I knew plain as day that she thought she was feeling what everybody else in the world felt. She hadn't any idea she was different.

"You know," she said, "how it is when you sit quiet, you know it's there—something good, it floods all over you. It's like people you love make you feel, only more. Just like something beautiful that can get right inside your heart!"

Now this may seem queer to you, for Moira was only a little girl of twelve, but there was a look on her face of just sheer, wonderful love, the way you see a girl look sometimes, or a young mother. It was so beautiful that it brought tears to my eyes. That was the last time I worried about Moira for a long time, for, think I, anything as beautiful as that is holy even if it ain't regular.

I told Mis' MacFarland about our talk.

"What do you think she means when she says 'her good'? Is it like feeling God's near?" I asked. She shook her head.

"I don't believe it," she said. "It's more human than that. I think it's someone *out there* that Moira loves—"

"How you talk!" I said. "Someone out there! If you keep on like this you'll be fey, as my old grandmother used to call it."

"Well," she said, "when you get to where I am, lots of things that seem curious at first thought don't seem a mite more curious than birth or death. Not as curious even, when you come to think about it. What's there so curious I'd like to know, Jane McQuarry, about sensing the feelings of somebody else off to a distance? How about your own mother, the night your brother was lost at sea; didn't she know that and hadn't you all mourned him dead for two months before the real word came to you?"

I couldn't deny this, and I felt that the wind was taken out of my sails. I suppose it was all along with that feeling of hers, with not making a difference between those that were dead and those that were not. All the world was mysterious, and she had a sense of the wonder of the least blade of grass in it, so the things that were not so usual as you might say didn't disturb her any.

"Why," says she, "sometimes I sit in a maze just to look at this room."

"Why, what ails this room?" said I.

'Twas a room like many you've seen hereabouts, with a good horse-hair sofy and the mahogany furniture nice and shiny from being varnished every spring, and over the sofy was thrown a fur rug made in lozenges of harp seal and some other fur and a dark fur border. It was real pretty—it was always wonderful to me that folks like Eskimos can make the things they do. There was some little walrus ivory carvings on the what-not, and on the mantel a row of pink mounted shells, and the model of her father's barkentine when he was in the China trade was on the wall in a glass case.

There's many rooms alike here in this town, with the furniture kept so nice and the things the men's brought back with 'em from the north and south, as you'd expect in a seafaring town—

"What ails this room?" I said.

"Why, it's the folks who made it," says she. "So many and from so far. The whole world's here!" She went on like that until it seemed to me the room was full of folks— savages and Eskimos and seafaring men dead a long while ago, all of 'em. It was wonderful if you looked at it that way.

"So," she said, jumping out on me sudden, "what's there strange about Moira feeling like she does when there's rooms like this? It's less common, but it's no more wonderful."

I saw what she meant, though at the time her explanation of Moira seemed just nonsense to me. Though I'll say I could tell myself when Moira lost what she called "her good." She'd be like a lost child; she'd be like a plant without water and without sun.

Except for that she grew up just like any other girl, a favorite with the children, and a lovely dancer. Only there it was—she had something that other children didn't. It came and went, and when it went away she would grow dim like a smoky lamp. I got so used to it that it just seemed to me like a part of Moira. Nothing that marked her off from nobody, or that gave you anything like a queer and creepy feeling about her. Quite the contrary. She just seemed to have an abiding loveliness about her that everybody else ought to have but didn't, not so much.

When Kenneth Everett came along, "Well," thinks I, "I might have saved myself the worry." For worry I always had for fear that this other feeling of hers would cut her off from the regular things in life. It would have been all very well in another time in the world when a girl could go off and be a saint, but there was no such place for a girl to go in a town like ours.

There was no one but Moira for Kenneth from the first. He was as dark as she was fair; sunlight and starshine they seemed to me. It used to make me happy just to see him come storming in calling out, "Moira!" from the time he passed the Rose of Sharon bush at the gate.

Things in those days seemed right to me. Maybe I didn't see far enough; maybe I wanted too much for her—all the things it seems to me a woman in this life ought to have—and that I hadn't understood what made Moira the way she was. No wonder he loved her. I wish I could make you feel the way Moira looked. You had to feel it in your heart some way. She was fair and her face was tanned with the wind to a lovely golden color and her cheeks were smooth like ripe fruit and her eyes were blue and steady, so dark sometimes they seemed black—seeing eyes, that looked beyond what Mis' MacFarland called "the veil of things." She always seemed to me as if the spirit of the sea and the dunes between them was more her father and mother than anything else. That's a fanciful idea, but she gave you thoughts like that. She was the kind that makes even plain bodies like me fanciful.

There was days when she looked to me like something out of a lovely dream—if you can imagine a girl that's been dreamed by the sea and the dunes come true.

I can't quite tell when I first sensed what Kenneth felt about the times Moira was *away*, for as she went to the back country—you know how wild and secret that back country behind the town is—so there was what you might call the back country of the spirit she used to go to. I guess I found out how he felt one afternoon when he was waiting for her to come back from the dunes. She flew in as if she was helped by wings and she was *listening*—I'd got so used to it by now, it was so part of her, that I forgot how it might strike lots of folks.

He jumped toward her. "Oh, I've been waiting such a time, Moira! I'm so glad you're back!"

I knew he'd seen she was "away" and he was putting himself between her and whatever it was. For a moment she stood looking at him puzzled, as if it had taken her a minute to come back, and then she was as glad to see him as he was her.

"Well," thinks I, "when she gets married all her odd ways will go."

I took to watching them, and then and again I'd see him, as you might say, bring her back to real earth from the shining spot to which her thoughts went. Then sometimes after he'd go she'd be restless like she was when she was little when she'd lost "her good."

I could tell Mis' MacFarland was watching her, too, as she'd sit there praying like she did so much of the time, though it often seemed to me that her prayers wasn't so much prayers as a kind of getting near to those she loved.

I was sure then, as I ever was of anything, that Moira loved Kenneth. At the sound of his voice, light would come to her eyes and color to her face and her hand would fly to her breast as if there wasn't enough air in the world for her to breathe. Yet there was something else, too. She was always sort of escaping from him and then coming back to him like a half-tamed bird, and all the time he came nearer and nearer to her heart. All the time he had more of her thoughts. He fought for them.

He loved her. It seemed he understood her. He sensed all that was in her heart, the way one does with those we love. He'd look at her sometimes with such anxious eyes as if he was afraid for her, as if he wanted to save her from something. I couldn't blame him. I'd felt that way myself, but I'd gotten used to her ways.

Now I saw all over again that there was strange thoughts in her heart—thoughts that don't rightly belong in the kind of world we live in now.

It seems queer to you, I suppose, and kind of crazy, but I couldn't someway see what would become of Moira without "her good." If you'd lived with her the way I did all those years you'd have seen something beautiful reflected in her like the reflection of a star in a little pool at evening, only I couldn't see the star myself, just the reflection of it, she saw the star.

I couldn't blame Kenneth; he wanted for her all the things I'd wanted for her always—and I couldn't bring myself to feel that the reflection of a star was better than the warm light of the fire from the hearth, but it was the star that had made her so lovely.

All this time Mis' MacFarland talked liked nothing was going on and all the time I knew she was watchin'. I'd try and sound her and she'd manage not to answer.

There came a time when I couldn't hold in. Moira'd been out all day on the dunes and toward night the fog had swept over us.

She came back out of the fog with a look on her face like a lost soul. I knew what had happened—I knew what was wrong—yet I couldn't help crying out:

"What's the matter?"

She just looked at me the way animals do when they suffer and can't understand. Her mouth was white and her eyes were dark, as if she was in pain, and when Kenneth came she ran to him as if she would have thrown herself in his arms to hide. They went out on the porch and that was when I could hold in no longer.

"What do you think about it?" I asked Mis' MacFarland right plain out.

"About what?" she asked.

I looked to where they was sitting. 'Twas a wet night; the windows and trees seemed like they was crying. The great drops that fell from them, plop—plop, was like tears. There was a rainbow around the street light that made it look like the moon had dropped down close. Mis' MacFarland looked at them and she just shut her mouth and she shook her head and I could tell she wasn't pleased. Then says she:

"Look!"

The light fell on Moira's face and she was seeing out into the night and I knew she was *out there*. Kenneth spoke and she answered and yet she wasn't with him.

He got up and walked up and down. He spoke again, and again she answered, but Moira's voice answered without Moira. Her face was shining like silver.

She'd heard—she'd found it again.

Then he stood in front of her and said in a strange sort of a voice:

"Moira, what are you doing?"

"Dreaming," she said.

"What are you dreaming about?"

"I don't know—"

"It's not about me, it's nothing about me. Moira, look at me!"

I tell you his tone made my heart bleed. She didn't answer, but looked out into the fog in that absorbed, happy way of hers.

"Moira," he said again, "Moira!" He couldn't get her; he couldn't reach her, any more than if she'd stepped into another world. He put his hands on her shoulders and turned her to him.

"Moira!" he said; his voice was husky with fear. "What do you find out there?" She turned to him as in a dream. She looked at him and she looked like some spirit when she spoke.

"I find the one I love!" she said.

"What do you mean?" he said. "What do you mean?"

"The one I love," she said again.

"Do you mean there's someone you love better than you do me?"

She nodded, with that flooding look of wonder on her face.

"I didn't know," she said next. "I didn't know—not—until now—all about it."

"All about it?" he cried.

"Yes, the meaning of what I felt—that it's someone as real as you, as real as me— that I love someone out there—someone I can't see."

"Moira!" His voice sent shivers down my back. "You're crazy—you're mad— you mean—you mean—you love someone you've never met—someone you *can't see*?" She nodded.

"I've loved him always," she said. "All my life I've known him for ever and ever—I know him more than anything in the world—from the time I could think he has lived in my heart—I didn't know him until now—I only suffered when he wasn't there, and went wandering and searching for him—and you've kept me from him—for I didn't know—"

"Moira," he called to her in his pain, "don't think these things—don't feel these things—"

But she only looked at him kindly and as if she were a long way off.

"I love him," she said, "better than life."

He stared at her then, and I saw what was in his mind. He thought she was crazy—stark, staring crazy. Next he said, "Good night, Moira—my darling, Moira." And he stumbled out into the fog like a man that's been struck blind.

But I knew she wasn't crazy. Maybe 'twas living with Mis' MacFarland made me believe things like that. Maybe 'twas Moira herself. But I didn't feel she was any more crazy than I do when I've heard folks recite, "I know that my Redeemer liveth."

But this isn't the end—this isn't the strangest part! Listen to what happened next.

There was a storm after the fog and strange vessels came into the port—and Moira came to Mis' MacFarland and her eyes were starry and says she:

"I'm going to get 'em to put me aboard that vessel," and she points to a bark which is a rare thing to see nowadays in these waters.

"He's out there," says she.

I didn't doubt her—I didn't doubt her any more than if she'd said the sun was shining when my own eyes were blinded by the light of it.

"Go, then," says Mis' MacFarland.

I tell you Moira was dragged out of that house as by a magnet. The sky had cleared and lay far off and cold, and the wrack of the broken clouds was burning itself up in the west when I saw a dory cast off from the vessel.

It was a queer procession came up our path, some foreign-looking sailors, and they carried a man on a sort of stretcher, and Moira walked alongside of him. I saw three things about him the same way you see a whole country in a flash of lightning.

One was that he was the strangest, the most beautiful man I had ever looked on, and I saw that he was dying.

Then in the next breath I knew he belonged to Moira more than anyone on earth ever had or would. Then all of a sudden it was as if a hand caught hold of my heart and squeezed the blood from it like water out of a sponge, for all at the same time I saw that they hadn't been born at the right time for each other and that they had only a moment to look into each other's faces—before the darkness of death could swallow him.

I couldn't bear it. I wanted to cry out to God that this miracle had come to pass only to be wiped out like a mark in the sand. He was as different from anyone I'd ever seen as Moira was. How can I say to you what I saw and felt. I knew that he belonged to Moira and Moira belonged to him. If I'd have met him at the ends of the earth I'd have known that they belonged together. We all dream about things like this when we're young—about there being a perfect love for us somewhere on earth—but there isn't, because we're not good enough.

The perfect flower can't bloom in most gardens. What these two had was love beyond love—the thing that poor, blundering mankind's been working for and straining toward all down the ages.

Love was what they had, not dimmed and tarnished, not the little flicker that comes for a moment and is gone, like in most of our lives, but the pure fire. The love that mankind tries to find in God—the final wonder. Some of us, at most, have a day or hour—a vision that's as far off and dim as northern lights.

Mis' MacFarland and me looked at each other and, without saying anything, we walked from the room. I saw tears streaming down her face and then I realized that I couldn't see for my own, I was crying the way you may do twice in your life, if you're lucky, because you've seen something so beautiful, poor, weak human nature can't bear it.

After a long time Mis' MacFarland spoke.

"It has to happen on earth, once in a while," she said, "the heart's desire to millions and millions of people living and dead—the dream of all who know the meaning of love. Sometimes it must come true."

That's how it made me feel, and I've always wanted to be a witness to what I saw— but there aren't many to whom you dare to tell it.

After a time we went back and he was lying there, his face shining like Moira's had when she'd found him in the dark spaces where she'd had to search for him. His hair was like dark silver, and his eyes were young like Moira's and blue as the sea at dawn. Wisdom was what was in his face, and love—and he lay there, quiet, holding Moira's hand in his.

But even as I looked a change came over him and I saw the end wasn't far away, and Moira saw it and clung fast to him.

"Take me with you," she said. "I have found you and can't leave you. I've looked for you so often and I couldn't find you. We lost each other so many times and the road together was so blind."

"It's all the same," he said, "she knows." He nodded to Mis' MacFarland. "It's all the same."

Mis' MacFarland motioned to me and I came to her and I was trembling like a leaf. "It's only walking into another room," she said.

Moira sat beside him, his hand in hers, pleading with her eyes. He turned to Mis' MacFarland—"You make her understand," he said, "we all have to wait our turn. You make her understand that we're all the same."

And we knew that he was talking about life and death. And then, as I watched, I saw the life of him was ebbing out and saw that Moira knew it. And then he was gone, just like the slow turning out of a light.

Moira turned to Mis' MacFarland and looked at her, and then I saw she'd gotten to the other side of grief, to where Mis' MacFarland was—to the place where there wasn't any death.

OVER THE WIRES

MRS. H. D. EVERETT

ERNEST CARRINGTON, CAPTAIN IN THE "OLD CONTEMPTIBLES," WAS IN ENGLAND on his first leave from the front. There he had a special errand, hoping to trace a family of the name of Regnier, which had been swept away in the exodus from Belgium, then of recent date. Two old people, brother and sister, harmless folk who had shown him the kindest hospitality before their home was wrecked and burned; and with them their niece Isabeau, who was his chosen love and his betrothed wife. He had endured agonies in these last weeks, receiving no news of them, though he fully believed they had escaped to England: it was more than strange that Isabeau did not write, as she knew his address, though he was ignorant of hers.

A friend in London had made inquiry for him where the thronging refugees were registered and their needs dealt with, but nothing seemed to be known of the Regniers. Now he would be on the spot, and could himself besiege the authorities. Hay might have been lukewarm over the quest, but it seemed impossible that he, Carrington, could fail. His friend Hay, with whom he was to have stayed, had just been transferred from Middlesex to the coast defence of Scotland, but had placed at Carrington's disposal his small flat, and the old family servant who was caretaker.

The flat was a plain little place, but it seemed luxurious indeed to Carrington that first evening, in sharp contrast to his recent experiences roughing it in the campaign. His brain was still in a whirl after the hurried journey, and it was too late to embark upon his quest that night; but the next morning, the very next morning, he would begin the search for Isabeau.

Only one item in Hay's room demands description. There was a telephone installation in one corner; and twice while Carrington's dinner was being served, there came upon it a sharp summons, answered first by the servant, and secondly by himself. Major Hay was wanted, and it had to be detailed how Major Hay had departed upon sudden orders for Scotland only that morning.

Now the meal was over and cleared away, and the outer door closed, shutting Carrington in for the night. Left alone, his thoughts returned to the channel in which they had flowed for many days and nights. Isabeau—his Isabeau: did the living world still hold his lost treasure, and under what conditions and where? And—maddening reflection—what might she not have suffered of privation, outrage, while he was held apart by his soldier's duty, ignorant, impotent to succour! He could picture her as at their last meeting when they exchanged tokens, the light in her eyes, the sweetness of her lips: the image was perfect before him, down to every fold of her white dress, and every ripple of her hair. His own then, pledged to him, and now vanished into blank invisibility and silence. What could have happened: what dread calamity had torn her from him? Terrible as knowledge might be when gained, it was his earnest prayer that he might know.

A groan burst from his lips, and he cried out her name in a passion of appeal.

"Isabeau, where are you? Speak to me, dead or alive!"

Was it in answer that the telephone call began to ring?—not sharply and loudly, like those demands for Major Hay, but thin and faint like their echo. But without doubt it rang, and Carrington turned to the instrument and took down the receiver.

"Yes," he called back. "What is it?"

Great Heaven! it was Isabeau's voice that answered, a voice he could but just hear, as it seemed to be speaking from far away. "Ernest—Ernest," she cried, "have you forgotten me? I have forgotten many things since I was tortured, but not you—never you."

"I am here, my darling. I have come to England seeking you, with no other thought in mind. Tell me, for God's sake, where I can find you. Can I come to-night?"

There was a pause, and then the remote voice began again, now a little stronger and clearer.

"Ernest—is it really you? I can die happy, now you tell me that you love me still. That is all I wanted, just the assurance. All I may have in this world—now."

"Darling, of course I love you: you are all in all to me. Where are you speaking from? Tell me, and I will come?"

"No, no: it is all I wanted, what you have just said. It will be easy now to die. I could never have looked you in the face again—after— I am not fit. But soon I shall be washed clean. What does it say—washed? And they gave them white robes—!"

The voice failed, dying away, and when Carrington spoke there was no answer. He called to her by name, begging her to say if she was in London or where, but either the connection had been cut off, or she did not hear. Then after an interval he rang up the exchange. Who was it who had just used the line? But the clerk was stupid or sleepy, thought there had been no call, but was only just on after the shift, and could not say.

It was extraordinary, that she could know where he was to be found that night, and call to him. And how was it that the voice had ceased without giving him a clue? But surely, surely, it would come again.

To seek his bed, tired as he was, seemed now to be impossible. He waited in the living-room, sometimes pacing up and down, sometimes sitting moodily, his head bent on his hands: could he rest or sleep when a further call might come, and, if unheard, a chance be lost. And a call did come a couple of hours later; the same thin reedy vibration of the wire. In a moment he was at the instrument, the receiver at his ear, and again it was Isabeau's voice that spoke.

"Ernest, can you hear me? Will you say it over again: say that you love me still, in spite of all?"

"Dearest, I love you with all my heart and soul. And I entreat you to tell me where you are, so that I can find you."

"You will be told—quite soon. They are so kind—the people here, but they want to know my name. I cannot tell them any more than Isabeau; I have forgotten what name came after. What was my name when you knew me?"

"My darling, you were Isabeau Regnier. And you were living at Martel, with your old uncle Antoine Regnier, and his sister, Mademoiselle Elise. Surely you remember?"

"Yes; yes. I remember now. I remember all. I was Isabeau Regnier then, and now I am lost—lost—lost! Poor old uncle Antoine! They set him up against the wall and shot him, because they said he resisted; and they dragged the Tante and me away. But the Tante could not go fast enough to please them. They stabbed her in the back with their bayonets, and left her bleeding and moaning, lying in the road to die. Oh, if only they had killed me too. Don't ask me—never ask me—what they did to me!"

"Do not think of it, Isabeau dearest. Think only that I have come to seek you, and that you are safe in England and will be my wife. But I must know where you are, and when I can come to see you."

"I will tell you some time, but not now. The nurse says I must not go on talking; that I am making myself more ill. She's wrong, for it cannot make me ill to speak to you; but I must do as I am bidden. Tell me that you love me; just once again. That you love what I was: you cannot love what I have become."

"Darling, I loved you then, I love you now, and shall love you always. But tell me—you must tell me where—"

She did not answer. This seemed to be the end, for, though he still watched and listened, the wire did not vibrate again that night, nor for many following hours.

He did not spend those hours in inaction. He was early at the London office, and then took the express to Folkestone, but at neither place was there knowledge of the name of Regnier. Nor had he better fortune at the other seaports, which he visited the day following. But where there had been such thronging numbers, despite the organisation vigilance, was it wonderful that a single name had dropped unnoted? And if what had been told him was correct, about the murder of her uncle and aunt, she must have reached England alone.

His next resort was to a private inquiry office, and there an appointment was arranged for him at three o'clock on Friday afternoon.

He had arrived in London on the Monday, and it was on Monday evening and night that those communications from Isabeau came over the wire. Each of the following nights, Tuesday, Wednesday and Thursday, he had spent in Hay's rooms, but from the installed telephone there was no sound or sign.

No sign came until mid-day on Friday, when he was just debating whether to go out to lunch, or have it brought to him from the service down below. The thin, echo-like call sounded again, and he was at once at the receiver.

"Isabeau! Is it you? Speak!"

"Yes, it is I." It was Isabeau's voice that answered, and yet her voice with a difference: it was firmer and clearer than on Monday night, although remote—so remote!

"Where are you? Tell me, that I may come to you. I am seeking you everywhere."

"I do not know where I am. It is all strange and new. But I rejoice in this: I have left behind what was soiled. I would tell you more, but something stops the words. I want you to do something for me: I have a fancy. You have done much, dear Ernest, but this is one thing more."

"What is it, dearest? You have only to ask."

"Go to the end of this street at two o'clock. That is in an hour from now; and wait there till I pass by. I shall not look as I used to do, but I will give you a flower—"

Here the voice failed; he could scarcely distinguish the last words. Strange, that one thing could be said and not another, never what he craved to know. But in an hour he would see her—speak to her, and their separation would be at an end. Not as she used to look! Did she mean changed by what she had suffered? But not so changed, surely, that he would not know, that she would need to identify herself by the gift of a flower. And was the change she spoke of, of the body or the mind? A chill doubt as to the latter, which had assailed him before, crept over him again. But even if it were so, there would be means of healing. She was ill now, shaken by what she had suffered: with love and care, and returning health, all would be well.

He was punctual at the place of appointment. A draughty corner this street-end; but what did he, campaign-hardened, care for chill winds, or for the flying gusts of rain? The passers-by were few for a London street; but each one was carefully scrutinized and each umbrella looked under—that is, if a woman carried it. There was not one, however, that remotely resembled Isabeau. Taxis went by, now and then horse-drawn vehicles; presently a funeral came up the crossing street. A glass hearse with a coffin in it, probably a woman's coffin by its size. A cross of violets lay upon it within, but a couple of white wreaths had been placed outside, next to the driver's seat. A hired brougham was the only following.

They had done better to put the wreaths under shelter, but perhaps no one was in charge who greatly cared. As the cortège came level with the corner, a sharper gust than before tore a white spray from the exposed wreath, and whirled it over towards him; it struck him on the chest, and fell on the wet pavement at his feet. He stooped to pick it up: he loved flowers too well to see it trodden in the mud: and as he did so, a great fear for the first time pierced him through. What might it not signify, this funeral flower? But no, death was not possible: scarcely an hour ago he had heard her living voice.

He waited long at the rendezvous, the flower held in his hand, but no one resembling her came by. Then, chilled and dispirited, but still holding the flower, he turned back to his lodging. It was time and over for his appointment at the inquiry office, but the rain had soaked him through, and he must change to a dry coat.

The servant met him as he came in.

"A letter for you, sir. I am sorry for the delay. You should have had it before, but it must have been brushed off the table and not seen. I found it just now on the floor."

Could it be from Isabeau?—but no, the address was not in her writing. Carrington tore it open: it was from the Belgian central office, and bore date two days bade.

"We have at last received information respecting Mademoiselle Regnier. A young woman who appeared to have lost her memory, was charitably taken in by Mrs. Duckworth, in whose house she has remained through a recent serious illness, the hospitals being over full. She recovered memory last night, and now declares her name to be Isabeau Regnier, formerly of Martel. Mrs. Duckworth's address is 18, Silkmore Gardens, S. Kensington, and you will doubtless communicate with her."

Here at last was the information so long vainly sought, and it must have been from the Kensington house that Isabeau telephoned, though her voice sounded like a long-distance call. He would go thither at once; his application to the inquiry office was no longer needed: but still there was a chill at his heart as he looked at the white flower. Was some deep-down consciousness aware, in spite of his surface ignorance; and had it begun to whisper of the greater barrier which lay between?

As he approached the house in Silkmore Gardens, he might have noticed that a servant was going from room to room, drawing up blinds that had been lowered. At the door he asked for Mrs. Duckworth.

"I am not sure if my mistress can see you, sir," was the maid's answer. "She has been very much upset."

"Will you take in my card, and say my business is urgent. I shall be grateful if she will spare me even five minutes. I am a friend of Mademoiselle Regnier's."

Carrington was shown into a sitting-room at the back of the house, with windows to the ground and a vision of greenery beyond. It was not long before Mrs. Duckworth came to him; she wore a black gown, and looked as if she had been weeping.

"You knew Isabeau Regnier," she began with a certain abruptness. "Are you the Ernest of whom she used to speak?"

"I am. She is my affianced wife, so you see I inquire for her by right. I have been searching for her in the utmost distress, and until now in vain. I have but just heard that you out of your charity took her in, also that she has been ill. May I see her now, to-day?"

The lady's eyes filled again with tears, and she shrank back.

"Ah, you do not know what has happened. O, how sad, how dreadful to have to tell you! Isabeau is dead."

"What, just now, within this hour? She was speaking to me on the telephone only at mid-day."

"No—there is some mistake. That is impossible. She died last Tuesday, and was buried this afternoon. Her coffin left the house at a quarter before two, and my husband went with it to the cemetery. I would have gone too, only that I have been ill."

At first he could only repeat her words: "Dead—Tuesday—Isabeau dead!" She was frightened by the look of his face—the look of a man who is in close touch with despair.

"Oh, I'm so sorry. Oh do sit down, Mr. Carrington. This has been too much for you."

He sank into a chair, and she went hurriedly out, and returned with a glass in her hand.

"Drink this: nay, you must. I am sorry; oh, I am sorry. I wish my husband were here; he would tell you all about it better than I. It has been a grief to us all, to every one in the house; we all grew fond of her. And we began quite to hope she would get well. When she came to us her memory was a blank, except for the wrong that had been done her. That seemed to have blotted out all that was behind, except her love for Ernest—you. But she said she could never look Ernest in the face again, and she wanted to be lost. She took an interest in things here after a while, and she was kind and helpful, like a daughter in the house—we have no children. And then her illness came on again; it was something the matter with the brain, caused by the shock she had sustained. She was very ill, but we could not get her into any hospital, all were too full. But she had every care with us, you may be sure of that, and I think she was happier to be here to the last. So it went on, up and down, sometimes a little better, sometimes worse. Last Monday evening delirium set in. She fancied Ernest was here—you—and she was talking to you all the time. It was as if she heard you answering."

"Have you a telephone installed? Could she get up and go to the telephone?"

"We have a telephone—yes, certainly. But she had not strength enough to leave her bed, and the installation is downstairs in the study."

"I declare to you on my most solemn word that she spoke to me over the telephone—twice on Monday night, and once to-day. It is beyond comprehension. Can you tell me what she said, speaking as she thought to Ernest?"

"She asked you to remind her of her forgotten name. We did not get Regnier till then, nor Martel where she lived; it was as if she heard the words spoken by you. I wrote at once to the organising people to say we had found out: I had no idea then that her death was so near. With the recollection of her name came back—horrors, and she was telling them to you. It seems she lived with an old uncle and aunt: would that be right for the girl you knew? They shot her uncle, the Germans did, when they burnt the house, and stabbed her poor old aunt and left her to die. I can show you a photograph of Isabeau, if that will help to identify. It is only an amateur snapshot, taken in our garden, at the time she was so much better, and, we hoped, recovering. It is very like her as she was then."

Mrs. Duckworth opened the drawer of a cabinet, and took out a small square photograph of a girl in a white dress sitting under a tree, and looking out of the picture with sad, appealing eyes.

Carrington looked at it, and at first he could not speak. Presently he said, answering a question of Mrs. Duckworth's:

"Yes, there can be no doubt."

He had heard enough. Mrs. Duckworth would fain have asked further about the marvel of the voice, but he got up to take leave.

"I will come again if you will permit," he said. "Another day I shall be able to thank you better for all you did for her—for all your kindness. You will then tell me where she is laid, and let me take on myself—all expense. Now I must be alone."

There was ready sympathy in the little woman's face; tears were running down, though her words of response were few. Carrington still held the photograph.

"May I take this?" he said, and she gave an immediate assent. Then he pressed the hand she held out in farewell, and in another moment was gone.

The sequel to this episode is unknown. Carrington sat long that night with the picture before him, the pathetic little picture of his lost love; and cried aloud to her in his solitude: "Isabeau, speak to me, come to me. Death did not make it impossible before: why should it now? Do not think I would shrink from you or fear you. Nothing is in my heart but a great longing—a great love—a great pity. Speak again—speak!"

But no answer came. The telephone in the corner remained silent, and that curious far-off tremor of the wire sounded for him no more.

THE OWL'S EAR

ERCKMANN-CHATRIAN

ON THE 29TH OF JULY, 1835, KASPER BOECK, A SHEPHERD OF THE LITTLE VILLAGE of Hirschwiller, with his large felt hat tipped back, his wallet of stringy sackcloth hanging at his hip, and his great tawny dog at his heels, presented himself at about nine o'clock in the evening at the house of the burgomaster, Petrus Mauerer, who had just finished supper and was taking a little glass of kirchwasser to facilitate digestion.

This burgomaster was a tall, thin man, and wore a bushy gray mustache. He had seen service in the armies of the Archduke Charles. He had a jovial disposition, and ruled the village, it is said, with his finger and with the rod.

"Mr. Burgomaster," cried the shepherd in evident excitement.

But Petrus Mauerer, without awaiting the end of his speech, frowned and said:

"Kasper Boeck, begin by taking off your hat, put your dog out of the room, and then speak distinctly, intelligibly, without stammering, so that I may understand you."

Hereupon the burgomaster, standing near the table, tranquilly emptied his little glass and wiped his great gray mustachios indifferently.

Kasper put his dog out, and came back with his hat off.

"Well!" said Petrus, seeing that he was silent, "what has happened?"

"It happens that the *spirit* has appeared again in the ruins of Geierstein!"

"Ha! I doubt it. You've seen it yourself?"

"Very clearly, Mr. Burgomaster."

"Without closing your eyes?"

"Yes, Mr. Burgomaster—my eyes were wide open. There was plenty of moonlight."

"What form did it have?"

"The form of a small man."

"Good!"

And turning toward a glass door at the left:

"Katel!" cried the burgomaster.

An old serving woman opened the door.

"Sir?"

"I am going out for a walk—on the hillside—sit up for me until ten o'clock. Here's the key."

"Yes, sir."

Then the old soldier took down his gun from the hook over the door, examined the priming, and slung it over his shoulder; then he addressed Kasper Boeck:

"Go and tell the rural guard to meet me in the holly path, and tell him behind the mill. Your *spirit* must be some marauder. But if it's a fox, I'll make a fine hood of it, with long earlaps."

Master Petrus Mauerer and humble Kasper then went out. The weather was superb, the stars innumerable. While the shepherd went to knock at the rural guard's door, the burgomaster plunged among the elder bushes, in a little lane that wound around behind the old church.

Two minutes later Kasper and Hans Goerner, whinger at his side, by running overtook Master Petrus in the holly path.

All three made their way together toward the ruins of Geierstein.

These ruins, which are twenty minutes' walk from the village, seem to be insignificant enough; they consist of the ridges of a few decrepit walls, from four to six feet high, which extend among the brier bushes. Archaeologists call them the aqueducts of Seranus, the Roman camp of Holderlock, or vestiges of Theodoric, according to their fantasy. The only thing about these ruins which could be considered remarkable is a stairway to a cistern cut in the rock. Inside of this spiral staircase, instead of concentric circles which twist around with each complete turn, the involutions become wider as they proceed, in such a way that the bottom of the pit is three times as large as the opening. Is it an architectural freak, or did some reasonable cause determine such an odd construction? It matters little to us. The result was to cause in the cistern that vague reverberation which anyone may hear upon placing a shell at his ear, and to make you aware of steps on the gravel path, murmurs of the air, rustling of the leaves, and even distant words spoken by people passing the foot of the hill.

Our three personages then followed the pathway between the vineyards and gardens of Hirschwiller.

"I see nothing," the burgomaster would say, turning up his nose derisively.

"Nor I either," the rural guard would repeat, imitating the other's tone.

"It's down in the hole," muttered the shepherd.

"We shall see, we shall see," returned the burgomaster. It was in this fashion, after a quarter of an hour, that they came upon the opening of the cistern. As I have said, the night was clear, limpid, and perfectly still.

The moon portrayed, as far as the eye could reach, one of those nocturnal landscapes in bluish lines, studded with slim trees, the shadows of which seemed to have been drawn with a black crayon. The blooming brier and broom perfumed the air with a rather sharp odor, and the frogs of a neighboring swamp sang their oily anthem, interspersed with silences. But all these details escaped the notice of our good rustics; they thought of nothing but laying hands on the *spirit*.

When they had reached the stairway, all three stopped and listened, then gazed into the dark shadows. Nothing appeared—nothing stirred.

"The devil!" said the burgomaster, "we forgot to bring a bit of candle. Descend, Kasper, you know the way better than I—I'll follow you."

At this proposition the shepherd recoiled promptly. If he had consulted his inclinations the poor man would have taken to flight; his pitiful expression made the burgomaster burst out laughing.

"Well, Hans, since he doesn't want to go down, show me the way," he said to the game warden.

"But, Mr. Burgomaster," said the latter, "you know very well that steps are missing; we should risk breaking our necks."

"Then what's to be done?"

"Yes, what's to be done?"

"Send your dog," replied Petrus.

The shepherd whistled to his dog, showed him the stairway, urged him—but he did not wish to take the chances any more than the others.

At this moment, a bright idea struck the rural guardsman.

"Ha! Mr. Burgomaster," said he, "if you should fire your gun inside."

"Faith," cried the other, "you're right, we shall catch a glimpse at least."

And without hesitating the worthy man approached the stairway and leveled his gun.

But, by the acoustic effect which I have already pointed out, the *spirit*, the marauder, the individual who chanced to be actually in the cistern, had heard everything. The idea of stopping a gunshot did not strike him as amusing, for in a shrill, piercing voice he cried:

"Stop! Don't fire—I'm coming."

Then the three functionaries looked at each other and laughed softly, and the burgomaster, leaning over the opening again, cried rudely:

"Be quick about it, you varlet, or I'll shoot! Be quick about it!"

He cocked his gun, and the click seemed to hasten the ascent of the mysterious person; they heard him rolling down some stones. Nevertheless it still took him another minute before he appeared, the cistern being at a depth of sixty feet.

What was this man doing in such deep darkness? He must be some great criminal! So at least thought Petrus Mauerer and his acolytes.

At last a vague form could be discerned in the dark, then slowly, by degrees, a little man, four and a half feet high at the most, frail, ragged, his face withered and yellow, his eye gleaming like a magpie's, and his hair tangled, came out shouting:

"By what right do you come to disturb my studies, wretched creatures?"

This grandiose apostrophe was scarcely in accord with his costume and physiognomy. Accordingly the burgomaster indignantly replied:

"Try to show that you're honest, you knave, or I'll begin by administering a correction."

"A correction!" said the little man, leaping with anger, and drawing himself up under the nose of the burgomaster.

"Yes," replied the other, who, nevertheless, did not fail to admire the pygmy's courage; "if you do not answer the questions satisfactorily I am going to put to you. I am the burgomaster of Hirschwiller; here are the rural guard, the shepherd and his dog. We are stronger than you—be wise and tell me peaceably who you are, what you are doing here, and why you do not dare to appear in broad daylight. Then we shall see what's to be done with you."

"All that's none of your business," replied the little man in his cracked voice. "I shall not answer."

"In that case, forward, march," ordered the burgomaster, who grasped him firmly by the nape of the neck; "you are going to sleep in prison."

The little man writhed like a weasel; he even tried to bite, and the dog was sniffing at the calves of his legs, when, quite exhausted, he said, not without a certain dignity:

"Let go, sir, I surrender to superior force—I'm yours!"

The burgomaster, who was not entirely lacking in good breeding, became calmer.

"Do you promise?" said he.

"I promise!"

"Very well—walk in front."

And that is how, on the night of the 29th of July, 1835, the burgomaster took captive a little red-haired man, issuing from the cavern of Geierstein.

Upon arriving at Hirschwiller the rural guard ran to find the key of the prison and the vagabond was locked in and double-locked, not to forget the outside bolt and padlock.

Everyone then could repose after his fatigues, and Petrus Mauerer went to bed and dreamed till midnight of this singular adventure.

On the morrow, toward nine o'clock, Hans Goerner, the rural guard, having been ordered to bring the prisoner to the town house for another examination, repaired to the cooler with four husky daredevils. They opened the door, all of them curious to look upon the Will-o'-the-wisp. But imagine their astonishment upon seeing him hanging from the bars of the window by his necktie! Some said that he was still writhing; others that he was already stiff. However that may be, they ran to Petrus Mauerer's house to inform him of the fact, and what is certain is that upon the latter's arrival the little man had breathed his last.

The justice of the peace and the doctor of Hirschwiller drew up a formal statement of the catastrophe; then they buried the unknown in a field of meadow grass and it was all over!

Now about three weeks after these occurrences, I went to see my cousin, Petrus Mauerer, whose nearest relative I was, and consequently his heir. This circumstance sustained an intimate acquaintance between us. We were at dinner, talking on indifferent matters, when the burgomaster recounted the foregoing little story, as I have just reported it.

"'Tis strange, cousin," said I, "truly strange. And you have no other information concerning the unknown?"

"None."

"And you have found nothing which could give you a clew as to his purpose?"

"Absolutely nothing, Christian."

"But, as a matter of fact, what could he have been doing in the cistern? On what did he live?"

The burgomaster shrugged his shoulders, refilled our glasses, and replied with:

"To your health, cousin."

"To yours."

We remained silent a few minutes. It was impossible for me to accept the abrupt conclusion of the adventure, and, in spite of myself, I mused with some melancholy on the sad fate of certain men who appear and disappear in this world like the grass of the field, without leaving the least memory or the least regret.

"Cousin," I resumed, "how far may it be from here to the ruins of Geierstein?"

"Twenty minutes' walk at the most. Why?"

"Because I should like to see them."

"You know that we have a meeting of the municipal council, and that I can't accompany you."

"Oh! I can find them by myself."

"No, the rural guard will show you the way; he has nothing better to do."

And my worthy cousin, having rapped on his glass, called his servant:

"Katel, go and find Hans Goerner—let him hurry, and get here by two o'clock. I must be going."

The servant went out and the rural guard was not tardy in coming.

He was directed to take me to the ruins.

While the burgomaster proceeded gravely toward the hall of the municipal council, we were already climbing the hill. Hans Goerner, with a wave of the hand, indicated the remains of the aqueduct. At the same moment the rocky ribs of the plateau, the blue distances of Hundsrück, the sad crumbling walls covered with somber ivy, the tolling of the Hirschwiller bell summoning the notables to the council, the rural guardsman panting and catching at the brambles—assumed in my eyes a sad and severe tinge, for which I could not account: it was the story of the hanged man which took the color out of the prospect.

The cistern staircase struck me as being exceedingly curious, with its elegant spiral. The bushes bristling in the fissures at every step, the deserted aspect of its surroundings, all harmonized with my sadness. We descended, and soon the luminous point of the opening, which seemed to contract more and more, and to take the shape of a star with curved rays, alone sent us its pale light. When we attained the very bottom of the cistern, we found a superb sight was to be had of all those steps, lighted from above and cutting off their shadows with marvelous precision. I then heard the hum of which I have already spoken: the immense granite conch had as many echoes as stones!

"Has nobody been down here since the little man?" I asked the rural guardsman.

"No, sir. The peasants are afraid. They imagine that the hanged man will return."

"And you?"

"I—oh, I'm not curious."

"But the justice of the peace? His duty was to—"

"Ha! What could he have come to the *Owl's Ear* for?"

"They call this the *Owl's Ear*?"

"Yes."

"That's pretty near it," said I, raising my eyes. "This reversed vault forms the *pavilion* well enough; the under side of the steps makes the covering of the *tympanum*, and the winding of the staircase the *cochlea*, the *labyrinth*, and *vestibule* of the ear. That is the cause of the murmur which we hear: we are at the back of a colossal ear."

"It's very likely," said Hans Goerner, who did not seem to have understood my observations.

We started up again, and I had ascended the first steps when I felt something crush under my foot; I stopped to see what it could be, and at that moment perceived a white object before me. It was a torn sheet of paper. As for the hard object, which I had felt grinding up, I recognized it as a sort of glazed earthenware jug.

"Aha!" I said to myself; "this may clear up the burgomaster's story."

I rejoined Hans Goerner, who was now waiting for me at the edge of the pit.

"Now, sir," cried he, "where would you like to go?"

"First, let's sit down for a while. We shall see presently."

I sat down on a large stone, while the rural guard cast his falcon eyes over the village to see if there chanced to be any trespassers in the gardens. I carefully examined the glazed vase, of which nothing but splinters remained. These fragments presented the appearance of a funnel, lined with wool. It was impossible for me to perceive its purpose. I then read the piece of a letter, written in an easy running and firm hand. I transcribe it here below, word for word. It seems to follow the other half of the sheet, for which I looked vainly all about the ruins:

"My *micracoustic* ear trumpet thus has the double advantage of infinitely multiplying the intensity of sounds, and of introducing them into the ear without causing the observer the least discomfort. You would never have imagined, dear master, the charm which one feels in perceiving these thousands of imperceptible sounds which are confounded, on a fine summer day, in an immense murmuring. The bumble-bee has his song as well as the nightingale, the honey-bee is the warbler of the mosses, the cricket is the lark of the tall grass, the maggot is the wren—it has only a sigh, but the sigh is melodious!

"This discovery, from the point of view of sentiment, which makes us live in the universal life, surpasses in its importance all that I could say on the matter.

"After so much suffering, privations, and weariness, how happy it makes one to reap the rewards of all his labors! How the soul soars toward the divine Author of all these microscopic worlds, the magnificence of which is revealed to us! Where now are the long hours of anguish, hunger, contempt, which overwhelmed us before? Gone, sir, gone! Tears of gratitude moisten our eyes. One is proud to have achieved, through suffering, new joys for humanity and to have contributed to its mental development. But howsoever vast, howsoever admirable may be the first fruits of my *micracoustic* ear trumpet, these do not delimit its advantages. There are more positive ones, more material, and ones which may be expressed in figures.

"Just as the telescope brought the discovery of myriads of worlds performing their harmonious revolutions in infinite space—so also will my *micracoustic* ear trumpet extend the sense of the unhearable beyond all possible bounds. Thus, sir, the circulation of the blood and the fluids of the body will not give me pause; you shall hear them flow with the impetuosity of cataracts; you shall perceive them so distinctly as to startle you; the slightest irregularity of the pulse, the least obstacle, is striking, and produces the same effect as a rock against which the waves of a torrent are dashing!

"It is doubtless an immense conquest in the development of our knowledge of physiology and pathology, but this is not the point on which I would emphasize.

Upon applying your ear to the ground, sir, you may hear the mineral waters springing up at immeasurable depths; you may judge of their volume, their currents, and
the obstacles which they meet!

"Do you wish to go further? Enter a subterranean vault which is so constructed
as to gather a quantity of loud sounds; then at night when the world sleeps, when
nothing will be confused with the interior noises of our globe—listen!

"Sir, all that it is possible for me to tell you at the present moment—for in the
midst of my profound misery, of my privations, and often of my despair, I am
left only a few lucid instants to pursue my geological observations—all that I can
affirm is that the seething of glow worms, the explosions of boiling fluids, is something terrifying and sublime, which can only be compared to the impression of the
astronomer whose glass fathoms depths of limitless extent.

"Nevertheless, I must avow that these impressions should be studied further
and classified in a methodical manner, in order that definite conclusions may be
derived therefrom. Likewise, as soon as you shall have deigned, dear and noble
master, to transmit the little sum for use at Neustadt as I asked, to supply my first
needs, we shall see our way to an understanding in regard to the establishment of
three great subterranean observatories, one in the valley of Catania, another in
Iceland, then a third in Capac-Uren, Songay, or Cayembé-Uren, the deepest of the
Cordilleras, and consequently—"

Here the letter stopped.

I let my hands fall in stupefaction. Had I read the conceptions of an idiot—or
the inspirations of a genius which had been realized? What am I to say? to think?
So this man, this miserable creature, living at the bottom of a burrow like a fox,
dying of hunger, had had perhaps one of those inspirations which the Supreme
Being sends on earth to enlighten future generations!

And this man had hanged himself in disgust, despair! No one had answered his
prayer, though he asked only for a crust of bread in exchange for his discovery. It
was horrible. Long, long I sat there dreaming, thanking Heaven for having limited
my intelligence to the needs of ordinary life—for not having desired to make me a
superior man in the community of martyrs. At length the rural guardsman, seeing
me with fixed gaze and mouth agape, made so bold as to touch me on the shoulder.

"Mr. Christian," said he, "see—it's getting late—the burgomaster must have
come back from the council."

"Ha! That's a fact," cried I, crumpling up the paper, "come on."

We descended the hill.

My worthy cousin met me, with a smiling face, at the threshold of his house.

"Well! well! Christian, so you've found no trace of the imbecile who hanged himself?"

"No."

"I thought as much. He was some lunatic who escaped from Stefansfeld or some-where— Faith, he did well to hang himself. When one is good for nothing, that's the simplest way for it."

The following day I left Hirschwiller. I shall never return.

PASSEUR

ROBERT W. CHAMBERS

Because man goeth to his long home,
And the mourners go about the streets.

WHEN HE HAD FINISHED HIS PIPE HE TAPPED THE BRIER BOWL AGAINST THE CHIM-
ney until the ashes powdered the charred log smouldering across the andirons. Then he
sank back in his chair, absently touching the hot pipe-bowl with the tip of each finger
until it grew cool enough to be dropped into his coat pocket.

Twice he raised his eyes to the little American clock ticking upon the mantel. He
had half an hour to wait.

The three candles that lighted the room might be trimmed to advantage; this
would give him something to do. A pair of scissors lay open upon the bureau, and
he rose and picked them up. For a while he stood dreamily shutting and opening the
scissors, his eyes roaming about the room. There was an easel in the corner, and a
pile of dusty canvases behind it; behind the canvases there was a shadow—that gray,
menacing shadow that never moved.

When he had trimmed each candle he wiped the smoky scissors on a paint rag and
flung them on the bureau again. The clock pointed to ten; he had been occupied exactly
three minutes.

The bureau was littered with neckties, pipes, combs and brushes, matches, reels
and flybooks, collars, shirt studs, a new pair of Scotch shooting stockings, and a woman's workbasket.

He picked out all the neckties, folded them once, and hung them over a bit of twine
that stretched across the looking-glass; the shirt studs he shovelled into the top drawer
along with brushes, combs, and stockings; the reels and fly-books he dusted with his
handkerchief and placed methodically along the mantel shelf. Twice he stretched out
his hand toward the woman's workbasket, but his hand fell to his side again, and he
turned away into the room staring at the dying fire.

Outside the snow-sealed window a shutter broke loose and banged monotonously, until
he flung open the panes and fastened it. The soft, wet snow, that had choked the window-panes all day, was frozen hard now, and he had to break the polished crust before
he could find the rusty shutter hinge.

He leaned out for a moment, his numbed hands resting on the snow, the roar of a rising snow-squall in his ears; and out across the desolate garden and stark hedgerow he saw the flat black river spreading through the gloom.

A candle sputtered and snapped behind him; a sheet of drawing-paper fluttered across the floor, and he closed the panes and turned back into the room, both hands in his worn pockets.

The little American clock on the mantel ticked and ticked, but the hands lagged, for he had not been occupied five minutes in all. He went up to the mantel and watched the hands of the clock. A minute—longer than a year to him—crept by.

Around the room the furniture stood ranged—a chair or two of yellow pine, a table, the easel, and in one corner the broad curtained bed; and behind each lay shadows, menacing shadows that never moved.

A little pale flame started up from the smoking log on the andirons; the room sang with the sudden hiss of escaping wood gases. After a little the back of the log caught fire; jets of blue flared up here and there with mellow sounds like the lighting of gas-burners in a row, and in a moment a thin sheet of yellow flame wrapped the whole charred log.

Then the shadows moved; not the shadows behind the furniture—they never moved—but other shadows, thin, gray, confusing, that came and spread their slim patterns all around him, and trembled and trembled.

He dared not step or tread upon them, they were too real; they meshed the floor around his feet, they ensnared his knees, they fell across his breast like ropes. Some night, in the silence of the moors, when wind and river were still, he feared these strands of shadow might tighten—creep higher around his throat and tighten. But even then he knew that those other shadows would never move, those gray shapes that knelt crouching in every corner.

When he looked up at the clock again ten minutes had straggled past. Time was disturbed in the room; the strands of shadow seemed entangled among the hands of the clock, dragging them back from their rotation. He wondered if the shadows would strangle Time, some still night when the wind and the flat river were silent.

There grew a sudden chill across the floor; the cracks of the boards let it in. He leaned down and drew his sabots toward him from their place near the andirons, and slipped them over his chaussons; and as he straightened up, his eyes mechanically sought the mantel above, where in the dusk another pair of sabots stood, little, slender, delicate sabots, carved from red beach. A year's dust grayed their surface; a year's rust dulled the silver band across the instep. He said this to himself aloud, knowing that it was within a few minutes of the year.

His own sabots came from Mort-Dieu; they were shaved square and banded with steel. But in days past he had thought that no sabot in Mort-Dieu was delicate enough to touch the instep of the Mort-Dieu passeur. So he sent to the shore lighthouse, and they sent to Lorient, where the women are coquettish and show their hair under the coiffe, and wear dainty sabots; and in this town, where vanity corrupts and there is much lace on coiffe and collarette, a pair of delicate sabots was found, banded with silver and chiselled in red beach. The sabots stood on the mantel above the fire now, dusty and tarnished.

There was a sound from the window, the soft murmur of snow blotting glass panes. The wind, too, muttered under the roof eaves. Presently it would begin to whisper to him from the chimney—he knew it—and he held his hands over his ears and stared at the clock.

In the hamlet of Mort-Dieu the pines sing all day of the sea secrets, but in the night the ghosts of little gray birds fill the branches, singing of the sunshine of past years. He heard the song as he sat, and he crushed his hands over his ears; but the gray birds joined with the wind in the chimney, and he heard all that he dared not hear, and he thought all that he dared not hope or think, and the swift tears scalded his eyes.

In Mort-Dieu the nights are longer than anywhere on earth; he knew it—why should he not know? This had been so for a year; it was different before. There were so many things different before; days and nights vanished like minutes then; the pines told no secrets of the sea, and the gray birds had not yet come to Mort-Dieu. Also, there was Jeanne, passeur at the Carmes.

When he first saw her she was poling the square, flat-bottomed ferry skiff from the Carmes to Mort-Dieu, a red handkerchief bound across her silky black hair, a red skirt fluttering just below her knees. The next time he saw her he had to call to her across the placid river, "Ohé! Ohé, passeur!" She came, poling the flat skiff, her deep blue eyes fixed pensively on him, the scarlet skirt and kerchief idly flapping in the April wind. Then day followed day when the far call "Passeur!" grew clearer and more joyous, and the faint answering cry, "I come!" rippled across the water like music tinged with laughter. Then spring came, and with spring came love—love, carried free across the ferry from the Carmes to Mort-Dieu.

The flame above the charred log whistled, flickered, and went out in a jet of wood vapour, only to play like lightning above the gas and relight again. The clock ticked more loudly, and the song from the pines filled the room. But in his straining eyes a summer landscape was reflected, where white clouds sailed and white foam curled under the square bow of a little skiff. And he pressed his numbed hands tighter to his ears to drown the cry, "Passeur! Passeur!"

And now for a moment the clock ceased ticking. It was time to go—who but he should know it, he who went out into the night swinging his lantern? And he went. He had gone each night from the first—from that first strange winter evening when a strange voice had answered him across the river, the voice of the new passeur. He had never heard *her* voice again.

So he passed down the windy wooden stairs, lantern hanging lighted in his hand, and stepped out into the storm. Through sheets of drifting snow, over heaps of frozen seaweed and icy drift he moved, shifting his lantern right and left, until its glimmer on the water warned him. Then he called out into the night, "Passeur!" The frozen spray spattered his face and crusted the lantern; he heard the distant boom of breakers beyond the bar, and the noise of mighty winds among the seaward cliffs.

"Passeur!"

Across the broad flat river, black as a sea of pitch, a tiny light sparkled a moment. Again he cried, "Passeur!"

"I come!"

He turned ghastly white, for it was her voice—or was he crazy?—and he sprang waist deep into the icy current and cried out again, but his voice ended in a sob.

Slowly through the snow the flat skiff took shape, creeping nearer and nearer. But she was not at the pole—he saw that; there was only a tall, thin man, shrouded to the eyes in oilskin; and he leaped into the boat and bade the ferryman hasten.

Halfway across he rose in the skiff, and called, "Jeanne!" But the roar of the storm and the thrashing of icy waves drowned his voice. Yet he heard her again, and she called to him by name.

When at last the boat grated upon the invisible shore, he lifted his lantern, trembling, stumbling among the rocks, and calling to her, as though his voice could silence the voice that had spoken a year ago that night. And it could not. He sank shivering upon his knees, and looked out into the darkness, where an ocean rolled across a world. Then his stiff lips moved, and he repeated her name; but the hand of the ferryman fell gently upon his head.

And when he raised his eyes he saw that the ferryman was Death.

POST-MORTEM

ARTHUR RANSOME

DERSLY AND I WENT TO THE *SÉANCE* TOGETHER, THOUGH NEITHER OF US HELD ANY very vivid faith in the possibilities of spiritualism. The tickets had been sent us by one of those people who are never happy until they feel that their own beliefs are shared by their acquaintances. Our faith in the performance was of no fanatic order. It was no more than the general open-eyed interest of young scientific men. He is a young doctor, and I, well, for the last twelve years I have been looking about me, interested in everything, and enjoying things in my own way.

The hall was full of people. There was the indefinable stir of black coats, white collars, and pale dresses, and the crackle of stiff frocks that makes a crowd felt even in a dim room. On a low platform, completely surrounded by the chairs of the spectators, sat two mediums and a demonstrator in the light of a little red-shaded lamp. They seemed just the intense, ostentatiously earnest folk I had imagined such people would be.

Presently, the demonstrator, an ugly little, bristle-haired fellow, with a bulging waistcoat, stood up and explained what was about to happen. He was to send one of the mediums into a trance, when it was not unlikely that in some way or other the spirit world would make itself manifest. He asked for a serious demeanour on the part of the audience, and hoped that, by concentrating their goodwill for the success of the experiment, the spectators would lessen the difficulties of the medium.

One of the mediums, a blonde and vacant-looking girl, had seated herself in readiness at the side of a little table where pencils and paper had been laid. He turned towards her, spoke to her, and made a few passes over her, and, so suddenly that even in the faint light it was noticeable by the audience, her body seemed to relax and lie passive in the chair, leaning over a little towards the table. Throughout the room there was a low murmur of excited petticoats. It was impossible not to watch with considerable curiosity.

The little demonstrator moved the girl's arm round on the table, and we could see under the faint red light of the lamp that her fingers were trembling limply, and that her hand moved at the wrist. He put a pencil in her fingers, and, after one or two failures to place the paper in the right position, he so managed that the girl half lay across the table, with the pencil in her hand just resting on the white sheets.

And then she began to write. Hesitatingly at first, the pencil moved in her limp hand, and then with greater certainty, and increasing speed, until it seemed to fly over the paper.

"It's a fraud," Dersly whispered to me, but I could tell that he was as much affected by the uncanny business as I was myself.

All over the room a faint hiss of whispers rose, until they were silenced by a warning movement of the demonstrator, and succeeded by a stir of petticoats. What were those words traced without effort, and apparently without understanding, by that limp figure on the platform? What meant this message from some being whom not one of us had seen? Or, perhaps, had one of us known the writer? Or, again, was it certain that the writer was not the girl herself, well trained in simulating complete unconsciousness? All these questions were expressed in the rustling murmur of frocks that defied the silencing gestures of the bristle-headed little man on the stage.

At last the hand fell limp again, and the writing stopped. The demonstrator picked up the sheets of paper that he had been laying one by one beneath the quickly moving pencil, and woke the medium with a series of rapid passes. He gave a signal, and the attendants turned on the electric lights, so that we blinked after the gloom. Sorting the papers into order, he read them through, and read them once again with eyebrows raised. Then he rose and spoke hurriedly, in a voice that trembled with excitement.

"Ladies and gentlemen," he said, "in the whole course of my career as an experimenter I have never witnessed the arrival of so extraordinary a message from that world which the ancients knew, and of which we have for so long allowed ourselves to remain in ignorance. I doubt if any spirit document so long, so coherent, so amazing as this has ever been received before. Ladies and gentlemen, we are fortunate in having been present to-night at the reception of the extraordinary communication that I am about to read. Extraordinary as it is, there is a logical sequence in its sentences that shows it to be of far more importance than those futile babblings that have more than once been accepted by men even eminent as revelations from the spirit world. If we cannot, as I confess I cannot, believe in the actuality of the events described in this statement, I think we are justified in assuming that it contains a meaning for us. If it is not a narrative of fact, it is a noble allegory. Who can tell what great truth may not be found in the words I am about to read? Ladies and gentlemen, this is the proudest moment of my life."

He read:—

". . . a man of very strong will [the manuscript opens like that; it is clear that some words were missed by the recording medium]. Having enough money to be able to live my own life, I did so, and spent all my days from my seventeenth year in the study of human nature, and in the development of the powers that I believe to be latent in every strong personality. I travelled in India and in other parts of the East, and continued my studies under the guidance of Hindoo sages, and a Japanese priest. Under their tuition, I came gradually towards that perfect control of the body by the spirit that is the object of the Eastern Yogis and Mahatmas. Only, while by its means they wish to attain peace, I desired only knowledge. Desire of knowledge filled my life with a perpetual thirst. I could not talk to a man for a moment in a railway station without experiencing an overpowering longing to enter into his life, and to understand it as fully, as clearly, as I had brought myself to comprehend my own. I knew that by the same means that win for the Oriental sages their nonchalant peace I should be able to obtain my supreme desire, and by freeing my spirit completely from the thraldom of the body, be able to enter at will into the existences of others.

"With this end constantly before me, I sustained the severe discipline of my teachers, until my powers were as complete as theirs; and, indeed, I liked to fancy, greater. I was able by an effort of will to dissociate my spirit absolutely from my flesh. I was able to go where I wished by the simple effort of will, and to return instantaneously to my body and ordinary existence, when I willed that it should be so. . . ."

The little demonstrator stopped reading for a moment, and looked round the room on the faces of his audience. There was an instant murmur of interest and surprise that died into the breathless silence of expectancy, when he turned again to the sheets in his hand.

". . . . When my powers had reached this state, I returned to England alone. I told no one of my powers. I told no one of what I had been doing. I was too interested in mankind to care to interest it in myself. I took a small house in ——, one of the southern suburbs of London. (Here Dersly nudged my arm. The man had mentioned the district where his practice lay. I nudged him back, and we continued listening.) I settled here in this small house that I furnished very simply. Externals were of no importance to me whatever. I continued my life of investigation.

"One of the rooms of the house I kept absolutely for my own use. The old housekeeper I had engaged was forbidden on pain of dismissal to meddle with it, or even to open its door. She was a trustworthy person up to a point, and I allowed her so much money a week, and left the management of the house to her sole control. Twice every day she laid a simple meal for me in one of the ordinary rooms. I would come out of my privacy, eat it, and again retire. If I did not appear, she had orders to make no inquiries, but to lay the next meal as if I had been present at the one preceding. To make myself doubly secure I had a double door built to my private room. (At this point Dersly made a convulsive movement, which I attributed to his interest in the document.)

"In my private room I would sit and meditate, and perform those other ceremonies prescribed by the wisdom of the East for those who seek to prepare themselves for the exercise of spiritual powers. Then, when I wished to pursue my researches in the motives of men, I would lock both doors, to secure myself from any possible interruption, and then, putting the keys in my pocket, and lying on the sofa make the supreme effort of personality for which my training had prepared me, and leave my body where it lay.

"I had only to will to be in the place where I wished to experiment. To India, Italy, America, to any country on earth I could transport myself by a moment of passionate desire. Each wish was an agony, so great was its intensity. But each wish was gratified for the same reason. I could go to any place, and enter the life of any person, watching the actions of a mind, and understanding them as though they were my own. I had all the joys of a God, and none of the responsibility.

"My only care was to return before curiosity or other motive had induced meddle-some persons to discover my body, which lay dead on my sofa, until I chose to re-enter it. When I was ready to return I merely willed myself again in the flesh, and immediately reassumed command of my body, got up from the sofa, took the keys from my pocket, and passed out again to meet the complaining looks of my housekeeper on those occa-sions when by my tardy return I had given her the trouble of cooking a meal for nothing.

"Several years passed in this way. I made my spiritual excursions as often as twice a week during almost the whole of the time, though, for the reasons I have mentioned, I was always careful to limit the durations of my absences from the flesh. There came a time, however, when my zeal for knowledge, my unbridled curiosity I will now call it, for I know I sought a worthless thing, got the better of my discretion.

"I had become particularly interested in the relations between different coloured races. Not politically, of course, but from an individualistic standpoint. I had watched cases of inter-marriage between persons of different religions, and noticed the pulsa-tions of revulsion between them. I was now interested in the inter-marriage of race. I had watched marriages between black and yellow, African and Malay, and observed the conjugal life of Western women and Turkish men, and many similar examples, in every case, I must remind you, studying not from without, but from within the minds of the characters concerned.

"My attention was caught by an American girl, who was on very friendly terms with a quadroon negro. I entered the negro's mind, and understood that he was pas-sionately attracted by the girl, and was only restraining his emotions by continual remembrance of the bar of race between himself and her. It was inevitable that feel-ings as powerful as his should sooner or later break away the dam of his will, and carry him violently towards the object of his affections. I wished to be present in the mind of the girl, to watch the sudden revulsion that I knew must come, when her coloured friend should force her to think of him in a new, and, as I was pretty nearly assured, repugnant light. I devoted three successive of my spiritual journeys to the examination of these two, and found at the fourth that the moment I wished to observe was very near at hand. The quadroon, a very clever young fellow, respected in spite of his colour, was staying in the same house as the girl. They were constantly together, discussing various problems of social reform, and kept by this interest alone continually in each other's mind. Every moment I thought the girl would realise the meaning of the man's devotion to her. Every moment I might expect the movement of revulsion that I wanted to notice. I associated myself with the girl's mind, lived in her, sharing with her her every thought, dreaming with her her very dreams, for I could not be sure that the moment of understanding would not come to her asleep.

"The moment came. She understood, and, as I had foreseen, was disgusted at the idea that came before her imagination. I watched the frightened activity of her mind, and saw her resolve to leave the house at once, and then, after perhaps the most perfect of all my experiments, I willed my return to the flesh. I had been five days and nights out of my body. The effort of will that was needed to bring me back was greater than it had ever been before. It was a terrible paroxysm of concentrated desire. . .

"I awoke in torture. A thousand thousand pricking pains ran through my body. My veins burned my flesh like white hot platinum wires. A deep booming sound filled my ears, which gradually formed itself into hammer-like throbbings, which, even in my agony, I counted—one, two, and three. I could not speak, or make any sound at all. With a tremendous effort that seemed to loose another myriad demons to twist the skein of painful threads of which my body seemed to be made, I raised my head, and knew that I lay naked on a table. I saw a man with a knife turning towards me. I felt that even my power of will was slipping from me in the torture that plucked at my nerves and scorched my flesh. With all the life that was left to me I compelled my spirit to the mastery of the man with the knife. I drew him with my eyes. . . ."

Dersly suddenly stood up swaying, with his mouth opened as if he were trying to cry aloud. Two women in the audience shrieked, and he collapsed towards the floor.

"Stop that," I shouted at the demonstrator on the platform, not knowing quite what I shouted, or why; and then, with the help of a man who was sitting near us, carried my friend out of the hall. There was a little lavatory outside, where we bathed his forehead. Presently he was sufficiently recovered to get into a cab, when we drove to my rooms, which were not far away.

I helped him to a chair in my study, poured a stiff whisky and soda into him, poured out another, and placed it by his side. He sat there as if half asleep. I have seen more than one man in a moment of strong physical fear, and more than one in the cruellest of mental torture, but I have never seen such a look as Dersly gave me when he opened his eyes. It was like a terrible memory that stares at one, whether one will or no, and will not be forgotten. His eyes, usually merry, alert, eager with the bright energy of the scientist, were like the eyes of an unfortunate madman whom I once saw, possessed by a mania that kept the fear of murder and sudden death his constant companion. I could not look away, and his eyes stared at me. I tell you I felt better when I realised that he did not see me. He put his hands together before his face, and moved them suddenly outwards, as if pushing from him some terrible vision that sought to crowd itself into his brain.

"Dersly!" I said; and again, "Dersly! Dersly!"

The whole of his body shook, from head to foot, and then he seemed to take himself by force and pull himself together. He moved suddenly in the chair, and drank off the glass with sobbing gulps.

"Allegory," he said. "My God, it was true!" The words seemed to shudder on his lips.

"What was true?" I asked, thinking to soothe him, and pouring out another glass for him, clinking the bottle and the glass together with my trembling hands.

"I was the man in the room," he whispered; and then, drinking off the third glass, sat bolt upright in the chair.

"The room had double doors. There could be no other."

"I do not understand," I said. "Tell me another time."

"No, no, no!" he almost shouted; and I saw that it would relieve him to share the thing that was on his mind. He spoke on rapidly.

"Five years ago a very extraordinary man lived in a house in my own district. He lived alone with a housekeeper, and had an odd habit of locking himself in a room, for as long as a whole day at a time. The room had double doors, and the housekeeper was forbidden to open them. For some years this lonely man's life continued, and then, after going into the room one morning, he did not return for lunch or dinner, and did not go to his bedroom at night. The housekeeper, who thought him mad, took no notice, thinking it, as she told me, as much as her place was worth to meddle with the double doors. But when he did not appear next morning, and had not come back at night again, she did the only thing she could, and communicated with the police. They broke open the door, and found the man lying dead on the sofa. The keys of the room were in his coat pocket. There was nothing to show how he had died, but he was too healthy a man, and the circumstances of the case were too unusual, to allow his death to be certified in the ordinary way. A post-mortem was ordered, and I was the surgeon called in to perform it.

"I had already opened his stomach and removed the intestines, preparatory to chemical examination. I had exposed the heart, and had turned aside for a moment to wipe my instruments, when I heard a slight stir on the table. I thought it was no more than the motion of a linen cloth lifted by a draught of air. Then I turned round. It was very hot weather, and for a moment I thought the heat was playing tricks with my brain. For the man's nerves had resumed their sensitiveness. A live nerve is a very different-looking thing from a dead one, you know. The blood that had congealed in the veins had broken out again. The inside of the body, that I had cleaned, perspired with crimson drops. The pale bags of the lungs were feebly throbbing. And then, as I looked, the man moved his head, and I saw into his eyes. He was alive.

"He was alive, and in the most acute pain that it is possible to conceive. He was alive, and would remain alive for minutes, perhaps hours, until the torture exhausted his vitality. It was impossible to save him.

"And then I saw his eyes, drawing me against myself. I knew what he desired. I saw the wild, fierce pain looking out of them, and I knew that in this man there was one thing stronger than the pain. His eyes, tortured as he was, drew me, drew me, though I held back, a weak and little thing in the presence of that tortured indomitable will. Suddenly, he conquered. I picked up a lancet and punctured his heart as it beat before me in his breast.

"When next I knew anything, I was standing holding tight to the edge of the table. Some time must have passed, for the body had again assumed, this time with reality, the appearance of a corpse.

"I certified his death from heart failure, and, until to-night, I had forced myself to think that it was a dream, that I had slept standing by the operating table. I could not let myself believe that I had killed a man. I could not let myself believe that I had seen that . . . that thing. . . ."

And Dersly fainted again.

Powers of Darkness

Alice Perrin

THE TRAIN FLEW ALONG, HEEDLESS, TRIUMPHANT, DRIVING THROUGH THE CLEAR morning sunshine of the English spring as we left behind us the rows of smoke-blackened houses, and their slits of back-yards littered with bottles, boxes, broken china, rusty cans, and squalor indescribable; also the subsequent suburb tapering off into a pathetically respectable line of little villas, some finished and inhabited, others still skeletons within scaffolding.

We had got into the real country, and now we swung swiftly through a fruitful landscape—villages, orchards, sparkling streams, and sloping woods tinted with the tender green of new-born leaves. Through the white smoke that writhed past the carriage-windows we caught flashes of purple heath, the gold of perfumed gorse, unmown meadows powdered with weed-flowers, hedges snowed with hawthorn blossom, cattle red and white in the pastures. It was all so soothing, so peaceful, so contentedly happy, and I had left India recently enough to take the keenest pleasure in the prospect, though, at the same time, I was craving for a pipe, and the compartment into which I had flung myself at the last moment was not labelled "Smoking."

I glanced tentatively at my neighbour, the only other occupant of the carriage, but perceived that she was clearly not the sort of person to encourage smoking, whether lawful or otherwise, in her presence. "Old Maid" was stamped legibly upon her person, from the ginger-coloured felt hat tilted over her nose, to the square-toed, heelless kid boots that protruded from beneath a brown skirt of some harsh material. She was afflicted with a troublesome throat cough which she made no effort to control, and she ignored my existence severely. Presently she drew off a pair of grey cotton gloves, opened a small basket shaped like a hand-bag, and ate a sandwich with care; then she drank what looked like toast-and-water from a medicine bottle, closed the basket neatly, resumed her gloves, and retired coughing behind a magazine with a blue-green cover.

The shape, the colour, and the design on the outside of this periodical seemed vaguely familiar to me. I gazed with curiosity, and saw that it was a missionary publication entitled *The Toiler*. The name called up with violence a memory that for years had been at rest, and in a moment I was back in India, standing heated, irritable, weary, on the platform of a little railway halting-place in the plains, with a copy of *The Toiler* in my hand. What followed now paraded itself through my mind as vividly as though it had only happened yesterday.

It was when I was still junior in the civil service, and had charge of a jungly district away from trains, thinly populated, unfertile, and horribly unhealthy. Naturally I escaped from it whenever I could, though I had to drive forty miles to the nearest railway station—the same little roadside halting-place—where mail trains up and down stopped only at long intervals in the twenty-four hours. I had wanted to catch the up-mail that morning in the height of a terrific hot-weather, when I was snatching ten days' privilege leave to the hills, but owing to a break-down on the road I had missed my train, and found myself at the station at four o'clock in the afternoon with a wait of three hours before me.

The situation was depressing. There was no waiting-room, no rest-house; the walls of the little white-washed building gave out a furnace heat, the masses of bougainvillia creeper that hung to them were gray with dust. The tall yellow grass, through which cut the railway line, rustled like paper in the hot wind, and though a water-carrier came and sprinkled the platform the drops dried even as they fell hissing to the ground. I looked about me with resigned despair. Baking in the hazy distance lay a mud village, behind it rose the spire of a little temple, and the round, heavy outline of a mango-grove. Otherwise there was nothing in sight but miles of dry, crackling grass the height of a man, stretching everywhere like a dreary, drab-coloured sea. A couple of melancholy coolies were squatting by the wall, a mangy pariah dog had curled itself up in the middle of the railway track, and over the whole squalid, desolate scene the sun poured with insufferable heat, scorching, blistering, blinding. I knew it must be two hours at the least before the fierce intensity would relax.

The station babu came out of his little ticket-office.

"Good day, sah!" he said pompously. His sleek black hair glistened with oil, his round face and fat limbs with perspiration; he was wrapped, toga-wise, in a white garment with a red border, and his arms and legs were bare. His feet were thrust into yellow leather slippers that clapped on the ground as he walked.

"This will be a long wait of nonconvenience," he continued with solicitude, as I returned his greeting, "here in such contemptible spot there is want of arrangement for traveller waiting, but they are not often. All the same 'when rain pours it falls'; yesterday two passengers have emerge, though not entirely of European peoples, still of Christian persuasions. They have depart in bullock vehicle of the country to one village afar off, and have discard a literature which, if sir would wish perusal, I can produce."

By this I gathered that some one had left in the station an English paper, or magazine, which the babu thoughtfully imagined might help me to pass the time;

and as I had nothing with me to read I accepted the offer with gratitude. He shuffled back to the ticket-office, and brought out a copy of *The Toiler*—the first I had ever seen— which he presented with a low bow, and apologies for leaving me.

"It is recreation hours," he said solemnly, "and having absence of work at this time your obedient servant seeks benefit of seclusion under marital roof. But I shall kill a bird with two stones, and use all endeavour to cause pleasantness to yourself, sir, beforehand."

He hailed the water-carrier, and in Hindustani admonished him with babu arrogance to be extra lavish with the water; he summoned the two coolies and directed them to place a bench for me in comparative shade, and then he locked up the office and departed.

I opened my tiffin-basket and drank a bottle of soda-water, and then sat alternately fanning myself with *The Toiler*, and studying its pages. I read moving stories of converted ayahs, pathetic accounts of Hindu wives, youths, and maidens, persecuted and outcast for turning Christian, stirring descriptions of martyred missionaries, and of miracles wrought by prayer. Then my attention wandered; the heat was awful, and I began to think of apoplexy, sun-stroke, heart-failure, and recall instances of men dying in a few minutes from the heat even when surrounded with punkahs, ice, thermantidotes, and doctors. I made the "bhistie" pour water on my head, and sat with a wet towel bound about my temples, while the time dragged mercilessly, and the heat seemed to grow worse instead of slackening as the sunset hour came on.

At last the creaking of cart-wheels attracted me to the station entrance, thankful for a diversion of any nature, and I was surprised to see a woman in English dress and a large sun-hat climbing out of a clumsy country cart that was drawn by a couple of lean white bullocks. She was a respectable looking Eurasian—the type of tidy, middle-aged person, not very dark, who might be a teacher in a Government native school, or perhaps the wife of a prosperous subordinate. One sees many hundreds like her in India. But what arrested my notice was the expression on her face—her eyes were strained and wild, and full of terror. She hurried towards me.

"Oh! when does thee train goh?" she demanded in excited "chi-chi," looking about her as if in a panic.

I explained that the up-mail was due at seven o'clock, and the down-mail two hours later. Which did she want?

"The down—the down—oh! if only I could get away more quickly. It is only— what?—five o'clock now! and still four hours to wait!" She went past me on to the platform, wringing her hands. I followed, and inquired if she were ill, or if I could do anything to help her, but at first I got no coherent reply. Then I offered her whisky, which she refused, and soda-water, which she accepted after some argument and persuasion, and when she had drunk it she grew a little calmer.

"Now come and sit down in the shade," I urged, "and tell me what has happened to upset you like this."

She allowed me to guide her to the bench, and when she saw *The Toiler* on the ground she began to cry with noisy unrestraint.

"Oh! there is my *Toiler*!"—she stooped and picked up the paper—"we left it here yesterday—only yesterday. We were so well, and happee, and the Pastor was making Christian jokes and all. I can see him now giving this paper to the station babu, and he said: 'Read this, babu-ji, feast on it till we return; it will do you more good than all the curry, and dal-bat, and ghee!' Now here I have come back without him, and it was only yesterday—" She wailed again.

What a piteous figure she looked in her dusty black gown, her sun-hat, which was too large for her, pushed to the back of her head, the tears trickling down her brown face, and her dull dark eyes in their yellow settings still open wide with the memory of some recent horror. Something had frightened the woman almost to the verge of dementia.

I seated myself by her side and made a few patient inquiries; she appeared to accept my presence and my interest in her plight without question, and after a little while she began to talk more connectedly. In the tiny jungle railway station, amidst the heat and dust and dry crackling grass, I listened to a queer story told in the high-pitched, jerky accents of the Eurasian.

It seemed that her name was de Castro, "Emilee de Castro," and that she was a missionary. "I began by just being Bible-woman, and reading in the Zenanas," she said querulously; "but we have so few workers, and I was promoted to teacher in the villages, itinerating. We converted a whole village two years ago,"—she shuddered—"the village I have just come from. It is many hours' journey from here by cart."

She pointed over the flat landscape, and turned her restless eyes towards me. I nodded.

"It is only a small jungle village," and she mentioned a place not in my district, "the people all gypsies and worshipping a low form of Kali." She shivered again. "They had been led into the right path by our efforts, they were repentant and ashamed of their idolatry, and they had promised our Evangelist they would no longer bow down to the graven image. But we have so few workers, and so much to do, and we were forced to leave them for a time to themselves. They could not be given more than their share of pastoral care, you see. This year there was nobody to spare but me and a native pastor; and we were so proud to be sent! He was a very good man, though black, of course, and so earnest,—and we went out there only yesterday, only yesterday, and now it seems years, not hours, ago."

She paused and looked over her shoulder nervously. "Did you hear a laugh?" she asked, and listened. I assured her that neither she nor I had heard a laugh, and, soothed, she went on with her story in a monotonous sing-song.

"We came here by train, and then got a cart from the nearest village, leaving at dawn with our Bibles and books, and a little tent for me. The pastor said he could sleep under a tree, or anywhere. We had a box, too, with some food and tea and cooking-vessels, and we knew we could get eggs and milk in the village. It was a very hot journey, but we were full of hope and trust, for we had orders to stay a week to preach and teach. But when we got to the village we found that all the good work had been undone by a wicked priest, that where our people had raised the altar of Christ there was now a heathen shrine, with a stone god. The priest was there looking, oh! so evil, with ashes rubbed on his face and body, and his hair hanging down like black snakes, and his eyes all red and fierce; and the people were worshipping, and sacrificing fowls, and offering money, and flowers, and food—"

Miss de Castro pressed her hand to her throat as though the remembrance sickened her, and again she glanced furtively over her shoulder. "Was there any one standing behind me?" she whispered.

"No one," I said steadily; "there is no one near us at all. Tell me, what did the villagers do when they saw you?"

"The people? Oh! they looked ashamed, but the priest was defiant and angry, and there was a great to-do. The pastor and I pleaded with the people, and asked them in sorrow why they had done this thing. They said they were offended with our God, because rain had not fallen on their crops at the right season, and they were in danger of famine. One woman cried out that a wild boar had attacked her husband when they were cutting grass in the jungle, and that though she had called on Christ He had not saved her man from death—and all sorts of foolish things like that. Therefore they had sent for this priest and built the altar to Kali. Then we prayed and preached and warned, we on the one side of the heathen shrine and the priest standing by on the other, scowling. The people listened, and at last some of them came up and told us they would return to Christianity and forego the idol; the rest slunk away to their houses without speaking, for they were afraid of the priest, who all the while said nothing—only looked. The pastor and I sang a hymn of praise, and we asked those that remained with us to destroy the shrine with the image upon it, but, seeing the priest standing there, they were reluctant. So the brave pastor went up and overthrew the idol, and pulled the sinful little altar all to pieces—"

She stopped suddenly, and threw up one arm before her face. "I did not touch it!" she screamed in a shrill, terrified voice; "I did not *touch* it!"

"Hush, hush," I said, with pity; "what is it that has frightened you so, poor thing? Try to tell me quietly—see, you are perfectly safe here, nobody can come near you without my knowing it."

She trembled, but grew reasonable again. "Yes, yes, I am foolish, but I cannot help it: you do not know; how can you, when you were not there? When the pastor destroyed the altar, at first the priest said nothing. Then he came near and held up his arms and cried that Kali would seek vengeance on us. His face was awful to see. But the pastor was not daunted; he said he did not fear Kali, and he called out in a loud voice that if Kali had the power she might prove it by killing him that very night! The people were frightened, but the priest laughed and said: 'Take care, Padresahib, remember that thou art a black man also, and that the gods of thy people are older than the gods of the Feringhees, and, maybe, as mighty in their own way!' But the pastor paid no heed, and we went about amongst the people and prayed with them and tried to give them faith and strength, for our time was short, and we knew it might be long before we could come to them again.

"We were astonished that the priest did not meddle; he just sat down under a tree and watched us, smiling, and saying nothing. Then we pitched the little tent and paid the cart man and let him go, for we knew we could hire another in the village to take us back to the station at the end of our week. We settled our things, and the pastor seemed tired, so I made him some tea, but he would not let me get milk or any supplies from the village in case there should be any attempt to poison us. So we arranged our meal somehow, and afterwards we sat on our campstools till it was dusk and sang hymns in Hindustani to the women and children that gathered round us, and all the time the priest was watching us. Darkness came, and he was still sitting under the tree a little distance from the tent, and when the moon rose I saw that he had not gone, but was there, quiet and not moving, just as if he was made of stone like his idol.

"I was very weary with the heat and the long day, and I needed sleep badly, but the pastor said he did not feel tired now, and he stayed up talking as though he did not wish me to leave him. He said: 'Look at that priest still there. I wish he would go away and not watch us. For hours he has never stirred, and I do not like it!' He seemed to get uneasy, and sat with his back to the priest; and he began asking me some queer things, such as, had I ever heard that the early Christians believed in devils? and he said the old idea was that the heathen idols really were gods, only bad gods—devils. Then he wanted to know what I thought was meant by Powers of Darkness in one of the hymns we had been singing. I said: 'Of course, Sin.' He said: 'Perhaps, but more likely the power of Evil,' and he looked behind him and began muttering.

"I suggested he should lie down and go to sleep, or we should not be rested for the next day's work, but he said: 'How can I sleep with that idolater sitting there staring at me?' and before I could answer he told me a tale of how a fakir had cursed three Englishmen for building a house on his piece of ground, and they had all died. I reproached him, and said I thought he had got fever or a touch of the sun to talk such nonsense, and with that I went into my tent, feeling annoyed. After I had said my prayers and laid down on my little camp-bed, I thought I had been perhaps un-Christian in my heart, so I got up and looked out to wish the pastor good-night. He was lying on the ground with a pillow, and his head was rolled up in a sheet native-fashion, so I did not disturb him. The moon was very bright, and I saw the priest still sitting: the ashes looked white on his face and chest, and his eyes were gleaming. Suddenly I felt afraid. I thought of what the pastor had said about Powers of Darkness, and I felt so alone and helpless, and although it was so hot I shivered. I held my Bible in my hand and prayed, and laid down again on my bed, but I could not sleep for the noises in the jungle so near, and the mosquitos, and knowing that the priest was there, awake and watching.

"I cannot tell how long time had passed when I thought I heard the pastor speaking. I got up and looked out. He was standing in the moonlight, his head was bare, and he was naked to the waist; and as I looked at him he called upon Kali in a loud voice and bowed himself three times to the earth. It was horrible—horrible—and what could I do? I put on some clothes quickly and ran to him. I cried: 'Pastor, what are you doing —you a Christian and all. What does it mean?' He turned to me, and his face looked gray in the moonlight as if he had rubbed it with ashes, like the priest. 'I know I am a Christian and a pastor,' he said; 'I know all that as well as you do. But also do I know that I am a native, and that the gods of my people have power, the Power of Darkness!' He bowed himself again towards where the priest was sitting, and cried: 'Kali! Kali! Kali!'

"I ran to get brandy, which we may use as medicine, for I was sure he was very ill, but when I tried to make him take it he pushed it away, and looking into my face told me to remember that I too had the blood of India in my veins (which is true, though there is only a little touch). I argued and prayed and wept, but he would not listen, and just as though he could not help it he moved towards where the priest sat, all the time bowing to the ground and saying prayers to Kali, the idol, in Hindustani. When he came before the priest he fell on his face and lay still. I ran to him and knelt by his side, and the priest got up and salaamed to me and laughed. He said: 'Hath Kali no power then?' and walked away into the jungle.

"I raised the pastor's head, I cried to him, I roused the villagers, and poured water on his face, and put brandy into his mouth, but it was no use. He was dead—he was dead—and I—I was afraid—I was afraid of the priest, and of Kali, and of the dead man. I was afraid of the Powers of Darkness—and I fled from the place as if I was mad. All the rest of the night I walked and walked along the rough cart-track, and when I had got miles away I rested in a village. I found the cart had also stopped there that brought us from the station, and when the man was ready to move on I came in it as quickly as it could take me. Now I shall have to go back to the Mission and tell them all, and what will they say? They will call me a coward because I left the pastor's body, and the tent, and all the things, and ran away in fear! But I cannot help it. I was afraid, and still I am afraid. Always shall I be afraid now, always shall I see that priest and hear him laugh, and feel the dread of Kali, the Powers of Darkness—"

The poor creature's words were lost in a scream, and she hid her face in her hands shuddering and sobbing convulsively. I did my best to quiet and comfort her, but her self-control was gone, and who can wonder? At last I persuaded her to raise her head, to drink a little more soda-water, to eat a biscuit, and finally to walk up and down the platform in the slackening sunshine, for the evening had begun, the dusty atmosphere was red with sunset, and a sense of release was everywhere.

The babu came back to his ticket-office just before my train was signalled. I took him on one side and bade him see to the comfort of the passenger who was waiting for the down-mail.

"She seems ill, babu," I said confidentially; "let her have your chair to sit on, will you?—till her train goes. I am giving her my pillow. Something has happened to frighten her, and she has left all her things behind."

The babu gazed at the limp figure on the bench.

"It is one of the passengers of yesterday, and she is Eurasian," he remarked without sympathy.

"Well, never mind that; do your best for her, and see her into the down-mail when it comes. My train's just due, and I don't want to lose it."

I mentioned, significantly, that the Traffic Superintendent of the railway was a friend of mine, and instantly the babu was ready to lie down and permit the despised Eurasian to walk over him if she so desired.

Then I went back to Miss de Castro, and ascertained that her return ticket was in her pocket and a little money also. "My train will be here soon," I added, "and you have only two hours to wait for yours, but I want to see that you are comfortable before I leave. Come and sit in the babu's chair, and he will look after you."

She followed me inertly, and I settled her in the clumsy, cane-bottomed chair, with my pillow at her back, and some biscuits and *The Toiler* in her lap. She murmured her gratitude, but still her eyes looked up at me strained with fear from a face that was ashen and drawn. It haunted me long after the train had carried me away into the dusk.

Throughout my journey I thought much of Miss de Castro, and of that which had happened in the jungle village. Then for a brief space the cool climate and distractions of a hill-station blotted her from my mind. I remembered her again when I returned to the heat and my work *via* the hideous little railway halting-place from which I had to drive to my headquarters. A few natives got out of the train, and straggled away towards the neighbouring village, and when the sound of their talk had ceased the place relapsed into its hot, desolate silence. There was the bench upon which I had sat and listened to Miss de Castro's extraordinary story, and behind it the dusty masses of bougainvillia hanging to the wall. The dry grass rustled and crackled, the mud village lay baking in the hazy distance, and presently the babu stood before me, salaaming, with a small bundle of tickets in his hand.

"I wish you happy return to-day," he began rapidly, "and have honour to report that death of missionary Eurasian female was none of the fault of your obedient servant—"

"Heavens, babu!" I interrupted, "what are you talking about?"

"It was not here that she breathed her last," he continued, in haste to exonerate himself from any possible blame. "I myself used all endeavour to keep up her pecker, supplying every assiduous attention, and she depart from here in the train living, but was expire at next station. Since then English religious ones have come here and go on journey into jungle. For the rest I am quite in camera, but lest your honour should think I fail in care towards Eurasian female, and make report to Traffic Superintendent, I have commit facts to paper—"

I waved away the coarse yellow sheets of office paper covered with copperplate handwriting, and questioned the babu closely. Yes; Miss de Castro had gone off by the down-mail alive, and at the next station she had been discovered in her compartment dead. A doctor travelling by the same train had taken charge of the body to its destination, the down-country station which was the headquarters of Miss de Castro's mission. More than this the babu did not know, and more than this I never heard myself.

Just as I was leaving the railway station in a dak-gharry, or post-chaise of the country, the babu ran after me and threw into my lap a paper in a blue-green cover.

"This was remainder of Eurasian female's presence!" he gasped; and the dust swallowed him up as the gharry whirled along the dry road.

It was the copy of *The Toiler*, and I flung it from me, for it could only recall the gray, stricken face and haunted eyes of the half-caste missionary woman, and her terrible story of the Powers of Darkness. What had killed those people? I speculated,

as we rattled and bumped over the uneven ground; and Reason answered "Fear"—
for I remembered that one of them had been a native and the other partly so, with
instinctive belief in the Powers of Darkness handed down to them as heritage
through countless generations.

The English landscape became hidden by engine-houses, trucks, and the paraphernalia
of a large junction. The train slackened, and my companion gathered up her brown
waterproof, her hand-bag-basket, and homely umbrella. She left the compartment
without a glance in my direction.

"Pardon me," I called after her, as I too got out, "you have left something behind
you"; for *The Toiler* lay on the carriage floor.

But she was gone; and I abandoned to its fate the blue-green paper that had called
up such unpleasant memories.

A Psychological Experiment

Richard Marsh

The conversation had been of murders and of suicides. It had almost seemed as if each speaker had felt constrained to cap the preceding speaker's tale of horror. As the talk went on, Mr. Howitt had drawn farther and farther into a corner of the room, as if the subject were little to his liking. Now that all the speakers but one had quitted the smoking-room, he came forward from his corner, in the hope, possibly, that with this last remaining individual, who, like himself, had been a silent listener, he might find himself in more congenial society.

"Dreadful stuff those fellows have been talking!"

Mr. Howitt was thin and he was tall. He seemed shorter than he really was, owing to what might be described as a persistent cringe rather than a stoop. He had a deferential, almost frightened air. His pallid face was lighted by a smile which one felt might, in a moment, change into a stare of terror. He rubbed his hands together softly, as if suffering from a chronic attack of nerves; he kept giving furtive glances round the room.

In reply to Mr. Howitt's observation the stranger nodded his head. There was something in the gesture, and indeed in the man's whole appearance, which caused Mr. Howitt to regard him more attentively. The stranger's size was monstrous. By him on the table was a curious-looking box, about eighteen inches square, painted in hideously alternating stripes of blue and green and yellow; and although it was spring, and the smoking-room was warm, he wore his overcoat and a soft felt hat. So far as one could judge from his appearance, seated, he was at least six feet in height. As to girth, his dimensions were bewildering. One could only guess wildly at his weight. To add to the peculiarity of his appearance, he wore a huge black beard, which not only hung over his chest, but grew so high up his cheeks as almost to conceal his eyes.

Mr. Howitt took the chair which was in front of the stranger. His eyes were never for a moment still, resting, as they passed, upon the bearded giant in front of him, then flashing quickly hither and thither about the room.

"Do you stay in Jersey long?"

"No."

The reply was monosyllabic, but, though it was heard so briefly, at the sound of the stranger's voice Mr. Howitt half rose, grasped the arm of his chair, and gasped. The stranger seemed surprised.

"What's the matter?"

Mr. Howitt dropped back on to his seat. He took out his handkerchief to wipe his forehead. His smile, which had changed into a stare of terror on its reappearance, assumed a sickly hue.

"Nothing. Only a curious similarity."

"Similarity? What do you mean?"

Whatever Mr. Howitt might mean, every time the stranger opened his mouth it seemed to give him another shock. It was a moment or two before he regained sufficient control over himself to enable him to answer.

"Your voice reminds me of one which I used to hear. It's a mere fugitive resemblance." "Whose voice does mine remind you of?"

"A friend's."

"What was his name?"

"His name was—Cookson." Mr. Howitt spoke with a perceptible stammer.

"Cookson? I see."

There was silence. For some cause, Mr. Howitt seemed on a sudden to have gone all limp. He sat in a sort of heap on his chair. He smoothed his hands together, as if with unconscious volition. His sickly smile had degenerated into a fatuous grin. His shifty eyes kept recurring to the stranger's face in front of him. It was the stranger who was the next to speak.

"Did you hear what those men were talking about?"

"Yes."

"They were talking of murders."

"Yes."

"I heard rather a curious story of a murder as I came down to Weymouth in the train."

"It's a sort of talk I do not care for."

"No. Perhaps not; but this was rather a singular tale. It was about a murder which took place the other day at Exeter."

Mr. Howitt started. "At Exeter?"

"Yes; at Exeter."

The stranger stood up. As he did so, one realised how grotesquely unwieldy was his bulk. It seemed to be as much as he could do to move. The three pockets in the front of his overcoat were protected by buttoned flaps. He undid the buttons. As he did so the flaps began to move. Something peeped out. Then hideous things began to creep from his pockets—efts, newts, lizards, various crawling creatures. Mr. Howitt's eyes ceased to stray. They were fastened on the crawling creatures. The hideous things wriggled and writhed in all directions over the stranger. The huge man gave himself a shake. They all fell from him to the floor. They lay for a second as if stupefied by the fall. Then they began to move to all four quarters of the room. Mr. Howitt drew his legs under his chair.

"Pretty creatures, aren't they?" said the stranger. "I like to carry them about with me wherever I go. Don't let them touch you. Some of them are nasty if they bite."

Mr. Howitt tucked his long legs still further under his chair. He regarded the creatures which were wriggling on the floor with a degree of aversion which was painful to witness. The stranger went on.

"About this murder at Exeter, which I was speaking of. It was a case of two solicitors who occupied offices together on Fore Street Hill."

Mr. Howitt glanced up at the stranger, then back again at the writhing newts. He rather gasped than spoke.

"Fore Street Hill?"

"Yes—they were partners. The name of one of them was Rolt—Andrew Rolt. By the way, I like to know with whom I am talking. May I inquire what your name is?"

This time Mr. Howitt was staring at the stranger with wide-open eyes, momentarily forgetful even of the creatures which were actually crawling beneath his chair. He stammered and he stuttered.

"My name's—Howitt. You'll see it in the hotel register."

"Howitt?—I see—I'm glad I have met you, Mr. Howitt. It seems that this man, Andrew Rolt, murdered his partner, a man named Douglas Colston."

Mr. Howitt was altogether oblivious of the things upon the floor. He clutched at the arms of his chair. His voice was shrill.

"Murdered! How do they know he murdered him?"

"It seems they have some shrewd ideas upon the point, from this."

The stranger took from an inner pocket of his overcoat what proved, when he had unfolded it, to be a double-crown poster. He held it up in front of Mr. Howitt. It was headed in large letters, "MURDER! £100 REWARD."

"You see, they are offering £100 reward for the apprehension of this man, Andrew Rolt. That looks as if someone had suspicions. Here is his description: Tall, thin, stoops; has sandy hair, thin on top, parted in the middle; restless grey eyes; wide mouth, bad teeth, thin lips; white face; speaks in a low, soft voice; has a nervous trick of rubbing his hands together." The stranger ceased reading from the placard to look at Mr. Howitt. "Are you aware, sir, that this description is very much like you?"

Mr. Howitt's eyes were riveted on the placard. They had followed the stranger as he read. His manner was feverishly strained. "It's not. Nothing of the sort. It's your imagination. It's not in the least like me."

"Pardon me, but the more I look at you the more clearly I perceive how strong is the resemblance. It is you to the life. As a detective"—he paused, Mr. Howitt held his breath—"I mean supposing I were a detective, which I am not"—he paused again, Mr. Howitt gave a gasp of relief—"I should feel almost justified in arresting you and claiming the reward. You are so made in the likeness of Andrew Rolt."

"I'm not. I deny it! It's a lie!" Mr. Howitt stood up. His voice rose to a shriek. A fit of trembling came over him. It constrained him to sit down again. The stranger seemed amused.

"My dear sir! I entreat you to be calm. I was not suggesting for one moment that you had any actual connection with the miscreant Rolt. The resemblance must be accidental. Did you not tell me your name was Howitt?"

"Yes; that's my name, Howitt—William Howitt."

"Any relation to the poet?"

"Poet?" Mr. Howitt seemed mystified; then, to make a dash at it, "Yes; my great-uncle."

"I congratulate you, Mr. Howitt, on your relationship. I have always been a great admirer of your great-uncle's works. Perhaps I had better put this poster away. It may be useful for future reference."

The stranger, folding up the placard, replaced it in his pocket. With a quick movement of his fingers he did something which detached what had seemed to be the inner lining of his overcoat from the coat itself—splitting the garment, as it were, and making it into two. As he did so, there fell from all sides of him another horde of crawling creatures. They dropped like lumps of jelly on to the floor, and remained for some seconds, a wriggling mass. Then, like their forerunners, they began to make incursions towards all the points of the compass. Mr. Howitt, already in a condition of considerable agitation, stared at these ungainly forms in a state of mind which seemed to approach to stupefaction.

"More of my pretty things, you perceive. I'm very fond of reptiles. I always have been. Don't allow any of them to touch you. They might do you an injury. Reptiles sometimes do." He turned a little away from Mr. Howitt. "I heard some particulars of this affair at Exeter. It seems that these two men, Rolt and Colston, were not only partners in the profession of the law, they were also partners in the profession of swindling. Thorough-paced rogues, both of them. Unfortunately, there is not a doubt of it. But it appears that the man Rolt was not only false to the world at large, he was false even to his partner. Don't you think, Mr. Howitt, that it is odd that a man should be false to his partner?"

The inquiry was unheeded. Mr. Howitt was gazing at the crawling creatures which seemed to be clustering about his chair.

"Ring the bell!" he gasped. "Ring the bell! Have them taken away!"

"Have what taken away? My pretty playthings? My dear sir, to touch them would be dangerous. If you are very careful not to move from your seat, I think I may guarantee that you will be safe. You did not notice my question. Don't you think it odd that a man should be false to his partner?"

"Eh?—Oh!—Yes; very."

The stranger eyed the other intently. There was something in Mr. Howitt's demeanour which, to say the least of it, was singular.

"I thought you would think it was odd. It appears that one night the two men agreed that they would divide spoils. They proceeded to do so then and there. Colston, wholly unsuspicious of evil, was seated at a table, making up a partnership account. Rolt, stealing up behind him, stupefied him with chloroform."

"It wasn't chloroform."

"Not chloroform? May I ask how you know?"

"I—I guessed it."

"For a stranger, rather a curious subject on which to hazard a guess, don't you think so? However, allowing your guess, we will say it was not chloroform. Whatever it was it stupefied Colston. Rolt, when he perceived Colston was senseless, produced a knife—like this."

The stranger flourished in the air a big steel blade, which was shaped like a hunting-knife. As he did so, throwing his overcoat from him on to the floor, he turned right round towards Mr. Howitt. Mr. Howitt stared at him voiceless. It was not so much at the sufficiently ugly weapon he was holding in his hand at which he stared, as at the man himself. The stranger, indeed, presented an extraordinary spectacle. The upper portion of his body was enveloped in some sort of oilskin—such as sailors wear in dirty weather. The oilskin was inflated to such an extent that the upper half of him resembled nothing so much as a huge ill-shaped bladder. That it was inflated was evident, with something, too, that was conspicuously alive. The oilskin writhed and twisted, surged and heaved, in a fashion that was anything but pleasant to behold.

"You look at me! See here!"

The stranger dashed the knife he held into his own breast, or he seemed to. He cut the oilskin open from top to bottom. And there gushed forth, not his heart's blood, but an amazing mass of hissing, struggling, twisting serpents. They fell, all sorts and sizes, in a confused, furious, frenzied heap, upon the floor. In a moment the room seemed to be alive with snakes. They dashed hither and thither, in and out, round and round, in search either of refuge or revenge. And, as the snakes came on, the efts, the newts, the lizards, and the other creeping things, in their desire to escape them, crawled up the curtains, and the doors, and the walls.

Mr. Howitt gave utterance to a sort of strangled exclamation. He retained suf-ficient presence of mind to spring upon the seat of his chair, and to sit upon the back of it. The stranger remained standing, apparently wholly unmoved, in the midst of the seeming pandemonium of creepy things.

"Do you not like snakes, Mr. Howitt? I do! They appeal to me strongly. This is part of my collection. I rather pride myself on the ingenuity of the contrivance which enables me to carry my pets about with me wherever I may go. At the same time you are wise in removing your feet from the floor. Not all of them are poison-ous. Possibly the more poisonous ones may not be able to reach you where you are. You see this knife?" The stranger extended it towards Mr. Howitt. "This is the knife with which, when he had stupefied him, Andrew Rolt slashed Douglas Colston about the head and face and throat like this!"

The removal of his overcoat, and, still more, the vomiting forth of the nest of serpents, had decreased the stranger's bulk by more than one-half. Disembarrassing himself of the remnants of his oilskins, he removed his soft felt hat, and, tearing off his huge black beard, stood revealed as a tall, upstanding, muscularly-built man, whose head and face and neck were almost entirely concealed by strips of plaster, which crossed and recrossed each other in all possible and impossible directions.

There was silence. The two men stared at each other. With a gasp Mr. Howitt found his voice.

"Douglas!"

"Andrew!"

"I thought you were dead."

"I am risen from the grave."

"I am glad you are not dead."

"Why?"

Mr. Howitt paused as if to moisten his parched lips. "I never meant to kill you."

"In that case, Andrew, your meaning was unfortunate. I do mean to kill you—now."

"Don't kill me, Douglas."

"A reason, Andrew?"

"If you knew what I have suffered since I thought I had killed you, you would not wish to take upon yourself the burden which I have had to bear."

"My nerves, Andrew, are stronger than yours. What would crush you to the ground would not weigh on me at all. Surely you knew that before." Mr. Howitt fidgeted on the back of his chair. "It was not that you did not mean to kill me. You lacked the courage. You gashed me like some frenzied cur. Then, afraid of your own handiwork, you ran to save your skin. You dared not wait to see if what you had meant to do was done. Why, Andrew, as soon as the effects of your drug had gone, I sat up. I heard you running down the stairs, I saw your knife lying at my side, all stained with my own blood—see, Andrew, the stains are on it still! I even picked up this scrap of paper which had fallen from your pocket on to the floor."

He held out a piece of paper towards Mr. Howitt.

"It is the advertisement of an hotel—Hotel de la Couronne d'Or, St. Hélier's, Jersey. I said to myself, I wonder if that is where Andrew is gone. I will go and see. And if I find him I will kill him. I have found you, and behold, your heart has so melted within you that already you feel something of the pangs of death." Mr. Howitt did seem to be more dead than alive. His face was bloodless. He was shivering as if with cold.

"These melodramatic and, indeed, slightly absurd details"—the stranger waved his hand towards the efts, and newts, and snakes, and lizards—"were planned for your especial benefit. I was aware what a horror you had of creeping things. I take it, it is constitutional. I knew I had but to spring on you half a bushel or so of reptiles, and all the little courage you ever had would vanish. As it has done."

The stranger stopped. He looked, with evident enjoyment of his misery, at the miserable creature squatted on the back of the chair in front of him. Mr. Howitt tried to speak. Two or three times he opened his mouth, but there came forth no sound. At last he said, in curiously husky tones, "Douglas?"

"Andrew?"

"If you do it they are sure to have you. It is not easy to get away from Jersey."

"How kind of you, Andrew, and how thoughtful! But you might have spared yourself your thought. I have arranged all that. There is a cattle-boat leaves for St. Malo in half an hour on the tide. You will be dead in less than half an hour—so I go in that."

Again there were movements of Mr. Howitt's lips. But no words were audible. The stranger continued.

"The question which I have had to ask myself has been, how shall I kill you? I might kill you with the knife with which you endeavoured to kill me." As he spoke, he tested the keenness of the blade with his fingers. "With it I might slit your throat from ear to ear, or I might use it in half a hundred different ways. Or I might shoot you like a dog." Producing a revolver, he pointed it at Mr. Howitt's head. "Sit quite still, Andrew, or I may be tempted to flatten your nose with a bullet. You know I can shoot straight. Or I might avail myself of this."

Still keeping the revolver pointed at Mr. Howitt's head, he took from his waistcoat pocket a small syringe.

"This, Andrew, is a hypodermic syringe. I have but to take firm hold of you, thrust the point into one of the blood-vessels of your neck, and inject the contents; you will at once endure exquisite tortures which, after two or three minutes, which will seem to you like centuries, will result in death. But I have resolved to do myself, and you, this service, with neither of the three."

Again the stranger stopped. This time Mr. Howitt made no attempt to speak. He was not a pleasant object to contemplate. As the other had said, to judge from his appearance he already seemed to be suffering some of the pangs of death. All the manhood had gone from him. Only the shell of what was meant to be a man remained. The exhibition of his pitiful cowardice afforded his whilom partner unqualified pleasure.

"Have you ever heard of an author named De Quincey? He wrote on murder considered as a fine art. It is as a fine art I have had to consider it. In that connection I have had to consider three things: 1. That you must be killed. 2. That you must be killed in such a manner that you shall suffer the greatest possible amount of pain. 3.—and not the least essential—That you must be killed in such a manner that under no circumstances can I be found guilty of having caused your death. I have given these three points my careful consideration, and I think that I have been able to find something which will satisfy all the requirements. That something is in this box."

The stranger went to the box which was on the table—the square box which had, as ornamentation, the hideously alternating stripes of blue and green and yellow. He rapped on it with his knuckles. As he did so, from within it there came a peculiar sound like a sullen murmur.

"You hear? It is death calling to you from the box. It awaits its prey. It bids you come."

He struck the box a little bit harder. There proceeded from it, as if responsive to his touch, what seemed to be a series of sharp and angry screeches.

"Again! It loses patience. It grows angry. It bids you hasten. Ah!"

He brought his hand down heavily upon the top of the box. Immediately the room was filled with a discord of sounds, cries, yelpings, screams, snarls, the tumult dying away in what seemed to be an intermittent, sullen roaring. The noise served to rouse the snakes, and efts, and lizards to renewed activity. The room seemed again to be alive with them. As he listened, Mr. Howitt became livid. He was, apparently, becoming imbecile with terror.

His aforetime partner, turning to him, pointed to the box with outstretched hand.

"What a row it makes! What a rage it's in! Your death screams out to you, with a ravening longing—the most awful death that a man can die. Andrew—to die! And such a death as this!"

Again he struck the box. Again there came from it that dreadful discord.

"Stand up!"

Mr. Howitt looked at him, as a drivelling idiot might look at a keeper whom he fears. It seemed as if he made an effort to frame his lips for the utterance of speech. But he had lost the control of his muscles. With every fibre of his being he seemed to make a dumb appeal for mercy to the man in front of him. The appeal was made in vain. The command was repeated.

"Get off your chair, and stand upon the floor."

Like some trembling automaton Mr. Howitt did as he was told. He stood there like some lunatic deaf mute. It seemed as if he could not move, save at the bidding of his master. That master was careful not to loosen, by so much as a hair's-breadth, the hold he had of him.

"I now proceed to put into execution the most exquisite part of my whole scheme. Were I to unfasten the box and let death loose upon you, some time or other it might come out—these things do come out at times—and it might then appear that the deed had, after all, been mine. I would avoid such risks. So you shall be your own slayer, Andrew. You shall yourself unloose the box, and you shall yourself give death its freedom, so that it may work on you its will. The most awful death that a man can die! Come to me, here!"

And the man went to him, moving with a curious, stiff gait, such as one might expect from an automaton. The creatures writhing on the floor went unheeded, even though he trod on them.

"Stand still in front of the box." The man stood still. "Kneel down."

The man did hesitate. There did seem to come to him some consciousness that he should himself be the originator of his own volition. There did come on to his distorted visage an agony of supplication which it was terrible to witness.

The only result was an emphasised renewal of the command.

"Kneel down upon the floor."

And the man knelt down. His face was within a few inches of the painted box. As he knelt the stranger struck the box once more with the knuckles of his hand. And again there came from it that strange tumult of discordant sounds.

"Quick, Andrew, quick, quick! Press your finger on the spring! Unfasten the box!"

The man did as he was bid. And, in an instant, like a conjurer's trick, the box fell all to pieces, and there sprang from it, right into Mr. Howitt's face, with a dreadful noise, some dreadful thing which enfolded his head in its hideous embraces.

There was a silence.

Then the stranger laughed. He called softly, "Andrew!" All was still. "Andrew!" Again there was none that answered. The laughter was renewed.

"I do believe he's dead. I had always supposed that the stories about being able to frighten a man to death were all apocryphal. But that a man could be frightened to death by a thing like this—a toy!"

He touched the creature which concealed Mr. Howitt's head and face. As he said, it was a toy. A development of the old-fashioned jack-in-the-box. A dreadful development, and a dreadful toy. Made in the image of some creature of the squid class, painted in livid hues, provided with a dozen long, quivering tentacles, each actuated by a spring of its own. It was these tentacles which had enfolded Mr. Howitt's head in their embraces.

As the stranger put them from him, Mr. Howitt's head fell, face foremost, on to the table. His partner, lifting it up, gazed down at him.

Had the creature actually been what it was intended to represent it could not have worked more summary execution. The look which was on the dead man's face as his partner turned it upwards was terrible to see.

Remorseless Vengeance

Guy Boothby

To use that expressive South Sea phrase, I have had the misfortune to be "on the beach" in a variety of places in my time. There are people who say that it is worse to be stranded in Trafalgar Square than, shall we say, Honolulu or Rangoon. Be that as it may, the worst time I ever had was that of which I am now going to tell you. I had crossed the Pacific from San Francisco before the mast on an American mail boat, had left her in Hong Kong, and had made my way down to Singapore on a collier. As matters did not look very bright there, I signed aboard a Dutch boat for Batavia, intending to work my way on to Australia. It was in Batavia, however, that the real trouble began. As soon as I arrived I fell ill, and the little money I had managed to scrape together melted like snow before the mid-day sun. What to do I knew not—I was on my beam ends. I had nothing to sell, even if there were anyone to buy, and horrible visions of Dutch gaols began to obtrude themselves upon me.

It was on the night of the 23rd of December, such a night as I'll be bound they were not having in the old country. There was not a cloud in the sky, and the stars shone like the lamps along the Thames Embankment when you look at them from Waterloo Bridge. I was smoking in the brick-paved verandah of the hotel and wondering how I was going to pay my bill, when a man entered the gates of the hotel and walked across the garden and along the verandah towards where I was seated. I noticed that he was very tall, very broad-shouldered, and that he carried himself like a man who liked his own way and generally managed to get it.

"I wonder who he can be?" I said to myself, and half expected that he would pass me and proceed in the direction of the manager's office. My astonishment may be imagined, therefore, when he picked up a chair from beside the wall and seated himself at my side.

"Good evening," he said, as calmly as you might address a friend on the top of a 'bus.

"Good evening," I replied in the same tone.

"Frank Riddington is your name, I believe?" he continued, still with the same composure.

"I believe so," I answered, "but I don't know how you became aware of it."

"That's neither here nor there," he answered; "putting other matters aside for the moment, let me give you some news."

He paused for a moment and puffed meditatively at his cigar.

"I don't know whether you're aware that there's an amiable plot on hand in this hotel to kick you into the street in the morning," he went on. "The proprietor seems to think it unlikely that you will be able to settle your account."

"And, by Jove, he is not far wrong," I replied. "It's Christmas time, I know, and I am probably in bed and dreaming. You're undoubtedly the fairy godmother sent to help me out of my difficulty."

He laughed—a short, sharp laugh.

"How do you propose to do it?"

"By putting a piece of business in your way. I want your assistance, and if you will give it me I am prepared to hand you sufficient money not only to settle your bill, but to leave a bit over. What's more, you can leave Batavia, if you like."

"Provided the business of which you speak is satisfactory," I replied, "you can call it settled. What am I to do?"

He took several long puffs at his cigar.

"You have heard of General Van der Vaal?"

"The man who, until lately, has been commanding the Dutch forces up in Achin?"

"The same. He arrived in Batavia three days ago. His house is situated on the King's Plain, three-quarters of a mile or so from here."

"Well, what about him?"

Leaning a little towards me, and sinking his voice, he continued:

"I want General Van der Vaal—badly—and to-night!"

For a moment I had doubts as to his sanity.

"I'm afraid I haven't quite grasped the situation," I said. "Do I understand that you are going to abduct General Van der Vaal?"

"Exactly!" he replied. "I am going to deport him from the island. You need not ask why, at this stage of the proceedings. I shouldn't have brought you into the matter at all, but that my mate fell ill, and I had to find a substitute."

"You haven't told me your name yet," I replied.

"It slipped my memory," he answered. "But you are welcome to it now. I am Captain Berringer!"

You may imagine my surprise. Here I was sitting talking face to face with the notorious Captain Berringer, whose doings were known from Rangoon to Vladivostock—from Nagasaki to Sourabaya. He and his brother—of whom, by the way, nothing had been heard for some time past—had been more than suspected of flagrant acts of piracy. They were well known to the Dutch as pearl stealers in prohibited waters. The Russians had threatened to hang them for seal-stealing in Behring Straits, while the French had some charges against them in Tonkin that

would ensure them a considerable sojourn there should they appear in that neighbourhood again.

"Well, what do you say to my proposal?" he asked. "It will be as easy to accomplish as it will be for them to turn you into the street in the morning."

I knew this well enough, but I saw that if he happened to fail I should, in all probability, be even worse off than before.

"Where's your vessel," I asked, feeling sure that he had one near at hand.

"Dodging about off the coast," he said. "We'll pick her up before daylight."

"And you'll take me with you?"

"That's as you please," he answered.

"I'll come right enough. Batavia will be too hot for me after to-night. But first you
must hand over the money. I must settle with that little beast of a proprietor to-night."

"I like your honesty," he said, with a sneer. "Under the circumstances it is so easy
to run away without paying."

"Captain Berringer," said I, "whatever I may be now, I was once a gentleman."

A quarter-of-an-hour later the bill was paid, and I had made my arrangements
to meet my employer outside the Harmonic Club punctually at midnight. I am not
going to say that I was not nervous, for it would not be the truth. Van der Vaal's
reputation was a cruel one, and if he got the upper hand of us we should be likely
to receive but scant mercy. Punctually to the minute I reached the rendezvous,
where I found the captain awaiting me. Then we set off in the direction of the
King's Plain, as you may suppose keeping well in the shadow of the trees. We
had not walked very far before Berringer placed a revolver into my hand, which
I slipped into my pocket.

"Let's hope we shan't have to use them," he said; "but there's nothing like
being prepared."

By the time we had climbed the wall and were approaching the house, still keeping
in the shadow of the trees, I was beginning to think I had had enough of the adventure, but it was too late to draw back, even had the Captain permitted such a thing.

Suddenly the Captain laid his hand on my arm.

"His room is at the end on this side," he whispered. "He sleeps with his window
open, and his bed is in the furthest corner. His lamp is still burning, but let us hope that
he is asleep. If he gives the alarm we're done for."

I won't deny that I was too frightened to answer him. My fear, however, did not
prevent me from following him into the clump of trees near the steps that led to the
verandah. Here we slipped off our boots, made our preparations, and then tiptoed
with the utmost care across the path, up the steps, and in the direction of the General's

room. That he was a strict disciplinarian we were aware, and that, in consequence, we knew that his watchman was likely to be a watchman in the real sense of the word.

The heavy breathing that came from the further corner of the room told us that the man we wanted was fast asleep. A faint light, from a wick which floated in a bowl of cocoanut oil, illuminated the room, and showed us a large bed of the Dutch pattern, closely veiled with mosquito curtains. Towards this we made our way. On it, stretched out at full length, was the figure of a man. I lifted the netting while the Captain prepared for the struggle. A moment later he leapt upon his victim, seized him by the throat and pinioned him. A gag was quickly thrust into his mouth, whilst I took hold of his wrists. In less time than it takes to tell he was bound hand and foot, unable either to resist or to summon help.

"Bundle up some of his clothes," whispered Berringer, pointing to some garments on a chair. "Then pick up his heels, while I'll take his shoulders. But not a sound as you love your life."

In less than ten minutes we had carried him across the grounds, had lifted him over the wall, where we found a native cart waiting for us, and had stowed him and ourselves away in it.

"Now for Tanjong Prick," said the Captain. "We must be out of the island before daybreak."

At a prearranged spot some four or five miles from the port we pulled up beneath a small tope of palms.

"Are you still bent upon accompanying me?" asked the Captain, as we lifted the inanimate General from the cart and placed him on the ground.

"More than ever," I replied. "Java shall see me no more."

Berringer consulted his watch, and found the time to be exactly half-past two. A second later a shrill whistle reached us from the beach.

"That's the boat," said Berringer. "Now let's carry him down to her."

We accordingly set off in the direction indicated. It was not, however, until we were alongside a smart-looking brig, and I was clambering aboard, that I felt in any way easy in my mind.

"Pick him up and bring him aft to the cuddy," said the skipper to two of the hands, indicating the prostrate General. Then turning to the second mate, who was standing by, he added: "Make sail, and let's get out of this. Follow me, Mr. Riddington."

I accompanied him along the deck, and from it into the cuddy, the two sailors and their heavy burden preceding us. Once there the wretched man's bonds were loosed. They had been tight enough, goodness knows, for when we released him he was so weak that he could not stand, but sank down on one of the seats beside the table, and buried his face in his hands.

"What does this mean?" he asked at last, looking up at us with a pitiable assumption of dignity. "Why have you brought me here?"

"That's easily told," said the Captain. "Last Christmas you were commanding in Achin. Do you remember an Englishman named Bernard Watson who threw in his lot with them?"

"I hanged him on Christmas Day," said the other, with a touch of his old spirit.

"Exactly," said Berringer. "And that's why you're here to-night. He was my brother. We will cry 'quits' when I hang you on the yard-arm on Christmas morning."

"Good heavens, Captain!" I cried, "you're surely not going to do this?"

"I am," he answered, with a firmness there was no mistaking. The idea was too horrible to contemplate. I tried to convince myself that, had I known what the end would be, I should have taken no part in it.

A cabin had already been prepared for the General, and to it he was forthwith conducted. The door having been closed and locked upon him, the Captain and I were left alone together. I implored him to reconsider his decision.

"I never reconsider my decisions," he answered. "The man shall hang at sunrise the day after tomorrow. He hanged my brother in cold blood, and I'll do the same for him. That's enough. Now I must go and look at my mate; he's been ailing this week past. If you want food the steward will bring it to you, and if you want a bunk—well, you can help yourself."

With that he turned on his heel, and left me.

Here I was in a nice position. To all intents and purposes I had aided and abetted a murder, and if any of Berringer's crew should care to turn Queen's evidence I should find myself in the dock, a convicted murderer. In vain I set my wits to work to try and find some scheme which might save the wretched man and myself. I could discover none, however.

All the next day we sailed on, heading for the Northern Australian Coast, so it seemed to me. I met the Captain at meals, and upon the deck, but he appeared morose and sullen, gave his orders in peremptory jerks, and never once, so far as I heard, alluded to the unhappy man below. I attempted to broach the subject to the mate, in the hope that he might take the same view of it as I did, but I soon found that my advances in that quarter were not likely to be favourably received. The crew, as I soon discovered, were Kanakas, with two exceptions, and devoted to their Captain. I was quite certain that they would do nothing but what he wished. Such a Christmas Eve I sincerely trust I may never spend again.

Late in the afternoon I bearded the Captain in his cabin, and once more endeavoured to induce him to think well before committing such an act. Ten minutes later I was back in the cuddy, a wiser and sadder man. From that moment I resigned myself to the inevitable.

At half-past six that evening the Captain and I dined together in solitary state. Afterwards I went on deck. It was a beautiful moonlight night, with scarcely enough wind to fill the canvas. The sea was as smooth as glass, with a long train of phosphorous light in our wake. I had seen nothing of the skipper since eight bells. At about ten o'clock, however, and just as I was thinking of turning in, he emerged from the companion. A few strides brought him to my side.

"A fine night, Riddington," he said, in a strange, hard voice, very unlike his usual tone.

"A very fine night," I answered.

"Riddington," he began again, with sudden vehemence, "do you believe in ghosts?"

"I have never thought much about the matter," I answered. "Why do you ask?"

"Because I've seen a ghost to-night," he replied. "The ghost of my brother Bernard, who was hanged by that man locked in the cabin below, exactly a year ago, at daybreak. Don't make any mistake about what I'm saying. You can feel my pulse, if you like, and you will find it beating as steady as ever it has done in my life. I haven't touched a drop of liquor to-day, and I honestly believe I'm as sane a man as there is in the world. Yet I tell you that, not a quarter of an hour ago, my brother stood beside me in my cabin."

Not knowing what answer to make, I held my tongue for the moment. At last I spoke."Did he say anything?" I inquired.

"He told me that I should not be permitted to execute my vengeance on Van der Vaal! It was to be left to him to deal with him. But I've passed my word, and I'll not depart from it. Ghost or no ghost, he hangs at sunrise."

So saying, he turned and walked away from me, and went below.

I am not going to pretend that I slept that night. Of one thing I am quite certain, and that is that the Captain did not leave his cabin all night. Half an hour before daybreak, however, he came to my cabin.

"Come on deck," he said. "The time is up."

I followed him, to find all the ghastly preparations complete. Once more I pleaded for mercy with all the strength at my command, and once more I failed to move him. Even the vision he had declared he had seen seemed now to be forgotten.

"Bring him on deck," he said at last, turning to the mate and handing him the key of the cabin as he spoke. The other disappeared, and I, unable to control myself, went to the side of the vessel and looked down at the still water below. The brig was scarcely moving. Presently I heard the noise of feet in the companion, and turning, with a white face, no doubt, I saw the mate and two of the hands emerge from the hatchway. They approached the Captain, who seemed not to see them. To the amazement of everyone, he was looking straight before him across the poop, with an expression of indescribable terror on his face. Then, with a crash, he lost his balance and fell forward upon the deck. We ran to his assistance, but were too late. He was dead.

Who shall say what he had seen in that terrible half-minute? The mate and I looked at each other in stupefied bewilderment. I was the first to find my voice.

"The General?"

"Dead," the other replied. "He died as we entered the cabin to fetch him out. God help me—you never saw such a sight! It looked as if he were fighting with someone whom we could not see, and was being slowly strangled."

I waited to hear no more, but turned and walked aft. I am not a superstitious man, but I felt that the Captain's brother had been right after all, when he had said that he would take the matter of revenge into his own hands.

THE SHADOW OF
A MIDNIGHT

MAURICE BARING

IT WAS NINE O'CLOCK IN THE EVENING. SASHA, THE MAID, HAD BROUGHT IN THE samovar and placed it at the head of the long table. Marie Nikolaevna, our hostess, poured out the tea. Her husband was playing Vindt with his daughter, the doctor, and his son-in-law in another corner of the room. And Jameson, who had just finished his Russian lesson—he was working for the Civil Service examination—was reading the last number of the *Rouskoe Slovo*.

"Have you found anything interesting, Frantz Frantzovitch?" said Marie Nikolaevna to Jameson, as she handed him a glass of tea.

"Yes, I have," answered the Englishman, looking up. His eyes had a clear dreaminess about them, which generally belongs only to fanatics or visionaries, and I had no reason to believe that Jameson, who seemed to be common sense personified, was either one or the other. "At least," he continued, "it interests me. And it's odd—very odd."

"What is it?" asked Marie Nikolaevna.

"Well, to tell you what it is would mean a long story which you wouldn't believe," said Jameson; "only it's odd—very odd."

"Tell us the story," I said.

"As you won't believe a word of it," Jameson repeated, "it's not much use my telling it."

We insisted on hearing the story, so Jameson lit a cigarette, and began:—

"Two years ago," he said, "I was at Heidelberg, at the University, and I made friends with a young fellow called Braun. His parents were German, but he had lived five or six years in America, and he was practically an American. I made his acquaintance by chance at a lecture, when I first arrived, and he helped me in a number of ways. He was an energetic and kind-hearted fellow, and we became great friends. He was a student, but he did not belong to any *Korps* or *Bursenschaft*, as he was working hard then. Afterwards he became an engineer. When the summer *Semester* came to an end, we both stayed on at Heidelberg. One day Braun suggested that we should go for a walking tour and explore the country. I was only too pleased, and we started. It was glorious weather, and we enjoyed ourselves hugely. On the third night after we had started we arrived at a village called Salzheim. It was a picturesque little place, and there was a

curious old church in it with some interesting tombs and relics of the Thirty Years
War. But the inn where we put up for the night was even more picturesque than the
church. It had once been a convent for nuns, only the greater part of it had been
burnt, and only a quaint gabled house, and a kind of tower covered with ivy, which
I suppose had once been the belfry, remained. We had an excellent supper and went
to bed early. We had been given two bedrooms, which were airy and clean, and
altogether we were satisfied. My bedroom opened into Braun's, which was beyond
it, and had no other door of its own. It was a hot night in July, and Braun asked me
to leave the door open. I did—we opened both the windows. Braun went to bed and
fell asleep almost directly, for very soon I heard his snores.

"I had imagined that I was longing for sleep, but no sooner had I got into bed than
all my sleepiness left me. This was odd, because we had walked a good many miles,
and it had been a blazing hot day, and up till then I had slept like a log the moment
I got into bed. I lit a candle and began reading a small volume of Heine I carried with
me. I heard the clock strike ten, and then eleven, and still I felt that sleep was out of
the question. I said to myself: 'I will read till twelve and then I will stop.' My watch
was on a chair by my bedside, and when the clock struck eleven I noticed that it was
five minutes slow, and set it right. I could see the church tower from my window, and
every time the clock struck—and it struck the quarters—the noise boomed through
the room.

"When the clock struck a quarter to twelve I yawned for the first time, and I felt
thankful that sleep seemed at last to be coming to me. I left off reading, and taking my watch in my hand I waited for midnight to strike. This quarter of an hour
seemed an eternity. At last the hands of my watch showed that it was one minute to
twelve. I put out my candle and began counting sixty, waiting for the clock to strike.
I had counted a hundred and sixty, and still the clock had not struck. I counted up
to four hundred; then I thought I must have made a mistake. I lit my candle again,
and looked at my watch: it was two minutes past twelve. And still the clock had
not struck!

"A curious uncomfortable feeling came over me, and I sat up in bed with my
watch in my hand and longed to call Braun, who was peacefully snoring, but I did
not like to. I sat like this till a quarter past twelve; the clock struck the quarter as
usual. I made up my mind that the clock must have struck twelve, and that I must
have slept for a minute—at the same time I knew I had not slept—and I put out my
candle. I must have fallen asleep almost directly.

"The next thing I remember was waking with a start. It seemed to me that some
one had shut the door between my room and Braun's. I felt for the matches. The

match-box was empty. Up to that moment—I cannot tell why—something—an unaccountable dread—had prevented me looking at the door. I made an effort and looked. It was shut, and through the cracks and through the keyhole I saw the glimmer of a light. Braun had lit his candle. I called him, not very loudly: there was no answer. I called again more loudly: there was still no answer.

"Then I got out of bed and walked to the door. As I went, it was gently and slightly opened, just enough to show me a thin streak of light. At that moment I felt that some one was looking at me. Then it was instantly shut once more, as softly as it had been opened. There was not a sound to be heard. I walked on tiptoe towards the door, but it seemed to me that I had taken a hundred years to cross the room. And when at last I reached the door I felt I could not open it. I was simply paralysed with fear. And still I saw the glimmer through the key-hole and the cracks.

"Suddenly, as I was standing transfixed with fright in front of the door, I heard sounds coming from Braun's room, a shuffle of footsteps, and voices talking low but distinctly in a language I could not understand. It was not Italian, Spanish, nor French. The voices grew all at once louder; I heard the noise of a struggle and a cry which ended in a stifled groan, very painful and horrible to hear. Then, whether I regained my self-control, or whether it was excess of fright which prompted me, I don't know, but I flew to the door and tried to open it. Some one or something was pressing with all its might against it. Then I screamed at the top of my voice, and as I screamed I heard the cock crow.

"The door gave, and I almost fell into Braun's room. It was quite dark. But Braun was waked by my screams and quietly lit a match. He asked me gently what on earth was the matter. The room was empty and everything was in its place. Outside the first greyness of dawn was in the sky.

"I said I had had a nightmare, and asked him if he had not had one as well; but Braun said he had never slept better in his life.

"The next day we went on with our walking tour, and when we got back to Heidelberg Braun sailed for America. I never saw him again, although we corresponded frequently, and only last week I had a letter from him, dated Nijni Novgorod, saying he would be at Moscow before the end of the month.

"And now I suppose you are all wondering what this can have to do with anything that's in the newspaper. Well, listen," and he read out the following paragraph from the *Rouskoe Slovo*:—

> *Samara, II, ix.*—In the centre of the town, in the Hotel ——, a band of armed swindlers attacked a German engineer named Braun and demanded money. On his refusal one of the robbers stabbed Braun

with a knife. The robbers, taking the money which was on him, amounting to 500 roubles, got away. Braun called for assistance, but died of his wounds in the night. It appears that he had met the swindlers at a restaurant.

"Since I have been in Russia," Jameson added, "I have often thought that I knew what language it was that was talked behind the door that night in the inn at Salzheim, but now I know it was Russian."

The Shape of Fear

Elia W. Peattie

Tim O'Connor—who was descended from the O'Conors with one N—started life as a poet and an enthusiast. His mother had designed him for the priesthood, and at the age of fifteen, most of his verses had an ecclesiastical tinge, but, somehow or other, he got into the newspaper business instead, and became a pessimistic gentleman, with a literary style of great beauty and an income of modest proportions. He fell in with men who talked of art for art's sake,—though what right they had to speak of art at all nobody knew,—and little by little his view of life and love became more or less profane. He met a woman who sucked his heart's blood, and he knew it and made no protest; nay, to the great amusement of the fellows who talked of art for art's sake, he went the length of marrying her. He could not in decency explain that he had the traditions of fine gentlemen behind him and so had to do as he did, because his friends might not have understood. He laughed at the days when he had thought of the priesthood, blushed when he ran across any of those tender and exquisite old verses he had written in his youth, and became addicted to absinthe and other less peculiar drinks, and to gaming a little to escape a madness of *ennui*.

As the years went by he avoided, with more and more scorn, that part of the world which he denominated Philistine, and consorted only with the fellows who flocked about Jim O'Malley's saloon. He was pleased with solitude, or with these convivial wits, and with not very much else beside. Jim O'Malley was a sort of Irish poem, set to inspiring measure. He was, in fact, a Hibernian Mæcenas, who knew better than to put bad whiskey before a man of talent, or tell a trite tale in the presence of a wit. The recountal of his disquisitions on politics and other current matters had enabled no less than three men to acquire national reputations; and a number of wretches, having gone the way of men who talk of art for art's sake, and dying in foreign lands, or hospitals, or asylums, having no one else to be homesick for, had been homesick for Jim O'Malley, and wept for the sound of his voice and the grasp of his hearty hand.

When Tim O'Connor turned his back upon most of the things he was born to and took up with the life which he consistently lived till the unspeakable end, he was unable to get rid of certain peculiarities. For example, in spite of all his debauchery, he continued to look like the Beloved Apostle. Notwithstanding abject friendships he wrote limpid and noble English. Purity seemed to dog his heels, no matter how violently he attempted to escape from her. He was never so drunk that he was not an exquisite, and even his creditors, who had become inured to his deceptions, confessed it was a privilege to meet so perfect a gentleman. The creature who held him in bondage, body and soul, actually came to love him for his gentleness, and for some quality which baffled her, and made her ache with a strange longing which she could not define. Not that she ever defined anything, poor little beast! She had skin the color of pale gold, and yellow eyes with brown lights in them, and great plaits of straw-colored hair. About her lips was a fatal and sensuous smile, which, when it got hold of a man's imagination, would not let it go, but held to it, and mocked it till the day of his death. She was the incarnation of the Eternal Feminine, with all the wifeliness and the maternity left out—she was ancient, yet ever young, and familiar as joy or tears or sin.

She took good care of Tim in some ways: fed him well, nursed him back to reason after a period of hard drinking, saw that he put on overshoes when the walks were wet, and looked after his money. She even prized his brain, for she discovered that it was a delicate little machine which produced gold. By association with him and his friends, she learned that a number of apparently useless things had value in the eyes of certain convenient fools, and so she treasured the autographs of distinguished persons who wrote to him—autographs which he disdainfully tossed in the waste basket. She was careful with presentation copies from authors, and she went the length of urging Tim to write a book himself. But at that he balked.

"Write a book!" he cried to her, his gentle face suddenly white with passion. "Who am I to commit such a profanation?"

She didn't know what he meant, but she had a theory that it was dangerous to excite him, and so she sat up till midnight to cook a chop for him when he came home that night.

He preferred to have her sitting up for him, and he wanted every electric light in their apartments turned to the full. If, by any chance, they returned together to a dark house, he would not enter till she touched the button in the hall, and illuminated the room. Or if it so happened that the lights were turned off in the night time, and he awoke to find himself in darkness, he shrieked till the woman came running to his relief, and, with derisive laughter, turned them on again. But when she found that after these frights he lay trembling and white in his bed, she began to be alarmed for the clever, gold-making little machine, and to renew her assiduities, and to horde more tenaciously than ever, those valuable curios on which she some day expected to realize when he was out of the way, and no longer in a position to object to their barter.

O'Connor's idiosyncrasy of fear was a source of much amusement among the boys at the office where he worked. They made open sport of it, and yet, recognizing him for a sensitive plant, and granting that genius was entitled to whimsicalities, it was their custom when they called for him after work hours, to permit him to reach the lighted corridor before they turned out the gas over his desk. This, they reasoned, was but a slight service to perform for the most enchanting beggar in the world.

"Dear fellow," said Rick Dodson, who loved him, "is it the Devil you expect to see? And if so, why are you averse? Surely the Devil is not such a bad old chap."

"You haven't found him so?"

"Tim, by heaven, you know, you ought to explain to me. A citizen of the world and a student of its purlieus, like myself, ought to know what there is to know! Now you're a man of sense, in spite of a few bad habits—such as myself, for example. Is this fad of yours madness?—which would be quite to your credit,—for gadzooks, I like a lunatic! Or is it the complaint of a man who has gathered too much data on the subject of Old Rye? Or is it, as I suspect, something more occult, and therefore more interesting?"

"Rick, boy," said Tim, "you're too—inquiring!" And he turned to his desk with a look of delicate hauteur.

It was the very next night that these two tippling pessimists spent together talking about certain disgruntled but immortal gentlemen, who, having said their say and made the world quite uncomfortable, had now journeyed on to inquire into the nothingness which they postulated. The dawn was breaking in the muggy east; the bottles were empty, the cigars burnt out. Tim turned toward his friend with a sharp breaking of sociable silence.

"Rick," he said, "do you know that Fear has a Shape?"

"And so has my nose!"

"You asked me the other night what I feared. Holy father, I make my confession to you. What I fear is Fear."

"That's because you've drunk too much—or not enough.

> "'Come, fill the cup, and in the fire of Spring
>   Your winter garment of repentance fling—'"

"My costume then would be too nebulous for this weather, dear boy. But it's true what I was saying. I am afraid of ghosts."

"For an agnostic that seems a bit—"

"Agnostic! Yes, so completely an agnostic that I do not even know that I do not know! God, man, do you mean you have no ghosts—no—no things which shape themselves? Why, there are things I have done—"

"Don't think of them, my boy! See, 'night's candles are burnt out, and jocund day stands tiptoe on the misty mountain top.'"

Tim looked about him with a sickly smile. He looked behind him and there was nothing there; stared at the blank window, where the smoky dawn showed its offensive face, and there was nothing there. He pushed away the moist hair from his haggard face—that face which would look like the blessed St. John, and leaned heavily back in his chair.

"'Yon light is not daylight, I know it, I,'" he murmured drowsily, "'it is some meteor which the sun exhales, to be to thee this night—'"

The words floated off in languid nothingness, and he slept. Dodson arose preparatory to stretching himself on his couch. But first he bent over his friend with a sense of tragic appreciation.

"Damned by the skin of his teeth!" he muttered. "A little more, and he would have gone right, and the Devil would have lost a good fellow. As it is"—he smiled with his usual conceited delight in his own sayings, even when they were uttered in soliloquy—"he is merely one of those splendid gentlemen one will meet with in hell." Then Dodson had a momentary nostalgia for goodness himself, but he soon overcame it, and stretching himself on his sofa, he, too, slept.

That night he and O'Connor went together to hear "Faust" sung, and returning to the office, Dodson prepared to write his criticism. Except for the distant clatter of telegraph instruments, or the peremptory cries of "copy" from an upper room, the office was still. Dodson wrote and smoked his interminable cigarettes; O'Connor rested his head in his hands on the desk, and sat in perfect silence. He did not know when Dodson finished, or when, arising, and absent-mindedly extinguishing the lights, he moved to the door with his copy in his hands. Dodson gathered up the hats and coats as he passed them where they lay on a chair, and called:

"It is done, Tim. Come, let's get out of this."

There was no answer, and he thought Tim was following, but after he had handed his criticism to the city editor, he saw he was still alone, and returned to the room for his friend. He advanced no further than the doorway, for, as he stood in the dusky corridor and looked within the darkened room, he saw before his friend a Shape, white, of perfect loveliness, divinely delicate and pure and ethereal, which seemed as the embodiment of all goodness. From it came a soft radiance and a perfume softer than the wind when "it breathes upon a bank of violets stealing and giving odor." Staring at it, with eyes immovable, sat his friend.

It was strange that at sight of a thing so unspeakably fair, a coldness like that which comes from the jewel-blue lips of a Muir crevasse should have fallen upon Dodson, or that it was only by summoning all the manhood that was left in him, that he was able to restore light to the room, and to rush to his friend. When he reached poor Tim he was stone-still with paralysis. They took him home to the woman, who nursed him out of that attack—and later on worried him into another.

When he was able to sit up and jeer at things a little again, and help himself to the quail the woman broiled for him, Dodson, sitting beside him, said:

"Did you call that little exhibition of yours legerdemain, Tim, you sweep? Or are you really the Devil's bairn?"

"It was the Shape of Fear," said Tim, quite seriously.

"But it seemed mild as mother's milk."

"It was compounded of the good I might have done. It is that which I fear."

He would explain no more. Later—many months later—he died patiently and sweetly in the madhouse, praying for rest. The little beast with the yellow eyes had high mass celebrated for him, which, all things considered, was almost as pathetic as it was amusing.

Dodson was in Vienna when he heard of it.

"Sa, sa!" cried he. "I wish it wasn't so dark in the tomb! What do you suppose Tim is looking at?"

As for Jim O'Malley, he was with difficulty kept from illuminating the grave with electricity.

THE SOUL THAT WOULD NOT BE BORN

DION FORTUNE

CONTRARY TO HIS USUAL CUSTOM, TAVERNER DID NOT INSIST ON SEEING HIS patient alone, for the sufficient reason that no information could be extracted from her. It was to the mother, a Mrs. Cailey, we turned for the case history, and she, poor anxious woman, gave us such scanty details as an onlooker might observe; but of the viewpoint and feelings of the patient we learnt nothing, for there was nothing to learn.

She sat before us in the big leather armchair; her body was a tenement for the soul of a princess, but it was, alas, untenanted. The fine dark eyes, utterly expressionless, looked into space while we discussed her as if she had been an inanimate object, which practically she was.

"She was never like ordinary children," said the mother. "When they put her in my arms after she was born she looked up at me with the most extraordinary expression in her eyes; they were not a baby's eyes at all, Doctor, they were the eyes of a woman, and an experienced woman too. She didn't cry, she never made a sound, but she looked as if she had all the troubles of the world upon her shoulders. That baby's face was a tragedy; perhaps she knew what was coming."

"Perhaps she did," said Taverner.

"In a few hours, however," continued the mother, "she looked quite like an ordinary baby, but from that time to this she has never changed, except in her body."

We looked at the girl in the chair, and she gazed back at us with the unblinking stolidity of a very young infant.

"We have taken her to everybody we could hear of, but they all say the same—that it is a hopeless case of mental deficiency; but when we heard of you, we thought you might say something different. We knew that your methods were not like those of most doctors. It does seem strange that it should be impossible to do anything for her. We passed some children playing in the street as we came here in the car—bonny, bright little things, but in such rags and dirt. Why is it that those, whose mothers can do so little for them, should be so splendid, and Mona, for whom we would do anything, should be—as she is?"

The poor woman's eyes filled with tears, and neither Taverner nor I could reply.

"I will take her down to my nursing home and keep her under observation for a time, if you wish," said Taverner. "If the brain is at fault, I can do nothing, but if it is the mind itself that has failed to develop I might attempt the cure. These deficiency cases are so inaccessible—it is like ringing up on the telephone when the subscriber will not answer. If one could attract her attention, something might be done; the crux of the matter lies in the establishment of communications."

When they had gone, I turned to Taverner and said: "What hope have you in dealing with a case like that?"

"I cannot tell you just yet," he replied; "I shall have to find out what her previous incarnations have been. I invariably find that congenital troubles originate in a former life. Then I shall have to work out her horoscope and see whether the conditions are ripe for the paying off of whatever debt she may have incurred in a previous life. Do you still think I am a queer sort of charlatan, or are you beginning to get used to my ways?"

"I have long ceased to be astonished at anything," I replied. "I should accept the devil, horns, hoofs, and tail, if you undertook to prescribe for him."

Taverner chuckled.

"With regard to our present case, I am of the opinion that we shall find the law of reincarnation is the one we shall have to look to. Now tell me this Rhodes—supposing reincarnation is not a fact, supposing this life is the beginning and end of our existence and at its conclusion we proceed to flames or harps according to the use we have made of it, how do you account for Mona Cailey's condition? What did she do in the few hours between her birth and the onset of her disease to bring down such a judgement on herself? And at the end of her life, can she justly be said to have deserved hell or earned Heaven?"

"I don't know," said I.

"But supposing my theory is right; then, if we can recover the record of her past, we shall be able to find the cause of her present condition, and having found the cause we may be able to remedy it. At any rate, let us try.

"Would you like to see how I recover the records? I use various methods; sometimes I get them by hypnotizing the patients or by crystal-gazing, and sometimes I read them from the subconscious mind of Nature. You know, we believe that every thought and impulse in the world is recorded in the Akashic records. It is like consulting a reference library. I am going to use the latter method in the present case."

In a few moments, by methods known to himself, Taverner had shut out all outward impressions from his mind, and was concentrated upon the inner vision.

Confused mental pictures evidently danced before his eyes; then he got the focus and began to describe what he saw while I took down notes.

Egyptian and Grecian lives were dismissed with a few words; these were not what he sought; he was merely working his way down through the ages, but I gathered that we were dealing with a soul of ancient lineage and great opportunities. Life after life we heard the tale of royal birth or initiation into the priesthood, and yet, in its present life, the girl's soul was cut off from all communication with its physical vehicle. I wondered what abuse of opportunity had led to such a sentence of solitary confinement in the cell of its body.

Then we came to the level we sought, Italy in the fifteenth century, as it turned out. "Daughter of the reigning duke ———." I could not catch the name of his principality. "Her younger sister was beloved by Giovanni Sigmundi; she contrived to win the affections of her sister's lover, and then, a richer suitor offering for her own hand, she betrayed Sigmundi to his enemies in order to be free of his importunities."

"A true daughter of the Renaissance," said Taverner when he had returned to normal consciousness and read my notes, for he seldom retained any memory of what transpired during his subconscious states. "Now I think we can guess the cause of the trouble. I wonder whether you are aware of the mental processes that precede birth? Just before birth the soul sees a cinematograph film (as it were) of its future life; not all the details, but the broad outlines which are determined by its fate; these things it cannot alter, but according to its reaction to them, so will its future lives be planned. Thus it is that although we cannot alter our fate in this life, our future lies entirely in our own hands.

"Now we know the record, we can guess what manner of fate lies upon this girl. She owes a life debt to a man and a woman; the suffering she caused recoils upon her. There is no need for a specialized hell; each soul builds its own."

"But she is not suffering," I said; "she is merely in a passive condition. The only one who suffers is the mother."

"Ah," said Taverner, "therein lies the crux of the whole matter. When she had that brief glimpse of what lay before her, she rebelled against her fate and tried to repudiate her debt; her soul refused to take up the heavy burden. It was this momentary flash of knowledge which gave her eyes their strange, unchildlike look which so startled her mother."

"Do people always have this foreknowledge?" I asked.

"They always have that glimpse, but its memory usually lies dormant. Some people have vague premonitions, however, and occult training tends to recover these lost memories, together with others belonging to previous lives."

"Having found out the cause of Miss Cailey's trouble, what can you do to cure her?"

"Very little," said Taverner. "I can only wait and watch her. When the time is ripe for the settlement of the balance, the other actors in the old tragedy will come along and unconsciously claim the payment of their debt. She will be given the opportunity of making restitution and going on her way fate-free. If she is unable to fulfil it, then she will be taken out of life and rapidly forced back into it again for another attempt, but I think (since she has been brought to me) her soul is to be given another chance of entering its body. We will see."

I often used to watch Mona Cailey after she was installed at the Hindhead nursing home. In spite of its mask-like expressionlessness, her face had character. The clearly cut features, firm mouth, and fine eyes were fitting abode for a soul of no ordinary calibre— only that soul was not present.

It was Taverner's expectation that the other actors in the drama would appear upon the scene before very long, brought to the girl's vicinity by those strange currents that are for ever on the move beneath the surface of life. As each new patient arrived at the nursing home, I used to watch Mona Cailey narrowly, wondering whether the new-comer would demand of her the payment of the ancient debt that held her bound.

Spring passed into summer and nothing happened. Other cases distracted my atten-tion, and I had almost forgotten the girl and her problems when Taverner reminded me of them.

"It is time we began to watch Miss Cailey," he said. "I have been working out her horoscope, and a conjunction of planets is taking place towards the end of the month which would provide an opportunity for the working out of her fate—if we can get her to take it."

"Supposing she does not take it?"

"Then she will not be long in going out, for she will have failed to achieve the pur-pose of this incarnation."

"And supposing she takes it?"

"Then she will suffer, but she will be free, and she will soon rise again to the heights she had previously gained."

"She is hardly likely to belong to a royal house in this life," I said.

"She was more than royal; she was an Initiate," replied Taverner, and from the way he said the word I knew he spoke of a royalty that is not of this earth.

Our words were suddenly interrupted by a cry from one of the upper rooms. It was a shriek of utter terror such as a soul might give that had looked into chaos and seen forbidden horrors; it was the cry of a child in nightmare, only—and this added to its ghastliness—it came from the throat of a man.

We rushed upstairs; we had no need to ask whence that cry came; there was only one case that could have uttered it—a poor fellow suffering from shell-shock whom we were keeping in bed for a rest.

We found him standing in the middle of the floor, shaking from head to foot. At sight of us he rushed across the room and flung himself into Taverner's arms. It was the pathetic action of a frightened child, but carried out by the tall figure in striped pyjamas, it was extraordinarily distressing to witness.

Taverner soothed him as gently as a mother, and got him back to bed, sitting by him until he quieted down.

"I do not think we will keep him in bed any longer," said my colleague after we had left the room. "The inactivity is making him brood, and he is living over again the scenes of the trenches."

Accordingly, Howson appeared among the patients next day for the first time since his arrival, and seemed to benefit by the change.

This benefit was not of long duration, however; when once the novelty had worn off, he commenced his brooding again, going over mentally the horrors he had lived through, and ending each recall with an attack of panic terror, rushing to the nearest human being for protection.

It proved somewhat distressing to our other patients to have six feet of burly humanity hurled unexpectedly into their arms, so we segregated Howson in the portion of the garden we kept for cases that we could not mix with the rest. The only other occupant of this part of the garden was Mona Cailey, but we hardly counted her, for she sat motionless in the deck chair we placed for her, never stirring until she was fetched in to meals.

As I was walking one evening with Taverner in that part of the grounds, we heard the now familiar sound of poor Howson's nightmare shriek. He shot out of the summer-house and stood irresolutely on the lawn. The only people in sight were ourselves and Mona Cailey, passive in her chair; he was about halfway between the two. When a man's nerve is broken, he reverts either to the savage or the child, according to his temperament, and for the time being Howson was about four years old. Taverner hurried towards him over the intervening grass, but when a man reverts to the child, it is to the mother he turns, and, ignoring the approaching man, Howson ran across the lawn to Mona Cailey and buried his face in her lap.

The impact of the heavy man, flung upon her with utter abandonment, nearly sent the girl, chair and all, over backwards, and startled even her dim brain into some measure of response. I was about to run forward and extricate her from her embarrassing position, when Taverner caught my arm and stopped me.

"No, watch," he said. "See what she does. This may be the working out of her fate."

There was nothing offensive in Howson's behaviour, for he was so obviously a child and not a man. He always used to remind me of a mastiff that has been nursed as a puppy and cannot realize when it has ceased to be a lap-dog.

For several endless minutes we watched the dim brain trying to work, and then a hand, white and beautifully formed, but limp, as only the hands of the mentally afflicted are limp, was laid on the man's heaving shoulder. It was the first thought-out action that Mona Cailey had ever performed.

I thought Taverner would have danced upon the lawn in his delight.

"Look!" he said. "Watch her mind trying to work."

I watched. It was like nothing so much as rusty machinery being reluctantly turned over by hand. The girl's unlined forehead was contracted with effort as the thought-currents forced their way through the unopened channels. What dim mother instincts awoke I do not know, but she had evidently taken the big child at her feet under her protection.

In a few minutes Howson recovered his self-control and made his embarrassed apologies to the victim of his onslaught. The fine dark eyes gazed steadily back into his without a trace of expression, and realizing the state of affairs he stopped his apologies in the middle of a sentence and stared back at her.

"Oh well," he said, as much to himself as to her, "if you don't mind, I'm sure I'm thankful," and sitting at her feet he lit a cigarette with shaking hands.

From that time onwards the pair were inseparable during their waking hours. To Howson, the passive presence seemed to afford just the companionship he needed. She gave him a sense of human protection, and yet he did not feel that in her eyes he was making a fool of himself. This curious comradeship between the mindless girl and the alert intelligent man was a source of complete amusement to other inmates of the home, and I myself was inclined to regard it as one of those strange friendships that spring up between the most incongruous cases in such a house as ours, until my colleague put his hand on my shoulder one evening as the two were crossing the lawn towards the house.

"Who is that with Mona Cailey?" he asked.

"Howson, of course," I replied, surprised at the obviousness of such a question.

"So we call him now," said Taverner, watching the pair closely, "but I think there was a time when he answered to the name of Giovanni Sigmundi."

"You mean—?" I exclaimed.

"Exactly," said Taverner. "The wheel has come round the full circle. When he was dying by torture in the hands of those to whom she betrayed him, he called for her in his agony. Needless to say, she did not come. Now that he is in agony again, some strange law of mental habit carried the call for help along the old channels, and she has answered it. She has begun to repay her debt. If all goes well, we may see that soul come right back into its body, and it will not be a small soul that comes into the flesh if that happens."

I had thought that we were going to witness a romance of re-united lovers, but I was soon made aware that it was more likely to be a tragedy for one at least of them.

Next day Howson's fiancée arrived to visit him. I took her out to the secluded part of the garden where he spent his time, and there saw enacted a most pathetic little tragi-comedy. As usual, Howson was at Mona Cailey's side, smoking his interminable cigarettes. At sight of his fiancée he sprang to his feet; Mona Cailey also rose. In the eyes of the newcomer there were fear and distrust, perhaps occasioned by her unfamiliarity with mental cases, which are always distressing at first sight, but in the eyes of our defective there was a look which I can only describe as contempt. There was one flash of the astute ruthlessness of the fifteenth century Italian, and I guessed who the newcomer was.

Howson, forgetful of the other girl's presence, advanced eagerly to meet his fiancée and kissed her, and I thought for a moment we were going to be treated to one of those nasty outbursts of spitefulness of which defectives are capable, when a sudden change came over Mona Cailey, and I saw that marvellous thing, a soul enter and take possession of its body.

Intelligence slowly dawned in the misty eyes as she watched the scene being enacted before her. For a moment the issue hung in the balance; would she rush forward and tear them apart, or would she stand aside? Behind the oblivious lovers I poised myself for a spring, ready to catch her if necessary. For ages we waited thus while the unpractised brain moved reluctantly in its unaccustomed effort.

Then the girl turned away slowly. Over the grass she moved, silently, unnoticed by the other two, seeking the shelter of the shrubberies as a wounded animal seeks cover, but her movements were no longer those of unguided limbs; she moved as a woman moves who has walked before kings, but as a woman stricken to the heart.

I followed her as she passed under the trees and put my hand on her arm, instinctively speaking words of comfort, although I expected no response. She turned on me dark eyes full of unshed tears and luminous with a terrible knowledge.

"It has to be," she said distinctly, perfectly, the first words she had ever uttered. Then she withdrew her arm from my hand and went on alone.

During the days that followed we watched the soul swing in and out of the body. Sometimes we had the mindless imbecile, and sometimes we had one of those women who have made history. Save that her means of communication developed slowly, she was often in full possession of her faculties. And what faculties they were! I had read of the wonderful women of the Renaissance—now I saw one.

Then, sometimes, when the pain of her position became too great to be borne, the soul would slip out for a while and rest in some strange Elysian fields we know not of, leaving to us again the care of the mindless body. But each time it came back refreshed. Whom it had talked with, what help had been given, we never knew; but each time it faced the agony of reincarnation and took up its burden with renewed courage and knowledge.

The dim, newly-awakened mind understood Howson through and through; each twist and turn of him, conscious and subconscious, she could follow, and of course she was the most perfect nurse he could have had. The panic-stricken mind was never allowed to thrash about in outer darkness and the horror of death. Instinctively she sensed the approach of nightmare forms, and putting out her hand, pulled the wandering soul back into safety.

Thus protected from the wear and tear of his terrible storms, Howson's mind began to heal. Day by day the time drew nearer when he would be fit to leave the nursing home and marry the woman he was engaged to, and day by day, by her instinctive skill and watchful care, Mona Cailey quickened the approach of that time.

I have said that he would leave and marry the woman he was engaged to—not the woman he loved—for at that time had Mona Cailey chosen to lift one finger she could have brought the old memories into consciousness and drawn Howson to herself; and that she was fully aware of this, I who watched her, am convinced. An ignorant woman could not have steered round the pitfalls as skilfully as she did.

The night before he was to leave she had a bad relapse into her old condition. Hour after hour Taverner and I sat beside her while she scarcely seemed to breathe, so completely was the soul withdrawn from the body.

"She is shut up in her own subconsciousness, moving among the memories of the past," Taverner whispered to me, as slight twitchings ran through the motionless form on the bed.

Then a change took place.

"Ah," said Taverner, "she is out now!"

Slowly the long white hand was raised—the hand that I had watched change from a limp thing of disgust to firmness and strength, and a sequence of knocks was given upon the wall at the bedside that would have skinned the knuckles of an ordinary hand.

"She is claiming entrance to her Lodge," whispered Taverner. "She will give the Word as soon as the knocks are acknowledged."

From somewhere up near the ceiling the sequence of knocks was repeated, and then Taverner placed his hand across the girl's mouth. Through the guarding fingers came some muffled sound I could not make out.

"She will get what she has gone to seek," said Taverner. "It is a high Degree to which she is claiming admission."

What transpired during the workings of that strange Lodge which meets out of the body I had no means of knowing. I could see that Taverner, however, with his telepathic faculties, was able to follow the ritual, for he joined in the responses and salutes.

As the uncanny ceremony drew to its close we saw the soul that was known to us as Mona Cailey withdraw from the company of its brethren and, plane by plane, return to normal consciousness. On her face was that look of peace which I had never before seen in the living, and only on the faces of such of the dead as went straight out into the Light.

"She has gathered strength for her ordeal," said Taverner, "and it will indeed be an ordeal, for Howson's fiancée is fetching him in her car."

"Will it be wise to let Miss Cailey be present?" I asked.

"She must go through with it," said Taverner. "It is better to break than to miss an opportunity."

He was a man who never spared his patients when there was a question of fate to be worked out. He thought less of death than most people think of emigration; in fact, he seemed to regard it in exactly that light.

"Once you have had some memory glimpse, however dim, of your own past, you are certain of your future; therefore you cease to fear life. Supposing I make a mess of an experiment today, I clear up the mess, go to bed, sleep, and then, in the morning when I am rested, I start again. You do the same with your lives when once you are sure of reincarnation. It is only the man who does not realize as a personal fact the immortality of the soul who talks of a ruined life and opportunities gone never to return."

Mona Cailey, Taverner, and myself were on the doorstep to bid goodbye to Howson when his fiancée called to take him away. He thanked us both with evident feeling for what we had done for him, but Taverner waved a disclaiming hand towards the girl at his elbow.

"You have had nothing from me but board and lodging," he said. "There is your psychologist."

Howson took Mona's hand in both his. She stood absolutely passive, but not with her usual limp inertia; it was the motionlessness of extreme tension.

"Poor little Mona!" he said. "You are a lot better than you used to be. Go on getting better, and one of these days you may be a real girl and have a good time," and he kissed her lightly as one would kiss a child.

What memories that kiss awakened I cannot say, but I saw him change colour and look at her sharply. Had one glimmer of response lightened those dark eyes, the old love would have returned, but there was no change in the mask-like countenance of the woman who was paying her debt. He shivered. Perhaps some cold breath from the torturers' dungeon touched him. He got into the car beside the woman he was to marry, and she drove away.

"How will that marriage turn out?" I asked as the sounds of the car died in the distance.

"Like a good many others where only the emotions are mated. They will be in love for a year, then will come disillusionment, and after they have bumped through the crisis, held together by the pressure of social opinion, they will settle down to the mutual toleration which passes for a successful marriage. *But when he comes to die, he will remember this Mona Cailey and call for her, and as he crosses the threshold she will claim him, for they have made restitution, and the way is clear.*"

THE SPIDER

CLIVE PEMBERTON

MIDWAY DOWN THE ECHOING, STONE-FLAGGED CORRIDOR, I STOPPED AND CLUTCHED Doctor Hoxton by the arm, for, iron-nerved and seldom moved as I am, I was rudely startled.

"Good heavens!" I cried. "What was that?"

From the far end of the corridor there had suddenly sounded a series of dull, sickening thuds; then a voice—a human voice but so distorted as to retain but an echo of humanity—wailed up and in a wild shriek that curdled the blood with its suggestion of nightmare horror. The doctor gave me a reassuring glance and led the way forward.

"If you spent your days within the walls of a lunatic asylum, you would not be alarmed at sounds like that," he said. "What you just heard proceeds from the padded cell at the end there. One of the worst cases. You can see him if you like. It is a peculiar case—very peculiar, and somewhat inexplicable . . ."

In a few moments we reached the padded cell. There was a small grating close up to the ceiling, and adjusting a short flight of portable steps, Hoxton told me to look in. The maniac was crouching against the wall opposite the grating. Fierce pants heaved his chest and shook his frame; over his face the long, matted hair fell in shaggy locks, and behind them a pair of wild, shining eyes glared out with terrible intensity. Suddenly, and without any warning, he leapt up, almost touching the ceiling, and two words came in a scream from his foaming lips, again and again—

"The Spider! The Spider! The Spider!"

A shriek, pregnant with the ecstasy of terror, followed the reiterated words, and with the perspiration pouring down his distorted countenance, the wretched being crouched back in his former position, his eyes again staring in horror at the mental vision conjured up by a frenzied brain.

"Come to my room," said the doctor, leading me away from the dreadful cell. "If you are interested, I will tell you about Andrew Fleming—the poor creature you have just seen."

I was interested, and, comfortably seated in an easy chair in my friend's room, I listened to the strangest story I had ever heard.

"Six months ago," began Hoxton, looking at his cigar reflexively, "Andrew Fleming was as sane as you or I, and a good deal saner than many people I have come across.

He was steward to Sir Jasper Holyoake, the owner of 'Marshlands.' You have seen the house, perhaps—a big, square mansion standing alone in a large expanse of grounds on the hill opposite to this asylum?"

"Yes, I have seen it," I replied, "but I understand it was shut up—deserted."

"Quite so—I am coming to that," went on the doctor. "As a matter of fact, 'Marshlands' has not been occupied for twenty years or more. Old Jasper Holyoake had a rooted antipathy to the place, and never came near it. When he died, however, and his son entered into the title and estates, he at once announced his intention of living there for a portion of the year. He accordingly sent Fleming to get the place in order. Fleming was a widower with one child—a little girl some eight or nine years of age. Now comes the horrible and mysterious part of the story. It was about a week after Fleming and his little daughter had taken up their abode there. The weather was fine and summer-like, and it was a delight to see the child playing about the grounds which had been so long deserted and empty.

"One evening, about eight o'clock, the little one being safely in bed, Fleming went over the house as usual, locked all the doors carefully, and went into the village to make a few purchases. On the way home, he was beguiled into joining a sort of impromptu concert which some of the young men of the village had got up in the parlour of the inn, and it was eleven o'clock before he arrived back at the house. Having let himself in with his latch-key, he went upstairs, but before going to his own room, he entered the small chamber adjoining to see if the child was asleep, as she sometimes kept awake until he returned when he spent the evening out. The room was in darkness, and he stopped suddenly as a faint moaning sound came—not from the bed, but over by the window! He hurriedly struck a light, and saw that the bed was empty! In another moment a sight met his eyes calculated to make the reason of any father totter. Huddled up on the floor beneath the window—the pane of which was cracked and broken—was the child. She was quite unconscious when he lifted her in his arms and placed her on the bed. He just noticed that there were marks of blood on the white nightgown, then, without a second's hesitation, he flew out of the house and ran madly here, knowing that I was the nearest doctor for a long way round. Fortunately, I was up and dressed, and we were back at the house within a few minutes. Alas! We were too late—the fair little creature was dead. I could do nothing immediately towards discovering what had caused the child's death, for the father's grief and rage were frightful to witness. Gradually, however, he became calmer, and I then examined the frail little body. From the moment I entered the room, I had become aware of peculiar odour—a smell like that given out when a pile of dead, sodden leaves, which have remained untouched for some time, is turned over. I only gave it a passing thought, then set to work on my examination.

The first thing I noticed was a number of strange cuts on the child's right forearm and breast. An examination of the broken window betrayed a fact that deepened the terrible mystery. Somebody or something had endeavored to drag the child through the broken window! The blood stains on the broken glass edges and the wounds on the arm and breast of the child proved it! But yet a more horrible discovery awaited me, and one I shall ever look back upon with shuddering horror. Incredible as it may sound—terrible as it is in its suggestion of vague horror—the deadly fact was not to be questioned. The little body was bloodless!—the terrible agent that had caused the child's death had drained her body of its life-blood!"

"You horrify me, Hoxton!" I interposed. "And it turned the father's brain?"

"No, that alone did not do it," replied the doctor; "therein lies the bottom of the mystery. What actually happened and what he underwent will never be known. The night after the child's death, the pane of glass in the room Fleming slept in was found broken, and he—he crawling from room to room—a raving madman!"

"But the words I heard him speak?" I said. "What do they mean?"

"I don't know—nobody knows. For days together he is quiet—sullenness is his usual demeanor—then, quite suddenly, he becomes violent. He seems to see something that terrifies him, for he cries ceaselessly, 'The Spider, The Spider!' Perhaps he did see something that night! . . ."

I sat silently thinking over what I had just heard—the strangeness of the affair sending my thoughts into curious channels.

"What is your opinion about it, Hoxton?" I said at last. "What, in your opinion, could have caused the horrible death of that innocent child, and sent her father—a sane, intelligent man—raving mad?"

His face turned curiously white.

"I do not know—I dare not think," he answered. "It is a mystery—a terrible mystery, and likely to remain so for all time, for nobody will go near the place after sunset, despite the thousand pounds' reward—still unearned—which awaits the man who will spend a night there and probe to the bottom the horror of the house. Death or madness are terrible issues to risk. You have traveled about, Dunscombe; what do you make of it?"

"I make nothing of it at present," I replied, steadily; "but I will answer you—after I have spent a night there."

He looked at me aghast, the dawn of a great fear in his eyes.

"Good heavens!" he cried. "You don't mean that you are going to—? Are you mad?"

He expostulated, argued, pleaded—even threatened, but I was obdurate. At least, seeing that I was determined, he gave way, and ultimately consented to assist me in so far as he was able. I decided to spend the following night at "Marshlands"—alone. If I could only have known—!

The sun—a great fiery ball—was just sinking below the ridge of the hill the following night as I entered the grounds of the shunned house. In my left-hand pocket jangled the keys; in the other was a small case containing a tiny but deadly revolver which had been my inseparable companion during my years of travel abroad, and which had saved my life more than once. I felt no nervous qualms or the slightest feeling akin to fear as I stepped into the hall and the door clanged behind me. Ascending the stairs, I decided on the room in which to hold my vigil, and laying the revolver and a pocket electric lamp on a small table, I started on a tour of inspection through the rooms. A dank, musty smell, caused by disuse, pervaded every room, and the dust lay thick on carpets and furniture. In the room adjoining that in which I was to spend the night I pulled up short with a momentary chill. The window pane, was *broken*!—and, yes, there was a faint, yet unmistakable odour of decayed leaves! . . . The next moment I was smiling at my sudden disquiet. It was the room the steward had last slept in, and the broken window had not been replaced because nobody would enter the house. But the strange odour Hoxton had spoken of was plainly there. . . . Returning to the next room, I shut and locked the door, and drew a chair close up to the window. The lurid after-glow of the sunset had long since faded from the sky, and the full moon, riding proudly in the clear, opaline dome, was bathing everything in a silvery sheen. How still it was! Not the faintest sound broke the intense silence, and sitting there alone with the ghostly panorama spread out before me, I fell to thinking strange things. I was excited but not nervous. My heart did not hurry one beat; my muscles were as rigid as the steel of the weapon I held in my hand. Yet I could not divert my thoughts from the one channel. The horrible death and mutilation of the child came up before my mental vision; the sudden madness of the man—whose frenzied cry, "The Spider! The Spider!" yet rang in my ears—persistently clamored within me for explanation. What did that cry mean! Was it the voicing of a diseased mind's fantasy, or was it—?

Quite suddenly, and without warning, a strange feeling came over me—a feeling I find it difficult to describe and place on paper. My heart, which had been beating regularly and with quiet imperceptibility, gave a sickening leap, and then began to throb violently like it does when one is unexpectedly startled. At the same instant an irresistible desire possessed me to lift the window and look out. Almost mechanically I did so, the revolver gripped in my right hand which hung rigid at my side. Fifty feet below, the grounds lay stretched out as brilliantly lighted by the floating radiance of the moon as in day. Every tree, shrub, and object stood out as clear and distinct as a cameo, and my eyes remained fixed almost against my will and inclination on the stone coping and cover of the disused well. The moon shone full upon it, revealing every chip and mark on the stone work and cover. Suddenly I leant farther out of the window. Were my eyes going wrong, or had I really seen the wooden cover of the well *move*? Rigid as a status, and with the blood humming in my ears, I watched. A few moments passed, and then—and then—great Heaven! It was no delusion; the solid wooden top of the well was moving, oscillating, tilting up! Scarcely breathing, and with a nameless dread congealing my marrow, I watched the well with starting eyes. Higher and higher rose the cover; then, with hardly a sound, it overweighed and fell to the ground. A moment passed, and then—and then— Even now my brain reels at the recollection of what followed. From the dark interior of the well crept out something which I can only describe best as a monstrous spider! From its body, which was about the size of a small barrel, there branched out four whip-like arms which were covered like the body with a coarse red stubble. Its eyes—even at the distance that I could plainly see them—were at the end of its triangular body, and as I looked, they flashed emerald green in the moonlight. Frozen into inaction I watched it.

For a few moments it was motionless, save for a slight heaving of the body as it breathed, then, raising itself up until it stood on the tips of its four tentacles—it standing then about three feet high—it bunched itself together and sped towards the sheer wall with astonishing speed. In a sort of stupefaction I watched it. In less time than it takes to write it, it was against the wall immediately beneath the window I was leaning out of; then, with a horrible, creeping action, it began to scale the wall—scaling the perpendicular wall and making straight for *my* window! I waited to see no more, but, withdrawing my head, banged down the window and fumbled at the catch. In my hurry I dropped the revolver. I pressed the spring of the electric lamp, but, to my dismay, no light shone out. Dropping on my knees with the desperation of terror, I groped wildly about the floor. Minute after minute passed and still found my frenzied hands empty; I half sobbed as I thought of the horror outside that would reach the window at any moment. It was no physical fear that assailed me—it was rather a deadly nausea—a revolting of the soul inexplicable and impossible to adequately explain. Suddenly I leapt to my feet and dashed headlong to the door. Wildly I fumbled at the handle, but I had locked the door and the key was in my pocket. As my hand closed over it, there came a sharp crack from the window, and I suddenly became aware of an over-powering scent of wet, rotten leaves! I turned my head swiftly and looked at the window through which the moonlight was streaming. The pane was shivered in a thousand cracks, and there, glued to it, with its emerald eyes glaring balefully at me, was the Thing! One long, hairy tentacle was through the hole in the glass; it swept the air as far as it could reach, and behind it glared the flashing, emerald eyes. I saw the lipless mouth dropping saliva, and felt the subtle odour of decay swaying my senses; then, dashing the key madly in the lock, I tore open the door and plunged headlong down the stairs. Out into the moonlit night I sped, biting my lips till the blood flowed to keep back the screams of delirium that choked me. At the gate I looked back at the moon-silvered wall. A black blotch showed high up at one of the windows, then it suddenly disappeared! . . .

Shutting out the sight with my hand, I rushed blindly away. I must have run at headlong speed for many miles, and in the middle of a quiet meadow, I sank down on the dewy grass in merciful oblivion.

And that is the beginning and end of the mystery of "Marshlands." On reflection, I determined to lock the events of that night in my memory, for I had no wish to be thought a madman. I visited the deserted place some day after, and, in accordance with my instructions, a massive stone slab was placed over the well which, I saw with a deadly shudder in the morning light, was again covered by the wooden top. And when I had last seen it, it was uncovered! . . .

The house is still shunned and deserted; the horror still remains; but I—and I alone—know that it will never visit it again.

The Squaw

Bram Stoker

Nurnberg at the time was not so much exploited as it has been since then. Irving had not been playing *Faust*, and the very name of the old town was hardly known to the great bulk of the travelling public. My wife and I being in the second week of our honeymoon, naturally wanted someone else to join our party, so that when the cheery stranger, Elias P. Hutcheson, hailing from Isthmian City, Bleeding Gulch, Maple Tree County, Neb., turned up at the station at Frankfort, and casually remarked that he was going on to see the most all-fired old Methusaleh of a town in Yurrup, and that he guessed that so much travelling alone was enough to send an intelligent, active citizen into the melancholy ward of a daft house, we took the pretty broad hint and suggested that we should join forces. We found, on comparing notes afterwards, that we had each intended to speak with some diffidence or hesitation so as not to appear too eager, such not being a good compliment to the success of our married life; but the effect was entirely marred by our both beginning to speak at the same instant—stopping simultaneously and then going on together again. Anyhow, no matter how, it was done; and Elias P. Hutcheson became one of our party. Straightway Amelia and I found the pleasant benefit; instead of quarrelling, as we had been doing, we found that the restraining influence of a third party was such that we now took every opportunity of spooning in odd corners. Amelia declares that ever since she has, as the result of that experience, advised all her friends to take a friend on the honeymoon. Well, we "did" Nurnberg together, and much enjoyed the racy remarks of our Transatlantic friend, who, from his quaint speech and his wonderful stock of adventures, might have stepped out of a novel. We kept for the last object of interest in the city to be visited the Burg, and on the day appointed for the visit strolled round the outer wall of the city by the eastern side.

The Burg is seated on a rock dominating the town, and an immensely deep fosse guards it on the northern side. Nurnberg has been happy in that it was never sacked; had it been it would certainly not be so spick and span perfect as it is at present. The ditch has not been used for centuries, and now its base is spread with tea-gardens and orchards, of which some of the trees are of quite respectable growth. As we wandered round the wall, dawdling in the hot July sunshine, we often paused to admire the views spread before us, and in especial the great plain covered with towns and villages and bounded with a blue line of hills, like a landscape of Claude Lorraine. From this we always turned with new delight to the city itself, with its myriad of quaint old gables and acre-wide red roofs dotted with dormer windows, tier upon tier. A little to our right rose the towers of the Burg, and nearer still, standing grim, the Torture Tower, which was, and is, perhaps, the most interesting place in the city. For centuries the tradition of the Iron Virgin of Nurnberg has been handed down as an instance of the horrors of cruelty of which man is capable; we had long looked forward to seeing it; and here at last was its home.

In one of our pauses we leaned over the wall of the moat and looked down. The garden seemed quite fifty or sixty feet below us, and the sun pouring into it with an intense, moveless heat like that of an oven. Beyond rose the grey, grim wall seemingly of endless height, and losing itself right and left in the angles of bastion and counterscarp. Trees and bushes crowned the wall, and above again towered the lofty houses on whose massive beauty Time has only set the hand of approval. The sun was hot and we were lazy; time was our own, and we lingered, leaning on the wall. Just below us was a pretty sight—a great black cat lying stretched in the sun, whilst round her gambolled prettily a tiny black kitten. The mother would wave her tail for the kitten to play with, or would raise her feet and push away the little one as an encouragement to further play. They were just at the foot of the wall, and Elias P. Hutcheson, in order to help the play, stooped and took from the walk a moderate sized pebble.

"See!" he said, "I will drop it near the kitten, and they will both wonder where it came from."

"Oh, be careful," said my wife; "you might hit the dear little thing!"

"Not me, ma'am," said Elias P. "Why, I'm as tender as a Maine cherry-tree. Lor, bless ye, I wouldn't hurt the poor pooty little critter more'n I'd scalp a baby. An' you may bet your variegated socks on that! See, I'll drop it fur away on the outside so's not to go near her!" Thus saying, he leaned over and held his arm out at full length and dropped the stone. It may be that there is some attractive force which draws lesser matters to greater; or more probably that the wall was not plumb but sloped to its base—we not noticing the inclination from above; but the stone fell with a sickening thud that came up to us through the hot air, right on the kitten's head, and shattered out its little brains then and there. The black cat cast a swift upward glance, and we saw her eyes like green fire fixed an instant on Elias P. Hutcheson; and then her attention was given to the kitten, which lay still with just a quiver of her tiny limbs, whilst a thin red stream trickled from a gaping wound. With a muffled cry, such as a human being might give, she bent over the kitten, licking its wound and moaning. Suddenly she seemed to realise that it was dead, and again threw her eyes up at us. I shall never forget the sight, for she looked the perfect incarnation of hate. Her green eyes blazed with lurid fire, and the white, sharp teeth seemed to almost shine through the blood which dabbled her mouth and whiskers. She gnashed her teeth, and her claws stood out stark and at full length on every paw. Then she made a wild rush up the wall as if to reach us, but when the momentum ended fell back, and further added to her horrible appearance for she fell on the kitten, and rose with her black fur smeared with its brains and blood. Amelia turned quite faint, and I had to lift her back from the wall. There was a seat close by in shade of a spreading plane-tree, and here I placed her whilst she composed herself. Then I went back to Hutcheson, who stood without moving, looking down on the angry cat below.

As I joined him, he said:

"Wall, I guess that air the savagest beast I ever see—'cept once when an Apache squaw had an edge on a half-breed what they nicknamed 'Splinters' 'cos of the way he fixed up her papoose which he stole on a raid just to show that he appreciated the way they had given his mother the fire torture. She got that kinder look so set on her face that it jest seemed to grow there. She followed Splinters more'n three year till at last the braves got him and handed him over to her. They did say that no man, white or Injun, had ever been so long a-dying under the tortures of the Apaches. The only time I ever see her smile was when I wiped her out. I kem on the camp just in time to see Splinters pass in his checks, and he wasn't sorry to go either. He was a hard citizen, and though I never could shake with him after that papoose business—for it was bitter bad, and he should have been a white man, for he looked like one—I see he had got paid out in full. Durn me, but I took a piece of his hide from one of his skinnin' posts an' had it made into a pocket-book. It's here now!" and he slapped the breast pocket of his coat.

Whilst he was speaking the cat was continuing her frantic efforts to get up the wall. She would take a run back and then charge up, sometimes reaching an incredible height. She did not seem to mind the heavy fall which she got each time but started with renewed vigour; and at every tumble her appearance became more horrible. Hutcheson was a kind-hearted man—my wife and I had both noticed little acts of kindness to animals as well as to persons—and he seemed concerned at the state of fury to which the cat had wrought herself.

"Wall, now!" he said, "I du declare that that poor critter seems quite desperate. There! there I poor thing, it was all an accident—though that won't bring back your little one to you. Say! I wouldn't have had such a thing happen for a thousand! Just shows what a clumsy fool of a man can do when he tries to play! Seems I'm too darned slipperhanded to even play with a cat. Say Colonel!" it was a pleasant way he had to bestow titles freely—"I hope your wife don't hold no grudge against me on account of this unpleasantness? Why, I wouldn't have had it occur on no account."

He came over to Amelia and apologised profusely, and she with her usual kindness of heart hastened to assure him that she quite understood that it was an accident. Then we all went again to the wall and looked over.

The cat missing Hutcheson's face had drawn back across the moat, and was sitting on her haunches as though ready to spring. Indeed, the very instant she saw him she did spring, and with a blind unreasoning fury, which would have been grotesque, only that it was so frightfully real. She did not try to run up the wall, but simply launched herself at him as though hate and fury could lend her wings to pass straight through the great distance between them. Amelia, womanlike, got quite concerned, and said to Elias P. in a warning voice:

"Oh! you must be very careful. That animal would try to kill you if she were here; her eyes look like positive murder."

He laughed out jovially, "Excuse me, ma'am," he said, "but I can't help laughin'. Fancy a man that has fought grizzlies an' Injuns bein' careful of bein' murdered by a cat!"

When the cat heard him laugh, her whole demeanour seemed to change. She no longer tried to jump or run up the wall, but went quietly over, and sitting again beside the dead kitten began to lick and fondle it as though it were alive.

"See!" said I, "the effect of a really strong man. Even that animal in the midst of her fury recognises the voice of a master, and bows to him!"

"Like a squaw!" was the only comment of Elias P. Hutcheson, as we moved on our way round the city fosse. Every now and then we looked over the wall and each time saw the cat following us. At first she had kept going back to the dead kitten, and then as the distance grew greater took it in her mouth and so followed. After a while, however, she abandoned this, for we saw her following all alone; she had evidently hidden the body somewhere. Amelia's alarm grew at the cat's persistence, and more than once she repeated her warning; but the American always laughed with amusement, till finally, seeing that she was beginning to be worried, he said:

"I say, ma'am, you needn't be skeered over that cat. I go heeled, I du!" Here he slapped his pistol pocket at the back of his lumbar region. "Why sooner'n have you worried, I'll shoot the critter, right here, an' risk the police interferin' with a citizen of the United States for carryin' arms contrairy to regulations!" As he spoke he looked over the wall, but the cat, on seeing him, retreated, with a growl, into a bed of tall flowers, and was hidden. He went on: "Blest if that ar critter ain't got more sense of what's good for her than most Christians. I guess we've seen the last of her! You bet, she'll go back now to that busted kitten and have a private funeral of it, all to herself!"

Amelia did not like to say more, lest he might, in mistaken kindness to her, fulfil his threat of shooting the cat: and so we went on and crossed the little wooden bridge leading to the gateway whence ran the steep paved roadway between the Burg and the pentagonal Torture Tower. As we crossed the bridge we saw the cat again down below us. When she saw us her fury seemed to return, and she made frantic efforts to get up the steep wall. Hutcheson laughed as he looked down at her, and said:

"Good-bye, old girl. Sorry I in-jured your feelin's, but you'll get over it in time! So long!" And then we passed through the long, dim archway and came to the gate of the Burg.

When we came out again after our survey of this most beautiful old place which not even the well-intentioned efforts of the Gothic restorers of forty years ago have been able to spoil—though their restoration was then glaring white—we seemed to have quite forgotten the unpleasant episode of the morning. The old lime tree with its great trunk gnarled with the passing of nearly nine centuries, the deep well cut through the heart of the rock by those captives of old, and the lovely view from the city wall whence we heard, spread over almost a full quarter of an hour, the multitudinous chimes of the city, had all helped to wipe out from our minds the incident of the slain kitten.

We were the only visitors who had entered the Torture Tower that morning—so at least said the old custodian—and as we had the place all to ourselves were able to make a minute and more satisfactory survey than would have otherwise been possible. The custodian, looking to us as the sole source of his gains for the day, was willing to meet our wishes in any way. The Torture Tower is truly a grim place, even now when many thousands of visitors have sent a stream of life, and the joy that follows life, into the place; but at the time I mention it wore its grimmest and most gruesome aspect. The dust of ages seemed to have settled on it, and the darkness and the horror of its memories seem to have become sentient in a way that would have satisfied the Pantheistic souls of Philo or Spinoza. The lower chamber where we entered was seemingly, in its normal state, filled with incarnate darkness; even the hot sunlight streaming in through the door seemed to be lost in the vast thickness of the walls, and only showed the masonry rough as when the builder's scaffolding had come down, but coated with dust and marked here and there with patches of dark stain which, if walls could speak, could have given their own dread memories of fear and pain. We were glad to pass up the dusty wooden staircase, the custodian leaving the outer door open to light us somewhat on our way; for to our eyes the one long-wick'd, evil-smelling candle stuck in a sconce on the wall gave an inadequate light. When we came up through the open trap in the corner of the chamber overhead, Amelia held on to me so tightly that I could actually feel her heart beat. I must say for my own part that I was not surprised at her fear, for this room was even more gruesome than that below. Here there was certainly more light, but only just sufficient to realise the horrible surroundings of the place. The builders of the tower had evidently intended that only they who should gain the top should have any of the joys of light and prospect. There, as we had noticed from below, were ranges of windows, albeit of mediæval smallness, but elsewhere in the tower were only a very few narrow slits such as were habitual in places of mediæval defence. A few of these only lit the chamber, and these so high up in the wall that from no part could the sky be seen through the thickness of the walls. In racks, and leaning in disorder against the walls, were a number of headsmen's swords, great double-handed weapons with broad blade and keen edge. Hard by were several blocks whereon the necks of the victims had lain, with here and there deep notches where the steel had bitten through the guard of flesh and shored into the wood. Round the chamber, placed in all sorts of irregular ways, were many implements of torture which made one's heart ache to see—chairs full of spikes which gave instant and excruciating pain; chairs and couches with dull knobs whose torture was seemingly less, but which, though slower, were equally efficacious; racks, belts, boots, gloves, collars, all made for compressing at will; steel baskets in which the head could be slowly crushed into a pulp if necessary; watchmen's hooks with long handle and knife that cut at resistance—this a specialty of the old Nurnberg police system; and many, many other devices for man's injury to man. Amelia grew quite pale with the horror of the things, but fortunately did not faint, for being a little overcome she sat down on a torture chair, but jumped up again with a shriek, all tendency to faint gone. We both pretended that it was the injury done to her dress by the dust of the chair, and the rusty spikes which had upset her, and Mr. Hutcheson acquiesced in accepting the explanation with a kind-hearted laugh.

But the central object in the whole of this chamber of horrors was the engine known as the Iron Virgin, which stood near the centre of the room. It was a rudely-shaped figure of a woman, something of the bell order, or, to make a closer comparison, of the figure of Mrs. Noah in the children's Ark, but without that slimness of waist and perfect *rondeur* of hip which marks the aesthetic type of the Noah family. One would hardly have recognised it as intended for a human figure at all had not the founder shaped on the forehead a rude semblance of a woman's face. This machine was coated with rust without, and covered with dust; a rope was fastened to a ring in the front of the figure, about where the waist should have been, and was drawn through a pulley, fastened on the wooden pillar which sustained the flooring above. The custodian pulling this rope showed that a section of the front was hinged like a door at one side; we then saw that the engine was of considerable thickness, leaving just room enough inside for a man to be placed. The door was of equal thickness and of great weight, for it took the custodian all his strength, aided though he was by the contrivance of the pulley, to open it. This weight was partly due to the fact that the door was of manifest purpose hung so as to throw its weight downwards, so that it might shut of its own accord when the strain was released. The inside was honeycombed with rust—nay more, the rust alone that comes through time would hardly have eaten so deep into the iron walls; the rust of the cruel stains was deep indeed! It was only, however, when we came to look at the inside of the door that the diabolical intention was manifest to the full. Here were several long spikes, square and massive, broad at the base and sharp at the points, placed in such a position that when the door should close the upper ones would pierce the eyes of the victim, and the lower ones his heart and vitals. The sight was too much for poor Amelia, and this time she fainted dead off, and I had to carry her down the stairs, and place her on a bench outside till she recovered. That she felt it to the quick was afterwards shown by the fact that my eldest son bears to this day a rude birthmark on his breast, which has, by family consent, been accepted as representing the Nurnberg Virgin.

When we got back to the chamber we found Hutcheson still opposite the Iron Virgin; he had been evidently philosophising, and now gave us the benefit of his thought in the shape of a sort of exordium.

"Wall, I guess I've been learnin' somethin' here while madam has been gettin' over her faint. 'Pears to me that we're a long way behind the times on our side of the big drink. We uster think out on the plains that the Injun could give us points in tryin' to make a man oncomfortable; but I guess your old mediæval law-and-order party could raise him every time. Splinters was pretty good in his bluff on the squaw, but this here young miss held a straight flush all high on him. The points of them spikes air sharp enough still, though even the edges air eaten out by what uster be on them. It'd be a good thing for our Indian section to get some specimens of this here play-toy to send round to the Reservations jest to knock the stuffin' out of the bucks, and the squaws too, by showing them as how old civilisation lays over them at their best. Guess but I'll get in that box a minute jest to see how it feels!"

"Oh no! no!" said Amelia. "It is too terrible!"

"Guess, ma'am, nothin's too terrible to the explorin' mind. I've been in some queer places in my time. Spent a night inside a dead horse while a prairie fire swept over me in Montana Territory—an' another time slept inside a dead buffler when the Comanches was on the war path an' I didn't keer to leave my kyard on them. I've been two days in a caved-in tunnel in the Billy Broncho gold mine in New Mexico, an' was one of the four shut up for three parts of a day in the caisson what slid over on her side when we was settin' the foundations of the Buffalo Bridge. I've not funked an odd experience yet, an' I don't propose to begin now!"

We saw that he was set on the experiment, so I said: "Well, hurry up, old man, and get through it quick?"

"All right, General," said he, "but I calculate we ain't quite ready yet. The gentlemen, my predecessors, what stood in that thar canister didn't volunteer for the office—not much! And I guess there was some ornamental tyin' up before the big stroke was made. I want to go into this thing fair and square, so I must get fixed up proper first. I dare say this old galoot can rise some string and tie me up accordin' to sample?"

This was said interrogatively to the old custodian, but the latter, who understood the drift of his speech, though perhaps not appreciating to the full the niceties of dialect and imagery, shook his head. His protest was, however, only formal and made to be overcome. The American thrust a gold piece into his hand, saying, "Take it, pard! it's your pot; and don't be skeer'd. This ain't no necktie party that you're asked to assist in!" He produced some thin frayed rope and proceeded to bind our companion with sufficient strictness for the purpose. When the upper part of his body was bound, Hutcheson said:

"Hold on a moment, Judge. Guess I'm too heavy for you to tote into the canister. You jest let me walk in, and then you can wash up regardin' my legs!"

Whilst speaking he had backed himself into the opening which was just enough to hold him. It was a close fit and no mistake. Amelia looked on with fear in her eyes, but she evidently did not like to say anything. Then the custodian completed his task by tying the American's feet together so that he was now absolutely helpless and fixed in his voluntary prison. He seemed to really enjoy it, and the incipient smile which was habitual to his face blossomed into actuality as he said:

"Guess this here Eve was made out of the rib of a dwarf! There ain't much room for a full-grown citizen of the United States to hustle. We uster make our coffins more roomier in Idaho territory. Now, Judge, you jest begin to let this door down, slow, on to me. I want to feel the same pleasure as the other jays had when those spikes began to move toward their eyes!"

"Oh no! no! no!" broke in Amelia hysterically. "It is too terrible! I can't bear to see it!—I can't! I can't!"

But the American was obdurate. "Say, Colonel," said he, "Why not take Madame for a little promenade? I wouldn't hurt her feelin's for the world; but now that I am here, havin' kem eight thousand miles, wouldn't it be too hard to give up the very experience I've been pinin' an' pantin' fur? A man can't get to feel like canned goods every time! Me and the Judge here'll fix up this thing in no time, an' then you'll come back, an' we'll all laugh together!"

Once more the resolution that is born of curiosity triumphed, and Amelia stayed holding tight to my arm and shivering whilst the custodian began to slacken slowly

inch by inch the rope that held back the iron door. Hutcheson's face was positively radiant as his eyes followed the first movement of the spikes.

"Wall!" he said, "I guess I've not had enjoyment like this since I left Noo York. Bar
a scrap with a French sailor at Wapping—an' that warn't much of a picnic neither—
I've not had a show fur real pleasure in this dod-rotted Continent, where there ain't no
b'ars nor no Injuns, an wheer nary man goes heeled. Slow there, Judge! Don't you rush
this business! I want a show for my money this game—I du!"

The custodian must have had in him some of the blood of his predecessors in
that ghastly tower, for he worked the engine with a deliberate and excruciating
slowness which after five minutes, in which the outer edge of the door had not
moved half as many inches, began to overcome Amelia. I saw her lips whiten, and
felt her hold upon my arm relax. I looked around an instant for a place whereon
to lay her, and when I looked at her again found that her eye had become fixed on
the side of the Virgin. Following its direction I saw the black cat crouching out of
sight. Her green eyes shone like danger lamps in the gloom of the place, and their
colour was heightened by the blood which still smeared her coat and reddened her
mouth. I cried out:

"The cat! look out for the cat!" for even then she sprang out before the engine. At
this moment she looked like a triumphant demon. Her eyes blazed with ferocity, her
hair bristled out till she seemed twice her normal size, and her tail lashed about as does
a tiger's when the quarry is before it. Elias P. Hutcheson when he saw her was amused,
and his eyes positively sparkled with fun as he said:

"Darned if the squaw hain't got on all her war paint! Jest give her a shove off if she
comes any of her tricks on me, for I'm so fixed everlastingly by the boss, that durn my
skin if I can keep my eyes from her if she wants them! Easy there, Judge! don't you slack
that ar rope or I'm euchered!"

At this moment Amelia completed her faint, and I had to clutch hold of her round
the waist or she would have fallen to the floor. Whilst attending to her I saw the black
cat crouching for a spring, and jumped up to turn the creature out.

But at that instant, with a sort of hellish scream, she hurled herself, not as we
expected at Hutcheson, but straight at the face of the custodian. Her claws seemed
to be tearing wildly as one sees in the Chinese drawings of the dragon rampant, and
as I looked I saw one of them light on the poor man's eye, and actually tear through
it and down his cheek, leaving a wide band of red where the blood seemed to spurt
from every vein.

With a yell of sheer terror which came quicker than even his sense of pain, the man
leaped back, dropping as he did so the rope which held back the iron door. I jumped

for it, but was too late, for the cord ran like lightning through the pulley-block, and the heavy mass fell forward from its own weight.

As the door closed I caught a glimpse of our poor companion's face. He seemed frozen with terror. His eyes stared with a horrible anguish as if dazed, and no sound came from his lips.

And then the spikes did their work. Happily the end was quick, for when I wrenched open the door they had pierced so deep that they had locked in the bones of the skull through which they had crushed, and actually tore him—it—out of his iron prison till, bound as he was, he fell at full length with a sickly thud upon the floor, the face turning upward as he fell.

I rushed to my wife, lifted her up and carried her out, for I feared for her very reason if she should wake from her faint to such a scene. I laid her on the bench outside and ran back. Leaning against the wooden column was the custodian moaning in pain whilst he held his reddening handkerchief to his eyes. And sitting on the head of the poor American was the cat, purring loudly as she licked the blood which trickled through the gashed socket of his eyes.

I think no one will call me cruel because I seized one of the old executioner's swords and shore her in two as she sat.

Sredni Vashtar

Saki

Conradin was ten years old, and the doctor had pronounced his professional opinion that the boy would not live another five years. The doctor was silky and effete, and counted for little, but his opinion was endorsed by Mrs. de Ropp, who counted for nearly everything. Mrs. de Ropp was Conradin's cousin and guardian, and in his eyes she represented those three-fifths of the world that are necessary and disagreeable and real; the other two-fifths, in perpetual antagonism to the foregoing, were summed up in himself and his imagination. One of these days Conradin supposed he would succumb to the mastering pressure of wearisome necessary things—such as illnesses and coddling restrictions and drawn-out dulness. Without his imagination, which was rampant under the spur of loneliness, he would have succumbed long ago.

Mrs. de Ropp would never, in her honestest moments, have confessed to herself that she disliked Conradin, though she might have been dimly aware that thwarting him "for his good" was a duty which she did not find particularly irksome. Conradin hated her with a desperate sincerity which he was perfectly able to mask. Such few pleasures as he could contrive for himself gained an added relish from the likelihood that they would be displeasing to his guardian, and from the realm of his imagination she was locked out—an unclean thing, which should find no entrance.

In the dull, cheerless garden, overlooked by so many windows that were ready to open with a message not to do this or that, or a reminder that medicines were due, he found little attraction. The few fruit-trees that it contained were set jealously apart from his plucking, as though they were rare specimens of their kind blooming in an arid waste; it would probably have been difficult to find a market-gardener who would have offered ten shillings for their entire yearly produce. In a forgotten corner, however, almost hidden behind a dismal shrubbery, was a disused tool-shed of respectable proportions, and within its walls Conradin found a haven, something that took on the varying aspects of a playroom and a cathedral. He had peopled it with a legion of familiar phantoms, evoked partly from fragments of history and partly from his own brain, but it also boasted two inmates of flesh and blood. In one corner lived a ragged-plumaged Houdan hen, on which the boy lavished an affection that had scarcely another outlet. Further back in the gloom stood a large hutch, divided into two compartments, one of which was fronted with close iron bars. This was the abode of a large polecat-ferret, which a friendly butcher-boy had once smuggled, cage and all, into its present quarters, in exchange for a long-secreted hoard of small silver. Conradin was dreadfully afraid of the lithe, sharp-fanged beast, but it was his most treasured possession. Its very presence in the tool-shed was a secret and fearful joy, to be kept scrupulously from the knowledge of the Woman, as he privately dubbed his cousin. And one day, out of Heaven knows what material, he spun the beast a wonderful name, and from that moment it grew into a god and a religion. The Woman indulged in religion once a week at a church near by, and took Conradin with her, but to him the church service was an alien rite in the House of Rimmon. Every Thursday, in the dim and musty silence of the tool-shed, he worshipped with mystic and elaborate ceremonial before the wooden hutch where dwelt Sredni Vashtar, the great ferret. Red flowers in their season and scarlet berries in the winter-time were offered at his shrine, for he was a god who laid some special stress on the fierce impatient side of things, as opposed to the Woman's religion, which, as far as Conradin could observe, went to great lengths in the contrary direction. And on great festivals powdered nutmeg was strewn in front of his hutch, an important feature of the offering being that the nutmeg had to be stolen. These festivals were of irregular occurrence, and were chiefly appointed to celebrate some passing event. On one occasion, when Mrs. de Ropp suffered from acute toothache for three days, Conradin kept up the festival during the entire three days, and almost succeeded in persuading himself that Sredni Vashtar was personally responsible for the toothache. If the malady had lasted for another day the supply of nutmeg would have given out.

The Houdan hen was never drawn into the cult of Sredni Vashtar. Conradin had long ago settled that she was an Anabaptist. He did not pretend to have the remotest knowledge as to what an Anabaptist was, but he privately hoped that it was dashing and not very respectable. Mrs. de Ropp was the ground-plan on which he based and detested all respectability.

After a while Conradin's absorption in the tool-shed began to attract the notice of his guardian. "It is not good for him to be pottering down there in all weathers," she promptly decided, and at breakfast one morning she announced that the Houdan hen had been sold and taken away overnight. With her short-sighted eyes she peered at Conradin, waiting for an outbreak of rage and sorrow, which she was ready to rebuke with a flow of excellent precepts and reasoning. But Conradin said nothing; there was nothing to be said. Something perhaps in his white set face gave her a momentary qualm, for at tea that afternoon there was toast on the table, a delicacy which she usually banned on the ground that it was bad for him; also because the making of it "gave trouble," a deadly offence in the middle-class feminine eye.

"I thought you liked toast," she exclaimed, with an injured air, observing that he did not touch it.

"Sometimes," said Conradin.

In the shed that evening there was an innovation in the worship of the hutch-god. Conradin had been wont to chant his praises, to-night he asked a boon.

"Do one thing for me, Sredni Vashtar."

The thing was not specified. As Sredni Vashtar was a god he must be supposed to know. And choking back a sob as he looked at that other empty corner, Conradin went back to the world he so hated.

And every night, in the welcome darkness of his bedroom, and every evening in the dusk of the tool-shed, Conradin's bitter litany went up: "Do one thing for me, Sredni Vashtar."

Mrs. de Ropp noticed that the visits to the shed did not cease, and one day she made a further journey of inspection.

"What are you keeping in that locked hutch?" she asked. "I believe it's guinea-pigs. I'll have them all cleared away."

Conradin shut his lips tight, but the Woman ransacked his bedroom till she found the carefully hidden key, and forthwith marched down to the shed to complete her discovery. It was a cold afternoon, and Conradin had been bidden to keep to the house. From the furthest window of the dining-room the door of the shed could just be seen beyond the corner of the shrubbery, and there Conradin stationed himself. He saw the Woman enter, and then he imagined her opening the door of the sacred hutch and peering down with her short-sighted eyes into the thick straw bed where his god lay hidden. Perhaps she would prod at the straw in her clumsy impatience. And Conradin fervently breathed his prayer for the last time. But he knew as he prayed that he did not believe. He knew that the Woman would come out presently with that pursed smile he loathed so well on her face, and that in an hour or two the gardener would carry away his wonderful god, a god no longer, but a simple brown ferret in a hutch. And he knew that the Woman would triumph always as she triumphed now, and that he would grow ever more sickly under her pestering and domineering and superior wisdom, till one day nothing would matter much more with him, and the doctor would be proved right. And in the sting and misery of his defeat, he began to chant loudly and defiantly the hymn of his threatened idol:—

> SREDNI VASHTAR WENT FORTH,
> HIS THOUGHTS WERE RED THOUGHTS AND HIS TEETH WERE WHITE.
> HIS ENEMIES CALLED FOR PEACE BUT HE BROUGHT THEM DEATH,
> SREDNI VASHTAR THE BEAUTIFUL.

And then of a sudden he stopped his chanting and drew closer to the window-pane. The door of the shed still stood ajar as it had been left, and the minutes were slipping by. They were long minutes, but they slipped by nevertheless. He watched the starlings running and flying in little parties across the lawn; he counted them over and over again, with one eye always on that swinging door. A sour-faced maid came in to lay the table for tea, and still Conradin stood and waited and watched. Hope had crept by inches into his heart, and now a look of triumph began to blaze in his eyes that had only known the wistful patience of defeat. Under his breath, with a furtive exultation, he began once again the paean of victory and devastation. And presently his eyes were rewarded; out through that doorway came a long, low, yellow-and-brown beast, with eyes a-blink at the waning daylight, and dark wet stains around the fur of jaws and throat. Conradin dropped on his knees. The great polecat-ferret made its way down to a small brook at the foot of the garden, drank for a moment, then crossed a little plank bridge and was lost to sight in the bushes. Such was the passing of Sredni Vashtar.

"Tea is ready," said the sour-faced maid; "where is the mistress?"

"She went down to the shed some time ago," said Conradin.

And while the maid went to summon her mistress to tea Conradin fished a toasting-fork out of the sideboard drawer and proceeded to toast himself a piece of bread. And during the toasting of it and the buttering of it with much butter and the slow enjoyment of eating it, Conradin listened to the noises and silences which fell in quick spasms beyond the dining-room door. The loud foolish screaming of the maid, the answering chorus of wondering ejaculations from the kitchen region, the scuttering footsteps and hurried embassies for outside help, and then after a lull, the scared sobbings and the shuffling tread of those who bore a heavy burden into the house.

"Whoever will break it to the poor child? I couldn't for the life of me!" exclaimed a shrill voice. And while they debated the matter among themselves Conradin made himself another piece of toast.

The Story of No. 1, Karma Crescent

E. and H. Heron

THE FOLLOWING STORY IS THE FIRST FULL RELATION OF THE EXTRAORDINARY features of the case connected with the house in South London, that at one time occupied so large a portion of the public attention. It may be remembered that several mysterious deaths took place within a few months of each other in a certain new suburb. In each instance the same unaccountable symptoms were present, and the successive inquests gave rise to a quite remarkable amount of discussion in the Press as the evidence furnished points of peculiar interest for the Psychical Societies.

It is a recognised fact that the public will die patiently, and to a large percentage, of any known and preventable epidemic before they trouble to make a stir about it, but they resent instantly and bitterly the removal of half-a-dozen individuals, provided these die from some unknown and, therefore, unpreventable cause. Thus the fate of the victims at No. 1, Karma Crescent, raised a storm of comment, conjecture, and vague accusation; in time this died away, however, and the whole business was forgotten, or only recalled to serve as an example of the many dark and sinister mysteries London carries in her unfathomed heart.

As many people may not be able to recall the details to mind, a brief *résumé* of the chief incidents is given below, together with additional information supplied later by Flaxman Low, the well-known psychical investigator.

Karma Crescent is one of several similar terraces planned and partially built upon a newly-opened estate in an outlying suburb of London. The locality is good, though not fashionable, hence the houses, though of fair size, are offered at moderate rentals. Karma Crescent has never been completed. It consists of six or seven houses, most of which were let when Colonel Simpson B. Hendriks and his son walked over from the railway station to inspect No. 1. This was a detached corner house, overlooking an untidy spread of building and, beyond which railway sheds and a network of lines on a rather high level rose against the sky. To the right of the house an old country lane, deeply rutted, led away between ragged hedges to a congeries of small houses about half a mile distant. These houses form the outer crust of a poor district, of which no more need be said than that it provides a certain amount of dock labour.

The Americans were, however, not deterred by the dreary surroundings; they had come to London on business, and since No. 1 was cheap, commodious, and well-furnished, they closed with the agent who showed them over. It was only when the lease was signed, and they had begun to inquire for servants, that the distinctive characteristics of the abode they had chosen was borne in upon them. Upon making inquiry they gathered that the house had been occupied by three successive sets of tenants, all of whom complained that it was haunted by a dark, evil, whispering face, that lurked in dusky corners, met them in lonely rooms, or hung over the beds, terrifying the awakened sleepers.

This silent, flitting presence foretold death, for each family had left hurriedly and in deep distress upon the loss of one of its members, but as the drains and the roof were sound, and it has been definitely decided that the English law can take no account of ghosts, the Hendriks were obliged to stick to their bargain. Finally, the Colonel, who was a widower, secured the services of a gaunt Scotch housekeeper, professing herself well acquainted with the habits of ghosts, and took up his residence with his son at No. 1, being fully persuaded that a free use of shooting-irons was likely to prove as good a preventive against hauntings as against any other form of annoyance.

Three days later, on the 5th February, the first symptoms of disturbance set in. The Hendriks had been out very late, and on their return in the small hours, found their housekeeper scared and shaking, and with a circumstantial story to tell of the apparition. She said she had been awakened from sleep by the touch of a death-cold hand. Opening her eyes, she saw a fearsome, whispering face hanging over her; she could not catch the meaning of the words it said, but was persuaded that they were threatening.

A faint light flickered about the face, "like I've seen brandy on a dish of raisins," continued Miss Anderson, "and I could see it was wrapped up in its winding-sheet, gone yellow wi' age and lying by. At last the light went out wi' a flash, and I lay trembling in the dairk till I heard the latch-keys in the door, for I was fair frechtened at yon ghaist." One further detail she added, to the effect that on going to bed she had locked the door and put the key under her pillow, where she found it safe after the visit of the apparition, although the door was still fast locked when she tried to leave the room an hour later.

After this experience the Americans had all the bolts and locks of the house examined and strengthened, also one or other of them remained at home every evening.

It was in the course of the following week that young Lamartine Hendriks went out to a theatre, leaving his father at home. He was absent something over three hours and a half. When he returned between eleven and twelve o'clock, he found Colonel Hendriks sitting at the table in the dining-room, his body swollen to an enormous size, his face of a livid indigo, and quite dead. Calling down the housekeeper, the young man went for a doctor. He recollected having seen a doctor's plate on the door of a house in a shabby street close by. Dr. Mulroon was at home, a big powerful Irishman, rather the worse for liquor, but with the deep eye and square jaw that indicate ability. Hendriks hurried him round to Karma Crescent. On the way Mulroon asked no questions, he walked silently into the dining-room and looked steadily to the Colonel. Then he shook his head.

"Bedad! It's just what I expected!" he said.

"What?" asked Hendriks sharply.

Mulroon was sober enough by this time.

"It's the old story," he replied with a strong brogue. "This makes the fourth case of this kind I've been called in to see in this house during the last eighteen months."

"In this neighbourhood?"

"In this house, faith, and nowhere else! Didn't ye know it was haunted? Haven't you heard of the 'Strange Deaths in South London'? The papers had them in capitals an inch long."

Hendriks leant against the table and spoke hoarsely.

"We have just come from America, and I can recall something of what you mention, but I did not connect them with this house. As you have attended similar cases, tell me what is the cause of death?"

"The Public Analyst himself couldn't do that! Not in the way you want to hear it. I made an examination in each case as well as he, and maybe I'm as capable as he, perhaps more so! For I swept off every medal and honour that came in my way at Dublin, and—but what's the use of talking? No man living can tell you more than this. The blue colour of the tissues and the swelling are produced by a change in the condition of the blood, though the most exhaustive examination has failed to discover any reason or cause for such a change. The result is death, that is the only certainty about it."

A long silence ensued, and then Hendriks said quietly: "If it takes me to the last day of my life, I'll get at this business from the inside. I'll never give it up until I know everything!"

"Well, now, look here, Mr. Hendriks, will you take my advice? The police and the doctors have done their living best over this business, and they're just where they were at the beginning. There's only one man in Europe can help you—Flaxman Low, the psychologist."

But Hendriks demurred on the ground of having seen enough of such gentry in the States.

"Low is not like any of them. He is as sensible and as practical a man as you or I. I know what he can do and how he sets about it, for I was in practice in the country four or five years ago, and he came down there and cleared up a mystery that had bothered the neighbourhood for above ten years. Leave this room exactly as it is. Wire for him first—you can get the police in after."

The upshot of this conversation was that Mr. Low arrived at Karma Crescent soon after it became light, having been fetched by Mulroon in person.

The dining-room was a square room opening on to the garden by a French window. It was richly furnished, everything was in order, there was no sign of a struggle. At the table about ten feet from the glass doors sat the dead man—a disfigured and horrible spectacle. The body was inclined to the left side, the head dropped rather forward on the left shoulder, the left arm hanging straight down at his side, and the left trouser leg slightly turned up. Low bent over him and looked at the puffed blue lips.

"Does the attitude suggest anything to you?" asked Flaxman Low after some time.

"He was bending forward to get his breath," returned Mulroon.

"On the contrary he had been stooping forward and to the left, but leant back for relief when the final spasm seized him," said Low. "Whatever may have been the cause of death, its action was rapid. Now can you give me the details of the former deaths which have taken place here?"

"I can do that same." Mulroon drew out a pocket-book. "Here you are.

"The first tenant of this house was Dr. Philipson Vines (D.D., you understand). On the 16th November, 1889, he was found dead sitting in that same chair by the servants at 6:30 A.M. A fine edition of Froissart was open on the table before him. He had evidently been dead for several hours. His age was fifty-three, the body was well nourished, and all the organs healthy.

"Next, Richard Stephen Holding, a retired linen-draper, with a large family, took the house. On the 3rd February, 1890, he was found dead by his wife at 2 A.M. He was also seated at the table, and in the same attitude as you have noticed in Colonel Hendriks's case. Like the Colonel, he was still warm. His age was sixty-three, and a progressive heart trouble existed—which was not, however, the cause of death.

"Next, the house was taken by a widow lady named Findlater, with one daughter and an invalid son. The son kept to his bedroom during the first fortnight of their stay, but one warm May morning he ventured down here. His sister left him in an armchair at 11:45 in the forenoon, and on returning half-an-hour after to bring him some beef-tea, she found him seated at the table, blue and swollen and dead, just like the others. Findlater was twenty-seven, and must in any case have died shortly from phthisis."

"Can you recollect the attitudes of the bodies when you saw them?"

"Only in the case of Holding. The two others had been laid on the couch before my arrival," answered Mulroon.

"Have you not noticed this left trouser leg?" continued Low.

"Yes; it was the same with Holding's. Probably a convulsive clutch at the last moment, and, no doubt, involuntary."

Some further conversation having taken place, it was eventually arranged that Mr. Low should return in the evening to spend a few days with young Hendriks, and to study the surroundings.

After he had gone notice of the death was given and the usual formalities were carried out. The police examined the whole house, but as far as could be judged by prolonged searching, no one from outside could have got in, yet Colonel Hendriks had been done to death although no wound appeared upon the body.

The evidence of Miss Anderson at the inquest excited much attention. Several persons interested in psychical mysteries were present and made copious notes, besides cross-examining the housekeeper subsequently at great length. But no one, police, doctors, or psychists, had any workable theory to offer. Miss Anderson stated before the coroner that she wished to leave No. 1, Karma Crescent, at once, as she was firmly persuaded that the malignant whispering face, which hung over her while she lay in bed, was the face of the "Wicked One."

The jury returned an open verdict, and Hendriks walked back to his house feeling very dejected. His father's unaccountable death weighed upon him. He could not rid himself of the remembrance of the hideously changed aspect of the keen, handsome face that had been so much to him from his boyhood.

He knew that Flaxman Low had been present unofficially at the inquest, and resolved to question him on arrival. But when Low came, he declined to commit himself to any opinion, though he went so far as to say that he hoped some further information might soon be forthcoming. And with this Hendriks had to be satisfied.

"I should like to occupy your late housekeeper's room, where, I understand, several manifestations have taken place," continued Mr. Low, "and if you would allow it to be understood that I am merely a servant, whom you have hired for the time being to attend upon you, I think it might be a wise precaution."

During the next few days Flaxman Low was busy. He had brought with him a number of solid and peculiar bolts, which he fixed on the various doors and windows, it seemed, almost at random. He shut off the basement very securely, and put another bolt on the outside of the shutters inclosing the glass doors leading from the dining-room into the garden. Yet, after all, Hendriks noticed that he went to bed for several nights leaving one or other of these fittings unbolted.

Meanwhile, Low loitered about the garden, and inside and outside the house. He walked over to the railway junction, and lingered in the little lane. He visited the unpleasant colony of houses by the river, and altogether gained a pretty thorough knowledge of the neighbourhood.

"Has that garden door from the lane been much used since you came here?" he asked Hendriks one morning.

"No; my father thought that, under the circumstances, it had better be secured. It was never used. And, as there is no cellarage, I don't see how any persons can enter the house except after the ordinary style of the burglar."

Mulroon dropped in very often to see them, and one night he inquired of Flaxman Low if the apparition had made its appearance.

To his astonishment, Mr. Low replied in the affirmative.

"What did you do?" asked Mulroon.

"Nothing," replied Mr. Low. "My plans do not admit of any overt action yet. But I can assure you that Miss Anderson is a good observer, she gave us a very correct description of its appearance."

"Then it was an evil spirit?"

Mr. Flaxman Low smiled a little. "Undoubtedly," he said.

That night Mr. Low securely locked off the basement from the upper floor. He had since his coming insisted that no one but himself should enter the dining-room at any time or for any purpose. He begged that it should be neither ventilated nor aired, but left closed and unopened. Every day he went in and remained for some time, morning and evening. On this occasion he paid the room his usual nightly visit, and Hendriks from the hall could hear him locking the French windows.

"Won't you draw your patent safety bolt outside, too?" he called out. "You've forgotten that every night."

"I think I may leave that for the present," was Low's reply.

"There's nothing to be got out of you, Mr. Low," said Hendriks with some irritation.

"Not yet, but I hope soon to have something to say for myself," Flaxman Low answered.

On the next day Mr. Low did not visit the dining-room until the afternoon. He opened the doors to air the room and lit the fire, after which he locked the French windows, and, shutting the door behind him, went to speak to Hendriks in the next room.

"I am going out for a short time," he said. "Will you be good enough not to enter the dining-room during my absence? Mulroon will probably come round. Please warn him also."

It was already growing dark when Mr. Low left the house. He remained away but a short time, and on his return was much disturbed by hearing Muldoon's big voice arguing with Hendriks in the dining-room. He opened the door. Mulroon was sitting in the same high-backed chair. He was a little tipsy, and in consequence, annoyingly obstinate

Mr. Low laid down the basket he held in his hand.

"For Heaven's sake, Mulroon, don't move! If you do, you're a dead man!" he said, approaching him. "Now, keep your legs straight—so, and rise gently."

Mulroon, grumbling a good deal, but partially sobered by Flaxman Low's manifest alarm, did as he was told.

"Now," added Low, "if you will kindly leave me for a few minutes alone, I will join you later."

Mulroon, however, had patients to attend to, and left, so that when Mr. Low followed Hendriks into the drawing-room a quarter of an hour afterwards, he found the American alone.

"There were two questions which I set myself to answer when I came to this house," said Low. "One was—Why did these persons die? There was a peculiar and obscure cause, of which we saw the effects. The second was—By what agency were these persons subjected to the cause of death? I have partially solved one problem to-night. To-morrow I have some hope of reaching the other. To begin with, I have already satisfied myself as to the precise manner of death. To-morrow night, if you and Mulroon will meet me here, I will tell you, as far as I can, how the whole mystery may be solved."

All the next day Flaxman Low and Hendriks kept close to the house. After dark Flaxman Low disappeared, and had not returned by eleven o'clock. Mulroon and Hendriks sat waiting for him in the drawing-room, until presently he walked into the room, and threw himself into an arm chair.

"I think now," he said, "that I may venture to say that I have something to show you.

"To begin at the beginning, this house was declared by successive tenants to be haunted. Further, the manifestations were said to be connected in some way with the deaths that took place after the apparitions had been seen—in all cases by some member of the household other than the victim. Whether these saw or heard anything prior to death was naturally beyond the power of their relatives to discover. But I fancy I can now answer that question. I have fairly good proof that they did not see any apparition."

"There never was any sign of a struggle or disturbance," put in Mulroon. "And that reminds me of what an old Irish charwoman, who worked here in the Findlaters' time, told me—that many cases had been known in her part of Ireland where the sight of a ghost turned the blood in the veins of the beholder. To be sure, we only smile at such sayings, but if you can give me any better reason why these men died, I'll thank you."

"This is exactly the point I hope to make," replied Low. "But to return to the manifestations. Miss Anderson's account of the ghost tallies with the stories of other residents. It nearly always appeared to the servants, by the way. The thing was evil and whispered, and each was convinced they could have understood what it said had they not been too frightened to do so. Then all agreed in saying it wore its winding-sheet. This added strength to my first conclusion and the further I pushed my inquiries the more I was confirmed in my theory."

"But the deaths. You cannot account for them?" asked Hendriks. "You can't persuade me that any whispering face killed my father. He would have put a bullet through it on sight."

"Pray be patient," said Flaxman Low. "You must remember that I had very little data to go upon. In all cases the postmortem aspect was the same—the terribly distended bodies, the puffy lips, the bluish skin. Something had brought about this aspect with its concurrent effect—death, but no one could find out anything more. Knowledge stopped at the ultimate fact of death. It appeared to be impossible to get behind that last wall."

Hendriks made a movement of impatience.

"Yes, yes, but where do the ghosts come in?"

"Nowhere," replied Flaxman Low decisively. "At a very early stage of the business I entirely cast aside all thoughts of spiritual phenomena. Two points I noticed in connection with Colonel Hendriks's appearance aided me—the turning up of the left trouser leg and the position of the body in the chair. From these two facts the conclusion was obvious. I then knew why the people had died. There was, of course, no ghost at all. They had simply been murdered!"

"By whom? I shall be glad to meet that man," said Hendriks suddenly.

"But allow me to ask you what you deduced from the winding-sheet and the whisperings?" asked Mulroon.

"Taken in conjunction with the manner of death of the inmates of this house," said Flaxman Low, "I deduced a Chinaman. The winding-sheet meant simply loose garments, which might readily be nothing more than the formless wide-sleeved jacket of dirty yellow worn by the Chinese. Upon this I searched the whole neighbourhood for a yellow skin, and came upon a furtive little colony down by the riverside."

"But we had this house secured in all sorts of ways. How could this fellow have gained an entrance, and what grudge can he bear against us? Then, as you know, there was no struggle."

"The reason of the haunting and the murders are evident. Certain persons wanted to keep this house empty. They have some means of entering from the basement, and they are in possession of duplicate keys for every lock, a matter which reduces the haunting to a very simple process. If you remember one of my very first steps was to fix bolts—which cannot be unlocked—upon some of the doors. I bolted off the basement for two nights after my arrival and consequently I slept in peace. On the third night I left the dividing door locked only, and I was at once favoured with a glimpse of the whispering face lit up by the usual phosphorescent trick. As I expected, the face was of the Malay cast, and it threatened in mumbling pidgin English.

"You told me, Mr. Hendriks, that the garden door had not been opened since your tenancy began—that it was in fact secured. I had reason to think otherwise, and made certain of the correctness by tying a thread across the doorway on the inner side, which was broken more than once. From the garden door to the French window in the dining-room was a natural step in my theory."

"But that bolt you put upon the outside of the wooden shutters?" said Mulroon.

"It suited my plans to put it there; in fact, I hope it is holding well at this moment. Knowing that duplicate keys existed, I presumed that someone would enter the dining-room shortly, for a purpose which I will presently explain. I, therefore, put up my little thread-detective, and it also gave satisfactory evidence. Someone had entered the room, and to make sure of their motive for doing so, I purchased a rat, which I brought back in a basket with me last evening, but Mulroon very nearly saved me the trouble of trying any experiment on my own part by sitting down in the chair which seems to be the fatal one here."

Mulroon turned pale, and laughed in a forced manner.

"Well, well," he said; "the drink makes fools of us all, but my luck stood to me. How did I escape, Mr. Low?"

"You had the luck of long legs, that is all. When you sat in the chair, the backs of your knees did not come against the frame of the seat; if they had, you would have been in your coffin by now."

"Then you have discovered how my father met his death?" exclaimed Hendriks.

"Yes. In examining the chair, I found the legs had been neatly cut, so as to tilt back the chair at a slight angle, and any person sitting in it would naturally sit far back in consequence, thus bringing the back of the knees against the wooden bar in front of the seat. To the left of this bar I found a tiny splinter of steel fixed in, and I tried its effect last night upon a rat, with the result that it died almost immediately, its body being dreadfully swollen in the course of a few minutes. The turned-up trouser on the left leg led me directly to this discovery. To take the case of Colonel Hendriks, he felt the prick on the inner side of the left knee, and was turning up his trouser when the poison took effect, and he died in the act."

"I remember now that at the post-mortem examination you pointed out a hardly visible mark on the Colonel's knee," said Mulroon; "but it seemed too faint and tiny to afford any clue. But as you are in a position to prove that the persons who have died here have died of poison, can you account for the fact that no trace of poison has been discovered in any of the bodies?"

"Other known poisons disappear from the system in a similar manner. In this instance, guided by my supposition that the perpetrators of the murders were Chinese, I naturally set about finding out as much as possible upon the subject of Chinese poisons. I cannot tell you the name, much less the specific nature of the poison used here, but I am prepared to show proofs that similar results have been recorded with regard to the victims of a certain dreaded secret society in China, which owes much of its power and prestige to the fact that it can strike its opponents with the dreaded 'Blue Death.'"

"But we are as far as ever from finding the murderer," objected Hendriks. "To find him and punish him is all that I care for. Nothing else has the slightest interest for me."

"I calculated," began Low, when this outburst was over, "I calculated that as the murderer had not yet accomplished his purpose of driving us out of the house, he would return to his diabolical work sooner or later. Hence I was quite cheered when the ghost visited me. I had identified my man two days ago, but I waited to get an opportunity of bringing his crimes home to him. Will you come with me into the dining-room?"

Hendriks and Mulroon followed Flaxman Low, who carried a candle. For a second he listened at the door of the dining-room, but dead silence reigned. "I bolted the shutters of the windows on the outside after I had seen my man enter to renew the supply of poison on the steel point," said Flaxman Low. "I hope we may find him still here. He will probably make a dash at us. Will you be careful?"

"All right," said Hendriks, showing his revolver.

Low opened the door. Nothing moved inside the room, but sitting at the table was a huddled figure. The hat had fallen off, the head with its coiled pig-tail lay upon the outstretched arms. Another moment made it clear that the man was dead. They lit the candles on the mantel-piece, and proceeded to examine the dead body.

The yellow face was puffed beyond recognition, the whole man was strangely and quiescently horrible. On the table before him lay a small lacquered box containing a scrap of a dark ointment, and in the man's forefinger was found a splinter of steel. Finding himself trapped, he had made away with himself rather than face his captors.

At this stage of the proceedings, Flaxman Low retired from the affair.

The police managed to hush up the business—the death of a Chinaman more or less makes little stir at any time—and they had further investigations of importance to make, which they wished to keep quiet.

It was, indeed, ultimately proved that No. 1, Karma Crescent, formed a very convenient head-quarters for Chinese and other ruffianism, being situated as it was near a junction, near the river, and near a low part of London. It was found that extensive excavations had been made in communication with the house and a well-built tunnel opened by a cleverly masked entrance into the lane. Thus by Flaxman Low's efforts a very distinct danger had been warded off, for the society in question were making very alarming headway in London, chiefly by allying themselves with other bands of criminals in this country, to whom they offered a secure place of hiding.

The Story of
the Rippling Train

Mrs. Molesworth

"Let's tell ghost stories, then," said Gladys.

"Aren't you tired of them? One hears nothing else nowadays. And they're all 'authentic,' really vouched for, only you never see the person who saw or heard or felt the ghost. It is always somebody's sister or cousin, or friend's friend," objected young Mrs. Snowdon, another of the guests at the Quarries.

"I don't know that that is quite a reasonable ground for discrediting them *en masse*," said her husband. "It is natural enough, indeed inevitable, that the principal or principals in such cases should be much more rarely come across than the stories themselves. A hundred people can repeat the story, but the author, or rather hero, of it, can't be in a hundred places at once. You don't disbelieve in any other statement or narrative merely because you have never seen the prime mover in it?"

"But I didn't say I discredited them on that account," said Mrs. Snowdon. "You take one up so, Archie. I'm not logical and reasonable; I don't pretend to be. If I meant anything, it was that a ghost story would have a great pull over other ghost stories if one could see the person it happened to. One does get rather provoked at *never* coming across him or her," she added a little petulantly.

She was tired; they were all rather tired, for it was the first evening since the party had assembled at the large country house known as "the Quarries" on which there was not to be dancing, with the additional fatigue of "ten miles there and ten back again"; and three or four evenings of such doings without intermission tell even on the young and vigorous.

To-night various less energetic ways of passing the evening had been proposed,— music, games, reading aloud, recitation,—none had found favour in everybody's sight, and now Gladys Lloyd's proposal that they should "tell ghost stories" seemed likely to fall flat also.

For a moment or two no one answered Mrs. Snowdon's last remarks. Then, somewhat to everybody's surprise, the young daughter of the house turned to her mother.

"Mamma," she said, "don't be vexed with me—I know you warned me once to be careful how I spoke of it; but *wouldn't* it be nice if Uncle Paul would tell us his ghost story? And then, Mrs. Snowdon," she went on, "you could always say you had heard *one* ghost story at or from—which should I say?—headquarters."

Lady Denholme glanced round half nervously before she replied.

"Locally speaking, it would not be *at* headquarters, Nina," she said. "The Quarries was not the scene of your uncle's ghost story. But I almost think it is better not to speak about it—I am not sure that he would like it mentioned, and he will be coming in a moment. He had only a note to write."

"I do wish he would tell it to us," said Nina regretfully. "Don't you think, mamma, I might just run to the study and ask him, and if he did not like the idea he might say so to me, and no one would seem to know anything about it? Uncle Paul is so kind—I'm never afraid of asking him any favour."

"Thank you, Nina, for your good opinion of me; you see there is no rule without exceptions; listeners do sometimes hear pleasant things of themselves," said Mr. Marischal, as he at that moment came round the screen which half concealed the doorway. "What is the special favour you were thinking of asking me?"

Nina looked rather taken aback.

"How softly you opened the door, Uncle Paul," she said. "I would not have spoken of you if I had known you were there."

"But after all you were saying no harm," observed her brother Michael. "And for my part I don't believe Uncle Paul would mind our asking him what we were speaking of."

"What was it?" asked Mr. Marischal. "I think, as I have heard so much, you may as well tell me the whole."

"It was only—" began Nina, but her mother interrupted her.

"I have told Nina not to speak of it, Paul," she said anxiously; "but—it was only that all these young people are talking about ghost stories, and they want you to tell them your own strange experience. You must not be vexed with them."

"Vexed!" said Mr. Marischal, "not in the least." But for a moment or two he said no more, and even pretty, spoilt Mrs. Snowdon looked a little uneasy.

"You shouldn't have persisted, Nina," she whispered.

Mr. Marischal must have had unusually quick ears. He looked up and smiled.

"I really don't mind telling you all there is to hear," he said. "At one time I had a sort of dislike to mentioning the story, for the sake of others. The details would have led to its being recognised—and it might have been painful. But there is no one now living to whom it would matter—you know," he added, turning to his sister; "her husband is dead too."

Lady Denholme shook her head.

"No," she said, "I did not hear."

"Yes," said her brother, "I saw his death in the papers last year. He had married again, I believe. There is not now, therefore, any reason why I should not tell the story, if it will interest you," he went on, turning to the others. "And there is not very much to tell. Not worth making such a preamble about. It was—let me see—yes, it must be nearly fifteen years ago."

"Wait a moment, Uncle Paul," said Nina. "Yes, that's all right, Gladys. You and I will hold each other's hands, and pinch hard if we get very frightened."

"Thank you," Miss Lloyd replied. "On the whole I should prefer for you not to hold my hand."

"But I won't pinch you so as to hurt," said Nina reassuringly; "and it isn't as if we were in the dark."

"Shall I turn down the lamps?" asked Mr. Snowdon.

"No, no," exclaimed his wife.

"There really is nothing frightening—scarcely even 'creepy,' in my story at all," said Mr. Marischal, half apologetically. "You make me feel like an impostor."

"Oh no, Uncle Paul, don't say that. It is all my fault for interrupting," said Nina. "Now go on, please. I have Gladys's hand all the same," she added *sotto voce*, "it's just as well to be prepared."

"Well, then," began Mr. Marischal once more, "it must be nearly fifteen years ago; and I had not seen her for fully ten years before that again! I was not thinking of her in the least; in a sense I had really forgotten her: she had quite gone out of my life; that has always struck me as a very curious point in the story," he added parenthetically.

"Won't you tell us who 'she' was, Uncle Paul?" asked Nina half shyly.

"Oh yes, I was going to do so. I am not skilled in story-telling, you see. She was, at the time I first knew her—at the only time, indeed, that I knew her—a very sweet and attractive girl, named Maud Bertram. She was very pretty—more than pretty, for she had remarkably regular features—her profile was always admired, and a tall and grace-ful figure. And she was a bright and happy creature too; that, perhaps, was almost her greatest charm. You will wonder—I see the question hovering on your lips, Miss Lloyd, and on yours too, Mrs. Snowdon—why, if I admired her and liked her so much, I did not go further. And I will tell you frankly that I did not because I dared not. I had then no prospect of being able to marry for years to come, and I was not very young. I was already nearly thirty, and Maud was quite ten years younger. I was wise enough and old enough to realise the situation thoroughly, and to be on my guard."

"And Maud?" asked Mrs. Snowdon.

"She was surrounded by admirers; it seemed to me then that it would have been insufferable conceit to have even asked myself if it could matter to her. It was only in the light of after events that the possibility of my having been mistaken occurred to me. And I don't even now see that I could have acted otherwise—" Here Uncle Paul sighed a little. "We were the best of friends. She knew that I admired her, and she seemed to take a frank pleasure in its being so. I had always hoped that she really liked and trusted me as a friend, but no more. The last time I saw her was just before I started for Portugal, where I remained three years. When I returned to London Maud had been married for two years, and had gone straight out to India on her marriage, and except by some few friends who had known us both intimately, I seldom heard her mentioned. And time passed. I cannot say I had exactly forgotten her, but she was not much or often in my thoughts. I was a busy and much-absorbed man, and life had proved a serious matter to me. Now and then some passing resemblance would recall her to my mind—once especially when I had been asked to look in to see the young wife of one of my cousins in her court-dress; something in her figure and bearing brought back Maud to my memory, for it was thus, in full dress, that I had last seen her, and thus perhaps, unconsciously, her image had remained photographed on my brain. But as far as I can recollect at the time when the occurrence I am going to relate to you happened, I had not been thinking of Maud Bertram for months. I was in London just then, staying with my brother, my eldest brother, who had been married for several years, and lived in our own old town-house in —— Square. It was in April, a clear spring day, with no fog or half-lights about, and it was not yet four o'clock in the afternoon—not very ghost-like circumstances, you will admit. I had come home early from my club—it was a sort of holiday-time with me just then for a few weeks—intending to get some letters written which had been on my mind for some days, and I had sauntered into the library, a pleasant, fair-sized room lined with books, on the first-floor. Before setting to work I sat down for a moment or two in an easy-chair by the fire, for it was still cool enough weather to make a fire desirable, and began thinking over my letters. No thought, no shadow of a thought of my old friend Miss Bertram was present with me; of that I am perfectly certain. The door was on the same side of the room as the fireplace; as I sat there, half facing the fire, I also half faced the door. I had not shut it properly on coming in—I had only closed it without turning the handle—and I did not feel surprised when it slowly and noiselessly swung open, till it stood right out into the room, concealing the actual doorway from my view. You will perhaps understand the position better if you think of the door as just then acting like a screen to the doorway. From where I sat I could not have seen any one entering the room till he or she had got beyond the door itself. I glanced up, half expecting to see some one come in, but there was no one; the door had swung open of itself. For the moment I sat on, with only the vague thought passing through my mind, 'I must shut it before I begin to write.'

"But suddenly I found my eyes fixing themselves on the carpet; something had come within their range of vision, compelling their attention in a mechanical sort of way. What was it?

"'Smoke,' was my first idea. 'Can there be anything on fire?' But I dismissed the notion almost as soon as it suggested itself. The something, faint and shadowy, that came slowly rippling itself in as it were beyond the dark wood of the open door, was yet too material for 'smoke.' My next idea was a curious one. 'It looks like soapy water,' I said to myself; 'can one of the housemaids have been scrubbing, and upset a pail on the stairs?' For the stair to the next floor almost faced the library door. But—no; I rubbed my eyes and looked again; the soapy water theory gave way. The wavy something that kept gliding, rippling in, gradually assumed a more substantial appearance. It was— yes, I suddenly became convinced of it—it was ripples of soft silken stuff, creeping in as if in some mysterious way unfolded or unrolled, not jerkily or irregularly, but glidingly and smoothly, like little wavelets on the sea-shore.

"And I sat there and gazed. 'Why did you not jump up and look behind the door to see what it was?' you may reasonably ask. That question I cannot answer. Why I sat still, as if bewitched, or under some irresistible influence, I cannot tell, but so it was.

"And it—came always rippling in, till at last it began to rise as it still came on, and I saw that a figure—a tall, graceful woman's figure—was slowly advancing, backwards of course, into the room, and that the waves of pale silk—a very delicate shade of pearly gray I think it must have been—were in fact the lower portion of a long court-train, the upper part of which hung in deep folds from the lady's waist. She moved in—I cannot describe the motion, it was not like ordinary walking or stepping backwards—till the whole of her figure and the clear profile of her face and head were distinctly visible, and when at last she stopped and stood there full in my view just, but only just beyond the door, I saw—it came upon me like a flash— that she was no stranger to me, this mysterious visitant! I recognised, unchanged it seemed to me since the day, ten years ago, when I had last seen her, the beautiful features of Maud Bertram."

Mr. Marischal stopped a moment. Nobody spoke. Then he went on again.

"I should not have said 'unchanged.' There was one great change in the sweet face. You remember my telling you that one of my girl-friend's greatest charms was her bright sunny happiness—she never seemed gloomy or depressed or dissatisfied, seldom even pensive. But in this respect the face I sat there gazing at was utterly unlike Maud Bertram's. Its expression, as she—or 'it'—stood there looking, not towards me, but out beyond, as if at some one or something outside the doorway, was of the profoundest sadness. Anything *so* sad I had never seen in a human face, and I trust I never may. But I sat on, as motionless almost as she, gazing at her fixedly, with no desire, no power perhaps, to move or approach more nearly to the phantom. I was not in the least frightened. I knew it *was* a phantom, but I felt paralysed, and as if I myself had somehow got outside of ordinary conditions. And there I sat—staring at Maud, and there she stood, gazing before her with that terrible, unspeakable sadness in her face, which, even though I felt no *fear*, seemed to freeze me with a kind of unutterable pity.

"I don't know how long I had sat thus, or how long I might have continued to sit there, almost as if in a trance, when suddenly I heard the front-door bell ring. It seemed to awaken me. I started up and glanced round, half-expecting that I should find the vision dispelled. But no; she was still there, and I sank back into my seat just as I heard my brother coming quickly upstairs. He came towards the library, and seeing the door wide open walked in, and I, still gazing, saw his figure *pass through that of the woman in the doorway* as you may walk through a wreath of mist or smoke—only, don't misunderstand me, the figure of Maud till that moment had had nothing unsubstantial about it. She had looked to me, as she stood there, literally and exactly like a living woman—the shade of her dress, the colour of her hair, the few ornaments she wore, all were as defined and clear as yours, Nina, at the present moment, and remained so, or perhaps became so again as soon as my brother was well within the room. He came forward addressing me by name, but I answered him in a whisper, begging him to be silent and to sit down on the seat opposite me for a moment or two. He did so, though he was taken aback by my strange manner, for I still kept my eyes fixed on the door. I had a queer consciousness that if I looked away *it* would fade, and I wanted to keep cool and see what would happen. I asked Herbert in a low voice if *he* saw nothing, but though he mechanically followed the direction of my eyes, he shook his head in bewilderment. And for a moment or two he remained thus. Then I began to notice that the figure was growing less clear, as if it were receding, yet without growing smaller to the sight; it grew fainter and vaguer, the colours grew hazy. I rubbed my eyes once or twice with a half idea that my long watching was making them misty, but it was not so. My eyes were not at fault—slowly but surely Maud Bertram, or her ghost, melted away, till all trace of her had gone. I saw again the familiar pattern of the carpet where she had stood and the objects of the room that had been hidden by her draperies—all again in the most commonplace way, but she was gone, quite gone.

"Then Herbert, seeing me relax my intense gaze, began to question me. I told him exactly what I have told you. He answered, as every 'common-sensible' person of course would, that it was strange, but that such things did happen sometimes and were classed by the wise under the head of 'optical delusions.' I was not well, perhaps, he suggested. Been over-working? Had I not better see a doctor? But I shook my head. I was quite well, and I said so. And perhaps he was right, it might be an optical delusion only. I had never had any experience of such things.

"'All the same,' I said, 'I shall mark down the date.'

"Herbert laughed and said that was what people always did in such cases. If he knew where Mrs. —— then was he would write to her, just for the fun of the thing, and ask her to be so good as to look up her diary, if she kept one, and let us know what she had been doing on that particular day—'the 6th of April, isn't it?' he said—when I would have it her wraith had paid me a visit. I let him talk. It seemed to remove the strange painful impression—painful because of that terrible sadness in the sweet face. But we neither of us knew where she was, we scarcely remembered her married name! And so there was nothing to be done—except, what I did at once in spite of Herbert's rallying, to mark down the day and hour with scrupulous exactness in *my* diary.

"Time passed. I had not forgotten my strange experience, but of course the impression of it lessened by degrees till it seemed more like a curious dream than anything more real, when one day I *did* hear of poor Maud again. 'Poor' Maud I cannot help calling her. I heard of her indirectly, and probably, but for the sadness of her story, I should never have heard it at all. It was a friend of her husband's family who had mentioned the circumstances in the hearing of a friend of mine, and one day something brought round the conversation to old times, and he startled me by suddenly inquiring if I remembered Maud Bertram. I said, of course I did. Did he know anything of her? And then he told me.

"She was dead—she had died some months ago after a long and trying illness, the result of a terrible accident. She had caught fire one evening when dressed for some grand entertainment or other, and though her injuries did not seem likely to be fatal at the time, she had never recovered the shock.

"'She was so pretty,' my friend said, 'and one of the saddest parts of it was that I hear she was terrifically disfigured, and she took this most sadly to heart. The right side of her face was utterly ruined, and the sight of the right eye lost, though, strange to say, the left side entirely escaped, and seeing her in profile one would have had no notion of what had happened. Was it not sad? She was such a sweet, bright creature.'

"I did not tell him *my* story, for I did not want it chattered about, but a strange sort of shiver ran through me at his words. *It was the left side of her face only* that the wraith of my poor friend had allowed me to see."

"Oh, Uncle Paul!" exclaimed Nina.

"And—as to the dates?" inquired Mr. Snowdon.

"I never knew the exact date of the accident," said Mr. Marischal, "but that of her death was fully six months after I had seen her. And in my own mind, I have never made any doubt that it was at or about, probably a short time after, the accident, that she came to me. It seemed a kind of appeal for sympathy—and—a farewell also, poor child."

They all sat silent for some little time, and then Mr. Marischal got up and went off to his own quarters, saying something vaguely about seeing if his letters had gone.

"What a touching story!" said Gladys Lloyd. "I am afraid, after all, it has been more painful than he realised for Mr. Marischal to tell it. Did you know anything of Maud's husband, dear Lady Denholme? Was he kind to her? Was she happy?"

"We never heard much about her married life," her hostess replied. "But I have no reason to think she was unhappy. Her husband married again two or three years after her death, but that says nothing."

"N—no," said Nina. "All the same, mamma, I am sure she really did love Uncle Paul very much,—much more than he had any idea of. Poor Maud!"

"And he has never married," added Gladys.

"No," said Lady Denholme, "but there have been many practical difficulties in the way of his doing so. He has had a most absorbingly busy life, and now that he is more at leisure he feels himself too old to form new ties."

"But," persisted Nina, "if he had had any idea at the time that Maud cared for him so?"

"Ah well," Lady Denholme allowed, "in that case, in spite of the practical difficulties, things would probably have been different."

And again Nina repeated softly, "Poor Maud!"

THE STRANGE ORCHID

H. G. WELLS

THE BUYING OF ORCHIDS ALWAYS HAS IN IT A CERTAIN SPECULATIVE FLAVOUR. You have before you the brown shrivelled lump of tissue, and for the rest you must trust your judgment, or the auctioneer, or your good-luck, as your taste may incline. The plant may be moribund or dead, or it may be just a respectable purchase, fair value for your money, or perhaps—for the thing has happened again and again—there slowly unfolds before the delighted eyes of the happy purchaser, day after day, some new variety, some novel richness, a strange twist of the labellum, or some subtler colouration or unexpected mimicry. Pride, beauty, and profit blossom together on one delicate green spike, and, it may be, even immortality. For the new miracle of Nature may stand in need of a new specific name, and what so convenient as that of its discoverer? "Johnsmithia"! There have been worse names.

It was perhaps the hope of some such happy discovery that made Winter-Wedderburn such a frequent attendant at these sales—that hope, and also, maybe, the fact that he had nothing else of the slightest interest to do in the world. He was a shy, lonely, rather ineffectual man, provided with just enough income to keep off the spur of necessity, and not enough nervous energy to make him seek any exacting employments. He might have collected stamps or coins, or translated Horace, or bound books, or invented new species of diatoms. But, as it happened, he grew orchids, and had one ambitious little hothouse.

"I have a fancy," he said over his coffee, "that something is going to happen to me to-day." He spoke—as he moved and thought—slowly.

"Oh, don't say *that*!" said his housekeeper—who was also his remote cousin. For "something happening" was a euphemism that meant only one thing to her.

"You misunderstand me. I mean nothing unpleasant—though what I do mean I scarcely know."

"To-day," he continued after a pause, "Peters are going to sell a batch of plants from the Andamans and the Indies. I shall go up and see what they have. It may be I shall buy something good, unawares. That may be it."

He passed his cup for his second cupful of coffee.

"Are these the things collected by that poor young fellow you told me of the other day?" asked his cousin as she filled his cup.

"Yes," he said, and became meditative over a piece of toast.

"Nothing ever does happen to me," he remarked presently, beginning to think aloud. "I wonder why? Things enough happen to other people. There is Harvey. Only the other week, on Monday he picked up sixpence, on Wednesday his chicks all had the staggers, on Friday his cousin came home from Australia, and on Saturday he broke his ankle. What a whirl of excitement!—compared to me."

"I think I would rather be without so much excitement," said his housekeeper. "It can't be good for you."

"I suppose it's troublesome. Still—you see, nothing ever happens to me. When I was a little boy I never had accidents. I never fell in love as I grew up. Never married—I wonder how it feels to have something happen to you, something really remarkable.

"That orchid-collector was only thirty-six—twenty years younger than myself—when he died. And he had been married twice and divorced once; he had had malarial fever four times, and once he broke his thigh. He killed a Malay once, and once he was wounded by a poisoned dart. And in the end he was killed by jungle-leeches. It must have all been very troublesome, but then it must have been very interesting, you know—except, perhaps, the leeches."

"I am sure it was not good for him," said the lady, with conviction.

"Perhaps not." And then Wedderburn looked at his watch. "Twenty-three minutes past eight. I am going up by the quarter to twelve train, so that there is plenty of time. I think I shall wear my alpaca jacket—it is quite warm enough—and my grey felt hat and brown shoes. I suppose—"

He glanced out of the window at the serene sky and sunlit garden, and then nervously at his cousin's face.

"I think you had better take an umbrella if you are going to London," she said in a voice that admitted of no denial. "There's all between here and the station coming back."

When he returned he was in a state of mild excitement. He had made a purchase. It was rare that he could make up his mind quickly enough to buy, but this time he had done so.

"There are Vandas," he said, "and a Dendrobe and some Palæonophis." He surveyed his purchases lovingly as he consumed his soup. They were laid out on the spotless tablecloth before him, and he was telling his cousin all about them as he slowly meandered through his dinner. It was his custom to live all his visits to London over again in the evening for her and his own entertainment.

"I knew something would happen to-day. And I have bought all these. Some of them—some of them—I feel sure, do you know, that some of them will be remarkable.

I don't know how it is, but I feel just as sure as if some one had told me that some of these will turn out remarkable.

"That one"—he pointed to a shrivelled rhizome—"was not identified. It may be a Palæonophis—or it may not. It may be a new species, or even a new genus. And it was the last that poor Batten ever collected."

"I don't like the look of it," said his housekeeper. "It's such an ugly shape."

"To me it scarcely seems to have a shape."

"I don't like those things that stick out," said his housekeeper.

"It shall be put away in a pot to-morrow."

"It looks," said the housekeeper, "like a spider shamming dead."

Wedderburn smiled and surveyed the root with his head on one side. "It is certainly not a pretty lump of stuff. But you can never judge of these things from their dry appearance. It may turn out to be a very beautiful orchid indeed. How busy I shall be to-morrow! I must see tonight just exactly what to do with these things, and to-morrow I shall set to work.

"They found poor Batten lying dead, or dying, in a mangrove swamp—I forget which," he began again presently, "with one of these very orchids crushed up under his body. He had been unwell for some days with some kind of native fever, and I suppose he fainted. These mangrove swamps are very unwholesome. Every drop of blood, they say, was taken out of him by the jungle-leeches. It may be that very plant that cost him his life to obtain."

"I think none the better of it for that."

"Men must work though women may weep," said Wedderburn, with profound gravity.

"Fancy dying away from every comfort in a nasty swamp! Fancy being ill of fever with nothing to take but chlorodyne and quinine—if men were left to themselves they would live on chlorodyne and quinine—and no one round you but horrible natives! They say the Andaman islanders are most disgusting wretches—and, anyhow, they can scarcely make good nurses, not having the necessary training. And just for people in England to have orchids!"

"I don't suppose it was comfortable, but some men seem to enjoy that kind of thing," said Wedderburn. "Anyhow, the natives of his party were sufficiently civilised to take care of all his collection until his colleague, who was an ornithologist, came back again from the interior; though they could not tell the species of the orchid, and had let it wither. And it makes these things more interesting."

"It makes them disgusting. I should be afraid of some of the malaria clinging to them. And just think, there has been a dead body lying across that ugly thing! I never thought of that before. There! I declare I cannot eat another mouthful of dinner."

"I will take them off the table if you like, and put them in the window-seat. I can see them just as well there."

The next few days he was indeed singularly busy in his steamy little hothouse, fussing about with charcoal, lumps of teak, moss, and all the other mysteries of the orchid cultivator. He considered he was having a wonderfully eventful time. In the evening he would talk about these new orchids to his friends, and over and over again he reverted to his expectation of something strange.

Several of the Vandas and the Dendrobium died under his care, but presently the strange orchid began to show signs of life. He was delighted, and took his housekeeper right away from jam-making to see it at once, directly he made the discovery.

"That is a bud," he said, "and presently there will be a lot of leaves there, and those little things coming out here are aërial rootlets."

"They look to me like little white fingers poking out of the brown. I don't like them," said his housekeeper.

"Why not?"

"I don't know. They look like fingers trying to get at you. I can't help my likes and dislikes."

"I don't know for certain, but I don't *think* there are any orchids I know that have aerial rootlets quite like that. It may be my fancy, of course. You see they are a little flattened at the ends."

"I don't like 'em," said his housekeeper, suddenly shivering and turning away. "I know it's very silly of me—and I'm very sorry, particularly as you like the thing so much. But I can't help thinking of that corpse."

"But it may not be that particular plant. That was merely a guess of mine."

His housekeeper shrugged her shoulders.

"Anyhow I don't like it," she said.

Wedderburn felt a little hurt at her dislike to the plant. But that did not prevent his talking to her about orchids generally, and this orchid in particular, whenever he felt inclined.

"There are such queer things about orchids," he said one day; "such possibilities of surprises. You know, Darwin studied their fertilisation, and showed that the whole structure of an ordinary orchid-flower was contrived in order that moths might carry the pollen from plant to plant. Well, it seems that there are lots of orchids known the flower of which cannot possibly be used for fertilisation in that way. Some of the Cypripediums, for instance; there are no insects known that can possibly fertilise them, and some of them have never been found with seed."

"But how do they form new plants?"

"By runners and tubers, and that kind of outgrowth. That is easily explained. The puzzle is, what are the flowers for?

"Very likely," he added, "*my* orchid may be something extraordinary in that way. If so, I shall study it. I have often thought of making researches as Darwin did. But hitherto I have not found the time, or something else has happened to prevent it. The leaves are beginning to unfold now. I do wish you would come and see them!"

But she said that the orchid-house was so hot it gave her the headache. She had seen the plant once again, and the aërial rootlets, which were now some of them more than a foot long, had unfortunately reminded her of tentacles reaching out after something; and they got into her dreams, growing after her with incredible rapidity. So that she had settled to her entire satisfaction that she would not see that plant again, and Wedderburn had to admire its leaves alone. They were of the ordinary broad form, and a deep glossy green, with splashes and dots of deep red towards the base. He knew of no other leaves quite like them. The plant was placed on a low bench near the thermometer, and close by was a simple arrangement by which a tap dripped on the hot-water pipes and kept the air steamy. And he spent his afternoons now with some regularity meditating on the approaching flowering of this strange plant.

And at last the great thing happened. Directly he entered the little glass house he knew that the spike had burst out, although his great *Palæonophis Lowii* hid the corner where his new darling stood. There was a new odour in the air, a rich, intensely sweet scent, that overpowered every other in that crowded, steaming little greenhouse.

Directly he noticed this he hurried down to the strange orchid. And, behold! the trailing green spikes bore now three great splashes of blossom, from which this over-powering sweetness proceeded. He stopped before them in an ecstasy of admiration.

The flowers were white, with streaks of golden orange upon the petals; the heavy labellum was coiled into an intricate projection, and a wonderful bluish purple mingled there with the gold. He could see at once that the genus was altogether a new one. And the insufferable scent! How hot the place was! The blossoms swam before his eyes.

He would see if the temperature was right. He made a step towards the thermometer. Suddenly everything appeared unsteady. The bricks on the floor were dancing up and down. Then the white blossoms, the green leaves behind them, the whole greenhouse, seemed to sweep sideways, and then in a curve upward.

At half-past four his cousin made the tea, according to their invariable custom. But Wedderburn did not come in for his tea.

"He is worshipping that horrid orchid," she told herself, and waited ten minutes. "His watch must have stopped. I will go and call him."

She went straight to the hothouse, and, opening the door, called his name. There was no reply. She noticed that the air was very close, and loaded with an intense perfume. Then she saw something lying on the bricks between the hot-water pipes.

For a minute, perhaps, she stood motionless.

He was lying, face upward, at the foot of the strange orchid. The tentacle-like aërial rootlets no longer swayed freely in the air, but were crowded together, a tangle of grey ropes, and stretched tight with their ends closely applied to his chin and neck and hands.

She did not understand. Then she saw from under one of the exultant tentacles upon his cheek there trickled a little thread of blood.

With an inarticulate cry she ran towards him, and tried to pull him away from the leech-like suckers. She snapped two of these tentacles, and their sap dripped red.

Then the overpowering scent of the blossom began to make her head reel. How they clung to him! She tore at the tough ropes, and he and the white inflorescence swam about her. She felt she was fainting, knew she must not. She left him and hastily opened the nearest door, and, after she had panted for a moment in the fresh air, she had a brilliant inspiration. She caught up a flower-pot and smashed in the windows at the end of the greenhouse. Then she re-entered. She tugged now with renewed strength at Wedderburn's motionless body, and brought the strange orchid crashing to the floor. It still clung with the grimmest tenacity to its victim. In a frenzy, she lugged it and him into the open air.

Then she thought of tearing through the sucker rootlets one by one, and in another minute she had released him and was dragging him away from the horror.

He was white and bleeding from a dozen circular patches.

The odd-job man was coming up the garden, amazed at the smashing of glass, and saw her emerge, hauling the inanimate body with red-stained hands. For a moment he thought impossible things.

"Bring some water!" she cried, and her voice dispelled his fancies. When, with unnatural alacrity, he returned with the water, he found her weeping with excitement, and with Wedderburn's head upon her knee, wiping the blood from his face.

"What's the matter?" said Wedderburn, opening his eyes feebly, and closing them again at once.

"Go and tell Annie to come out here to me, and then go for Dr. Haddon at once," she said to the odd-job man so soon as he brought the water; and added, seeing he hesitated, "I will tell you all about it when you come back."

Presently Wedderburn opened his eyes again, and, seeing that he was troubled by the puzzle of his position, she explained to him, "You fainted in the hothouse."

"And the orchid?"

"I will see to that," she said.

Wedderburn had lost a good deal of blood, but beyond that he had suffered no very great injury. They gave him brandy mixed with some pink extract of meat, and carried him upstairs to bed. His housekeeper told her incredible story in fragments to Dr. Haddon. "Come to the orchid-house and see," she said.

The cold outer air was blowing in through the open door, and the sickly perfume was almost dispelled. Most of the torn aërial rootlets lay already withered amidst a number of dark stains upon the bricks. The stem of the inflorescence was broken by the fall of the plant, and the flowers were growing limp and brown at the edges of the petals. The doctor stooped towards it, then saw that one of the aërial rootlets still stirred feebly, and hesitated.

The next morning the strange orchid still lay there, black now and putrescent. The door banged intermittently in the morning breeze, and all the array of Wedderburn's orchids was shrivelled and prostrate. But Wedderburn himself was bright and garrulous upstairs in the story of his strange adventure.

THE STRANGE STORY
OF OUR VILLA

MARY E. PENN

"'VILLA DE L'ORIENT, AVENUE DES CITRONNIERS, NICE'—REALLY, OUR ADDRESS looks uncommonly well at the head of a letter," remarked Mrs. Brandon, contemplating, with her head on one side, the effect of the words she had just written.

"It really does," we agreed in chorus. We always agreed with Mrs. Brandon; it saved trouble.

We were three "lone-lorn" females—two spinsters and a widow—who had agreed to share a house—or, rather, part of a house, for we occupied but one story—at Nice for the winter.

First there was Mrs. Brandon—our chaperon, housekeeper, and directress in chief—tall, blonde, majestic, with a calm, suave manner, and a quietly distinct voice, which always made itself heard and obeyed; then came Miss Lucy Lester, a plump, good-tempered little lady of a certain age, with a round, smiling face, kindly blue eyes, and not an angle about her, either moral or physical. Lastly there was the present writer, who modestly prefers to leave her portrait to the reader's imagination, trusting that he will paint it in the most attractive colours at his disposal.

The supplementary members of the party were Mrs. Brandon's daughter Georgie, an over-grown school-girl of thirteen; Georgie's inseparable companion, "Chum," a small, sharp, and extremely impudent fox-terrier; and Joséphine, our stout French *bonne*, who inhabited a microscopic kitchen, which her capacious person entirely filled.

In spite of its name there was nothing in the least Oriental about the appearance of "our villa." It was simply a good-sized, square, pink-and-white house, looking, Georgie said, as if it were built of *nougat*, with green balconies and shutters, and a semi-circular flight of steps to the front door. It stood in the midst of an extensive garden, planted with orange and lemon trees, and sheltered on one side by a rocky hill, which rose above it, sheer and straight, like a natural wall. At the end of the garden was a rustic bench, sheltered by a gnarled old olive-tree.

The house was furnished with remarkable taste. The house agent, through whom we took our *appartement*, informed us that the landlord, M. de Valeyre—a gentleman of good birth, though not of large means, who was now on a shoot-ing tour in Corsica—had spent many years of his life in the East, and our rooms contained not a few souvenirs of his travels in the shape of ornaments, rugs, and draperies, to say nothing of his own clever oil-sketches of Oriental life and scenery which adorned the walls.

The rooms, though decidedly small, were bright and airy, and the outlook on the garden, where the oranges were ripening under their glossy leaves, delightful. Altogether we felt we might congratulate ourselves on our good fortune.

"Yes," proceeded our "chief," glancing complacently around her—we were sit-ting in the dining-room after lunch on the third day of our arrival—"it is really a *trouvaille*. So charmingly situated, so well furnished, and so cheap! We might have looked all over Nice and found nothing to suit us so well."

"We might, indeed," assented Lucy Lester, who generally echoed the last speaker. "One could wish, perhaps, that the bedrooms were a little larger—"

"And that they did not open one out of the other like a nest of boxes, of which mine is the inside box," I ventured to add.

Mrs. Brandon glanced at me austerely over her eyeglass.

"If we, whom you disturb by passing through our rooms, do not object to that, I think *you* need not," she observed reprovingly.

"But it seems you do object," I returned. "Every morning I am greeted with anathemas 'not loud, but deep,' half smothered under the bed-clothes."

"Why will you persist in getting up at such unearthly hours, waking people out of their beauty sleep?"

"I don't mind that," put in Georgie, who was teaching Chum to balance a pencil on his nose; "but I do wish the woman upstairs would not make such a noise at night; I can't go to sleep for her. The ceilings are so thin, one hears every sound."

"The woman upstairs?" her mother repeated. "What do you mean, child? There is no one in the house but ourselves. The upper stories and the ground floor are unlet."

"There is some one in the room above mine all the same," Georgie persisted. "She keeps me awake by walking about overhead, sometimes muttering and laugh-ing to herself, and sometimes sobbing as if her heart would break. Last night I stood up on the bed and rapped the ceiling with my umbrella to silence her, but she kept on all the same. Chum heard her too—didn't you, sir?"

Chum, glad of any interruption to his lesson, barked an emphatic assent.

"Well, now, that is very strange," Miss Lester remarked, dropping her knitting. "I have fancied, myself, do you know, that I heard some one moving about, overhead; not only at night, but in the daytime."

"Perhaps there is some servant or caretaker left in charge of the rooms," Mrs. Brandon said after a pause; "I will ask M. Gillet when next I see him."

We saw M. Gillet, the house-agent, the following day. He called, as he explained politely, to ask after the health of "these ladies," and to ascertain if we were satisfied with our "installation."

He was a round, fat, oily man of middle age, with a bland manner and a propitiatory smile.

"We are quite well and perfectly satisfied," Mrs. Brandon replied graciously, answering for us all, as usual. "But I thought you told us, M. Gillet, that the upstairs rooms were unoccupied?"

"So they are, madame. There is no one in the house but yourselves and your servant."

"Then who is it my daughter hears at night in the room above hers?" He raised his eyebrows, glancing inquiringly at Georgie.

"I hear a woman walking about and talking to herself," she explained. "I can't understand what she says; it is not French."

"Ah!" His face changed from smiling incredulity to startled gravity. He drew in his lips and looked perturbed.

"It must be Madame de Valeyre," he muttered; "it can be no one else. Just like her to turn up again in this mysterious fashion without a word of warning! Monsieur will be furious when he knows she is here, and I shall certainly think it my duty to inform him at once."

"Are you speaking of our landlord's wife?" I inquired. He assented.

"But why should he be displeased? Has she not a right to occupy her own house?"

"Well—no—that is just it. When they separated by mutual consent a year ago it was expressly stipulated, as a condition of his making her an allowance, that she should not return here, or in any way molest him. I had it from his own lips."

"Why did they separate?" Miss Lester inquired, curiously.

He shrugged his shoulders.

"'Incompatibility of temper' was the reason given, but, of course, there were others. The fact is, it was one of those madly romantic marriages which never do turn out well—except in novels. She was an Arab girl whom he picked up somewhere in Algeria, and insisted on marrying, to the scandal of his family and friends—that is her portrait," he added, nodding towards a picture on the wall; "painted by Monsieur himself, soon after his marriage."

We looked with interest at the canvas; a slight but clever oil-sketch of a young Arab girl, with an oval olive-tinted face of striking beauty, and strange passionate dark eyes with a smouldering fire in their depths. Under it was written "Ayesha," and a date.

"Yes, she was handsome, then," he admitted, in answer to our comments, "but half a savage, and more than half a heathen, though supposed to have been converted. I heard that in the early days of their marriage she spent most of her time concocting charms and potions 'to keep her husband's love.' Apparently they were not the right sort," he added drily; "he soon wearied of her; then there were scenes, tears, upbraidings. Madame was jealous—(with cause, if report spoke truly); Monsieur had a temper— *enfin*, no one was surprised when, just a year ago, M. de Valeyre announced that they had separated by mutual consent, and that Madame had returned to her friends. Since then he has been travelling, and no doubt is much happier without her."

"While she, poor soul, is fretting her heart out," Mrs. Brandon put in; "though I have no doubt he was a brute to her."

The agent shrugged his shoulders with a deprecating smile.

"There were faults on both sides, Madame; but it was hardly possible for any man to live in peace with such a *toquée* as she is."

"*Toquée?*" Mrs. Brandon repeated; "do you mean that she is mad? If so, it is certainly not pleasant to have her in the house."

"*Mais non, Madame!*" he protested; "she is not mad; only eccentric, erratic, capricious. Her returning in this mysterious way is a proof of it. Of course I have no right to interfere with her, but I shall certainly let M. de Valeyre know at once that she is here. You must not be subjected to this annoyance."

After a few more words he took his leave.

The days that followed were fully and pleasantly occupied in exploring Nice and its environs, which were new to all of us. We sunned ourselves on the Promenade des Anglais; drove on the Cornice Road; heard the band in the Jardin Public, and loitered among the tempting shops on the Place Masséna; all in due course. The weather was glorious. Sunny days and moonlit nights succeeded each other in uninterrupted splendour, and made it difficult for us to believe that we were actually within a few weeks of Christmas.

The presence of the mysterious Madame de Valeyre in the house was no longer a matter of doubt. Not only had we all heard her restless footsteps overhead, and the unintelligible muttering which sounded so strangely uncanny, but more than once we had caught sight of her—a tall slender figure clad in a loose white wrapper—pacing to and fro in the shadowy garden alleys, or sitting on the bench under the gnarled old olive-tree. Once, at dusk, I met her on the stair-case flitting silently upstairs to her own lonely rooms, but she passed me quickly without returning my salutation, or even glancing at me.

"*C'est drôle!*" Joséphine often remarked; "to shut herself up like that, without even a servant. And how does she get her food? she never seems to go beyond the gates."

We agreed that it *was* "drôle," but did not trouble ourselves greatly about the matter, having more interesting occupation for our thoughts.

One evening, in the third week of our tenancy, the others were gone to the theatre, and I, pleading letters to write, had remained at home with no companion but "Chum," having given Joséphine permission to go out.

Chum, by the way, was the only one of the party who did not appear to like his winter quarters. He had not been in his usual rude health and spirits since we came to the Villa, but seemed restless and depressed. Even now, as he lay curled up on my gown, he could not sleep quietly, but kept waking up with a start and a shiver, looking uneasily about him.

I sat in the dining-room, out of which the other rooms opened. To the right was the curtained doorway (doors there were none) of the *salon*—to the left, that which admitted to Mrs. Brandon's bed-room, leading out of which was Miss Lester's. The dressing-room of the latter had been converted into a bed-room for Georgie, and the last of the suite was my own chamber.

The evening was warm and very still. Glancing through the open window, which was shaded by a tall eucalyptus, I caught a glimpse of a sky full of stars, and over the tree-tops a line of tremulous silver showed where the sea lay sleeping.

As I lowered my head to my writing again, my eye was arrested by a slight movement of the *portière* which screened the drawing-room doorway. I looked up quickly, but seeing nothing unusual, concluded I had been mistaken. I was writing busily again, when the dog stirred uneasily, growled, then suddenly sprang to his feet, gazing, with dilated eyes and ears erect, towards the door. As I involuntarily looked again in the same direction, I was startled to see a hand, the long slender hand of a woman, put forth from within to draw the curtain back. For a moment it remained motionless, grasping the *portière,* and I had time to note every detail of its form and colour; the fine but dusky skin, the delicate taper fingers, on one of which gleamed a quaint snake-shaped gold ring. Then the curtain was abruptly withdrawn, and a figure appeared in the opening: a tall, slender woman, enveloped in a loose wrapper of some gauzy Algerian stuff.

It was Madame de Valeyre. I had never had a full view of her face before, but I recognised her at once as the original of the portrait: thinner, older, with a wild and troubled look in her lovely dark eyes, but the same.

Too startled to speak, I stared at her, and she looked back as silently and as fixedly at me. Then, before I could rise or address her, my strange visitor crossed the room with a calm and leisurely step, and passed through the opposite doorway.

Recovering from my surprise, I caught up the lamp and followed her. She had already traversed Mrs. Brandon's bedroom, and was passing into the one beyond.

"Pardon, Madame——" I called after her; but she neither paused nor turned till she reached the threshold of my own room, the inner one of the suite.

Drawing back the *portière* with one hand, she looked at me over her shoulder—a look that thrilled me, so earnest it was, so imperious, so fraught with meaning to which I had not the clue—but uttered not a word. Then she passed in, and the heavy curtain dropped behind her.

In a second's space I had followed her into the room.

To my utter astonishment she was not there. I looked round blankly, raising the lamp above my head. There was no other door but that by which she had entered; no closet, no cupboard, no recess in which she could be concealed. And yet she was gone, vanished, it seemed, into thin air. For a moment I stood, looking about me in utter bewilderment; then a sort of panic seized me—an irrational fear of I knew not what or whom.

I hurried back through the empty and silent rooms, not daring to cast a glance behind me; and feeling a sudden distaste for the dining-room, took refuge in the tiny kitchen, where I sat with Chum on my lap, starting nervously at every sound, till the others returned.

I had decided to say nothing of what had occurred to Miss Lester or Georgie, lest it should alarm them, but Mrs. Brandon I must tell, for the relief of my own mind, though I hardly expected she would believe my story. In fact it seemed, even to myself, so incredible that I could well excuse her scepticism.

It was as I anticipated. She heard me out with a look of mingled astonishment and incredulity.

"My dear Edith," she said when I had finished; "excuse me, but—are you quite sure you did not fall asleep and dream all this?"

"I am quite sure that I was as wide awake then as I am now."

"But it is so utterly unaccountable," she objected; "not only her disappearance, but her appearance. How did she get into the drawing-room in the first instance? She was not there when we went out I am certain, and she could not have entered it afterwards without your seeing her. Why did you not ask her what she wanted— what she meant by it?"

"I was too startled at first, and when I recovered myself she had vanished."

"Well, I hope I shall encounter her myself," Mrs. Brandon remarked resolutely; "she shall not 'vanish' again till she has explained the matter, I promise you. We can't have her prowling about our rooms like a Banshee."

But the days passed on, and we caught no further glimpse of Madame de Valeyre.

It was the last day of the old year—a day so brilliant, so warm, serene, and sunny, that it would not have disgraced an English midsummer. Long after Georgie had retired for the night, we three elders sat round the handful of wood fire which we kept in more for the sake of cheerfulness than warmth, talking of old times, old friends and old scenes, in that retrospective mood which falls on most of us at such seasons.

"I wonder if that poor woman upstairs will have any one to wish her 'Bonne Année' to-morrow?" Miss Lester remarked during a pause in the conversation. "Fancy how triste to be spending New Year's Eve alone! I thought I heard her crying just now."

We listened, and sure enough a sound of suppressed sobbing, inexpressibly sad and forlorn, reached us from the room above.

"Poor soul!" Mrs. Brandon exclaimed compassionately. "I feel strongly inclined to go upstairs and see if there is anything I can do to help or comfort her, but there is no knowing how she might take it. She is evidently more than a little *toquée*, as M. Gillet told us. If that husband of hers—"

She left the sentence unfinished, and we all started as a sound of wheels reached us, coming rapidly up the garden drive, and stopping at the door. The next moment there was a loud peal at the bell.

"Who can it be at this hour? it is past eleven o'clock!" I exclaimed.

"Perhaps it is Monsieur de Valeyre," Lucy Lester suggested suddenly. I rose, and, cautiously opening the window, glanced down into the garden. The moonlight showed me a tall man's figure just alighting from a *fiacre*, the driver of which was handing down a gun-case and a portmanteau.

"It is our landlord, sure enough," I said, closing the window. "Monsieur Gillet's information has brought him home, I suppose. I hope there will be no 'scene' upstairs."

"Dear me, I hope not!" Lucy echoed; though the anticipated excitement seemed not altogether unpleasing to her.

"He is evidently not remarkable for patience," was Mrs. Brandon's comment, as another still louder peal rang though the house. "If Madame does not choose to admit him one of us must go down. Joséphine is in bed long ago."

I volunteered for the task, and, Lucy offering to accompany me, we descended, noisily escorted by Chum.

The *fiacre* was driving away as we opened the door, and the visitor stood on the step, looking out at the moonlit garden.

He turned, and, expecting no doubt to see a servant, was beginning an impatient exclamation at the delay, but checked himself on perceiving us.

"A hundred pardons, Mesdames, for disturbing you at this untimely hour," he said, raising his hat; "but I have only just arrived from Corsica. I am Monsieur de Valeyre," he added.

I bowed, and drew back to admit him, trying in vain to silence Chum, whose bark was now exchanged for a low, angry growl.

The visitor was a tall, well-built, bronze-complexioned man of six or seven and thirty, with a face which would have been strikingly handsome but for its worn and haggard look, and something repellent in the expression of the bold dark eyes.

"Your dog objects to strangers, apparently," he said, with a glance of no great favour at the terrier, who responded with a snarl which showed all his little sharp white teeth.

"He is a capital watch-dog," I said, apologetically; "he would soon let us know if there were thieves in the house."

"Ah, that reminds me—" He turned as he spoke, to put up the door-chain. "I hear from Gillet, my agent, that you were alarmed on your arrival by strange noises in the upper rooms. Do they still continue?"

"We were not alarmed exactly, but they puzzled us till we knew that Madame de Valeyre had returned."

He let fall the door-chain and turned to look at me.

"Madame de Valeyre?" he repeated.

"Yes; did not M. Gillet tell you, Monsieur, that she was here?"

"He told me you had said so, but I could not believe it; I cannot believe it now. She—my wife—is with her family at Algiers, and it is not likely she would have returned without letting me know."

"She is in the house at this moment," I said, quietly; "she has been here for the last month. We have not only heard but seen her repeatedly—have we not?" I added, turning to my companion, who echoed, "Repeatedly!"

He looked from one to the other of us with a frown, but said nothing; and, having secured the fastening of the door, took up his portmanteau and followed us upstairs.

"May I ask you to lend me your light for a moment?" he said, when we reached the landing; "I will return it presently."

Nearly a quarter of an hour elapsed before he descended. We heard him going from room to room, opening and shutting doors and windows, but no sound of voices reached us.

At last he reappeared at the open door of our sitting-room, candle in hand. Mrs. Brandon herself went forward to take it from him, looking at him scrutinizingly as she did so.

"Many thanks, Madame," he said, relinquishing it to her with a bow. Then, turning to me, he added, coldly: "You were mistaken in supposing that my wife had returned. There is no living creature in the rooms upstairs, nor have they been entered since I left them."

"But we have seen her——" I began.

"Whoever you may have seen, it was certainly not my wife," was his reply.

Before I could speak again, he added:

"I have the honour to wish you good-evening, Mesdames," and, with a comprehensive bow which included us all, he left the room.

We looked at each other bewilderedly. What did it mean? What had become of the woman?

"She must have heard his voice, and hidden herself somewhere, in fear of him," Miss Lester suggested.

"Depend upon it, she has reason to fear him," Mrs. Brandon remarked. "He looks like a man who would use his power mercilessly. It is dreadful to think of that poor half-demented creature being left unprotected to his anger, perhaps violence."

Lucy Lester drew her shawl closer round her with a shiver.

"I feel as if something terrible was going to happen," she said nervously.

The same uneasy presentiment weighed on my own mind, together with some other shadowy fear which I could not have put into words.

Feeling too anxious and excited to go to bed, we gathered round the fire again, talking in whispers, and listening apprehensively to every sound from above. For a time we heard M. de Valeyre moving about; then there was silence, only interrupted when the time-piece, chiming midnight, reminded us to wish each other a Happy New Year.

After that I must have fallen into a doze, from which I was roused by a touch on my arm.

"Edith," Mrs. Brandon whispered, "do you hear?"

I started and sat upright, looking about me in the confusion of a sudden awakening. "What is it?" I asked.

Keeping her hand on my arm, she pointed upwards. The light restless footsteps we had grown to know so well, were once more pacing to and fro overhead, and we heard the low intermittent murmur of a woman's voice. Suddenly it was interrupted by a cry—a man's hoarse cry of mortal anguish or terror, such as I trust I may never hear again.

Mingling with the cry, came a peal of eldritch laughter, then the sound of a struggle, and a heavy fall which shook the house.

"Come, or there will be murder done," Mrs. Brandon exclaimed, and she hurried from the room and upstairs, followed by Miss Lester and myself.

We found the outer door of M. de Valeyre's apartments closed, but not locked, and passing through the ante-chamber, entered the first room of the suite. A lamp on the chimney-piece showed that it was in strange disorder; the furniture displaced, the carpet upturned, the cloth half-dragged from the table.

Its only present occupant was the master of the house, who crouched against the wall at the further end, in an attitude of abject terror.

Never while I live shall I forget the face he turned towards us when we entered. With strained dilated eyes, and parted lips, it looked like an image of incarnate Fear. I stopped short over the threshold, feeling a shrinking reluctance to enter, but Mrs. Brandon without hesitation advanced to his side.

"What is the matter? what has happened?" she asked.

He looked at her vaguely, but seemed incapable of uttering a word, and put his hand to his throat as if suffocating. There was a carafe of brandy on the table. She filled a liqueur glass and held it to his lips. Presently he drew a deep sobbing breath, and half raised himself, glancing round the room with a haggard look of dread.

"Is she—gone?" he asked hoarsely.

"There is no one here but ourselves," Mrs. Brandon replied. "You—" She broke off, recoiling from him with a stifled cry.

He had started convulsively, and was gazing with a look of speechless terror at some object on the opposite side of the room. Involuntarily we followed the direction of his eyes, but to us nothing was visible.

"There she is—look!" he gasped. "My wife—dead, yet living. Keep her from me—keep her hands from my throat! Ayesha—mercy—pardon! Oh, Heaven."

He crouched against the wall again, putting out both hands to repel some invisible assailant; struggling desperately as if with an actual bodily antagonist, and apparently using all his strength to keep the murderous fingers from his throat.

Mrs. Brandon had fled from him in a panic, and we all three stood on the threshold, watching with horror-struck eyes that ghastly struggle. It did not last long. With a dreadful choking cry he dropped his arms; his whole figure collapsed and fell in a heap, face downwards, on the floor.

Strangely enough my fear had now utterly passed away. While the others hesitated I approached him and lifted his head, and turned his face to the light. After one glance I laid it down again with a shudder. "Has he fainted again?" they asked me. "He is dead," I answered, as I rose.

Yes, he was dead; but *how* had he died? What was the meaning of those livid finger-marks, which, for a moment, I had seen plainly printed on his throat? That is a mystery which has never been solved.

The sudden death of the master of the Villa de l'Orient caused a sensation in Nice, where he was well known, and it was intensified by a rumour that Madame de Valeyre had mysteriously disappeared. There was no trace of her recent presence in the house, and it was ascertained that her relatives in Algeria had had no news of her for more than a year. Some other facts came to light which threw a sinister suspicion on the dead man. Search was made in the garden and grounds, and finally her body was discovered buried under the old olive-tree. An Algerian scarf, tightly knotted round her throat, showed what had been the manner of her death.

It need hardly be said that we took flight as soon as possible from the ill-omened house, which was shortly afterwards demolished by order of the Valeyre family, so that not a vestige now remains of what we once called "our villa."

A Stray Reveler

Emma Francis Dawson

> "Who hath known the ways and the wrath.
> The sleepless spirit, the root
> And blossom of evil will?"

"Which is the room, and which is the picture?" I asked my friend Aura, when she received me after my long absence abroad, during which I heard she had fallen heir to a fortune, but found her looking pinched and wan.

The picture filled nearly one side of the room, which was arranged as an exact copy of it, even having a lattice-window opening lengthwise, put in to match the painted one. Carpet, Navajo rugs, chairs, tables, draperies were alike. A strip of carpet hid the lower part of the frame, so that one might fancy he saw double parlors instead of one room and a painting. The screen in the room stood at just such an angle as just such a screen stood in the painted scene. Tall Japanese vases, low bookcase, hanging shelves filled with rare, odd trifles, were all thus doubled.

"Yes," she said, seeing me glance to and fro, "I felt impelled to copy everything painted there, and to banish all my room held before. That knotted rope under glass on the mantel? Well, no; that was neither in the picture nor here, till now; the fact is, I hold the property Penniel left me only by keeping that there. Two of his friends, Dacre and Chartram, received bequests on condition of calling here unexpectedly at irregular intervals to see that I let it remain always in my sight."

"I don't like it there."

"Nor I; but there is nothing puzzling about it as about the picture, finished just before he—he died. That is a legacy I have often pondered over. Why did he call it prophetic? I always wonder where the window in it looks, and that inner door ajar, showing a banquet-scene. Is it a Christmas revel?"

"One of the female figures resembles you—why, it is meant for you!"

"Don't, don't say so! It makes me uneasy, and angry, too; for I will not believe in the 'mystic' nonsense of his scribbling, painting, and acting tribe."

"Yet you always let them hang round you."

"Because they are amusing, often handsome, and sometimes have money. But few come now, except Chartram and Dacre, in their uncertain visits. I am no longer gay enough company."

"Pshaw! as if the influence of one who is dead could thus last!"

"If not, how could there be so many true tales of curses which have followed individuals or families through generation after generation. I never used to believe any such thing. I am forced to keep the picture under the terms of Penniel's will, and I cannot help studying it."

"Did Penniel paint it?"

"Yes. He put me in that festive scene because I am yet alive. He once spoke of ghosts as stray revelers after life's banquet. The vacant seat beside me was to signify his absence. 'Not eternal,' he wrote; 'I shall come back when you least expect it.'"

"You make me shiver. Let us talk of other things. What a pretty inlaid table—wild-fowl flying over a marsh—isn't it? Ah! it is just like that one in the picture, even to a manuscript lying upon it spread open under a horseshoe paper-weight."

"You see," said Aura, "one drifts inevitably to that painting. What the manuscript there represents I have often asked myself. The one beside you, Dacre wrote. Read it."

It was:

A FLIGHT OF FANCY

In single file wild-ducks drift by.
Dyed red by western glow.
Belated swallows lonely fly,
And strange birds trooping go.

Though flown from forest-pine remote,
Or from near orchard-pear,
Along the water-depths they float,
As on the heights of air.

The lake, with mirror-surface spread,
Bronzed by the day's bright close,
To each wayfarer overhead,
A shadowy double shows.

Ah! thus reflected in my soul
What flitting thoughts will stray
From hidden source — ancestors' dole,
Or sunshine of my day.

Fantastic shapes that, circling, throng,
Some charming, some unblest;

> I snare one in this fragile song,
> I cannot count the rest.

I made another effort to divert her mind. "What is behind your lovely screen?" I asked.

"Nothing. What is behind that one?" she asked, pointing to the pictured one. "That question haunts me like the indefinite meaning of some passage in Browning or Rossetti."

"What have you learned by your study of it?"

"What do you discover by examining that screen near you?"

"Masses of interwoven flowers with trailing vines and lights and shadows athwart the whole. Who painted it?"

"Chartram; and while he was doing it he and I suddenly detected amid those apparently random dashes of color eleven letters. Look again—begin at the lower left-hand corner and cross diagonally—here are lilies of the valley, then eschscholtzias, a branch of xanthoxylum fraxineum, tuberoses, azalias, lobelia, iris-lilies, oleander blossoms, Neapolitan violets, ixia-lilies, and stephanotis flowers."

"Well?"

"Don't you see? Two words not merely spelled by the first letter of the plants' names, as the old-fashioned 'regard' rings were set with ruby, emerald, garnet, amethyst, ruby, and diamond, but by looking carefully you can discern, in the seemingly careless spray or cluster, the letter in indistinct and fanciful form."

As she spoke and I gazed at the screen, I was surprised to distinguish so plainly now the words, Lex talionis! so skillfully placed as to elude a careless glance. "The law of revenge!" I cried. "Was this more of your old coquetries?"

"No; I did not tire of Penniel as usual. He had one charm all my other lovers had lacked: a stronger will than mine."

I looked at her inquiringly.

"When you went away you remember I was starving—genteelly starving. I met Penniel; he was engaged to an heiress. I reasoned with myself that she did not need his money as I did. I used every art to win him from her."

"Oh, Aura!"

"I did, I did! I may own it now, since both are dead."

"Both?"

"Yes; he broke the engagement on account of something I told him about her. She died soon after, some say broken-hearted; but, of course, we know that is a mere phrase. I presume she got a cold, or something."

"And your refusal of him killed him?"

"No; I accepted him. All went well until one night we went on horseback with a party of friends, on a moonlight trip to the Cliff House. While there, he overheard me own my worship for money. '*Not* marry for it?' I said. 'It is a woman's duty.' And he met there that night some old friend who completely disproved all I had told him about Helen Rothsay, the girl who died. Oh, how angry he was!—his eyes were lurid, he never spoke to me again. Next day he sent back to me these verses he had found that Dacre had written for me to give him as mine, though you know there is nothing nonsensical about me."

She gave me to read a

VILLANELLE

What clouds of laughing little Loves arise—
On buoyant wing are all about me blown!
I dream within the night of his dark eyes.

How blest to be, though but in flower guise,
Worn on his heart until my life were flown!
What clouds of laughing little Loves arise!

Forgotten is the sun, to-day's blue skies,
I know nor time nor space nor any zone;
I dream within the night of his dark eyes—

By fancied blisses borne to Paradise,
Like some translated saint that Art has shown.
What clouds of laughing little Loves arise!

Such lotos-eating lures until one dies,
No poppy-petals such nepenthe own;
I dream within the night of his dark eyes.

For him my passion waxes crescent-wise;
Will wind and tide of Fate its sway disown?
What clouds of laughing little Loves arise!
I dream within the night of his dark eyes.

"He also sent me a letter telling me of these discoveries and taking leave. 'I shall avenge Helen's wrongs,' he wrote, 'I shall avenge my own wrongs, but in my own time and in my own way. You shall suffer for what you have done, if I have to come back from the next world to make you. Poor or rich, old or young, sad or gay, remember that *I have not forgotten.*'"

"He died soon after?"

"Yes; in a year and a day from the time we first met, which was Christmas Eve."

Company came, and I could hear no more.

Two weeks later, on Christmas Eve, Aura sent for me. I found her in the same room, looking thinner and more depressed, and studying the painting.

"Don't!" I said; "you will dream of it."

"I did. I have been in the picture, gathered a leaf from that graceful clump of ferns growing in the odd jar, sat in that antique chair, and looked from that open window."

I could not understand my hitherto matter-of-fact friend. "What did you see?" I asked.

"The same grand sunrise that thrilled us, Penniel, Dacre, Chartram, and I, as we returned from a New Year's Eve ball. A sunrise Penniel wrote about."

She showed me these lines:

NEW-YEAR'S DAWN

Through fog that veils both sky and bay there gleam
The sun and wraith, red glowing;
So interblended that one flame they seem
As if dread portent showing.

Where will it lead us through the year untried,
Through what vast desert places,
Vague tracts of time whose misty margins glide
Within eternal spaces?

I, weary pilgrim in Life's caravan,
That pillared fire must follow
Past pyramid and sphinx of Doubt and Ban,
Mirage of Hope, how hollow!

Palm-shaded wells of joy, too far apart,
Long leagues through changeful weather,
Unless that foe in ambush, my own heart,
Leaps, and we fall together!

"What else happened?" I asked.

"Nothing. I was dimly conscious of coming from that room into this. I want to stay here. Tell me about your travels, and divert me."

I talked to her a long while; then she brewed rich chocolate, which we sipped as we sat silently listening to the sounds of mirth from a party given by boarders in the opposite room, listening to the fog-horn and the wind, till drowsiness stole over us insensibly as the fog crept round the house, as if forming an impalpable barrier around a region enchanted.

Suddenly Aura started out of her doze with a piercing cry, and sat trembling from head to foot. "I have been there again," she said.

"You have not left your chair." I murmured, half-awake; "you dropped asleep."

"Perhaps you think so; but I have been in the picture." She shuddered as she turned her head to look at it. "There were *two* vacant places at the table. I no longer sat there, but wandered about the outer room while the guests at supper were watching and whispering and pointing, and a murmur of '*Lex talionis!*' ran from mouth to mouth. I felt that some horror waited for me and drew me to that screen, but I tried not to go. I went to the window, but the view was changed to the blackness of midnight. I looked in the mirror, yet saw nothing reflected but the room behind me. I was not to be seen. I noticed the perfume of the flowers in the bouquet on the table. I saw this room, with our figures sitting before the fire, with our chocolate-tray between us, as a picture on the wall of that room. I took the manuscript from the table, and found it to be verses, as we thought. I can repeat them:

BALLADE OF THE SEA OF SLEEP

When from far headland of the Night I slip,
What potent force within the rising tide
Bears me resistless as the billows dip,
To meet their shifting wonders, eager-eyed,
Or float, half-conscious what stars watch me glide,
To fear when nightmare monster's weight o'erpowers,
Or laugh with nymphs and mermen in their bowers—
Through blinding tempest toss on breakers steep,
Or fall for countless fathoms past what lowers
Below the dream waves of the sea of Sleep!

I trace, with sails all set, the unbuilt ship,
And sunken treasure, ere the waves subside;
Find here the wrecked craft making phantom trip;
Define the misty bounds: upon this side,
The mighty mountains of the Dark abide;
On that, the realms of Light expand like flowers;

There, 'tis the rocky coast of Death that towers;
Here, on the shoals, Life must its lighthouse keep.
Who is it that vague terror thus empowers
Below the dream-waves of the sea of Sleep?

On shore all day I find slight fellowship,
But in those surges fain would plunge and hide;
Those depths hold joys that none above outstrip.
Perchance—I cannot choose what shall betide—
Friend flown afar I clasp, dread foe deride,
Forget that sorrow all my heart devours,
Avenge the wrongs that Fate upon me showers.
Not my control can lift the tide at neap,
Nor quell its rise. Who thus my will deflours
Below the dream-waves of the sea of Sleep?

ENVOY

Archangels, princes, thrones, dominions, powers!
Which of ye dwarf the centuries to hours,
Or swell the moments into eons' sweep?
Is it the Prince of Darkness, then, who cowers
Below the dream-waves of the sea of Sleep?

"I was full of indecision and fear about looking behind the screen, but, at last, I did look—"

Her voice failed. I gave her some wine.

"What did you think you saw?"

"Think! I *saw* it."

"What?"

"Don't ask me!" she cried, shuddering. "I cannot describe it. Can you imagine the aspect of a corpse, long dead, mouldering, luminous, all blue light, and threads and tatters of its burial robe? O God, save us!" Her glance rested on the mantel. "I will not keep that rope. I will *not*! I *will* not! Curses on him and his memory!"

She snatched down the glass case, broke it, and flung the rope in the grate. We watched it as the fire consumed it and for a few moments held its charred outlines as it had fallen in a distinct semblance of a closed hand with index-finger pointing toward the screen! Our eyes met above it. "Do poets and artists possess an extra sense?" she muttered, grasping my arm in awe.

"But the property!" I stammered in sudden alarm. "What will you do without that?"

"No one need know at present of this conflagration. I will lock up and go abroad. I will start to-morrow!"

Just then we heard the voices of Dacre and Chartram in the hall. We stared at each other in dismay. "They must not come here!" she cried, and hurrying toward the next room disappeared behind the screen. The next instant a blood-curdling shriek rang through the room, rooting me to the spot where I stood. Before I knew anything more, Dacre and Chartram were standing by me, asking what was the matter. I could not speak. Weighed down by a sense of dread, I could only point to the screen. As they turned it aside, throwing another part of the room into shadow, the picture vanished in gloom, but the room took a more picturesque aspect. The door ajar showed, across the narrow hall, the open door where the merry-makers paused, leaning forward with startled faces and anxious gestures. Aura was lying full length on the carpet, dead! Her face was full of terror. Was it only a shadow, that livid line around her neck as if she had been strangled? As we turned away in horror, Dacre uttered a cry of surprise, and touching Chartram, pointed to the vacant space on the mantel.

"The rope?" they cried with one voice, like the chorus to a tragic opera.

"She had just burned it," I stammered.

They looked at each other. "Did she furnish Penniel with the means to destroy her?" Dacre asked Chartram.

"Tell me," I begged, "what is the mystery of that rope?"

There was a moment's delay. Then Chartram gave the startling reply: "It was the one with which Penniel hung himself."

THE STRIDING PLACE

GERTRUDE ATHERTON

WEIGALL, CONTINENTAL AND DETACHED, TIRED EARLY OF GROUSE-SHOOTING. To stand propped against a sod fence while his host's workmen routed up the birds with long poles and drove them towards the waiting guns, made him feel himself a parody on the ancestors who had roamed the moors and forests of this West Riding of Yorkshire in hot pursuit of game worth the killing. But when in England in August he always accepted whatever proffered for the season, and invited his host to shoot pheasants on his estates in the South. The amusements of life, he argued, should be accepted with the same philosophy as its ills.

It had been a bad day. A heavy rain had made the moor so spongy that it fairly sprang beneath the feet. Whether or not the grouse had haunts of their own, wherein they were immune from rheumatism, the bag had been small. The women, too, were an unusually dull lot, with the exception of a new-minded *débutante* who bothered Weigall at dinner by demanding the verbal restoration of the vague paintings on the vaulted roof above them.

But it was no one of these things that sat on Weigall's mind as, when the other men went up to bed, he let himself out of the castle and sauntered down to the river. His intimate friend, the companion of his boyhood, the chum of his college days, his fellow-traveller in many lands, the man for whom he possessed stronger affection than for all men, had mysteriously disappeared two days ago, and his track might have sprung to the upper air for all trace he had left behind him. He had been a guest on the adjoining estate during the past week, shooting with the fervor of the true sportsman, making love in the intervals to Adeline Cavan, and apparently in the best of spirits. As far as was known there was nothing to lower his mental mercury, for his rent-roll was a large one, Miss Cavan blushed whenever he looked at her, and, being one of the best shots in England, he was never happier than in August. The suicide theory was preposterous, all agreed, and there was as little reason to believe him murdered. Nevertheless, he had walked out of March Abbey two nights ago without hat or overcoat, and had not been seen since.

The country was being patrolled night and day. A hundred keepers and workmen were beating the woods and poking the bogs on the moors, but as yet not so much as a handkerchief had been found.

Weigall did not believe for a moment that Wyatt Gifford was dead, and although it was impossible not to be affected by the general uneasiness, he was disposed to be more angry than frightened. At Cambridge Gifford had been an incorrigible practical joker, and by no means had outgrown the habit; it would be like him to cut across the country in his evening clothes, board a cattle-train, and amuse himself touching up the picture of the sensation in West Riding.

However, Weigall's affection for his friend was too deep to companion with tranquillity in the present state of doubt, and, instead of going to bed early with the other men, he determined to walk until ready for sleep. He went down to the river and followed the path through the woods. There was no moon, but the stars sprinkled their cold light upon the pretty belt of water flowing placidly past wood and ruin, between green masses of overhanging rocks or sloping banks tangled with tree and shrub, leaping occasionally over stones with the harsh notes of an angry scold, to recover its equanimity the moment the way was clear again.

It was very dark in the depths where Weigall trod. He smiled as he recalled a remark of Gifford's: "An English wood is like a good many other things in life—very promising at a distance, but a hollow mockery when you get within. You see daylight on both sides, and the sun freckles the very bracken. Our woods need the night to make them seem what they ought to be—what they once were, before our ancestors' descendants demanded so much more money, in these so much more various days."

Weigall strolled along, smoking, and thinking of his friend, his pranks—many of which had done more credit to his imagination than this—and recalling conversations that had lasted the night through. Just before the end of the London season they had walked the streets one hot night after a party, discussing the various theories of the soul's destiny. That afternoon they had met at the coffin of a college friend whose mind had been a blank for the past three years. Some months previously they had called at the asylum to see him. His expression had been senile, his face imprinted with the record of debauchery. In death the face was placid, intelligent, without ignoble lineation—the face of the man they had known at college. Weigall and Gifford had had no time to comment there, and the afternoon and evening were full; but, coming forth from the house of festivity together, they had reverted almost at once to the topic.

"I cherish the theory," Gifford had said, "that the soul sometimes lingers in the body after death. During madness, of course, it is an impotent prisoner, albeit a conscious one. Fancy its agony, and its horror! What more natural than that, when the life-spark goes out, the tortured soul should take possession of the vacant skull and triumph once more for a few hours while old friends look their last? It has had time to repent while compelled to crouch and behold the result of its work, and it has shrived itself into a state of comparative purity. If I had my way, I should stay inside my bones until the coffin had gone into its niche, that I might obviate for my poor old comrade the tragic impersonality of death. And I should like to see justice done to it, as it were—to see it lowered among its ancestors with the ceremony and solemnity that are its due. I am afraid that if I dissevered myself too quickly, I should yield to curiosity and hasten to investigate the mysteries of space."

"You believe in the soul as an independent entity, then—that it and the vital principle are not one and the same?"

"Absolutely. The body and soul are twins, life comrades—sometimes friends, sometimes enemies, but always loyal in the last instance. Some day, when I am tired of the world, I shall go to India and become a mahatma, solely for the pleasure of receiving proof during life of this independent relationship."

"Suppose you were not sealed up properly, and returned after one of your astral flights to find your earthly part unfit for habitation? It is an experiment I don't think I should care to try, unless even juggling with soul and flesh had palled."

"That would not be an uninteresting predicament. I should rather enjoy experimenting with broken machinery."

The high wild roar of water smote suddenly upon Weigall's ear and checked his memories. He left the wood and walked out on the huge slippery stones which nearly close the River Wharfe at this point, and watched the waters boil down into the narrow pass with their furious untiring energy. The black quiet of the woods rose high on either side. The stars seemed colder and whiter just above. On either hand the perspective of the river might have run into a rayless cavern. There was no lonelier spot in England, nor one which had the right to claim so many ghosts, if ghosts there were.

Weigall was not a coward, but he recalled uncomfortably the tales of those that had been done to death in the Strid.[1] Wordsworth's Boy of Egremond had been disposed of by the practical Whitaker; but countless others, more venturesome than wise, had gone down into that narrow boiling course, never to appear in the still pool a few yards beyond. Below the great rocks which form the walls of the Strid was believed to be a natural vault, on to whose shelves the dead were drawn. The spot had an ugly fascination. Weigall stood, visioning skeletons, uncoffined and green, the home of the eyeless things which had devoured all that had covered and filled that rattling symbol of man's

---

1.   "This striding place is called the 'Strid,'
    A name which it took of yore;
    A thousand years hath it borne the name,
    And it shall a thousand more."

mortality; then fell to wondering if any one had attempted to leap the Strid of late. It was covered with slime; he had never seen it look so treacherous.

He shuddered and turned away, impelled, despite his manhood, to flee the spot. As he did so, something tossing in the foam below the fall—something as white, yet independent of it—caught his eye and arrested his step. Then he saw that it was describing a contrary motion to the rushing water—an upward backward motion. Weigall stood rigid, breathless; he fancied he heard the crackling of his hair. Was that a hand? It thrust itself still higher above the boiling foam, turned sidewise, and four frantic fingers were distinctly visible against the black rock beyond.

Weigall's superstitious terror left him. A man was there, struggling to free himself from the suction beneath the Strid, swept down, doubtless, but a moment before his arrival, perhaps as he stood with his back to the current.

He stepped as close to the edge as he dared. The hand doubled as if in imprecation, shaking savagely in the face of that force which leaves its creatures to immutable law; then spread wide again, clutching, expanding, crying for help as audibly as the human voice.

Weigall dashed to the nearest tree, dragged and twisted off a branch with his strong arms, and returned as swiftly to the Strid. The hand was in the same place, still gesticulating as wildly; the body was undoubtedly caught in the rocks below, perhaps already half-way along one of those hideous shelves. Weigall let himself down upon a lower rock, braced his shoulder against the mass beside him, then, leaning out over the water, thrust the branch into the hand. The fingers clutched it convulsively. Weigall tugged powerfully, his own feet dragged perilously near the edge. For a moment he produced no impression, then an arm shot above the waters.

The blood sprang to Weigall's head; he was choked with the impression that the Strid had him in her roaring hold, and he saw nothing. Then the mist cleared. The hand and arm were nearer, although the rest of the body was still concealed by the foam. Weigall peered out with distended eyes. The meagre light revealed in the cuffs links of a peculiar device. The fingers clutching the branch were as familiar.

Weigall forgot the slippery stones, the terrible death if he stepped too far. He pulled with passionate will and muscle. Memories flung themselves into the hot light of his brain, trooping rapidly upon each other's heels, as in the thought of the drowning. Most of the pleasures of his life, good and bad, were identified in some way with this friend. Scenes of college days, of travel, where they had deliberately sought adventure and stood between one another and death upon more occasions than one, of hours of delightful companionship among the treasures of art, and others in the pursuit of pleasure, flashed like the changing particles of a kaleidoscope. Weigall had loved several women; but he would have flouted in these moments the thought that he had ever loved any woman as he loved Wyatt Gifford. There were so many charming women in the world, and in the thirty-two years of his life he had never known another man to whom he had cared to give his intimate friendship.

He threw himself on his face. His wrists were cracking, the skin was torn from his hands. The fingers still gripped the stick. There was life in them yet.

Suddenly something gave way. The hand swung about, tearing the branch from Weigall's grasp. The body had been liberated and flung outward, though still submerged by the foam and spray.

Weigall scrambled to his feet and sprang along the rocks, knowing that the danger from suction was over and that Gifford must be carried straight to the quiet pool. Gifford was a fish in the water and could live under it longer than most men. If he survived this, it would not be the first time that his pluck and science had saved him from drowning.

Weigall reached the pool. A man in his evening clothes floated on it, his face turned towards a projecting rock over which his arm had fallen, upholding the body. The hand that had held the branch hung limply over the rock, its white reflection visible in the black water. Weigall plunged into the shallow pool, lifted Gifford in his arms and returned to the bank. He laid the body down and threw off his coat that he might be the freer to practise the methods of resuscitation. He was glad of the moment's respite. The valiant life in the man might have been exhausted in that last struggle. He had not dared to look at his face, to put his ear to the heart. The hesitation lasted but a moment. There was no time to lose.

He turned to his prostrate friend. As he did so, something strange and disagreeable smote his senses. For a half-moment he did not appreciate its nature. Then his teeth clacked together, his feet, his outstretched arms pointed towards the woods. But he sprang to the side of the man and bent down and peered into his face. There was no face.

A Terrible Night

Fitz-James O'Brien

"By Jove! Dick, I'm nearly done up."

"So am I. Did any one ever see such a confounded forest, Charley?"

"I am not alone weak, but hungry. Oh for a steak of moose, with a bottle of old red wine to wash it down!"

"Charley! beware. Take care how you conjure up such visions in my mind. I am already nearly starving, and if you increase my appetite much more it will go hard with me if I don't dine off of you. You are young, and Bertha says you're tender—"

"Hearted, she meant. Well, so I am, if loving Bertha be any proof of it. Do you know, Dick, I have often wondered that you, who love your sister so passionately, were not jealous of her attachment to me."

"So I was, my dear fellow, at first—furiously jealous. But then I reflected that Bertha must one day or the other marry, and I must lose my sister, so I thought it better that she should marry my old college chum and early friend, Charley Costarre, than any one else. So you see there was a little selfishness in my calculations, Charley."

"Dick, we were friends at school, and friends at college, and I thought at both those places that nothing could shorten the link that bound us together, but I was mistaken. Since my love for, and engagement to your sister, I feel as if you were fifty times the friend that you were before. Dick, we three will never part!"

"So he married the king's daughter, and they all lived together as happy as the days are long," shouted Dick with a laugh, quoting from nursery tale.

The foregoing is a slice out the conversation with which Dick Linton and myself endeavored to beguile the way, as we tramped through one of the forests of Northern New York. Dick was an artist, and I was a sportsman, so when one fine autumn day he announced his intention going into the woods for a week to study Nature, it seemed to me an excellent opportunity for me to exercise my legs and my trigger finger at the same time. Dick had some backwoods friend who lived in a log-hut on the shores of Eckford Lake, and there we determined to take up our quarters. Dick, who said he knew the forest thoroughly, was to be the guide, and we accordingly, with our guns on our shoulders, started on foot from Root's, a tavern known to tourists, and situated on the boundaries of Essex and Warren counties. It was a desperate walk; but as we started by daybreak, and had great faith in our pedestrian qualities, we expected to reach the nearest of the Eckford lakes by nightfall. The forest through which we traveled was of the densest description. Overhead the branches of spruce and pine shut out the day, while beneath our feet lay a frightful soil, composed principally of jagged shingle, cunningly concealed by an almost impenetrable brush. As the day wore on, our hopes of reaching our destination grew fainter and fainter, and I could almost fancy, from the anxious glances that Dick cast around him, that in spite of his boasted knowledge of the woods he had lost his way. It was not, however, until night actually fell, and that we were both sinking from hunger and exhaustion, that I could get him to acknowledge it.

"We're in a nice pickle, Master Dick," said I, rather crossly, for an empty stomach does much to destroy a man's natural amiability. "Confound your assurance that led you to set up as a guide. Of all men painters are the most conceited."

"Come, Charley," answered Dick, good-humoredly, "there's no use in growling so loudly. You'll bring the bears and panthers on us if you do. We must make the best of a bad job, and sleep in a tree."

"It's easy to talk, my good fellow. I'm not a partridge, and don't know how to roost on a bough."

"Well, you'll have to learn then; for if you sleep on the ground, the chances are ten to one but you will have the wolves nibbling at your toes before daylight."

"I'm hanged if I'll do either!" said I, desperately. "I'm going to walk all night, and I'll drop before I'll lie down."

"Come, come, Charley, don't be a fool!"

"I was a fool only when I consented to let you assume the *rôle* of guide."

"Well, Charley, if you are determined to go on, let it be so. We'll go together. After all, it's only an adventure."

"I say, Dick, don't you see a light?"

"By Jove, so there is! Come, you see Providence intervenes between us and wolves and hunger. That must be some squatter's hut."

The light to which I had so suddenly called Dick's attention was very faint, and seemed to be about half a mile distant. It glimmered through the dark branches of the hemlock and spruce trees, and weak as the light was, I hailed it as a mariner without a compass hails the star by which he steers. We instantly set out in the direction of our beacon. In a moment it seemed as if all fatigue had vanished, and we walked as if our muscles were as tense as iron, and our joints oily as a piston-shaft.

We soon arrived at what in the dusk seemed to be a clearing of about five acres, but it may have been larger, for the tall forest rising up around it must have diminished its apparent size, giving it the appearance of a square pit rather than a farm. Toward one corner of the clearing, we discerned the dusky outline of a log-hut, through whose single end window a faint light was streaming. With a sigh of relief we hastened to the door and knocked. It was opened immediately, and a man appeared on the threshold. We explained our condition, and were instantly invited to walk in and make ourselves at home. All our host said he could offer us were some cold Indian corn cakes, and a slice of dried deer's-flesh, to all of which we were heartily welcome. These viands in our starving condition were luxuries to us, and we literally reveled in anticipation of a full meal.

The hut into which we had so unceremoniously entered was of the most poverty-stricken order. It consisted of but one room, with a rude brick fire-place at one end. Some deer- skins and old blankets stretched out by way of a bed at the other extremity of the apartment, and the only seats visible were two sections of a large pine trunk that stood close to the fire-place. There was no vestige of a table, and the rest of the furniture was embodied in a long Tennessee rifle that hung close to the rough wall.

If the hut was remarkable, its proprietor was still more so. He was, I think, the most villainous looking man I ever beheld. About six feet two inches in height, proportionately broad across the shoulders, and with a hand large enough to pick up a fifty-six pound shot, he seemed to be a combination of extraordinary strength and agility. His head was narrow, and oblong in shape. His straight Indian-like hair fell smoothly over his low forehead as if it had been plastered with soap. And his black, bead-like eyes were set obliquely, and slanted downward toward his nose, giving him a mingled expression of ferocity and cunning. As I examined his features attentively, in which I thought I could trace almost every bad passion, I confess I experienced a certain feeling of apprehension and distrust that I could not shake off.

While he was getting us the promised food, we tried, by questioning him, to draw him into conversation. He seemed very taciturn and reserved. He said he lived entirely alone, and had cleared the spot he occupied with his own hands. He said his name was Joel; but when we hinted that he must have some other name, he pretended not to hear us, though I saw his brows knit, and his small black eyes flash angrily. My suspicions of this man were further aroused by observing a pair of shoes lying in a corner of the hut. These shoes were at least three sizes smaller than those that our gigantic host wore, and yet he had distinctly replied that he lived entirely alone. If those shoes were not his, whose were they? The more I reflected on this circumstance the more uneasy I felt, and apprehensions were still further aroused, when Joel, as he called himself, took both our fowling-pieces, and, in order to have them out of the way, as he said, hung them on crooks from the wall, at a height that neither Dick or I could reach without getting on a stool. I smiled inwardly, however, as I felt the smooth barrel of my revolver that was slung in the hollow of my back, by its leathern belt, and thought to myself, if this fellow has any bad designs, the more unprotected he thinks us the more incautious he will be, so I made no effort to retain our guns. Dick also had a revolver, and was one of those men who I knew would use it well when the time came.

My suspicions of our host grew at last to such a pitch that I determined to communicate them to Dick. Nothing would be easier than for this villainous half-breed—for I felt convinced he had Indian blood in him—nothing would be easier than, with the aid of an accomplice, to cut our throats or shoot us while we were asleep, and so get our guns, watches, and whatever money we carried. Who, in those lonely woods, would hear the shot, or hear our cries for help? What emissary of the law, however sharp, could point out our graves in those wild woods, or bring the murder home to those who committed it? Linton at first laughed; then grew serious; and gradually became a convert to my apprehensions. We hurriedly agreed that, while one slept, the other should watch, and so take it in turns through the night.

Joel had surrendered to us his couch of deer-skin and his blanket; he himself said he could sleep quite as well on the floor, near the fire. As Dick and I were both very tired, we were anxious to get our rest as soon as possible. So after a hearty meal of deer-steak and tough cakes, washed down by a good draught from our brandy flask, I, being the youngest, got the first hour's sleep, and flung myself on the couch of skins. As my eyes gradually closed, I saw a dim picture of Dick seated sternly watching by the fire, and the long shape of the half-breed stretching out like a huge shadow upon the floor.

After what I could have sworn to be only a three-minute doze, Dick woke me, and in- formed me that my hour was out; and turning me out of my warm nest, lay down without any ceremony, and in a few seconds was heavily snoring. I rubbed my eyes, felt for my revolver, and seating myself on one of the pine-stumps, commenced my watch. The half-breed appeared to be buried in a profound slumber, and in the half-weird light cast by the wood embers, his enormous figure seemed almost Titanic in its proportions. I confess I felt that in a struggle for life he was more than a match for Dick and myself. I then looked at the fire, and began a favorite amusement of mine—shaping forms in the embers. All sorts of figures defined themselves before me. Battles, tempests at sea, familiar faces, and above all shone, ever returning, the dear features of Bertha Linton, my affianced bride. She seemed to me to smile at me through a burning haze, and I could almost fancy I heard her say, "While you are watching in the lonely forest I am thinking of you, and praying for your safety."

A slight movement on the part of the slumbering half-breed here recalled me from those sweet dreams. He turned on his side, lifted himself slowly on his elbow, and gazed attentively at me. I did not stir. Still retaining my stooping attitude, I half closed my eyes, and remained motionless. Doubtless he thought I was asleep, for in a moment or two he rose noiselessly, and creeping with a stealthy step across the floor, passed out of the hut. I listened—Oh, how eagerly! It seemed to me that, through the imperfectly-joined crevices of the log-walls, I could plainly hear voices whispering. I would have given worlds to have crept nearer to listen, but I was fearful of disturbing the fancied security of our host, who I now felt certain had sinister designs upon us. So I remained perfectly still. The whispering suddenly ceased. The half-breed re-entered the hut in the same stealthy way in which he had quitted it, and after giving a scrutiniz-ing glance at me, once more stretched himself upon the floor and affected to sleep. In a few moments I pretended to awake—yawned, looked at my watch, and finding that my hour had more than expired, proceeded to wake Dick. As I turned him out of bed I whispered in his ear, "Don't take your eyes off that fellow, Dick. He has accomplices outside; be careful!" Dick gave a meaning glance, carelessly touched his revolver, as much as to say, "Here's something to interfere with his little arrangements," and took his seat on the pine-stump, in such a position as to command a view of the sleeping half-breed and the doorway at the same time.

This time, though horribly tired, I could not sleep. A horrible load seemed pressing on my chest, and every five minutes I would start up to see if Dick was keeping his watch faithfully. My nerves were strung to a frightful pitch of tensity; my heart beat at every sound, and my head seemed to throb until I thought my temples would burst. The more I reflected on the conduct of the half-breed, the more assured I was that he intended murder. Full of this idea, I took my revolver from its sling, and held it in my hand, ready to shoot him down at the first movement that appeared at all dangerous. A haze seemed now to pass across my eyes. Fatigued with long watching and excite-ment, I passed into that semi-conscious state, in which I seemed perfectly aware of every thing that passed, although objects were dim and dull in outline, and did not appear so sharply defined as in one's waking moments. I was apparently roused from this state by a slight crackling sound. I started, and raised myself on my elbow. My heart almost ceased to beat at what I saw. The half-breed had lit some species of dried herb, which sent out a strong aromatic odor as it burned. This herb he was holding directly under Dick's nostrils, who I now perceived, to my horror, was wrapped in a profound slumber. The smoke of this mysterious herb appeared to deprive him of all consciousness, for he rolled gently off of the pine-log, and lay stretched upon the floor. The half-breed now stole to the door, and opened it gently. Three sinister heads peered in out of the gloom. I saw the long barrels of rifles, and the huge brawny hands that clasped them. The half-breed pointed significantly to where I lay with his long bony finger, then drawing a large, thirsty-looking knife from his breast, moved toward me. The time was come. My blood stopped—my heart ceased to beat. The half-breed was within a foot of my bed; the knife was raised; another instant and it would have been buried in my heart, when, with a hand as cold as ice, I lifted my revolver, took deadly aim, and fired!

A stunning report, a dull groan, a huge cloud of smoke curling around me, and I found myself standing upright, with a dark mass lying at my feet.

"Great God! what have you done, Sir?" cried the half-breed, rushing toward me. "You have killed him! He was just about to wake you."

I staggered against the wall. My senses, until then immersed in sleep, suddenly recovered their activity. The frightful truth burst upon me in a flash. I had shot Dick Linton while under the influence of a nightmare! Then every thing seemed to fade away, and I remember no more.

There was a trial, I believe. The lawyers were learned, and proved by physicians that it was a case of what is called *Somnolentia,* or sleep-drunkenness; but of the proceedings I took no heed. One form haunted me, lying black and heavy on the hut floor; and one pale face was ever present—a face I saw once after the terrible catastrophe, and never saw again—the wild, despairing face of Bertha Linton, my promised bride!

The Thing in the Forest

Bernard Capes

Into the snow-locked forests of Upper Hungary steal wolves in winter; but there is a footfall worse than theirs to knock upon the heart of the lonely traveller.

One December evening Elspet, the young, newly-wedded wife of the woodman Stefan, came hurrying over the lower slopes of the White Mountains from the town where she had been all day marketing. She carried a basket with provisions on her arm; her plump cheeks were like a couple of cold apples; her breath spoke short, but more from nervousness than exhaustion. It was nearing dusk, and she was glad to see the little lonely church in the hollow below, the hub, as it were, of many radiating paths through the trees, one of which was the road to her own warm cottage yet a half-mile away.

She paused a moment at the foot of the slope, undecided about entering the little chill, silent building and making her plea for protection to the great battered stone image of Our Lady of Succour which stood within by the confessional box; but the stillness and the growing darkness decided her, and she went on. A spark of fire glowing through the presbytery window seemed to repel rather than attract her, and she was glad when the convolutions of the path hid it from her sight. Being new to the district, she had seen very little of Father Ruhl as yet, and somehow the penetrating knowledge and burning eyes of the pastor made her feel uncomfortable.

The soft drift, the lane of tall, motionless pines, stretched on in a quiet like death. Somewhere the sun, like a dead fire, had fallen into opalescent embers faintly luminous: they were enough only to touch the shadows with a ghastlier pallor. It was so still that the light crunch in the snow of the girl's own footfalls trod on her heart like a desecration.

Suddenly there was something near her that had not been before. It had come like a shadow, without more sound or warning. It was here—there,—behind her. She turned, in mortal panic, and saw a wolf. With a strangled cry and trembling limbs she strove to hurry on her way; and always she knew, though there was no whisper of pursuit, that the gliding shadow followed in her wake. Desperate in her terror, she stopped once more and faced it.

A wolf!—was it a wolf? O who could doubt it! Yet the wild expression in those famished eyes, so lost, so pitiful, so mingled of insatiable hunger and human need! Condemned, for its unspeakable sins, to take this form with sunset, and so howl and snuffle about the doors of men until the blessed day released it. A werewolf—not a wolf.

That terrific realisation of the truth smote the girl as with a knife out of darkness: for an instant she came near fainting. And then a low moan broke into her heart and flooded it with pity. So lost, so infinitely hopeless. And so pitiful—yes, in spite of all, so pitiful. It had sinned, beyond any sinning that her innocence knew or her experience could gauge; but she was a woman, very blest, very happy, in her store of comforts and her surety of love. She knew that it was forbidden to succour these damned and nameless outcasts, to help or sympathise with them in any way. But—

There was good store of meat in her basket, and who need ever know or tell? With shaking hands she found and threw a sop to the desolate brute—then, turning, sped upon her way.

But at home her secret sin stood up before her, and, interposing between her husband and herself, threw its shadow upon both their faces. What had she dared—what done? By her own act forfeited her birthright of innocence; by her own act placed herself in the power of the evil to which she had ministered. All that night she lay in shame and horror, and all the next day, until Stefan had come about his dinner and gone again, she moved in a dumb agony. Then, driven unendurably by the memory of his troubled, bewildered face, as twilight threatened she put on her cloak and went down to the little church in the hollow to confess her sin.

"Mother, forgive, and save me," she whispered, as she passed the statue.

After ringing the bell for the confessor, she had not knelt long at the confessional box in the dim chapel, cold and empty as a waiting vault, when the chancel rail clicked, and the footsteps of Father Ruhl were heard rustling over the stones. He came, he took his seat behind the grating; and, with many sighs and falterings, Elspet avowed her guilt. And as, with bowed head, she ended, a strange sound answered her—it was like a little laugh, and yet not so much like a laugh as a snarl. With a shock as of death she raised her face. It was Father Ruhl who sat there—and yet it was not Father Ruhl. In that time of twilight his face was already changing, narrowing, becoming wolfish—the eyes rounded and the jaw slavered. She gasped, and shrunk back; and at that, barking and snapping at the grating, with a wicked look he dropped—and she heard him coming. Sheer horror lent her wings. With a scream she sprang to her feet and fled. Her cloak caught in something—there was a wrench and crash and, like a flood, oblivion overswept her.

It was the old deaf and near senile sacristan who found them lying there, the woman unhurt but insensible, the priest crushed out of life by the fall of the ancient statue, long tottering to its collapse. She recovered, for her part: for his, no one knows where he lies buried. But there were dark stories of a baying pack that night, and of an empty, blood-stained pavement when they came to seek it for the body.

"The Toll-House"

W. W. Jacobs

"It's all nonsense," said Jack Barnes. "Of course people have died in the house; people die in every house. As for the noises—wind in the chimney and rats in the wainscot are very convincing to a nervous man. Give me another cup of tea, Meagle."

"Lester and White are first," said Meagle, who was presiding at the tea-table of the Three Feathers Inn. "You've had two."

Lester and White finished their cups with irritating slowness, pausing between sips to sniff the aroma, and to discover the sex and dates of arrival of the "strangers" which floated in some numbers in the beverage. Mr. Meagle served them to the brim, and then, turning to the grimly expectant Mr. Barnes, blandly requested him to ring for hot water.

"We'll try and keep your nerves in their present healthy condition," he remarked. "For my part I have a sort of half-and-half belief in the supernatural."

"All sensible people have," said Lester. "An aunt of mine saw a ghost once."

White nodded.

"I had an uncle that saw one," he said.

"It always is somebody else that sees them," said Barnes.

"Well, there is a house," said Meagle, "a large house at an absurdly low rent, and nobody will take it. It has taken toll of at least one life of every family that has lived there—however short the time—and since it has stood empty caretaker after caretaker has died there. The last caretaker died fifteen years ago."

"Exactly," said Barnes. "Long enough ago for legends to accumulate."

"I'll bet you a sovereign you won't spend the night there alone, for all your talk," said White, suddenly.

"And I," said Lester.

"No," said Barnes slowly. "I don't believe in ghosts nor in any supernatural things whatever; all the same I admit that I should not care to pass a night there alone."

"But why not?" inquired White.

"Wind in the chimney," said Meagle with a grin.

"Rats in the wainscot," chimed in Lester.

"As you like," said Barnes coloring.

"Suppose we all go," said Meagle. "Start after supper, and get there about eleven. We have been walking for ten days now without an adventure—except Barnes's discovery that ditchwater smells longest. It will be a novelty, at any rate, and, if we break the spell by all surviving, the grateful owner ought to come down handsome."

"Let's see what the landlord has to say about it first," said Lester. "There is no fun in passing a night in an ordinary empty house. Let us make sure that it is haunted."

He rang the bell, and, sending for the landlord, appealed to him in the name of our common humanity not to let them waste a night watching in a house in which spectres and hobgoblins had no part. The reply was more than reassuring, and the landlord, after describing with considerable art the exact appearance of a head which had been seen hanging out of a window in the moonlight, wound up with a polite but urgent request that they would settle his bill before they went.

"It's all very well for you young gentlemen to have your fun," he said indulgently; "but supposing as how you are all found dead in the morning, what about me? It ain't called the Toll-House for nothing, you know."

"Who died there last?" inquired Barnes, with an air of polite derision.

"A tramp," was the reply. "He went there for the sake of half a crown, and they found him next morning hanging from the balusters, dead."

"Suicide," said Barnes. "Unsound mind."

The landlord nodded. "That's what the jury brought it in," he said slowly; "but his mind was sound enough when he went in there. I'd known him, off and on, for years. I'm a poor man, but I wouldn't spend the night in that house for a hundred pounds."

He repeated this remark as they started on their expedition a few hours later. They left as the inn was closing for the night; bolts shot noisily behind them, and, as the regular customers trudged slowly homewards, they set off at a brisk pace in the direction of the house. Most of the cottages were already in darkness, and lights in others went out as they passed.

"It seems rather hard that we have got to lose a night's rest in order to convince Barnes of the existence of ghosts," said White.

"It's in a good cause," said Meagle. "A most worthy object; and something seems to tell me that we shall succeed. You didn't forget the candles, Lester?"

"I have brought two," was the reply; "all the old man could spare."

There was but little moon, and the night was cloudy. The road between high hedges was dark, and in one place, where it ran through a wood, so black that they twice stumbled in the uneven ground at the side of it.

"Fancy leaving our comfortable beds for this!" said White again. "Let me see; this desirable residential sepulchre lies to the right, doesn't it?"

"Farther on," said Meagle.

They walked on for some time in silence, broken only by White's tribute to the softness, the cleanliness, and the comfort of the bed which was receding farther and farther into the distance. Under Meagle's guidance they turned off at last to the right, and, after a walk of a quarter of a mile, saw the gates of the house before them.

The lodge was almost hidden by overgrown shrubs and the drive was choked with rank growths. Meagle leading, they pushed through it until the dark pile of the house loomed above them.

"There is a window at the back where we can get in, so the landlord says," said Lester, as they stood before the hall door.

"Window?" said Meagle. "Nonsense. Let's do the thing properly. Where's the knocker?"

He felt for it in the darkness and gave a thundering rat-tat-tat at the door.

"Don't play the fool," said Barnes crossly.

"Ghostly servants are all asleep," said Meagle gravely, "but *I'll* wake them up before I've done with them. It's scandalous keeping us out here in the dark."

He plied the knocker again, and the noise volleyed in the emptiness beyond. Then with a sudden exclamation he put out his hands and stumbled forward.

"Why, it was open all the time," he said, with an odd catch in his voice. "Come on."

"I don't believe it was open," said Lester, hanging back. "Somebody is playing us a trick."

"Nonsense," said Meagle sharply. "Give me a candle. Thanks. Who's got a match?"

Barnes produced a box and struck one, and Meagle, shielding the candle with his hand, led the way forward to the foot of the stairs. "Shut the door, somebody," he said, "there's too much draught."

"It is shut," said White, glancing behind him.

Meagle fingered his chin. "Who shut it?" he inquired, looking from one to the other. "Who came in last?"

"I did," said Lester, "but I don't remember shutting it—perhaps I did, though."

Meagle, about to speak, thought better of it, and, still carefully guarding the flame, began to explore the house, with the others close behind. Shadows danced on the walls and lurked in the corners as they proceeded. At the end of the passage they found a second staircase, and ascending it slowly gained the first floor.

"Careful!" said Meagle, as they gained the landing.

He held the candle forward and showed where the balusters had broken away. Then he peered curiously into the void beneath.

"This is where the tramp hanged himself, I suppose," he said thoughtfully.

"You've got an unwholesome mind," said White, as they walked on. "This place is quite creepy enough without your remembering that. Now let's find a comfortable room and have a little nip of whiskey apiece and a pipe. How will this do?"

He opened a door at the end of the passage and revealed a small square room. Meagle led the way with the candle, and, first melting a drop or two of tallow, stuck it on the mantelpiece. The others seated themselves on the floor and watched pleasantly as White drew from his pocket a small bottle of whiskey and a tin cup.

"H'm! I've forgotten the water," he exclaimed.

"I'll soon get some," said Meagle.

He tugged violently at the bell-handle, and the rusty jangling of a bell sounded from a distant kitchen. He rang again.

"Don't play the fool," said Barnes roughly.

Meagle laughed. "I only wanted to convince you," he said kindly. "There ought to be, at any rate, one ghost in the servants' hall."

Barnes held up his hand for silence.

"Yes?" said Meagle with a grin at the other two. "Is anybody coming?"

"Suppose we drop this game and go back," said Barnes suddenly. "I don't believe in spirits, but nerves are outside anybody's command. You may laugh as you like, but it really seemed to me that I heard a door open below and steps on the stairs."

His voice was drowned in a roar of laughter.

"He is coming round," said Meagle with a smirk. "By the time I have done with him he will be a confirmed believer. Well, who will go and get some water? Will you, Barnes?"

"No," was the reply.

"If there is any it might not be safe to drink after all these years," said Lester. "We must do without it."

Meagle nodded, and taking a seat on the floor held out his hand for the cup. Pipes were lit and the clean, wholesome smell of tobacco filled the room. White produced a pack of cards; talk and laughter rang through the room and died away reluctantly in distant corridors.

"Empty rooms always delude me into the belief that I possess a deep voice," said Meagle. "Tomorrow I—"

He started up with a smothered exclamation as the light went out suddenly and something struck him on the head. The others sprang to their feet. Then Meagle laughed.

"It's the candle," he exclaimed. "I didn't stick it enough."

Barnes struck a match and relighting the candle stuck it on the mantelpiece, and sitting down took up his cards again.

"What was I going to say?" said Meagle. "Oh, I know; to-morrow I—"

"Listen!" said White, laying his hand on the other's sleeve. "Upon my word I really thought I heard a laugh."

"Look here!" said Barnes. "What do you say to going back? I've had enough of this. I keep fancying that I hear things too; sounds of something moving about in the passage outside. I know it's only fancy, but it's uncomfortable."

"You go if you want to," said Meagle, "and we will play dummy. Or you might ask the tramp to take your hand for you, as you go downstairs."

Barnes shivered and exclaimed angrily. He got up and, walking to the half-closed door, listened.

"Go outside," said Meagle, winking at the other two. "I'll dare you to go down to the hall door and back by yourself."

Barnes came back and, bending forward, lit his pipe at the candle.

"I am nervous but rational," he said, blowing out a thin cloud of smoke. "My nerves tell me that there is something prowling up and down the long passage outside; my reason tells me that it is all nonsense. Where are my cards?"

He sat down again, and taking up his hand, looked through it carefully and led.

"Your play, White," he said after a pause.

White made no sign.

"Why, he is asleep," said Meagle. "Wake up, old man. Wake up and play."

Lester, who was sitting next to him, took the sleeping man by the arm and shook him, gently at first and then with some roughness; but White, with his back against the wall and his head bowed, made no sign. Meagle bawled in his ear and then turned a puzzled face to the others.

"He sleeps like the dead," he said, grimacing. "Well, there are still three of us to keep each other company."

"Yes," said Lester, nodding. "Unless— Good Lord! suppose—"

He broke off and eyed them trembling.

"Suppose what?" inquired Meagle.

"Nothing," stammered Lester. "Let's wake him. Try him again. *White! White!*"

"It's no good," said Meagle seriously; "there's something wrong about that sleep."

"That's what I meant," said Lester; "and if *he* goes to sleep like that, why shouldn't—"

Meagle sprang to his feet. "Nonsense," he said roughly. "He's tired out; that's all. Still, let's take him up and clear out. You take his legs and Barnes will lead the way with the candle. *Yes? Who's that?*"

He looked up quickly towards the door. "Thought I heard somebody tap," he said with a shamefaced laugh. "Now, Lester, up with him. One, two— Lester! Lester!"

He sprang forward too late; Lester, with his face buried in his arms, had rolled over on the floor fast asleep, and his utmost efforts failed to awaken him.

"He—is—asleep," he stammered. "Asleep!"

Barnes, who had taken the candle from the mantelpiece, stood peering at the sleepers in silence and dropping tallow over the floor.

"We must get out of this," said Meagle. "Quick!"

Barnes hesitated. "We can't leave them here——" he began.

"We must," said Meagle in strident tones. "If you go to sleep I shall go— Quick! Come."

He seized the other by the arm and strove to drag him to the door. Barnes shook him off, and putting the candle back on the mantelpiece, tried again to arouse the sleepers.

"It's no good," he said at last, and, turning from them, watched Meagle. "Don't you go to sleep," he said anxiously.

Meagle shook his head, and they stood for some time in uneasy silence. "May as well shut the door," said Barnes at last.

He crossed over and closed it gently. Then at a scuffling noise behind him he turned and saw Meagle in a heap on the hearthstone.

With a sharp catch in his breath he stood motionless. Inside the room the candle, fluttering in the draught, showed dimly the grotesque attitudes of the sleepers. Beyond the door there seemed to his overwrought imagination a strange and stealthy unrest. He tried to whistle, but his lips were parched, and in a mechanical fashion he stooped, and began to pick up the cards which littered the floor.

He stopped once or twice and stood with bent head listening. The unrest outside seemed to increase; a loud creaking sounded from the stairs.

"Who is there?" he cried loudly.

The creaking ceased. He crossed to the door and flinging it open, strode out into the corridor. As he walked his fears left him suddenly.

"Come on!" he cried with a low laugh. "All of you! All of you! Show your faces— your infernal ugly faces! Don't skulk!"

He laughed again and walked on; and the heap in the fireplace put out his head tortoise fashion and listened in horror to the retreating footsteps. Not until they had become inaudible in the distance did the listeners' features relax.

"Good Lord, Lester, we've driven him mad," he said in a frightened whisper. "We must go after him."

There was no reply. Meagle sprung to his feet.

"Do you hear?" he cried. "Stop your fooling now; this is serious. White! Lester! Do you hear?"

He bent and surveyed them in angry bewilderment. "All right," he said in a trembling voice. "You won't frighten me, you know."

He turned away and walked with exaggerated carelessness in the direction of the door. He even went outside and peeped through the crack, but the sleepers did not stir. He glanced into the blackness behind, and then came hastily into the room again.

He stood for a few seconds regarding them. The stillness in the house was horrible; he could not even hear them breathe. With a sudden resolution he snatched the candle from the mantelpiece and held the flame to White's finger. Then as he reeled back stupefied the footsteps again became audible.

He stood with the candle in his shaking hand listening. He heard them ascending the farther staircase, but they stopped suddenly as he went to the door. He walked a little way along the passage, and they went scurrying down the stairs and then at a jog-trot along the corridor below. He went back to the main staircase, and they ceased again.

For a time he hung over the balusters, listening and trying to pierce the blackness below; then slowly, step by step, he made his way downstairs, and, holding the candle above his head, peered about him.

"Barnes!" he called. "Where are you?"

Shaking with fright, he made his way along the passage, and summoning up all his courage pushed open doors and gazed fearfully into empty rooms. Then, quite suddenly, he heard the footsteps in front of him.

He followed slowly for fear of extinguishing the candle, until they led him at last into a vast bare kitchen with damp walls and a broken floor. In front of him a door leading into an inside room had just closed. He ran towards it and flung it open, and a cold air blew out the candle. He stood aghast.

"Barnes!" he cried again. "Don't be afraid! It is I—Meagle!"

There was no answer. He stood gazing into the darkness, and all the time the idea of something close at hand watching was upon him. Then suddenly the steps broke out overhead again.

He drew back hastily, and passing through the kitchen groped his way along the narrow passages. He could now see better in the darkness, and finding himself at last at the foot of the staircase began to ascend it noiselessly. He reached the landing just in time to see a figure disappear round the angle of a wall. Still careful to make no noise, he followed the sound of the steps until they led him to the top floor, and he cornered the chase at the end of a short passage.

"Barnes!" he whispered. "Barnes!"

Something stirred in the darkness. A small circular window at the end of the passage just softened the blackness and revealed the dim outlines of a motionless figure. Meagle, in place of advancing, stood almost as still as a sudden horrible doubt took possession of him. With his eyes fixed on the shape in front he fell back slowly and, as it advanced upon him, burst into a terrible cry.

"Barnes! For God's sake! Is it *you*?"

The echoes of his voice left the air quivering, but the figure before him paid no heed. For a moment he tried to brace his courage up to endure its approach, then with a smothered cry he turned and fled.

The passages wound like a maze, and he threaded them blindly in a vain search for the stairs. If he could get down and open the hall door—

He caught his breath in a sob; the steps had begun again. At a lumbering trot they clattered up and down the bare passages, in and out, up and down, as though in search of him. He stood appalled, and then as they drew near entered a small room and stood behind the door as they rushed by. He came out and ran swiftly and noiselessly in the other direction, and in a moment the steps were after him. He found the long corridor and raced along it at top speed. The stairs he knew were at the end, and with the steps close behind he descended them in blind haste. The steps gained on him, and he shrank to the side to let them pass, still continuing his headlong flight. Then suddenly he seemed to slip off the earth into space.

Lester awoke in the morning to find the sunshine streaming into the room, and White sitting up and regarding with some perplexity a badly blistered finger.

"Where are the others?" inquired Lester.

"Gone, I suppose," said White. "We must have been asleep."

Lester arose, and stretching his stiffened limbs, dusted his clothes with his hands, and went out into the corridor. White followed. At the noise of their approach a figure which had been lying asleep at the other end sat up and revealed the face of Barnes. "Why, I've been asleep," he said in surprise. "I don't remember coming here. How did I get here?"

"Nice place to come for a nap," said Lester, severely, as he pointed to the gap in the balusters. "Look there! Another yard and where would you have been?"

He walked carelessly to the edge and looked over. In response to his startled cry the others drew near, and all three stood gazing at the dead man below.

The Torture by Hope

Villiers de l'Isle Adam

In the official dungeons of Saragossa, long ago, at nightfall, the aged Pedro Arbez d'Espila, sixth Dominican Prior of Segovia, third Grand Inquisitor of Spain, followed by a "brother of the redemption" (a master torturer), and preceded by two secret servants (familiars) of the Holy Office, bearing lanterns, descended toward a condemned cell. The lock of the massive door grated; and they made their way into a mephitic *in-pace*, where the lingering daylight from above revealed, between rings riveted to the wall, a rack black with blood, a chafing-dish, a pitcher. On a muck bed, shackled, an iron collar on his neck, sat a haggard man in tatters, of an age from henceforward never to be distinguished.

This prisoner was no other than Rabbi Aser Abarbanel, a Jew of Aragon, convicted of usury and pitiless disregard of the poor, who had for over a year been put upon the rack daily. And yet, his "blindness being as hard as his hide," he had refused to abjure.

Proud of a stock dating back by the thousand years, boasting his ancient ancestry,—for all Jews worthy the name are jealous of their race,—he traced descent from Othniel, and consequently from Ipsibea, wife of this last judge of Israel, a circumstance which had sustained his courage beneath the hardest of his incessant tortures.

It was with tears in his eyes at the thought that so firm a soul should shut itself out from salvation that the aged Pedro Arbez d'Espila, approaching the trembling Rabbi, pronounced the following words:

"Rejoice, my son. Behold, your trials here below are about to end! If, in face of your stubbornness, I have felt it my duty to employ so much rigor, yet my task of fraternal correction has limits. You are the withered fig-tree which, so many times found barren, is cut down and cast into the fire. But God alone is able to judge your soul. Mayhap the Infinite Clemency will shine upon you at the supreme moment. We should trust so. There have been cases—so may it be! Rest, then, this evening in peace. You will take part to-morrow in the *auto-da-fé*; that is, you will be exposed to the *quemadero*, the fire premonitory of eternal flames. It burns, as you know, only at a distance, my son, and death has at least two hours (often three) to come, because of the wet and ice-cold bandages with which we take care to shield the foreheads and hearts of the holocausts. There will be but forty-three of you. Remember that you, being placed in the last rank, will have time to invoke God and to offer Him that baptism by fire which is of the Holy Ghost. Trust, then, in the Light, and sleep."

While finishing this discourse, Don Arbez, having by a sign caused the wretch to be freed from his chains, embraced him tenderly. Then it was the turn of the brother of the redemption, who in a low voice begged the Jew to pardon him that to which he had submitted him in order to redeem him; then the two familiars embraced him, their kisses made silent by their hoods. This ceremony ended, the captive was left condemned and alone in the darkness.

Rabbi Aser Abarbanel, his mouth dry, his face stupefied with suffering, regarded, at first without exact attention, the closed door. "Closed?" That word quite unconsciously awakened within his confused thoughts a dream. It was that for an instant he still beheld the light from the lanterns in the opening between the wall and the door. A morbid idea of hope, due to the enfeebling of his brain, possessed him. He dragged himself toward the unusual thing appearing. And very gently sliding a finger, with slow precaution, along the opening, he pulled the door toward him— oh, astounding! By an extraordinary chance the servant who had closed it had turned the great key a little before he had shut it to between the stone doorposts, so that the rusty bolt not having entered its socket, the door moved again when it was pushed.

The Rabbi risked a glance outside.

By means of a sort of livid obscurity, he distinguished at first a half-circle of earthy wall pierced by spiral stairs, and paramount, in front of him, five or six stone steps, a kind of black porch, giving access to a vast corridor of which he could perceive from below only the first arches.

Stretching himself along, he crawled to the level of this entrance. Yes, it was indeed a corridor, but of an immeasurable length. A wan light illumined it, glimmering as in a dream from the night-lamps hung from the vaulted roof and burning blue, at times, through the dull air. The distance beyond was darkness. Not a door on the side in all the length! Only on one side, at his left, vent-holes barred with iron in recesses of the wall allowed the passage of a twilight which should be that of evening, from the redness of the rays striking from afar athwart the flagging. And what a frightful stillness! Nevertheless, below there, in the depths of that veiled gloom, an outlet might open upon liberty. The tremulous hope of the Jew was tenacious, for it was his last.

Without hesitating, then, he ventured across the pavement, skirting the wall by the vent-holes, striving to blend himself in with the shadowy tinge of the long walls. He advanced slowly, dragging himself on his breast, and keeping himself from crying out when a wound recently lacerated twinged.

Suddenly the sound of a sandal approaching reached him in the echo of the stone corridor. Shivers shook him; anxiety suffocated him; his sight dimmed. So, then, all was ended, doubtless. He effaced himself, crouching on his haunches in a recess, and waited, half-dead.

It was a familiar of the Inquisition hurrying by. He passed rapidly, a thumb-screw in his grip, his hood lowered, terrible,—and disappeared. The seizure whose constraint the Rabbi had suffered having, as it were, suspended the functions of life, he remained for nearly an hour unable to make a stir. Fearing increased torture if he were seized, the idea came to him to go back into his hole. But the old hope whispered in his soul, the divine "perhaps" which comforts the worst distress. A miracle was to occur. He could no longer doubt it. He set himself then to creep toward the possible escape. Attenuated by hunger and suffering, trembling with anguish, he advanced. The sepulchral corridor seemed to lengthen mysteriously; and he himself, never finishing his advance, seemed to gaze forever at the shadows down there, where there ought to be salvation.

Oh, oh! Steps sound again, but this time slower and more hopeless. Shapes white and black, with long hats with rolled brims, appear before him, two inquisitors emerging upon the dull air down below. They chat in a low voice, and seem to be in controversy upon some important point, for their hands are gesticulating.

At this sight Rabbi Aser Abarbanel shut his eyes; his heart beat as if to kill him; his rags were saturated with the cold sweat of his agony; he remained gaping, motionless, stretched the length of the wall under the rays of a lamp, praying the God of David.

Having arrived opposite to him, the two inquisitors stopped under the light of the lamp, this, by a chance, doubtless, growing out of their discussion. One of them, while listening to his interlocutor, found himself regarding the Rabbi. And beneath this look, whose abstracted expression he did not at first comprehend, the unfortunate Rabbi believed he felt the warm pincers bite his poor flesh again: he was going again then to become a wail and a wound! Faltering, not able to breathe, his eyeballs pulsing, he shivered at the grazing of that robe. But—thing both strange and natural—the eyes of the inquisitor were evidently those of a man deeply preoccupied with what he is going to reply, absorbed by the idea to which he was listening. The pupils were fixed, and seemed to regard the Jew without seeing him.

In fact, after some minutes, the two sinister disputants pursued their way by slow steps, and still talking in a low voice, toward the central passage whence the captive had escaped. *They had not seen him!* In the horrible disarray of his sensations the idea crossed his brain, "Am I already dead, that they do not see me?"

A hideous impression roused him from his lethargy. While looking at the wall close by his own face, he thought he saw, opposite his own, two ferocious eyes observing him. He drew back his head in a sudden and desperate fright, his hair on end. But no, no! His hand, feeling the stones, brought him a true account: it was the reflection of the inquisitor's eyes that he had yet on his retina, and that he had refracted upon two spots on the wall.

On, then! He must hasten toward the end that he imagined (morbidly, no doubt) to be deliverance—toward those shadows from which he was distant no more than about thirty steps; again he took, more quickly, on his knees, on his hands, on his belly, his dolorous way; and soon he entered the darkest part of this frightful corridor. All at once the wretch felt cold *upon* his hands, which were resting on the flags; that was to be accounted for by a violent draught of air rushing under a little door on which the two walls abutted. Ah, God! if that door should open outdoors! His whole frame broke loose into a vertigo of hope. He examined it from top to bottom without being able to determine surely in the gloom around him. He felt. No bolts, no lock! A latch! He tried it. The latch yielded under his thumb; the silent door opened before him.

"Alleluia!" murmured the Rabbi, with an immense sigh of relief and thanks, now standing on the sill in sight of what appeared before him.

The door had opened upon a garden, beneath a starry night, upon spring, liberty, life! Thence the country beyond extended toward the Sierras, whose sinuous blue lines were silhouetted on the horizon. There salvation was! Oh, to flee thither! He would run all night under the citron woods whose perfume reached him. Once in the mountains he would be safe. He breathed the good, blessed air; the wind reanimated him; his lungs revived. He heard in his dilated heart the "Come forth!" of Lazarus. And that he might bless God again, who had accorded him this mercy, he stretched out his arms before him, raising his eyes to the sky. It was ecstasy.

Then he thought he saw the shadow of his own arms turn back upon himself; he thought he felt those shadowy arms surround him, enlace him, and that he was pressed tenderly against a breast. A tall form was, indeed, near him. Confidingly he cast his eyes upon it, and stood gasping, doting, dejected, throbbing, his cheeks distended, drivelling with fright.

Horror! he was in the arms of the Grand Inquisitor himself, the venerable Pedro Arbez d'Espila, who gazed upon him with his eyes full of big tears, and with the air of a good shepherd finding again his lost sheep.

The gloomy priest pressed the luckless Jew to his heart with an outburst of affection so fervent that the points of the monkish haircloth under the frock pricked the Dominican's chest; and while Rabbi Aser Abarbanel, his eyes drawn up under his lids, was convulsed with anguish in the arms of the ascetic Don Arbez, understanding confusedly that all the incidents of that evening were but a prepared torture,—the torture by hope!—the Grand Inquisitor, with an accent of poignant reproach and a glance of consternation, murmured in his ear, with ardor heightened by fasting,—

"Eh! what, my child? On the evening, perhaps, of salvation, you would, then, leave us?"

A Tough Tussle

Ambrose Bierce

ONE NIGHT IN THE AUTUMN OF 1861 A MAN SAT ALONE IN THE HEART OF A FOREST in western Virginia. The region was one of the wildest on the continent—the Cheat Mountain country. There was no lack of people close at hand, however; within a mile of where the man sat was the now silent camp of a whole Federal brigade. Somewhere about—it might be still nearer—was a force of the enemy, the numbers unknown. It was this uncertainty as to its numbers and position that accounted for the man's presence in that lonely spot; he was a young officer of a Federal infantry regiment and his business there was to guard his sleeping comrades in the camp against a surprise. He was in command of a detachment of men constituting a picket-guard. These men he had stationed just at nightfall in an irregular line, determined by the nature of the ground, several hundred yards in front of where he now sat. The line ran through the forest, among the rocks and laurel thickets, the men fifteen or twenty paces apart, all in concealment and under injunction of strict silence and unremitting vigilance. In four hours, if nothing occurred, they would be relieved by a fresh detachment from the reserve now resting in care of its captain some distance away to the left and rear. Before stationing his men the young officer of whom we are writing had pointed out to his two sergeants the spot at which he would be found if it should be necessary to consult him, or if his presence at the front line should be required.

It was a quiet enough spot—the fork of an old wood-road, on the two branches of which, prolonging themselves deviously forward in the dim moonlight, the sergeants were themselves stationed, a few paces in rear of the line. If driven sharply back by a sudden onset of the enemy—and pickets are not expected to make a stand after firing—the men would come into the converging roads and naturally following them to their point of intersection could be rallied and "formed." In his small way the author of these dispositions was something of a strategist; if Napoleon had planned as intelligently at Waterloo he would have won that memorable battle and been overthrown later.

Second-Lieutenant Brainerd Byring was a brave and efficient officer, young and comparatively inexperienced as he was in the business of killing his fellow-men. He had enlisted in the very first days of the war as a private, with no military knowledge whatever, had been made first-sergeant of his company on account of his education and engaging manner, and had been lucky enough to lose his captain by a Confederate bullet; in the resulting promotions he had gained a commission. He had been in several engagements, such as they were—at Philippi, Rich Mountain, Carrick's Ford and Greenbrier—and had borne himself with such gallantry as not to attract the attention of his superior officers. The exhilaration of battle was agreeable to him, but the sight of the dead, with their clay faces, blank eyes and stiff bodies, which when not unnaturally shrunken were unnaturally swollen, had always intolerably affected him. He felt toward them a kind of reasonless antipathy that was something more than the physical and spiritual repugnance common to us all. Doubtless this feeling was due to his unusually acute sensibilities—his keen sense of the beautiful, which these hideous things outraged. Whatever may have been the cause, he could not look upon a dead body without a loathing which had in it an element of resentment. What others have respected as the dignity of death had to him no existence—was altogether unthinkable. Death was a thing to be hated. It was not picturesque, it had no tender and solemn side—a dismal thing, hideous in all its manifestations and suggestions. Lieutenant Byring was a braver man than anybody knew, for nobody knew his horror of that which he was ever ready to incur.

Having posted his men, instructed his sergeants and retired to his station, he seated himself on a log, and with senses all alert began his vigil. For greater ease he loosened his sword-belt and taking his heavy revolver from his holster laid it on the log beside him. He felt very comfortable, though he hardly gave the fact a thought, so intently did he listen for any sound from the front which might have a menacing significance—a shout, a shot, or the footfall of one of his sergeants coming to apprise him of something worth knowing. From the vast, invisible ocean of moonlight overhead fell, here and there, a slender, broken stream that seemed to plash against the intercepting branches and trickle to earth, forming small white pools among the clumps of laurel. But these leaks were few and served only to accentuate the blackness of his environment, which his imagination found it easy to people with all manner of unfamiliar shapes, menacing, uncanny, or merely grotesque.

He to whom the portentous conspiracy of night and solitude and silence in the heart of a great forest is not an unknown experience needs not to be told what another world it all is—how even the most commonplace and familiar objects take on another character. The trees group themselves differently; they draw closer together, as if in fear. The very silence has another quality than the silence

of the day. And it is full of half-heard whispers—whispers that startle—ghosts
of sounds long dead. There are living sounds, too, such as are never heard under
other conditions: notes of strange night-birds, the cries of small animals in sudden
encounters with stealthy foes or in their dreams, a rustling in the dead leaves—it
may be the leap of a wood-rat, it may be the footfall of a panther. What caused
the breaking of that twig?—what the low, alarmed twittering in that bushful of
birds? There are sounds without a name, forms without substance, translations in
space of objects which have not been seen to move, movements wherein nothing
is observed to change its place. Ah, children of the sunlight and the gaslight, how
little you know of the world in which you live!

Surrounded at a little distance by armed and watchful friends, Byring felt
utterly alone. Yielding himself to the solemn and mysterious spirit of the time
and place, he had forgotten the nature of his connection with the visible and
audible aspects and phases of the night. The forest was boundless; men and the
habitations of men did not exist. The universe was one primeval mystery of darkness, without form and void, himself the sole, dumb questioner of its eternal
secret. Absorbed in thoughts born of this mood, he suffered the time to slip away
unnoted. Meantime the infrequent patches of white light lying amongst the tree-
trunks had undergone changes of size, form and place. In one of them near by, just
at the roadside, his eye fell upon an object that he had not previously observed.
It was almost before his face as he sat; he could have sworn that it had not before
been there. It was partly covered in shadow, but he could see that it was a human
figure. Instinctively he adjusted the clasp of his sword-belt and laid hold of his
pistol—again he was in a world of war, by occupation an assassin.

The figure did not move. Rising, pistol in hand, he approached. The figure lay
upon its back, its upper part in shadow, but standing above it and looking down
upon the face, he saw that it was a dead body. He shuddered and turned from it
with a feeling of sickness and disgust, resumed his seat upon the log, and forgetting military prudence struck a match and lit a cigar. In the sudden blackness that
followed the extinction of the flame he felt a sense of relief; he could no longer
see the object of his aversion. Nevertheless, he kept his eyes set in that direction
until it appeared again with growing distinctness. It seemed to have moved a
trifle nearer.

"Damn the thing!" he muttered. "What does it want?"

It did not appear to be in need of anything but a soul.

Byring turned away his eyes and began humming a tune, but he broke off in
the middle of a bar and looked at the dead body. Its presence annoyed him, though

he could hardly have had a quieter neighbor. He was conscious, too, of a vague, indefinable feeling that was new to him. It was not fear, but rather a sense of the supernatural—in which he did not at all believe.

"I have inherited it," he said to himself. "I suppose it will require a thousand ages—perhaps ten thousand—for humanity to outgrow this feeling. Where and when did it originate? Away back, probably, in what is called the cradle of the human race—the plains of Central Asia. What we inherit as a superstition our barbarous ancestors must have held as a reasonable conviction. Doubtless they believe themselves justified by facts whose nature we cannot even conjecture in thinking a dead body a malign thing endowed with some strange power of mischief, with perhaps a will and a purpose to exert it. Possibly they had some awful form of religion of which that was one of the chief doctrines, sedulously taught by their priesthood, as ours teach the immortality of the soul. As the Aryans moved slowly on, to and through the Caucasus passes, and spread over Europe, new conditions of life must have resulted in the formulation of new religions. The old belief in the malevolence of the dead body was lost from the creeds and even perished from tradition, but it left its heritage of terror, which is transmitted from generation to generation—is as much a part of us as are our blood and bones."

In following out his thought he had forgotten that which suggested it; but now his eye fell again upon the corpse. The shadow had now altogether uncovered it. He saw the sharp profile, the chin in the air, the whole face, ghastly white in the moonlight. The clothing was gray, the uniform of a Confederate soldier. The coat and waistcoat, unbuttoned, had fallen away on each side, exposing the white shirt. The chest seemed unnaturally prominent, but the abdomen had sunk in, leaving a sharp projection at the line of the lower ribs. The arms were extended, the left knee was thrust upward. The whole posture impressed Byring as having been studied with a view to the horrible.

"Bah!" he exclaimed; "he was an actor—he knows how to be dead."

He drew away his eyes, directing them resolutely along one of the roads leading to the front, and resumed his philosophizing where he had left off.

"It may be that our Central Asian ancestors had not the custom of burial. In that case it is easy to understand their fear of the dead, who really were a menace and an evil. They bred pestilences. Children were taught to avoid the places where they lay, and to run away if by inadvertence they came near a corpse. I think, indeed, I'd better go away from this chap."

He half rose to do so, then remembered that he had told his men in front and the officer in the rear who was to relieve him that he could at any time be found at that spot. It was a matter of pride, too. If he abandoned his post he feared they would think he feared the corpse. He was no coward and he was unwilling to incur anybody's ridicule. So he again seated himself, and to prove his courage looked boldly at the body. The right arm—the one farthest from him—was now in shadow. He could barely see the hand which, he had before observed, lay at the root of a clump of laurel. There had been no change, a fact which gave him a certain comfort, he could not have said why. He did not at once remove his eyes; that which we do not wish to see has a strange fascination, sometimes irresistible. Of the woman who covers her eyes with her hands and looks between the fingers let it be said that the wits have dealt with her not altogether justly.

Byring suddenly became conscious of a pain in his right hand. He withdrew his eyes from his enemy and looked at it. He was grasping the hilt of his drawn sword so tightly that it hurt him. He observed, too, that he was leaning forward in a strained attitude—crouching like a gladiator ready to spring at the throat of an antagonist. His teeth were clenched and he was breathing hard. This matter was soon set right, and as his muscles relaxed and he drew a long breath he felt keenly enough the ludicrousness of the incident. It affected him to laughter. Heavens! what sound was that? what mindless devil was uttering an unholy glee in mockery of human merriment? He sprang to his feet and looked about him, not recognizing his own laugh.

He could no longer conceal from himself the horrible fact of his cowardice; he was thoroughly frightened. He would have run from the spot, but his legs refused their office; they gave way beneath him and he sat again upon the log, violently trembling. His face was wet, his whole body bathed in a chill perspiration. He could not even cry out. Distinctly he heard behind him a stealthy tread, as of some wild animal, and dared not look over his shoulder. Had the soulless living joined forces with the soulless dead?—was it an animal? Ah, if he could but be assured of that! But by no effort of will could he now unfix his gaze from the face of the dead man.

I repeat that Lieutenant Byring was a brave and intelligent man. But what would you have? Shall a man cope, single-handed, with so monstrous an alliance, as that of night and solitude and silence and the dead,—while an incalculable host of his own ancestors shriek into the ear of his spirit their coward counsel, sing their doleful death-songs in his heart, and disarm his very blood of all its iron? The odds are too great—courage was not made for so rough use as that.

One sole conviction now had the man in possession: that the body had moved. It lay nearer to the edge of its plot of light—there could be no doubt of it. It had also moved its arms, for, look, they are both in the shadow! A breath of cold air struck Byring full in the face; the boughs of trees above him stirred and moaned. A strongly defined shadow passed across the face of the dead, left it luminous, passed back upon it and left it half obscured. The horrible thing was visibly moving! At that moment a single shot rang out upon the picket-line—a lonelier and louder, though more distant, shot than ever had been heard by mortal ear! It broke the spell of that enchanted man; it slew the silence and the solitude, dispersed the hindering host from Central Asia and released his modern manhood. With a cry like that of some great bird pouncing upon its prey he sprang forward, hot-hearted for action!

Shot after shot now came from the front. There were shoutings and confusion, hoof-beats and desultory cheers. Away to the rear, in the sleeping camp, were a singing of bugles and grumble of drums. Pushing through the thickets on either side the roads came the Federal pickets, in full retreat, firing backward at random as they ran. A straggling group that had followed back one of the roads, as instructed, suddenly sprang away into the bushes as half a hundred horsemen thundered by them, striking wildly with their sabres as they passed. At headlong speed these mounted madmen shot past the spot where Byring had sat, and vanished round an angle of the road, shouting and firing their pistols. A moment later there was a roar of musketry, followed by dropping shots—they had encountered the reserve-guard in line; and back they came in dire confusion, with here and there an empty saddle and many a maddened horse, bullet-stung, snorting and plunging with pain. It was all over—"an affair of out-posts."

The line was reëstablished with fresh men, the roll called, the stragglers were re-formed. The Federal commander with a part of his staff, imperfectly clad, appeared upon the scene, asked a few questions, looked exceedingly wise and retired. After standing at arms for an hour the brigade in camp "swore a prayer or two" and went to bed.

Early the next morning a fatigue-party, commanded by a captain and accompanied by a surgeon, searched the ground for dead and wounded. At the fork of the road, a little to one side, they found two bodies lying close together—that of a Federal officer and that of a Confederate private. The officer had died of a sword-thrust through the heart, but not, apparently, until he had inflicted upon his enemy no fewer than five dreadful wounds. The dead officer lay on his face in a pool of blood, the weapon still in his breast. They turned him on his back and the surgeon removed it.

"Gad!" said the captain—"It is Byring!"—adding, with a glance at the other, "They had a tough tussle."

The surgeon was examining the sword. It was that of a line officer of Federal infantry—exactly like the one worn by the captain. It was, in fact, Byring's own. The only other weapon discovered was an undischarged revolver in the dead officer's belt.

The surgeon laid down the sword and approached the other body. It was frightfully gashed and stabbed, but there was no blood. He took hold of the left foot and tried to straighten the leg. In the effort the body was displaced. The dead do not wish to be moved—it protested with a faint, sickening odor. Where it had lain were a few maggots, manifesting an imbecile activity.

The surgeon looked at the captain. The captain looked at the surgeon.

THE TRAVELLER

R. H. BENSON

ON ONE OF THESE EVENINGS AS WE SAT TOGETHER AFTER DINNER IN FRONT OF THE wide open fireplace in the central room of the house, we began to talk on that old subject—the relation of Science to Faith.

"It is no wonder," said the priest, "if their conclusions appear to differ, to shallow minds who think that the last words are being said on both sides; because their standpoints are so different. The scientific view is that you are not justified in committing yourself one inch ahead of your intellectual evidence: the religious view is that in order to find out anything worth knowing your faith must always be a little in advance of your evidence; you must advance *en* échelon. There is the principle of our Lord's promises. 'Act as if it were true, and light will be given.' The scientist on the other hand says, 'Do not presume to commit yourself until light is given.' The difference between the methods lies, of course, in the fact that Religion admits the heart and the whole man to the witness-box, while Science only admits the head—scarcely even the senses. Yet surely the evidence of experience is on the side of Religion. Every really great achievement is inspired by motives of the heart, and not of the head; by feeling and passion, not by a calculation of probabilities. And so are the mysteries of God unveiled by those who carry them first by assault; 'The Kingdom of Heaven suffereth violence; and the violent take it by force.'

"For example," he continued after a moment, "the scientific view of haunted houses is that there is no evidence for them beyond that which may be accounted for by telepathy, a kind of thought-reading. Yet if you can penetrate that veneer of scientific thought that is so common now, you find that by far the larger part of mankind still believes in them. Practically not one of us really accepts the scientific view as an adequate one."

"Have you ever had an experience of that kind yourself?" I asked.

"Well," said the priest, smiling, "you are sure you will not laugh at it? There is nothing commoner than to think such things a subject for humour; and that I cannot bear. Each such story is sacred to one person at the very least, and therefore should be to all reverent people."

I assured him that I would not treat his story with disrespect.

"Well," he answered, "I do not think you will, and I will tell you. It only happened a very few years ago. This was how it began:

"A friend of mine was, and is still, in charge of a church in Kent, which I will not name; but it is within twenty miles of Canterbury. The district fell into Catholic hands a good many years ago. I received a telegram, in this house, a day or two before Christmas, from my friend, saying that he had been suddenly seized with a very bad attack of influenza, which was devastating Kent at that time; and asking me to come down, if possible at once, and take his place over Christmas. I had only lately given up active work, owing to growing infirmity, but it was impossible to resist this appeal; so Parker packed my things and we went together by the next train.

"I found my friend really ill, and quite incapable of doing anything; so I assured him that I could manage perfectly, and that he need not be anxious.

"On the next day, a Wednesday, and Christmas Eve, I went down to the little church to hear confessions. It was a beautiful old church, though tiny, and full of interesting things: the old altar had been set up again; there was a rood-loft with a staircase leading on to it; and an awmbry on the north of the sanctuary had been fitted up as a receptacle for the Most Holy Sacrament, instead of the old hanging pyx. One of the most interesting discoveries made in the church was that of the old confessional. In the lower half of the rood-screen, on the south side, a square hole had been found, filled up with an insertion of oak; but an antiquarian of the Alcuin Club, whom my friend had asked to examine the church, declared that this without doubt was the place where in the pre-Reformation times confessions were heard. So it had been restored, and put to its ancient use; and now on this Christmas Eve I sat within the chancel in the dim fragrant light, while penitents came and knelt outside the screen on the single step, and made their confessions through the old opening.

"I know this is a great platitude, but I never can look at a piece of old furniture without a curious thrill at a thing that has been so much saturated with human emotion; but, above all that I have ever seen, I think that this old confessional moved me. Through that little opening had come so many thousands of sins, great and little, weighted with sorrow; and back again, in Divine exchange for those burdens, had returned the balm of the Saviour's blood. 'Behold! a door opened in heaven,' through which that strange commerce of sin and grace may be carried on—grace pressed down and running over, given into the bosom in exchange for sin! *O bonum commercium!*"

The priest was silent for a moment, his eyes glowing. Then he went on,

"Well, Christmas Day and the three following festivals passed away very happily. On the Sunday night after service, as I came out of the vestry, I saw a child waiting. She told me, when I asked her if she wanted me, that her father and others of her family wished to make their confessions on the following evening about six o'clock. They had

had influenza in the house, and had not been able to come out before; but the father was going to work next day, as he was so much better, and would come, if it pleased me, and some of his children to make their confessions in the evening and their communions the following morning.

"Monday dawned, and I offered the Holy Sacrifice as usual, and spent the morning chiefly with my friend, who was now able to sit up and talk a good deal, though he was not yet allowed to leave his bed.

"In the afternoon I went for a walk.

"All the morning there had rested a depression on my soul such as I have not often felt; it was of a peculiar quality. Every soul that tries, however poorly, to serve God, knows by experience those heavinesses by which our Lord tests and confirms His own: but it was not like that. An element of terror mingled with it, as of impending evil.

"As I started for my walk along the high road this depression deepened. There seemed no physical reason for it that I could perceive. I was well myself, and the weather was fair; yet air and exercise did not affect it. I turned at last, about half-past three o'clock, at a milestone that marked sixteen miles to Canterbury.

"I rested there for a moment, looking to the south-east, and saw that far on the horizon heavy clouds were gathering; and then I started homewards. As I went I heard a far-away boom, as of distant guns, and I thought at first that there was some sea-fort to the south where artillery practice was being held; but presently I noticed that it was too irregular and prolonged for the report of a gun; and then it was with a sense of relief that I came to the conclusion it was a far-away thunderstorm, for I felt that the state of the atmosphere might explain away this depression that so troubled me. The thunder seemed to come nearer, pealed more loudly three or four times and ceased.

"But I felt no relief. When I reached home a little after four Parker brought me in some tea, and I fell asleep afterwards in a chair before the fire. I was wakened after a troubled and unhappy dream by Parker bringing in my coat and telling me it was time to keep my appointment at the church. I could not remember what my dream was, but it was sinister and suggestive of evil, and, with the shreds of it still clinging to me, I looked at Parker with something of fear as he stood silently by my chair holding the coat.

"The church stood only a few steps away, for the garden and churchyard adjoined one another. As I went down carrying the lantern that Parker had lighted for me, I remember hearing far away to the south, beyond the village, the beat of a horse's hoofs. The horse seemed to be in a gallop, but presently the noise died away behind a ridge.

"When I entered the church I found that the sacristan had lighted a candle or two as I had asked him, and I could just make out the kneeling figures of three or four people in the north aisle.

"When I was ready I took my seat in the chair set beyond the screen, at the place I have described; and then, one by one, the labourer and his children came up and made their confessions. I remember feeling again, as on Christmas Eve, the strange charm of this old place of penitence, so redolent of God and man, each in his tenderest character of Saviour and penitent; with the red light burning like a luminous flower in the dark before me, to remind me how God was indeed tabernacling with men, and was their God.

"Now I do not know how long I had been there, when again I heard the beat of a horse's hoofs, but this time in the village just below the churchyard; then again there fell a sudden silence. Then presently a gust of wind flung the door wide, and the candles began to gutter and flare in the draught. One of the girls went and closed the door.

"Presently the boy who was kneeling by me at that time finished his confession, received absolution and went down the church, and I waited for the next, not knowing how many there were.

"After waiting a minute or two I turned in my seat, and was about to get up, thinking there was no one else, when a voice whispered sharply through the hole a single sentence. I could not catch the words, but I supposed they were the usual formula for asking a blessing, so I gave the blessing and waited, a little astonished at not having heard the penitent come up.

"Then the voice began again."

The priest stopped a moment and looked round, and I could see that he was trembling a little.

"Would you rather not go on?" I said. "I think it disturbs you to tell me."

"No, no," he said; "it is all right, but it was very dreadful—very dreadful.

"Well, the voice began again in a loud quick whisper, but the odd thing was that I could hardly understand a word; there were just phrases here and there, like the name of God and of our Lady, that I could catch. Then there were a few old French words that I knew; '*le roy*' came over and over again. Just at first I thought it must be some extreme form of dialect unknown to me; then I thought it must be a very old man who was deaf, because when I tried, after a few sentences, to explain that I could not understand, the penitent paid no attention, but whispered on quickly without a pause. Presently I could perceive that he was in a terrible state of mind; the voice broke and sobbed, and then almost cried out but still in this loud whisper; then on the other side of the screen I could hear fingers working and moving uneasily, as if entreating admittance at some barred door. Then at last there was silence for a moment, and then plainly some closing formula was repeated, which gradually grew lower and ceased. Then, as I rose, meaning to come round and explain that I had not been able to hear, a loud moan or two came from the penitent. I stood up quickly and looked through the upper part of the screen, and there was no one there.

"I can give you no idea of what a shock that was to me. I stood there glaring, I suppose, through the screen down at the empty step for a moment or two, and perhaps I said something aloud, for I heard a voice from the end of the church.

"'Did you call, sir?' And there stood the sacristan, with his keys and lantern, ready to lock up.

"I still stood without answering for a moment, and then I spoke; my voice sounded oddly in my ears.

"'Is there any one else, Williams? Are they all gone?' or something like that.

"Williams lifted his lantern and looked round the dusky church.

"'No, sir; there is no one.'

"I crossed the chancel to go to the vestry, but as I was half-way, suddenly again in the quiet village there broke out the desperate gallop of a horse.

"'There! there!' I cried, 'do you hear that?'

"Williams came up the church towards me.

"'Are you ill, sir?' he said. 'Shall I fetch your servant?'

"I made an effort and told him it was nothing; but he insisted on seeing me home: I did not like to ask him whether he had heard the gallop of the horse; for, after all, I thought, perhaps there was no connection between that and the voice that whispered.

"I felt very much shaken and disturbed; and after dinner, which I took alone of course, I thought I would go to bed very soon. On my way up, however, I looked into my friend's room for a few minutes. He seemed very bright and eager to talk, and I stayed very much longer than I had intended. I said nothing of what had happened in the church; but listened to him while he talked about the village and the neighbourhood. Finally, as I was on the point of bidding him good-night, he said something like this:

"'Well, I mustn't keep you, but I've been thinking while you've been in church of an old story that is told by antiquarians about this place. They say that one of St. Thomas à Becket's murderers came here on the very evening of the murder. It is his day, to-day, you know, and that is what put me in mind of it, I suppose.'

"While my friend said this, my old heart began to beat furiously; but, with a strong effort of self-control, I told him I should like to hear the story.

"'Oh! there's nothing much to tell,' said my friend; 'and they don't know who it's supposed to have been; but it is said to have been either one of the four knights, or one of the men-at-arms.'

"'But how did he come here?' I asked, 'and what for?'

"'Oh! he's supposed to have been in terror for his soul, and that he rushed here to get absolution, which, of course, was impossible.'

"'But tell me,' I said. 'Did he come here alone, or how?'

"'Well, you know, after the murder they ransacked the Archbishop's house and stables: and it is said that this man got one of the fastest horses and rode like a madman, not knowing where he was going: and that he dashed into the village, and into the church where the priest was: and then afterwards, mounted again and rode off. The priest, too, is buried in the chancel, somewhere, I believe. You see it's a very vague and improbable story. At the Gatehouse at Malling, too, you know, they say that one of the knights slept there the night after the murder.'

"I said nothing more; but I suppose I looked strange, because my friend began to look at me with some anxiety, and then ordered me off to bed: so I took my candle and went.

"Now," said the priest, turning to me, "that is the story. I need not say that I have thought about it a great deal ever since: and there are only two theories which appear to me credible, and two others, which would no doubt be suggested, which appear to me incredible.

"First, you may say that I was obviously unwell: my previous depression and dreaming showed that, and therefore that I dreamt the whole thing. If you wish to think that—well, you must think it.

"Secondly, you may say, with the Psychical Research Society, that the whole thing was transmitted from my friend's brain to mine; that his was in an energetic, and mine in a passive state, or something of the kind.

"These two theories would be called 'scientific,' which term means that they are not a hair's-breadth in advance of the facts with which the intellect, a poor instrument at the best, is capable of dealing. And these two 'scientific' theories create in their turn a new brood of insoluble difficulties.

"Or you may take your stand upon the spiritual world, and use the faculties which God has given you for dealing with it, and then you will no longer be helplessly puzzled, and your intellect will no longer overstrain itself at a task for which it was never made. And you may say, I think, that you prefer one of two theories.

"First, that human emotion has a power of influencing or saturating inanimate nature. Of course this is only the old familiar sacramental principle of all creation. The expressions of your face, for instance, caused by the shifting of the chemical particles of which it is composed vary with your varying emotions. Thus we might say that the violent passions of hatred, anger, terror, remorse, of this poor murderer, seven hundred years ago, combined to make a potent spiritual fluid that bit so deep into the very place where it was all poured out, that under certain circumstances it is reproduced. A phonograph for example, is a very coarse parallel, in which the vibrations of sound translate themselves first into terms of wax, and then re-emerge again as vibrations when certain conditions are fulfilled.

"Or, secondly, you may be old-fashioned and simple, and say that by some law, vast and inexorable, beyond our perception, the personal spirit of the very man is chained to the place, and forced to expiate his sin again and again, year by year, by attempting to express his grief and to seek forgiveness, without the possibility of receiving it. Of course we do not know who he was; whether one of the knights who afterwards did receive absolution, which possibly was not ratified by God; or one of the men-at-arms who assisted, and who, as an anonymous chronicle says, '*sine confessione et viatico subito rapti sunt.*'

"There is nothing materialistic, I think, in believing that spiritual beings may be bound to express themselves within limits of time and space; and that inanimate nature, as well as animate, may be the vehicles of the unseen. Arguments against such possibilities have surely, once for all, been silenced, for Christians at any rate, by the Incarnation and the Sacramental system, of which the whole principle is that the Infinite and Eternal did once, and does still, express Itself under forms of inanimate nature, in terms of time and space.

"With regard to another point, perhaps I need not remind you that a thunderstorm broke over Canterbury on the day and hour of the actual murder of the Archbishop."

A Tropical Horror

William Hope Hodgson

We are a hundred thirty days out from Melbourne, and for three weeks we have lain in this sweltering calm.

It is midnight, and our watch on deck until four A.M. I go out and sit on the hatch. A minute later, Joky, our youngest 'prentice, joins me for a chatter. Many are the hours we have sat thus and talked in the night watches; though, to be sure, it is Joky who does the talking. I am content to smoke and listen, giving an occasional grunt at seasons to show that I am attentive.

Joky has been silent for some time, his head bent in meditation. Suddenly he looks up, evidently with the intention of making some remark. As he does so, I see his face stiffen with a nameless horror. He crouches back, his eyes staring past me at some unseen fear. Then his mouth opens. He gives forth a strangulated cry and topples backward off the hatch, striking his head against the deck. Fearing I know not what, I turn to look.

Great Heavens! Rising above the bulwarks, seen plainly in the bright moonlight, is a vast slobbering mouth a fathom across. From the huge dripping lips hang great tentacles. As I look the Thing comes further over the rail. It is rising, rising, higher and higher. There are no eyes visible; only that fearful slobbering mouth set on the tremendous trunk-like neck; which, even as I watch, is curling inboard with the stealthy celerity of an enormous eel. Over it comes in vast heaving folds. Will it never end? The ship gives a slow, sullen roll to starboard as she feels the weight. Then the tail, a broad, flat-shaped mass, slips over the teak rail and falls with a loud slump to the deck.

For a few seconds the hideous creature lies heaped in writhing, slimy coils. Then, with quick darting movements, the monstrous head travels along the deck. Close by the mainmast stand the harness casks, and alongside of these a freshly opened cask of salt beef with the top loosely replaced. The smell of the meat seems to attract the monster, and I can hear it sniffing with a vast indrawing breath. Then those lips open, displaying four huge fangs; there is a quick forward motion of the head, a sudden crashing, crunching sound, and beef and barrel have disappeared. The noise brings one of the ordinary seamen out of the fo'cas'le. Coming into the night, he can see nothing for a moment. Then, as he gets further aft, he *sees*, and with horrified cries rushes forward. Too late! From the mouth of the Thing there flashes forth a long, broad blade of glistening white, set with fierce teeth. I avert my eyes, but cannot shut out the sickening "Glut! Glut!" that follows.

The man on the "look-out," attracted by the disturbance, has witnessed the tragedy, and flies for refuge into the fo'cas'le, flinging to the heavy iron door after him.

The carpenter and sailmaker come running out from the half-deck in their drawers. Seeing the awful Thing, they rush aft to the cabin with shouts of fear. The second mate, after one glance over the break of the poop, runs down the companion-way with the helmsman after him. I can hear them barring the scuttle, and abruptly *I realise that I am on the main deck alone.*

So far I have forgotten my own danger. The past few minutes seem like a portion of an awful dream. Now, however, I comprehend my position and, shaking off the horror that has held me, turn to seek safety. As I do so my eyes fall upon Joky, lying huddled and senseless with fright where he has fallen. I cannot leave him there. Close by stands the empty half-deck—a little steel-built house with iron doors. The lee one is hooked open. Once inside I am safe.

Up to the present the Thing has seemed to be unconscious of my presence. Now, however, the huge barrel-like head sways in my direction; then comes a muffled bellow, and the great tongue flickers in and out as the brute turns and swirls aft to meet me. I know there is not a moment to lose, and, picking up the helpless lad, I make a run for the open door. It is only distant a few yards, but that awful shape is coming down the deck to me in great wreathing coils. I reach the house and tumble in with my burden; then out on deck again to unhook and close the door. Even as I do so something white curls round the end of the house. With a bound I am inside and the door is shut and bolted. Through the thick glass of the ports I see the Thing sweep round the house, in vain search for me.

Joky has not moved yet; so, kneeling down, I loosen his shirt collar and sprinkle some water from the breaker over his face. While I am doing this I hear Morgan shout something; then comes a great shriek of terror, and again that sickening "Glut! Glut!"

Joky stirs uneasily, rubs his eyes, and sits up suddenly.

"Was that Morgan shouting—?" He breaks off with a cry. "Where are we? I have had such awful dreams!"

At this instant there is a sound of running footsteps on the deck and I hear Morgan's voice at the door.

"Tom, open—!"

He stops abruptly and gives an awful cry of despair. Then I hear him rush forward. Through the porthole, I see him spring into the fore rigging and scramble madly aloft. Something steals up after him. It shows white in the moonlight. It wraps itself around his right ankle. Morgan stops dead, plucks out his sheath-knife, and hacks fiercely at the fiendish thing. It lets go, and in a second he is over the top and running for dear life up t'gallant rigging.

A time of quietness follows, and presently I see that the day is breaking. Not a sound can be heard save the heavy gasping breathing of the Thing. As the sun rises higher the creature stretches itself out along the deck and seems to enjoy the warmth. Still no sound, either from the men forward or the officers aft. I can only suppose that they are afraid of attracting its attention. Yet, a little later, I hear the report of a pistol away aft, and looking out I see the serpent raise its huge head as though listening. As it does so I get a good view of the fore part, and in the daylight see what the night has hidden.

There, right about the mouth, is a pair of little pig-eyes, that seem to twinkle with a diabolical intelligence. It is swaying its head slowly from side to side; then, without warning, it turns quickly and looks right in through the port. I dodge out of sight; but not soon enough. It has seen me, and brings its great mouth up against the glass.

I hold my breath. My God! If it breaks the glass! I cower, horrified. From the direction of the port there comes a loud, harsh, scraping sound. I shiver. Then I remember that there are little iron doors to shut over the ports in bad weather. Without a moment's waste of time I rise to my feet and slam to the door over the port. Then I go round to the others and do the same. We are now in darkness, and I tell Joky in a whisper to light the lamp, which, after some fumbling, he does.

About an hour before midnight I fall asleep. I am awakened suddenly some hours later by a scream of agony and the rattle of a water-dipper. There is a slight scuffling sound; then that soul-revolting "Glut! Glut!"

I guess what has happened. One of the men forrad has slipped out of the fo'cas'le to try and get a little water. Evidently he has trusted to the darkness to hide his movements. Poor beggar! He has paid for his attempt with his life!

After this I cannot sleep, though the rest of the night passes quietly enough. Towards morning I doze a bit, but wake every few minutes with a start. Joky is sleeping peacefully; indeed, he seems worn out with the terrible strain of the past twenty-four hours. About eight A.M. I call him, and we make a light breakfast off the dry ship's biscuit and water. Of the latter happily we have a good supply. Joky seems more himself, and starts to talk a little—possibly somewhat louder than is safe; for, as he chatters on, wondering how it will end, there comes a tremendous blow against the side of the house, making it ring again. After this Joky is very silent. As we sit there I cannot but wonder what all the rest are doing, and how the poor beggars forrard are faring, cooped up without water, as the tragedy of the night has proved.

Towards noon, I hear a loud bang, followed by a terrific bellowing. Then comes a great smashing of woodwork, and the cries of men in pain. Vainly I ask myself what has happened. I begin to reason. By the sound of the report it was evidently something much heavier than a rifle or pistol, and judging from the mad roaring of the Thing, the shot must have done some execution. On thinking it over further, I become convinced that, by some means, those aft have got hold of the small signal cannon we carry, and though I know that some have been hurt, perhaps killed, yet a feeling of exultation seizes me as I listen to the roars of the Thing, and realise that it is badly wounded, perhaps mortally. After a while, however, the bellowing dies away, and only an occasional roar, denoting more of anger than aught else, is heard.

Presently I become aware, by the ship's canting over to starboard, that the creature has gone over to that side, and a great hope springs up within me that possibly it has had enough of us and is going over the rail into the sea. For a time all is silent and my hope grows stronger. I lean across and nudge Joky, who is sleeping with his head on the table. He starts up sharply with a loud cry.

"Hush!" I whisper hoarsely. "I'm not certain, but I do believe it's gone."

Joky's face brightens wonderfully, and he questions me eagerly. We wait another hour or so, with hope ever rising. Our confidence is returning fast. Not a sound can we hear, not even the breathing of the Beast. I get out some biscuits, and Joky, after rummaging in the locker, produces a small piece of pork and a bottle of ship's vinegar. We fall to with a relish. After our long abstinence from food the meal acts on us like wine, and what must Joky do but insist on opening the door, to make sure the Thing has gone. This I will not allow, telling him that at least it will be safer to open the iron port-covers first and have a look out. Joky argues, but I am immovable. He becomes excited. I believe the youngster is light-headed. Then, as I turn to unscrew one of the after-covers, Joky makes a dash at the door. Before he can undo the bolts I have him, and after a short struggle lead him back to the table. Even as I endeavour to quieten him there comes at the starboard door—the door that Joky has tried to open—a sharp, loud sniff, sniff, followed immediately by a thunderous grunting howl and a foul stench of putrid breath sweeps in under the door. A great trembling takes me, and were it not for the carpenter's tool-chest I should fall. Joky turns very white and is violently sick, after which he is seized by a hopeless fit of sobbing.

Hour after hour passes, and, weary to death, I lie down on the chest upon which I have been sitting, and try to rest.

It must be about half-past two in the morning, after a somewhat longer doze, that I am suddenly awakened by a most tremendous uproar away forrad—men's voices shrieking, cursing, praying; but in spite of the terror expressed, so weak and feeble;

while in the midst, and at times broken off short with that hellishly suggestive "Glut! Glut!" is the unearthly bellowing of the Thing. Fear incarnate seizes me, and I can only fall on my knees and pray. Too well I know what is happening.

Joky has slept through it all, and I am thankful.

Presently, under the door there steals a narrow riband of light, and I know that the day has broken on the second morning of our imprisonment. I let Joky sleep on. I will let him have peace while he may. Time passes, but I take little notice. The Thing is quiet, probably sleeping. About midday I eat a little biscuit and drink some of the water. Joky still sleeps. It is best so.

A sound breaks the stillness. The ship gives a slight heave, and I know that once more the Thing is awake. Round the deck it moves, causing the ship to roll perceptibly. Once it goes forrard—I fancy to again explore the fo'cas'le. Evidently it finds nothing, for it returns almost immediately. It pauses a moment at the house, then goes on further aft. Up aloft, somewhere in the fore-rigging, there rings out a peal of wild laughter, though sounding very faint and far away. The Horror stops suddenly. I listen intently, but hear nothing save a sharp creaking beyond the after end of the house, as though a strain had come upon the main rigging.

A minute later I hear a cry aloft, followed almost instantly by a loud crash on deck that seems to shake the ship. I wait in anxious fear. What is happening? The minutes pass slowly. Then comes another frightened shout. It ceases suddenly. The suspense has become terrible, and I am no longer able to bear it. Very cautiously I open one of the after port-covers, and peep out to see a fearful sight. There, with its tail upon the deck and its vast body curled round the mainmast, is the monster, its head above the topsail yard, and its great claw-armed tentacle waving in the air. It is the first proper sight that I have had of the Thing. Good Heavens! It must weigh a hundred tons! Knowing that I shall have time, I open the port itself, then crane my head out and look up. There on the extreme end of the lower topsail yard I see one of the able seamen. Even down here I note the staring horror of his face. At this moment he sees me and gives a weak, hoarse cry for help. I can do nothing for him. As I look the great tongue shoots out and licks him off the yard, much as might a dog a fly off the window-pane.

Higher still, but happily out of reach, are two more of the men. As far as I can judge they are lashed to the mast above the royal yard. The Thing attempts to reach them, but after a futile effort it ceases, and starts to slide down, coil on coil, to the deck. While doing this I notice a great gaping wound on its body some twenty feet above the tail.

I drop my gaze from aloft and look aft. The cabin door is torn from its hinges, and the bulkhead—which, unlike the half-deck, is of teak wood—is partly broken down. With a shudder I realise the cause of those cries after the cannon-shot. Turning I screw my head round and try to see the foremast, but cannot. The sun, I notice, is low, and the night is near. Then I draw in my head and fasten up both port and cover.

How will it end? Oh! how will it end?

After a while Joky wakes up. He is very restless, yet though he has eaten nothing during the day I cannot get him to touch anything.

Night draws on. We are too weary—too dispirited to talk. I lie down, but not to sleep . . . Time passes.

A ventilator rattles violently somewhere on the main deck, and there sounds constantly that slurring, gritty noise. Later I hear a cat's agonised howl, and then again all is quiet. Some time after comes a great splash alongside. Then, for some hours all is silent as the grave. Occasionally I sit up on the chest and listen, yet never a whisper of noise comes to me. There is an absolute silence, even the monotonous creak of the gear has died away entirely, and at last a real hope is springing up within me. That splash, this silence—surely I am justified in hoping. I do not wake Joky this time. I will prove first for myself that all is safe. Still I wait. I will run no unnecessary risks. After a time I creep to the after-port and will listen; but there is no sound. I put up my hand and feel at the screw, then again I hesitate, yet not for long. Noiselessly I begin to unscrew the fastening of the heavy shield. It swings loose on its hinge, and I pull it back and peer out. My heart is beating madly. Everything seems strangely dark outside. Perhaps the moon has gone behind a cloud. Suddenly a beam of moonlight enters through the port, and goes as quickly. I stare out. Something moves. Again the light streams in, and now I seem to be looking into a great cavern, at the bottom of which quivers and curls something palely white.

My heart seems to stand still! It is the Horror! I start back and seize the iron port-flap to slam it to. As I do so, something strikes the glass like a steam ran, shatters it to atoms, and flicks past me into the berth. I scream and spring away. The port is quite filled with it. The lamp shows it dimly. It is circling and twisting here and there. It is as thick as a tree, and covered with a smooth slimy skin. At the end is a great claw, like a lobster's, only a thousand times larger. I cower down into the farthest corner . . . It has broken the tool-chest to pieces with one click of those frightful mandibles. Joky has crawled under a bunk. The Thing sweeps round in my direction. I feel a drop of sweat trickle slowly down my face—it tastes salty. Nearer comes that awful death . . . Crash! I roll over backwards. It has crushed the water breaker against which I leant, and I am rolling in the water across the floor. The claw drives up, then down, with a quick uncertain movement, striking the deck a dull, heavy blow, a foot from my head. Joky gives a little gasp of horror. Slowly the Thing rises and starts feeling its way round the berth. It plunges into a bunk and pulls out a bolster, nips it in half and drops it, then moves on. It is feeling along the deck. As it does so it comes across a half of the bolster. It seems to toy with it, then picks it up and takes it out through the port . . .

A wave of putrid air fills the berth. There is a grating sound, and something enters the port again—something white and tapering and set with teeth. Hither and thither it curls, rasping over the bunks, ceiling, and deck, with a noise like that of a great saw at work. Twice it flickers above my head, and I close my eyes. Then off it goes again. It sounds now on the opposite side of the berth and nearer to Joky. Suddenly the harsh, raspy noise becomes muffled, as though the teeth were passing across some soft substance. Joky gives a horrid little scream, that breaks off into a bubbling, whistling sound. I open my eyes. The tip of the vast tongue is curled tightly round something that drips, then is quickly withdrawn, allowing the moonbeams to steal again into the berth. I rise to my feet. Looking round, I note in a mechanical sort of way the wrecked state of the berth—the shattered chests, dismantled bunks, and something else—

"Joky!" I cry, and tingle all over.

There is that awful Thing again at the port. I glance round for a weapon. I will revenge Joky. Ah! there, right under the lamp, where the wreck of the carpenter's chest strews the floor, lies a small hatchet. I spring forward and seize it. It is small, but so keen—so keen! I feel its razor edge lovingly. Then I am back at the port. I stand to one side and raise my weapon. The great tongue is feeling its way to those fearsome remains. It reaches them. As it does so, with a scream of "Joky! Joky!" I strike savagely again and again and again, gasping as I strike; once more, and the monstrous mass falls to the deck, writhing like a hideous eel. A vast, warm flood rushes in through the porthold. There is a sound of breaking steel and an enormous bellowing. A singing comes in my ears and grows louder—louder. Then the berth grows indistinct and suddenly dark.

EXTRACT FROM THE LOG OF THE STEAMSHIP *HISPANIOLA*.

June 24.—Lat.—N. Long.—W. 11 A.M.—Sighted four-masted barque about four points on the port bow, flying signal of distress. Ran down to her and sent a boat aboard. She proved to be the *Glen Doon*, homeward bound from Melbourne to London. Found things in a terrible state. Decks covered with blood and slime. Steel deck-house stove in. Broke open door, and discovered youth of about nineteen in last stage of inanition, also part remains of boy about fourteen years of age. There was a great quantity of blood in the place, and a huge curled-up mass of whitish flesh, weighing about half a ton, one end of which appeared to have been hacked through with a sharp instrument. Found forecastle door open and hanging from one hinge. Doorway bulged, as though something had been forced through. Went inside. Terrible state of affairs, blood everywhere, broken chests, smashed bunks, but no men nor remains. Went aft again and found youth showing signs of recovery. When he came round, gave the name of Thompson. Said they had been attacked by a huge serpent—thought it must have been sea-serpent. He was too weak to say much, but told us there were some men up the mainmast. Sent a hand aloft, who reported them lashed to the royal mast, and quite dead. Went aft to the cabin. Here we found the bulkhead smashed to pieces, and the cabin-door lying on the deck near the after-hatch. Found body of captain down lazarette, but no officers. Noticed amongst the wreckage part of the carriage of a small cannon. Came aboard again.

Have sent the second mate with six men to work her into port. Thompson is with us. He has written out his version of the affair. We certainly consider that the state of the ship, as we found her, bears out in every respect his story. (Signed)

William Norton (Master).
Tom Briggs (1st Mate).

THE TRUTH, THE WHOLE TRUTH, AND NOTHING BUT THE TRUTH

RHODA BROUGHTON

MRS. DE WYNT TO MRS. MONTRESOR

18, Eccleston Square,
May 5th

My Dearest Cecilia,

Talk of the friendships of Orestes and Pylades, of Julie and Claire, what are they to ours? Did Pylades ever go *ventre à terre*, half over London on a day more broiling than any but an *âme damnée* could even imagine, in order that Orestes might be comfortably housed for the season?

Did Claire ever hold sweet converse with from fifty to one hundred house agents, in order that Julie might have three windows to her drawing-room and a pretty *portière*? You see I am determined not to be done out of my full meed of gratitude.

Well, my friend, I had no idea till yesterday how closely we were packed in this great smoky beehive, as tightly as herrings in a barrel. Don't be frightened, however. By dint of squeezing and crowding, we have managed to make room for two more herrings in our barrel, and those two are yourself and your other self, *i.e.* your husband. Let me begin at the beginning. After having looked over, I verily believe, every undesirable residence in West London; after having seen nothing intermediate between what was suited to the means of a duke, and what was suited to the needs of a chimney-sweep; after having felt bed-ticking, and explored kitchen-ranges till my brain reeled under my accumulated experience, I arrived at about half-past five yesterday afternoon at 32, —— Street, May Fair.

"Failure No. 253, I don't doubt," I said to myself, as I toiled up the steps with my soul athirst for afternoon tea, and feeling as ill-tempered as you please. So much for my spirit of prophecy. Fate, I have noticed, is often fond of contradicting us flat, and giving the lie to our little predictions. Once inside, I thought I had got into a small compartment of Heaven by mistake. Fresh as a daisy, clean as a cherry, bright as a seraph's face, it is all these, and a hundred more, only that my limited stock of similes is exhausted. Two drawing-rooms as pretty as ever woman crammed with people she did not care two straws about; white curtains with rose-coloured ones underneath, festooned in the sweetest way; marvellously, *immorally* becoming, my dear, as I ascertained entirely for your benefit, in the mirrors, of which there are about a dozen and a half; Persian mats, easy chairs, and lounges suited to every possible physical conformation, from the Apollo Belvedere to Miss Biffin; and a thousand of the important little trivialities that make up the sum of a woman's life: peacock fans, Japanese screens, naked boys and *décolletée* shepherdesses; not to speak of a family of china pugs, with blue ribbons round their necks, which ought of themselves to have added fifty pounds a year to the rent. Apropos, I asked, in fear and trembling, what the rent might be—"Three hundred pounds a year." A feather would have knocked me down. I could hardly believe my ears, and made the woman repeat it several times, that there might be no mistake. To this hour it is a mystery to me.

With that suspiciousness which is so characteristic of you, you will immediately begin to hint that there must be some terrible unaccountable smell, or some odious inexplicable noise haunting the reception-rooms. Nothing of the kind, the woman assured me, and she did not look as if she were telling stories. You will next suggest—remembering the rose-coloured curtains—that its last occupant was a member of the demi-monde. Wrong again. Its last occupant was an elderly and unexceptionable Indian officer, without a liver, and with a most lawful wife. They did not stay long, it is true, but then, as the housekeeper told me, he was a deplorable old hypochondriac, who never could bear to stay a fortnight in any one place. So lay aside that scepticism, which is your besetting sin, and give unfeigned thanks to St. Brigitta, or St. Gengulpha, or St. Catherine of Siena, or whoever is your tutelar saint, for having provided you with a palace at the cost of a hovel, and for having sent you such an invaluable friend as

Your attached,

Elizabeth De Wynt

P.S.—I am so sorry I shall not be in town to witness your first raptures, but dear Artie looks so pale and thin and tall after the hooping-cough, that I am sending him off at once to the sea, and as I cannot bear the child out of my sight, I am going into banishment likewise.

MRS. MONTRESOR TO MRS. DE WYNT

32, —— Street, May Fair,

May 14th

Dearest Bessy,

Why did not dear little Artie defer his hooping-cough convalescence &c., till August? It is very odd, to me, the perverse way in which children always fix upon the most inconvenient times and seasons for their diseases. Here we are installed in our Paradise, and have searched high and low, in every hole and corner, for the serpent, without succeeding in catching a glimpse of his spotted tail. Most things in this world are disappointing, but 32, —— Street, May Fair, is not. The mystery of the rent is still a mystery. I have been for my first ride in the Row this morning; my horse was a little fidgety; I am half afraid that my nerve is not what it was. I saw heaps of people I knew. Do you recollect Florence Watson? What a wealth of red hair she had last year! Well, that same wealth is black as the raven's wing this year! I wonder how people can make such walking impositions of themselves, don't you? Adela comes to us next week; I am so glad. It is dull driving by oneself of an afternoon; and I always think that one young woman alone in a brougham, or with only a dog beside her, does not look *good*. We sent round our cards a fortnight before we came up, and have been already deluged with callers. Considering that we have been two years exiled from civilised life, and that London memories are not generally of the longest, we shall do pretty well, I think. Ralph Gordon came to see me on Sunday; he is in the ——th Hussars now. He has grown up such a dear fellow, and so good-looking! Just my style, large and fair and whiskerless! Most men nowadays make themselves as like monkeys, or Scotch terriers, as they possibly can. I intend to be quite a mother to him. Dresses are gored to as *indecent* an extent as ever; short skirts are rampant. I am sorry; I hate them. They make tall women look *lank*, and short ones insignificant. A knock! Peace is a word that might as well be expunged from one's London dictionary.

Yours affectionately,

Cecilia Montresor

MRS. DE WYNT TO MRS. MONTRESOR

The Lord Warden, Dover,

May 18th

Dearest Cecilia,

You will perceive that I am about to devote only one small sheet of note-paper to you. This is from no dearth of time, Heaven knows! time is a drug in the market here, but from a total dearth of ideas. Any ideas that I ever have, come to me from without, from external objects; I am not clever enough to generate any within myself. My life here is not an eminently suggestive one. It is spent digging with a wooden spade, and eating prawns. Those are my employments at least; my relaxation is going down to the Pier, to see the Calais boat come in. When one is miserable oneself, it is decidedly consolatory to see someone more miserable still; and wretched and bored, and reluctant vegetable as I am, I am not *sea-sick*. I always feel my spirits rise after having seen that peevish, draggled procession of blue, green and yellow fellow-Christians file past me. There is a wind here *always*, in comparison of which the wind that behaved so violently to the corners of Job's house was a mere zephyr. There are heights to climb which require more daring perseverance than ever Wolfe displayed, with his paltry heights of Abraham. There are glaring white houses, glaring white roads, glaring white cliffs. If any one knew how unpatriotically I detest the chalk-cliffs of Albion! Having grumbled through my two little pages—I have actually been reduced to writing very large in order to fill even them—I will send off my dreary little billet. How I wish I could get into the envelope myself too, and whirl up with it to dear, beautiful, filthy London. Not more heavily could Madame de Staël have sighed for Paris from among the shades of Coppet.

Your disconsolate,

Bessy

MRS. MONTRESOR TO MRS. DE WYNT

32, —— Street, May Fair,

May 27th

Oh, my dearest Bessy, how I wish we were out of this dreadful, dreadful house! Please don't think me very ungrateful for saying this, after your taking such pains to provide us with a Heaven upon earth, as you thought.

What has happened could, of course, have been neither foretold, nor guarded against, by any human being. About ten days ago, Benson (my maid) came to me with a very long face, and said, "If you please, 'm, did you know that this house was haunted?" I was *so* startled: you know what a coward I am. I said, "Good Heavens! No! is it?" "Well, 'm, I'm pretty nigh sure it is," she said, and the expression of her countenance was about as lively as an undertaker's; and then she told me that cook had been that morning to order groceries from a shop in the neighbourhood, and on her giving the man the direction where to send the things to, he had said, with a very peculiar smile, "No. 32, —— Street, eh? h'm? I wonder how long *you'll* stand it; last lot held out just a fortnight." He looked so odd that she asked him what he meant, but he only said, "Oh! nothing! only that parties never *do* stay long at 32." He had known parties go in one day, and out the next, and during the last four years he had never known any remain over the month. Feeling a good deal alarmed by this information, she naturally inquired the reason; but he declined to give it, saying that if she had not found it out for herself, she had much better leave it alone, as it would only frighten her out of her wits; and on her insisting and urging him, she could only extract from him, that the house had such a villainously bad name, that the owners were glad to let it for a mere song. You know how firmly I believe in apparitions, and what an unutterable fear I have of them: anything material, tangible, that I can lay hold of—anything of the same fibre, blood, and bone as myself, I could, I think, confront bravely enough; but the mere thought of being brought face to face with the "bodiless dead," makes my brain unsteady. The moment Henry came in, I ran to him, and told him; but he pooh-poohed the whole story, laughed at me, and asked whether we should turn out of the prettiest house in London, at the very height of the season, because a grocer said it had a bad name. Most good things that had ever been in the world had had a bad name in their day; and, moreover, the man had probably a motive for taking away the house's character, some friend for whom he coveted the charming situation and the low rent. He derided my "babyish fears," as he called them, to such an extent that I felt half ashamed, and yet not quite comfortable either; and then came the usual rush of London engagements, during which one has no time to think of anything but how to speak, and act, and look for the moment then present. Adela was to arrive yesterday, and in the morning our weekly hamper of flowers, fruit, and vegetables arrived from home. I always dress the flower vases myself, servants are so tasteless; and as I was arranging them, it occurred to me—you know Adela's passion for flowers—to carry up one particular cornucopia of roses and mignonette and set it on her toilet-table, as a pleasant surprise for her. As I came downstairs, I had seen the housemaid—a fresh, round-faced country girl— go into the room, which was being prepared for Adela, with a pair of sheets that had been airing over her arm. I went upstairs very slowly, as my cornucopia was full of water, and I was afraid of spilling some. I turned the handle of the bedroom-door and entered, keeping my eyes fixed on my flowers, to see how they bore the transit, and whether any of them had fallen out. Suddenly a sort of shiver passed over me; and feeling frightened—I did not know why—I looked up quickly. The girl was standing by the bed, leaning forward a little with her hands clenched in each other, rigid, every nerve tense; her eyes, wide open, starting out of her head, and a look of unutterable stony horror in them; her cheeks and mouth not pale, but livid as those of one that died awhile ago in mortal pain. As I looked at her, her lips moved a little, and an awful hoarse voice, not like hers in the least, said, "Oh! my God, I have seen it!" and then she fell down suddenly, like a log, with a heavy noise. Hearing the noise, loudly audible all through the thin walls and floors of a London house, Benson came running in, and between us we managed to lift her on to the bed, and tried to bring her to herself by rubbing her feet and hands, and holding strong salts to her nostrils. And all the while we kept glancing over our shoulders, in a vague cold terror of seeing some awful, shapeless apparition. Two long hours she lay in a state of utter unconsciousness. Meanwhile Harry, who had been down to his club, returned. At the end of two hours we succeeded in bringing her back to sensation and life, but only to make the awful discovery that she was raving mad. She became so violent that it required all the combined strength of Harry and Phillips (our butler) to hold her down in the bed. Of course, we sent off instantly for a doctor, who on her growing a little calmer towards evening, removed her in a cab to his own house. He has just been here to tell me that she is now pretty quiet, not from any return to sanity, but from sheer exhaustion. We are, of course, utterly in the dark as to *what* she saw, and her ravings are far too disconnected and unintelligible to afford us the slightest clue. I feel so completely shattered and upset by this awful occurrence, that you will excuse me, dear, I'm sure, if I write incoherently. One thing I need hardly tell you, and that is, that no earthly consideration would induce me to allow Adela to occupy that terrible room. I shudder and run by quickly as I pass the door.

Yours, in great agitation,
Cecilia

Mrs. De Wynt to Mrs. Montresor
The Lord Warden, Dover,
May 28th

Dearest Cecilia,

Yours just come; how very dreadful! But I am still unconvinced as to house being in fault. You know I feel a sort of godmother to it, and responsible for its good behaviour. Don't you think that what the girl had might have been a fit? Why not? I myself have a cousin who is subject to seizures of the kind, and immediately on being attacked his whole body becomes rigid, his eyes glassy and staring, his complexion livid, exactly as in the case you describe. Or, if not a fit, are you sure that she has not been subject to fits of madness? *Please* be sure and ascertain whether there is not insanity in her family. It is so common nowadays, and so much on the increase, that nothing is more likely. You know my utter disbelief in ghosts. I am convinced that most of them, if run to earth, would turn out about as genuine as the famed Cock Lane one. But even allowing the possibility, nay, the actual unquestioned existence of ghosts in the abstract, is it likely that there should be anything to be seen so horribly fear-inspiring, as to send a perfectly sane person *in one instant* raving mad, which you, after three weeks' residence in the house, have never caught a glimpse of? According to your hypothesis, your whole household ought, by this time, to be stark staring mad. Let me implore you not to give way to a panic which may, possibly, probably prove utterly groundless. Oh, how I wish I were with you, to make you listen to reason!

Artie ought to be the best prop ever woman's old age was furnished with, to indemnify me for all he and his hooping-cough have made me suffer. Write immediately, please, and tell me how the poor patient progresses. Oh, had I the wings of a dove! I shall be on wires till I hear again.

Yours,

Bessy

MRS. MONTRESOR TO MRS. DE WYNT

No. 5, Bolton Street, Piccadilly,

June 12th

Dearest Bessy,

You will see that we have left that terrible, hateful, fatal house. How I wish we had escaped from it sooner! Oh, my dear Bessy, I shall never be the same woman again if I live to be a hundred. Let me try to be coherent, and to tell you connectedly what has happened. And first, as to the housemaid, she has been removed to a lunatic asylum, where she remains in much the same state. She has had several lucid intervals, and during them has been closely, pressingly questioned as to what it was she saw; but she has maintained an absolute, hopeless silence, and only shudders, moans, and hides her face in her hands when the subject is broached. Three days ago I went to see her, and on my return was sitting resting in the drawing-room, before going to dress for dinner, talking to Adela about my visit, when Ralph Gordon walked in. He has always been walking in the last ten days, and Adela has always flushed up and looked very happy, poor little cat, whenever he made his appearance. He looked very handsome, dear fellow, just come in from the park; seemed in tremendous spirits, and was as sceptical as even you could be, as to the ghostly origin of Sarah's seizure. "Let me come here to-night and sleep in that room; *do*, Mrs. Montresor," he said, looking very eager and excited. "With the gas lit and a poker, I'll engage to exorcise every demon that shows his ugly nose; even if I should find—

"Seven white ghostisses

Sitting on seven white postisses."

"You don't mean really?" I asked, incredulously. "Don't I? that's all," he answered emphatically. "I should like nothing better. Well, is it a bargain?" Adela turned quite pale. "Oh, don't," she said, hurriedly, *"please*, don't! why should you run such a risk? How do you know that you might not be sent mad too?" He laughed very heartily, and coloured a little with pleasure at seeing the interest she took in his safety. "Never fear," he said, "it would take more than a whole squadron of departed ones, with the old gentleman at their head, to send me crazy." He was so eager, so persistent, so thoroughly in earnest, that I yielded at last, though with a certain strong reluctance, to his entreaties. Adela's blue eyes filled with tears, and she walked away hastily to the conservatory, and stood picking bits of heliotrope to hide them. Nevertheless, Ralph got his own way; it was so difficult to refuse him anything. We gave up all our engagements for the evening, and he did the same with his. At about ten o'clock he arrived, accompanied by a friend and brother officer, Captain Burton, who was anxious to see the result of the experiment. "Let me go up at once," he said, looking very happy and animated. "I don't know when I have felt in such good tune; a new sensation is a luxury not to be had every day of one's life; turn the gas up as high as it will go; provide a good stout poker, and leave the issue to Providence and me." We did as he bid. "It's all ready now," Henry said, coming downstairs after having obeyed his orders; "the room is nearly as light as day. Well, good luck to you, old fellow!" "Good-bye, Miss Bruce," Ralph said, going over to Adela, and taking her hand with a look, half laughing, half sentimental—

> "Fare thee well, and if for ever,
> Then for ever, fare thee well,

that is my last dying speech and confession. Now mind," he went on, standing by the table, and addressing us all; "if I ring once, *don't* come. I may be flurried, and lay hold of the bell without thinking; if I ring twice, *come*." Then he went, jumping up the stairs three steps at a time, and humming a tune. As for us, we sat in different attitudes of expectation and listening about the drawing-room. At first we tried to talk a little, but it would not do; our whole souls seemed to have passed into our ears. The clock's ticking sounded as loud as a great church bell close to one's ear. Addy lay on the sofa, with her dear little white face hidden in the cushions. So we sat for exactly an hour; but it seemed like two years, and just as the clock began to strike eleven, a sharp ting, ting, ting, rang clear and shrill through the house. "Let us go," said Addy, starting up and running to the door. "Let us go," I cried too, following her. But Captain Burton stood in the way, and intercepted our progress. "No," he said, decisively, "you must not go; remember Gordon told us distinctly, if he rang once not to come. I know the sort of fellow he is, and that nothing would annoy him more than having his directions disregarded."

"Oh, nonsense!" Addy cried passionately, "he would never have rung if he had not seen something dreadful; do, *do* let us go!" she ended, clasping her hands. But she was overruled, and we all went back to our seats. Ten minutes more of suspense, next door to unendurable; I felt a lump in my throat, a gasping for breath;—ten minutes on the clock, but a thousand centuries on our hearts. Then again, loud, sudden, violent, the bell rang! We made a simultaneous rush to the door. I don't think we were one second flying upstairs. Addy was first. Almost simultaneously she and I burst into the room. There he was, standing in the middle of the floor, rigid, petrified, with that same look—that look that is burnt into my heart in letters of fire—of awful, unspeakable, stony fear on his brave young face. For one instant he stood thus; then stretching out his arms stiffly before him, he groaned in a terrible, husky voice, "Oh, my God! I have seen it!" and fell down *dead*. Yes, *dead*. Not in a swoon or in a fit, but *dead*. Vainly we tried to bring back the life to that strong young heart; it will never come back again till that day when the earth and the sea give up the dead that are therein. I cannot see the page for the tears that are blinding me; he was such a dear fellow! I can't write any more to-day.

Your broken-hearted
Cecilia

This is a true story.

The Tunnel

John Metcalfe

With an unspoken curse Pietro Succi gave his head a downward, peck-like jerk, twisted his shoulder round and bit his upper arm. The fit of coughing which he stifled in his sleeve convulsed his frame, passed, then returned more violently. And each time that he coughed Pietro bit.

At last the paroxysm left him. He raised his head and with a cautious venom spat out the earth which filled his mouth, gritted between his teeth. His body was damp with sweat. He was weak and panting from strenuous exertion and from his smothered rage against the cough which nearly had betrayed him.

The narrow tunnel at one end of which he crouched was perhaps twelve yards long, but Succi reckoned it in years. Two yards a year, that made six years. That was the time it took a man to burrow downwards through the earthen flooring of his cell, to drive a level passage underneath the prison wall, to start at last with feverish hands and wildly beating heart upon the upward trending slope that led towards freedom and the light of day.

Humped half-asquat within the elbow of this gradual ascent, Succi could catch the glimmer of the lamp that shone all night outside his cell. The light had to pass through the grating over his door, to filter downwards through the boards that screened the opening of his burrow, to struggle finally along the horizontal passage. Yet by this niggard radiance Succi could see as plainly as most men in the daylight. He could see the knots in the boards which he had used to revet the sides of his tunnel, could even see the blood that dulled the glitter of the nail upon a lacerated finger. He had developed the eyes of a bat or of a mole.

With a curious illusion of remoteness the shadowy vista of his burrow stretched in a dwindling ring towards the grudging trickle of the light, but closer, at a little further than his hand might reach, the upper portion of its circle was occluded by a straight black edge. That was the bottom of the prison wall, he thought. He looked at it and frowned.

Even now, with liberty, fresh air, a bare two yards maybe above his head, the thing dismayed and baffled him. Hardly a board that stayed the tunnel's sides of which he should not know the form and feel by heart, hardly a scar upon the stubborn soil to which he might not give a proper story and a date, yet of the grave miscalculation which had brought him up against the lower courses of the wall instead of several feet beneath it he could remember nothing. It must have added at the least a fortnight to his tale of strenuous days, for it entailed an awkward dip and, till he worked beyond it, a painful cramping of the limbs. Strange that he should have so forgotten! For some moments he regarded it perplexedly, then with a sudden passionate intake of the breath he turned. Enough that it was passed. Another hour and he should be free. Feverishly he recommenced his labouring.

He was still panting from excitement and from the violence of his toil. The sweat which had chilled upon his body made him shiver till his renewed exertion warmed him once again. He worked with both hands clasped about the handle of a chisel, prising and clawing, using his fingers to tear out the loosened clods. The earth fell pattering round him in a chilly, softly crumbling shower, matting his hair, tickling inside his loosely fitting shirt, filling his eyes and nose, making him choke and grunt. Once, in a frozen rage, he stopped again to clap his mouth against his sleeve, fearing a fresh attack of coughing, but presently the irritation passed and he continued. A cough now, he fancied, so short a distance from the surface, might well be heard above. The sound might carry upwards. . . . And then, perhaps, detection and the wrecking of the work of years, a thing for him far worse than death, a thing to crack the heart.

He strove in desperate haste, for he had burned his boats behind him. It was now or never. The work that he should do tonight would, at an earlier age, have taken him six months. He had calculated matters to a nicety. Now, on the final lap, it was no longer necessary to carry back the earth laboriously to his cell, plaster it evenly upon the floor and cover it with straw. He had merely to let it fall about him, packing it roughly downwards with his feet. Unless he had seriously underestimated his distance from the surface there would always be an opening left to breathe by.

The tunnel took increasingly an upward trend. Behind him lay the little pile of boards which he had brought to prop the sides. They were the last the Governor had sent him, the remnants of a packing-case. After the first two years he had been allowed to occupy his time in fashioning as best he might from rude material such as this a host of worthless trifles—brackets and little cabinets, a table even and an ornamental stool. Of what became of them he had no notion, nor was he curious to inquire. They were removed as soon as made, gravely, without comment, but with the suggestion of a stern pity, by the sphinx-like warder who carried him the wood. Enough that they had served his turn, they and the chisel. As for the boards, he would hardly need them now. In half an hour or less the burrow should be vertical, and then . . . .

With a tightening at his chest, a curious prickling and tingling of his skin, he realised that at last the time had come, the moment he had longed for, the distant goal of years, the crowning of his days of planning, stolen nights of toil. Already he was actually outside the prison wall, even his toes had passed that fatal boundary. The earth rained round him in a steady and increasing shower. It was much softer to work than he had thought. The going was strangely, unexpectedly easy. For a second he stood puzzled, vaguely disconcerted.

Then, with a bracing of his muscles for the ultimate assault, he began again to battle upwards, and as his body strove and struggled, Pietro's mind, released, fled skimming backwards.

In a kind of vivid dream he saw himself as he had stood eight years ago, desolate for the first time within his cell, gazing with unseeing eyes upon the truckle bed, the freshly littered straw, listening in a dry anguish of despair to the fading echoes of his gaoler's tread.

For an unreckoned time his mind had frozen in a curious suspension of emotion. Within it none the less the feverishly imaged details of his trial had revolved grotesquely.

He came of humble but aspiring stock. At twenty-five he had inherited from his father one of the small quicksilver mines by Veggia. He had married, bought a villa near the coast. The mine was managed by a Sardinian named Torriani, a bitter, yellow-visaged man, whom gossip credited with a passion for Pietro's wife. One morning Torriani vanished, but a fortnight later his battered body was discovered at the bottom of a disused shaft. Pietro was arrested.

His trial dragged throughout the flaming heat of a Sicilian summer towards a pre-destined end. A thousand nothings had declared his guilt—forgotten jests that turned bewilderingly to subtle threats, the raked-up story of some fatuous, years-old altercation over cards, innumerable significant and sinister mischances. . . . Pietro, calm throughout three torturing months, broke down at last before his lawyer. "But," he had cried, "they don't understand! You see? They don't understand. I'm innocent, I proclaim it, innocent!" The lawyer, shrugging wryly, had with a bitter smile replied: "Ah, well, as it happens you're a lucky one. I can tell you that you've escaped the life term. They're commuting it to forty years." That irony, however, was lost upon Pietro.

Now, as his fingers tore away the over-roofing earth in their exultant fury, he felt a dim amazement for these early days. What had his life been like, how had he lived at all without this hope, this secret and engrossing dream of liberty, to nourish and sustain him?

Quite plainly he recalled the birth of his idea. Two years or more had passed since his conviction and he was busy hoeing a bed of garlic in the Governor's garden. Such jobs were granted in reward for good behaviour. Raising his eyes a moment from his work he had looked up and seen the sunlight glitter on a pane. He had been long enough within the prison to realise that a little further to the rear beneath this pane was situated his own cell. In a flash it had come to him. He could be no more than twenty paces from the outer wall. Some day he would escape!

Reflection, while it brought to light unreckoned difficulties, had strengthened his resolve. A number of circumstances favoured the attempt. For one thing, the wood and mallet and the precious chisel! Besides that, the prison was old and anti-quated. Upon the mainland it could never have existed. It had been extemporised half a century ago from the ruined stronghold of some fallen noble house and served since then for the incarceration of *ladrones* and occasional *banditti* from the hills. His own cell had an earthen floor. . . .

It was in the night that he had worked. At first he had used a nail and after that the taper of the chisel blade which he had pulled from out its wooden socket. The blunting and thrusting of the other end would have aroused suspicion. A hundred pitfalls lay in wait for an unwary step, a hundred far-off chances of detection had had to be envisaged. The smallest things disclosed a lurking menace, the veriest trifle might betray him instantly. Even the cleansing of the chisel-end, still more of his own person, required elaborate thought and preparation. Impossible to use his drinking water; he had had to lick and afterwards to spit.

With the deepening of his burrow fresh obstacles arose. The opening had to be covered with boards and then with straw. It became increasingly an arduous task to free his clothes and body of the soil that covered them. Finally he feigned a liking for lying on the earth to cool himself. His warder, fortunately, was an unsuspicious giant from the plains of Lombardy.

There came one day the rumour of an inspection of the prison. In each cell old straw was to be removed and fresh laid down. Pietro spent a night in the meticulous plas-tering and levelling of earth upon the boards that hid his tunnel. It was not, however, until week had lengthened into weary week that the inspection finally took place. And meanwhile all his work was at a standstill. The matter cost him full two months' delay.

So through six years of striving, planning, had he toiled on undaunted towards his distant goal. Beneath the semblance of a bowed dejection he had developed an amazing cunning. True, he had made the tunnel, but truer that the tunnel had made him. He had given it of his best, and as requital had acquired courage and enterprise, resource and swift prevision. His wits were tempered danger-sharp.

Of dire necessity he had achieved the very refinement of dissimulation. Amongst his keepers he was held to be a man whose spirit had been broken by his troubles. He had overheard them once as they discussed him. Their words had made him chuckle. He, broken! He who had wrought a tunnel with the sweat of brain and body, the ungrudging agony of years! He was above them all, the clods, the fat-cheeked, swine-fed dolts! He worked more gleefully that night for knowing how he had outwitted them.

Thus with the steady lengthening of the tunnel a secret and increasing pride had burned within the soul of its creator. Pride—and another and intenser feeling of which the man himself was unaware.

Slowly, unconsciously, the focus of his powers had shifted. The tunnel, from being a means to an end, had grown itself to be an overmastering passion, filling his days and nights, absorbing his whole being. Like a difficult and ungrateful child it called unceasingly upon his time, his labour and his loving care. His life was dedicated to its service. He was become its creature and its slave.

Once there has been excitement in the prison. A man was pardoned. He had been a convict longer than Pietro—fifteen years. Fresh evidence had come to light and he was free. A miracle! There had been a glimpse of him as he passed unsteadily along a corridor in a grey shirt and trousers, his face vacant, staring. He did not look happy. Liberty had merely dazed, bewildered him. Pietro felt no envy. Not thus to him should freedom come at length. Not as a gift—Pietro should command it!

And now, at last, the time had come, the time towards which his every thought had strained, his every energy been bent. . . . A few more moments and he would have left the tunnel. It would be no longer his. In the midst of his feverish labours a sudden chill passed down his spine, a shudder almost of dismay.

His tunnel! Like the recurring motive of some splendid symphony it had run through his life, informing, unifying. He had served it as an artist served his art, a priest his faith, a worshipper, a devotee. For years on end he had assessed each day by nothing but the handfuls of brown earth he carried backwards to his cell. Those strenuous, troglodytic hours had done their work on him. He was becoming the slave of one idea, a scheming, resolute brain directing hands that clawed and tore, a man no longer, only a Creature that could Tunnel.

Yet now was not the time to waver, falter. The work which he had carried almost to completion awaited coronation. Success alone would set a seal upon endeavour. To fail was to be false to what his strength and skill had fashioned, to prove unworthy of the masterpiece he had created. Besides, the moments sped. He must be free three hours before sunrise at the least. The nights just now were very cold. He knew the country well. With any luck he would have gained the forest-covered foot-hills before the dawn had broken. And then, by stealth and fleetness to the Northern coast, running by night, hiding throughout the day. He wondered how his wife would welcome him. He pictured her surprise. . . .

Suddenly he paused. His heart gave a wild beat. A clod, untouched, came tumbling of itself upon his feet. He put a hand upon the place from which it fell. Just for a second the crumbling earth seemed to strike faintly warm upon his finger-tips.

His brain swam. Save for his cramped position in the tunnel he would have fallen. After a while he felt again. The warmth was nothing, only his imagination. Yet no! Placing his fingers on the earth a little lower down he thought he could detect a difference in the temperature. The lower soil was cooler by a shade.

He struggled to collect himself, but as his hand had felt the earth his heart had given a sick drop. He was curiously weak, exhausted, not by his savage toil so much as by some strange and clutching terror, a vague and haunting fear, that sapped his strength and drained his energy. A sense of ominous impendence weighed him down. In vain he tried to grapple with he knew not what. The thing evaded capture like a dream that mocked him.

In the close silence of the tunnel's end he waited, listening, and, as he waited, something crept and stirred minutely in his brain. He could hear the hammering of his heart—it sounded like the beating of a drum. He could hear the drive and surge of blood against his ears, the tiny whispering of the damp and wounded earth about his head. And now between these sounds, a voice, a memory. . . .

His haunting dream had slowly gathered shape. A threatening image rose before his eyes. He saw the bottom of the prison wall, its ruled and level edge, that wall that should not have been there. He saw himself as he had stood dismayed a moment gone, his hand upon the earth that had seemed warm. He saw at last a vacant, goggling face, the face of someone passing down a corridor, the tautly white and staring face of one whom liberty had terrified. . . .

He turned and in a final frenzy tore wildly at the soil above his head. He struggled, but the presage of some imminent disaster sucked his strength. A foreboding, black as death, had gripped his soul, a baffling, nightmare sense of unreality.

He had dropped the chisel and was working with his hands alone. There were stones now and suddenly the blood ran trickling warm about his fingers. A smother of earth fell blinding, choking, in his eyes and mouth, but still he battled upwards. As from some frightful dream that holds its victim still upon the parting brink of sleep he struggled to awake. Once and again his brain had tottered, bursting, on that fatal verge. . . .

He realised that he was shouting, cursing, but his outcry did not cease. A blind unreasoning fury had possessed him.

Suddenly the earth above him stirred. It fell upon his neck, his shoulders, in a murderous, crushing weight. He gasped for breath. As by degrees he fought his upward way he felt a burning heat. His eyes were blinded by a torturing light. Something was roaring, booming, in his ears. Surely the sound of voices.

And, why, it was broad day!

He sank exhausted, dazed, upon the ground. He rubbed his eyes and, blinking, looked about him. Where was the prison, where? Whose were those faces peering at him through a fence?

For a while he sat, bewildered and dismayed, then, as he heard a step behind and felt a touch upon his shoulder, his confusion ended. Of course, he could remember now, remember perfectly. This was his joke, the little joke he played so well. These were the people who had come to watch him and applaud.

The fire left his eyes. His frenzy was replaced by an abashed docility. Upon his grimed and bleeding face there broke the flicker of a wistful smile. A pair of unseen hands assisted him to rise.

He shuffled slowly off, dropping upon that firm and friendly arm. He was weary, weary, and very hungry.

Presently he knew that they would give him supper.

His smile attained a preternatural tenderness.

For a short time after he had vanished the little crowd that had collected to watch Pietro Succi's exit from his burrow stood chattering by the fence. It was rare fun to see that shouting, frenzied thing with whirling, flail-lIke arms come thrashing upwards from the ground. Good fun, and nobody the worse for peeping, although his people did make such a fuss. It was worth ten lire any day to watch. Besides, it only happened about once a month.

After the rest had scattered, two peasant lads remained beside an opening in the fence.

"And now, you see," said one, "that's how he always does it. Just like a badger, isn't he, or else an earth-bear from the forest? They only start the tunnel for him and he finishes. He thinks that he's escaping from the prison. Seven times I've seen it. The greatest sight in Veggia—or anywhere in Sicily they say. Why, once there was a man who came to see him do it from Palermo."

"But why," inquired the other, "why does he want to tunnel? And was he really in a prison once?"

"Yes. He was eight years in the prison. They thought he murdered someone. He was just escaping by his tunnel when they pardoned him. It made him mad. And now he always has to burrow."

For a while they hung fascinated, staring upon the place from which the madman had emerged. Then, with a final shuddering glance, they slowly turned away.

Twilight:

Lucrezia Borgia, Duchess d'Este

Marjorie Bowen

THREE WOMEN STOOD BEFORE A MARBLE-MARGINED POOL IN THE GROUNDS OF THE Ducal palace at Ferrara; behind them three cypresses waved against a purple sky from which the sun was beginning to fade; at the base of these trees grew laurel, ilex, and rose bushes. Round the pool was a sweep of smooth green across which the light wind lifted and chased the red, white and pink rose leaves.

Beyond the pool the gardens descended, terrace on terrace of opulent trees and flowers; behind the pool the square strength of the palace rose, with winding steps leading to balustraded balconies. Further still, beyond palace and garden, hung vineyard and cornfield in the last warm maze of heat.

All was spacious, noble, silent; ambrosial scents rose from the heated earth— the scent of pine, lily, rose and grape.

The centre woman of the three who stood by the pool was the Spanish Duchess, Lucrezia, daughter of the Borgia Pope. The other two held her up under the arms, for her limbs were weak beneath her.

The pool was spread with the thick-veined leaves of water-lilies and upright plants with succulent stalks broke the surface of the water. In between the sky was reflected placidly, and the Duchess looked down at the counterfeit of her face as clearly given as if in a hand-mirror.

It was no longer a young face; beauty was painted on it skilfully; false red, false white, bleached hair cunningly dyed, faded eyes darkened on brow and lash, lips glistening with red ointment, the lost loveliness of throat and shoulders concealed under a lace of gold and pearls, made her look like a portrait of a fair woman, painted crudely.

And, also like one composed for her picture, her face was expressionless save for a certain air of gentleness, which seemed as false as everything else about her— false and exquisite, inscrutable and alluring—alluring still with a certain sickly and tainted charm, slightly revolting as were the perfumes of her unguents when compared to the pure scents of trees and flowers. Her women had painted faces, too, but they were plainly gowned, one in violet, one in crimson, while the Duchess blazed in every device of splendour.

Her dress, of citron-coloured velvet, trailed about her in huge folds, her bodice and her enormous sleeves sparkled with tight-sewn jewels; her hair was twisted into plaits and curls and ringlets; in her ears were pearls so large that they touched her shoulders.

She trembled in her splendour and her knees bent; the two women stood silent, holding her up—they were little more than slaves.

She continued to gaze at the reflection of herself; in the water she was fair enough. Presently she moistened her painted lips with a quick movement of her tongue.

"Will you go in, Madonna?" asked one of the women.

The Duchess shook her head; the pearls tinkled among the dyed curls.

"Leave me here," she said.

She drew herself from their support and sank heavily and wearily on the marble rim of the pool.

"Bring me my cloak."

They fetched it from a seat among the laurels; it was white velvet, unwieldy with silver and crimson embroidery.

Lucrezia drew it round her shoulders with a little shudder.

"Leave me here," she repeated.

They moved obediently across the soft grass and disappeared up the laurel-shaded steps that led to the terraces before the high-built palace.

The Duchess lifted her stiff fingers, that were rendered almost useless by the load of gems on them, to her breast.

Trails of pink vapour, mere wraiths of clouds began to float about the west; the long Italian twilight had fallen.

A young man parted the bushes and stepped on to the grass; he carried a lute slung by a red ribbon across his violet jacket; he moved delicately, as if reverent of the great beauty of the hour.

Lucrezia turned her head and watched him with weary eyes.

He came lightly nearer, not seeing her. A flock of homing doves passed over his head; he swung on his heel to look at them and the reluctantly departing sunshine was golden on his upturned face.

Lucrezia still watched him, intently, narrowly; he came nearer again, saw her, and paused in confusion, pulling off his black velvet cap.

"Come here," she said in a chill, hoarse voice. He obeyed with an exquisite swiftness and fell on one knee before her; his dropped hand touched the ground a pace beyond the furthest-flung edge of her gown.

"Who are you?" she asked. "Ormfredo Orsini, one of the Duke's gentlemen, Madonna," he answered.

He looked at her frankly surprised to see her alone in the garden at the turn of the day. He was used to see her surrounded by her poets, her courtiers, her women; she was the goddess of a cultured court and persistently worshipped.

"One of the Orsini," she said. "Get up from your knees."

He thought she was thinking of her degraded lineage, of the bad, bad blood in her veins. As he rose he considered these things for the first time. She had lived decorously at Ferrara for twenty-one years, nearly the whole of his lifetime; but he had heard tales, though he had never dwelt on them.

"You look as if you were afraid of me——"

"Afraid of you—I, Madonna?"

"Sit down," she said.

He seated himself on the marble rim and stared at her; his fresh face wore a puzzled expression.

"What do you want of me, Madonna?" he asked.

"Ahè!" she cried. "How very young you are, Orsini!"

Her eyes flickered over him impatiently, greedily; the twilight was beginning to fall over her, a merciful veil; but he saw her for the first time as an old woman. Slightly he drew back, and his lute touched the marble rim as he moved, and the strings jangled.

"When I was your age," she said, "I had been betrothed to one man and married to another, and soon I was wedded to a third. I have forgotten all of them."

"You have been so long our lady here," he answered. "You may well have forgotten the world, Madonna, beyond Ferrara."

"You are a Roman?"

"Yes, Madonna."

She put out her right hand and clasped his arm.

"Oh, for an hour of Rome!—in the old days!"

Her whole face, with its artificial beauty and undisguisable look of age, was close to his; he felt the sense of her as the sense of something evil.

She was no longer the honoured Duchess of Ferrara, but Lucrezia, the Borgia's lure, Cesare's sister, Alessandro's daughter, the heroine of a thousand orgies, the inspiration of a hundred crimes.

The force with which this feeling came over him made him shiver; he shrank beneath her hand.

"Have you heard things of me?" she asked in a piercing voice.

"There is no one in Italy who has not heard of you, Madonna."

"That is no answer, Orsini. And I do not want your barren flatteries."

"You are the Duke's wife," he said, "and I am the servant of the Duke."

"Does that mean that you must lie to me?"

She leant even nearer to him; her whitened chin, circled by the stiff goldwork of her collar, touched his shoulder.

"Tell me I am beautiful," she said. "I must hear that once more—from young lips."

"You are beautiful. Madonna."

She moved back and her eyes flared.

"Did I not say I would not have your flatteries?"

"What, then, was your meaning?"

"Ten years ago you would not have asked; no man would have asked. I am old. Lucrezia old!—ah, Gods above!"

"You are beautiful," he repeated. "But how should I dare to touch you with my mouth?"

"You would have dared, if you had thought me desirable," she answered hoarsely. "You cannot guess how beautiful I was—before you were born, Orsini."

He felt a sudden pity for her; the glamour of her fame clung round her and gilded her. Was not this a woman who had been the fairest in Italy seated beside him?

He raised her hand and kissed the palm, the only part that was not hidden with jewels.

"You are sorry for me," she said.

Orsini started at her quick reading of his thoughts.

"I am the last of my family," she added. "And sick. Did you know that I was sick, Orsini?"

"Nay, Madonna."

"For weeks I have been sick. And wearying for Rome."

"Rome," he ventured, "is different now, Madonna."

"Ahè!" she wailed. "And I am different also."

Her hand lay on his knee; he looked at it and wondered if the things he had heard of her were true. She had been the beloved child of her father, the old Pope, rotten with bitter wickedness; she had been the friend of her brother, the dreadful Cesare—her other brother, Francesco, and her second husband—was it not supposed that she knew how both had died?

But for twenty-one years she had lived in Ferrara, patroness of poet and painter, companion of such as the courteous gentle Venetian, Pietro Bembo.

And Alfonso d'Este, her husband, had found no fault with her; as far as the world could see, there had been no fault to find.

Ormfredo Orsini stared at the hand sparking on his knee and wondered.

"Suppose that I was to make you my father confessor?" she said. The white mantle had fallen apart and the bosom of her gown glittered, even in the twilight.

"What sins have you to confess, Madonna?" he questioned.

She peered at him sideways.

"A Pope's daughter should not be afraid of the Judgment of God," she answered. "And I am not. I shall relate my sins at the bar of Heaven and say I have repented—Ahè—if I was young again!"

"Your Highness has enjoyed the world," said Orsini.

"Yea, the sun," she replied, "but not the twilight."

"The twilight?"

"It has been twilight now for many years," she said, "ever since I came to Ferrara."

The moon was rising behind the cypress trees, a slip of glowing light. Lucrezia took her chin in her hand and stared before her; a soft breeze stirred the tall reeds in the pool behind her and gently ruffled the surface of the water.

The breath of the night-smelling flowers pierced the slumbrous air; the palace showed a faint shape, a marvellous tint; remote it looked and uncertain in outline.

Lucrezia was motionless; her garments were dim, yet glittering, her face a blur; she seemed the ruin of beauty and graciousness, a fair thing dropped suddenly into decay.

Orsini rose and stepped away from her; the perfume of her unguents offended him. He found something horrible in the memory of former allurement that clung to her; ghosts seemed to crowd round her and pluck at her, like fierce birds at carrion.

He caught the glitter of her eyes through the dusk; she was surely evil, bad to the inmost core of her heart; her stale beauty reeked of dead abomination. . . . Why had he never noticed it before?

The ready wit of his rank and blood failed him; he turned away towards the cypress trees.

The Duchess made no attempt to detain him; she did not move from her crouching, watchful attitude.

When he reached the belt of laurels he looked back and saw her dark shape still against the waters of the pool that were beginning to be touched with the argent glimmer of the rising moon. He hurried on, continually catching the strings of his lute against the boughs of the flowering shrubs; he tried to laugh at himself for being afraid of an old, sick woman; he tried to ridicule himself for believing that the admired Duchess, for so long a decorous great lady, could in truth be a creature of evil.

But the conviction flashed into his heart was too deep to be uprooted.

She had not spoken to him like a Duchess of Ferrara, but rather as the wanton Spaniard whose excesses had bewildered and sickened Rome.

A notable misgiving was upon him; he had heard great men praise her, Ludovico Ariosto, Cardinal Ippolito's secretary and the noble Venetian Bembo; he had himself admired her remote and refined splendour. Yet, because of these few moments of close talk with her, because of a near gaze into her face, he felt that she was something horrible, the poisoned offshoot of a bad race.

He thought that there was death on her glistening painted lips, and that if he had kissed them he would have died, as so many of her lovers were reputed to have died.

He parted the cool leaves and blossoms and came on to the borders of a lake that lay placid under the darkling sky.

It was very lonely; bats twinkled past with a black flap of wings; the moon had burnt the heavens clear of stars; her pure light began to fill the dusk. Orsini moved softly, with no comfort in his heart.

The stillness was intense; he could hear his own footfall, the soft leather on the soft grass. He looked up and down the silence of the lake.

Then suddenly he glanced over his shoulder. Lucrezia Borgia was standing close behind him; when he turned her face looked straight into his.

He moaned with terror and stood rigid; awful it seemed to him that she should track him so stealthily and be so near to him in this silence and he never know of her presence.

"Eh, Madonna!" he said.

"Eh, Orsini," she answered in a thin voice, and at the sound of it he stepped away, till his foot was almost in the lake.

His unwarrantable horror of her increased, as he found that the glowing twilight had confused him; for, whereas at first he had thought she was the same as when he had left her seated by the pool, royal in dress and bearing, he saw now that she was leaning on a stick, that her figure had fallen together, that her face was yellow as a church candle, and that her head was bound with plasters, from the under edge of which her eyes twinkled, small and lurid.

She wore a loose gown of scarlet brocade that hung open on her arms that showed lean and dry; the round bones at her wrist gleamed white under the tight skin, and she wore no rings.

"Madonna, you are ill," muttered Ormfredo Orsini. He wondered how long he had been wandering in the garden.

"Very ill," she said. "But talk to me of Rome. You are the only Roman at the Court, Orsini."

"Madonna, I know nothing of Rome," he answered, "save our palace there and sundry streets—"

She raised one hand from the stick and clutched his arm.

"Will you hear me confess?" she asked. "All my beautiful sins that I cannot tell the priest? All we did in those days of youth before this dimness at Ferrara?"

"Confess to God," he answered, trembling violently.

Lucrezia drew nearer.

"All the secrets Cesare taught me," she whispered. "Shall I make you heir to them?"

"Christ save me," he said, "from the Duke of Valentinois' secrets!"

"Who taught you to fear my family!" she questioned with a cunning accent. "Will you hear how the Pope feasted with his Hebes and Ganymedes? Will you hear how we lived in the Vatican?"

Orsini tried to shake her arm off; anger rose to equal his fear.

"Weed without root or flower, fruitless uselessness!" he said hoarsely. "Let me free of your spells!"

She loosed his arm and seemed to recede from him without movement; the plasters round her head showed ghastly white, and he saw all the wrinkles round her drooped lips and the bleached ugliness of her bare throat.

"Will you not hear of Rome?" she insisted in a wailing whisper. He fled from her, crashing through the bushes.

Swiftly and desperately he ran across the lawns and groves, up the winding steps to the terraces before the palace, beating the twilight with his outstretched hands as if it was an obstacle in his way.

Stumbling and breathless, he gained the painted corridors that were lit with a hasty blaze of wax light. Women were running to and fro, and he saw a priest carrying the Holy Eucharist cross a distant door.

One of these women he stopped.

"The Duchess—" he began, panting.

She laid her finger on her lip.

"They carried her in from the garden an hour ago; they bled and plastered her, but she died—before she could swallow the wafer—(hush! she was not thinking of holy things, Orsini!)—ten minutes ago—"

A Twilight Experience

G. M. Robins

Let me not slur over any of my weaknesses! Needs must I then begin with an admission that I do worse than write bad verses—I paint bad pictures.

One cannot tell why. I am without the motive that inspired Dante on the historic occasion when he began to paint an angel. It is a mere superfluity of naughtiness, for which no excuse can be found, and for which indulgence must be humbly craved.

There lies a district in the extreme west of Dorsetshire, near the coast, which appeals to my inmost being in a way I can only account for by supposing that it must have been the scene of a remote previous incarnation. It is beautiful, of course. The hills are wild, the combes deep, the poor soil only lavish of pine, larch, heather, and golden broom; but other places as beautiful make not the same appeal.

This is a land desolate and forsaken, of dwindling villages, ruined cottages, vast tracts of solitude, and hints of bygone races in cairn and castrum.

There is one particular spot which, when you reach it, at the summit of a sheer sharp climb, emerging from the dense shadow of a pine-hanger, gives the effect of a vast natural amphitheatre. Before you lies a circular basin of broken moorland; the opposite rim makes your horizon, lifting jagged edges like crenulations against the dead eastern evening sky.

Rabbits and juniper, whortleberry and bramble, patches of heather, some bare sandy scars where the loose land has slipped a little—this is all; yet the effect is tremendous.

It was sunset when I first reached it. Mrs. Vyell, the wife of the squire who owned the old red house in the fertile neighbouring combe, had given me the hint to seek it out.

A spot more separate, more completely isolated from all life, one could not conjure up in thought. Sketching-material was with me; the place was absolutely unsketchable. But it held me with a powerful, compelling hand, the solitude reaching out mighty arms to clutch me. I sat down and drank in the impression of desolation, paint-box and palette idle beside me.

Wild, sterile land! There was not even pasture for sheep. How few feet, since the dawn of history, must have trod its inhospitable acres! No trace of farming, no shed, no barn, not even a gate, wherever I turned my eyes.

The sun went down as I sat lost in musings. I knew the moon would soon be up, and that she would rise in the east, right before me. It became a necessity to wait, gazing

into the purple August twilight until the disc of yellowed silver should emerge, a radiant surprise, from behind the rim of my amphitheatre, to hang lamenting above the
silence and emptiness.

Just where would she appear? Behind that bit of crumbled wall? Behind the beech-
clump next to it? Over the castellated edge of rabbit-levelled turf? I must wait and see.
No human being could or would intrude. It led no whither, this wild cup in the heart of
the hills. Loneliness had immemorially claimed it wholly; it belonged "to darkness and
to me" in the uttermost sense of those magic words.

And even as the thought was framed, I became aware of some movement in the
depth of the hollow beneath me, down far below, where winter torrents had washed
and broken the ground into fantastic shapes, finding only partial outlet, and in summer
settling down to be soft emerald morass.

Something, someone, flitted behind a big bramble-bush, then emerged, and
moved upwards, away from me, but nearer to the level of my line of vision. It was
a man, carrying a bundle over his shoulder—a shepherd, as I guessed, slowly and
with toil ascending the eastern slope of the amphitheatre, exactly opposite my point
of view.

I wondered whence he came and whither he went; and as the moon tarried and
nothing else diverted my eye, I watched him with careful eagerness in the fading
light, and it seemed that as he moved, a very narrow track which he was following
became perceptible on the rugged slopes. Up he went, slowly but steadily, never
glancing behind, making evidently for a given point; and now that the pink flush
had wholly died away from the hillside, it suddenly became apparent that what had
seemed only a bit of broken wall on the horizon line, was in fact a solitary dwelling—a cottage with a thatched roof. So soon had my fantastic conception of utter
loneliness received its contradiction!

That cottage was doubtless the wayfarer's bourne. Here, careless of the awful
dead weight of isolation, unmoved by the power of the spirit of the hills, he dwelt, and
brought up children, and rested, all unconscious of the awful forces of nature, and faced
without flinching the terrors which were real to his forefathers, simply because he did
not understand them.

In a few minutes he would reach his home, and in a few minutes more a light would
appear in that remote window, which I saw now only as a small square of shadow.

Yes, I was right. He had reached the cottage; he had paused, or hesitated,—he was
too far off for me to divine why,—and now he had gone in at the door.

But all was still dark within. More and more densely the shadow of night fell upon
the hills; the brooding peace was broken only by the wheeling flight of a white owl

around my head. Ah, there at last! A bright gleam was shining through the window-square. It grew larger as I gazed; the aperture was very gradually filling with light—a dazzling, pure, white light.

Something like a shock overcame me as I suddenly realised the truth. It was the moon I saw—the moon, which had stolen up behind the hill, and now showed me the weird fact that the cottage was a ruin, a hollow shell. Its broken lineaments were now plainly visible against the radiance behind.

What did the shepherd seek there at this hour?

An unaccountable tremor seized me—a desire for human society and a warm hearth; the spirits of the hills were too strong for me. The shepherd might have no nerves, but I was the child of my age, and I promptly packed up my things and went home through the murky recesses of the pine-hanger, and then by way of lanes which human feet had lately trodden, and where one saw occasionally behind drawn curtains the twinkle of a light more homely, if less brilliant, than that of the queenly moon.

But next evening the influences of the place drew me there again at sunset; and again at the same hour I saw the same man taking the same course up the hillside to the cottage. It was, of course, later that evening before the moon came up; but though I waited till then, I did not see the man come out.

I was consumed with a vast curiosity—a curiosity to know what he did there alone without a light in the ruin. I laughed at my own folly, too. He kept his tools there; he was storing peat, or bringing up a lamb by hand. But none of these obvious reasons satisfied me. Deep down in my heart blossomed the hope that he might turn out to be a recluse, a real lover of solitude, a person capable of sympathising with me.

I formed a plan to intercept him. The next night I would come early, walk round to the ruined cottage, confront him on his arrival, and have a talk—perhaps become the recipient of some quaint bit of history or folklore. The idea so formed was quickly carried out. The spell of glorious weather waxed with the waxing moon; nothing on the following day intervened to prevent my solitary evening ramble.

The cottage was a long way off; it took a surprisingly long time to reach it. Perched on the brow of the hill, it overlooked another combe as desolate as this one, and also commanded a view of the sea.

It had evidently been a dwelling-house; in a square walled-in garden-patch were still traces of cultivation. It was built of solid stone, but the decay of the roof had left it at the mercy of the wild weather, and it was sadly fallen to ruin. There were four rooms—two upstairs, two down. One walked straight into the kitchen, with its wide fireplace and mouldering remnant of dresser-shelves, and ladder-like stair communicating with rooms above. From the kitchen a communicating doorway opened into an inner parlour.

Among the scattered ashes on the hearth bloomed a yellow sea-poppy; no fire, then, had been recently kindled there. The soft summer breeze blew lightly through the hollow shell, and swayed a jagged end of rope that dangled in the doorway between kitchen and parlour.

I tried the narrow stair. It creaked and groaned, but it was of Dorset oak and it bore my weight. Above were two bedrooms, empty and half unroofed. Nothing to be seen or found there. A search around the back of the premises revealed no more; there were no stores, no wood-pile, no sign of human industry, no apparent reason of any kind why a man should visit the place.

Piqued curiosity began to stimulate imagination, and sought to invent a motive for lonely twilight seeking of such a spot. It might be a tryst; there might be a second party, as yet unseen, who came over the brow of the hill to meet her lover as he ascended from the valley. Or it might be a place to hide treasure—though I could find no indication of a cellar. As gloaming fell, romance awoke, and various possibilities suggested themselves. It seemed very long before I saw the figure of my friend, as I secretly called him, working his way up the hillside, his bundle as usual on his shoulder.

I had taken up my station in the little square bit of garden-ground in front of the cottage. The gate had entirely disappeared, the gateway through which the approaching figure must enter was about three yards to my left. I sat on the low stone wall, and watched him come.

It was not dark. I could see him plainly; it followed, therefore, that he could see me also. But even when he drew near enough for his features to be recognisable, he took no notice.

Pausing, he fumbled at the yawning gateway in the place where no latch was. Such light as remained was behind him, so his face was not distinctly visible. It was dark and bearded. He seemed a powerful man in the prime of life.

His indifference was curiously annoying, I had been awaiting his appearance so long and so anxiously.

"Good-evening, friend," I said heartily.

He neither started nor turned; he simply took no notice whatever.

A queer feeling of chill crept over me. He had passed by in such a notable silence; his feet upon the weed-grown shingle pathway made no sound; he had slipped into the gloom of the interior like a shadow.

Again the curious agitation of the nerves which had possessed me when first I saw the moonlight glint through the ruin!

I had no matches with me, and I confess, to the detriment of my reputation for courage, that until the moon rose, I simply dared not enter the cottage.

There was no method of getting out at the back; he could hardly leave the place without my seeing him. My pipe, lit with my last match, was mercifully not out. I sat down to wait. No sound came from the darkness inside. It might have been hard to say which was the more completely silent, he within or I without.

Slowly, slowly, the showering radiance of the moonlight stole over the dusky wall. Her coming illuminated all things, sharp, well-edged, splendidly massed into lights and darks. I delayed no longer, but stepped up the pathway and looked into the cottage.

All was still. In the kitchen there was not much light, for there was no window in the opposite wall; but to the right, beyond the doorway that led to the parlour, a vivid moonbeam streamed across the floor, throwing into clear relief some object that swung from the jagged rope's end—something drooping, limp, inhuman, with a head that lolled horribly to one side. I faced it for several appreciable seconds. I heard my own heart-beats as there gradually awoke a tingling repulsion, a rush of shame at my callous, cowardly waiting outside while inside this man had unhindered inflicted upon himself the death which apparently he had contemplated for the past two nights, without the courage to accomplish it. It was not cowardice, but an instinct stronger than I,—it may have been reverence,—that caused me to cover my eyes a moment before snatching out my knife and advancing.

In that moment the delusion had vanished: no dark form hung in the void space where still the jagged rope's end swung to and fro on the idle breeze. I saw the empty oblong of the doorway, like a dark picture-frame, filled with moonlight. Some madness had seized my senses; there was nothing there.

I made no further investigations, but just turned on my heel and hurried away—not to say bolted—over the hillside, plunging through the thick trees, down to where nestled the old red manor-house of Barton Fitzroy.

It was late for a call, but the squire and Mrs. Vyell were kind enough to overlook the irregularity. It was explained that night had overtaken me rambling on the hillside; and when a glass of Madeira and a good cigar had tranquillised the nerves which, it must be owned, were somewhat jarred, and I felt pretty sure of being able to control the vocal chords, I said lightly:

"What a curiously solitary place is that little circular combe of which you told me!"

"Ah, you have been there!"

Pretty Mrs. Vyell was interested.

"More than once," I confessed, with eyes fixed upon my cigar.

"Did you happen to notice a ruined cottage on the brow of the hill?"

"Yes, I thought it the most lonely human habitation I have met with in England."

"It has never been inhabited since I remember," she said softly, gazing into the fire. "About thirty years ago there was a tragedy there."

"Will you tell me about it?"

"Francis knows more about it than I do," she said, with a glance at her husband. "He's a native of these parts, you see. Tell it, Francis. Mr. Rivers won't accuse a man of exaggeration; women have all the credit of a lively imagination."

The squire looked reminiscent for a few moments.

"There was a man in this village," he suddenly began, "when I was quite a youngster, named Israels. He was a miller's son, and they had Portuguese blood in them. Young Israels was a big, handsome fellow, but moody and restless, with the fever of the sea adventurer in his veins. He would have nothing to do with the mill, but was always a rover. When he was about thirty years old, he came home from a voyage, wooed Kitty Eusden, our local belle, and married her, under the very nose of Larking, a good, respectable fellow, to whom she was betrothed.

"Israels' marriage developed in him a new trait—a jealousy that was almost mania; he may have had more reasons for it than we knew of, but the fact is certain that the men of the village hardly dared pass the time of day with his wife, for fear of getting their teeth knocked down their throats.

"When they had been two or three years wed, the yearning to wander came upon him again. He was torn between the ever-growing restlessness and his fear of leaving his wife behind. So he set to work to build that cottage—far from the village—far from everything that might have helped her to bear her solitude; settled her in it, with provision of all he could think of for her comfort, and was off, leaving her, though this he did not know, within six months of becoming a mother for the first time.

"She was fond of him, and she was not a bad girl, not by any means, though shallow. Her conduct at first was exemplary, and had the baby lived I believe all might have gone well. But the baby died, and there came on the top of this desolation a period when she heard not a word from her absent husband. Her loneliness must have been hard to bear, and poor Larking used to go and see her.

"The place was so remote that nobody knew what was going on, until, when Israels had been two years absent, they went away together. A week after their departure the wanderer returned.

"He went up to the cottage, found it forsaken, and came down to the vicarage for information. All they could do was to show him his baby's grave in the churchyard, and tell him that his wife was gone. The vicar was a good man, but hard; he told Israels that he deserved his fate. The wretched creature went back to the deserted cottage on the hillside, and hanged himself in the doorway between the kitchen and the parlour.

There, a month later, his corpse was found by Larking, who had come back to get some things for Kitty.

"Of course no one would rent the cottage after that. It was lonely before; now were added all the horrors of superstition, and people have been actually known to declare that Israels still haunts the hillside. A shepherd told me seriously about fifteen years ago that his dog saw him, and bolted off some miles across the countryside, half mad with fear. These superstitions come of living too far from a railway: the inhabitants of these combes live, as one might say, some centuries behind the times."

What could I say after that? I could not own to what I had seen. The squire would have been quite polite about it, but from that moment he would have considered me an unreliable person. One must preserve one's character for veracity even at the expense of truth, concluded the Minor Poet sadly. Therefore I held my tongue; but for all that, I did see what I have told you, and I consider it the most curious experience of my life.

TWO DOCTORS

M. R. JAMES

IT IS A VERY COMMON THING, IN MY EXPERIENCE, TO FIND PAPERS SHUT UP IN OLD books; but one of the rarest things to come across any such that are at all interesting. Still it does happen, and one should never destroy them unlooked at. Now it was a practice of mine before the war occasionally to buy old ledgers of which the paper was good, and which possessed a good many blank leaves, and to extract these and use them for my own notes and writings. One such I purchased for a small sum in 1911. It was tightly clasped, and its boards were warped by having for years been obliged to embrace a number of extraneous sheets. Three-quarters of this inserted matter had lost all vestige of importance for any living human being: one bundle had not. That it belonged to a lawyer is certain, for it is endorsed: *The strangest case I have yet met*, and bears initials, and an address in Gray's Inn. It is only materials for a case, and consists of statements by possible witnesses. The man who would have been the defendant or prisoner seems never to have appeared. The *dossier* is not complete, but, such as it is, it furnishes a riddle in which the supernatural appears to play a part. You must see what you can make of it.

The following is the setting and the tale as I elicit it.

Dr. Abell was walking in his garden one afternoon waiting for his horse to be brought round that he might set out on his visits for the day. As the place was Islington, the month June, and the year 1718, we conceive the surroundings as being countrified and pleasant. To him entered his confidential servant, Luke Jennett, who had been with him twenty years.

"I said I wished to speak to him, and what I had to say might take some quarter of an hour. He accordingly bade me go into his study, which was a room opening on the terrace path where he was walking, and came in himself and sat down. I told him that, much against my will, I must look out for another place. He inquired what was my reason, in consideration I had been so long with him. I said if he would excuse me he would do me a great kindness, because (this appears to have been common form even in 1718) I was one that always liked to have everything pleasant about me. As well as I can remember, he said that was his case likewise, but he would wish to know why I should change my mind after so many years, and, says he, 'you know there can be no talk of a remembrance of you in my will if you leave my service now.' I said I had made my reckoning of that.

"'Then,' says he, 'you must have some complaint to make, and if I could I would willingly set it right.' And at that I told him, not seeing how I could keep it back, the matter of my former affidavit and of the bedstaff in the dispensing-room, and said that a house where such things happened was no place for me. At which he, looking very black upon me, said no more, but called me fool, and said he would pay what was owing me in the morning; and so, his horse being waiting, went out. So for that night I lodged with my sister's husband near Battle Bridge and came early next morning to my late master, who then made a great matter that I had not lain in his house and stopped a crown out of my wages owing.

"After that I took service here and there, not for long at a time, and saw no more of him till I came to be Dr. Quinn's man at Dodds Hall in Islington."

There is one very obscure part in this statement, namely, the reference to the former affidavit and the matter of the bedstaff. The former affidavit is not in the bundle of papers. It is to be feared that it was taken out to be read because of its special oddity, and not put back. Of what nature the story was may be guessed later, but as yet no clue has been put into our hands.

The Rector of Islington, Jonathan Pratt, is the next to step forward. He furnishes particulars of the standing and reputation of Dr. Abell and Dr. Quinn, both of whom lived and practised in his parish.

"It is not to be supposed," he says, "that a physician should be a regular attendant at morning and evening prayers, or at the Wednesday lectures, but within the measure of their ability I would say that both these persons fulfilled their obligations as loyal members of the Church of England. At the same time (as you desire my private mind) I must say, in the language of the schools, *distinguo*. Dr. A. was to me a source of perplexity, Dr. Q. to my eye a plain, honest believer, not inquiring over closely into points of belief, but squaring his practice to what lights he had. The other interested himself in questions to which Providence, as I hold, designs no answer to be given us in this state: he would ask me, for example, what place I believed those beings now to hold in the scheme of creation which by some are thought neither to have stood fast when the rebel angels fell, nor to have joined with them to the full pitch of their transgression.

"As was suitable, my first answer to him was a question, What warrant he had for supposing any such beings to exist? for that there was none in Scripture I took it he was aware. It appeared—for as I am on the subject, the whole tale may be given—that he grounded himself on such passages as that of the satyr which Jerome tells us conversed with Antony; but thought too that some parts of Scripture might be cited in support. 'And besides,' said he, 'you know 'tis the universal belief among those that spend their days and nights abroad, and I would add that if your calling took you so continuously as it does me about the country lanes by night, you might not be so surprised as I see you to be by my suggestion.' 'You are then of John Milton's mind,' I said, 'and hold that

> 'Millions of spiritual creatures walk the earth
> Unseen, both when we wake and when we sleep.'

"'I do not know,' he said, 'why Milton should take upon himself to say "unseen"; though to be sure he was blind when he wrote that. But for the rest, why, yes, I think he was in the right.' 'Well,' I said, 'though not so often as you, I am not seldom called abroad pretty late; but I have no mind of meeting a satyr in our Islington lanes in all the years I have been here; and if you have had the better luck, I am sure the Royal Society would be glad to know of it.'

"I am reminded of these trifling expressions because Dr. A. took them so ill, stamping out of the room in a huff with some such word as that these high and dry parsons had no eyes but for a prayerbook or a pint of wine.

"But this was not the only time that our conversation took a remarkable turn. There was an evening when he came in, at first seeming gay and in good spirits, but afterwards as he sat and smoked by the fire falling into a musing way; out of which to rouse him I said pleasantly that I supposed he had had no meetings of late with his odd friends. A question which did effectually arouse him, for he looked most wildly, and as if scared, upon me, and said, '*You* were never there? I did not see you. Who brought you?' And then in a more collected tone, 'What was this about a meeting? I believe I must have been in a doze.' To which I answered that I was thinking of fauns and centaurs in the dark lane, and not of a witches' Sabbath; but it seemed he took it differently.

"'Well,' said he, 'I can plead guilty to neither; but I find you very much more of a sceptic than becomes your cloth. If you care to know about the dark lane you might do worse than ask my housekeeper that lived at the other end of it when she was a child.' 'Yes,' said I, 'and the old women in the almshouse and the children in the kennel. If I were you, I would send to your brother Quinn for a bolus to clear your brain.' 'Damn Quinn,' says he; 'talk no more of him: he has embezzled four of my best patients this month; I believe it is that cursed man of his, Jennett, that used to be with me, his tongue is never still; it should be nailed to the pillory if he had his deserts.' This, I may say, was the only time of his showing me that he had any grudge against either Dr. Quinn or Jennett, and as was my business, I did my best to persuade him he was mistaken in them. Yet it could not be denied that some respectable families in the parish had given him the cold shoulder, and for no reason that they were willing to allege. The end was that he said he had not done so ill at Islington but that he could afford to live at ease elsewhere when he chose, and anyhow he bore Dr. Quinn no malice. I think I now remember what observation of mine drew him into the train of thought which he next pursued. It was, I believe, my mentioning some juggling tricks which my brother in the East Indies had seen at the court of the Rajah of Mysore. 'A convenient thing enough,' said Dr. Abell to me, 'if by some arrangement a man could get the power of communicating motion and energy to inanimate objects.' 'As if the axe should move itself against him that lifts it; something of that kind?' 'Well, I don't know that that was in my mind so much; but if you could summon such a volume from your shelf or even order it to open at the right page.'

"He was sitting by the fire—it was a cold evening—and stretched out his hand that way, and just then the fire-irons, or at least the poker, fell over towards him with a great clatter, and I did not hear what else he said. But I told him that I could not easily conceive of an arrangement, as he called it, of such a kind that would not include as one of its conditions a heavier payment than any Christian would care to make; to which he assented. 'But,' he said, 'I have no doubt these bargains can be made very tempting, very persuasive. Still, you would not favour them, eh, Doctor? No, I suppose not.'

"This is as much as I know of Dr. Abell's mind, and the feeling between these men. Dr. Quinn, as I said, was a plain, honest creature, and a man to whom I would have gone—indeed I have before now gone to him for advice on matters of business. He was, however, every now and again, and particularly of late, not exempt from troublesome fancies. There was certainly a time when he was so much harassed by his dreams that he could not keep them to himself, but would tell them to his acquaintances and among them to me. I was at supper at his house, and he was not inclined to let me leave him at my usual time. 'If you go,' he said, 'there will be nothing for it but I must go to bed and dream of the chrysalis.' 'You might be worse off,' said I. 'I do not think it,' he said, and he shook himself like a man who is displeased with the complexion of his thoughts. 'I only meant,' said I, 'that a chrysalis is an innocent thing.' 'This one is not,' he said, 'and I do not care to think of it.'

"However, sooner than lose my company he was fain to tell me (for I pressed him) that this was a dream which had come to him several times of late, and even more than once in a night. It was to this effect, that he seemed to himself to wake under an extreme compulsion to rise and go out of doors. So he would dress himself and go down to his garden door. By the door there stood a spade which he must take, and go out into the garden, and at a particular place in the shrubbery somewhat clear and upon which the moon shone, for there was always in his dream a full moon, he would feel himself forced to dig. And after some time the spade would uncover something light-coloured, which he would perceive to be a stuff, linen or woollen, and this he must clear with his hands. It was always the same: of the size of a man and shaped like the chrysalis of a moth, with the folds showing a promise of an opening at one end.

"He could not describe how gladly he would have left all at this stage and run to the house, but he must not escape so easily. So with many groans, and knowing only too well what to expect, he parted these folds of stuff, or, as it sometimes seemed to be, membrane, and disclosed a head covered with a smooth pink skin, which breaking as the creature stirred, showed him his own face in a state of death. The telling of this so much disturbed him that I was forced out of mere compassion to sit with him the greater part of the night and talk with him upon indifferent subjects. He said that upon every recurrence of this dream he woke and found himself, as it were, fighting for his breath."

Another extract from Luke Jennett's long continuous statement comes in at this point.

"I never told tales of my master, Dr. Abell, to anybody in the neighbourhood. When I was in another service I remember to have spoken to my fellow-servants about the matter of the bedstaff, but I am sure I never said either I or he were the persons concerned, and it met with so little credit that I was affronted and thought best to keep it to myself. And when I came back to Islington and found Dr. Abell still there, who I was told had left the parish, I was clear that it behoved me to use great discretion, for indeed I was afraid of the man, and it is certain I was no party to spreading any ill report of him. My master, Dr. Quinn, was a very just, honest man, and no maker of mischief. I am sure he never stirred a finger nor said a word by way of inducement to a soul to make them leave going to Dr. Abell and come to him; nay, he would hardly be persuaded to attend them that came, until he was convinced that if he did not they would send into the town for a physician rather than do as they had hitherto done.

"I believe it may be proved that Dr. Abell came into my master's house more than once. We had a new chambermaid out of Hertfordshire, and she asked me who was the gentleman that was looking after the master, that is Dr. Quinn, when he was out, and seemed so disappointed that he was out. She said whoever he was he knew the way of the house well, running at once into the study and then into the dispensing-room, and last into the bed-chamber. I made her tell me what he was like, and what she said was suitable enough to Dr. Abell; but besides she told me she saw the same man at church and some one told her that was the Doctor.

"It was just after this that my master began to have his bad nights, and complained to me and other persons, and in particular what discomfort he suffered from his pillow and bedclothes. He said he must buy some to suit him, and should do his own marketing. And accordingly brought home a parcel which he said was of the right quality, but where he bought it we had then no knowledge, only they were marked in thread with a coronet and a bird. The women said they were of a sort not commonly met with and very fine, and my master said they were the comfortablest he ever used, and he slept now both soft and deep. Also the feather pillows were the best sorted and his head would sink into them as if they were a cloud: which I have myself remarked several times when I came to wake him of a morning, his face being almost hid by the pillow closing over it.

"I had never any communication with Dr. Abell after I came back to Islington, but one day when he passed me in the street and asked me whether I was not looking for another service, to which I answered I was very well suited where I was, but he said I was a tickle-minded fellow and he doubted not he should soon hear I was on the world again, which indeed proved true."

Dr. Pratt is next taken up where he left off.

"On the 16th I was called up out of my bed soon after it was light—that is about five— with a message that Dr. Quinn was dead or dying. Making my way to his house I found there was no doubt which was the truth. All the persons in the house except the one that let me in were already in his chamber and standing about his bed, but none touching him. He was stretched in the midst of the bed, on his back, without any disorder, and indeed had the appearance of one ready laid out for burial. His hands, I think, were even crossed on his breast. The only thing not usual was that nothing was to be seen of his face, the two ends of the pillow or bolster appearing to be closed quite over it. These I immediately pulled apart, at the same time rebuking those present, and especially the man, for not at once coming to the assistance of his master. He, however, only looked at me and shook his head, having evidently no more hope than myself that there was anything but a corpse before us.

"Indeed it was plain to any one possessed of the least experience that he was not only dead, but had died of suffocation. Nor could it be conceived that his death was accidentally caused by the mere folding of the pillow over his face. How should he not, feeling the oppression, have lifted his hands to put it away? whereas not a fold of the sheet which was closely gathered about him, as I now observed, was disordered. The next thing was to procure a physician. I had bethought me of this on leaving my house, and sent on the messenger who had come to me to Dr. Abell; but I now heard that he was away from home, and the nearest surgeon was got, who however could tell no more, at least without opening the body, than we already knew.

"As to any person entering the room with evil purpose (which was the next point to be cleared), it was visible that the bolts of the door were burst from their stanchions, and the stanchions broken away from the door-post by main force; and there was a sufficient body of witness, the smith among them, to testify that this had been done but a few minutes before I came. The chamber being moreover at the top of the house, the window was neither easy of access nor did it show any sign of an exit made that way, either by marks upon the sill or footprints below upon soft mould."

The surgeon's evidence forms of course part of the report of the inquest, but since it has nothing but remarks upon the healthy state of the larger organs and the coagulation of blood in various parts of the body, it need not be reproduced. The verdict was "Death by the visitation of God."

Annexed to the other papers is one which I was at first inclined to suppose had made its way among them by mistake. Upon further consideration I think I can divine a reason for its presence.

It relates to the rifling of a mausoleum in Middlesex which stood in a park (now broken up), the property of a noble family which I will not name. The outrage was not that of an ordinary resurrection man. The object, it seemed likely, was theft. The account is blunt and terrible. I shall not quote it. A dealer in the North of London suffered heavy penalties as a receiver of stolen goods in connexion with the affair.

The Vampire

Jan Neruda

THE EXCURSION STEAMER HAD BROUGHT US FROM CONSTANTINOPLE TO THE SHORE of the island Prinkipo, and we disembarked. There were not many in the party. A Polish family, father, mother, daughter, and the daughter's husband, then we two. And I must not forget to mention that we had been joined on the wooden bridge leading across the Golden Horn in Constantinople by a Greek, quite a young man; a painter perhaps, to judge by the portfolio which he carried under his arm. Long black tresses flowed over his shoulders, his face was pale, his dark eyes deeply sunken in their sockets. At first he interested me, especially because of his readiness to oblige and his familiarity with local affairs. But he had a good deal too much to say, and I soon turned away from him.

I found the Polish family all the more pleasant. The father and mother were worthy, kindly folk, the husband an elegant young man of unassuming and polished manners. They were travelling to Prinkipo, with the object of spending the summer months there for the sake of the daughter, who was slightly ailing. From the pallor of the beautiful girl it appeared either that she was just recovering from a severe illness, or that she was about to be attacked by one. She leaned upon her husband, showed a fondness for sitting down, and a frequent, dry cough interrupted her whispering. Whenever she coughed, her escort stood still in concern. He kept looking at her pityingly, and she at him, as much as to say: "There is really nothing the matter,— how happy I am!" They were clearly convinced of recovery and happiness.

On the recommendation of the Greek, who had left us immediately by the landing stage, the family had hired a lodging at the inn which stands on the hill. The inn-keeper was a Frenchman, and his whole house, in accordance with French style, was arranged comfortably and neatly.

We lunched together, and when the heat of noon had abated a little, we all made our way up the hill to a pine-grove where we could refresh ourselves with the view. Scarcely had we discovered a suitable spot and had settled down, than the Greek once more made his appearance. He greeted us in an off-hand way, looked around him, and sat down only a few paces from us. He opened his portfolio and began to draw.

"I believe he has purposely sat close against the rock so that we can't look at his drawing," I said.

"We need not look," observed the young Pole, "we can see quite enough in front of us." And after a while he added: "It seems to me that he is including us in the fore-ground of his drawing,—let him!"

Truly, there was enough for us to see. There is no fairer and happier nook in the world than this Prinkipo. The political female martyr, Irene, a contemporary of Charlemagne, spent a month there "in banishment"—if I could pass a single month of my life there, the memory of it would make me happy for all the remainder of my days. Even that single day I spent there I shall never forget.

The air was as clear as diamond, so soft, so delightful, that it lapped all one's soul afar. On the right, beyond the sea, towered the brown summits of Asia, on the left, the steep shore of Europe faded into the bluish distance. Close by, Chalki, one of the nine islands that form the "archipelago of the prince," rose up with its cypress woods into the silent height like a mournful dream, crowned with a large building,—this, a refuge for the infirm of spirit.

The waters of the Sea of Marmora were only slightly ruffled, and played in all colours like a sparkling opal. In the distance was the ocean, white as milk, then rose-tinted, then between two islands like a glowing orange, and beneath us of a beautiful greenish-blue like a transparent sapphire. It was alone in its beauty; no large vessels were to be seen. Only two small craft with English flags were slipping along hard by the shore. One was a steam-boat, the size of a watchman's booth, the other was manned by about twelve rowers, and when all their oars were lifted at the same time, it was as if molten silver were trickling from them. Artless dolphins were moving in their midst, and flew in long curves above the surface of the water. From time to time across the blue sky peaceful eagles soared, measuring out a boundary between two portions of the world.

The whole slope beneath us was hidden by blossoming roses, with whose fragrance the air was saturated. From the café near the sea, music, muffled by the distance, vibrated through the stainless air.

The impression was overwhelming. We all grew silent and sated our whole being with the prospect which savoured of paradise. The young Polish lady was lying on the turf with her head resting in her husband's lap. The pale oval of her delicate face gained a slight colour and tears suddenly began to flow from her blue eyes. Her husband understood; he bent forward and kissed tear upon tear. Her mother also began to shed tears, and I myself was strangely moved.

"Mind and body must needs be healed here," whispered the girl. "What a happy place!"

"God knows, I have no enemies, but if I had, here I would forgive them!" declared the father with trembling voice.

And again all were silent. A feeling of beauty, of inexpressible sweetness, came upon all. Each one felt within him a whole world of happiness, and each one would have shared his happiness with the whole world. Each one felt the same, and so none jarred upon the other. We did not even notice that the Greek, after some hour or so, had arisen, closed his portfolio, and after greeting us again, had gently departed. We remained.

Finally, after some hours, when the distance was hiding itself in a dusky violet hue, which in the South is so magically lovely, the mother urged us to make our way back. We arose and strolled down to the inn, our steps as free and elastic as those of children without a care in the world.

Scarcely had we sat down than we heard quarrelling and abuse under the veranda. Our Greek was quarrelling there with the inn-keeper and we listened for our amusement.

The quarrel did not last long. "If I had no other guests here—" growled the inn-keeper, and came up the steps towards us.

"Would you kindly tell me, sir," asked the young Pole of the inn-keeper, as he came along, "who this gentleman is, and what his name is?"

"Oh, who knows what the fellow's name is," growled the inn-keeper, giving a vicious glance downwards. "We call him the Vampire."

"A painter?"

"A fine trade! He only paints corpses. If anybody in Constantinople or round about here dies, he always has a portrait of the corpse ready on the same day. The fellow paints in advance, and he never makes a mistake, the vulture."

The old Polish lady gave a cry of horror,—in her arms lay the daughter, swooning, white as a sheet.

And at the same instant the husband leaped down the small flight of steps, seized the Greek by the throat with one hand, and with the other clutched at the portfolio.

We quickly ran down after him. The two men were already scuffling in the sand.

The portfolio was flung down, and on one leaf, sketched in pencil, was the head of the young Polish girl,—her eyes closed, a sprig of myrtle around her brow.

THE VILLA DÉSIRÉE

MAY SINCLAIR

I

He had arranged it all for her. She was to stay a week in Cannes with her aunt, and then to go on to Roquebrune by herself, and he was to follow her there. She, Mildred Eve, supposed he could follow her anywhere, since they were engaged now.

There had been difficulties, but Louis Carson had got over all of them by lending her the Villa Désirée. She would be all right there, he said. The caretakers, Narcisse and Armandine, would look after her—Armandine was an excellent cook—and she wouldn't be five hundred yards from her friends, the Derings. It was so like him to think of it, to plan it all out for her. And when he came down? Oh, when he came down he would go to the Cap Martin Hotel, of course.

He understood everything without any tiresome explaining. She couldn't afford the hotels at Cap Martin and Monte Carlo; and though the Derings had asked her to stay with them, she really couldn't dump herself down on them like that, almost in the middle of their honeymoon.

Their honeymoon—she could have bitten her tongue out for saying it, for not remembering. It was awful of her to go talking to Louis Carson about honeymoons, after the appalling tragedy of *his*.

There were things she hadn't been told, that she hadn't liked to ask: Where it had happened? And how? And how long ago? She only knew it was on his wedding night, that he had gone in to the poor little girl of a bride and found her dead there, in the bed.

They say she had died in a sort of a fit.

You had only to look at him to see that something terrible had happened to him at some time. You saw it when his face was doing nothing: a queer, agonised look that made it strange to her while it lasted. It was more than suffering; it was almost as if he could be cruel, only he never was, he never could be. *People* were cruel, if you liked; they said it put them off. Mildred could see what they meant. It might have put *her* off, perhaps, if she hadn't known what he had gone through. But the first time she had met him he had been pointed out to her as the man to whom just that appalling thing had happened. So far from putting her off that was what had drawn her to him from the beginning, made her pity him first, then love him. Their engagement had come quickly, in the third week of their acquaintance.

When she asked herself: "After all, what do I know about him," she had her answer, "I know *that*." She felt that already she had entered into a mystical union with him through compassion. She *liked* the strangeness that kept other people away and left him to her altogether. He was more her own that way.

There was (Mildred Eve didn't deny it) his personal magic, the fascination of his almost abnormal beauty. His black, white, and blue. The intensely blue eyes under the straight black bars of the eyebrows, the perfect, pure, white face suddenly masked by the black moustache and small, black, pointed beard. And the rich, vivid smile he had for her, the lighting up of the blue, the flash of white teeth in the black mask.

He had smiled then at her embarrassment as the awful words leaped out at him. He had taken it from her and turned the sharp edge of it.

"It would never do," he had said, "to spoil the *honeymoon*. You'd much better have my villa. Some day, quite soon, it'll be yours too. You know I like anticipating things."

That was always the excuse he made for his generosities. He had said it again when he engaged her seat in the *train de luxe* from Paris and wouldn't let her pay for it. (She had wanted to travel third class.) He was only anticipating, he said.

He was seeing her off now at the Gare de Lyons, standing on the platform with a great sheaf of blush roses in his arms. She, on the high step of the railway carriage, stood above him, swinging in the open doorway. His face was on a level with her feet; they gleamed white through the fine black stockings. Suddenly he thrust his face forwards and kissed her feet. As the train moved he ran beside it and tossed the roses into her lap.

And then she sat in the hurrying train, holding the great sheaf of blush roses in her lap, and smiling at them as she dreamed. She was on the Riviera Express; the Riviera Express. Next week she would be in Roquebrune, at the Villa Désirée. She read the three letters woven into the edges of the grey cloth cushions: P.L.M.: Paris-Lyons-Méditerranée, Paris-Lyons-Méditerranée, over and over again. They sang themselves to the rhythm of the wheels; they wove their pattern into her dream. Every now and then, when the other passengers weren't looking, she lifted the roses to her face and kissed them.

She hardly knew how she dragged herself through the long dull week with her aunt at Cannes.

And now it was over and she was by herself at Roquebrune.

The steep narrow lane went past the Derings' house and up the face of the hill. It led up into a little olive wood, and above the wood she saw the garden terraces. The sunlight beat in and out of their golden yellow walls. Tier above tier, the blazing terraces rose, holding up their ranks of spindle-stemmed lemon and orange trees. On the topmost terrace the Villa Désirée stood white and hushed between two palms, two tall poles each topped by a head of dark-green curving, sharp-pointed blades. A grey scrub of olive-trees straggled up the hill behind it and on each side.

Rolf and Martha Dering waited for her with Narcisse and Armandine on the steps of the veranda.

"Why on earth didn't you come to us?" they said.

"I didn't want to spoil your honeymoon."

"Honeymoon, what rot! We've got over that silliness. Anyhow, it's our third week of it."

They were detached and cool in their happiness.

She went in with them, led by Narcisse and Armandine. The caretakers, subservient to Mildred Eve and visibly inimical to the Derings, left them together in the *salon*. It was very bright and French and fragile and worn, all faded grey and old, greenish gilt; the gilt chairs and settees carved like picture frames round the gilded cane. The hot light beat in through the long windows open to the terrace, drawing up a faint powdery smell from the old floor.

Rolf Dering stared at the room, sniffing, with fine nostrils in a sort of bleak disgust.

"You'd much better have come to us," he said.

"Oh, but, —it's charming."

"Do you *think* so?" Martha said. She was looking at her intently.

Mildred saw that they expected her to feel something, she wasn't sure what, something that they felt. They were subtle and fastidious.

"It does look a little queer and—unlived in," she said, straining for the precise impression.

"I should say," said Martha, "it had been too much lived in, if you ask me."

"Oh, no. That's only dust you smell. I think, perhaps, the windows haven't been open very long."

She resented this criticism of Louis' villa.

Armandine appeared at the doorway. Her little slant, Chinesy eyes were screwed up and smiling. She wanted to know if Madame wouldn't like to go up and look at her room.

"We'll all go up and look at it," said Rolf.

They followed Armandine up the steep, slender, curling staircase. A closed door faced them on the landing. Armandine opened it, and the hot golden light streamed out to them again.

The room was all golden white; it was like a great white tank filled with blond water where things shimmered, submerged in the stream; the white-painted chairs and dressing-table, the high white-painted bed, the pink-and-white striped ottoman at its foot; all vivid and still, yet quivering in the stillness, with the hot throb, throb of the light.

"*Voilà*, Madame," said Armandine.

They didn't answer. They stood, fixed in the room, held by the stillness, staring, all three of them, at the high white bed that rose up, enormous, with its piled mattresses and pillows, the long white counterpane hanging straight and steep, like a curtain, to the floor.

Rolf turned to Armandine.

"Why have you given Madame this room?"

Armandine shrugged her fat shoulders. Her small Chinesy eyes blinked at him, slanting, inimical.

"Monsieur's orders, Monsieur. It is the best room in the house. It was Madame's room."

"I know. That's *why*—"

"But no, Monsieur. Nobody would dislike to sleep in Madame's room. The poor little thing, she was so pretty, so sweet, so young, Monsieur. Surely Madame will not dislike the room."

"Who *was*—Madame?"

"But, Monsieur's wife, Madame. Madame Carson. Poor Monsieur, it was so sad—"

"Rolf," said Mildred, "did he bring her here—on their honeymoon?"

"Yes."

"Yes, Madame. She died here. It was so sad. Is there anything I can do for Madame?"

"No, thank you, Armandine."

"Then I will get ready the tea."

She turned again in the doorway, crooning in her thick, Provençal voice. "*Madame* does not dislike her room?"

"No, Armandine. No. It's a beautiful room."

The door closed on Armandine. Martha opened it again to see whether she was listening on the landing. Then she broke out.

"Mildred—you know you loathe it. It's beastly. The whole place is beastly."

"You can't stay in it," said Rolf.

"Why not? Do you mean, because of Madame?"

Martha and Rolf were looking at each other, as if they were both asking what they should say. They said nothing.

"Oh, her poor little ghost won't hurt me, if that's what you mean."

"Nonsense," Martha said. "Of course it isn't."

"What is it, then?"

"It's so beastly lonely, Mildred," said Rolf.

"Not with Narcisse and Armandine."

"Well, I wouldn't sleep a night in the place," Martha said, "if there wasn't any other on the Riviera. I don't like the look of it."

Mildred went to the open lattice, turning her back on the high, rather frightening bed. Down there below the terraces she saw the grey flicker of the olive woods and, beyond them, the sea. Martha was wrong. The place was beautiful; it was adorable. She wasn't going to be afraid of poor little Madame. Louis had loved her. He loved the place. That was why he had lent it to her.

She turned. Rolf had gone down again. She was alone with Martha. Martha was saying something.

"Mildred—where's Mr. Carson?"

"In Paris. Why?"

"I thought he was coming here."

"So he is, later on."

"To the villa?"

"No. Of course not. To Cap Martin." She laughed. "So *that's* what you're thinking of, is it?"

She could understand her friend's fear of haunted houses, but not these previsions of impropriety.

Martha looked shy and ashamed.

"Yes," she said. "I suppose so."

"How horrid of you! You might have trusted me."

"I do trust you." Martha held her a minute with her clear, loving eyes. "Are you sure you can trust *him*?"

"Trust him? Do *you* trust Rolf?"

"Ah—if it was like that, Mildred—"

"It *is* like that."

"You're really not afraid?"

"What is there to be afraid of? Poor little Madame?"

"I didn't mean Madame. I meant Monsieur."

"Oh—wait till you've seen him."

"Is he *very* beautiful?"

"Yes. But it isn't *that*, Martha. I can't tell you what it is."

They went downstairs, hand in hand, in the streaming light. Rolf waited for them on the verandah. They were taking Mildred back to dine with them.

"Won't you let me tell Armandine you're stopping the night?" he said.

"No, I won't. I don't want Armandine to think I'm frightened."

She meant she didn't want Louis to think she was frightened. Besides, she was not frightened.

"Well, if you find you don't like it, you must come to us," he said.

And they showed her the little spare room next to theirs with its camp-bed made up, the bed-clothes turned back, all ready for her, any time of the night, in case she changed her mind. The front door was on the latch.

"You've only to open it, and creep in here and be safe," Rolf said.

II

Armandine—subservient and no longer inimical, now that the Derings were not there—Armandine had put the candle and matches on the night-table and the bell which, she said, would summon her if Madame wanted anything in the night. And she had left her.

As the door closed softly behind Armandine, Mildred drew in her breath with a light gasp. Her face in the looking-glass, between the tall lighted candles, showed its mouth half open, and she was aware that her heart shook slightly in its beating. She was angry with the face in the glass with its foolish mouth gaping. She said to herself, Is it possible I'm frightened? It was not possible. Rolf and Martha had made her walk too fast up the hill, that was all. Her heart always did that when she walked too fast up hill, and she supposed that her mouth always gaped when it did it.

She clenched her teeth and let her heart choke her till it stopped shaking.

She was quiet now. But the test would come when she had blown out the candles and had to cross the room in the dark to the bed.

The flame bent backwards before the light puff she gave, and righted itself. She blew harder, twice, with a sense of spinning out the time. The flame writhed and went out. She extinguished the other candle at one breath. The red point of the wick pricked the darkness for a second and died, too, with a small crackling sound. At the far end of the room the high bed glimmered. She thought: Martha was right. The bed *is* awful.

She could feel her mouth set in a hard grin of defiance as she went to it, slowly, too proud to be frightened. And then suddenly, half way, she thought about Madame.

The awful thing was, climbing into that high funeral bed that Madame had died in. Your back felt so undefended. But once she was safe between the bedclothes it would be all right. It would be all right so long as she didn't think about Madame. Very well, then, she wouldn't think about her. You could frighten yourself into anything by thinking.

Deliberately, by an intense effort of her will, she turned the sad image of Madame out of her mind and found herself thinking about Louis Carson.

This was Louis' house, the place he used to come to when he wanted to be happy. She made out that he had sent her there because he wanted to be happy in it again. She was there to drive away the unhappiness, the memory of poor little Madame. Or, perhaps, because the place was sacred to him; because they were both so sacred, she and the young dead bride who hadn't been his wife. Perhaps he didn't think about her as dead at all; he didn't want her to be driven away. The room she had died in was not awful to him. He had the faithfulness for which death doesn't exist. She wouldn't have loved him if he hadn't been faithful. You could be faithful and yet marry again.

She was convinced that whatever she was there for, it was for some beautiful reason. Anything that Louis did, anything he thought or felt or wanted, would be beautiful. She thought of Louis standing on the platform in the Paris station, his beautiful face looking up at her; its sudden darting forward to kiss her feet. She drifted again into her happy, hypnotising dream, and was fast asleep before midnight.

She woke with a sense of intolerable compulsion, as if she were being dragged violently up out of her sleep. The room was grey in the twilight of the unrisen moon.

And she was not alone.

She knew that there was something there. Something that gave up the secret of the room and made it frightful and obscene. The greyness was frightful and obscene. It shut her in gathered itself together; it was became the containing shell of the horror.

The thing that had waked her was there with her in the room.

For she knew she was awake. Apart from her supernatural certainty, one physical sense, detached from the horror, was alert. It heard the ticking of the clock on the chimney-piece, the hard, sharp shirring of the palm-leaves outside, as the wind rubbed their knife-blades together. These sounds were witnesses to the fact that she was awake, and that therefore the thing that was going to happen would be real. At the first sight of the greyness she had shut her eyes again, afraid to look into the room, because she knew that what she would see there was real. But she had no more power over her eyelids than she had had over her sleep. They opened under the same intolerable compulsion. And the supernatural thing forced itself now on her sight.

It stood a little in front of her by the bedside. From the breasts downwards its body was unfinished, rudimentary, not quite born. The grey shell was still pregnant with its loathsome shapelessness. But the face—the face was perfect in absolute horror. And it was Louis Carson's face.

Between the black bars of the eyebrows and the black pointed beard she saw it, drawn back, distorted in an obscene agony, corrupt and malignant. The face and the body, flesh and yet not flesh, they were the essence made manifest of untold, unearthly abominations.

It came on to her, bending over her, peering at her, so close that the piled mattresses now hid the lower half of its body. And the frightful thing about it was that it was blind, parted from all controlling and absolving clarity, flesh and yet not flesh. It looked for her without seeing her; and she knew that unless she could save herself that instant, it would find what it looked for. Even now, behind the barrier of the piled-up mattresses, the unfinished form defined and completed itself; she could feel it shake with the agitation of its birth.

Her heart staggered and stopped in her breast, as if her breast had been clamped down on to her backbone. She struggled against wave after wave of faintness; for the moment that she lost consciousness the appalling presence there would have its way with her. All her will rose up against it. She dragged herself upright in the bed suddenly and spoke to it.

"Louis! What are you doing there?"

At her cry it went, without moving; sucked, back into the greyness that had borne it. She thought: "It'll come back. Even if I don't see it I shall know it's in the room."

She knew what she would do. She would get up and go to the Derings. She longed for the open air, for Rolf and Martha, for the strong earth under her feet.

She lit the candle on the night-table and got up. She still felt that It was there, and that standing up on the floor she was more vulnerable, more exposed to it. Her terror was too extreme for her to stay and dress herself. She thrust her bare feet into her shoes, slipped her travelling coat over her nightgown and went downstairs and out through the house door, sliding back the bolts without a sound. She remembered that Rolf had left a lantern for her in the verandah, in case she should want it—as if they had known.

She lit the lantern and made her way down the villa garden, stumbling from terrace to terrace, through the olive wood and the steep lane to the Derings' house. Far down the hill she could see a light in the window of the spare room. The house door was on the latch. She went through and on into the lamp-lit room that waited for her.

She knew again what she would do. She would go away before Louis Carson could come to her. She would go away to-morrow, and never come back again. Rolf and Martha would bring her things down from the villa; he would take her into Italy in his car. She would get away from Louis Carson for ever. She would get away up through Italy.

III

Rolf had come back from the villa with her things and he had brought her a letter. It had been sent up that morning from Cap Martin.

It was from Louis Carson.

> MY DARLING MILDRED:
>
> You see I couldn't wait a fortnight without seeing you. I had to come. I'm here at the Cap Martin Hotel.
>
> I'll be with you some time between half-past ten and eleven—

Below, at the bottom of the lane, Rolf's car waited. It was half-past ten. If they went now they would meet Carson coming up the lane. They must wait till he had passed the house and gone up through the olive wood.

Martha had brought hot coffee and rolls. They sat down at the other side of the table and looked at her with kind, anxious eyes as she turned sideways, watching the lane.

"Rolf," she said suddenly, "do you know anything about Louis Carson?"

She could see them looking now at each other.

"Nothing. Only the things the people here say."

"What sort of things?"

"Don't tell her, Rolf."

"Yes. He *must* tell me. I've got to know."

She had no feeling left but horror, horror that nothing could intensify.

"There's not much. Except that he was always having women with him up there. Not particularly nice women. He seems," Rolf said, "to have been rather an appalling beast."

"Must have been," said Martha, "to have brought his poor little wife there, after—"

"Rolf, what did Mrs. Carson die of?"

"Don't ask *me*," he said.

But Martha answered. "She died of fright. She saw something. I told you the place was beastly."

Rolf shrugged his shoulders.

"Why, you said you felt it yourself. We both felt it."

"Because we knew about the beastly things he did there."

"*She* didn't know. I tell you, she saw something."

Mildred turned her white face to them.

"I saw it too."

"You?"

"What? What did you see?"

"Him. Louis Carson."

"He must be dead, then, if you saw his ghost."

"The ghosts of poor dead people don't kill you. It was what he *is*. All that beastliness in a face. A face."

She could hear them draw in their breath short and sharp. "Where?"

"There. In that room. Close by the bed. It was looking for me. I saw what *she* saw."

She could see them frown now, incredulous, forcing themselves to disbelieve. She could hear them talking, their voices beating off the horror.

"Oh, but she couldn't. He wasn't there."

"He heard her scream first."

"Yes. He was in the other room, you know."

"*It* wasn't. He can't keep it back."

"Keep it back?"

"No. He was waiting to go to her."

Her voice was dull and heavy with realisation. She felt herself struggling, helpless, against their stolidity, their unbelief.

"Look at that," she said. She pushed Carson's letter across to them.

"He was waiting to go to her," she repeated. "And—last night—he was waiting to come to me."

They stared at her, stupefied.

"Oh, can't you *see*?" she cried. "It didn't wait. It got there before him."

THE VOICE IN THE NIGHT

WILLIAM J. WINTLE

JOHN BARRON WAS FRANKLY PUZZLED. HE COULD NOT MAKE IT OUT AT ALL. HE HAD lived in the place all his life—save for the few years spent at Rugby and Oxford—and nothing of the sort had happened to him before. His people had occupied the estate for generations past; and there was neither record nor tradition of anything of the kind. He did not like it at all. It seemed like an intrusion upon the respectability of his family. And John Barron had a very good opinion of his family.

Certainly he was entitled to have a good opinion of it. He came from a good stock; his ancestry was one to be proud of; his coat of arms had quarterings that few could display; and his immediate forbears had kept up the reputation of their ancestors. He himself could boast a career without reproach: the short time he had spent at the bar was marked by considerable success and still more promise—a promise cut short by the death of his father and his recall to Bannerton to take up the duties of squire, magistrate, and county magnate.

In the eyes of his friends and of people generally, he was a man to be envied. He had an ample fortune, a delightful house and estate, hosts of friends, and the best of health. What could a man wish for more? The ladies of the neighbourhood said that he lacked only one thing, and that was a wife. But it may be that they were not entirely unprejudiced judges—the unmarried ones, at any rate. But up till the time of our story John Barron had shown no sign of marrying. He used to boast that he was neither married, nor engaged, nor courting, nor had he his eye on anyone.

And now this annoyance had come to trouble and puzzle him! What had he done to deserve it? True, he might take the comfort to his soul that it was no immediate concern of his. The affair had not happened to any member of his family or household. Why then should he not mind his own business? But he felt that it was his business. It had happened within the bounds of his manor and almost within sight of his windows. If anything tangible could be connected with it, he was the magistrate whose duty it would be to investigate the matter. But up till the present there was nothing tangible for him to deal with.

The whole business was a mystery: and John Barron disapproved of mysteries. Mysteries savoured of detectives and the police court. When unravelled they usually proved to be sordid and undesirable; and when not unravelled they brought with them a vague sense of discomfort and of danger. As a lawyer he held that mysteries had no right to exist. That they should continue to exist was a sort of reflection on the profession, as well as upon the public intelligence.

And yet here was the parish of Bannerton in the hands of a mystery of the first water. As a magistrate, John Barron had officially looked into the matter; and, as a lawyer, he had spent some hours in carefully considering it; but entirely without any practical result. The mystery was not merely unsolved: it had even thickened!

This was the history with which he was faced. A fortnight before, the occupants of a cottage on the outskirts of the village—a gardener and his wife—had left their little daughter of three years old in the house while they went on an errand. The child was soundly asleep in its cot; and they locked the door as they went out. They were absent about twenty minutes; and were nearing the house when they heard the screams of a child. The father rushed forward, unlocked the door, and the two parents entered together.

The child's cot was in the living room into which the front door opened. As they went in, the screams ceased and a terrible gasping sound took their place. Then they saw that the cot was hidden by some dark body that seemed to be lying on it. This they hardly saw, though they were quite clear that it was there, for it seemed to melt away like a mist when they rushed into the room. Certainly it was nothing solid, for it completely disappeared without a sound. It could not have dashed out through the door, for the parents were hardly clear of the door when it vanished.

They had returned only just in time to save the life of the child. At first it was doubtful if they were in time, for the doctor held out little hope. But after a day or two, the child took a turn for the better, and was now out of danger. It had evidently been attacked by some kind of savage animal, which had torn at its throat and had only just failed to sever the arteries of the neck. In the opinion of the doctor and of John Barron himself, the wounds suggested that the assailant had been a very large dog. But it was strange that a dog of such size had not done far worse damage. One might have expected that it would have killed the child with a single bite.

But was it a dog? If so, how did it enter the house? The door in front was locked, as we have seen; that at the back was bolted; and all the windows were shut and fastened. There was no apparent way by which it could possibly have got into the house. And we have already seen that its way of going was equally mysterious.

The most careful examination of the room and of the premises generally failed to yield the smallest clue. Nothing had been disturbed or damaged, and there were no footprints. The only thing at all unusual was the presence of an earthy or mouldy odour which was noticed by the doctor when he entered the room and also by some other persons who were on the scene soon afterwards. John Barron had the same impression when he went to the cottage some hours later, but the odour was then so faint that he could not be at all sure about its existence.

By way of embroidery to the story came two or three items of local gossip of the usual sort. An old woman nearby said that she was looking out of her window to see the state of the weather a little earlier in the evening, when she saw a huge black dog run across the lane and go in the direction of the cottage. According to her tale, the dog limped as if lame or very much tired.

Three people said they had been disturbed for two or three nights previous by the howling of a dog in the distance; and a farmer in the parish complained that his sheep had apparently been chased about the field during the night by some wandering dog. He loudly vowed vengeance on dogs in general; but, as none of the sheep had been worried, nobody took much notice. All these tales came to the ears of John Barron; but to a man accustomed to weigh evidence they were negligible.

But he attached much more importance to another piece of evidence, if such it might be called. As the injured child began to get better, and was able to talk, an attempt was made to find out if it could give any information about the attack. As it had been asleep when attacked, it did not see the arrival of its assailant; and the only thing it could tell was, "Nasty, ugly lady bit me!" This seemed absurd; but, when asked about the dog, it persisted in saying, "No dog. Nasty ugly lady!"

The parents were inclined to laugh at what they thought a mere childish fancy; but the trained lawyer was considerably impressed by it. To him there were three facts available. The wounds seemed to have been caused by a large dog; the child said she had been bitten by an ugly lady; and the parents had actually seen the form of the assailant. Unfortunately it had disappeared before they could make out any details; but they said it was about the size of a very large dog, and was dark in colour.

The local gossip was of small importance and was such as might be expected under the circumstances. But, for what it was worth, it all pointed to a dog or dog-like animal. But how could it have entered the closed house; how did it get away; and why did the child persist in her story of an ugly lady? The only theory that would at all fit the case was that supplied by the old Norse legends of the werewolf. But who believes such stories now?

So it was not to be wondered at that John Barron was puzzled. He was rather annoyed too. Bannerton had its average amount of crime; but it was in a small way and could generally be disposed of at the petty sessions. It was not often that a case had to be sent to the assizes, and the newspapers seldom got any sensational copy from the quiet little place. He reflected with some small satisfaction that it was lucky the child had not died; for in that case there must have been an inquest and the inevitable publicity. If his suspicions were well founded, the case would have yielded something far more sensational than generally falls to the lot of the local reporter.

But a day or two later he had more to ponder over. Things had developed—and in a way that he did not like. The farmer had again complained that his sheep had been chased about the field during the night; and this time more damage had been done. Two of the sheep had died; but the strange thing was that they had hardly been bitten at all. Their wounds were so slight that their death could only be attributed to fright and exhaustion. It was very curious that the dog—if dog it was—had not mauled them worse and made a meal of them. The suggestion that it was some very small dog was negatived by the fact that what wounds there were must have been made by a large animal. It really looked as if the animal had not sufficient strength to finish its evil work.

But John Barron had another item of evidence which he was keeping to himself for the present. During each of the two past nights he had woke up without any apparent reason soon after midnight. And each time he had heard the Cry in the Night. It was a voice borne on the night air which he never expected to hear in England; and least of all in Bannerton. The voice came from the moor that stood above the little hamlet; and it rose and fell on the silence like the cry of a spirit in distress. It began with a low wail of unspeakable sadness; then rose and fell in lamentable ululations; and then died away into sobs and silence.

The voice came at intervals for more than an hour: and the second night it was stronger and seemed nearer than the first. John Barron had no difficulty in recognising that long-drawn cry. He had heard it before when travelling in the wilder parts of Russia. It was the howling of a wolf!

But there are no wolves in England. True, it might have been an escaped animal from some travelling menagerie; but such an animal would have made worse havoc of the sheep. And if this was the assailant of the little child, how did it get in; how did it get away; and why did the child still persist in saying that it was not a dog but a lady who bit her?

The next few days saw the plot thicken. Other people heard the voice in the night, and put it down to a stray dog out on the moor. Another farmer's sheep were worried, and this time one of them was partly eaten. So a chase was arranged, and all the local farmers and many other people banded together to hunt the sheep-killer. For two days the moor was scoured, and the adjacent woods thoroughly beaten, but without coming across any signs of the miscreant.

But John Barron heard a story from one of the farmers that set him thinking. He noticed that this man seemed to avoid a little thicket beside the moor, suggesting that there was a better path at some distance from it; and after some pressing he explained the real reason for this. But he was careful to add that of course he was not himself superstitious, but his wife had queer notions and had begged him to avoid the place.

It seemed that not long before, some wandering gipsies who from time to time camped on the moor, had secretly buried an old woman in the thicket and had never returned to the moor since. Of course there were the inevitable additions to a tale of this sort. The old lady was alleged to have been the queen of the gipsy tribe; and she was also said to have been a witch of the most malignant kind; and these were supposed to have been the reasons for her secret burial in this lonely spot. It did not seem to occur to the farmer that the gipsies thus saved the expense of a regular funeral. Very few people knew the story, and they thought it well to hold their peace. It was not worth while to make enemies of the gipsies, who could so easily have their revenge by robbing hen-roosts or even by driving cattle; to say nothing of the more mysterious doings with which they were credited.

John Barron began to put things together. The whole business had a distinct resemblance to the tales of the werewolf in the Scandinavian literature of the Middle Ages. Here we had a woman of suspicious reputation buried in a lonely place without Christian rites; and soon afterwards a mysterious wolf roams the district in search of blood—just like the werewolf. But who believed such stories now, except a few ghost-ridden cranks with shattered nerves and unbalanced minds? The whole thing was absurd.

Still, the mystery had to be cleared up; for John Barron had not the slightest intention of letting it simply slide into the refuse heap of unsolved problems. He kept his own counsel; but he meant to get to the bottom of it. Perhaps if he had realised the horror that lay at the bottom of it, he would have let it alone.

In the meantime the farmers had taken their own steps to deal with the sheep-worrying nuisance. Tempting morsels, judiciously seasoned with poison, were laid about; but with the sole result of causing the untimely death of a valued sheep-dog. Night after night the younger men, armed with guns, sat up and watched; but without success. Nothing happened, the sheep were undisturbed, and it really seemed as if the invader had left the neighbourhood. But John Barron knew that once a dog had taken to worrying sheep, it can never be cured. If the mysterious visitor was a dog, he would most certainly return if still alive and able to travel: if it was not a dog—well, anything might happen. So he continued to watch even after the general hunt for the dog had ceased.

Soon he had his reward. One very dark and stormy night, he again heard the distant voice in the night. It came very faintly rising and falling on the air, for the breeze was strong and the sound had to travel against the wind. Then he left the house, carrying his gun, and took up his post on rising ground that commanded the road that led from the moor.

Presently the cry came nearer, and then nearer still, till it was evident that the wolf had left the moor and was approaching the farms. Several dogs barked; but they were not the barks of challenge and defiance, but rather the timid yelps of fear. Then the howling came from a turn in the road so close at hand that John Barron, who was by no means a timid or nervous man, could hardly resist a shudder.

He silently cocked his gun, crept softly from behind the hedge into the road, and waited. Then a small, shrivelled old woman came into sight, walking with the aid of a stick. She hobbled along with surprising briskness for so old a woman until a turn in the road brought her suddenly face to face with him. And then something happened.

He was not a man addicted to fancies; nor was he at all lacking in powers of description as a rule; but he could never state quite clearly what it was that really happened. Probably it was because he did not quite know. He could only speak of an impression rather than of certain experience. According to him, the old woman gave him one glance of unspeakable malignancy; and then he seemed to become dazed or semi-conscious for a moment. It could have been only a matter of a second or two: but during that short space of time the old woman vanished. John Barron pulled himself together just in time to see a large wolf disappear round the turn of the road.

Naturally enough, he was somewhat confused by his startling experience. But there was no doubt about the presence of the wolf. He only just saw it; but he saw it quite clearly for about a second of time. Whether the wolf accompanied the old woman, or the old woman turned into a wolf, he neither saw nor could know. But each supposition was open to many obvious objections.

John Barron spent some time next day in thinking the thing out; and then it suddenly occurred to him to visit the thicket by the moorside and see the grave of the gipsy. He did not expect that there would be anything to see; but still it might be worth while to take a look at the place.

So he strolled in that direction early in the afternoon.

The thicket occupied a kind of little dell lying under the edge of the moor and was densely filled with small trees and undergrowth. But a scarcely visible path led into it; and, pushing his way through, he found that there was a small open space in the middle. Evidently this was the site of the gipsy grave.

And there he found it: but he found more than he expected. Not only was the grave there, but it lay open! The loose earth was heaped up on either side, and had the appearance of having been scraped out by some animal. And, sure enough, the foot-prints of a very large dog or wolf were to be seen in several places.

John Barron was simply horrified to find that the grave had been thus desecrated—and apparently in a manner that suggested an even worse horror. But, after a moment of hesitation, he stepped to the edge of the grave and looked in. What he saw was less appalling than he feared. There lay the coffin, exposed to view; but there was no sign that it had been opened or tampered with in any way.

There was evidently only one thing to be done, and that was to cover up the coffin decently and fill in the grave again. He would borrow a spade at the nearest cottage on some pretence and get the job done. He turned away to do this; but as he went through the thicket he could have sworn that he heard a sound like muffled laughter! And he could not get away from the notion that the laughter had some quality closely resem-bling the howling of a wolf. He called himself a fool for thinking such a thing—but he thought it all the same.

He borrowed the spade and filled the grave, beating the earth down as hard as he could; and again, as he turned away after completing the task, he heard that muffled laugh. But this time it was even less distinct than before, and somehow it sounded underground. He was rather glad to get away.

It may well be imagined that he had plenty to occupy his thoughts for the rest of the day; and even when he sought to sleep he could not. He lay tossing uneasily, thinking all the time of the mysterious grave and the events that certainly seemed now to be connected with it. Then, soon after midnight, he heard the voice in the night again. The wolf howled a long way off at first; then came a long interval of silence; and then the voice sounded so close to the house that Barron started up in alarm and he heard his dog give a cry of fear. Then the silence fell again; and some time later the howling was again heard in the distance.

Next morning he found his favourite dog lying dead beside his kennel; and it was only too evident how he had met his end. His neck was almost severed by one fearful bite; but the strange thing was that there was very little blood to be seen. A closer examination showed that the dog had bled to death; but where was the blood? Natural wolves tear their prey and devour it. They do not suck its blood. What kind of a wolf could this be?

John Barron found the answer next day. He was walking in the direction of the moor late in the afternoon, as it grew towards dusk, when he heard shrieks of terror coming from a little side lane. He ran to the rescue, and there he saw a little child of the village lying on the ground, with a huge wolf in the act of tearing at its throat.

Fortunately he had his gun with him; and, as the wolf sprang off its victim when he shouted, he fired. The range was a short one, and the beast got the full force of the charge. It bounded into the air and fell in a heap. But it got up again, and went off in a limping gallop in the way that wolves will often do even when mortally wounded. It made for the moor.

John Barron saw that it had received its death wound, and so gave it no further attention for the moment. Some men came running up at his shouts, and with their assistance he took the wounded child to the local doctor. Happily he had been in time to save its life.

Then he reloaded his gun, took a man with him, and followed the track of the wolf. It was not difficult to follow, for blood-stains on the road at frequent intervals showed plainly enough that it was severely wounded. As Barron expected, the track led straight to the thicket and entered it.

The two men followed cautiously; but they found no wolf. In the midst of the thicket lay the grave once more uncovered. And there beside it lay the body of a little old woman, drenched with blood. She was quite dead, and the terrible gunshot wound in her side told its own story. And the two men noticed that her canine teeth projected slightly beyond her lips on each side—like those of a snarling wolf—and they were blood-stained.

THE WEREWOLF OF RANNOCH

ELLEN SCRYSMOUR

IT WAS A CHILL NIGHT IN LATE JANUARY. THE SNOW LAY THICK UPON THE GROUND; the wind howled among the trees; and the full moon shone down on a desolate wilderness.

Half-a-mile from the little village of Dhuvhair—a village situated in the very heart and desolation of Rannoch—stood the little unpretentious house tenanted by Doctor Chisholm and his sister. It was a wild, dreary spot in which to live, and the mystery and horrors which had fallen upon the little community were in keeping with the weirdness of the place itself.

For some months Dhuvhair had suffered from an "evil visitation," to put it in the words of the "Wee Free Meenister." Cattle and sheep had been found dead in their pens, bloody and torn. Horses in their stalls had not escaped, pigs in their sties, dogs in their kennels, chickens in their runs had all suffered. And the manner of the kill was always the same, the throat of the victim was lacerated and bleeding, and the bowels torn from the body were left partly devoured.

"It's a Killer," said the Moorland folk. "It's a Killer. Keep your cattle under lock and key."

For a Killer is a dread thing among the shepherds and cottars of the North. By a Killer they mean a sheep-dog that has gone mad for blood; a dog that can no longer be trusted to look after the sheep, but one that will steal away as soon as darkness falls, and will slay the very creatures he is trained to guard.

But when children disappeared, and grown men and women, and their bodies were afterwards found torn and bleeding, lacerated with savage toothmarks, the people looked at each other timidly, and kept behind bolted doors at night, and prayed with the minister in the kirk on the Sabbath that "the visitation" might be lifted from them.

And it was the Reverend Evan MacIntosh himself who wrote to Shiela Crerar and asked her to come and investigate the mystery that surrounded Dhuvhair; for he had known her since she was a little girl, and had heard of her marvellous successes. She had accepted, and Miss Chisholm had offered to put her up, as the manse was only a bachelor establishment.

So Shiela arrived at the little Highland clachan, situated in the heart of remote Rannoch Moor, and set to work on perhaps the most gruesome mystery she ever had to solve.

The days passed, and she was still unsuccessful. Each morning she chose a new theory upon which to work, and each night had to abandon it as being either impossible or absurd.

There was certainly the element of the unreal about the visitation. Crofters averred they saw "a shaggy shape with eyes like burning coal, slinking about the hillside at the full of the moon." And always, after the creature had been seen, there was a Kill. Children were kept indoors at night and came screaming from the "ben" room, saying they had seen the face of a wolf at the window. The whole countryside was in a ferment of terror, and Shiela felt powerless to cope with it. She followed up clue after clue that proved useless, and all her nerves were on edge.

Doctor Chisholm, her host, a cheery soul of sixty-odd years, gave her all the help in his power, but he was openly sceptical about her theory that the Killer was possessed of a supernatural element. "I am sure we shall find that it is simply some mad dog loose on the country, Miss Crerar. What else can it be?"

"Have you never heard of werewolves, Doctor?" she asked, quietly.

"Yes," he replied, "but I don't think I am quite sure in my own mind as to what they are supposed to be."

"They are men with dual personalities, Doctor, who have the power to change themselves into the form of a wolf or some other carnivorous animal."

"My dear Miss Crerar—" smiled the Doctor, genially, and ran his hand through his snowy hair.

"Oh, I believe in it, Doctor. It is another form of the 'Jekyll and Hyde' theory, that's all, only a much worse form. The astral spirit leaves the body in a sleeping condition, while it assumes an animal shape itself. Thus free, it roams round the world at will, and lengthens its existence by drinking fresh, warm blood drawn from a new kill."

"Surely that is quite a mediaeval superstition, Miss Crerar," protested the Doctor again. "We are in the prosaic twentieth century, and—"

But Shiela refused to answer. She had been in touch with the unreal too often to doubt. She knew the power of the spirits from the other world—the tangibility of the elemental—she had come across the very essence of witchcraft. Nothing was impossible.

And that night, as she stood at the garden gate after dinner and enjoyed the glory of a white earth under a full moon, she caught sight of a shadowy grey shape creeping among the trees. It was her first glimpse of the Killer. Without a thought of fear she bounded after it—hatless, coatless, breathless, she followed it. It turned its head—its eyes gleamed viciously, and it snarled angrily. Shiela pulled a branch of whitethorn—a protection against witchcraft—and held it high above her head. The wolf leapt at her, but as it touched the tree, it whined, slunk round a corner, and when Shiela moved a second later it had vanished from sight. There was no place in which it could hide, yet it had gone completely, and the only living thing in sight was a man who was walking quickly into the distance. She hurried after him, but the space between them never seemed to lessen. His walk, his figure, his manner seemed familiar to her, but there suddenly came a flash, and when she opened her eyes, he, too, was gone. She walked back slowly and ran into Doctor Chisholm.

"I've proved my theory," she said, with quiet concentration. "The visitant *is* a Werewolf. I have seen it tonight, and I must now set to work to discover who it is that is the menace to this little place. I believe some men have no knowledge that they possess this power, and while their astral spirit is absent, they are asleep and unconscious of their evil doings. This Werewolf is different. I am convinced he knows his own powers."

"Why, what makes you think that?"

"Because just now he appeared as a wolf—a second later the animal had gone, but a man had taken his place. I tried to reach the man. At first I didn't realise that the change had taken place, but when I drew near he used his magical powers, blinded me with a light for a moment, and when I could see, he too had vanished."

"Have you any idea who this—this man is?"

"Not the slightest at present. Although he seemed familiar to me, I find I am unable to place him. But I shall work hard to discover him, and then—" She left the sentence unfinished, and the kindly doctor tucked his arm though hers, and led the way back to his house.

But although Shiela saw the ominous grey shape many times, she was never able to track it to its lair.

"Will you watch with me tonight, Doctor?" she asked one day. "I want to try and discover the direction from which the Werewolf comes. Let us hide in the bushes by the churchyard. We shall be safe there on consecrated ground."

So they waited that night at the edge of the little graveyard—a spot eerie and forlorn.

"Get behind that tombstone," said the Doctor genially, "and I'll wait here."

"But I can't see you, Doctor."

"Never mind. I can see you."

So they waited. The moon was hidden beneath heavy clouds, the wind was piercing, and heavy flakes of snow cut Shiela's face and made it smart. Suddenly, as the clock in the church tower boomed twelve, there came the sound of ghostly laughter—laughter that seemed to come from the regions of the damned.

Shiela felt her blood run cold, and, as she watched, she heard the baying of hounds in the distance—and knew them to be the ghostly hounds of the wicked dead. Nearer they drew, and nearer. Shiela watched their approach, and counted them mechanically. Five—six—seven—eight. And they strained at a leash that was held taut by their invisible master. And even as they passed her Shiela heard the crack of a whip, and saw the quiver of the flesh that was flayed—yet of the whip itself there was nothing to be seen. As they passed, leaving a luminous trail behind them, she saw the "grey hulking shapes" speed swiftly by, there was the snapping of hungry jaws, a cry of pain, and the ghostly pack only numbered seven! They had passed, and all was still and quiet.

"Doctor, Doctor! Don't say now that you don't believe!" said Shiela.

"Doctor, Doctor!" she cried again.

"Doctor Chisholm, are you there?" and a frightened note crept into her voice.

But the genial doctor answered her, his voice grave and low.

"Forgive me, Miss Crerar, I scarcely realised you were speaking. I was carried away by the scene."

Shiela left her hiding-place and crossed to him. He was rising from the shelter of a large whin bush, and the girl cried out in dismay.

"Oh, Doctor, thank God you are safe!"

"Why, what is the matter, Miss Crerar?"

"Do you realise you have not been on consecrated ground at all? You were on the path that separates the graveyard from the flower gardens that surround it."

He gave a little wry smile.

"Then it was your presence that no doubt saved me from harm, my dear."

Then one day Shiela saw the Werewolf lurking in the meadow near the Chisholms' byre. With the protecting whitethorn spray, she tracked it, but it disappeared behind the building itself, and as she turned the corner she came face to face with Doctor Chisholm's partner. They passed with a curt "Good night," and Shiela thought no more about the incident.

A week later it was, however, brought back to her mind. She was waiting again in the churchyard, but this time alone. Midnight boomed out, and the Killer passed. But even as he vanished from sight the Doctor's partner appeared from the copse at the side of the road. This time she passed him without speaking, for the moment her eyes lighted upon him a wild possibility suggested itself to her mind, and she felt at last that she had a clue—that at last she was on the right track.

When she had first met Doctor Chisholm's partner she had taken a dislike to him. He was a Dane—Olaf Sylmak by name—a dark, taciturn man of late middle life. She felt sorry he was an inmate of Cnoc-na-Ruaidh, as the Chisholm's house was called. She never spoke to him more than courtesy demanded of her.

She read craft in his expression, cruelty in his tight, thin lips, and shivered at the touch of his damp, flaccid hand. And now—well, she hoped the *dénouement* was not far off. The Killer was always abroad when the moon was full, and tonight she would try and track the malefactor to its lair.

"Well," said Doctor Chisholm genially, as she said good night, "you have not discovered the identity of our unpleasant visitor yet?"

"Not yet. But I think I am at last on his track."

The old man's eyes twinkled, and he gave an exaggerated little shudder.

"Oh, you modern women! You dabble in science and medicine, you dabble in politics and law, and now you dabble in the occult. What else is there left for mere man?"

"Well, Doctor, you'll be glad if this mysterious horror is satisfactorily cleared up, won't you?"

"Of course I shall, my dear young lady—and so will Mary." He nodded affectionately at his sister. "Why, Mary scarcely ever sleeps a wink at nights now, do you?"

Miss Chisholm, a delicate spinster, many years her brother's junior, looked up flutteringly.

"Indeed, Miss Crerar, I have not. If it were not for Doctor Sylmak's kindness to me, his cheery presence, and the wonderful tonic he had made up for me for nerves, I am sure I should have had a breakdown long ago. The suspense is terrible, not to know from one minute to the next whether the—the Killer will make his visitation here."

Shiela looked grave. "You like Doctor Sylmak, don't you, Miss Chisholm?"

The little lady flushed.

"It is quite a secret. My brother, of course, knows; but if Doctor Sylmak is successful in a big experiment he is making, we are to be married."

Shiela was unable to look into the candid eyes of the little young-old lady.

"I—I hope he—he will be successful," she murmured, and then she not only surprised herself by bending over the spinster and kissing her on the forehead, saying, "But, above all, I hope you will be happy."

When she reached her room she muttered angrily to herself, "If I am right in my conjectures, I shall bring unhappiness on that poor little soul who trusts him. Yet better one heart broken than distress and desolation on many."

It was a bitterly cold night, and she wrapped herself up very warmly, put on snow-shoes, and pulled a woollen cap close about her ears. She loaded a little automatic revolver, and carefully opened a French window that led from her room to the outside stair, so prevalent in Scottish houses. Quickly she descended it, and crept into the shadow of a holly bush, and remained waiting—waiting.

It was an eerie night. The moon was brilliant, but the huge rings round it foretold stormy weather. The wind moaned and whistled, and Shiela drew her cloak close around her. She looked at her watch, and saw that it wanted but a few seconds to midnight, when she suddenly stiffened and her nostrils quivered. She had caught the scent of her prey!

There was a crunch! crunch! on the frozen snow, and a great grey beast slunk round the corner of the house. His nose was high in the air, and his red eyes gleamed banefully. The foam dropped from his slobbering jowl, and the steam rose from his heated body. She raised her revolver, and the beast seemed to scent danger, for with a whimper of fear it slunk into the shadows and vanished from sight. Quickly Shiela followed the direction it had taken. Among the trees she saw a grey shape flitting. It was the malevolent beast she knew to be responsible for the killings.

Night after night she had waited for it; tracked it among the peat hags and morasses of the moor; had followed it along the banks of lochs and peaty tarns; across heathery hummocks and granite boulders. But always the uncanny brute had evaded her. But now she had seen it come from the shadow of Cnoc-na-Ruaidh, and she felt that the Doctor's house was indeed the lair of the Werewolf—a thing loathsome, treacherous, vile. And even as she sped after it she shook with anger at the thought of the gentle spinster who had given her heart to Olaf Sylmak—the Wolf-man. Shiela had no doubts now—she had been suspicious of him from the first; but she had now to prove that he and the Killer were one.

As she crossed the dreary wasteland she heard a choking cry of pain—a cry that was hideous in the silence of the night. Still on she went, and at last came on the body of a stag. It was the beautiful creature that had cried out in its death agony. Its throat was completely gone, its body ripped open, and its entrails partly devoured. Drops of crimson stained the whiteness of the snow, and Shiela followed the bloody track. On it went across the uneven moorland, and at last came to a sudden stop, and Shiela saw the marks on the snow where the brute had wiped its jaws after its ghoulish meal.

The girl found she had journeyed to the edge of the moor. The spot was unfamiliar to her. A rugged mountain rose precipitously from the side of a melancholy loch. Her quest was done for the night. She could trail the beast no further, and she turned back to Cnoc-na-Ruaidh.

And even as she came in sight of the house she caught a glimpse of a hulking grey form crossing the front lawn. It seemed unconscious of the watchful eyes upon it, and stealthily crept beneath the shelter of a half-opened lobby window. For a second or two it remained quite quiet, then even as the girl watched it, it disappeared, and a moment later she saw the window shut and heard it latched from the inside.

Next day, as soon as breakfast was over, she retraced her steps of the previous night. The body of the stag was still in the same place, and the bloodstains, faint and blurred, still directed her. At the edge of the loch she hesitated and wondered which way to turn. A quarter way up the mountain side a huge lichen-covered boulder jutted out. At its base grew thick bushes of stunted holly, and Shiela's practised eye told her that some massive body had crept hastily beneath the shelter of the low branches. She climbed swiftly up to it, and peered beneath. There was an opening at the foot of the rock, and, fearless as ever, she crept into the passage-way. The way proved to be very narrow, and ran perhaps thirty feet down into a large cavern. As Shiela entered it she gave a cry of excited pleasure. She had found the Wolf-man's lair!

The place was full of strange devices and mechanical appliances, the use of which she did not know. High up the rocky wall was a tiny ledge. Quickly she tried to reach it. It was an arduous task, but she was sure-footed, the rocky wall gave her foothold, and she reached it safely. It was in reality the mouth of a tiny cave, and she could stay there in safety, and watch all unseen anyone who might be down below. It commanded a perfect view of the whole cavern.

She hurried home and rested, preparing for her nocturnal adventure; but she was not destined to go out that night. A sudden storm came on, the rain came down in torrents, and she knew it would be a physical impossibility to walk the five miles alone. She went to bed early, however, and quivered with indignation as she saw Dr. Sylmak bend tenderly over the gentle spinster, who looked with such trust into his eyes.

He was a Werewolf! A man whose astral spirit took on the form of a wolf, and prowled at night in search of prey! A man who left his body in his chamber while his real self gorged on cannibalistic feasts. It was terrible—horrible—abhorrent!

Shiela was restless in her sleep, her dreams were uneasy, and she tossed from side to side in the large canopied bed. Suddenly she realised she was awake, and listened. There was a soft pad-padding outside her door, and she heard the snuffling of an animal, followed by a tiny whimper. Now, there were no animals at Cnoc-na-Ruaidh—neither cat nor dog nor bird. The house possessed no pets.

She lit her candle and looked round quickly, and gave a sigh of relief as she saw the branch of whitethorn by her side. She caught it up in her hand and opened her door. There was nothing outside. She felt a little mystified. She expected an encounter with the ghostly creature itself, and was a little disappointed. She shut her door and listened. Again she heard the whimper. This time she crept behind the door and waited. Slowly the door opened, yet neither handle turned nor lock clicked. It seemed to glide through rather than open, and through the crack in the hinges she saw the Wolf outside. There was no mistaking it! Its little red eyes gleamed with hatred, and its tongue lolled out of its mouth hungrily. It entered her bedchamber. Round and round it stalked, and she, ever watchful, held the whitethorn high above her head. It was a mighty duel of wits and strength.

The great grey shape crouched at her feet. Its breath was foetid and vile, and its coat gave forth a sulphurous vapour. Its murderous little eyes seemed to laugh as it saw the effort Shiela had to make to keep her arms above her head. How long they faced each other she never knew. She felt at any moment she must let her arms drop for very weariness. The stench of the creature was unbearable; the fumes from its body choked and nauseated her.

She saw her little revolver on her dressing-table, but was unable to reach it. Her eyes grew dim—her head ached. Then suddenly the Wolf was gone, and a pure white kitten clawed at her skirts and mewed piteously. Its foot was hurt, and in the prettiest way imaginable it lifted up its little paw. For a moment only Shiela hesitated, then with a swift movement she slashed viciously at the pretty little creature with her weapon of whitethorn, and the same instant reached her revolver. When she looked again there was no pretty white kitten, but a hideous grey creature, that whined savagely and licked the blood that oozed from a jagged wound across its body.

At that moment Shiela fired, and, with a cry, the Wolf leapt out of the door, and she realised she had missed it.

But had she, after all?

Dr. Sylmak appeared at her door, and there was blood upon his hand.

"What is the matter, Miss Crerar? I heard a noise, and came to see what it was. At that minute you must have fired, for see—the bullet just grazed my little finger."

Shiela gazed at him in horror. Then she had touched the grey shape after all. She thought she had missed; but was there not such a thing as repercussion?

If she wounded the Wolf, would not the man also suffer? If she killed the Wolf, would not the man die in a like manner? Although she had levelled the revolver at the Wolf, Olaf Sylmak had received the discharge. It was indeed curious!

But she did not mean to show her hand yet.

"Pray accept my apology," she said sweetly. "I thought I saw a burglar. I woke from a bad dream. I do hope I have not hurt you much?"

"Nothing to worry about, Miss Crerar. Go back to bed, and sleep better. Good night."

"Good night."

But Shiela did not intend delaying further, and directly after dinner the next night she slipped out of her room and started on her walk to the Wolf-man's cave. She had plenty of time; it was still before nine. She reached the place in safety, climbed the rocky wall, and waited.

It was very dreary in that place of fear, and she wished she had told Dr. Chisholm of her discovery, and invited him to accompany her. Time dragged. She must have fallen asleep, for suddenly she realised the place was lighted by huge torches that were fitted in brackets on the wall. In the centre of the cavern a brazier burned, its flames blue and red. A hooded man in a red gown, covered in strange hieroglyphics, stood over it, muttering in a monotone as he sprinkled a powder on the glowing coals that caused the flames to shoot up about the feet, assuming the colours of the rainbow.

A faint cry came from a darkened corner, and Shiela gazed in horror as she saw the magician stoop down and lift up in his arms a tiny naked child of perhaps two years. The plump little body squirmed and struggled with fear, but the man held it deftly while he anointed it with oils and sweet-smelling spices. Suddenly he held a knife aloft, and Shiela buried her face in her hands. There was an agonising cry—a cry that ended with a muffled, choking moan—and silence!

The girl felt too sick to watch; but the scene had its fascination as well as its horror, and tightly clasped in her hand was her loaded revolver. She would make no mistake tonight! But the wizard had not yet finished his revels. He dragged a stool in front of the brazier, and on it he placed two quaint figures. Subconsciously Shiela realised they were familiar. She peered cautiously down from her hiding-place, and realised that one was dressed like Miss Chisholm, while the other was wrapped round in a black hood, the exact counterpart of the one she was wearing at that moment.

The figure below raised the effigy of Miss Chisholm, and in a low voice called on Satan the Mighty, and Shiela knew she was looking at a *corp chréidh*[1] ceremony. She did not know that the practice still existed: the cult of fashioning a body in clay, and by aid of ghastly spells and prayers to the devil, working harm through its medium upon the person it represented.

The sorcerer held the little clay figure in one hand, and with a long, pincer-shaped instrument twisted off the right hand from the wrist. And as he did so, a cry

---

1. Gaelic for clay body.

of pain came from the effigy, and a second later Shiela heard Miss Chisholm's voice cry out, "It hurts! It hurts!"

Then the image was flung contemptuously aside, and the man picked up the one dressed in the likeness of Shiela.

He lifted the *corp chréidh* in his hand, and with muffled words of hatred, bent over it for a moment before he plunged the entire left arm into the flames. And as the limb was shrivelled up by the furnace it uttered a wail of agony.

But Shiela had turned white and deadly faint, and she realised she was suffering the pain of burns. She hesitated no longer, and fired twice in quick succession at the monster below.

A piercing shriek broke the stillness of the night, and the man below had vanished; but Shiela saw a grey shape lift up its muzzle in the air and howl dismally, and even as it did so, it, too, disappeared from her ken.

Shiela, trembling and terror-stricken, crept home in the grey morning. Her arm was painful, but she had bound it up with strips torn from her petticoat. In the dim light she saw great blisters had risen from the inflamed flesh. She was worn out and tired, and hoped to creep into her room unseen. But she found the house full of excitement and trouble. Miss Chisholm was in the dining-room, weeping convulsively. Dr. Olaf Sylmak was bending over her, and soothing her.

"Why, whatever is the matter?" asked Shiela.

"My—my brother!" sobbed the woman. "He—he is dead!"

"What?" And as she spoke she noticed Miss Chisholm's right hand was bandaged.

"Shot twice through the heart, Miss Crerar. I heard the sound of a revolver fired twice in quick succession, and when I rushed into Dr. Chisholm's room—he was quite dead."

Shiela looked full into Olaf Sylmak's eyes, and read the truth there.

"May I see him?" she asked quietly.

It was Dr. Sylmak himself who led her into the darkened death-chamber. The face of Robert Chisholm had lost its benignity—its contour. The lips were drawn back, and revealed sharp fangs—fangs that scarcely seemed to belong to a human creature.

"There will be no more killings now, Miss Crerar," said Olaf Sylmak softly.

"You knew?" breathed Shiela.

The man nodded.

"I suspected it some time ago. I've been watching."

"Forgive me! Oh, forgive me!" cried the girl.

But Olaf Sylmak never knew what she meant.

THE WITCHES' SABBATH

JAMES PLATT

OUR SCENE IS ONE OF THOSE TERRIFIC PEAKS SET APART BY TRADITION AS THE trysting place of wizards and witches, and of every kind of folk that prefers dark to day.

It might have been Mount Elias, or the Brocken, associated with Doctor Faustus. It might have been the Horsel or Venusberg of Tannhaeuser, or the Black Forest. Enough that it was one of these.

Not a star wrinkled the brow of night. Only in the distance the twinkling lights of some town could be seen. Low down in the skirts of the mountain rode a knight, followed closely by his page. We say a knight, because he had once owned that distinction. But a wild and bloody youth had tarnished his ancient shield, the while it kept bright and busy his ancestral sword. Behold him now, little better than a highwayman. Latterly he had wandered from border to border, without finding where to rest his faithful steed. All authority was in arms against him; Hageck, the wild knight, was posted throughout Germany. More money was set upon his head than had ever been put into his pocket. Pikemen and pistoliers had dispersed his following. None remained to him whom he could call his own, save this stripling who still rode sturdily at the tail of his horse. Him also, the outlaw had besought, even with tears, to abandon one so ostensibly cursed by stars and men. But in vain. The boy protested that he would have no home, save in his master's shadow.

They were an ill-assorted pair. The leader was all war-worn and weather-worn. Sin had marked him for its own and for the wages of sin. The page was young and slight, and marble pale. He would have looked more at home at the silken train of some great lady, than following at these heels from which the gilded spurs had long been hacked. Nevertheless, the music of the spheres themselves sings not more sweetly in accord than did these two hearts.

The wild knight, Hageck, had ascended the mountain as far as was possible to four-legged roadsters. Therefore he reined in his horse and dismounted, and addressed his companion. His voice was now quite gentle, which on occasion could quench mutiny, and in due season dry up the taste of blood in the mouths of desperate men.

"Time is that we must part, Enno."

"Master, you told me we need never part."

"Let be, child, do you not understand me? I hope with your own heart's hope that we shall meet again to-morrow in this same tarrying place. But I have not brought you to so cursed a place without some object. When I say that we must part, I mean that you must take charge of our horses while I go further up the mountain upon business, which for your own sake you must never share."

"And is this your reading of the oath of our brotherhood which we swore together?"

"The oath of our brotherhood, I fear, was writ in water. You are, in fact, the only one of all my company that has kept faith with me. For that very reason I would not spare your neck from the halter, nor your limbs from the wheel. But also for that very reason I will not set your immortal soul in jeopardy."

"My immortal soul! Is this business then unhallowed that you go upon? Now I remember me that this mountain at certain seasons is said to be haunted by evil spirits. Master, you also are bound by our oath to tell me all."

"You shall know all, Enno, were oaths even cheaper than they are. You have deserved by your devotion to be the confessor of your friend."

"Friend is no name for companionship such as ours. I am sure you would die for me. I believe I could die for you, Hageck."

"Enough, you have been more than brother to me. I had a brother once, after the fashion of this world, and it is his envious hand which has placed me where I stand. That was before I knew you, Enno, and it is some sweets in my cup at any rate, that had he not betrayed me I should never have known you. Nevertheless, you will admit that since he robbed me of the girl I loved, even your loyal heart is a poor set off for what fate and fraternity took from me. In fine, we both loved the same girl, but she loved me, and would have none of my brother. She was beautiful, Enno—how beautiful you can never guess that have not yet loved."

"I have never conceived any other love than that I bear you."

"Tush, boy, you know not what you say. But to return to my story. One day that I was walking with her my brother would have stabbed me. She threw herself between and was killed upon my breast."

He tore open his clothes at the throat and showed a great faded stain upon his skin.

"The hangman's brand shall fade," he cried, "ere that wash out. Accursed be the mother that bore me seeing that she also first bore him! The devil squat down with him in his resting, lie with him in his sleeping, as the devil has sat and slept with me every noon and night since that deed was done. Never give way to love of woman, Enno, lest you lose the one you love, and with her lose the balance of your life."

"Alas! Hageck, I fear I never shall."

"Since that miscalled day, blacker than any night, you know as well as any one the sort of death in life I led. I had the good or evil luck to fall in with some broken men like myself, fortune's foes and foes of all whom fortune cherishes, you among them. Red blood, red gold for a while ran through our fingers. Then a turn of the wheel, and, presto, my men are squandered to every wind that blows—I am a fugitive with a price upon my head!"

"And with one comrade whom, believe me, wealth is too poor to buy."

"A heart above rubies. Even so. To such alone would I confide my present purpose. You must know that my brother was a student of magic of no mean repute, and before we quarrelled had given me some insight into its mysteries. Now that I near the end of my tether I have summed up all the little I knew, and am resolved to make a desperate cast in this mountain of despair. In a word, I intend to hold converse with my dead sweetheart before I die. The devil shall help me to it for the love he bears me."

"You would invoke the enemy of all mankind?"

"Him and none other. Aye, shudder not, nor seek to turn me from it. I have gone over it again and again. The gates of Hell are set no firmer than this resolve."

"God keep Hell far from you when you call it!"

"I had feared my science was of too elementary an order to conduct an exorcism under any but the most favourable circumstances. Hence our journey hither. This place is one of those where parliaments of evil are held, where dead and living meet on equal ground. To-night is the appointed night of one of these great Sabbaths. I propose to leave you here with the horses. I shall climb to the topmost peak, draw a circle that I may stand in for my defence, and with all the vehemence of love deferred, pray for my desire."

"May all good angels speed you!"

"Nay, I have broken with such. Your good wish, Enno, is enough."

"But did we not hear talk in the town about a hermit that spent his life upon the mountain top, atoning for some sin in day-long prayer and mortification? Can this evil fellowship of which you speak still hold its meetings upon a spot which has been attached in the name of Heaven by one good man?"

"Of this hermit I knew nothing until we reached the town. It was then too late to seek another workshop. Should what you say be correct, and this holy man have purged this plague spot, I can do no worse than pass the night with him, and return to you. But should the practices of witch and wizard continue as of yore, then the powers of evil shall draw my love to me, be she where she may. Aye, be it in that most secret nook of heaven where God retires when He would weep, and where even archangels are never suffered to tread."

"O all good go with you!"

"Farewell, Enno, and if I never return count my soul not so lost but what you may say a prayer for it now and again, when you have leisure."

"I will not outlive you!"

The passionate words were lost on Hageck, who had already climbed so far as to be out of hearing. He only knew vaguely that something was shouted to him, and waved his hand above his head for a reply. On and on he climbed. Time passed. The way grew harder. At last exhausted, but fed with inward exaltation, he reached the summit. It was of considerable extent and extremely uneven. The first thing our hero noticed was the cave of the hermit. It could be nothing else, although it was closed with an iron door. A new departure, thought Hageck to himself, as he hammered upon it with the pommel of his sword, for a hermit's cell to be locked in like a fortress.

"Open, friend," he cried, "in heaven's name, or in that of the other place if you like it better."

The noise came from within of a bar being removed. The door opened. It revealed a mere hole in the rock, though large enough, it is true, to hold a considerable number of persons. Furniture was conspicuous by its absence. There was no sign even of a bed, unless a coffin that grinned in one corner served the occupant's needs. A skull, a scourge, a crucifix, a knife for his food, what more does such a hermit want? His feet were bare, his head was tonsured, but his eyebrows were long and matted, and fell like a screen over burning maniacal eyes. A fanatic, every inch of him. He scrutinised the invader from top to toe. Apparently the result was unsatisfactory. He frowned.

"A traveller," said he, "and at this unholy hour. Back, back, do you not know the sinister reputation of this time and place?"

"I know your reputation to be of the highest, reverend father; I could not credit what rumour circulates about this mountain top when I understood that one of such sanctity had taken up a perpetual abode here."

"My abode is fixed here for the very reason that it is a realm of untold horror. My task is to win back, if I can, to the dominion of the church this corner, which has been so long unloved that it cries aloud to God and man. This position of my own choice is no sinecure. Hither at stated times the full brunt of the Sabbath sweeps to its rendezvous. Here I defy the Sabbath. You see that mighty door?"

"I had wondered, but feared to ask, what purpose such a barrier could serve in such a miserable place."

"You may be glad to crouch behind it if you stay here much longer. At midnight, Legion, with all the swirl of all the hells at his back, will sweep this summit like a tornado. Were you of the stuff that never trembles, yet you shall hear such sounds as shall melt your backbone. Avoid hence while there is yet time."

"But you, if you remain here, why not I?"

"I remain here as a penance for a crime I did, a crime which almost takes prisoner my reason, so different was it from the crime I set out to do, so deadly death to all my hopes. I am on my knees throughout the whole duration of this pandemonium that I tell you of, and count thick and fast my beads during the whole time. Did I cease for one second to pray, that second would be my last. The roof of my cavern would descend and efface body and soul. But you, what would you do here?"

"I seek my own ends, for which I am fully prepared. To confer with a shade from the other world I place my own soul in jeopardy. For the short time that must elapse, before the hour arrives when I can work, I ask but a trifle of your light and fire."

"The will-o'-the-wisp be your light, Saint Anthony's your fire! Do you not recognise me?"

The wild knight bent forward and gazed into the hermit's inmost eye, then started back, and would have fallen had his head not struck the iron door. This recalled him to his senses, and after a moment he stood firm again, and murmured between his teeth, "My brother!"

"Your brother," repeated the holy man, "your brother, whose sweetheart you stole and drove me to madness and crime."

"I drove you to no madness, I drove you to no crime. The madness, the crime you expiate here, were all of your own making. She loved me, and me alone—you shed her blood, by accident I confess, yet you shed it, and not all the prayers of your lifetime can gather up one drop of it. What soaked into my own brain remains there for ever, though I have sought to wash it out with an ocean of other men's blood."

"And I," replied the hermit, and he tore his coarse frock off his shoulders, "I have sought to drown it with an ocean of my own."

He spoke truth. Blood still oozed from his naked flesh, ploughed into furrows by the scourge.

"You, that have committed so many murders," he continued, "and who have reproached me so bitterly for one, all the curses of your dying victims, all the curses I showered upon you before I became reformed have not availed to send you yet to the gibbet or to the wheel. You are one that, like the basil plant, grows ever the rifer for cursing. I remember I tried to lame you, after you left home, by driving a rusty nail into one of your footsteps, but the charm refused to work. You were never the worse for it that I could hear. They say the devil's children have the devil's luck. Yet some day shall death trip up your heels."

"Peace, peace," cried the wild horseman, "let ill-will be dead between us, and the bitterness of death be passed, as befits your sacred calling. Even if I see her for one moment to-night, by the aid of the science you once taught me, will you not see her for eternity in heaven some near day?"

"In heaven," cried the hermit, "do I want to see her in heaven? On earth would I gladly see her again and account that moment cheap if weighed against my newly discovered soul! But that can never be. Not the art you speak of, not all the dark powers which move men to sin, can restore her to either of us as she was that day. And she loved you. She died to save you. You have nothing to complain of. But to me she was like some chaste impossible star."

"I loved her most," muttered the outlaw.

"You loved her most," screamed the hermit. "Hell sit upon your eyes! Put it to the test. Look around. Do you see anything of her here?"

The other Hageck gazed eagerly round the cave, but without fixing upon anything.

"I see nothing," he was forced to confess.

The hermit seized the skull and held it in front of his eyes.

"This is her dear head," he cried, "fairer far than living red and white to me!"

The wild knight recoiled with a gasp of horror, snatched the ghastly relic from the hand of his brother, and hurled it over the precipice. He put his fingers over his eyes and fell to shaking like an aspen. For a moment the hermit scarcely seemed to grasp his loss. Then with a howl of rage he seized his brother by the throat.

"You have murdered her," he shrieked in tones scarcely recognisable, "she will be dashed to a hundred pieces by such a fall!"

He threw the outlaw to the ground and, retreating to his cave, slammed the door behind him, but his heart-broken sobs could still be heard distinctly. It was very evident that he was no longer in his right mind. The wild knight rose somewhat painfully and limped to a little distance where he perceived a favourable spot for erecting his circle. The sobbing of the crazed hermit presently ceased. He was aware that his rival had entered upon his operations. The hermit re-opened his door that he might more clearly catch the sound of what his foe was engaged upon. Every step was of an absorbing interest to the solitary as to the man who made it. Anon the hermit started to his feet. He fancied he heard another voice replying to his brother. Yes, it was a voice he seemed to know. He rushed out of the cave. A girlish figure clad in a stained dress was clasped in his brother's arms. Kiss after kiss the wild knight was showering upon brow, and eye, and cheek, and lip. The girl responded as the hermit had surely seen her do once before. He flew to his cave. He grasped the knife he used for his food. He darted like an arrow upon the startled pair. The woman tried to throw herself in front of her lover, but the hermit with a coarse laugh, "Not twice the dagger seeks the same breast," plunged it into the heart of her companion. The wild knight threw up his arms and without a cry fell to the ground. The girl uttered a shriek that seemed to rive the skies and flung herself across her dead. The hermit gazed at it stupidly and rubbed his eyes. He seemed like one dazed, but slowly recovering his senses. Suddenly he started, came as it were to himself, and pulled the girl by the shoulder.

"We have not a minute to lose," he cried, "the great Sabbath is all but due. If his body remains out here one second after the stroke of twelve, his soul will be lost to all eternity. It will be snatched by the fiends who even now are bound to it. Do you not see yon shadowy hosts—but I forget, you are not a witch."

"I see nothing," she replied, sullenly, rising up and peering round. The night was clear, but starless.

"I have been a wizard," he answered, "and once a wizard always a wizard, though I now fight upon the other side. Take my hand and you will see."

She took his hand, and screamed as she did so. For at the instant there became visible to her these clouds of loathsome beings that were speeding thither from every point of the compass. Warlock, and witch, and wizard rode post on every conceivable graceless mount. Their motion was like the lightning of heaven, and their varied cries—owlet hoot, caterwaul, dragon-shout—the horn of the Wild Hunter, and the hurly of risen dead—vied with the bay of Cerberus to the seldseen moon. A forest of whips was flourished aloft. The whirr of wings raised dozing echoes. The accustomed mountain shook and shivered like a jelly, with the fear of their onset.

The girl dropped his hand and immediately lost the power of seeing them. She had learned at any rate that what he said was true.

"Help me to carry the body to the cave," cried he, and in a moment it was done. The corpse was placed in the coffin of his murderer. Then the hermit crashed his door to its place. Up went bolts and bars. Some loose rocks that were probably the hermit's chairs and tables were rolled up to afford additional security.

"And now," demanded the man, "now that we have a moment of breathing space, tell me what woman-kind are you whom I find here with my brother? That you are not her I know (woe is me that I have good reason to know) yet you are as like her as any flower that blows. I loved her, and I murdered her, and I have the right to ask, who and what are you that come to disturb my peace?"

"I am her sister."

"Her sister! Yes, I remember you. You were a child in those days. Neither I nor my brother (God rest his soul!), neither of us noticed you."

"No, he never took much notice of me. Yet I loved him as well as she did."

"You, too, loved him," whispered the hermit, as if to himself; "what did he do to be loved by two such women?"

"Yes, I loved him, though he never knew it, but I may confess it now, for you are a priest of a sort, are you not, you that shrive with steel?"

"You are bitter, like your sister. She was always so with me."

"I owe you my story," she replied more gently; "when she died and he fell into evil courses and went adrift with bad companions, I found I could not live without him, nor with anyone else, and I determined to become one of them. I dressed in boy's clothes and sought enlistment into his company of free lances. He would have driven me from him, saying it was no work for such as I, yet at last I wheedled it from him. I think there was something in my face (all undeveloped as it was and stained with walnut juice) that reminded him of her he had lost. I followed him faithfully through good and evil, cringing for a look or word from him. We were at last broken up (as you know) and I alone of all his sworn riders remained to staunch his wounds. He brought me hither that he might wager all the soul that was left to him on the chance of evoking her spirit. I had with me the dress my sister died in, that I had cherished through all my wanderings, as my sole reminder of her life and death. I put it on after he had left me, and followed him as fast as my strength would allow me. My object was to beguile him with what sorry pleasure I could, while at the same time saving him from committing the sin of disturbing the dead. God forgive me if there was mixed with it the wholly selfish yearning to be kissed by him once, only once, in my true character as loving woman, rid of my hated disguise! I have had my desire, and it has turned to apples of Sodom on my lips. You are right. All we can do now is to preserve his soul alive."

She fell on her knees beside the coffin. The hermit pressed his crucifix into her hands.

"Pray!" he cried, and at the same moment the distant clock struck twelve. There came a rush of feet, a thunder at the iron door, the cave rocked like a ship's cabin abruptly launched into the trough of a storm. An infernal whooping and hallooing filled the air outside, mixed with it imprecations that made the strong man blanch. The banner of Destruction was unfurled. All the horned heads were upon them. Thrones and Dominions, Virtues, Princes, Powers. All hell was loose that night, and the outskirts of Hell.

The siege had begun. The hermit told his beads with feverish rapidity. One Latin prayer after another rolled off his tongue in drops of sweat. The girl, to whom these were unintelligible, tried in vain to think of prayers. All she could say, as she pressed the Christ to her lips, was "Lord of my life! My Love." She scarcely heard the hurly-burly that raged outside. Crash after crash resounded against the door, but good steel tempered with holy water is bad to beat. Showers of small pieces of rock fell from the ceiling and the cave was soon filled with dust. Peals of hellish cachinnation resounded after each unsuccessful attempt to break down that defence. Living battering rams pressed it hard, dragon's spur, serpent's coil, cloven hoof, foot of clay. Tall Iniquities set their backs to it, names of terror, girt with earthquake. All the swart crew dashed their huge bulk against it, rakehelly riders, humans and superhumans, sin and its paymasters. The winds well nigh split their sides with hounding of them on. Evil stars in their courses fought against it. The seas threw up their dead. Haunted houses were no more haunted that night. Graveyards steamed. Gibbets were empty. The ghoul left his half-gnawn corpse, the vampire his victim's throat. Buried treasures rose to earth's surface that their ghostly guardians might swell the fray. Yet the hermit prayed on, and the woman wept, and the door kept its face to the foe. Will the hour of release never strike? Crested Satans now lead the van. Even steel cannot hold out for ever against those in whose veins instead of blood, runs fire. At last it bends ever so little, and the devilish hubbub is increased tenfold.

"Should they break open the door—" yelled the hermit, making a trumpet of his hands, yet she could not hear what he shouted above the abominable din, nor had he time to complete his instructions. For the door did give, and that suddenly, with a clang that was heard from far off in the town, and made many a burgher think the last trump had come. The rocks that had been rolled against the door flew off in every direction, and a surging host—and the horror of it was that they were invisible to the girl—swept in.

The hermit tore his rosary asunder, and scattered the loose beads in the faces of the fiends.

"Hold fast the corpse!" he yelled, as he was trampled under foot, and this time he made himself heard. The girl seized the long hair of her lover, pressed it convulsively, and swooned.

Years afterwards (as it seemed to her) she awakened and found the chamber still as death, and—yes—this was the hair of death which she still clutched in her dead hand. She kissed it a hundred times before it brought back to her where she was and what had passed. She looked round then for the hermit. He, poor man, was lying as if also dead. But when she could bring herself to release her hoarded treasure, she speedily brought him to some sort of consciousness. He sat up, not without difficulty, and looked around. But his mind, already half way to madness, had been totally overturned by what had occurred that woeful night.

"We have saved his soul between us," she cried. "What do I not owe you for standing by me in that fell hour?"

He regarded her in evident perplexity. "I cannot think how you come to be wearing that blood-stained dress of hers," was all he replied.

"I have told you," she said, gently, "but you have forgotten that I cherished it through all my wanderings as my sole memento of her glorious death. She laid down the last drop of her blood for him. She chose the better part. But I! my God! what in the world is to become of me?"

"I had a memento of her once," he muttered. "I had her beautiful head, but I have lost it."

"That settles it," she said, "you shall cut off mine."

Witch In-Grain

R. Murray Gilchrist

Of late Michal had been much engrossed in the reading of the black-letter books that Philosopher Bale brought from France. As you know I am no Latinist—though one while she was earnest in her desire to instruct me; but the open air had ever greater charms for me than had the dry precincts of a library. So I grudged the time she spent apart, and throughout the spring I would have been all day at her side, talking such foolery as lovers use. But ever she must steal away and hide herself amongst dead volumes.

Yestereven I crossed the Roods, and entered the garden, to find the girl sitting under a yew-tree. Her face was haggard and her eyes sunken: for the time it seemed as if many years had passed over her head, but somehow the change had only added to her beauty. And I marvelled greatly, but ere I could speak a huge bird, whose plumage was as the brightest gold, fluttered out of her lap from under the silken apron; and looking on her uncovered bosom I saw that his beak had pierced her tender flesh. I cried aloud, and would have caught the thing, but it rose slowly, laughing like a man, and, beating upwards, passed out of sight in the quincunx. Then Michal drew long breaths, and her youth came back in some measure. But she frowned, and said, "What is it, sweetheart? Why hast awakened me? I dreamed that I fed the Dragon of the Hesperidean Garden." Meanwhile, her gaze set on the place whither the bird had flown.

"Thou hast chosen a filthy mammet," I said. "Tell me how came it hither?"

She rose without reply, and kissed her hands to the gaudy wings, which were nearing through the trees. Then, lifting up a great tome that had lain at her feet, she turned towards the house. But ere she had reached the end of the maze she stopped, and smiled with strange subtlety.

"How camest *thou* hither, O satyr?" she cried. "Even when the Dragon slept, and the fruit hung naked to my touch. . . . The gates fell to."

Perplexed and sore adread, I followed to the hall; and found in the herb garden the men struggling with an ancient woman—a foul crone, brown and puckered as a rotten costard. At sight of Michal she thrust out her hands, crying, "Save me, mistress!" The girl cowered, and ran up the perron and indoors. But for me, I questioned Simon, who stood well out of reach of the wretch's nails, as to the wherefore of this hurly-burly.

His underlings bound the runnion with cords, and haled her to the closet in the banqueting gallery. Then, her beldering being stilled, Simon entreated me to compel Michal to prick her arm. So I went down to the library, and found my sweetheart sitting by the window, tranced with seeing that goblin fowl go tumbling on the lawn.

My heart was full of terror and anguish. "Dearest Michal," I prayed, "for the sake of our passion let me command. Here is a knife." I took a poniard from Sir Roger's stand of arms. "Come with me now; I will tell you all."

Her gaze still shed her heart upon the popinjay; and when I took her hand and drew her from the room, she strove hard to escape. In the gallery I pressed her fingers round the haft, and knowing that the witch was bound, flung open the door so that they faced each other. But Mother Benmusk's eyes glared like fire, so that Michal was withered up, and sank swooning into my arms. And a chuckle of disdain leaped from the hag's ragged lips. Simon and the others came hurrying, and when Michal had found her life, we begged her to cut into one of those knotted arms. Yet she would none of it, but turned her face and signed no—no—she would not. And as we strove to prevail with her, word came that one of the Bishop's horses had cast a shoe in the village, and that his lordship craved the hospitality of Ford, until the smith had mended the mishap. Nigh at the heels of his message came the divine, and having heard and pondered our tale, he would fain speak with her.

I took her to the withdrawing-room, where at the sight of him she burst into such a loud fit of laughter that the old man rose in fear and went away.

"Surely it is an obsession," he cried; "nought can be done until the witch takes back her spells!"

So I bade the servants carry Benmusk to the mere, and cast her in the muddy part thereof where her head would lie above water. That was fifteen hours ago, but methinks I still hear her screams clanging through the stagnant air. Never was hag so fierce and full of strength! All along the garden I saw a track of uprooted flowers. Amongst the sedges the turmoil grew and grew till every heron fled. They threw her in, and the whole mere seethed as if the floor of it were hell. For full an hour she cursed us fearsomely: then, finding that every time she neared the land the men thrust her back again, her spirit waxed abject, and she fell to whimpering. Two hours before twelve she cried that she would tell all she knew. So we landed her, and she was loosened of her bonds and she mumbled in my ear: "I swear by Satan that I am innocent of this harm! I ha' none but pawtry secrets. Go at midnight to the lows and watch Baldus's tomb. There thou shalt find all."

The beldam tottered away, her bemired petticoats clapping her legs; and I bade them let her rest in peace until I had certainly proved her guilt. With this I returned to the house; but, finding that Michal had retired for the night, I sat by the fire, waiting for the time to pass. A clock struck the half before eleven, and I set out for King Baldus's grave, whither, had not such a great matter been at stake, I dared not have ventured after dark. I stole from the garden and through the first copse. The moon lay against a brazen curtain; little snail-like clouds were crawling underneath, and the horns of them pricked her face.

As I neared the lane to the waste, a most unholy dawn broke behind the fringe of pines, looping the boles with strings of grey-golden light. Surely a figure moved there? I ran. A curious motley and a noisy swarmed forth at me. Another moment, and I was in the midst of a host of weasels and hares and such-like creatures, all flying from the precincts of the tomb. I quaked with dread, and the hair of my flesh stood upright. But I thrust on, and parted the thorn boughs, and looked up at the mound.

On the summit thereof sat Michal, triumphing, invested with flames. And the Shape approached, and wrapped her in his blackness.

XÉLUCHA

M. P. SHIEL

He goeth after her . . . and knoweth not . . .

[FROM A DIARY]

THREE DAYS AGO! BY HEAVEN, IT SEEMS AN AGE. BUT I AM SHAKEN—MY REASON IS debauched. A while since, I fell into a momentary coma precisely resembling an attack of *petit mal*. "Tombs, and worms, and epitaphs"—that is my dream. At my age, with my physique, to walk staggery, like a man stricken! But all that will pass: I must collect myself—my reason is debauched. Three days ago! it seems an age! I sat on the floor before an old cista full of letters. I lighted upon a packet of Cosmo's. Why, I had forgotten them! they are turning sere! Truly, I can no more call myself a young man. I sat reading, listlessly, rapt back by memory. To muse is to be lost! of *that* evil habit I must wring the neck, or look to perish. Once more I threaded the mazy sphere-harmony of the minuet, reeled in the waltz, long pomps of candelabra, the noonday of the bacchanal, about me. Cosmo was the very tsar and maharajah of the Sybarites! the Priap of the *détraqués*! In every unexpected alcove of the Roman Villa was a couch, raised high, with necessary foot-stool, flanked and canopied with *mirrors* of clarified gold. Consumption fastened upon him; reclining at last at table, he could, till warmed, scarce lift the wine! his eyes were like two fat glow-worms, coiled together! they seemed haloed with vaporous emanations of phosphorus! Desperate, one could see, was the secret struggle with the Devourer. But to the end the princely smile persisted calm; to the end—to the last day—he continued among that comic crew unchallenged choragus of all the rites, I will not say of Paphos, but of Chemos! and Baal-Peor! Warmed, he did not refuse the revel, the dance, the darkened chamber. It was utterly black, rayless; approached by a secret passage; in shape circular; the air hot, haunted always by odours of balms, bdellium, hints of dulcimer and flute; and radiated round with a hundred thick-strewn ottomans of Morocco. Here Lucy Hill stabbed to the heart Caccofogo, mistaking the scar of his back for the scar of Soriac. In a bath of malachite the Princess Egla, waking late one morning, found Cosmo lying stiffly dead, the water covering him wholly.

"But in God's name, Mérimée!" (so he wrote), "to think of Xélucha dead! Xélucha! Can a moon-beam, then, perish of suppurations? Can the rainbow be eaten by worms? Ha! ha! ha! laugh with me, my friend: *'elle dérangera l'Enfer'*! She will introduce the *pas de tarantule* into Tophet! Xélucha, the feminine! Xélucha recalling the splendid harlots of history! Weep with me—manat rara meas lacrima per genas! expert as Thargelia; cultured as Aspatia; purple as Semiramis. She comprehended the human tabernacle, my friend, its secret springs and tempers, more intimately than any *savant* of Salamanca who breathes. *Tarare*—but Xélucha is not dead! Vitality is not mortal; you cannot wrap flame in a shroud. Xélucha! where then is she? Translated, perhaps—rapt to a constellation like the daughter of Leda. She journeyed to Hindostan, accompanied by the train and appurtenance of a Begum, threatening descent upon the Emperor of Tartary. I spoke of the desolation of the West; she kissed me, and promised return. Mentioned you, too, Mérimée—'her Conqueror'—'Mérimée, Destroyer of Woman.' A breath from the conservatory rioted among the ambery whiffs of her forelocks, sending it singly a-wave over that thulite tint you know. Costumed cap-à-pie, she had, my friend, the dainty little completeness of a daisy mirrored bright in the eye of the browsing ox. A simile of Milton had for years, she said, inflamed the lust of her Eye: 'The barren plains of Sericana, where Chineses drive with sails and wind their cany wagons light.' I, and the Sabæans, she assured me, wrongly considered Flame the whole of being; the other half of things being Aristotle's quintessential light. In the Ourania Hierarchia and the Faust-book you meet a completeness: burning Seraph, Cherûb full of eyes. Xélucha combined them. She would reconquer the Orient for Dionysius, and return. I heard of her blazing at Delhi; drawn in a chariot by lions. Then this rumour—probably false. Indeed, it comes from a source somewhat turgid. Like Odin, Arthur, and the rest, Xélucha—will reappear."

Soon subsequently, Cosmo lay down in his balneum of malachite, and slept, having drawn over him the water as a coverlet. I, in England, heard little of Xélucha: first that she was alive, then dead, then alighted at old Tadmor in the Wilderness, Palmyra now. Nor did I greatly care, Xélucha having long since turned to apples of Sodom in my mouth. Till I sat by the cista of letters and re-read Cosmo, she had for some years passed from my active memories.

The habit is now confirmed in me of spending the greater part of the day in sleep, while by night I wander far and wide through the city under the sedative influence of a tincture which has become necessary to my life. Such an existence of shadow is not without charm; nor, I think, could many minds be steadily subjected to its conditions without elevation, deepened awe. To travel alone with the Primordial cannot but be solemn. The moon is of the hue of the glow-worm; and Night of the sepulchre. Nux bore not less Thanatos than Hupuos, and the bitter tears of Isis redundulate to a flood. At three, if a cab rolls by, the sound has the augustness of thunder. Once, at two, near a corner, I came upon a priest, seated, dead, leering, his legs bent. One arm, supported on a knee, pointed with rigid accusing forefinger obliquely upward. By exact observation, I found that he indicated Betelgeux, the star "*a*" which shoulders the wet sword of Orion. He was hideously swollen, having perished of dropsy. Thus in all Supremes is a *grotesquerie*; and one of the sons of Night is—Buffo.

In a London square deserted, I should imagine, even in the day, I was aware of the metallic, silvery-clinking approach of little shoes. It was three in a heavy morning of winter, a day after my rediscovery of Cosmo. I had stood by the railing, regarding the clouds sail as under the sea-legged pilotage of a moon wrapped in cloaks of inclemency. Turning, I saw a little lady, very gloriously dressed. She had walked straight to me. Her head was bare, and crisped with the amber stream which rolled lax to a globe, kneaded thick with jewels, at her nape. In the redundance of her décolleté development, she resembled Parvati, mound-hipped love-goddess of the luscious fancy of the Brahmin.

She addressed to me the question:

"What are you doing there, darling?"

Her loveliness stirred me, and Night is *bon camarade*. I replied:

"Sunning myself by means of the moon."

"All that is borrowed lustre," she returned, "you have got it from old Drummond's *Flowers of Sion*."

Looking back, I cannot remember that this reply astonished me, though it should—of course—have done so. I said:

"On my soul, no; but you?"

"You might guess whence *I* come!"

"You are dazzling. You come from Paz."

"Oh, farther than that, my son! Say a subscription ball in Soho."

"Yes?. . . and alone? in the cold? on foot...?"

"Why, I am old, and a philosopher. I can pick you out riding Andromeda yonder from the ridden Ram. They are in error, M'sieur, who suppose an atmosphere on the broad side of the moon. I have reason to believe that on Mars dwells a race whose lids are transparent like glass; so that the eyes are visible during sleep; and every varying dream moves imaged forth to the beholder in tiny panorama on the limpid iris. You cannot imagine me a mere *fille*! To be escorted is to admit yourself a woman, and that is improper in Nowhere. Young Eos drives an *équipage à quatre*, but Artemis 'walks' alone. Get out of my borrowed light in the name of Diogenes! I am going home."

"Far?"

"Near Piccadilly."

"But a cab?"

"No cabs for *me*, thank you. The distance is a mere nothing. Come."

We walked forward. My companion at once put an interval between us, quoting from the *Spanish Curate* that the open is an enemy to love. The Talmudists, she twice insisted, rightly held the hand the sacredest part of the person, and at that point also contact was for the moment interdict. Her walk was extremely rapid. I followed. Not a cat was anywhere visible. We reached at length the door of a mansion in St. James's. There was no light. It seemed tenantless, the windows all uncurtained, pasted across, some of them, with the words, To Let. My companion, however, flitted up the steps, and, beckoning, passed inward. I, following, slammed the door, and was in darkness. I heard her ascend, and presently a region of glimmer above revealed a stairway of marble, curving broadly up. On the floor where I stood was no carpet, nor furniture: the dust was very thick. I had begun to mount when, to my surprise, she stood by my side, returned; and whispered:

"To the very top, darling."

She soared nimbly up, anticipating me. Higher, I could no longer doubt that the house was empty but for us. All was a vacuum full of dust and echoes. But at the top, light streamed from a door, and I entered a good-sized oval saloon, at about the centre of the house. I was completely dazzled by the sudden resplendence of the apartment. In the midst was a spread table, square, opulent with gold plate, fruit, dishes; three ponderous chandeliers of electric light above; and I noticed also (what was very *bizarre*) one little candlestick of common tin containing an old soiled curve of tallow, on the table. The impression of the whole chamber was one of gorgeousness not less than Assyrian. An ivory couch at the far end was made sun-like by a head-piece of chalcedony forming a sea for the sport of emerald ichthyotauri. Copper hangings, panelled with mirrors in iasperated crystal, corresponded with a dome of flame and copper; yet this latter, I now remember, produced upon my glance an impression of actual grime. My companion reclined on a small Sigma couch, raised high to the table-level in the Semitic manner, visible to her saffron slippers of satin. She pointed me a seat opposite. The incongruity of its presence in the middle of this arrogance of pomp so tickled me, that no power could have kept me from a smile: it was a grimy chair, mean, all wood, nor was I long in discovering one leg somewhat shorter than its fellows.

She indicated wine in a black glass bottle, and a tumbler, but herself made no pretence of drinking or eating. She lay on hip and elbow, *petite*, resplendent, and looked gravely upward. I, however, drank.

"You are tired," I said, "one sees that."

"It is precious little than *you* see!" she returned, dreamy, hardly glancing.

"How! your mood is changed, then? You are morose."

"You never, I think, saw a Norse passage-grave?"

"And abrupt."

"Never?"

"A passage-grave? No."

"It is worth a journey! They are circular or oblong chambers of stone, covered by great earthmounds, with a 'passage' of slabs connecting them with the outer air. All round the chamber the dead sit with head resting upon the bent knees, and consult together in silence."

"Drink wine with me, and be less Tartarean."

"You certainly seem to be a fool," she replied with perfect sardonic iciness. "Is it not, then, highly romantic? They belong, you know, to the Neolithic age. As the teeth fall, one by one, from the lipless mouths—they are caught by the lap. When the lap thins—they roll to the floor of stone. Thereafter, every tooth that drops all round the chamber sharply breaks the silence."

"Ha! ha! ha!"

"Yes. It is like a century-slow, circularly-successive dripping of slime in some cavern of the far subterrene."

"Ha! ha! This wine seems heady! They express themselves in a dialect largely dental."

"The Ape, on the other hand, in a language wholly guttural."

A town-clock tolled four. Our talk was holed with silences, and heavy-paced. The wine's yeasty exhalation reached my brain. I saw her through mist, dilating large, uncertain, shrinking again to dainty compactness. But amorousness had died within me.

"Do you know," she asked, "what has been discovered in one of the Danish *Kjökkenmöddings* by a little boy? It was ghastly. The skeleton of a huge fish with human—"

"You are most unhappy."

"Be silent."

"You are full of care."

"I think you a great fool."

"You are racked with misery."

"You are a child. You have not even an instinct of the meaning of the word."

"How! Am I not a man? I, too, miserable, careful?"

"You are not, really, *anything*—until you can create."

"Create what?"

"Matter."

"That is foppish. Matter cannot be created, nor destroyed."

"Truly, then, you must be a creature of unusually weak intellect. I see that now. Matter does not exist, then, there is no such thing, really—it is an appearance, a spectrum—every writer not imbecile from Plato to Fichte has, voluntary or involuntary, proved that for your good. To create it is to produce an impression of its reality upon the senses of others; to destroy it is to wipe a wet rag across a scribbled slate."

"Perhaps. I do not care. Since no one can do it."

"No one? You are mere embryo—"

"Who then?"

"*Anyone*, whose power of Will is equivalent to the gravitating force of a star of the First Magnitude."

"Ha! ha! ha! By heaven, you choose to be facetious. Are there then wills of such equivalence?"

"There have been three, the founders of religions. There was a fourth: a cobbler of Herculaneum, whose mere volition induced the cataclysm of Vesuvius in 79, in direct opposition to the gravity of Sirius. There are more fames than *you* have ever sung, you know. The greater number of disembodied spirits, too, I feel certain—"

"By heaven, I cannot but think you full of sorrow! Poor wight! come, drink with me. The wine is thick and boon. Is it not Setian? It makes you sway and swell before me, I swear, like a purple cloud of evening—"

"But you are mere clayey ponderance!—I did not know that!—you are no companion! your little interest revolves round the lowest centres."

"Come—forget your agonies—"

"What, think you, is the portion of the buried body first sought by the worm?"

"The eyes! the eyes!"

"You are *hideously* wrong—you are so *utterly* at sea—"

"My God!"

She had bent forward with such rage of contradiction as to approach me closely. A loose gown of amber silk, wide-sleeved, had replaced her ball attire, though at what opportunity I could not guess; wondering, I noticed it as she now placed her palms far forth upon the table. A sudden wafture as of spice and orange-flowers, mingled with the abhorrent faint odour of mortality over-ready for the tomb, greeted my sense. A chill crept upon my flesh.

"You are so *hopelessly* at fault—"

"For God's sake—"

"You are so *miserably* deluded! Not the eyes *at all*!"

"Then, in Heaven's name, what?"

Five tolled from a clock.

"*The Uvula*! the soft drop of mucous flesh, you know, suspended from the palate above the glottis. They eat through the face-cloth and cheek, or crawl by the lips through a broken tooth, filling the mouth. They make straight for it. It is the *deliciæ* of the vault."

At her horror of interest I grew sick, at her odour, and her words. Some unspeakable sense of insignificance, of debility, held me dumb.

"You say I am full of sorrows. You say I am racked with woe; that I gnash with anguish. Well, you are a mere child in intellect. You use words without realisation of meaning like those minds in what Leibnitz calls 'symbolical consciousness.' But suppose it were so—"

"It is so."

"You know nothing."

"I see you twist and grind. Your eyes are very pale. I thought they were hazel. They are of the faint bluishness of phosphorus shimmerings seen in darkness."

"That proves nothing."

"But the 'white' of the sclerotic is dyed to yellow. And you look inward. Why do you look so palely inward, so woe-worn, upon your soul? Why can you speak of nothing but the sepulchre, and its rottenness? Your eyes seem to me wan with centuries of vigil, with mysteries and millenniums of pain."

"Pain! but you know so *little* of it! you are wind and words! of its philosophy and *rationale* nothing!"

"Who knows?"

"I will give you a hint. It is the sub-consciousness in conscious creatures of Eternity, and of eternal loss. The least prick of a pin not Pæan and Æsculapius and the powers of heaven and hell can utterly heal. Of an everlasting loss of pristine wholeness the conscious body is sub-conscious, and 'pain' is its sigh at the tragedy. So with all pain—greater, the greater the loss. The hugest of losses is, of course, the loss of Time. If you lose that, any of it, you plunge at once into the transcendental-isms, the infinitudes, of Loss; if you lose *all of it*—"

"But you so wildly exaggerate! Ha! ha! You rant, I tell you, of commonplaces with the woe—"

"Hell is where a clear, untrammelled Spirit is sub-conscious of lost Time; where it boils and writhes with envy of the living world; *hating* it for ever, and all the sons of Life!"

"But curb yourself! Drink—I implore—I *implore*—for God's sake—but *once*—"

"To *hasten* to the snare—*that* is woe! to drive your ship upon the *lighthouse* rock—that is Marah! To wake, and feel it irrevocably true that you went after her—*and the dead were there*—and her guests were in the depths of hell—*and you did not know it!*—though you *might* have. Look out upon the houses of the city this dawning day: not one, I tell you, but in it haunts some soul—walking up and down the old theatre of its little Day—goading imagination by a thousand childish tricks, vraisemblances—elaborately duping itself into the momentary fantasy *that it still lives*, that the chance of life is not for ever and for ever lost—yet riving all the time with under-memories of the wasted Summer, the lapsed brief light between the two eternal glooms—riving I say and shriek to you!—riving, *Mérimée, you destroying fiend*—"

She had sprung—*tall* now, she seemed to me—between couch and table.

"Mérimée!" I screamed, "—*my* name, harlot, in your maniac mouth! By God, woman, you terrify me to death!"

I too sprang, the hairs of my head catching stiff horror from my fancies.

"Your name? Can you imagine me ignorant of your name, or anything concerning you? Mérimée! Why, did you not sit yesterday and read of me in a letter of Cosmo's?"

"Ah-h . . . ," hysteria bursting high in sob and laughter from my arid lips— "Ah! ha! ha! Xélucha! My memory grows palsied and grey, Xélucha! pity me—my walk is in the very valley of shadow!—senile and sere!—observe my hair, Xélucha, its grizzled growth—trepidant, Xélucha, clouded—I am not the man you knew, Xélucha, in the palaces—of Cosmo! You are Xélucha!"

"You rave, poor worm!" she cried, her face contorted by a species of malicious contempt. "Xélucha died of cholera ten years ago at Antioch. I wiped the froth from her lips. Her nose underwent a green decay before burial. So far sunken into the brain was the left eye—"

"You are—*you are Xélucha!*" I shrieked; "voices now of thunder howl it within my consciousness—and by the holy God, Xélucha, though you blight me with the breath of the hell you are, I shall clasp you,—living or damned—"

I rushed toward her. The word "Madman!" hissed as by the tongues of ten thousand serpents through the chamber, I heard; a belch of pestilent corruption puffed poisonous upon the putrid air; for a moment to my wildered eyes there seemed to rear itself, swelling high to the roof, a formless tower of ragged cloud, and before my projected arms had closed upon the very emptiness of insanity, I was tossed by the operation of some Behemoth potency far-circling backward to the utmost circumference of the oval, where, my head colliding, I fell, shocked, into insensibility.

When the sun was low toward night, I lay awake, and listlessly observed the grimy roof, and the sordid chair, and the candlestick of tin, and the bottle of which I had drunk. The table was small, filthy, of common deal, uncovered. All bore the appearance of having stood there for years. But for them, the room was void, the vision of luxury thinned to air. Sudden memory flashed upon me. I scrambled to my feet, and plunged and tottered, bawling, through the twilight into the street.